TENDER IS THE NIGHT

&

THE LAST TYCOON

Tender is the Night
&
The Last Tycoon

F. Scott Fitzgerald

with Introductions and Notes by
HENRY CLARIDGE

WORDSWORTH CLASSICS

For my husband
ANTHONY JOHN RANSON
with love from your wife, the publisher.
Eternally grateful for your unconditional love.

Readers who are interested in other titles from
Wordsworth Editions are invited to visit our website at
www.wordsworth-editions.com

This edition first published in 2011 by
Wordsworth Editions Limited
8B East Street, Ware, Hertfordshire SG12 9HJ

ISBN 978 1 84022 663 8

Text © Wordsworth Editions Limited 2011

Introductions and Notes © Henry Claridge 2011

Wordsworth® is a registered trade mark of
Wordsworth Editions Limited

Wordsworth Editions
is the company founded in 1987 by
MICHAEL TRAYLER

Typeset in Great Britain by Antony Gray
Printed and bound by Clays Ltd, St Ives plc

CONTENTS

GENERAL INTRODUCTION

Wordsworth Classics are inexpensive editions designed to appeal to the general reader and students. We commissioned teachers and specialists to write wide-ranging, jargon-free introductions and to provide notes that would assist the understanding of our readers, rather than interpret the stories for them. In the same spirit, because the pleasures of reading are inseparable from the surprises, secrets and revelations that all narratives contain, we strongly advise you to enjoy the book before turning to the Introduction.

General Advisor
KEITH CARABINE
Rutherford College, University of Kent

INTRODUCTION TO
TENDER IS THE NIGHT

With the obvious exception of *The Great Gatsby*, *Tender is the Night* is Fitzgerald's best-known novel. As with *The Great Gatsby*, its genesis lies in that period of the mid-1920s when Fitzgerald's creative talents were rescued from the temptations of writing 'primers' on adolescent sexual activity or guidebooks for would-be 'flappers', and from his attachment to the model of what he called the 'Wells-Shaw-Chesterton-Mackenzie combination' that he had identified as his fictional ideal while training as an officer at Fort Leavenworth, Kansas, in 1918. The more demanding models of Joseph Conrad and Anatole France inform the achievement of *The Great Gatsby*, particularly, of course, the 'discovery' of the sympathetic 'middle-man narrator' (*pace* Marlow in *Heart of Darkness*) who both edits his author's material and guides his readers' judgements. T. S. Eliot's encouragement of Fitzgerald in his letter to him of December 1925, where he writes of *The Great Gatsby* as 'the first step American fiction has taken since Henry James', may have led him to believe that a social novel, on a grander scale than *Gatsby* (whose 'world' feels, admittedly, larger than the 125 or so pages taken to evoke it), was well within his ability. Thus, in a letter of 1 May 1925 to his editor at Scribner's, Maxwell Perkins, written just after the publication of *The Great Gatsby*, he spoke ambitiously of his new novel as 'something really NEW in form, idea, structure – the model for the age that Joyce and Stein are searching for, that Conrad didn't find'. At this point in his life, given the extensive revisions he had effected to *The Great Gatsby* at galley stage, the 'new novel' could have been little more than the adumbration of a few ideas. In its original form *Tender is the Night* seems to have been conceived as a murder story (though not a detective novel). Like many of his contemporaries, Fitzgerald was fascinated by two celebrated contemporary murders, the Leopold–Loeb case of 1924 and Dorothy Ellingson's murder of her mother in 1925 after a heated argument over her daughter's wild and impulsive behaviour. The murder in Chicago of a boy of fourteen called Bobby Franks by two wealthy University of Chicago students, Nathan Leopold and Richard Loeb, seems especially to have intrigued him. Their 'explanation' of the crime was that they were trying to commit the perfect murder (Franks was selected randomly) and thus the whole thing was a kind of intellectual exercise in sensationalism. The details of the crime surfaced just before the Fitzgeralds left Long Island for the South of France and we know the degree of Fitzgerald's interest in the case from the fact that an article about it from *Liberty* magazine (in which one of his stories, 'The Sensible Thing', was about to be published) was filed among his papers. The finished novel suggests that his fascination with the case lay not with the genesis and execution of the murder itself, but rather with Leopold and Loeb as types of malign 'genius': both were intelligent and, to an extent, sensitive, but their wealthy backgrounds acted in ways that seemed to promote degenerate behaviour. In other words, they were victims of the social advantages secured by wealth. The fact, also, that so much of the testimony and evidence in the trial took on a psychiatric (and psychoanalytical) character might also have impressed upon Fitzgerald the degree to which actions of the most heinous kind were to be understood in a scientific vocabulary that owed little to the appeal of moral or religious certitudes of earlier generations, and was thus evidence of the very modernity that he had seen (and described) in the early 1920s.

Scholars describe various ur-versions of *Tender is the Night*, with titles such as *Our Type*, *The Melarky Case*, *The World's Fair* and *The Boy Who Killed His Mother*, in which a young man called Francis Melarky, evicted from West Point military academy, travels to Europe with a domineering mother and falls in with a group of expatriated Americans, whose influence over him, though at times charming and seemingly innocent, provokes an ineluctable process of degeneration. In one adumbration of the plot, inspired by Dorothy Ellingson's murder of her mother, Francis was finally to kill his mother. (We should be very thankful Fitzgerald never wrote this novel.) Though Fitzgerald told Perkins and Harold Ober in 1925 that he was making steady progress on his new novel and, indeed, promised it for serialisation in *Liberty* by June 1926, his work on it was fitful. *The Great Gatsby* was followed not by the new novel but by *All the Sad Young Men* (1926), his third collection of short stories, many of them from the period between 1922 and 1924.

Two years later, in July 1928, he told Perkins in a letter from Paris:'The novel goes fine. I think its [*sic*] quite wonderful & I think those who've seen it (for I've read it around a little) have been quite excited.' Clearly the new novel wasn't going 'fine', and his reference in the same letter to James Joyce's telling him that his new novel would be finished in 'three or four years' is a coded way of intimating to Perkins that he, too, may have to wait longer than he would like, despite Fitzgerald's unconvincing assurance that: 'Mine will be done *sure* in September.' In November 1928 Perkins wrote to Fitzgerald after having read two chapters of the novel, noting in passing that the second of the chapters 'contains some of the best writing you have ever done . . . ' But despite effusive promises this is all Perkins saw and one letter to him from Cannes in June 1929 is particularly telling; in it Fitzgerald wrote: 'I am working night & day on novel from new angle that I think will solve previous difficulties.' Five months later, in November 1929, he told Perkins: 'For the first time since August I see my way clear to a long stretch on the novel . . . ' There can be little doubt that what work Fitzgerald was doing on his novel, no matter how faltering or intermittent it was, was radically reshaping the original. He continued to publish short stories in this period, above all as a way of keeping his head above water financially, and many of them provide insights into the nature of his refashioning of the material of the novel with which he had begun. A man married to a jealous wife who discovers his infidelities is a situation common to both 'The Love Boat' (1927) and 'The Rough Crossing' (1929), the latter notable for the fact that the thirty-one-year-old playwright, Adrian

Smith, falls in love with a girl of eighteen. The story recalls Fitzgerald's fascination with the young American actress Lois Moran whom he met in 1927, and, of course, foreshadows the relationship between Dick Diver and Rosemary Hoyt in *Tender is the Night*. Another story, 'One Trip Abroad' (1930), plays out its drama of the disintegration of the marriage of a wealthy couple against the background of the expatriate community in the South of France. Here, the husband, Nelson Kelly, who has resigned his business interests in the hope of becoming a painter, and his wife, Nicole, are drawn into a world of moral dissolution (particularly drunkenness and infidelity) and violence. The 'new angle' of which Fitzgerald wrote in June 1929 seems to have had a striking similarity to this story. In the novel version, however, the characters become Lew and Nicole Kelly, the husband now a film director who becomes infatuated with a young American actress called Rosemary whom he meets on a transatlantic voyage to Europe.

Progress on the novel was now seriously interrupted by his wife's illness: in April 1930 Zelda suffered a nervous breakdown and Fitzgerald took her to a psychiatric clinic in Montreux, Switzerland, where she was diagnosed as schizophrenic. In July he wrote to Perkins from Switzerland that 'Zelda was sick as hell . . . ' and that he 'was so upset in June when hopes for her recovery were black that I could do practically no work and got behind . . . ' But the black cloud had a silver lining. Zelda's illness and his conversations with her doctors enabled him to reimagine the materials that had gone into the early drafts of *Tender is the Night* and the group of stories that had appeared, roughly, at mid-point in its gestation. The film director gives way to a doctor, not the physician of nineteenth-century fiction, but the 'new' doctor of the age of modernity, a psychiatrist/psychoanalyst. The work that emerged from this 'fusing' of Fitzgerald's new conception of his hero with the older material from ur-versions such as *The Melarky Case* and *The Boy Who Killed His Mother* now assumed the identity of *The Drunkard's Holiday*, a title we are pleased Fitzgerald did not finally adopt but one that for all its clumsiness adverts to the dangerous, indeed fatal, combination of excess and leisure that has led some critics to write about *Tender is the Night* as if it were an extended footnote to Thorstein Veblen's *The Theory of the Leisure Class* (1899). *The Drunkard's Holiday* mutated to *Dick Diver* and by now, that is sometime in the summer of 1932, Fitzgerald had a clear idea of what the finished novel would look like. In a handwritten 'Sketch' among his preliminary working notes for the novel he wrote:

The novel should do this. Show a man who is natural idealist, a spoiled priest, giving in for various causes to the ideas of the haute Burgeoise [*sic*], and in his rise to the top of the social world losing his idealism, his talent and turning to drink and dissipation. Background is one in which the leisure class is at their truly most brilliant and glamorous such as Murphys.

(The 'Murphys' were Gerald and Sara Murphy, wealthy expatriate American friends who lived in the South of France and to whom Fitzgerald dedicated the novel.) This theme now drove his renewed energies and a manuscript ready for submission was prepared by October 1933, though its new title was *Richard Diver* and *Tender is the Night* emerged only at a very late stage in Fitzgerald's revisions.

The 'new' novel – conceived at the height of the 'Roaring Twenties' only to see publication in one of the worst years of the Depression – was now finished. *Tender is the Night* was published serially in *Scribner's Magazine* in four parts January–April 1934, and then in book form on 12 April 1934. Sales of the novel, however, were poor, possibly because the serial publication had already attracted a substantial readership. The novel sold around thirteen thousand copies, but given the economic vagaries of Depression-era publishing these are not unrespectable figures. The issue of the novel's sales, however, and the income generated by them, influenced Fitzgerald's subsequent reconsideration of the novel's narrative structure.

The Novel

There can be no doubt that the long period of gestation had deleterious consequences for the finished work we read as *Tender is the Night*. Fitzgerald admitted as much in a letter of April 1934 to H. L. Mencken where he remarked that: 'The first part, the romantic introduction, is too long and too elaborated largely because of the fact that it has been written over a series of years with a varying plan . . . ' The simplest way in which we can recast the 'problem' of the novel is to point to its uncertainty of focus and this will, inevitably, lead us into some consideration of the competing merits of the two versions of the novel that I describe in my 'Note on the Text' below. What we know of the genesis and composition of the novel – the seventeen drafts that Fitzgerald's best textual scholar, Matthew J. Bruccoli, identifies – reveal how little resemblance Fitzgerald's original conception of the novel bears to the finished text. Dr Richard Diver emerges quite late in the chronology and then he has to be 'fitted into' a wealth of disparate materials that were conceived (and in many cases enacted) without his organising presence. It is this that explains why Fitzgerald was continually exercised about whether the novel had achieved 'the cohesion I aimed at'. In the original, 1934, version reprinted here, the world of the Divers is evoked through the point of view of Rosemary Hoyt, the eighteen-year-old American actress who is brought by her mother to the South of France; the girl's perspective yields both ironic and dramatic potential. The Divers are a family who seem to own part of the beach and the 'tanned prayer-mat' that Dick fashions from raking the pebbles and seaweed on the sand registers precisely the degree to which the Divers' world is invested with a kind of pseudo-religiosity, with Dick acting as the priestly overseer, or conductor, of its rituals and observances. Rosemary is too naïve and inexperienced to understand it in this way, but Fitzgerald's authorial interruptions and commentary allow him to hint at hidden forces at work in the Divers' marriage (and, indeed, in the world of their friends and acquaintances) while allowing Rosemary's overly romanticised response to the loveliness and refinement of what she sees (including Dick's physical attractiveness) to be rendered ironically. The effect is, of course, simultaneously dramatic, for the reader senses some inner sickness that discolours Rosemary's initial impressions, but the causes of this are obscure and the reader is drawn towards the unfolding of the materials of causation as if it were towards the explanation of a mystery. But the dramatic achievement comes at the expense of our 'placing' of the hero, for Rosemary's registrations are atmospheric and are, above all, responses to what Fitzgerald describes in Chapter 6 of Book One as 'the intensely calculated perfection of Villa Diana . . . ' Nicole, an important catalyst, if not the single cause, of Dick's decline is a largely silent figure, observed primarily in a social context. As Dick and Rosemary's relationship develops and she is drawn ever deeper into the world of the Divers and their friends, notably Abe and Mary North and Tommy Barban, so some of the superficial glamour to which she is attracted peels away, partly as a result of external disasters (such as the murder she witnesses while saying farewell to Abe at the Gare St-Lazare as he departs for New York), partly as a result of what I have described as the discoloration of her initial impressions. The problem with this is that it can (and for many readers does) cause some diminution in our sympathies for Dick Diver, who, as Rosemary sees him, is identified with – is almost co-extensive with – his world. I shall return to this issue when I come to look at the competing arguments for the original and revised editions of *Tender is the Night*.

These opening chapters of the novel (the 'romantic introduction') are modernist in character, for Fitzgerald is working according to the narrative methods of Joseph Conrad and Ford Madox Ford with their insistence on the artificiality, indeed unreality, of omniscient narration. But Rosemary is inadequate to the task Fitzgerald has set for himself in the novel. If *Tender is the Night* were a novel about the American expatriate rich idly passing the summer of 1925 (the height of the 'Jazz Age') at some of the most exclusive resorts on the French Riviera she would be ideal: she, after all, is a beautiful young actress, a creation of the age of cinema and someone aware, to an extent, of the 'commodification' of her sexuality (we learn, of course, through Collis Clay that her innocent cinematic image is complicated by sexual indiscretions), and she is uncritical of the expatriate community and its values. But this isn't the novel Fitzgerald is writing. It becomes apparent to us in Book One, partly during the visit to Paris in Chapter 12, more obviously during the visit to the battlefields of the World War 1 in the subsequent chapter, that a more profound intelligence is at work on this seemingly frivolous subject. These chapters begin a process by which Fitzgerald starts to generalise the significance of his story, both with respect to Dick's personal dissolution and decline, and how they might be understood naturalistically, and also with respect to socio-historical (though rarely political) realities. The brutalities of European war (brilliantly evoked by Dick when they stand overlooking the battlefield at Beaumont Hamel in Chapter 13) mark a significant moment of transition from the certitudes and securities of the Victorian age to the world of modernity. It is Abe North who ironically remarks in response to Dick's 'This was the last love battle', that Dick wants to 'hand over this battle to D. H. Lawrence'. The joke is a good one, but behind it lies the more profound realisation that, at bottom, the transition is ideological. As Dick reflects on the recent past we recall that the Russian Revolution followed in the wake of Russia's ignominious defeat by Germany in 1918, and that beyond the eastern borders of France are fascist Italy and an economically depressed proto-fascist Germany. But the war also marks a transitional moment in the history of consciousness: Dick's remark in this scene that he is 'an old romantic' serves to link him with the pre-war order that has shaped his sense of duty, moral responsibility and his commitment to the exacting demands of his profession. Fitzgerald himself was impressed, primarily through his reading, and rereading, of Joseph Conrad, with the moral seriousness of high art, and he has worked his understanding of a life of vocation (in Dick Diver's case to science, not art) into the portrait of his hero. But we don't see this aspect of him through Rosemary; instead it is Fitzgerald himself, in the authorial voice, who anticipates Dick's demise when he remarks, in Chapter 20 of Book One, of Dick's confused feelings about his relationship with Rosemary: 'He knew that what he was now doing marked a turning point in his life . . . ' The reader now understands that Dick's charming, civilised and successful exterior masks an inner turmoil. This theme recalls a sketch for *Tender is the Night* in one of its earlier 'incarnations':

> *The Drunkard's Holiday* will be a novel of our time showing the break-up of a fine personality. Unlike *The Beautiful and Damned* the break-up will be caused not by flabbiness but really tragic forces such as the inner conflicts of the idealist and the compromises forced on him by circumstances.

The 'circumstances' are complex and arise both from what Fitzgerald identifies as 'inner conflicts' and from the human and social contexts through which Dick Diver moves. His marriage to Nicole Warren, the daughter of a wealthy Chicago businessman who brings her for treatment to the clinic in Zurich where Dick works, sets in motion a chain of events that leads, with the inevitability of the 'tragic forces' of which Fitzgerald spoke, to his decline, his separation from Nicole, and his final return to the United States to take up work as a small-town doctor. His fall is in many ways precipitated by his marriage to Nicole, but Fitzgerald does not suggest that this is its sole cause. When Dick takes Nicole as his wife he gains access to the Warren fortune. With this come the temptations of luxury and indolence, and Dick struggles to keep his professional and personal probity untarnished by paying his own way and not drawing on Nicole's fortune. The bargain struck with the Warren family, particularly with Baby Warren, Nicole's older sister, who acts as her guardian, is to make Nicole better and this involves making her happy. Marriage to her, though he is warned against it and despite what he knows of Nicole's past condition, is part of the treatment and thus a world of material possessions is now made available to him without the necessity of its being worked for, and the 'pull' of his vocation now meets the 'counter pull' of what Fitzgerald subtly renders as the moral and spiritual desolation of the lives of the rich. But this isn't an adequate account of what explains his fall, for, as some critics have pointed out, it's not great wealth that unhinges Fitzgerald's male protagonists, it's great wealth in the hands of women (a theme we also find in *The Great Gatsby*). If Dick could just play doctor, or even nurse, to Nicole he would be immune to the dangers she presents. But as Fitzgerald makes clear in the middle of the novel (in Chapter 12 of Book Two): 'It was not so much fun. His work became confused with Nicole's problems; in addition, her income had increased so fast of late that it seemed to belittle his work.' As Nicole improves, so Dick's relationship to her becomes more tenuous, and, indeed, when there is no need for Dick as a doctor there is equally no need for him as a husband. It is one of the cruel, and powerful, ironies of *Tender is the Night* that as Nicole is cured so Dick becomes redundant, and her full recovery is marked by her submission to the conventional physical attractions of Tommy Barban. Interestingly, Fitzgerald writes of their relationship in epochal terms: Nicole and Tommy are the figures of modernity, and Dick, still possessing the idealism and illusions of his youth, is consigned to the past.

The depiction of the working life of a psychiatrist is one of the most striking aspects of *Tender is the Night*. The figure of the medical practitioner is, of course, familiar to us from nineteenth-century fiction: we think of Tertius Lydgate in George Eliot's *Middlemarch* or, at the opposite extreme, Charles Bovary in *Madame Bovary*. In the modern novel he is found in characters such as Andrew Manson in A. J. Cronin's *The Citadel* (1921) or Martin Arrowsmith in Sinclair Lewis's *Arrowsmith* (1925). The doctor was often invested with heroic qualities, not merely as a result of his abilities to diagnose and heal, but also because the medical practitioner represented the application of the great discoveries of nineteenth-century science to the world of human disorders. In his notes Fitzgerald emphasised that he sought 'suggestion' rather than overly detailed technical description in his account of Dick's professional activities, not wanting *Tender is the Night* to be 'like doctor's stories' where the interest might lie more with the presentation of Nicole's mental illness and less with the tragic inevitability of Dick's fall from intellectual and scientific brilliance. Dick's role in life is to cure, but Fitzgerald had done enough research into psychiatry and psychoanalysis (despite some caveats we may have about certain details) to know that both the nature of mental disorders and their treatment were matters of complex and intricate investigation, and that the results of psychiatric medicine were not conclusively scientific. Biographers have shown how much Fitzgerald profited from conversations he had with the doctors who treated Zelda's illness when she was hospitalised in Switzerland in April 1930. She was treated, in the main, by doctors of a Jungian persuasion, but in the novel Fitzgerald draws on the vocabulary and clinical methods of Sigmund Freud, and we assume that the book Dick Diver published in Zurich in 1920 (see Chapter 1 of Book Two) was heavily influenced by Freudian psychoanalysis. Nicole, diagnosed as schizophrenic (her illness is, in part, attributed to an incestuous relationship with her father), is treated by a process of 'transference', one of the clinical methods of psychoanalysis that distinguishes it from other forms of therapy, whereby psychological experiences are revived in analysis and are then 'transferred' to the person of the physician or analyst. The relationship between patient and analyst can assume a hostile character; in *Tender is the Night* it is one of dependency and love. Paradoxically, however, the 'transference' results in Nicole's liberation and release, whereas for Dick the 'counter-transference' brings only defeat and disillusion, and his 'imprisonment' in the little towns of western New York State with which the novel concludes. It is a measure of the novel's achievement in its portrayal of the working life of Dr Richard Diver that a review in the *Journal of Nervous and Mental Disease* of July 1935 remarked that for 'the psychiatrist and psychoanalyst the book is of special value as a probing story of some of the major dynamic interlockings in marriage which, conditioned by economic and psychobiological situations, have their innumerable counterparts in differences of degree rather than of kind'. The review concluded with the opinion that 'Mr Fitzgerald has written a book which is extremely valuable both as an understanding and sensitive record of human life, and as an accurate and fully prepared chronicle of European life *circa* 1917–1930.' It is a pity that there is no evidence that Fitzgerald ever read this encomium to his most ambitious and profound novel.

Fitzgerald was aware that in *Tender is the Night* he had written a novel very unlike its predecessor, *The Great Gatsby*. Of *Gatsby* he said the novel was 'selective', of *Tender* that it was 'full and comprehensive'. He wrote to H. L. Mencken in May 1925 of 'the elaborate and overlapping blankets of prose' in *The Great Gatsby* that served to disguise what he took as the novel's fundamental weakness, 'the lack of an emotional presentment of Daisy's attitude to Gatsby after their reunion . . . ' But *Tender is the Night*, as he explained in a letter to John Peale Bishop in April 1934, was shooting at something like *Vanity Fair*. The dramatic novel has canons quite different from the philosophical, now called psychological, novel. One is a kind of *tour de force* and the other a confession of faith. It would be like comparing a sonnet sequence with an epic.

The invocation of Thackeray's *Vanity Fair* reveals how strongly Fitzgerald sensed that he had written a novel in the manner of the great social-realist works of nineteenth-century fiction. Such a novel demands something other than the broad impressionist brush-strokes of *The Great Gatsby*. Instead it demands an attention to, and precision of, detail, and the composition of a densely actualised social, historical and geographical background against which the dramas of the characters' lives are played out (this alone explains why *Tender is the Night* is a more allusive novel than *The Great Gatsby*). We can think of few realist novels in which our sense of the characters' 'reality' is achieved without their being placed in a human and social context. Fitzgerald knew as much and his working notes for the novel (particularly those gathered around what Bruccoli calls the Third Version of *Tender is the Night*) are replete with reminders to himself of the importance of setting, chronology (especially of a character's age and growth) and historical moment. The richly particularised details about, among other things, World War I and contemporary conflicts such as those in Morocco and Asia Minor, the wealth of scientific, technological and medical facts, the use of lyrics from popular songs and the abundance of references to film stars and film directors, all lend to *Tender is the Night* a strong and vivid objective framework for the actions, and thoughts, of its characters.

It is the tension between *Tender is the Night* as a modernist novel and its harking back to the fictional model we associate with the great tradition of European social realism that is at the heart of the debate about the merits, and demerits, of the two versions of the novel, the original 1934 edition and Malcolm Cowley's revised edition of 1951. We can dismiss the scholarly argument for the revision on the simple grounds that the revision never bore Fitzgerald's *imprimatur* (see the Note on the Text below). But the critical case is more compelling and has to be addressed, in part because it will yield us some valuable final insights into the fictional experience the novel offers. Cowley argued (in his Introduction) that the opening pages of the novel confuse us, for we don't know 'whether the author had intended to write about a whole group of

Americans on the Riviera . . . or whether he had intended to write a psychological novel about the glory and decline of Richard Diver as a person'. If we begin, as in Cowley's version, at the beginning (that is, where chronology dictates) it becomes clear that the novel is psychological, that Dick is at its centre, and the force of his decline and dissolution is all the more powerful by virtue of our being made aware of how his early scientific brilliance gives way beneath the superficial and meretricious temptations of the indulgent and leisured lifestyle now afforded him by his marriage to Nicole. The dramatic and ironic effects of the original opening of the novel as seen through Rosemary's point of view are necessarily sacrificed, but the revision more clearly emphasises the 'dying fall' of which Fitzgerald spoke in a letter to H. L. Mencken shortly after the novel's publication, and lends it an overall symmetry that is lacking in the 1934 edition (a symmetry that, Cowley noted, turned in part on the image of General, later President, Ulysses S. Grant, in his family's general store in Galena, Illinois – see Notes). Cowley's critical preference for the revision gained support from Wayne C. Booth. In *The Rhetoric of Fiction*, Booth restated the case for a 'clean direct, old-fashioned presentation of his hero's initial pre-eminence and gradual decline'. This, he argued, could only be achieved by Fitzgerald's repudiation of the discoveries of modernism, for not every story demands the methods promoted by Conrad and Ford where a strong, vivid impression of the central character (such as, for example, the description of Jim Brown in the opening pages of *Lord Jim*) is registered and is then supplemented by materials that extend backwards and forwards over chronological time. Cowley's revision, Booth concluded, serves to correct 'a fault of over-distancing, a fault that springs from a method appropriate to other works at other times but not to the tragedy Fitzgerald wanted to write'.

Clearly there is much to be said for the arguments put forward by Cowley and Booth, and it is wrong to dismiss them, out of hand, as some critics have done (Brian Way is one of them) as harmful and misleading. In fact, it should be pointed out that the reader who reads both versions does not experience radically dissimilar novels: the characters are the same, the settings and scenes are the same, the incidents are the same, the characters speak the same words and feel the same emotions. The rearrangement of sections and scenes affects how we experience the novel as a sequence of moments of enlightenment and insight and our evaluation of its achievement as an aesthetic whole, but we are left with the much the same picture of Dick's decline and much the same understanding of its causes and consequences. Our aesthetic experience necessarily differs from one version to another and much of this (as I have shown above) arises from Fitzgerald's use of Rosemary. In the revision, as Cowley conceded, we know the truth about the Divers before Rosemary meets them and thus her discovery at the end of Book One (' . . . now she knew what Violet McKisco had seen in the bathroom at the Villa Diana') loses its dramatic force. But as we go back to the beginnings of Dick's career in Zurich in 1917 Rosemary has to be put aside and when she re-enters the narrative in Chapter 19 of Book Two (after Dick's return to Europe from his father's funeral) their affair is resumed, but with none of the pleasure of its conception, and by Book Three Rosemary recedes into the background. Cowley's revision doesn't overcome the difficulties Rosemary creates, since by moving to the second book what Fitzgerald in his notes entitled 'Rosemary's Angle' he possibly makes her seem an intrusion and an irrelevance; however, we arguably have a clearer sense, now that we have a picture of his scientific and vocational promise, that Dick's infatuation with her is both misguided and a debasement of his high ideals. Against this we can argue that our realisation of Nicole's mental illness is the more touching when refracted through Rosemary's perspective on the indulgent lifestyle of the American expatriate community on the Riviera. Thus, there is a critical case for Cowley's revision, but it is not conclusive and, given both the critical and scholarly arguments for the original edition, it is the 1934 version that is reprinted here.

It should be noted that from Chapter 11 of Book Two in this edition and Chapter Fourteen of Book Three in Cowley's revision, the two versions are, to all intents and purposes, identical.

A NOTE ON THE TEXT OF
TENDER IS THE NIGHT

Tender is the Night was published serially in *Scribner's Magazine* and then in book form by Charles Scribner's Sons on 12 April 1934. Fitzgerald was disappointed by the novel's sales and in August of 1936 he wrote to Bennett Cerf, then responsible for Random House's successful Modern Library series, and suggested revisions to the novel such as the realignment of certain scenes and the insertion of what he called 'sudden stops and part headings which would be to some extent explanatory . . . ' (here Fitzgerald is borrowing an idea from his first novel, *This Side of Paradise*). On Christmas Eve 1938, he wrote to Maxwell Perkins explaining that the novel's 'great fault is that the *true* beginning – the young psychiatrist in Switzerland – is tucked away in the middle of the book. If pages 151–212 were taken from their present place and put at the start the improvement in appeal would be enormous. In fact the mistake was noted and suggested by a dozen reviewers.' It is around this time, too, that he committed an 'Analysis of *Tender*' to his notebooks in which he divided the novel into five books instead of three and assembled the narrative in such a way that what is (in the present edition here) the beginning of Book Two is moved to the opening pages; thus we start with Richard Diver's arrival in Zurich in the spring of 1917 and the 'flashback' chapters of Book Two (Chapters 1–10) are presented in chronological sequence. 'Rosemary's section' or 'angle' (as Book One has come to be known) is moved to Book Two. Inside the front cover of his personal copy of *Tender is the Night*, with the alterations marked and various pages cut out and slipped into what would be their locations in the new version, Fitzgerald wrote: 'This is the *final version* of the book as I would like it.'

But Fitzgerald died (in December 1940) before seeing these revisions effected. Malcolm Cowley, however, a personal friend of Fitzgerald's and an influential critic, persuaded Scribner's to re-publish the novel in a revised form and he reassembled the narrative along the lines suggested in Fitzgerald's letters and notebooks. For about a decade or so this 'revised' version of *Tender is the Night* was the one most readers read. Scholarly and critical opinion has, however, reverted to the claims of the original 1934 edition (in part for the simple reason that no such revision was ever effected, authorised or approved by Fitzgerald) and Cowley's version has not been reprinted since the early 1970s. The present Wordsworth edition follows the text of the 1934 edition.

INTRODUCTION TO
THE LAST TYCOON

This new edition of *Tender is the Night* is accompanied by the incomplete text of *The Last Tycoon* that Fitzgerald left at his death on 21 December 1940. At that point Fitzgerald had completed seventeen episodes of a novel that began to take shape in September 1938 while he was on contract to Metro-Goldywn-Mayer. He had intended to write a novel of around 50,000–60,000 words, comparable in length to *The Great Gatsby*, and conceived structurally in much the same way, but the text of the novel his friend, the critic Edmund Wilson, published in 1941 (in an edition that included *The Great Gatsby* and selected stories) ran to about 70,000 words. Clearly Fitzgerald had underestimated the scope of his project and there are clear indications in both his correspondence and his various outline drafts that the finished work would have had a scale comparable to that of *Tender is the Night*. At the time of his death (he suffered a heart attack in November 1940 and a cardiac spasm and second heart attack on 20 December 1940), Sheilah Graham, his mistress, sent the unfinished manuscript and many of Fitzgerald's working notes to Max Perkins, Fitzgerald's editor at the publishing house of Charles Scribner's Sons in New York City. She asked Perkins to pay particular attention to a remark in which Fitzgerald spoke of his intention to recapture his readership and, indeed, of how his new novel was aimed at two generations of readers, 'for seventeen as symbolised by Scottie [his daughter, Frances Scott Fitzgerald, born in 1921] and for Edmund Wilson at forty-five'. Fitzgerald was aware that he had lost the readership he enjoyed in the 1920s; he was seen as a novelist of the pre-Depression era, the laureate of the Jazz Age, and in a decade of economic and political uncertainty and upheaval his identification with the lives of the rich and leisured classes (particularly as they had been dramatised in *Tender is the Night*) did not endear him to critics who thought of fiction as something co-extensive with social realism and political agitation. Reminiscing about Fitzgerald in his essay 'Fitzgerald in Hollywood', published shortly after Fitzgerald's death, Budd Schulberg, the novelist whose *The Disenchanted* (1950) is a fictional portrait of Fitzgerald's last years, wrote of how, when the Depression came, ' . . . we consciously and a little belligerently turned our backs on Fitzgerald'. Friends and colleagues, Schulberg recalls, 'protested that they couldn't read him'. And some 'had never heard of him'. Fitzgerald's intention to recapture his reader-ship, therefore, is evidence of his eagerness to find his fictional feet again after subordinating his talents to the demands of Hollywood, and of his understanding of his new novel as something different in kind from his earlier writings. At the end of January 1941 Perkins wrote to Graham to inform her that he had not yet decided what to do with Fitzgerald's manuscript. Conscious of the effort that Fitzgerald had put into the work during the prolonged periods of illness and depression that he experienced over the last few years of his life, Graham pleaded with Perkins to bring the novel to press. Perkins consulted the journalist and critic Gilbert Seldes, and Seldes was sufficiently impressed to recommend publication. Perkins reported his plans to publish *The Last Tycoon* to John Biggs, Fitzgerald's literary executor, noting in his letter to him that 'it has the same old magic that Scott got into a sentence, or a paragraph, or a phrase . . . It was to have been a very remarkable book.' His letter to Biggs counted the novel at around 56,000 words, but this might well have been a very cursory calculation. It was thought by Perkins and Seldes that Edmund Wilson, who had known Fitzgerald since their days together at Princeton University in 1915 and whose reviews of Fitzgerald had consistently articulated a sympathetic and perceptive response to his work, would be the person best-placed to write an explanatory introduction. Perkins further persuaded Wilson to edit the existing manuscript in such a way that it approached the form and structure of a finished work and to summarise, as far as was reasonably possible, how the novel would have unfolded. The novel was to be published along with *The Great Gatsby* and a selection of Fitzgerald's major short stories that included 'May Day', 'The Diamond as Big as the Ritz', 'The Rich Boy' and 'Crazy Sunday', all of them, other than 'Crazy Sunday', writings from the 1920s. The intention was clear, to reacquaint Fitzgerald with his readers by reprinting his greatest finished achievement in fiction alongside some of his greatest short stories in the company of a work that in Wilson's eyes, even in its unfinished state, was 'Fitz-gerald's most mature piece of work'. *The Last Tycoon: An Unfinished Novel, together with The Great Gatsby, and Selected Short Stories* was published in New York by Charles Scribner's Sons on 27 October 1941. By December 1941, a year after Fitzgerald's death, the novel had gone into its second printing and the critical response to his work, affirming, as is so often the case, Samuel Johnson's assertion in his *Preface to Shakespeare* that 'While an author is yet living we estimate his powers by his worst performance, and when he is dead we rate them by his best', was almost uniformly positive. There can be little doubt that the publication of *The Last Tycoon* was responsible for the 'Fitzgerald revival' and for what is his commanding presence in any history of twentieth-century American fiction.

Background and Genesis

Fitzgerald's connections with Hollywood began in 1923 when he sold the film rights for his first novel, *This Side of Paradise*, for $10,000. In December 1926 he was approached by United Artists Studios to work on a film about college life entitled *Lipstick*. The star was Constance Talmadge, one of the most popular actresses of the day, and Fitzgerald's salary of $12,000 for about ten week's work was equal to about eight times the average yearly salary for a skilled industrial worker ($3,500 was paid to Fitzgerald initially, however, the remainder only to be paid if the studio decided to use his script). The work was more demanding than he expected but one important consequence of his stay in California (though he could not at the time have realised it) was his meeting with Irving Thalberg, then, even at the young age of twenty-three, Second Vice-President and Supervisor of Productions at MGM Studios. MGM was in its 'golden age' and the studios' imaginative response to the moving image and its cultivation of a talented group of new actors, among them Clark Gable, Jean Harlow and Myrna Loy, had helped cement its centrality in a rapidly-expanding business. MGM had been the first studio to experiment with Technicolor and careful management of its considerable commercial assets ensured that it was the only Hollywood studio to pay dividends to its stockholders during the Depression years of the 1930s. Many of its films were sophisticated and urbane, intended for metropolitan audiences, and Thalberg, though conscious of the demands of a mass-entertainment industry, rarely compromised on artistic and literary matters. His name never appeared on any film credit but under his leadership MGM made the silent films of *Ben Hur* and *The Hunchback of Notre Dame*, and the sound films of *Marie Antoinette*, starring Thalberg's wife Norma Shearer, and Max Reinhardt's screen version of Shakespeare's *A Midsummer Night's Dream*. Fitzgerald made a second visit to Hollywood in November 1931 on a five-week contract with MGM to work on *Red-Headed Woman* at $1,200 a week. Again Thalberg was in charge but his introduction of the system whereby several screenwriters worked simultaneously on the same script, memorably recreated in Chapter 2 of *The Last Tycoon*, alienated Fitzgerald who had gone to California as, of course, a 'major' writer and who sensed that his talent was being debased by this new art form. But the figure of Thalberg loomed large in Fitzgerald's imagination and there is a fictional portrait of him in the 1932 story 'Crazy Sunday', selected, very appropriately, by Wilson for inclusion in the 1941 edition of the novel. Joel Coles, a Hollywood screenwriter, is clearly a self-portrait and his embarrassment at a party thrown by Miles Calman, a Hollywood producer, where he collapses in a drunken stupor, allegedly fictionalises Fitzgerald's own experience. Calman is a 'version' of Thalberg, and Fitzgerald's love-hate relationship with the producer is enacted in the somewhat contradictory tone of the story: Calman initially seems pathetic, his prejudice towards heavy drinkers a reaction generated by his ill-health, but after his death he assumes heroic proportions and Joel remarks of him that 'Everything he touched he did something magical to . . . ' Anticipating Stahr's death, Calman dies in a plane accident. The story is evidence of how a man like Thalberg was taking fictional shape in Fitzgerald's mind: 'At certain moments,' Fitzgerald remarked in his notes for *The Last Tycoon*, 'one man appropriates to himself the total significance of a time and place.' Clearly Thalberg was assuming, in the sense in which it is articulated by Ralph Waldo Emerson, the status of a 'Representative Man', and it was only after Thalberg's death from pneumonia (he had had rheumatic fever as a child and suffered a major heart attack in 1932) on 14 September 1936 that Fitzgerald grasped his intelligence, insight, diligence and executive talents, qualities that no doubt, in Fitzgerald's eyes, made him 'an epic figure', someone who could be appropriated to a sense of national destiny.

While recovering from an injury to his shoulder in 1936, Fitzgerald wrote to Maxwell Perkins of a new novel, and his biographers have speculated that Thalberg's death at the age of thirty-seven had prompted Fitzgerald to conceive a 'Hollywood novel' with a 'Conradian' hero at its centre, a great man whose fall is compounded both by personal, internal weaknesses and by the machinations of those immediately around him. Important evidence of the way in which Fitzgerald was to dramatise his hero comes in an (unsent) letter he wrote to the actress Norma Shearer, Thalberg's wife, after his death. Fitzgerald writes of his attempt to 'preserve something of Irving', of the 'dazzling effect' Thalberg had on him, and of his invention of a 'tragic story . . . Irving's life was, of course, not tragic except his struggle against ill health . . . because no one has written a tragedy about Hollywood . . . ' As Stahr took shape in his mind (at one point, tellingly, in his notes he refers to him as 'Irving'), so his epical and heroic qualities brought other great men to mind. Fitzgerald's reading as he worked on his novel included biographies of Julius Caesar, the Duke of Wellington, Robert E. Lee, Ulysses S. Grant and William Tecumseh Sherman, who was both soldier and businessman. In the novel this reading finds its outlet in the invocation of two great figures from American history: at the beginning while the plane *en route* to Los Angeles is grounded by the storm, the writer Wylie White drives the narrator, Cecilia, to the home of Andrew Jackson outside Nashville; later the developing analogy between Stahr and other great figures from American history is reinforced when Prince Agge, the Danish nobleman who is visiting the studio commissary, sees an actor dressed as Abraham Lincoln. The two presidents have been carefully chosen, Jackson for his strength and his ability to take on enemies in various camps, Lincoln for his compassion, his vision, and his understanding that enemies are best kept close, particularly if you want to anticipate their next move. One further aspect of the 'Lincolnian' qualities of Stahr is Fitzgerald's decision to make his hero's origins more lowly than they were in real life: Thalberg's background was solidly middle-class, his father a successful importer of lace, whilst Stahr's impoverished origins in the Bronx, a borough of New York City, more clearly identify him with the 'rags to riches' myth of Abraham Lincoln. The invocation of these two great figures further emphasises the tragedy of Stahr's death: they belong to an heroic age much as Stahr is an heroic figure in an age that has no demand for heroes beyond those it creates fantastically on the screen. By early 1940 Thalberg's 'reinvention' as Stahr had been fully realised and Fitzgerald could write of completing the first draft of the novel in the space of about a month, despite his suffering a cardiac spasm in late November. A second heart attack on 20 December, however, proved terminal and he died on 21 December 1940 at 5.15 p.m. leaving *The Last Tycoon* unfinished.

The Novel

Fitzgerald was confident about his new novel. At the end of his synopsis of the plot in his letter of 29 September 1939 to Kenneth Littauer, he concluded:

> There's nothing that worries me in the novel, nothing that seems uncertain. Unlike *Tender is the Night* it is not the story of deterioration – it is not depressing and not morbid in spite of the tragic ending. If one could ever be more 'like' another I should say it is more 'like' *The Great Gatsby* than any other of my books. But I hope it will be entirely different – I hope it will be something new, arouse new emotions, perhaps even a new way of looking at certain phenomena. I have set it safely in a period of five years ago to obtain detachment, but now that Europe is tumbling about our ears this also seems to be for the best. It is an escape into a lavish, romantic past that perhaps will not come again into our time. It is certainly a novel I would like to read. Shall I write it?

The enigmatic quality of some of the remarks here, ' a new way of looking at certain phenomena . . . ', 'an escape into a lavish, romantic past . . . ', might suggest that Fitzgerald was uncertain of his grip or his focus, but the verisimilitude and attention to detail in *The Last Tycoon* is evidence of how far he had progressed from the overt romanticising that had attended his characterisation of Amory Blaine in *This Side of Paradise* and Jay Gatsby in *The Great Gatsby*. Fitzgerald had warned himself against waking 'the Tarkington ghosts' in one of his notes to the novel, an injunction that he was to avoid the genteel sentimentalism and moral equivocations of the Indiana-born author, best known for *The Magnificent Ambersons*. Here his central character is as wholly convincing as the world in which he is embedded. The opening chapter, one of the most perfectly realised beginnings in Fitzgerald's fiction, exemplifies the mature control and rediscovered confidence of his writing at this late stage in his life. The narrator is Cecilia Brady, a junior-year student at Bennington College who is on her way home to Los Angeles for the summer. *En route*, the plane in which she is travelling is grounded in Nashville, Tennessee. Also on board the plane is a film producer: 'In the corridor of the plane I ran into Monroe Stahr and fell all over him, or wanted to.' Cecilia has known Stahr since she was seven when he joined her father's 'picture business' as a partner. She is both the daughter of Stahr's most

prominent antagonist and is half in love with him. As their plane
finally approaches Glendale Airport at the end of the chapter,
Cecilia, looking back equipped with her Conradian locution, 'Years
later . . . ', is able to understand the magnitude of Stahr's role both
narrowly in the rapidly growing industry of movie-making and,
more broadly, his place in the economic and social destiny of the
United States:

> The California moon was out, huge and orange over the Pacific.
> However I happened to feel about these things – and they were
> home, after all – I know that Stahr must have felt much more.
> These were the things I had first opened my eyes on, like the
> sheep on the back lot of the old Laemmle studio; but this was
> where Stahr had come to earth after that extraordinary illuminat-
> ing flight where he saw which way we were going, and how we
> looked doing it, and how much of it mattered. You could say that
> this was where an accidental wind blew him, but I don't think so. I
> would rather think that in a 'long shot' he saw a new way of
> measuring our jerky hopes and graceful rogueries and awkward
> sorrows, and that he came here from choice to be with us to the
> end. Like the plane coming down into the Glendale airport, into
> the warm darkness.   [p. 284]

What Cecilia says here, of course, enlarges our comprehension of
what Fitzgerald meant in his letter to Littaeur by 'a new way of
looking at certain phenomena . . . ' and 'a lavish, romantic past . . . '
for Stahr is both at the forefront of the business of modernity
embodied in the film industry and, as the adjective 'last' before
'tycoon' informs us, already on his final descent, as is symbolised
here as the plane drops into the airport. He is compared to 'the
Emperor and the Old Guard', a reference both to Napoleon
Bonaparte and to the Imperial Guard of veteran soldiers that made
up one of his elite divisions. Stahr, Cecilia informs us at the
conclusion of Chapter 2, 'was the hero', to his employees and
associates 'he was their man, the last of the princes'. But the 'old
loyalties' are under pressure, both from the economic downturn
brought on by the Great Depression and from the growing power
of the Hollywood unions and the internecine fighting for position
and influence in an industry whose youthful idealism and urgent
innovations had quickly deteriorated into a preoccupation with
money, competitive acquisition, and business corruption. Strikingly, in a symbolic geography that echoes that of *The Great Gatsby*,
Stahr is associated with the West while his antagonist Brady,

Cecilia's father, is associated with the East. And, equally strikingly, Stahr's 'Western qualities' make him the 'artist', an aesthetic frontiersman, deeply concerned with the quality of the films he makes and their role as a 'public art', while the East represents the 'merchant' concerned only with commercial rewards.

The narrative method Fitzgerald employs in *The Last Tycoon* took him back to the 'selective' method of *The Great Gatsby* and he spoke of *The Last Tycoon* as being 'more like *The Great Gatsby* than any of his other books'. Cecilia Brady's position is in many ways comparable to that of Nick Carraway, the narrator of *The Great Gatsby*, but the combination of involvement and detachment in her commentary offers her advantages that his earlier narrator did not enjoy. Unlike Nick, she plays a direct role in the unfolding plot for it she who tells her father of Stahr's secret affair with Kathleen, thus giving Brady the basis for his subsequent plans to blackmail Stahr. Her love for Stahr also enables her to avoid the kind of juvenile romanticism that occasionally attends on Nick's portrait of Gatsby, for while her emotional reactions guide us towards our sense of Stahr's heroism, even his 'fabulousness', she is equally able, and, indeed, intelligent enough, to chronicle a working day in Stahr's life with exactness and precision and the appropriate degree of observational detachment. What is apparent again in Fitzgerald's use of Cecilia is his indebtedness to Joseph Conrad (he put *Nostromo* sixth on his list of the ten novels he had most enjoyed). This was not merely a matter of his learning from Conrad the value of employing a 'middleman' narrator as a means by which to achieve 'selection' rather than 'saturation' in fiction. He was also drawn to Conrad's dramatisations of human aspirations and human destiny, and as we have seen, Stahr is in many ways conceived as a 'Conradian hero'. But it is clearly the 'technical' Conrad he is thinking of when he spoke in his synoptic letter to Littauer of granting himself 'the privilege, as Conrad did', of letting his narrator, Cecilia, imagine the actions of the characters. Some critics have argued that the reader may be disconcerted by the frequent interruptions of 'This is Cecilia taking up the narrative in person', but Fitzgerald's disarming honesty indicates how far he had come from the narrative uncertainty that accompanies the concluding three chapters (7–9) of *The Great Gatsby*, where his narrator Nick Carraway's absence from many of the important and dramatic events that drive the novel towards its conclusion finds Nick increasingly adopting, unsatisfactorily, the posture of an omniscient commentator. Here the alternating perspectives of the narrative as we move from Cecilia's first-person reporting to her quasi-omniscient recording of scenes and events where she is not present (for example, in Chapters 3 and 4) recalls the narrative method of *Under Western Eyes*. And, like Conrad's unnamed narrator in that novel, Cecilia looks back and 'fills in', gathering information from other participants in Stahr's life, from Wylie White, from Prince Agge, from Robinson, the 'cutter' or cameraman (who in an earlier version of the story was to have had an affair with Kathleen), and from one of the pilots mentioned in Chapter 1, so much so that Fitzgerald invites the reader to participate actively in the creation of his story, to become, in effect a co-creator with Cecilia. Academic criticism and scholarship makes far too much of the importance of the illusion of reality in fiction and the common reader is rarely exercised by the problems of reliability and perspective raised in theoretical commentary on the first-person narrator. The intelligent reader is always conscious of the artifice. Cecilia's narrative allows for the concentration, foreshortening and the kind of elliptical compression to the relationship between character and incident ('ACTION IS CHARACTER,' Fitzgerald had famously remarked in his notes to the novel) that gives the novel its concision and its dramatic urgency.

It should also be noted that one of the great achievements of *The Last Tycoon* is its evocation of the world of work and Edmund Wilson was right in his Foreword to his edition of the manuscript to state that it is marked off from Fitzgerald's 'other novels by the fact that it is the first to deal seriously with any profession or business'. The first five chapters take us into the world of the Hollywood studios and their executive offices, Fitzgerald concerning himself with the business of film-making rather than its effects on those who inhabit the underworld of Hollywood (as is the case with the other great Hollywood novel of the period, Nathanael West's *The Day of the Locust* [1939]) or that great amorphous mass of Americans who constituted its audience. In *Tender is the Night* we saw little of its protagonist, Dick Diver, a psychiatrist, at work; here we see Stahr working almost relentlessly and watch him orchestrate a complex and intricate world of writers, scriptwriters, cameramen, editors, actors, both famous and unknown, secretaries, stock-holders, investors and bankers. Few American novels of the period are as alive with the details of business and, as one critic remarked, 'every page is packed with things happening'. Stahr is identified by his work: we see him rushing from one activity to another with barely a pause for thought or contemplation; he works late into the evenings, and only gives up Sundays to cultivate his love affair with

Kathleen, and when he meets her he is 'breathless'. This emphasis on work, however, has a wider application: it lends Stahr that sense of purpose, perseverance and decisiveness that makes him an essentially Protestant hero, his links with his Bronx Jewish upbringing severed and replaced by the association of moral integrity and moral authority with the world of professional work, and in this respect it is tempting to see Fitzgerald's hero as, in part, autobiographical, expressing, somewhat tragically in the light of the novel's unfinished state, Fitzgerald own sense, shared no doubt with Conrad and his friend and contemporary Ernest Hemingway, that his importance in other men's eyes was to be judged on what he had created and that this final text was offered to the public as, in the old-fashioned sense, an act of labour, a piece of work.

The Last Tycoon has the unavoidable deficiencies that arise from an incomplete work and any attempt to infer the final shape of the novel from the partially completed manuscript and the plethora of notes, synopses, character sketches and outlines that Fitzgerald left at his death will almost certainly issue in a distorted vision of his achievement. The text that Edmund Wilson supplied resembled a partially finished work, whereas the working drafts indicate areas of uncertainty in emphasis, event, mood and tone that would, no doubt, have been polished and refined at a later stage. The very absence of a final title and the somewhat inchoate notes for the conclusion in the diagram of his last outline reinforce our sense that Fitzgerald had not yet settled many of the narrative questions his work had raised. But what we have here is conclusive proof that even the incomplete works of major writers have an aesthetic and moral value that goes well beyond many 'finished' works. The English novelist J. B. Priestley, reviewing *The Last Tycoon*, wrote: 'I would rather have written this unfinished novel than the total works of some widely admired American novelists.' But Max Perkins put the case for the novel more compellingly when he wrote to Sheilah Graham with his 'progress report' in January 1941: 'All I know is that it promised to be the most completely mature, and rich, and in a deep sense the most brilliant book he ever did. I think Stahr, though incomplete, is his best character . . . It would break a man's heart to see what this book would have been, and that it wasn't finished.'

HENRY CLARIDGE
University of Kent

BIBLIOGRAPHY

Bibliography

Matthew J. Bruccoli, *The Composition of 'Tender is the Night'*, University of Pittsburgh Press, 1963

Matthew J. Bruccoli, *F. Scott Fitzgerald: A Descriptive Bibliography*, University of Pittsburgh Press, 1987

Matthew J. Bruccoli and Judith S. Baughman, *Reader's Companion to F. Scott Fitzgerald's 'Tender is the Night'*, University of South Carolina Press, 1996

Robert L. Gale, *An F. Scott Fitzgerald Encyclopaedia*, Greenwood Press, London, 1998

Mary Jo Tate, *F. Scott Fitzgerald A to Z: The Essential Reference to His Life and Work*, Facts on File, New York, 1998

Biography and Letters

Matthew J. Bruccoli (ed.), *As Ever, Scott Fitz-: Letters Between F. Scott Fitzgerald and His Literary Agent, Harold Ober, 1919–1940*, Lippincott, New York, 1972

Matthew J. Bruccoli and Margaret Duggan (eds), *Correspondence of F. Scott Fitzgerald*, Random House, New York, 1980

Matthew J. Bruccoli, *Some Sort of Epic Grandeur: The Life of F. Scott Fitzgerald*, Carroll & Graf, New York, 1993

Matthew J. Bruccoli, *F. Scott Fitzgerald: A Life in Letters*, Charles Scribner's Sons, New York, 1994

Scott Donaldson, *Fool for Love*, Congdon & Weed, New York, 1983

Sheilah Graham, *College of One*, Viking Press, New York, 1967

Ernest Hemingway, *A Moveable Feast*, Jonathan Cape, London, 1964

John Kuehl and Jackson R. Bryer (eds), *Dear Scott/Dear Max: The Fitzgerald–Perkins Correspondence*, Charles Scribner's Sons, New York, 1971

André F. Le Vot, *F. Scott Fitzgerald: A Biography*, Doubleday & Co., New York, 1963

Sara Mayfield, *Exiles from Paradise: Zelda and Scott Fitzgerald*, Delacorte Press, New York, 1971

James R. Mellow, *Invented Lives: F. Scott & Zelda Fitzgerald*,
  Ballantine Books, New York, 1984

Linda Patterson Miller, *Letters from the Lost Generation: Gerald and
  Sara Murphy and Friends*, Rutgers University Press, New
  Brunswick, New Jersey, 1991

Arthur Mizener, *The Far Side of Paradise: A Biography of F. Scott
  Fitzgerald*, Houghton Mifflin, Boston, 1951

Ruth Prigozy, *F. Scott Fitzgerald*, Overlook Press, Woodstock, New
  York, 2001

Edward J. Reilly, *F Scott Fitzgerald: A Biography*, Greenwood Press,
  Westport, Connecticut, 2005

Andrew Turnbull, *Scott Fitzgerald*, Charles Scribner's Sons, New
  York, 1962

Andrew Turnbull (ed.), *The Letters of F. Scott Fitzgerald*, Charles
  Scribner's Sons, 1963

Critical Studies and Collections of Essays

Joan M. Allen, *Candles and Carnival Lights: The Catholic Sensibility of
  F. Scott Fitzgerald*, New York University Press, 1978

James Barbour and Tom Quirk (eds), *Writing the American Classics*,
  University of North Carolina Press, 1990

Wayne C. Booth, *The Rhetoric of Fiction*, University of Chicago
  Press, 1961

Matthew J. Bruccoli, *Last of the Novelists: F. Scott Fitzgerald and 'The
  Last Tycoon'*, Southern Illinois University Press, Carbondale,
  1977

Jackson R. Bryer, *The Critical Reputation of F. Scott Fitzgerald*,
  Archon Books, New Haven, 1967

Jackson R. Bryer (ed.), *F. Scott Fitzgerald: The Critical Reception*,
  Burt Franklin & Co. Ltd, New York, 1978

Jackson R. Bryer, Alan Margolies and Ruth Prigozy (eds), *F. Scott
  Fitzgerald: New Perspectives*, University of Georgia Press, Athens,
  Georgia, 2000

John F. Callahan, *The Illusions of Nation: Myth and History in the
  Novels of F. Scott Fitzgerald*, University of Illinois Press, Urbana,
  Illinois, 1972

John B. Chambers, *The Novels of F. Scott Fitzgerald*, Macmillan,
  London, 1990

Henry Claridge (ed.), *F. Scott Fitzgerald: Critical Assessments*, 4 vols, Helm Information, Robertsbridge, East Sussex, 1992

Malcolm Cowley, *Exile's Return*, Viking Press, New York, 1951

K. G. W. Cross, *F. Scott Fitzgerald*, Oliver and Boyd, Edinburgh, 1964

Kenneth Eble (ed.), *F. Scott Fitzgerald: A Collection of Criticism*, McGraw-Hill, New York, 1973

Andrew Hook, *F. Scott Fitzgerald*, Edward Arnold, London, 1992

Alfred Kazin (ed.), *F. Scott Fitzgerald: The Man and His Work*, World Publishing, Cleveland, 1951

J. Gerald Kennedy, *Imagining Paris: Exile, Writing, and American Identity*, Yale University Press, New Haven, 1993

J. Gerald Kennedy and Jackson R. Bryer (eds), *French Connections: Hemingway and Fitzgerald Abroad*, St Martin's Press, New York, 1998

Hugh Kenner, *A Homemade World: The American Modernist Writers*, Alfred A. Knopf, New York, 1975

A. Robert Lee (ed.), *F. Scott Fitzgerald: The Promises of Life*, Vision Press, London, 1989

Richard D. Lehan, *F. Scott Fitzgerald and the Craft of Fiction*, Southern Illinois University Press, Carbondale, Illinois, 1966

James E. Miller, *F. Scott Fitzgerald: His Art and Technique*, New York University Press, 1964

Arthur Mizener, *F. Scott Fitzgerald: A Collection of Critical Essays*, Prentice-Hall, Englewood Cliffs, New Jersey, 1963

Arthur Mizener, *Scott Fitzgerald and His World*, Thames and Hudson, London, 1972

Kathleen Parkinson, *'Tender is the Night': A Critical Study*, Penguin Books, Harmondsworth, 1986

Sergio Perosa, *The Art of F. Scott Fitzgerald*, University of Michigan Press, 1965

Larry W. Phillips (ed.), *F. Scott Fitzgerald on Writing*, Charles Scribner's Sons, New York, 1985

Henry Dan Piper, *F. Scott Fitzgerald: A Critical Portrait*, Bodley Head, London, 1965

Donald Pizer, *American Expatriate Writing and the Paris Moment*, Louisiana State University Press, Baton Rouge, 1996

Ruth Prigozy (ed.), *The Cambridge Companion to F. Scott Fitzgerald*, Cambridge University Press, 2001

Charles E. Shain, *F. Scott Fitzgerald*, University of Minnesota Press, 1961

Robert Sklar, *F. Scott Fitzgerald: The Last Laocoön*, Oxford University Press, 1967

Thomas J. Stavola, *F. Scott Fitzgerald: Crisis in an American Identity*, Vision Press, London, 1979

Milton R. Stern, *The Golden Moment: The Novels of F. Scott Fitzgerald*, University of Illinois Press, 1970

Milton R. Stern (ed.), *Critical Essays on F. Scott Fitzgerald's 'Tender is the Night'*, G. K. Hall, Boston, 1986

Milton R. Stern, *'Tender is the Night': The Broken Universe*, Twayne Publishers, New York, 1994

Brian Way, *F. Scott Fitzgerald and the Art of Social Fiction*, Edward Arnold, London, 1980

TENDER IS THE NIGHT

A Romance

◆

F. Scott Fitzgerald

Already with thee! tender is the night
      . . . But here there is no light,
Save what from heaven is with breezes blown
Through verdurous glooms and winding mossy ways.

'Ode to a Nightingale'[1]

TO
GERALD AND SARA

MANY FÊTES[2]

BOOK ONE

Chapter 1

ON THE PLEASANT SHORE of the French Riviera, about halfway between Marseilles and the Italian border, stands a large, proud, rose-coloured hotel. Deferential palms cool its flushed façade, and before it stretches a short dazzling beach. Lately it has become a summer resort of notable and fashionable people; a decade ago it was almost deserted after its English clientele went north in April. Now, many bungalows cluster near it, but when this story begins only the cupolas of a dozen old villas rotted like water-lilies among the massed pines between Gausse's Hôtel des Étrangers[3] and Cannes, five miles away.

The hotel and its bright tan prayer rug of a beach were one. In the early morning the distant image of Cannes, the pink and cream of old fortifications, the purple Alps that bounded Italy, were cast across the water and lay quavering in the ripples and rings sent up by sea-plants through the clear shallows. Before eight a man came down to the beach in a blue bathrobe and with much preliminary application to his person of the chilly water, and much grunting and loud breathing, floundered a minute in the sea. When he had gone, beach and bay were quiet for an hour. Merchantmen crawled westward on the horizon; bus boys shouted in the hotel court; the dew dried upon the pines. In another hour the horns of motors began to blow down from the winding road along the low range of the Maures,[4] which separates the littoral from true Provençal France.

A mile from the sea, where pines give way to dusty poplars, is an isolated railroad stop, whence one June morning in 1925 a victoria brought a woman and her daughter down to Gausse's Hôtel. The mother's face was of a fading prettiness that would soon be patted with broken veins; her expression was both tranquil and aware in a pleasant way. However, one's eyes moved on quickly to her daughter, who had magic in her pink palms and her cheeks lit to a lovely flame, like the thrilling flush of children after their cold bath in the evening.

Her fine high forehead sloped gently up to where her hair, bordering it like an armorial shield, burst into lovelocks and waves and curlicues of ash blonde and gold. Her eyes were bright, big, clear, wet, and shining, the colour of her cheeks was real, breaking close to the surface from the strong young pump of her heart. Her body hovered delicately on the last edge of childhood – she was almost eighteen, nearly complete, but the dew was still on her.

As sea and sky appeared below them in a thin, hot line the mother said: 'Something tells me we're not going to like this place.'

'I want to go home anyhow,' the girl answered.

They both spoke cheerfully but were obviously without direction and bored by the fact – moreover, just any direction would not do. They wanted high excitement, not from the necessity of stimulating jaded nerves but with the avidity of prize-winning schoolchildren who deserved their vacations.

'We'll stay three days and then go home. I'll wire right away for steamer tickets.'

At the hotel the girl made the reservation in idiomatic but rather flat French, like something remembered. When they were installed on the ground floor she walked into the glare of the French windows and out a few steps on to the stone veranda that ran the length of the hotel. When she walked she carried herself like a ballet-dancer, not slumped down on her hips but held up in the small of her back. Out there the hot light clipped close her shadow and she retreated – it was too bright to see. Fifty yards away the Mediterranean yielded up its pigments, moment by moment, to the brutal sunshine; below the balustrade a faded Buick cooked on the hotel drive.

Indeed, of all the region only the beach stirred with activity. Three British nannies sat knitting the slow pattern of Victorian England, the pattern of the forties, the sixties, and the eighties, into sweaters and socks, to the tune of gossip as formalised as incantation; closer to the sea a dozen persons kept house under striped umbrellas, while their dozen children pursued unintimidated fish through the shallows or lay naked and glistening with coconut oil out in the sun.

As Rosemary came on to the beach a boy of twelve ran past her and dashed into the sea with exultant cries. Feeling the impactive scrutiny of strange faces, she took off her bathrobe and followed. She floated face down for a few yards and finding it shallow staggered to her feet and plodded forward, dragging slim legs like weights against the resistance of the water. When it was about breast high, she glanced back towards the shore: a bald man in a monocle and a pair of tights, his tufted chest thrown out, his brash navel sucked in, was regarding her attentively. As Rosemary returned the gaze the man dislodged the monocle, which went into hiding amid the facetious whiskers of his chest, and poured himself a glass of something from a bottle in his hand.

Rosemary laid her face on the water and swam a choppy little four-beat crawl out to the raft. The water reached up for her, pulled her down tenderly out of the heat, seeped in her hair and ran into the corners of her body. She turned round and round in it, embracing it, wallowing in it. Reaching the raft she was out of breath, but a tanned woman with very white teeth looked down at her, and Rosemary, suddenly conscious of the raw whiteness of her own body, turned on her back and drifted towards the shore. The hairy man holding the bottle spoke to her as she came out.

'I say – they have sharks out behind the raft.' He was of indeterminate nationality, but spoke English with a slow Oxford drawl. 'Yesterday they devoured two British sailors from the *flotte* at Golfe Juan.'[5]

'Heavens!' exclaimed Rosemary.

'They come in for the refuse from the *flotte*.'

Glazing his eyes to indicate that he had only spoken in order to warn her, he minced off two steps and poured himself another drink.

Not unpleasantly self-conscious, since there had been a slight sway of attention towards her during this conversation, Rosemary looked for a place to sit. Obviously each family possessed the strip of sand immediately in front of its umbrella; besides there was much visiting and talking back and forth – the atmosphere of a community upon which it would be presumptuous to intrude. Farther up, where the beach was strewn with pebbles and dead seaweed, sat a group with flesh as white as her own. They lay under small hand-parasols instead of beach umbrellas and were obviously less indigenous to the place. Between the dark people and the light, Rosemary found room and spread out her peignoir on the sand.

Lying so, she first heard their voices and felt their feet skirt her body and their shapes pass between the sun and herself. The breath of an inquisitive dog blew warm and nervous on her neck; she could feel her skin broiling a little in the heat and hear the small exhausted wa-waa of the expiring waves. Presently her ear distinguished individual voices and she became aware that someone referred to scornfully as 'that North guy' had kidnapped a waiter from a café in Cannes last night in order to saw him in two. The sponsor of the story was a white-haired woman in full evening dress, obviously a relic of the previous evening, for a tiara still clung to her head and a discouraged orchid expired from her shoulder. Rosemary, forming a vague antipathy to her and her companions, turned away.

Nearest her, on the other side, a young woman lay under a roof of umbrellas making out a list of things from a book open on the sand. Her bathing suit was pulled off her shoulders, and her back, a ruddy, orange brown, set off by a string of creamy pearls, shone in the sun. Her face was hard and lovely and pitiful. Her eyes met Rosemary's but did not see her. Beyond her was a fine man in a jockey cap and red-striped tights; then the woman Rosemary had seen on the raft, and who looked back at her, seeing her; then a man with a long face and a golden, leonine head, with blue tights and no hat, talking very seriously to an unmistakably Latin young man in black tights, both of them picking at little pieces of seaweed in the sand. She thought they were mostly Americans, but something made them unlike the Americans she had known of late.

After a while she realised that the man in the jockey cap was giving a quiet little performance for this group; he moved gravely about with a rake, ostensibly removing gravel and meanwhile developing some esoteric burlesque held in suspension by his grave face. Its faintest ramification had become hilarious, until whatever he said released a burst of laughter. Even those who, like herself, were too far away to hear, sent out antennæ of attention until the only person on the beach not caught up in it was the young woman with the string of pearls. Perhaps from modesty of possession she responded to each salvo of amusement by bending closer over her list.

The man of the monocle and bottle spoke suddenly out of the sky above Rosemary.

'You are a ripping swimmer.'

She demurred.

'Jolly good. My name is Campion. Here is a lady who says she saw you in Sorrento last week and knows who you are and would so like to meet you.'

Glancing around with concealed annoyance Rosemary saw the untanned people were waiting. Reluctantly she got up and went over to them.

'Mrs Abrams – Mrs McKisco – Mr McKisco – Mr Dumphry – '

'We know who you are,' spoke up the woman in evening dress. 'You're Rosemary Hoyt and I recognised you in Sorrento and asked the hotel clerk and we all think you're perfectly marvellous and we want to know why you're not back in America making another marvellous moving picture.'

They made a superfluous gesture of moving over for her. The woman who had recognised her was not a Jewess, despite her name. She was one of those elderly 'good sports' preserved by an imperviousness to experience and a good digestion into another generation.

'We wanted to warn you about getting burned the first day,' she continued cheerily, 'because *your* skin is important, but there seems to be so darn much formality on this beach that we didn't know whether you'd mind.'

Chapter 2

'WE THOUGHT MAYBE you were in the plot,' said Mrs McKisco. She was a shabby-eyed, pretty young woman with a disheartening intensity. 'We don't know who's in the plot and who isn't. One man my husband had been particularly nice to turned out to be a chief character – practically the assistant hero.'

'The plot?' enquired Rosemary, half understanding. 'Is there a plot?'

'My dear, we don't *know*,' said Mrs Abrams, with a convulsive, stout woman's chuckle. 'We're not in it. We're the gallery.'

Mr Dumphry, a tow-headed, effeminate young man, remarked: 'Mama Abrams is a plot in herself,' and Campion shook his monocle at him, saying: 'Now, Royal, don't be too ghastly for words.' Rosemary looked at them all uncomfortably, wishing her mother had come down here with her. She did not like these people, especially in her immediate comparison of them with those who had interested her at the other end of the beach. Her mother's modest but compact social gift got them out of unwelcome situations swiftly and firmly. But Rosemary had been a celebrity for only six months, and sometimes the French manners of her early adolescence and the democratic manners of America, these latter superimposed, made a certain confusion and let her in for just such things.

Mr McKisco, a scrawny, freckle-and-red man of thirty, did not find the topic of the 'plot' amusing. He had been staring at the sea – now after a swift glance at his wife he turned to Rosemary and demanded aggressively: 'Been here long?'

'Only a day.'

'Oh.'

Evidently feeling that the subject had been thoroughly changed, he looked in turn at the others.

'Going to stay all summer?' asked Mrs McKisco, innocently. 'If you do you can watch the plot unfold.'

'For God's sake, Violet, drop the subject!' exploded her husband. 'Get a new joke, for God's sake!'

Mrs McKisco swayed towards Mrs Abrams and breathed audibly: 'He's nervous.'

'I'm not nervous,' disagreed McKisco. 'It just happens I'm not nervous at all.'

He was burning visibly – a greyish flush had spread over his face, dissolving all his expressions into a vast ineffectuality. Suddenly remotely conscious of his condition he got up to go in the water, followed by his wife, and seizing the opportunity Rosemary followed.

Mr McKisco drew a long breath, flung himself into the shallows and began a stiff-armed batting of the Mediterranean, obviously intended to suggest a crawl – his breath exhausted he rose and looked around with an expression of surprise that he was still in sight of shore.

'I haven't learned to breathe yet. I never quite understood how they breathed.' He looked at Rosemary enquiringly.

'I think you breathe out under water,' she explained. 'And every fourth beat you roll your head over for air.'

'The breathing's the hardest part for me. Shall we go to the raft?'

The man with the leonine head lay stretched out upon the raft, which tipped back and forth with the motion of the water. As Mrs McKisco reached for it a sudden tilt struck her arm up roughly, whereupon the man started up and pulled her on board.

'I was afraid it hit you.' His voice was slow and shy; he had one of the saddest faces Rosemary had ever seen, the high cheek-bones of an Indian, a longer upper lip, and enormous deep-set dark golden eyes. He had spoken out of the side of his mouth, as if he hoped his words would reach Mrs McKisco by a circuitous and unobtrusive route; in a minute he had shoved off into the water and his long body lay motionless towards the shore.

Rosemary and Mrs McKisco watched him. When he had exhausted his momentum he abruptly bent double, his thin thighs rose above the surface, and he disappeared totally, leaving scarcely a fleck of foam behind.

'He's a good swimmer,' Rosemary said.

Mrs McKisco's answer came with surprising violence.

'Well, he's a rotten musician.' She turned to her husband, who after two unsuccessful attempts had managed to climb on the raft, and having attained his balance was trying to make some kind of compensatory flourish, achieving only an extra stagger. 'I was just saying that Abe North may be a good swimmer but he's a rotten musician.'

'Yes,' agreed McKisco, grudgingly. Obviously he had created his wife's world, and allowed her few liberties in it.

'Antheil's my man.' Mrs McKisco turned challengingly to Rosemary, 'Antheil and Joyce.[6] I don't suppose you ever hear much about those sort of people in Hollywood, but my husband wrote the first criticism of *Ulysses*[7] that ever appeared in America.'

'I wish I had a cigarette,' said McKisco calmly. 'That's more important to me just now.'

'He's got insides – don't you think so, Albert?'

Her voice faded off suddenly. The woman of the pearls had joined her two children in the water, and now Abe North came up under one of them like a volcanic island, raising him on his shoulders. The child yelled with fear and delight and the woman watched with a lovely peace, without a smile.

'Is that his wife?' Rosemary asked.

'No, that's Mrs Diver. They're not at the hotel.' Her eyes, photographic, did not move from the woman's face. After a moment she turned vehemently to Rosemary.

'Have you been abroad before?'

'Yes – I went to school in Paris.'

'Oh! Well then you probably know that if you want to enjoy yourself here the thing is to get to know some real French families. What do these people get out of it?' She pointed her left shoulder towards the shore. 'They just stick around with each other in little cliques. Of course, we had letters of introduction and met all the best French artists and writers in Paris. That made it very nice.'

'I should think so.'

'My husband is finishing his first novel, you see.'

Rosemary said: 'Oh, he is?' She was not thinking anything special, except wondering whether her mother had got to sleep in this heat.

'It's on the idea of *Ulysses*,' continued Mrs McKisco. 'Only instead of taking twenty-four hours my husband takes a hundred years. He takes a decayed old French aristocrat and puts him in contrast with the mechanical age – '

'Oh, for God's sake, Violet, don't go telling everybody the idea,' protested McKisco. 'I don't want it to get all around before the book's published.'

Rosemary swam back to the shore, where she threw her peignoir over her already sore shoulders and lay down again in the sun. The man with the jockey cap was now going from umbrella to umbrella carrying a bottle and little glasses in his hands; presently he and his friends grew livelier and closer together and now they were all under a single assemblage of umbrellas – she gathered that someone was leaving and that this was a last drink on the beach. Even the children knew that excitement was generating under that umbrella and turned towards it – and it seemed to Rosemary that it all came from the man in the jockey cap.

Noon dominated sea and sky – even the white line of Cannes, five miles off, had faded to a mirage of what was fresh and cool; a robin-breasted sailing-boat pulled in behind it a strand from the outer, darker sea. It seemed that there was no life anywhere in all this expanse of coast except under the filtered sunlight of those umbrellas, where something went on amid the colour and the murmur.

Campion walked near her, stood a few feet away and Rosemary closed her eyes, pretending to be asleep; then she half-opened them and watched two dim, blurred pillars that were legs. The man tried to edge his way into a sand-coloured cloud, but the cloud floated off into the vast hot sky. Rosemary fell really asleep.

She awoke drenched with sweat to find the beach deserted save for the man in the jockey cap, who was folding a last umbrella. As Rosemary lay blinking, he walked nearer and said: 'I was going to wake you before I left. It's not good to get too burned right away.'

'Thank you.' Rosemary looked down at her crimson legs. 'Heavens!'

She laughed cheerfully, inviting him to talk, but Dick Diver was already carrying a tent and a beach umbrella up to a waiting car, so she went into the water to wash off the sweat. He came back and gathering up a rake, a shovel, and a sieve, stowed them in a crevice of a rock. He glanced up and down the beach to see if he had left anything.

'Do you know what time it is?' Rosemary asked.

'It's about half-past one.'

They faced the seascape together momentarily.

'It's not a bad time,' said Dick Diver, 'it's not one of the worst times of the day.'

He looked at her and for a moment she lived in the bright blue worlds of his eyes, eagerly and confidently. Then he shouldered his last piece of junk and went up to his car, and Rosemary came out of the water, shook out her peignoir and walked up to the hotel.

Chapter 3

IT WAS ALMOST TWO when they went into the dining-rooms. Back and forth over the deserted tables a heavy pattern of beams and shadows swayed with the motion of the pines outside. Two waiters, piling plates and talking loud Italian, fell silent when they came in and brought them a tired version of the table d'hôte luncheon.

'I fell in love on the beach,' said Rosemary.

'Who with?'

'First with a whole lot of people who looked nice. Then with one man.'

'Did you talk to him?'

'Just a little. Very handsome. With reddish hair.' She was eating, ravenously. 'He's married though – it's usually the way.'

Her mother was her best friend and had put every last possibility into the guiding of her, not so rare a thing in the theatrical profession, but rather special in that Mrs Elsie Speers was not recompensing herself for a defeat of her own. She had no personal bitterness or resentments about life – twice satisfactorily married and twice widowed, her cheerful stoicism had each time deepened. One of her husbands had been a cavalry officer and one an army doctor, and they both left something to her that she tried to present intact to Rosemary. By not sparing Rosemary she had made her hard – by not sparing her own labour and devotion she had cultivated an idealism in Rosemary, which at present was directed towards herself and saw the world through her eyes. So that while Rosemary was a 'simple' child she was protected by a double sheath of her mother's armour and her own – she had a mature distrust of the trivial, the facile and the vulgar. However, with Rosemary's sudden success in pictures Mrs Speers felt that it was time she were spiritually weaned; it would please rather than pain her if this somewhat bouncing, breathless and exigent idealism would focus on something except herself.

'Then you like it here?' she asked.

'It might be fun if we knew those people. There were some other people, but they weren't nice. They recognised me – no matter where we go everybody's seen *Daddy's Girl*.'[8]

Mrs Speers waited for the glow of egotism to subside; then she said in a matter-of-fact way: 'That reminds me, when are you going to see Earl Brady?'[9]

'I thought we might go this afternoon – if you're rested.'

'You go – I'm not going.'

'We'll wait till tomorrow then.'

'I want you to go alone. It's only a short way – it isn't as if you didn't speak French.'

'Mother – aren't there some things I don't have to do?'

'Oh, well, then go later – but some day before we leave.'

'All right, mother.'

After lunch they were both overwhelmed by the sudden flatness that comes over American travellers in quiet foreign places. No stimuli worked upon them, no voices called them from without, no fragments of their own thoughts came suddenly from the minds of others, and missing the clamour of Empire they felt that life was not continuing here.

'Let's only stay three days, mother,' Rosemary said when they were back in their rooms. Outside a light wind blew the heat around, straining it through the trees and sending little hot gusts through the shutters.

'How about the man you fell in love with on the beach?'

'I don't love anybody but you, mother, darling.'

Rosemary stopped in the lobby and spoke to Gausse *père* about trains. The concierge, lounging in light-brown khaki by the desk, stared at her rigidly, then suddenly remembered the manners of his *métier*. She took the bus and rode with a pair of obsequious waiters to the station, embarrassed by their deferential silence, waiting to urge them: 'Go on, talk, enjoy yourselves. It doesn't bother me.'

The first-class compartment was stifling; the vivid advertising cards of the railroad companies – the Pont du Gard at Arles, the Amphitheatre at Orange, winter sports at Chamonix[10] – were fresher than the long motionless sea outside. Unlike American trains that were absorbed in an intense destiny of their own, and scornful of people on another world less swift and breathless, this train was part of the country through which it passed. Its breath stirred the dust from the palm leaves, the cinders mingled with the dry dung in the gardens. Rosemary was sure she could lean from the window and pull flowers with her hand.

A dozen cabbies slept in their hacks outside the Cannes station. Over on the promenade the Casino, the smart shops, and the great hotels turned blank iron masks to the summer sea. It was unbelievable that there could ever have been a 'season', and Rosemary, half in the grip of fashion, became a little self-conscious, as though she were displaying an unhealthy taste for the moribund; as though people were wondering why she was here in the lull between the gaiety of last winter and next winter, while up north the true world thundered by.

As she came out of a drugstore with a bottle of coconut oil, a woman, whom she recognised as Mrs Diver, crossed her path with arms full of sofa cushions, and went to a car parked down the street. A long, low black dog barked at her, a dozing chauffeur woke with a start. She sat in the car, her lovely face set, controlled, her eyes brave and watchful, looking straight ahead towards nothing. Her dress was bright red and her brown legs were bare. She had thick, dark, gold hair like a chow's.

With half an hour to wait for her train Rosemary sat down in the Café des Alliés on the Croisette,[11] where the trees made a green twilight over the tables and an orchestra wooed an imaginary public of cosmopolites with the Nice Carnival Song and last year's American tune. She had bought *Le Temps* and the *Saturday Evening Post*[12] for her mother, and as she drank her citronade she opened the latter at the memoirs of a Russian princess, finding the dim conventions of the nineties realer and nearer than the headlines of the French paper. It was the same feeling that had oppressed her at the hotel – accustomed to seeing the starkest grotesqueries of a continent heavily underlined as comedy or tragedy, untrained to the task of separating out the essential for herself, she now began to feel that French life was empty and stale. This feeling was surcharged by listening to the sad tunes of the orchestra, reminiscent of the melancholy music played for acrobats in vaudeville. She was glad to go back to Gausse's Hôtel.

Her shoulders were too burned to swim with the next day, so she and her mother hired a car – after much haggling, for Rosemary had formed her valuation of money in France – and drove along the Riviera, the delta of many rivers. The chauffeur, a Russian Czar of the period of Ivan the Terrible,[13] was a self-appointed guide, and the resplendent names – Cannes, Nice, Monte Carlo – began to glow through their torpid camouflage, whispering of old kings come here to dine or die, of rajahs tossing Buddha's eyes to English ballerinas, of Russian princes turning the weeks into Baltic twilights in the lost caviare days. Most of all, there was the scent of the Russians along the coast – their closed bookshops and grocery stores. Ten years ago, when the season ended in April, the doors of the Orthodox Church were locked, and the sweet champagnes they favoured were put away until their return. 'We'll be back next season,' they said, but this was premature, for they were never coming back any more.

It was pleasant to drive back to the hotel in the late afternoon, above a sea as mysteriously coloured as the agates and cornelian of childhood, green as green milk, blue as laundry water, wine dark. It was pleasant to pass people eating outside their doors, and to hear the fierce mechanical pianos behind the vines of country estaminets.[14] When they turned off the Corniche d'Or[15] and down to Gausse's Hôtel through the darkening banks of trees, set one behind another in many greens, the moon already hovered over the ruins of the aqueducts . . .

Somewhere in the hills behind the hotel there was a dance, and Rosemary listened to the music through the ghostly moonshine of her mosquito net, realising that there was gaiety too somewhere about, and she thought of the nice people on the beach. She thought she might meet them in the morning, but they obviously formed a self-sufficient little group, and once their umbrellas, bamboo rugs, dogs, and children were set out in place that part of the plage[16] was literally fenced in. She resolved in any case not to spend her last two mornings with the other ones.

Chapter 4

THE MATTER WAS SOLVED for her. The McKiscos were not yet there and she had scarcely spread her peignoir when two men – the man with the jockey cap and the tall blond man, given to sawing waiters in two – left the group and came down towards her.

'Good-morning,' said Dick Diver. He broke down. 'Look – sunburn or no sunburn, why did you stay away yesterday? We worried about you.'

She sat up and her happy little laugh welcomed their intrusion.

'We wondered,' Dick Diver said, 'if you wouldn't come over this morning. We go in, we take food and drink, so it's a substantial invitation.'

He seemed kind and charming – his voice promised that he would take care of her, and that a little later he would open up whole new worlds for her, unroll an endless succession of magnificent possibilities. He managed the introduction so that her name wasn't mentioned and then let her know easily that everyone knew who she was but was respecting the completeness of her private life – a courtesy that Rosemary had not met with save from professional people since her success.

Nicole Diver, her brown back hanging from her pearls, was looking through a recipe book for chicken Maryland. She was about twenty-four, Rosemary guessed – her face could have been described in terms of conventional prettiness, but the effect was that it had been made first on the heroic scale with strong structure and marking, as if the features and vividness of brow and colouring, everything we associate with temperament and character, had been moulded with a Rodinesque[17] intention, and then chiselled away in the direction of prettiness to a point where a single slip would have irreparably diminished its force and quality. With the mouth the sculptor had taken desperate chances – it was the cupid's bow of a magazine cover, yet it shared the distinction of the rest.

'Are you here for a long time?' Nicole asked. Her voice was low, almost harsh.

Suddenly Rosemary let the possibility enter her mind that they might stay another week.

'Not very long,' she answered vaguely. 'We've been abroad a long time – we landed in Sicily in March and we've been slowly working our way north. I got pneumonia making a picture last January and I've been recuperating.'

'Mercy! How did that happen?'

'Well, it was from swimming.' Rosemary was rather reluctant at embarking upon personal revelations. 'One day I happened to have the grippe and didn't know it, and they were taking a scene where I dove into a canal in Venice. It was a very expensive set, so I had to dive and dive and dive all morning. Mother had a doctor right there, but it was no use – I got pneumonia.' She changed the subject determinedly before they could speak. 'Do you like it here – this place?'

'They have to like it,' said Abe North slowly. 'They invented it.' He turned his noble head slowly so that his eyes rested with tenderness and affection on the two Divers.

'Oh, did you?'

'This is only the second season that the hotel's been open in summer,' Nicole explained. 'We persuaded Gausse to keep on a cook and a *garçon* and a *chasseur*[18] – it paid its way and this year it's doing even better.'

'But you're not in the hotel.'

'We built a house, up at Tarmes.'

'The theory is,' said Dick, arranging an umbrella to clip a square of sunlight off Rosemary's shoulder, 'that all the northern places, like Deauville, were picked out by Russians and English who don't mind the cold, while half of us Americans come from tropical climates – that's why we're beginning to come here.'

The young man of Latin aspect had been turning the pages of the *New York Herald*.[19]

'Well, what nationality are these people?' he demanded, suddenly, and read with a slight French intonation, ' "Registered at the Hôtel Palace at Vevey are Mr Pandely Vlasco, Mme Bonneasse" – I don't exaggerate – "Corinna Medonca, Mme Pasche, Seraphim Tullio, Maria Amalia Roto Mais, Moises Teubel, Mme Paragoris, Apostle Alexandre, Yolanda Yosfuglu and Geneveva de Momus!" She attracts me most – Geneveva de Momus. Almost worth running up to Vevey to take a look at Geneveva de Momus.'

He stood up with sudden restlessness, stretching himself with one sharp movement. He was a few years younger than Diver or North. He was tall and his body was hard but overspare save for the bunched force gathered in his shoulders and upper arms. At first glance he seemed conventionally handsome – but there was a faint disgust always in his face which marred the full fierce lustre of his brown eyes. Yet one remembered them afterward, when one had forgotten the inability of the mouth to endure boredom and the young forehead with its furrows of fretful and unprofitable pain.

'We found some fine ones in the news of Americans last week,' said Nicole. 'Mrs Evelyn Oyster and – what were the others?'

'There was Mr S. Flesh,' said Diver, getting up also. He took his rake and began to work seriously at getting small stones out of the sand.

'Oh, yes – S. Flesh – doesn't he give you the creeps?'

It was quiet alone with Nicole – Rosemary found it even quieter than with her mother. Abe North and Barban, the Frenchman, were talking about Morocco, and Nicole having copied her recipe picked up a piece of sewing. Rosemary examined their appurtenances – four large parasols that made a canopy of shade, a portable bath-house for dressing, a pneumatic rubber horse, new things that Rosemary had never seen, from the first burst of luxury manufacturing after the war, and probably in the hands of the first of purchasers. She had gathered that they were fashionable people, but though her mother had brought her up to beware such people as drones, she did not feel that way here. Even in their absolute immobility, complete as that of the morning, she felt a purpose, a working over something, a direction, an act of creation different from any she had known. Her immature mind made no speculations upon the nature of their relation to each other, she was only concerned with their attitude towards herself – but she perceived the web of some pleasant interrelation, which she expressed with the thought that they seemed to have a very good time.

She looked in turn at the three men, temporarily expropriating them. All three were personable in different ways; all were of a special gentleness that she felt was part of their lives, past and future, not circumstanced by events, not at all like the company manners of actors, and she detected also a far-reaching delicacy that was different from the rough and ready good fellowship of directors, who represented the intellectuals in her life. Actors and directors – those were the only men she had ever known, those and the heterogeneous, indistinguishable mass of college boys, interested only in love at first sight, whom she had met at the Yale prom last fall.

These three were different. Barban was less civilised, more sceptical and scoffing, his manners were formal, even perfunctory. Abe North had, under his shyness, a desperate humour that amused but puzzled her. Her serious nature distrusted its ability to make a supreme impression on him.

But Dick Diver – he was all complete there. Silently she admired him. His complexion was reddish and weather-burned, so was his short hair – a light growth of it rolled down his arms and hands. His eyes were of a bright, hard blue. His nose was somewhat pointed and there was never any doubt at whom he was looking or talking – and this is a flattering attention, for who looks at us? – glances fall upon us, curious or disinterested, nothing more. His voice, with some faint Irish melody running through it, wooed the world, yet she felt the layer of hardness in him, of self-control and of self-discipline, her own virtues. Oh, she chose him, and Nicole, lifting her head, saw her choose him, heard the little sigh at the fact that he was already possessed.

Towards noon the McKiscos, Mrs Abrams, Mr Dumphry, and Señor Campion came on the beach. They had brought a new umbrella that they set up with side glances towards the Divers, and crept under with satisfied expressions – all save Mr McKisco, who remained derisively without. In his raking Dick had passed near them and now he returned to the umbrellas.

'The two young men are reading the Book of Etiquette[20] together,' he said in a low voice.

'Planning to mix wit' de quality,' said Abe.

Mary North, the very tanned young woman whom Rosemary had encountered the first day on the raft, came in from swimming and said with a smile that was a rakish gleam: 'So Mr and Mrs Neverquiver have arrived.'

'They're this man's friends,' Nicole reminded her, indicating Abe. 'Why doesn't he go and speak to them? Don't you think they're attractive?'

'I think they're very attractive,' Abe agreed. 'I just don't think they're attractive, that's all.'

'Well, I *have* felt there were too many people on the beach this summer,' Nicole admitted. '*Our* beach that Dick made out of a pebble pile.' She considered, and then lowering her voice out of the range of the trio of nannies who sat back under another umbrella, 'Still they're preferable to those British last summer who kept shouting about: "Isn't the sea blue? Isn't the sky white? Isn't little Nellie's nose red?"'

Rosemary thought she would not like to have Nicole for an enemy.

'But you didn't see the fight,' Nicole continued. 'The day before you came, the married man, the one with the name that sounds like a substitute for gasoline or butter – '

'McKisco?'

'Yes – well they were having words and she tossed some sand in his face. So naturally he sat on top of her and rubbed her face in the sand. We were – electrified. I wanted Dick to interfere.'

'I think,' said Dick Diver, staring down abstractedly at the straw mat, 'that I'll go over and invite them to dinner.'

'No, you won't,' Nicole told him quickly.

'I think it would be a very good thing. They're here – let's adjust ourselves.'

'We're very well adjusted,' she insisted, laughing. 'I'm not going to have *my* nose rubbed in the sand. I'm a mean, hard woman,' she explained to Rosemary, and then raising her voice: 'Children, put on your bathing suits!'

Rosemary felt that this swim would become the typical one of her life, the one that would always pop up in her memory at the mention of swimming. Simultaneously the whole party moved towards the water, super-ready from the long, forced inaction, passing from the heat to the cool with the *gourmandise* of a tingling curry eaten with chilled white wine. The Divers' day was spaced like the day of the older civilisations to yield the utmost from the materials at hand, and to give all the transitions their full value, and she did not know that there would be another transition presently from the utter absorption of the swim to the garrulity of the Provençal lunch hour. But again she had the sense that Dick was taking care of her, and she delighted in responding to the eventual movement as if it had been an order.

Nicole handed her husband the curious garment on which she had been working. He went into the dressing tent and inspired a commotion by appearing in a moment clad in transparent black lace drawers. Close inspection revealed that actually they were lined with flesh-coloured cloth.

'Well, if that isn't a pansy's trick!'[21] exclaimed Mr McKisco contemptuously – then turning quickly to Mr Dumphry and Mr Campion, he added, 'oh, I beg your pardon.'

Rosemary bubbled with delight at the trunks. Her naïveté responded wholeheartedly to the expensive simplicity of the Divers, unaware of its complexity and its lack of innocence, unaware that it was all a selection of quality rather than quantity from the run of the world's bazaar; and that the simplicity of behaviour also, the nursery-like peace and good will, the emphasis on the simpler virtues, was part of a desperate bargain with the gods and had been attained through struggles she could not have guessed at. At that moment the Divers represented externally the exact furthermost evolution of a class, so that most people seemed awkward beside them – in reality a qualitative change had already set in that was not at all apparent to Rosemary.

She stood with them as they took sherry and ate crackers. Dick Diver looked at her with cold blue eyes; his kind, strong mouth said thoughtfully and deliberately: 'You're the only girl I've seen for a long time that actually did look like something blooming.'

*　　*　　*

In her mother's lap afterward Rosemary cried and cried.

'I love him, mother, I'm desperately in love with him – I never knew I could feel that way about anybody. And he's married and I like her too – it's just hopeless. Oh, I love him so!'

'I'm curious to meet him.'

'She invited us to dinner Friday.'

'If you're in love it ought to make you happy. You ought to laugh.'

Rosemary looked up and gave a beautiful little shiver of her face and laughed. Her mother always had a great influence on her.

Chapter 5

ROSEMARY WENT TO MONTE CARLO feeling nearly as sulky as it was possible for her to be. She rode up the rugged hill to La Turbie,[22] to an old Gaumont lot[23] in process of reconstruction, and as she stood by the grilled entrance waiting for an answer to the message on her card, she might have been looking into Hollywood. The bizarre débris of some recent picture, a decayed street scene in India, a great cardboard whale, a monstrous tree bearing cherries large as basket-balls, bloomed there by exotic dispensation, autochthonous as the pale amaranth, mimosa, cork oak or dwarfed pine. There were a quick-lunch shack and two barnlike stages, and everywhere about the lot, groups of waiting, hopeful, painted faces.

After ten minutes a young man with hair the colour of canary feathers hurried down to the gate.

'Come in, Miss Hoyt, Mr Brady's on the set, but he's very anxious to see you. I'm sorry you were kept waiting, but you know some of these French dames are worse about pushing themselves in – '

The studio manager opened a small door in the blank wall of stage building and with sudden glad familiarity Rosemary followed him into half-darkness. Here and there figures spotted the twilight, turning up ashen faces to her like souls in purgatory watching the passage of a mortal through. There were whispers and soft voices and, apparently from afar, the gentle tremolo of a small organ. Turning the corner made by some flats, they came upon the white crackling glow of a stage, where a French actor – his shirt front, collar, and cuffs tinted a brilliant pink – and an American actress stood motionless face to face. They stared at each other with dogged eyes, as though they had been in the same position for hours; and still for a long time nothing happened, no one moved. A bank of lights went off with a savage hiss, went on again; the plaintive tap of a hammer begged admission to nowhere in the distance; a blue face appeared among the blinding lights above, called something unintelligible into the upper blackness. Then the silence was broken by a voice in front of Rosemary.

'Baby, you don't take off the stockings, you can spoil ten more pairs. That dress is fifteen pounds.'

Stepping backward the speaker ran against Rosemary, whereupon the studio manager said, 'Hey, Earl – Miss Hoyt.'

They were meeting for the first time. Brady was quick and

strenuous. As he took her hand she saw him look her over from head to foot, a gesture she recognised and that made her feel at home, but gave her always a faint feeling of superiority to whoever made it. If her person was property she could exercise whatever advantage was inherent in its ownership.

'I thought you'd be along any day now,' Brady said, in a voice that was just a little too compelling for private life, and that trailed with it a faintly defiant cockney accent. 'Have a good trip?'

'Yes, but we're glad to be going home.'

'No –o –o!' he protested. 'Stay awhile – I want to talk to you. Let me tell you that was some picture of yours – that *Daddy's Girl*. I saw it in Paris. I wired the coast right away to see if you were signed.'

'I just had – I'm sorry.'

'God, what a picture!'

Not wanting to smile in silly agreement Rosemary frowned.

'Nobody wants to be thought of forever for just one picture,' she said.

'Sure – that's right. What're your plans?'

'Mother thought I needed a rest. When I get back we'll probably either sign up with First National or keep on with Famous.'[24]

'Who's we?'

'My mother. She decides business matters. I couldn't do without her.'

Again he looked her over completely, and, as he did, something in Rosemary went out to him. It was not liking, not at all the spontaneous admiration she had felt for the man on the beach this morning. It was a click. He desired her and, so far as her virginal emotions went, she contemplated a surrender with equanimity. Yet she knew she would forget him half an hour after she left him – like an actor kissed in a picture.

'Where are you staying?' Brady asked. 'Oh, yes, at Gausse's. Well, my plans are made for this year, too, but that letter I wrote you still stands. Rather make a picture with you than any girl since Connie Talmadge[25] was a kid.'

'I feel the same way. Why don't you come back to Hollywood?'

'I can't stand the damn place. I'm fine here. Wait till after this shot and I'll show you around.'

Walking on to the set he began to talk to the French actor in a low, quiet voice.

Five minutes passed – Brady talked on, while from time to time the Frenchman shifted his feet and nodded. Abruptly, Brady broke off, calling something to the lights that startled them into a humming glare. Los Angeles was loud about Rosemary now. Unappalled she moved once more through the city of thin partitions, wanting to be back there. But she did not want to see Brady in the mood she sensed he would be in after he had finished and she left the lot with a spell still upon her. The Mediterranean world was less silent now that she knew the studio was there. She liked the people on the streets and bought herself a pair of espadrilles on the way to the train.

Her mother was pleased that she had done so accurately what she was told to do, but she still wanted to launch her out and away. Mrs Speers was fresh in appearance but she was tired; deathbeds make people tired indeed and she had watched beside a couple.

Chapter 6

FEELING GOOD from the rosy wine at lunch, Nicole Diver folded her arms high enough for the artificial camellia on her shoulder to touch her cheek, and went out into her lovely grassless garden. The garden was bounded on one side by the house, from which it flowed and into which it ran, on two sides by the old village, and on the last by the cliff falling by ledges to the sea.

Along the walls on the village side all was dusty, the wriggling vines, the lemon and eucalyptus trees, the casual wheelbarrow, left only a moment since, but already grown into the path, atrophied and faintly rotten. Nicole was invariably somewhat surprised that by turning in the other direction past a bed of peonies she walked into an area so green and cool that the leaves and petals were curled with tender damp.

Knotted at her throat she wore a lilac scarf that even in the achromatic sunshine cast its colour up to her face and down around her moving feet in a lilac shadow. Her face was hard, almost stern, save for the soft gleam of piteous doubt that looked from her green eyes. Her once fair hair had darkened, but she was lovelier now at twenty-four than she had been at eighteen, when her hair was brighter than she.

Following a walk marked by an intangible mist of bloom that followed the white border stones she came to a space overlooking the sea where there were lanterns asleep in the fig trees and a big table and wicker chairs and a great market umbrella from Sienna, all gathered about an enormous pine, the biggest tree in the garden. She paused there a moment, looking absently at a growth of nasturtiums and iris tangled at its foot, as though sprung from a careless handful of seeds, listening to the plaints and accusations of some nursery squabble in the house. When this died away on the summer air, she walked on, between kaleidoscopic peonies massed in pink clouds, black and brown tulips and fragile mauve-stemmed roses, transparent like sugar flowers in a confectioner's window – until, as if the scherzo of colour could reach no further intensity, it broke off suddenly in mid-air, and moist steps went down to a level five feet below.

Here there was a well with the boarding around it dank and slippery even on the brightest days. She went up the stairs on the other side and into the vegetable garden; she walked rather quickly; she liked to be active, though at times she gave an impression of repose that was at once static and evocative. This was because she knew few words and believed in none, and in the world she was rather silent, contributing just her share of urbane humour with a precision that approached meagreness. But at the moment when strangers tended to grow uncomfortable in the presence of this economy she would seize the topic and rush off with it, feverishly surprised with herself – then bring it back and relinquish it abruptly, almost timidly, like an obedient retriever, having been adequate and something more.

As she stood in the fuzzy green light of the vegetable garden, Dick crossed the path ahead of her going to his work house. Nicole waited silently till he had passed; then she went on through lines of prospective salads to a little menagerie where pigeons and rabbits and a parrot made a medley of insolent noises at her. Descending to another ledge she reached a low, curved wall and looked down seven hundred feet to the Mediterranean Sea.

She stood in the ancient hill village of Tarmes. The villa and its grounds were made out of a row of peasant dwellings that abutted on the cliff – five small houses had been combined to make the house and four destroyed to make the garden. The exterior walls were untouched so that from the road far below it was indistinguishable from the violet grey mass of the town.

For a moment Nicole stood looking down at the Mediterranean but there was nothing to do with that, even with her tireless hands. Presently Dick came out of his one-room house carrying a telescope and looked east towards Cannes. In a moment Nicole swam into his field of vision, whereupon he disappeared into his house and came out with a megaphone. He had many light mechanical devices.

'Nicole,' he shouted, 'I forgot to tell you that as a final apostolic gesture I invited Mrs Abrams, the woman with the white hair.'

'I suspected it. It's an outrage.'

The ease with which her reply reached him seemed to belittle his megaphone, so she raised her voice and called, 'Can you hear me?'

'Yes.' He lowered the megaphone and then raised it stubbornly. 'I'm going to invite some more people too. I'm going to invite the two young men.'

'All right,' she agreed placidly.

'I want to give a really *bad* party. I mean it. I want to give a party where there's a brawl and seductions and people going home with their feelings hurt and women passed out in the *cabinet de toilette*.[26] You wait and see.'

He went back into his house and Nicole saw that one of his most characteristic moods was upon him, the excitement that swept everyone up into it and was inevitably followed by his own form of melancholy, which he never displayed but at which she guessed. This excitement about things reached an intensity out of proportion to their importance, generating a really extraordinary virtuosity with people. Save among a few of the tough-minded and perennially suspicious, he had the power of arousing a fascinated and uncritical love. The reaction came when he realised the waste and extravagance involved. He sometimes looked back with awe at the carnivals of affection he had given, as a general might gaze upon a massacre he had ordered to satisfy an impersonal blood-lust.

But to be included in Dick Diver's world for a while was a remarkable experience: people believed he made special reservations about them, recognising the proud uniqueness of their destinies, buried under the compromises of how many years. He won everyone quickly with an exquisite consideration and a politeness that moved so fast and intuitively that it could be examined only in its effect. Then, without caution, lest the first bloom of the relation wither, he opened the gate to his amusing world. So long as they subscribed to it completely, their happiness was his preoccupation, but at the first flicker of doubt as to its all-inclusiveness he evaporated before their eyes, leaving little communicable memory of what he had said or done.

At eight-thirty that evening he came out to meet his first guests, his coat carried rather ceremoniously, rather promisingly, in his hand, like a toreador's cape. It was characteristic that after greeting Rosemary and her mother he waited for them to speak first, as if to allow them the reassurance of their own voices in the new surroundings.

To resume Rosemary's point of view it should be said that, under the spell of the climb to Tarmes and the fresher air, she and her mother looked about appreciatively. Just as the personal qualities of extraordinary people can make themselves plain in an unaccustomed change of expression, so the intensely calculated perfection of Villa Diana transpired all at once through such minute failures as the chance apparition of a maid in the background or the perversity of a cook. While the first guests arrived bringing with them the excitement of the night, the domestic activity of the day receded past them gently, symbolised by the Diver children and their governess still at supper on the terrace.

'What a beautiful garden!' Mrs Speers exclaimed.

'Nicole's garden,' said Dick. 'She won't let it alone – she nags it all the time, worries about its diseases. Any day now I expect to have her come down with Powdery Mildew or Fly Speck, or Late Blight.' He pointed his forefinger decisively at Rosemary, saying with a lightness seeming to conceal a paternal interest, 'I'm going to save your reason – I'm going to give you a hat to wear on the beach.'

He turned them from the garden to the terrace, where he poured a cocktail. Earl Brady arrived, discovering Rosemary with surprise. His manner was softer than at the studio, as if his differentness had been put on at the gate, and Rosemary, comparing him instantly with Dick Diver, swung sharply towards the latter. In comparison Earl Brady seemed faintly gross, faintly ill-bred; once more, though, she felt an electric response to his person.

He spoke familiarly to the children, who were getting up from their outdoor supper.

'Hello, Lanier, how about a song? Will you and Topsy sing me a song?'

'What shall we sing?' agreed the little boy, with the odd chanting accent of American children brought up in France.

'That song about *"Mon ami Pierrot"*.'²⁷

Brother and sister stood side by side without self-consciousness and their voices soared sweet and shrill upon the evening air.

> 'Au clair de la lune,
>   Mon ami Pierrot,
> Prête-moi ta plume
>   Pour écrire un mot.
> Ma chandelle est morte,
>   Je n'ai plus de feu,
> Ouvre-moi ta porte,
>   Pour l'amour de Dieu.'

The singing ceased and the children, their faces aglow with the late sunshine, stood smiling calmly at their success. Rosemary was thinking that the Villa Diana was the centre of the world. On such a stage some memorable thing was sure to happen. She lighted up higher as the gate tinkled open and the rest of the guests arrived in a body – the McKiscos, Mrs Abrams, Mr Dumphry, and Mr Campion came up to the terrace.

Rosemary had a sharp feeling of disappointment – she looked quickly at Dick, as though to ask an explanation of this incongruous mingling. But there was nothing unusual in his expression. He greeted his new guests with a proud bearing and an obvious defer-ence to their infinite and unknown possibilities. She believed in him so much that presently she accepted the rightness of the McKiscos' presence as if she had expected to meet them all along.

'I've met you in Paris,' McKisco said to Abe North, who with his wife had arrived on their heels, 'in fact I've met you twice.'

'Yes, I remember,' Abe said.

'Then where was it?' demanded McKisco, not content to let well enough alone.

'Why, I think – ' Abe got tired of the game, 'I can't remember.'

The interchange filled a pause and Rosemary's instinct was that something tactful should be said by somebody, but Dick made no attempt to break up the grouping formed by these late arrivals, not even to disarm Mrs McKisco of her air of supercilious amusement. He did not solve this social problem because he knew it was not of importance at the moment and would solve itself. He was saving his newness for a larger effort, waiting a more significant moment for his guests to be conscious of a good time.

Rosemary stood beside Tommy Barban – he was in a particularly scornful mood and there seemed to be some special stimulus working upon him. He was leaving in the morning.

'Going home?'

'Home? I have no home. I am going to a war.'

'What war?'

'What war? Any war. I haven't seen a paper lately but I suppose there's a war – there always is.'

'Don't you care what you fight for?'

'Not at all – so long as I'm well treated. When I'm in a rut I come to see the Divers, because then I know that in a few weeks I'll want to go to war.'

Rosemary stiffened.

'You like the Divers,' she reminded him.

'Of course – especially her – but they make me want to go to war.'

She considered this, to no avail. The Divers made her want to stay near them for ever.

'You're half American,' she said, as if that should solve the problem.

'Also I'm half French, and I was educated in England and since I was eighteen I've worn the uniforms of eight countries. But I hope I did not give you the impression that I am not fond of the Divers – I am, especially of Nicole.'

'How could anyone help it?' she said simply.

She felt far from him. The undertone of his words repelled her and she withdrew her adoration for the Divers from the profanity of his bitterness. She was glad he was not next to her at dinner and she was still thinking of his words 'especially her' as they moved towards the table in the garden.

For a moment now she was beside Dick Diver on the path. Alongside his hard, neat brightness everything faded into the surety that he knew everything. For a year, which was for ever, she had had money and a certain celebrity and contact with the celebrated, and these latter had presented themselves merely as powerful enlargements of the people with whom the doctor's widow and her daughter had associated in a hotel-pension in Paris. Rosemary was a romantic and her career had not provided many satisfactory opportunities on that score. Her mother, with the idea of a career for Rosemary, would not tolerate any such spurious substitutes as the excitations available on all sides, and indeed Rosemary was already beyond that – she was In the movies but not at all At them. So when she had seen approval of Dick Diver in her mother's face it meant that he was 'the real thing'; it meant permission to go as far as she could.

'I was watching you,' he said, and she knew he meant it. 'We've grown very fond of you.'

'I fell in love with you the first time I saw you,' she said quietly.

He pretended not to have heard, as if the compliment were purely formal.

'New friends,' he said, as if it were an important point, 'can often have a better time together than old friends.'

With that remark, which she did not understand precisely, she found herself at the table, picked out by slowly emerging lights against the dark dust. A chord of delight struck inside her when she saw that Dick had taken her mother on his right hand; for herself she was between Luis Campion and Brady.

Surcharged with her emotion she turned to Brady with the intention of confiding in him, but at her first mention of Dick a hard-boiled sparkle in his eyes gave her to understand that he refused the fatherly office. In turn she was equally firm when he tried to monopolise her hand, so they talked shop or rather she listened while he talked shop, her polite eyes never leaving his face, but her mind was so definitely elsewhere that she felt he must guess the fact. Intermittently she caught the gist of his sentences and supplied the rest from her subconscious, as one picks up the striking of a clock in the middle with only the rhythm of the first uncounted strokes lingering in the mind.

Chapter 7

IN A PAUSE Rosemary looked away and up the table where Nicole sat between Tommy Barban and Abe North, her chow's hair foaming and frothing in the candlelight. Rosemary listened, caught sharply by the rich clipped voice in infrequent speech: 'The poor man,' Nicole exclaimed. 'Why did you want to saw him in two?'

'Naturally I wanted to see what was inside a waiter. Wouldn't you like to know what was inside a waiter?'

'Old menus,' suggested Nicole with a short laugh. 'Pieces of broken china and tips and pencil stubs.'

'Exactly – but the thing was to prove it scientifically. And of course doing it with that musical saw would have eliminated any sordidness.'

'Did you intend to play the saw while you performed the operation?' Tommy enquired.

'We didn't get quite that far. We were alarmed by the screams. We thought he might rupture something.'

'All sounds very peculiar to me,' said Nicole. 'Any musician that'll use another musician's saw to – '

They had been at table half an hour and a perceptible change had set in – person by person had given up something, a preoccupation, an anxiety, a suspicion, and now they were only their best selves and the Divers' guests. Not to have been friendly and interested would have seemed to reflect on the Divers, so now they were all trying, and seeing this, Rosemary liked everyone – except McKisco, who had contrived to be the unassimilated member of the party. This was less from ill will than from his determination to sustain with wine the good spirit he had enjoyed on his arrival. Lying back in his place between Earl Brady, to whom he had addressed several withering remarks about the movies, and Mrs Abrams, to whom he said nothing, he stared at Dick Diver with an expression of devastating irony, the effect being occasionally interrupted by his attempts to engage Dick in a cater-cornered conversation across the table.

'Aren't you a friend of Van Buren Denby?'[28] he would say.

'I don't believe I know him.'

'I thought you were a friend of his,' he persisted irritably.

When the subject of Mr Denby fell of its own weight, he essayed other equally irrelevant themes, but each time the very deference of Dick's attention seemed to paralyse him, and after a moment's stark pause the conversation that he had interrupted would go on without him. He tried breaking into other dialogues, but it was like continually shaking hands with a glove from which the hand had been withdrawn – so finally, with a resigned air of being among children, he devoted his attention entirely to the champagne. Rosemary's glance moved at intervals around the table, eager for the others' enjoyment, as if they were her future stepchildren. A gracious table light, emanating from a bowl of spicy pinks, fell upon Mrs Abrams' face, cooked to a turn in Veuve Cliquot,[29] full of vigour, tolerance, adolescent good will; next to her sat Mr Royal Dumphry, his girl's comeliness less startling in the pleasure world of evening. Then Violet McKisco, whose prettiness had been piped to the surface of her, so that she ceased her struggle to make tangible to herself her shadowy position as the wife of an arriviste who had not arrived.

Then came Dick, with his arms full of the slack he had taken up from others, deeply merged in his own party.

Then her mother, for ever perfect.

Then Barban talking to her mother with an urbane fluency that made Rosemary like him again. Then Nicole. Rosemary saw her suddenly in a new way and found her one of the most beautiful people she had ever known. Her face, the face of a saint, a viking Madonna, shone through the faint motes that snowed across the candlelight, drew down its flush from the wine-coloured lanterns in the pine. She was still as still.

Abe North was talking to her about his moral code: 'Of course I've got one,' he insisted, ' – a man can't live without a moral code. Mine is that I'm against the burning of witches. Whenever they burn a witch I get all hot under the collar.' Rosemary knew from Brady that he was a musician who after a brilliant and precocious start had composed nothing for seven years.

Next was Campion, managing somehow to restrain his most blatant effeminacy, and even to visit upon those near him a certain disinterested motherliness. Then Mary North with a face so merry that it was impossible not to smile back into the white mirrors of her teeth – the whole area around her parted lips was a lovely little circle of delight.

Finally Brady, whose heartiness became, moment by moment, a social thing instead of a crude assertion and reassertion of his own mental health, and his preservation of it by a detachment from the frailties of others.

Rosemary, as dewy with belief as a child from one of Mrs Burnett's vicious tracts,[30] had a conviction of homecoming, of a return from the derisive and salacious improvisations of the frontier. There were fireflies riding on the dark air and a dog baying on some low and faraway ledge of the cliff. The table seemed to have risen a little towards the sky like a mechanical dancing platform, giving the people around it a sense of being alone with each other in the dark universe, nourished by its only good, warmed by its only lights. And, as if a curious hushed laugh from Mrs McKisco were a signal that such a detachment from the world had been attained, the two Divers began suddenly to warm and glow and expand, as if to make up to their guests, already so subtly assured of their importance, so flattered with politeness, for anything they might still miss from that country well left behind. Just for a moment they seemed to speak to every one at the table, singly and together, assuring them of their friendliness, their affection. And for a moment the faces turned up towards them were like the faces of poor children at a Christmas tree. Then abruptly the table broke up – the moment when the guests had been daringly lifted above conviviality into the rarer atmosphere of sentiment was over before it could be irreverently breathed, before they had half realised it was there.

But the diffused magic of the hot sweet South had withdrawn into them – the soft-pawed night and the ghostly wash of the Mediterranean far below – the magic left these things and melted into the two Divers and became part of them. Rosemary watched Nicole pressing upon her mother a yellow evening bag she had admired, saying, 'I think things ought to belong to the people that like them' – and then sweeping into it all the yellow articles she could find, a pencil, a lipstick, a little notebook, 'because they all go together.'

Nicole disappeared and presently Rosemary noticed that Dick was no longer there; the guests distributed themselves in the garden or drifted in towards the terrace.

'Do you want,' Violet McKisco asked Rosemary, 'to go to the bathroom?'

Not at that precise moment.

'I want,' insisted Mrs McKisco, 'to go to the bathroom.' As a frank outspoken woman she walked towards the house, dragging her secret after her, while Rosemary looked after with reprobation. Earl Brady proposed that they walk down to the sea wall but she felt that this was her time to have a share of Dick Diver when he reappeared, so she stalled, listening to McKisco quarrel with Barban.

'Why do you want to fight the Soviets?' McKisco said. 'The greatest experiment ever made by humanity? And the Riff?[31] It seems to me it would be more heroic to fight on the just side.'

'How do you find out which it is?' asked Barban dryly.

'Why – usually everybody intelligent knows.'

'Are you a Communist?'

'I'm a Socialist,' said McKisco, 'I sympathise with Russia.'

'Well, I'm a soldier,' Barban answered pleasantly. 'My business is to kill people. I fought against the Riff[32] because I am a European, and I have fought the Communists because they want to take my property from me.'

'Of all the narrow-minded excuses.' McKisco looked around to establish a derisive liaison with someone else, but without success. He had no idea what he was up against in Barban, neither of the simplicity of the other man's bag of ideas nor the complexity of his training. McKisco knew what ideas were, and as his mind grew he was able to recognise and sort an increasing number of them – but faced by a man whom he considered 'dumb', one in whom he found no ideas he could recognise as such, and yet to whom he could not feel personally superior, he jumped at the conclusion that Barban was the end product of an archaic world, and as such, worthless. McKisco's contacts with the princely classes in America had impressed upon him their uncertain and fumbling snobbery, their delight in ignorance and their deliberate rudeness, all lifted from the English with no regard paid to factors that make English philistinism and rudeness purposeful, and applied in a land where a little knowledge and civility buy more than they do anywhere else – an attitude which reached its apogee in the 'Harvard manner' of about 1900. He thought that this Barban was of that type, and being drunk rashly forgot that he was in awe of him – this led up to the trouble in which he presently found himself.

Feeling vaguely ashamed for McKisco, Rosemary waited, placid but inwardly on fire, for Dick Diver's return. From her chair at the deserted table with Barban, McKisco, and Abe she looked up along the path edged with shadowy myrtle and fern to the stone terrace, and falling in love with her mother's profile against a lighted door, was about to go there when Mrs McKisco came hurrying down from the house.

She exuded excitement. In the very silence with which she pulled out a chair and sat down, her eyes staring, her mouth working a little, they all recognised a person crop-full of news, and her husband's 'What's the matter, Vi?' came naturally, as all eyes turned towards her.

'My dear – ' she said at large, and then addressed Rosemary, 'my dear – it's nothing. I really can't say a word.'

'You are among friends,' said Abe.

'Well, upstairs I came upon a scene, my dears – '

Shaking her head cryptically she broke off just in time, for Tommy arose and addressed her politely but sharply: 'It's inadvisable to comment on what goes on in this house.'

Chapter 8

VIOLET BREATHED LOUD and hard once and with an effort brought another expression into her face.

Dick came finally and with a sure instinct he separated Barban and the McKiscos and became excessively ignorant and inquisitive about literature with McKisco – thus giving the latter the moment of superiority which he required. The others helped him carry lamps up – who would not be pleased at carrying lamps helpfully through the darkness? Rosemary helped, meanwhile responding patiently to Royal Dumphry's inexhaustible curiosity about Hollywood.

Now – she was thinking – I've earned a time alone with him. He must know that because his laws are like the laws mother taught me.

Rosemary was right – presently he detached her from the company on the terrace, and they were alone together, borne away from the house towards the seaside wall with what were less steps than irregularly spaced intervals through some of which she was pulled, through others blown.

They looked out over the Mediterranean. Far below, the last excursion boat from the Îles des Lérins[33] floated across the bay like a Fourth-of-July balloon footloose in the heavens. Between the black isles it floated, softly parting the dark tide.

'I understand why you speak as you do of your mother,' he said. 'Her attitude towards you is very fine, I think. She has a sort of wisdom that's rare in America.'

'Mother is perfect,' she prayed.

'I was talking to her about a plan I have – she told me that how long you both stayed in France depended on you.'

On *you*, Rosemary all but said aloud.

'So since things are over down here – '

'Over?' she enquired.

'Well, this is over – this part of the summer is over. Last week Nicole's sister left, tomorrow Tommy Barban leaves, Monday Abe and Mary North are leaving. Maybe we'll have more fun this summer but this particular fun is over. I want it to die violently instead of fading out sentimentally – that's why I gave this party. What I'm coming to is – Nicole and I are going up to Paris to see Abe North off for America – I wonder if you'd like to go with us.'

'What did mother say?'

'She seemed to think it would be fine. She doesn't want to go herself. She wants you to go alone.'

'I haven't seen Paris since I've been grown,' said Rosemary. 'I'd love to see it with you.'

'That's nice of you.' Did she imagine that his voice was suddenly metallic? 'Of course we've been excited about you from the moment you came on the beach. That vitality, we were sure it was professional – especially Nicole was. It'd never use itself up on any one person or group.'

Her instinct cried out to her that he was passing her along slowly towards Nicole and she put her own brakes on, saying with an equal hardness: 'I wanted to know all of you too – especially you. I told you I fell in love with you the first time I saw you.'

She was right going at it that way. But the space between heaven and earth had cooled his mind, destroyed the impulsiveness that had led him to bring her here, and made him aware of the too obvious appeal, the struggle with an unrehearsed scene and unfamiliar words.

He tried now to make her want to go back to the house and it was difficult, and he did not quite want to lose her. She felt only the draught blowing as he joked with her good-humouredly.

'You don't know what you want. You go and ask your mother what you want.'

She was stricken. She touched him, feeling the smooth cloth of his dark coat like a chasuble. She seemed about to fall to her knees – from that position she delivered her last shot.

'I think you're the most wonderful person I ever met – except my mother.'

'You have romantic eyes.'

His laughter swept them on up towards the terrace where he delivered her to Nicole . . .

Too soon it had become time to go and the Divers helped them all to go quickly. In the Divers' big Isotta[34] there would be Tommy Barban and his baggage – he was spending the night at the hotel to catch an early train – with Mrs Abrams, the McKiscos and Campion. Earl Brady was going to drop Rosemary and her mother on his way to Monte Carlo, and Royal Dumphry rode with them because the Divers' car was crowded. Down in the garden lanterns still glowed over the table where they had dined, as the Divers stood side by side in the gate, Nicole blooming away and filling the night with gracious-ness, and Dick bidding goodbye to everyone by name. To Rosemary it seemed very poignant to drive away and leave them in their house. Again she wondered what Mrs McKisco had seen in the bathroom.

Chapter 9

It was a limpid black night, hung as in a basket from a single dull star. The horn of the car ahead was muffled by the resistance of the thick air. Brady's chauffeur drove slowly; the tail-light of the other car appeared from time to time at turnings – then not at all. But after ten minutes it came into sight again, drawn up at the side of the road. Brady's chauffeur slowed up behind but immediately it began to roll forward slowly and they passed it. In the instant they passed it they heard a blur of voices from behind the reticence of the limousine and saw that the Divers' chauffeur was grinning. Then they went on, going fast through the alternating banks of darkness and thin night, descending at last in a series of roller-coaster swoops, to the great bulk of Gausse's Hôtel.

Rosemary dozed for three hours and then lay awake, suspended in the moonshine. Cloaked by the erotic darkness she exhausted the future quickly, with all the eventualities that might lead up to a kiss, but with the kiss itself as blurred as a kiss in pictures. She changed position in bed, deliberately, the first sign of insomnia she had ever had, and tried to think with her mother's mind about the question. In this process she was often acute beyond her experience, with remembered things from old conversations that had gone into her half-heard.

Rosemary had been brought up with the idea of work. Mrs Speers had spent the slim leavings of the men who had widowed her on her daughter's education, and when she blossomed out at sixteen with that extraordinary hair, rushed her to Aix-les-Bains[35] and marched her unannounced into the suite of an American producer who was recuperating there. When the producer went to New York they went too. Thus Rosemary had passed her entrance examinations. With the ensuing success and the promise of comparative stability that followed, Mrs Speers had felt free to tacitly imply tonight: 'You were brought up to work – not especially to marry. Now you've found your first nut to crack and it's a good nut – go ahead and put whatever happens down to experience. Wound yourself or him – whatever happens it can't spoil you because economically you're a boy, not a girl.'

Rosemary had never done much thinking, save about the illimitability of her mother's perfections, so this final severance of the umbilical cord disturbed her sleep. A false dawn sent the sky passing through the tall French windows, and getting up she walked out on the terrace, warm to her bare feet. There were secret noises in the air, an insistent bird achieved an ill-natured triumph with regularity in the trees above the tennis court; footfalls followed a round drive in the rear of the hotel, taking their tone in turn from the dust road, the crushed-stone walk, the cement steps, and then reversing the process in going away. Beyond the inky sea and far up that high, black shadow of a hill lived the Divers. She thought of them both together, heard them still singing faintly a song like rising smoke, like a hymn, very remote in time and far away. Their children slept, their gate was shut for the night.

She went inside and dressing in a light gown and espadrilles went out her window again and along the continuous terrace towards the front door, going fast since she found that other private rooms, exuding sleep, gave upon it. She stopped at the sight of a figure seated on the wide white stairway of the formal entrance – then she saw that it was Luis Campion and that he was weeping.

He was weeping hard and quietly and shaking in the same parts as a weeping woman. A scene in a role she had played last year swept over her irresistibly and advancing she touched him on the shoulder. He gave a little yelp before he recognised her.

'What is it?' Her eyes were level and kind and not slanted into him with hard curiosity. 'Can I help you?'

'Nobody can help me. I knew it. I have only myself to blame. It's always the same.'

'What is it – do you want to tell me?'

He looked at her to see.

'No,' he decided. 'When you're older you'll know what people who love suffer. The agony. It's better to be cold and young than to love. It's happened to me before but never like this – so accidental – just when everything was going well.'

His face was repulsive in the quickening light. Not by a flicker of her personality, a movement of the smallest muscle, did she betray her sudden disgust with whatever it was. But Campion's sensitivity realised it and he changed the subject rather suddenly.

'Abe North is around here somewhere.'

'Why, he's staying at the Divers'!'

'Yes, but he's up – don't you know what happened?'

A shutter opened suddenly in a room two storeys above and an English voice spat distinctly: 'Will you kaindlay stup tucking!'

Rosemary and Luis Campion went humbly down the steps and to a bench beside the road to the beach.

'Then you have no idea what's happened? My dear, the most extraordinary thing – ' He was warming up now, hanging on to his revelation. 'I've never seen a thing come so suddenly – I have always avoided violent people – they upset me so I sometimes have to go to bed for days.'

He looked at her triumphantly. She had no idea what he was talking about.

'My dear,' he burst forth, leaning towards her with his whole body as he touched her on the upper leg, to show it was no mere irresponsible venture of his hand – he was so sure of himself. 'There's going to be a duel.'

'Wh-at?'

'A duel with – we don't know what yet.'

'Who's going to duel?'

'I'll tell you from the beginning.' He drew a long breath and then said, as if it were rather to her discredit but he wouldn't hold it against her, 'Of course, you were in the other automobile. Well, in a way you were lucky – I lost at least two years of my life, it came so suddenly.'

'What came?' she demanded.

'I don't know what began it. First she began to talk – '

'Who?'

'Violet McKisco.' He lowered his voice as if there were people under the bench. 'But don't mention the Divers because he made threats against anybody who mentioned it.'

'Who did?'

'Tommy Barban, so don't you say I so much as mentioned them. None of us ever found out anyhow what it was Violet had to say because he kept interrupting her, and then her husband got into it and now, my dear, we have the duel. This morning – at five o'clock – in an hour.' He sighed, suddenly thinking of his own griefs. 'I almost

wish it were I. I might as well be killed now I have nothing to live for.'
He broke off and rocked to and fro with sorrow.

Again the iron shutter parted above and the same British voice said:
'Rilly, this must stup immejetely.'

Simultaneously Abe North, looking somewhat distracted, came
out of the hotel, perceived them against the sky, white over the sea.
Rosemary shook her head warningly before he could speak and they
moved to another bench further down the road. Rosemary saw that
Abe was a little tight.

'What are *you* doing up?' he demanded.

'I just got up.' She started to laugh, but remembering the voice
above, she restrained herself.

'Plagued by the nightingale,' Abe suggested, and repeated, 'probably
plagued by the nightingale. Has this sewing-circle member told you
what happened?'

Campion said with dignity: 'I only know what I heard with my own
ears.'

He got up and walked swiftly away; Abe sat down beside Rosemary.

'Why did you treat him so badly?'

'Did I?' he asked surprised. 'He's been weeping around here all
morning.'

'Well, maybe he's sad about something.'

'Maybe he is.'

'What about a duel? Who's going to duel? I thought there was
something strange in that car. Is it true?'

'It certainly is cuckoo[36] but it seems to be true.'

Chapter 10

THE TROUBLE BEGAN at the time Earl Brady's car passed the Divers'
car stopped on the road – Abe's account melted impersonally into
the thronged night – Violet McKisco was telling Mrs Abrams
something she had found out about the Divers – she had gone
upstairs in their house and she had come upon something there
which had made a great impression on her. But Tommy is a watch-
dog about the Divers. As a matter of fact she is inspiring and
formidable – but it's a mutual thing, and the fact of The Divers
together is more important to their friends than many of them
realise. Of course it's done at a certain sacrifice – sometimes they
seem just rather charming figures in a ballet, and worth just the
attention you give a ballet, but it's more than that – you'd have to

know the story. Anyhow Tommy is one of those men that Dick's passed along to Nicole and when Mrs McKisco kept hinting at her story, he called them on it. He said: 'Mrs McKisco, please don't talk further about Mrs Diver.'

'I wasn't talking to you,' she objected.

'I think it's better to leave them out.'

'Are they so sacred?'

'Leave them out. Talk about something else.'

He was sitting on one of the two little seats beside Campion. Campion told me the story.

'Well, you're pretty high-handed,' Violet came back.

You know how conversations are in cars late at night, some people murmuring and some not caring, giving up after the party, or bored or asleep. Well, none of them knew just what happened until the car stopped and Barban cried in a voice that shook everybody, a voice for cavalry.

'Do you want to step out here – we're only a mile from the hotel and you can walk it or I'll drag you there. *You've got to shut up and shut your wife up!*'

'You're a bully,' said McKisco. 'You know you're stronger muscularly than I am. But I'm not afraid of you – what they ought to have is the code duello – '[37]

There's where he made his mistake because Tommy, being French, leaned over and clapped him one, and then the chauffeur drove on. That was where you passed them. Then the women began. That was still the state of things when the car got to the hotel.

Tommy telephoned some man in Cannes to act as second and McKisco said he wasn't going to be seconded by Campion, who wasn't crazy for the job anyhow, so he telephoned me not to say anything but to come right down. Violet McKisco collapsed and Mrs Abrams took her to her room and gave her a bromide whereupon she fell comfortably asleep on the bed. When I got there I tried to argue with Tommy but the latter wouldn't accept anything short of an apology and McKisco rather spunkily wouldn't give it.

When Abe had finished, Rosemary asked thoughtfully: 'Do the Divers know it was about them?'

'No – and they're not ever going to know they had anything to do with it. That damn Campion had no business talking to you about it, but since he did – I told the chauffeur I'd get out the old musical saw if he opened his mouth about it. This fight's between two men – what Tommy needs is a good war.'

'I hope the Divers don't find out,' Rosemary said.

Abe peered at his watch.

'I've got to go up and see McKisco – do you want to come? – he feels sort of friendless – I bet he hasn't slept.'

Rosemary had a vision of the desperate vigil that high-strung, badly organised man had probably kept. After a moment balanced between pity and repugnance she agreed, and full of morning energy, bounced upstairs beside Abe.

McKisco was sitting on his bed with his alcoholic combativeness vanished, in spite of the glass of champagne in his hand. He seemed very puny and cross and white. Evidently he had been writing and drinking all night. He stared confusedly at Abe and Rosemary and asked: 'Is it time?'

'No, not for half an hour.'

The table was covered with papers which he assembled with some difficulty into a long letter; the writing on the last pages was very large and illegible. In the delicate light of electric lamps fading, he scrawled his name at the bottom, crammed it into an envelope and handed it to Abe. 'For my wife.'

'You better souse your head in cold water,' Abe suggested.

'You think I'd better?' enquired McKisco doubtfully. 'I don't want to get too sober.'

'Well, you look terrible now.'

Obediently McKisco went into the bathroom.

'I'm leaving everything in an awful mess,' he called. 'I don't know how Violet will get back to America. I don't carry any insurance. I never got around to it.'

'Don't talk nonsense, you'll be right here eating breakfast in an hour.'

'Sure, I know.' He came back with his hair wet and looked at Rosemary as if he saw her for the first time. Suddenly tears stood in his eyes. 'I never have finished my novel. That's what makes me so sore. You don't like me,' he said to Rosemary, 'but that can't be helped. I'm primarily a literary man.' He made a vague discouraged sound and shook his head helplessly. 'I've made lots of mistakes in my life – many of them. But I've been one of the most prominent – in some ways – '

He gave this up and puffed at a dead cigarette.

'I do like you,' said Rosemary, 'but I don't think you ought to fight a duel.'

'Yeah, I should have tried to beat him up, but it's done now. I've let myself be drawn into something that I had no right to be. I have a very violent temper – ' He looked closely at Abe as if he expected the statement to be challenged. Then with an aghast laugh he raised the cold cigarette butt towards his mouth. His breathing quickened.

'The trouble was I suggested the duel – if Violet had only kept her mouth shut I could have fixed it. Of course even now I can just leave, or sit back and laugh at the whole thing – but I don't think Violet would ever respect me again.'

'Yes, she would,' said Rosemary. 'She'd respect you more.'

'No – you don't know Violet. She's very hard when she gets an advantage over you. We've been married twelve years, we had a little girl seven years old and she died and after that you know how it is. We both played around on the side a little, nothing serious but drifting apart – she called me a coward out there tonight.'

Troubled, Rosemary didn't answer.

'Well, we'll see there's as little damage done as possible,' said Abe. He opened the leather case. 'These are Barban's duelling pistols – I borrowed them so you could get familiar with them. He carries them in his suitcase.' He weighed one of the archaic weapons in his hand. Rosemary gave an exclamation of uneasiness and McKisco looked at the pistols anxiously.

'Well – it isn't as if we were going to stand up and pot each other with forty-fives,'[38] he said.

'I don't know,' said Abe cruelly; 'the idea is you can sight better along a long barrel.'

'How about distance?' asked McKisco.

'I've enquired about that. If one or the other parties has to be definitely eliminated they make it eight paces, if they're just good and sore it's twenty paces, and if it's only to vindicate their honour it's forty paces. His second agreed with me to make it forty.'

'That's good.'

'There's a wonderful duel in a novel of Pushkin's,'[39] recollected Abe. 'Each man stood on the edge of a precipice, so if he was hit at all he was done for.'

This seemed very remote and academic to McKisco, who stared at him and said, 'What?'

'Do you want to take a quick dip and freshen up?'

'No – no, I couldn't swim.' He sighed. 'I don't see what it's all about,' he said helplessly. 'I don't see why I'm doing it.'

It was the first thing he had ever done in his life. Actually he was one of those for whom the sensual world does not exist, and faced with a concrete fact he brought to it a vast surprise.

'We might as well be going,' said Abe, seeing him fail a little.

'All right.' He drank off a stiff drink of brandy, put the flask in his pocket, and said with almost a savage air: 'What'll happen if I kill him – will they throw me in jail?'

'I'll run you over the Italian border.'

He glanced at Rosemary – and then said apologetically to Abe: 'Before we start there's one thing I'd like to see you about alone.'

'I hope neither of you gets hurt,' Rosemary said. 'I think it's very foolish and you ought to try to stop it.'

Chapter 11

SHE FOUND CAMPION downstairs in the deserted lobby. 'I saw you go upstairs,' he said excitedly. 'Is he all right? When is the duel going to be?'

'I don't know.' She resented his speaking of it as a circus, with McKisco as the tragic clown.

'Will you go with me?' he demanded, with the air of having seats. 'I've hired the hotel car.'

'I don't want to go.'

'Why not? I imagine it'll take years off my life but I wouldn't miss it for worlds. We could watch it from quite far away.'

'Why don't you get Mr Dumphry to go with you?'

His monocle fell out, with no whiskers to hide in – he drew himself up.

'I never want to see him again.'

'Well, I'm afraid I can't go. Mother wouldn't like it.'

As Rosemary entered her room Mrs Speers stirred sleepily and called to her: 'Where've you been?'

'I just couldn't sleep. You go back to sleep, mother.'

'Come in my room.' Hearing her sit up in bed, Rosemary went in and told her what had happened.

'Why don't you go and see it?' Mrs Speers suggested. 'You needn't go up close and you might be able to help afterwards.'

Rosemary did not like the picture of herself looking on and she demurred, but Mrs Speers' consciousness was still clogged with sleep and she was reminded of night calls to death and calamity when she was the wife of a doctor. 'I like you to go places and do things on your own initiative without me – you did much harder things for Rainy's publicity stunts.'

Still Rosemary did not see why she should go, but she obeyed the sure, clear voice that had sent her into the stage entrance of the

Odéon in Paris when she was twelve and greeted her when she came out again.

She thought she was reprieved when from the steps she saw Abe and McKisco drive away – but after a moment the hotel car came around the corner. Squealing delightedly Luis Campion pulled her in beside him.

'I hid there because they might not let us come. I've got my movie camera, you see.'

She laughed helplessly. He was so terrible that he was no longer terrible, only dehumanised.

'I wonder why Mrs McKisco didn't like the Divers?' she said. 'They were very nice to her.'

'Oh, it wasn't that. It was something she saw. We never did find exactly what it was because of Barban.'

'Then that wasn't what made you so sad.'

'Oh, no,' he said, his voice breaking, 'that was something else that happened when we got back to the hotel. But now I don't care – I wash my hands of it completely.'

They followed the other car east along the shore past Juan les Pins,[40] where the skeleton of the new Casino was rising. It was past four and under a blue-grey sky the first fishing-boats were creaking out into a glaucous sea. Then they turned off the main road and into the back country.

'It's the golf course,' cried Campion. 'I'm sure that's where it's going to be.'

He was right. When Abe's car pulled up ahead of them the east was crayoned red and yellow, promising a sultry day. Ordering the hotel car into a grove of pines Rosemary and Campion kept in the shadow of a wood and skirted the bleached fairway where Abe and McKisco, were walking up and down, the latter raising his head at intervals like a rabbit scenting. Presently there were moving figures over by a farther tree and the watchers made out Barban and his French second – the latter carried the box of pistols under his arm.

Somewhat appalled, McKisco slipped behind Abe and took a long swallow of brandy. He walked on choking and would have marched directly up into the other party, but Abe stopped him and went forward to talk to the Frenchman. The sun was over the horizon.

Campion grabbed Rosemary's arm.

'I can't stand it,' he squeaked, almost voiceless. 'It's too much. This will cost me – '

'Let go,' Rosemary said peremptorily. She breathed a frantic prayer in French.

The principals faced each other, Barban with the sleeve rolled up from his arm. His eyes gleamed restlessly in the sun, but his motion was deliberate as he wiped his palm on the seam of his trousers. McKisco reckless with brandy, pursed his lips in a whistle and pointed his long nose about nonchalantly, until Abe stepped forward with a handkerchief in his hand. The French second stood with his face turned away. Rosemary caught her breath in terrible pity and gritted her teeth with hatred for Barban; then: 'One – two – three!' Abe counted in a strained voice.

They fired at the same moment. McKisco swayed but recovered himself. Both shots had missed.

'Now, that's enough!' cried Abe.

The duellists walked in, and everyone looked at Barban enquiringly.

'I declare myself unsatisfied.'

'What? Sure you're satisfied,' said Abe impatiently. 'You just don't know it.'

'Your man refuses another shot?'

'You're damn right, Tommy. You insisted on this and my client went through with it.'

Tommy laughed scornfully.

'The distance was ridiculous,' he said. 'I'm not accustomed to such farces – your man must remember he's not now in America.'

'No use cracking at America,' said Abe rather sharply. And then, in a more conciliatory tone, 'This has gone far enough, Tommy.' They parleyed briskly for a moment – then Barban nodded and bowed coldly to his late antagonist.

'No shake hand?' suggested the French doctor.

'They already know each other,' said Abe.

He turned to McKisco.

'Come on, let's get out.'

As they strode off, McKisco, in exultation, gripped his arm.

'Wait a minute!' Abe said. 'Tommy wants his pistol back. He might need it again.'

McKisco handed it over.

'To hell with him,' he said in a tough voice. 'Tell him he can – '

'Shall I tell him you want another shot?'

'Well, I did it,' cried McKisco, as they went along. 'And I did it pretty well, didn't I? I wasn't yellow.'

'You were pretty drunk,' said Abe bluntly.

'No, I wasn't.'

'All right, then, you weren't.'

'Why would it make any difference if I had a drink or so?'

As his confidence mounted he looked resentfully at Abe.

'What difference does that make?' he repeated.

'If you can't see it, there's no use going into it.'

'Don't you know everybody was drunk all the time during the war?'

'Well, let's forget it.'

But the episode was not quite over. There were urgent footsteps in the heather behind them and the doctor drew up alongside.

'Pardon, Messieurs,' he panted. 'Voulez-vous régler mes honoraires? Naturellement c'est pour soins médicaux seulement. M Barban n'a qu'un billet de mille et ne peut pas les régler et l'autre a laissé son porte-monnaie chez lui.'[41]

'Trust a Frenchman to think of that,' said Abe, and then to the doctor. 'Combien?'[42]

'Let me pay this,' said McKisco.

'No, I've got it. We were all in about the same danger.'

Abe paid the doctor while McKisco suddenly turned into the bushes and was sick there. Then paler than before he strutted on with Abe towards the car through the now rosy morning.

Campion lay gasping on his back in the shrubbery, the only casualty of the duel, while Rosemary suddenly hysterical with laughter kept kicking at him with her espadrille. She did this persistently until she roused him – the only matter of importance to her now was that on the beach in a few hours she would see the person whom she still referred to in her mind as 'the Divers'.

Chapter 12

THEY WERE AT VOISINS[43] waiting for Nicole, six of them, Rosemary, the Norths, Dick Diver and two young French musicians. They were looking over the other patrons of the restaurant to see if they had repose – Dick said no American men had any repose, except himself, and they were seeking an example to confront him with. Things looked black for them – not a man had come into the restaurant for ten minutes without raising his hand to his face.

'We ought never to have given up waxed moustaches,' said Abe. 'Nevertheless Dick isn't the *only* man with repose – '

'Oh, yes, I am.'

' – but he may be the only sober man with repose.'

A well-dressed American had come in with two women who swooped and fluttered unself-consciously around a table. Suddenly, he perceived that he was being watched – whereupon his hand rose spasmodically and arranged a phantom bulge in his necktie. In another unseated party a man endlessly patted his shaven cheek with his palm, and his companion mechanically raised and lowered the stub of a cold cigar. The luckier ones fingered eyeglasses and facial hair, the unequipped stroked blank mouths, or even pulled desperately at the lobes of their ears.

A well-known general came in, and Abe, counting on the man's first year at West Point[44] – that year during which no cadet can resign and from which none ever recovers – made a bet with Dick of five dollars.

His hands hanging naturally at his sides, the general waited to be seated. Once his arms swung suddenly backward like a jumper's and Dick said, 'Ah!' supposing he had lost control, but the general recovered and they breathed again – the agony was nearly over, the *garçon* was pulling out his chair . . .

With a touch of fury the conqueror shot up his hand and scratched his grey immaculate head.

'You see,' said Dick smugly, 'I'm the only one.'

Rosemary was quite sure of it, and Dick, realising that he never had a better audience, made the group into so bright a unit that Rosemary felt an impatient disregard for all who were not at their table. They had been two days in Paris but actually they were still under the beach umbrella. When, as at the ball of the Corps des Pages the night before, the surroundings seemed formidable to Rosemary, who had yet to attend a Mayfair party in Hollywood,[45] Dick would bring the scene within range by greeting a few people, a sort of selection – the Divers seemed to have a large acquaintance, but it was always as if the person had not seen them for a long, long time, and was utterly bowled over, 'Why, where do you *keep* yourselves?' – and then re-create the unity of his own party by destroying the outsiders softly but permanently with an ironic *coup de grâce*. Presently Rosemary seemed to have known those people herself in some deplorable past, and then got on to them, rejected them, discarded them.

Their own party was overwhelmingly American and sometimes scarcely American at all. It was themselves he gave back to them, blurred by the compromises of how many years.

Into the dark, smoky restaurant, smelling of the rich raw foods on the buffet, slid Nicole's sky-blue suit like a stray segment of the weather outside. Seeing from their eyes how beautiful she was, she thanked them with a smile of radiant appreciation. They were all very nice people for a while, very courteous and all that. Then they grew tired of it and they were funny and bitter, and finally they made a lot of plans. They laughed at things that they would not remember clearly afterward – laughed a lot and the men drank three bottles of wine. The trio of women at the table were representative of the enormous flux of American life. Nicole was the granddaughter of a self-made American capitalist and the granddaughter of a Count of the House of Lippe Weissenfeld.[46] Mary North was the daughter of a journeyman paper-hanger and a descendant of President Tyler.[47] Rosemary was from the middle of the middle class, catapulted by her mother on to the uncharted heights of Hollywood. Their point of resemblance to each other and their difference from so many American women, lay in the fact that they were all happy to exist in a man's world – they preserved their individuality through men and not by opposition to them. They would all three have made alternatively good courtesans or good wives not by the accident of birth but through the greater accident of finding their man or not finding him.

So Rosemary found it a pleasant party, that luncheon, nicer in that there were only seven people, about the limit of a good party. Perhaps, too, the fact that she was new to their world acted as a sort of catalytic agent to precipitate out all their old reservations about one another. After the table broke up, a waiter directed Rosemary back into the dark hinterland of all French restaurants, where she looked up a phone number by a dim orange bulb, and called Franco-American Films.[48] Sure, they had a print of *Daddy's Girl* – it was out for the moment but they would run it off later in the week for her at 341 Rue des Saintes Anges – ask for Mr Crowder.

The semi-booth gave on the *vestiaire*[49] and as Rosemary hung up the receiver she heard two low voices not five feet from her on the other side of a row of coats.

' – So you love me?'

'Oh, *do* I!'

It was Nicole – Rosemary hesitated in the door of the booth – then she heard Dick say: 'I want you terribly – let's go to the hotel now.' Nicole gave a little gasping sigh. For a moment the words conveyed nothing at all to Rosemary – but the tone did. The vast secretiveness of it vibrated to herself.

'I want you.'

'I'll be at the hotel at four.'

Rosemary stood breathless as the voices moved away. She was at first astonished – she had seen them in their relation to each other as people without personal exigencies – as something cooler. Now a strong current of emotion flowed through her, profound and unidentified. She did not know whether she was attracted or repelled, but only that she was deeply moved. It made her feel very alone as she went back into the restaurant, but it was touching to look in upon, and the passionate gratitude of Nicole's 'Oh, *do I*!' echoed in her mind. The particular mood of the passage she had witnessed lay ahead of her; but however far she was from it her stomach told her it was all right – she had none of the aversion she had felt in the playing of certain love scenes in pictures.

Being far away from it she nevertheless irrevocably participated in it now, and shopping with Nicole she was much more conscious of the assignation than Nicole herself. She looked at Nicole in a new way, estimating her attractions. Certainly she was the most attractive woman Rosemary had ever met – with her hardness, her devotions and loyalties, and a certain elusiveness, which Rosemary, thinking now through her mother's middle-class mind, associated with her attitude about money. Rosemary spent money she had earned – she was here in Europe due to the fact that she had gone in the pool six times that January day with her temperature roving from ninety-nine degrees in the early morning to a hundred and three degrees, when her mother stopped it.

With Nicole's help Rosemary bought two dresses and two hats and four pairs of shoes with her money. Nicole bought from a great list that ran to two pages, and bought the things in the windows besides. Everything she liked that she couldn't possibly use herself, she bought as a present for a friend. She bought coloured beads, folding beach cushions, artificial flowers, honey, a guest bed, bags, scarfs, love-birds, miniatures for a doll's house, and three yards of some new cloth the colour of prawns. She bought a dozen bathing suits, a rubber alligator, a travelling chess set of gold and ivory, big linen handkerchiefs for Abe, two chamois leather jackets of kingfisher blue and burning bush from Hermès [50] – bought all these things not a bit like a high-class courtesan buying underwear and jewels, which were after all professional equipment and insurance – but with an entirely different point of view. Nicole was the product of much ingenuity and toil. For her sake trains began their run at Chicago and traversed the round belly of the continent to California; chicle factories fumed and link belts grew link by link in factories; men mixed toothpaste in vats and drew mouthwash out of copper hogsheads; girls canned tomatoes quickly in August or worked rudely at the Five-and-Tens [51] on Christmas Eve; half-breed Indians toiled on Brazilian coffee plantations and dreamers were muscled out of patent rights in new tractors – these were some of the people who gave a tithe to Nicole, and as the whole system swayed and thundered onward it lent a feverish bloom to such processes of hers as wholesale buying, like the flush of a fireman's face holding his post before a spreading blaze. She illustrated very simple principles, containing in herself her own doom, but illustrated them so accurately that there was grace in the procedure, and presently Rosemary would try to imitate it.

It was almost four. Nicole stood in a shop with a love-bird on her shoulder, and had one of her infrequent outbursts of speech.

'Well, what if you hadn't gone in that pool that day – I sometimes wonder about such things. Just before the war we were in Berlin – I was thirteen, it was just before mother died. My sister was going to a court ball and she had three of the royal princes on her dance card, all arranged by a chamberlain and everything. Half an hour before she was going to start she had a side ache and high fever. The doctor said it was appendicitis and she ought to be operated on. But mother had her plans made, so Baby went to the ball and danced till two with an ice pack strapped on under her evening dress. She was operated on at seven o'clock next morning.'

It was good to be hard, then; all nice people were hard on themselves. But it was four o'clock and Rosemary kept thinking of Dick waiting for Nicole now at the hotel. She must go there, she must not make him wait for her. She kept thinking, 'Why don't you go?' and then suddenly, 'or let me go if you don't want to.' But Nicole went to one more place to buy corsages for them both and sent one to Mary North. Only then she seemed to remember and with sudden abstraction she signalled for a taxi.

'Goodbye,' said Nicole. 'We had fun, didn't we?'

'Loads of fun,' said Rosemary. It was more difficult than she thought and her whole self protested as Nicole drove away.

Chapter 13

DICK TURNED THE CORNER of the traverse and continued along the trench walking on the duckboard. He came to a periscope, looked through it a moment, then he got up on the step and peered over the parapet. In front of him beneath a dingy sky was Beaumont-Hamel;[52] to his left the tragic hill of Thiepval.[53] Dick stared at them through his field-glasses, his throat straining with sadness.

He went on along the trench, and found the others waiting for him in the next traverse. He was full of excitement and he wanted to communicate it to them, to make them understand about this, though actually Abe North had seen battle service and he had not.

'This land here cost twenty lives a foot that summer,' he said to Rosemary. He looked out obediently at the rather bare green plain with its low trees of six years' growth. If Dick had added that they were now being shelled she would have believed him that afternoon. Her love had reached a point where now at last she was beginning to be unhappy, to be desperate. She didn't know what to do – she wanted to talk to her mother.

'There are lots of people dead since and we'll all be dead soon,' said Abe consolingly.

Rosemary waited tensely for Dick to continue.

'See that little stream – we could walk to it in two minutes. It took the British a month to walk to it – a whole empire walking very slowly, dying in front and pushing forward behind. And another empire walked very slowly backward a few inches a day, leaving the dead like a million bloody rugs. No Europeans will ever do that again in this generation.'

'Why, they've only just quit over in Turkey,'[54] said Abe. 'And in Morocco – '[55]

'That's different. This western-front business couldn't be done again, not for a long time. The young men think they could do it but they couldn't. They could fight the first Marne again[56] but not this. This took religion and years of plenty and tremendous sureties and the exact relation that existed between the classes. The Russians and Italians weren't any good on this front. You had to have a whole-souled sentimental equipment going back further than you could remember. You had to remember Christmas, and postcards of the Crown Prince and his fiancée, and little cafés in Valence and beer gardens in Unter den Linden and weddings at the *mairie*, and going to the Derby,[57] and your grandfather's whiskers.'

'General Grant invented this kind of battle at Petersburg[58] in sixty-five.'

'No, he didn't – he just invented mass butchery. This kind of battle was invented by Lewis Carroll[59] and Jules Verne[60] and whoever wrote *Undine*,[61] and country deacons bowling and *marraines*[62] in Marseilles and girls seduced in the back lanes of Württemberg and Westphalia. Why, this was a love battle – there was a century of middle-class love spent here. This was the last love battle.'

'You want to hand over this battle to D. H. Lawrence,'[63] said Abe.

'All my beautiful lovely safe world blew itself up here with a great gust of high explosive love,' Dick mourned persistently. 'Isn't that true, Rosemary?'

'I don't know,' she answered with a grave face. 'You know everything.'

They dropped behind the others. Suddenly a shower of earth gobs and pebbles came down on them and Abe yelled from the next traverse: 'The war spirit's getting into me again. I have a hundred years of Ohio love behind me and I'm going to bomb out this trench.' His head popped up over the embankment. 'You're dead – don't you know the rules? That was a grenade.'

Rosemary laughed and Dick picked up a retaliatory handful of stones and then put them down.

'I couldn't kid here,' he said rather apologetically. 'The silver cord is cut and the golden bowl is broken and all that, but an old romantic like me can't do anything about it.'

'I'm romantic too.'

They came out of the neat restored trench, and faced a memorial to the Newfoundland dead.[64] Reading the inscription Rosemary burst into sudden tears. Like most women, she liked to be told how she should feel, and she liked Dick's telling her which things were ludicrous and which things were sad. But most of all she wanted him to know how she loved him, now that the fact was upsetting everything, now that she was walking over the battlefield in a thrilling dream.

After that they got in their car and started back towards Amiens.[65] A thin warm rain was falling on the new scrubby woods and underbrush and they passed great funeral pyres of sorted duds, shells, bombs, grenades, and equipment, helmets, bayonets, gun stocks and rotten leather, abandoned six years in the ground. And suddenly around a bend the white caps of a great sea of graves. Dick asked the chauffeur to stop.

'There's that girl – and she still has her wreath.'

They watched as he got out and went over to the girl, who stood uncertainly by the gate with a wreath in her hand. Her taxi waited. She was a red-haired girl from Tennessee whom they had met on the train this morning, come from Knoxville to lay a memorial on her brother's grave. There were tears of vexation on her face.

'The War Department must have given me the wrong number,' she whimpered. 'It had another name on it. I been lookin' for it since two o'clock, and there's so many graves.'

'Then if I were you I'd just lay it on any grave without looking at the name,' Dick advised her.

'You reckon that's what I ought to do?'

'I think that's what he'd have wanted you to do.'

It was growing dark and the rain was coming down harder. She left the wreath on the first grave inside the gate, and accepted Dick's suggestion that she dismiss her taxi-cab and ride back to Amiens with them.

Rosemary shed tears again when she heard of the mishap – altogether it had been a watery day, but she felt that she had learned something, though exactly what it was she did not know. Later she remembered all the hours of the afternoon as happy – one of those uneventful times that seem at the moment only a link between past and future pleasure but turn out to have been the pleasure itself.

Amiens was an echoing purple town, still sad with the war, as some railroad stations were: the Gare du Nord and Waterloo Station[66] in London. In the daytime one is deflated by such towns, with their little trolley cars of twenty years ago crossing the great grey cobble-stoned squares in front of the cathedral, and the very weather seems to have a quality of the past, faded weather like that of old photographs. But after dark all that is most satisfactory in French life swims back into the picture – the sprightly tarts, the men arguing with a hundred *voilàs* in the cafés, the couples drifting, head to head, towards the satisfactory inexpensiveness of nowhere. Waiting for the train they sat in a big arcade, tall enough to release the smoke and chatter and music upward, and obligingly the orchestra launched into 'Yes, We Have No Bananas'[67] – they clapped, because the leader looked so pleased with himself. The Tennessee girl forgot her sorrow and enjoyed herself, even began flirtations of tropical eye-rollings and pawings, with Dick and Abe. They teased her gently.

Then, leaving infinitesimal sections of Württembergers, Prussian Guards, Chasseurs Alpins,[68] Manchester mill-hands and old Eto-nians to pursue their eternal dissolution under the warm rain, they took the train for Paris. They ate sandwiches of mortadella sausage and bel paese cheese made up in the station restaurant, and drank Beaujolais.[69] Nicole was abstracted, biting her lip restlessly and reading over the guidebooks to the battlefield that Dick had brought along – indeed, he had made a quick study of the whole affair, simplifying it always until it bore a faint resemblance to one of his own parties.

Chapter 14

WHEN THEY REACHED PARIS Nicole was too tired to go on to the grand illumination at the Decorative Arts Exposition[70] as they had planned. They left her at the Hôtel Roi George,[71] and as she disappeared between the intersecting planes made by lobby lights of the glass doors, Rosemary's oppression lifted. Nicole was a force – not necessarily well disposed or predictable like her mother – an incalculable force. Rosemary was somewhat afraid of her.

At eleven she sat with Dick and the Norths at a houseboat café just opened on the Seine. The river shimmered with lights from the bridges and cradled many cold moons. On Sundays sometimes when Rosemary and her mother had lived in Paris they had taken the little steamer up to Suresnes[72] and talked about plans for the future. They had little money, but Mrs Speers was so sure of Rosemary's beauty and had implanted in her so much ambition, that she was willing to gamble the money on 'advantages'; Rosemary in turn was to repay her mother when she got her start . . .

Since reaching Paris Abe North had had a thin vinous fur over him; his eyes were bloodshot from sun and wine. Rosemary realised for the first time that he was always stopping in places to get a drink, and she wondered how Mary North liked it. Mary was quiet, so quiet save for her frequent laughter that Rosemary had learned little about her. She liked the straight dark hair brushed back until it met some sort of natural cascade that took care of it – from time to time it eased with a jaunty slant over the corner of her temple, until it was almost in her eye when she tossed her head and caused it to fall sleek into place once more.

'We'll turn in early tonight, Abe, after this drink.' Mary's voice was light but it held a little flicker of anxiety. 'You don't want to be poured on the boat.'

'It's pretty late now,' Dick said. 'We'd all better go.'

The noble dignity of Abe's face took on a certain stubbornness, and he remarked with determination: 'Oh, no.' He paused gravely. 'Oh, no, not yet. We'll have another bottle of champagne.'

'No more for me,' said Dick.

'It's Rosemary I'm thinking of. She's a natural alcoholic – keeps a bottle of gin in the bathroom and all that – her mother told me.'

He emptied what was left of the first bottle into Rosemary's glass. She had made herself quite sick the first day in Paris with quarts of lemonade; after that she had taken nothing with them, but now she raised the champagne and drank at it.

'But what's this?' exclaimed Dick. 'You told me you didn't drink.'

'I didn't say I was never going to.'

'What about your mother?'

'I'm just going to drink this one glass.' She felt some necessity for it. Dick drank, not too much, but he drank, and perhaps it would bring her closer to him, be a part of the equipment for what she had to do. She drank it quickly, choked and then said, 'Besides, yesterday was my birthday – I was eighteen.'

'Why didn't you tell us?' they said indignantly.

'I knew you'd make a fuss over it and go to a lot of trouble.' She finished the champagne. 'So this is the celebration.'

'It most certainly is not,' Dick assured her. 'The dinner tomorrow night is your birthday party and don't forget it. Eighteen – why that's a terribly important age.'

'I used to think until you're eighteen nothing matters,' said Mary.

'That's right,' Abe agreed. 'And afterward it's the same way.'

'Abe feels that nothing matters till he gets on the boat,' said Mary. 'This time he really has got everything planned out when he gets to New York.' She spoke as though she were tired of saying things that no longer had a meaning for her, as if in reality the course that she and her husband followed, or failed to follow, had become merely an intention.

'He'll be writing music in America and I'll be working at singing in Munich, so when we get together again there'll be nothing we can't do.'

'That's wonderful,' agreed Rosemary, feeling the champagne.

'Meanwhile, another touch of champagne for Rosemary. Then she'll be more able to rationalise the acts of her lymphatic glands. They only begin to function at eighteen.'

Dick laughed indulgently at Abe, whom he loved, and in whom he had long lost hope: 'That's medically incorrect and we're going.' Catching the faint patronage Abe said lightly: 'Something tells me I'll have a new score on Broadway long before you've finished your scientific treatise.'

'I hope so,' said Dick evenly. 'I hope so. I may even abandon what you call my "scientific treatise".'

'Oh, Dick!' Mary's voice was startled, was shocked. Rosemary had never before seen Dick's face utterly expressionless; she felt that this announcement was something momentous and she was inclined to exclaim with Mary, 'Oh, Dick!'

But suddenly Dick laughed again, added to his remark ' – abandon it for another one,' and got up from the table.

'But Dick, sit down. I want to know – '

'I'll tell you some time. Good-night, Abe. Good-night, Mary.'

'Good-night, dear Dick.' Mary smiled as if she were going to be perfectly happy sitting there on the almost deserted boat. She was a brave, hopeful woman and she was following her husband somewhere, changing herself to this kind of person or that, without being able to lead him a step out of his path, and sometimes realising with discouragement how deep in him the guarded secret of her direction lay. And yet an air of luck clung about her, as if she were a sort of token.

Chapter 15

'WHAT IS IT YOU ARE GIVING UP?' demanded Rosemary, facing Dick earnestly in the taxi.

'Nothing of importance.'

'Are you a scientist?'

'I'm a doctor of medicine.'

'Oh-h!' she smiled delightedly. 'My father was a doctor too. Then why don't you – ' she stopped.

'There's no mystery. I didn't disgrace myself at the height of my career, and hide away on the Riviera. I'm just not practising. You can't tell, I'll probably practise again some day.'

Rosemary put up her face quietly to be kissed. He looked at her for a moment as if he didn't understand. Then holding her in the hollow of his arm he rubbed his cheek against her cheek's softness, and then looked down at her for another long moment.

'Such a lovely child,' he said gravely.

She smiled up at him; her hands playing conventionally with the lapels of his coat. 'I'm in love with you and Nicole. Actually that's my secret – I can't even talk about you to anybody because I don't want any more people to know how wonderful you are. Honestly – I love you and Nicole – I do.'

So many times he had heard this – even the formula was the same.

Suddenly she came towards him, her youth vanishing as she passed inside the focus of his eyes and he had kissed her breathlessly as if she were any age at all. Then she lay back against his arm and sighed.

'I've decided to give you up,' she said.

Dick started – had he said anything to imply that she possessed any part of him?

'But that's very mean,' he managed to say lightly, 'just when I was getting interested.'

'I've loved you so – ' As if it had been for years. She was weeping a little now. 'I've loved you s–o–o.'

Then he should have laughed, but he heard himself saying, 'Not only are you beautiful but you are somehow on the grand scale. Everything you do, like pretending to be in love or pretending to be shy, gets across.'

In the dark cave of the taxi, fragrant with the perfume Rosemary had bought with Nicole, she came close again, clinging to him. He kissed her without enjoying it. He knew that there was passion there, but there was no shadow of it in her eyes or on her mouth; there was a faint spray of champagne on her breath. She clung nearer desperately and once more he kissed her and was chilled by the innocence of her kiss, by the glance that at the moment of contact looked beyond him out into the darkness of the night, the darkness of the world. She did not know yet that splendour is something in the heart; at the moment when she realised that and melted into the passion of the universe he could take her without question or regret.

Her room in the hotel was diagonally across from theirs and nearer the elevator. When they reached the door she said suddenly: 'I know you don't love me – I don't expect it. But you said I should have told you about my birthday. Well, I did, and now for my birthday present I want you to come into my room a minute while I tell you something. Just one minute.'

They went in and he closed the door, and Rosemary stood close to him, not touching him. The night had drawn the colour from her face – she was pale as pale now, she was a white carnation left after a dance.

'When you smile – ' he had recovered his paternal attitude, perhaps because of Nicole's silent proximity – 'I always think I'll see a gap where you've lost some baby teeth.'

But he was too late – she came close up against him with a forlorn whisper.

'Take me.'

'Take you where?'

Astonishment froze him rigid.

'Go on,' she whispered. 'Oh, please go on, whatever they do. I don't care if I don't like it – I never expected to – I've always hated to think about it but now I don't. I want you to.'

She was astonished at herself – she had never imagined she could talk like that. She was calling on things she had read, seen, dreamed through a decade of convent hours. Suddenly she knew too that it was one of her greatest roles and she flung herself into it more passionately.

'This is not as it should be,' Dick deliberated. 'Isn't it just the champagne? Let's more or less forget it.'

'Oh, no, *now*. I want you to do it now, take me, show me, I'm absolutely yours and I want to be.'

'For one thing, have you thought how much it would hurt Nicole?'

'She won't know – this won't have anything to do with her.'

He continued kindly.

'Then there's the fact that I love Nicole.'

'But you can love more than just one person, can't you? Like I love mother and I love you – more. I love you more now.'

' – the fourth place you're not in love with me but you might be afterwards, and that would begin your life with a terrible mess.'

'No, I promise I'll never see you again. I'll get mother and go to America right away.'

He dismissed this. He was remembering too vividly the youth and freshness of her lips. He took another tone.

'You're just in that mood.'

'Oh, please, I don't care even if I had a baby. I could go into Mexico like a girl at the studio. Oh, this is so different from anything I ever thought – I used to hate it when they kissed me seriously.' He saw she was still under the impression that it must happen. 'Some of them had great big teeth, but you're all different and beautiful. I want you to do it.'

'I believe you think people just kiss some way and you want me to kiss you.'

'Oh, don't tease me – I'm not a baby. I know you're not in love with me.' She was suddenly humble and quiet. 'I didn't expect that much. I know I must seem just nothing to you.'

'Nonsense. But you seem young to me.' His thoughts added, ' – there'd be so much to teach you.'

Rosemary waited, breathing eagerly till Dick said: 'And lastly things aren't arranged so that this could be as you want.'

Her face drooped with dismay and disappointment and Dick said automatically, 'We'll have to simply – ' He stopped himself, followed her to the bed, sat down beside her while she wept. He was suddenly confused, not about the ethics of the matter, for the impossibility of it was sheerly indicated from all angles, but simply confused, and for a moment his usual grace, the tensile strength of his balance, was absent.

'I knew you wouldn't,' she sobbed. 'It was just a forlorn hope.'

He stood up.

'Good-night, child. This is a damn shame. Let's drop it out of the picture.' He gave her two lines of hospital patter to go to sleep on. 'So many people are going to love you and it might be nice to meet your first love all intact, emotionally too. That's an old-fashioned idea, isn't it?' She looked up at him as he took a step towards the door; she looked at him without the slightest idea as to what was in his head, she saw him take another step in slow motion, turn and look at her again, and she wanted for a moment to hold him and devour him, wanted his mouth, his ears, his coat collar, wanted to surround him and engulf him; she saw his hand fall on the doorknob. Then she gave up and sank back on the bed. When the door closed she got up and went to the mirror, where she began brushing her hair, sniffling a little. One hundred and fifty strokes Rosemary gave it, as usual, then a hundred and fifty more. She brushed it until her arm ached, then she changed arms and went on brushing.

Chapter 16

SHE WOKE UP COOLED and shamed. The sight of her beauty in the mirror did not reassure her but only awakened the ache of yesterday, and a letter, forwarded by her mother, from the boy who had taken her to the Yale prom last fall, which announced his presence in Paris, was no help – all that seemed far away. She emerged from her room for the ordeal of meeting the Divers weighted with a double trouble. But it was hidden by a sheath as impermeable as Nicole's when they met and went together to a series of fittings. It was consoling, though, when Nicole remarked, apropos of a distraught saleswoman: 'Most people think everybody feels about them much more violently than they actually do – they think other people's opinions of them swing through great arcs of approval or disapproval.' Yesterday in her expansiveness Rosemary would have resented that remark – today in her desire to minimise what had happened she welcomed it eagerly. She admired Nicole for her beauty and her wisdom, and also for the first time in her life she was jealous. Just before leaving Gausse's Hôtel her mother had said in that casual tone, which Rosemary knew concealed her most significant opinions, that Nicole was a great beauty, with the frank implication that Rosemary was not. This did not bother Rosemary, who had only recently been allowed to learn that she was even personable; so that her prettiness never seemed exactly her own but rather an acquirement, like her French. Nevertheless, in the taxi she looked at Nicole, matching herself against her. There were all the potentialities for romantic love in that lovely body and in the delicate mouth, sometimes tight, sometimes expectantly half open to the world. Nicole had been a beauty as a young girl and she would be a beauty later when her skin stretched tight over her high cheek-bones – the essential structure was there. She had been white-Saxon-blonde but she was more beautiful now that her hair had darkened than when it had been like a cloud and more beautiful than she.

'We lived there,' Rosemary suddenly pointed to a building in the Rue des Saints-Pères.[73]

'That's strange. Because when I was twelve mother and Baby and I once spent a winter there,' and she pointed to a hotel directly across the street. The two dingy fronts stared at them, grey echoes of girlhood.

'We'd just built our Lake Forest[74] house and we were economising,' Nicole continued. 'At least Baby and I and the governess economised and mother travelled.'

'We were economising too,' said Rosemary, realising that the word meant different things to them.

'Mother always spoke of it very carefully as a small hotel – ' Nicole gave her quick magnetic little laugh ' – I mean instead of saying a "cheap" hotel. If any swanky friends asked us our address we'd never say, "We're in a dingy little hole over in the apache quarter where we're glad of running water," – we'd say "We're in a small hotel." As if all the big ones were too noisy and vulgar for us. Of course the friends always saw through us and told everyone about it, but mother always said it showed we knew our way around Europe. She did, of course: she was born a German citizen. But her mother was American, and she was brought up in Chicago, and she was more American than European.'

They were meeting the others in two minutes, and Rosemary reconstructed herself once more as they got out of the taxi in the Rue Guynemer, across from the Luxembourg Gardens.[75] They were lunching in the Norths' already dismantled apartment high above the green mass of leaves. The day seemed different to Rosemary from the day before. When she saw him face to face their eyes met and brushed like birds' wings. After that everything was all right, everything was wonderful, she knew that he was beginning to fall in love with her. She felt wildly happy, felt the warm sap of emotion being pumped through her body. A cool, clear confidence deepened and sang in her. She scarcely looked at Dick but she knew everything was all right.

After luncheon the Divers and the Norths and Rosemary went to the Franco-American Films, to be joined by Collis Clay, her young man from New Haven,[76] to whom she had telephoned. He was a Georgian, with the peculiarly regular, even stencilled ideas of Southerners who are educated in the North. Last winter she had thought him attractive – once they held hands in an automobile going from New Haven to New York; now he no longer existed for her.

In the projection room she sat between Collis Clay and Dick while the mechanic mounted the reels of *Daddy's Girl* and a French executive fluttered about her trying to talk American slang. 'Yes, boy,' he said when there was trouble with the projector, 'I have not any benenas.' Then the lights went out, there was a sudden click and a flickering noise and she was alone with Dick at last. They looked at each other in the half-darkness.

'Dear Rosemary,' he murmured. Their shoulders touched. Nicole stirred restlessly at the end of the row and Abe coughed convulsively and blew his nose; then they all settled down and the picture ran.

There she was – the schoolgirl of a year ago, hair down her back and rippling out stiffly like the solid hair of a Tanagra[77] figure; there she was – *so* young and innocent – the product of her mother's loving care; there she was – embodying all the immaturity of the race, cutting a new cardboard paper doll to pass before its empty harlot's mind. She remembered how she had felt in that dress, especially fresh and new under the fresh young silk.

Daddy's girl. Was it a 'itty-bitty bravekins and did it suffer? Ooo-ooo-tweet, de tweetest thing, wasn't she dest too tweet?' Before her tiny fist the forces of lust and corruption rolled away; nay, the very march of destiny stopped; inevitably became evitable, syllogism, dialectic, all rationality fell away. Women would forget the dirty dishes at home and weep, even within the picture one woman wept so long that she almost stole the film away from Rosemary. She wept all over a set that cost a fortune, in a Duncan Phyfe[78] dining-room, in an aviation port, and during a yacht race that was only used in two flashes, in a subway and finally in a bathroom. But Rosemary triumphed. Her fineness of character, her courage and steadfastness intruded upon by the vulgarity of the world, and Rosemary showing what it took with a face that had not yet become mask-like – yet it was actually so moving that the emotions of the whole row of people went out to her at intervals during the picture. There was a break once and the light went on and after the chatter of applause Dick said to her sincerely: 'I'm simply astounded. You're going to be one of the best actresses on the stage.'

Then back to *Daddy's Girl*: happier days now, and a lovely shot of Rosemary and her parent united at the last in a father complex so apparent that Dick winced for all psychologists at the vicious sentimentality. The screen vanished, the lights went on, the moment had come.

'I've arranged one other thing,' announced Rosemary to the company at large, 'I've arranged a test for Dick.'

'A what?'

'A screen test, they'll take one now.'

There was an awful silence – then an irrepressible chortle from the Norths. Rosemary watched Dick comprehend what she meant, his face moving first in an Irish way; simultaneously she realised that she had made some mistake in the playing of her trump and still she did not suspect that the card was at fault.

'I don't want a test,' said Dick firmly; then, seeing the situation as a whole, he continued lightly, 'Rosemary, I'm disappointed. The pictures make a fine career for a woman – but my God, they can't photograph me. I'm an old scientist all wrapped up in his private life.'

Nicole and Mary urged him ironically to seize the opportunity; they teased him, both faintly annoyed at not having been asked for a sitting. But Dick closed the subject with a somewhat tart discussion of actors: 'The strongest guard is placed at the gateway to nothing,' he said. 'Maybe because the condition of emptiness is too shameful to be divulged.'

In the taxi with Dick and Collis Clay – they were dropping Collis, and Dick was taking Rosemary to a tea from which Nicole and the Norths had resigned in order to do the things Abe had left undone till the last – in the taxi Rosemary reproached him.

'I thought if the test turned out to be good I could take it to California with me. And then maybe if they liked it you'd come out and be my leading man in a picture.'

He was overwhelmed. 'It was a darn sweet thought, but I'd rather look at you. You were about the nicest sight I ever looked at.'

'That's a great picture,' said Collis. 'I've seen it four times. I know one boy at New Haven who's seen it a dozen times – he went all the way to Hartford to see it one time. And when I brought Rosemary up to New Haven he was so shy he wouldn't meet her. Can you beat that? This girl knocks them cold.'

Dick and Rosemary looked at each other, wanting to be alone, but Collis failed to understand.

'I'll drop you where you're going,' he suggested. 'I'm staying at the Lutetia.'[79]

'We'll drop you,' said Dick.

'It'll be easier for me to drop you. No trouble at all.'

'I think it will be better if we drop you.'

'But – ' began Collis; he grasped the situation at last and began discussing with Rosemary when he would see her again.

Finally, he was gone, with a shadowy unimportance but the offensive bulk of the third party. The car stopped unexpectedly, unsatisfactorily, at the address Dick had given. He drew a long breath.

'Shall we go in?'

'I don't care.' Rosemary said. 'I'll do anything you want.'

He considered.

'I almost have to go in – she wants to buy some pictures from a friend of mine who needs the money.'

Rosemary smoothed the brief expressive disarray of her hair.

'We'll stay just five minutes,' he decided. 'You're not going to like these people.'

She assumed that they were dull and stereotyped people, or gross and drunken people, or tiresome, insistent people, or any of the sorts of people that the Divers avoided. She was entirely unprepared for the impression that the scene made on her.

Chapter 17

IT WAS A HOUSE hewn from the frame of Cardinal de Retz's palace in the Rue Monsieur,[80] but once inside the door there was nothing of the past, nor of any present that Rosemary knew. The outer shell, the masonry, seemed rather to enclose the future so that it was an electric-like shock, a definite nervous experience, perverted as a breakfast of oatmeal and hashish, to cross that threshold, if it could be so called, into the long hall of blue steel, silver-gilt, and the myriad facets of many oddly bevelled mirrors. The effect was unlike that of any part of the Decorative Arts Exhibition – for there were people in it, not in front of it. Rosemary had the detached false-and-exalted feeling of being on a set and she guessed that everyone else present had that feeling too.

There were about thirty people, mostly women, and all fashioned by Louisa M. Alcott or Madame de Ségur;[81] and they functioned on this set as cautiously, as precisely, as does a human hand picking up jagged broken glass. Neither individually nor as a crowd could they be said to dominate the environment, as one comes to dominate a work of art he may possess, no matter how esoteric. No one knew what this room meant because it was evolving into something else, becoming everything a room was not; to exist in it was as difficult as walking on a highly polished moving stairway, and no one could succeed at all save with the aforementioned qualities of a hand moving among broken glass – which qualities limited and defined the majority of those present.

These were of two sorts. There were the Americans and English who had been dissipating all spring and summer, so that now everything they did had a purely nervous inspiration. They were very quiet and lethargic at certain hours and then they exploded into sudden quarrels and breakdowns and seductions. The other class, who might be called the exploiters, was formed by the spongers, who were sober, serious people by comparison, with a purpose in life and no time for fooling. These kept their balance best in that environment, and what tone there was beyond the apartment's novel organisation of light values came from them.

The Frankenstein took down Dick and Rosemary at a gulp – it separated them immediately and Rosemary suddenly discovered herself to be an insincere little person, living all in the upper registers of her throat and wishing the director would come. There was however such a wild beating of wings in the room that she did not feel her position was more incongruous than anyone else's. In addition, her training told and after a series of semi-military turns, shifts, and marches she found herself presumably talking to a neat, slick girl with a lovely boy's face, but actually absorbed by a conversation taking place on a sort of gun-metal ladder diagonally opposite her and four feet away.

There was a trio of young women sitting on the bench. They were all tall and slender with small heads groomed like mannequins' heads, and as they talked the heads waved gracefully about above their dark tailored suits, rather like long-stemmed flowers and rather like cobras' hoods.

'Oh, they give a good show,' said one of them, in a deep rich voice. 'Practically the best show in Paris – I'd be the last one to deny that. But after all – ' She sighed. 'Those phrases he uses over and over – "Oldest inhabitant gnawed by rodents." You laugh once.'

'I prefer people whose lives have more corrugated surfaces,' said the second, 'and I don't like her.'

'I've never really been able to get very excited about them, or their entourage either. Why, for example, the entirely liquid Mr North?'

'He's out,' said the first girl. 'But you must admit that the party in question can be one of the most charming human beings you have ever met.'

It was the first hint Rosemary had had that they were talking about the Divers, and her body grew tense with indignation. But the girl talking to her, in the starched blue shirt with the bright blue eyes and the red cheeks and the very grey suit, a poster of a girl, had begun to play up. Desperately she kept sweeping things from between them, afraid that Rosemary couldn't see her, sweeping them away until presently there was not so much as a veil of brittle humour hiding the girl, and with distaste Rosemary saw her plain.

'Couldn't you have lunch, or maybe dinner, or lunch the day after?' begged the girl. Rosemary looked about for Dick, finding him with the hostess, to whom he had been talking since they came in. Their eyes met and he nodded slightly, and simultaneously the three cobra women noticed her; their long necks darted towards her and they fixed finely critical glances upon her. She looked back at them defiantly, acknowledging that she had heard what they said. Then she threw off her exigent vis-à-vis with a polite but clipped parting that she had just learned from Dick, and went over to join him. The hostess – she was another tall rich American girl, promenading insouciantly upon the national prosperity – was asking Dick innumerable questions about Gausse's Hôtel, whither she evidently wanted to come, and battering persistently against his reluctance. Rosemary's presence reminded her that she had been recalcitrant as a hostess and glancing about she said: 'Have you met anyone amusing, have you met Mr – ' Her eyes groped for a male who might interest Rosemary, but Dick said they must go. They left immediately, moving over the brief threshold of the future to the sudden past of the stone façade without.

'Wasn't it terrible?' he said.

'Terrible,' she echoed obediently.

'Rosemary?'

She murmured, 'What?' in an awed voice.

'I feel terribly about this.'

She was shaken with audibly painful sobs. 'Have you got a hand-kerchief?' she faltered. But there was little time to cry, and lovers now they fell ravenously on the quick seconds, while outside the taxi windows the green and cream twilight faded, and the fire-red, gas-blue, ghost-green signs began to shine smokily through the tranquil rain. It was nearly six, the streets were in movement, the bistros gleamed, the Place de la Concorde[82] moved by in pink majesty as the cab turned north.

They looked at each other at last, murmuring names that were a spell. Softly the two names lingered on the air, died away more slowly than other words, other names, slower than music in the mind.

'I don't know what came over me last night,' Rosemary said. 'That glass of champagne? I've never done anything like that before.'

'You simply said you loved me.'

'I do love you – I can't change that.' It was time for Rosemary to cry, so she cried a little in her handkerchief.

'I'm afraid I'm in love with you,' said Dick, 'and that's not the best thing that could happen.'

Again the names – then they lurched together as if the taxi had swung them. Her breasts crushed flat against him, her mouth was all new and warm, owned in common. They stopped thinking with an almost painful relief, stopped seeing; they only breathed and sought each other. They were both in the grey gentle world of a mild hangover of fatigue when the nerves relax in bunches like piano strings, and crackle suddenly like wicker chairs. Nerves so raw and tender must surely join other nerves, lips to lips, breast to breast . . .

They were still in the happier stage of love. They were full of brave illusions about each other, tremendous illusions, so that the communion of self with self seemed to be on a plane where no other human relations mattered. They both seemed to have arrived there with an extraordinary innocence as though a series of pure accidents had driven them together, so many accidents that at last they were forced to conclude that they were for each other. They had arrived with clean hands, or so it seemed, after no traffic with the merely curious and clandestine.

But for Dick that portion of the road was short; the turning came before they reached the hotel.

'There's nothing to do about it,' he said, with a feeling of panic. 'I'm in love with you but it doesn't change what I said last night.'

'That doesn't matter now. I just wanted to make you love me – if you love me everything's all right.'

'Unfortunately I do. But Nicole mustn't know – she mustn't suspect even faintly. Nicole and I have got to go on together. In a way that's more important than just wanting to go on.'

'Kiss me once more.'

He kissed her, but momentarily he had left her.

'Nicole mustn't suffer – she loves me and I love her – you understand that.'

She did understand – it was the sort of thing she understood well, not hurting people. She knew the Divers loved each other because it had been her primary assumption. She had thought however that it was a rather cooled relation, and actually rather like the love of herself and her mother. When people have so much for outsiders didn't it indicate a lack of inner intensity?

'And I mean love,' he said, guessing her thoughts. 'Active love – it's more complicated than I can tell you. It was responsible for that crazy duel.'

'How did you know about the duel? I thought we were to keep it from you.'

'Do you think Abe can keep a secret?' He spoke with incisive irony. 'Tell a secret over the radio, publish it in a tabloid, but never tell it to a man who drinks more than three or four a day.'

She laughed in agreement, staying close to him.

'So you understand my relations with Nicole are complicated. She's not very strong – she looks strong but she isn't. And this makes rather a mess.'

'Oh, say that later! But kiss me now – love me now. I'll love you and never let Nicole see.'

'You darling.'

They reached the hotel and Rosemary walked a little behind him, to admire him, to adore him. His step was alert as if he had just come from some great doings and was hurrying on towards others. Organiser of private gaiety, curator of a richly incrusted happiness. His hat was a perfect hat and he carried a heavy stick and yellow gloves. She thought what a good time they would all have being with him tonight.

They walked upstairs – five flights. At the first landing they stopped and kissed; she was careful on the next landing, on the third more careful still. On the next – there were two more – she stopped halfway and kissed him fleetingly goodbye. At his urgency she walked down with him to the one below for a minute – and then up and up. Finally it was goodbye with their hands stretching to touch along the diagonal of the banister and then the fingers slipping apart. Dick went back downstairs to make some arrangements for the evening – Rosemary ran to her room and wrote a letter to her mother; she was conscience-stricken because she did not miss her mother at all.

Chapter 18

ALTHOUGH THE DIVERS were honestly apathetic to organised fashion, they were nevertheless too acute to abandon its contemporaneous rhythm and beat – Dick's parties were all concerned with excitement, and a chance breath of fresh night air was the more precious for being experienced in the intervals of the excitement.

The party that night moved with the speed of a slapstick comedy. They were twelve, they were sixteen, they were quartets in separate motors bound on a quick odyssey over Paris. Everything had been foreseen. People joined them as if by magic, accompanied them as specialists, almost guides, through a phase of the evening, dropped out and were succeeded by other people, so that it appeared as if the freshness of each one had been husbanded for them all day. Rosemary appreciated how different it was from any party in Hollywood, no matter how splendid in scale. There was, among many diversions, the car of the Shah of Persia.[83] Where Dick had commandeered this vehicle, what bribery was employed, these were facts of irrelevance. Rosemary accepted it as merely a new facet of the fabulous, which for two years had filled her life. The car had been built on a special chassis in America. Its wheels were of silver, so was the radiator. The inside of the body was inlaid with innumerable brilliants which would be replaced with true gems by the court jeweller when the car arrived in Teheran[84] the following week. There was only one real seat in back, because the Shah must ride alone, so they took turns riding in it and sitting on the marten fur that covered the floor.

But always there was Dick. Rosemary assured the image of her mother, ever carried with her, that never, never had she known anyone so nice, so thoroughly nice as Dick was that night. She compared him with the two Englishmen, whom Abe addressed conscientiously as 'Major Hengist and Mr Horsa',[85] and with the heir to a Scandinavian throne and the novelist just back from Russia, and with Abe, who was desperate and witty, and with Collis Clay, who joined them somewhere and stayed along – and felt there was no comparison. The enthusiasm, the selflessness behind the whole performance ravished her, the technique of moving many varied types, each as immobile, as dependent on supplies of attention as an infantry battalion is dependent on rations, appeared so effortless that he still had pieces of his own most personal self for everyone.

Afterward she remembered the times when she had felt the happiest. The first time was when she and Dick danced together and she felt her beauty sparkling bright against his tall, strong form as they floated, hovering like people in an amusing dream – he turned her here and there with such a delicacy of suggestion that she was like a bright bouquet, a piece of precious cloth being displayed before fifty eyes. There was a moment when they were not dancing at all, simply clinging together. Some time in the early morning they were alone, and her damp powdery young body came up close to him in a crush of tired cloth, and stayed there, crushed against a background of other people's hats and wraps . . .

The time she laughed most was later, when six of them, the best of them, noblest relics of the evening, stood in the dusky front lobby of the Ritz[86] telling the night concierge that General Pershing[87] was outside and wanted caviare and champagne. 'He brooks no delay. Every man, every gun is at his service.' Frantic waiters emerged from nowhere, a table was set in the lobby, and Abe came in representing General Pershing while they stood up and mumbled remembered fragments of war songs at him. In the waiter's injured reaction to this anticlimax they found themselves neglected, so they built a waiter trap – a huge and fantastic device constructed of all the furniture in the lobby and functioning like one of the bizarre machines of a Goldberg cartoon.[88] Abe shook his head doubtfully at it.

'Perhaps it would be better to steal a musical saw and – '

'That's enough,' Mary interrupted. 'When Abe begins bringing up that it's time to go home.' Anxiously she confided to Rosemary: 'I've got to get Abe home. His boat train leaves at eleven. It's so important – I feel the whole future depends on his catching it, but whenever I argue with him he does the exact opposite.'

'I'll try and persuade him,' offered Rosemary.

'Would you?' Mary said doubtfully. 'Maybe you could.'

Then Dick came up to Rosemary: 'Nicole and I are going home and we thought you'd want to go with us.'

Her face was pale with fatigue in the false dawn. Two wan dark spots in her cheek marked where the colour was by day.

'I can't,' she said. 'I promised Mary North to stay along with them – or Abe'll never go to bed. Maybe you could do something.'

'Don't you know you can't do anything about people?' he advised her. 'If Abe was my room-mate in college, tight for the first time, it'd be different. Now there's nothing to do.'

'Well, I've got to stay. He says he'll go to bed if we only come to the Halles[89] with him,' she said, almost defiantly.

He kissed the inside of her elbow quickly.

'Don't let Rosemary go home alone,' Nicole called to Mary as they left. 'We feel responsible to her mother.'

Later Rosemary and the Norths and a manufacturer of dolls' voices from Newark and ubiquitous Collis and a big splendidly dressed oil Indian named George T. Horse-protection were riding along on top of thousands of carrots in a market wagon. The earth in the carrot beards was fragrant and sweet in the darkness, and Rosemary was so high up in the load that she could hardly see the others in the long shadow between infrequent street lamps. Their voices came from far off, as if they were having experiences different from hers, different and far away, for she was with Dick in her heart, sorry she had come with the Norths, wishing she was at the hotel and him asleep across the hall, or that he was here beside her with the warm darkness streaming down.

'Don't come up,' she called to Collis, 'the carrots will all roll.' She threw one at Abe, who was sitting beside the driver, stiffly like an old man . . .

Later she was homeward bound at last in broad daylight, with the pigeons already breaking over Saint-Sulpice.[90] All of them began to laugh spontaneously because they knew it was still last night while the people in the streets had the delusion that it was bright hot morning.

'At last I've been on a wild party,' thought Rosemary, 'but it's no fun when Dick isn't there.'

She felt a little betrayed and sad, but presently a moving object came into sight. It was a huge horse-chestnut tree in full bloom bound for the Champs Élysées, strapped now into a long truck and simply shaking with laughter – like a lovely person in an undignified position yet confident none the less of being lovely. Looking at it with fascination Rosemary identified herself with it, and laughed cheerfully with it, and everything all at once seemed gorgeous.

Chapter 19

ABE LEFT FROM THE GARE SAINT-LAZARE[91] at eleven – he stood alone under the fouled glass dome, relic of the seventies, era of the Crystal Palace; his hands, of that vague grey colour that only twenty-four hours can produce, were in his coat pockets to conceal the trembling fingers. With his hat removed it was plain that only the top layer of his hair was brushed back – the lower levels were pointed resolutely sidewise. He was scarcely recognisable as the man who had swum upon Gausse's beach a fortnight ago.

He was early; he looked from left to right with his eyes only; it would have taken nervous forces out of his control to use any other part of his body. New-looking baggage went past him; presently prospective passengers, with dark little bodies, were calling: 'Jew-uls – *Hoo-oo!*' in dark piercing voices.

At the minute when he wondered whether or not he had time for a drink at the buffet, and began clutching at the soggy wad of thousand-franc notes in his pocket, one end of his pendulous glance came to rest upon the apparition of Nicole at the stairhead. He watched her – she was self-revelatory in her little expressions as people seem to someone waiting for them, who as yet is himself unobserved. She was frowning, thinking of her children, less gloating over them than merely animally counting them – a cat checking her cubs with a paw.

When she saw Abe, the mood passed out of her face; the glow of the morning skylight was sad, and Abe made a gloomy figure with dark circles that showed through the crimson tan under his eyes. They sat down on a bench.

'I came because you asked me,' said Nicole defensively. Abe seemed to have forgotten why he asked her and Nicole was quite content to look at the travellers passing by.

'That's going to be the belle of your boat – that one with all the men to say goodbye – you see why she bought that dress?' Nicole talked faster and faster. 'You see why nobody else would buy it except the belle of the world cruise? See? No? Wake up! That's a story dress – that extra material tells a story and somebody on a world cruise would be lonesome enough to want to hear it.'

She bit close her last words; she had talked too much for her; and Abe found it difficult to gather from her serious set face that she had spoken at all. With an effort he drew himself up to a posture that looked as if he were standing up while he was sitting down.

'The afternoon you took me to that funny ball – you know, St Genèvieve's[92] – ' he began.

'I remember. It was fun, wasn't it?'

'No fun for me. I haven't had fun seeing you this time. I'm tired of you both, but it doesn't show because you're even more tired of me – you know what I mean. If I had any enthusiasm, I'd go on to new people.'

There was a rough nap on Nicole's velvet gloves as she slapped him back: 'Seems rather foolish to be unpleasant, Abe. Anyhow you don't mean that. I can't see why you've given up about everything.'

Abe considered, trying hard not to cough or blow his nose.

'I suppose I got bored; and then it was such a long way to go back in order to get anywhere.'

Often a man can play the helpless child in front of a woman, but he can almost never bring it off when he feels most like a helpless child.

'No excuse for it,' Nicole said crisply.

Abe was feeling worse every minute – he could think of nothing but disagreeable and sheerly nervous remarks. Nicole thought that the correct attitude for her was to sit staring straight ahead, hands in her lap. For a while there was no communication between them – each was racing away from the other, breathing only insofar as there was blue space ahead, a sky not seen by the other. Unlike lovers, they possessed no past; unlike man and wife, they possessed no future; yet up to this morning Nicole had liked Abe better than anyone except Dick – and he had been heavy, belly-frightened, with love for her for years.

'Tired of women's worlds,' he spoke up suddenly.

'Then why don't you make a world of your own?'

'Tired of friends. The thing is to have sycophants.'

Nicole tried to force the minute hand around on the station clock, but, 'You agree?' he demanded.

'I am a woman and my business is to hold things together.'

'My business is to tear them apart.'

'When you get drunk you don't tear anything apart except yourself,' she said, cold now, and frightened and unconfident. The station was filling but no one she knew came. After a moment her eyes fell gratefully on a tall girl with straw hair like a helmet, who was dropping letters in the mail slot.

'A girl I have to speak to, Abe. Abe, wake up! You fool!'

Patiently Abe followed her with his eyes. The woman turned in a startled way to greet Nicole, and Abe recognised her as some one he had seen around Paris. He took advantage of Nicole's absence to cough hard and retchingly into his handkerchief, and to blow his nose loud. The morning was warmer and his underwear was soaked with sweat. His fingers trembled so violently that it took four matches to light a cigarette; it seemed absolutely necessary to make his way into the buffet for a drink, but immediately Nicole returned.

'That was a mistake,' she said with frosty humour. 'After begging me to come and see her, she gave me a good snubbing. She looked at me as if I were rotted.' Excited she did a little laugh, as with two fingers high in the scales. 'Let people come to you.'

Abe recovered from a cigarette cough and remarked: 'Trouble is when you're sober you don't want to see anybody, and when you're tight nobody wants to see you.'

'Who, me?' Nicole laughed again, for some reason the late encounter had cheered her.

'No – me.'

'Speak for yourself. I like people, a lot of people – I like – '

Rosemary and Mary North came in sight, walking slowly and searching for Abe, and Nicole burst forth grossly with 'Hey! Hi! Hey!' and laughed and waved the package of handkerchiefs she had bought for Abe.

They stood in an uncomfortable little group weighted down by Abe's gigantic presence: he lay athwart them like the wreck of a galleon, dominating with his presence his own weakness and self-indulgence, his narrowness and bitterness. All of them were conscious of the solemn dignity that flowed from him, of his achievement, fragmentary, suggestive and surpassed. But they were frightened at his survivant[93] will, once a will to live, now become a will to die.

Dick Diver came and brought with him a fine glowing surface on which the three women sprang like monkeys with cries of relief, perching on his shoulders, on the beautiful crown of his hat or the gold head of his cane. Now, for a moment, they could disregard the spectacle of Abe's gigantic obscenity. Dick saw the situation quickly and grasped it quietly. He pulled them out of themselves into the station, making plain its wonders. Nearby, some Americans were saying goodbye in voices that mimicked the cadence of water running into a large old bathtub. Standing in the station, with Paris in back of them, it seemed as if they were vicariously leaning a little over the ocean, already undergoing a sea-change, a shifting about of atoms to form the essential molecule of a new people.

So the well-to-do Americans poured through the station on to the platforms with frank new faces, intelligent, considerate, thoughtless, thought-for. An occasional English face among them seemed sharp and emergent. When there were enough Americans on the platform the first impression of their immaculacy and their money began to fade into a vague racial dusk that hindered and blinded both them and their observers.

Nicole seized Dick's arm crying, 'Look!' Dick turned in time to see what took place in half a minute. At a Pullman entrance[94] two cars off, a vivid scene detached itself from the tenor of many farewells. The young woman with the helmet-like hair to whom Nicole had spoken made an odd dodging little run away from the man to whom she was talking and plunged a frantic hand into her purse; then the sound of two revolver shots cracked the narrow air of the platform. Simultaneously the engine whistled sharply and the train began to move, momentarily dwarfing the shots in significance. Abe waved again from his window, oblivious to what had happened. But before the crowd closed in, the others had seen the shots take effect, seen the target sit down upon the platform.

Only after a hundred years did the train stop; Nicole, Mary, and Rosemary waited on the outskirts while Dick fought his way through. It was five minutes before he found them again – by this time the crowd had split into two sections, following, respectively, the man on a stretcher and the girl walking pale and firm between distraught gendarmes.

'It was Maria Wallis,' Dick said hurriedly. 'The man she shot was an Englishman – they had an awful time finding out who, because she shot him through his identification card.' They were walking quickly from the train, swayed along with the crowd. 'I found out what *poste de police*[95] they're taking her to so I'll go there – '

'But her sister lives in Paris,' Nicole objected. 'Why not phone her? Seems very peculiar nobody thought of that. She's married to a Frenchman, and he can do more than we can.'

Dick hesitated, shook his head and started off.

'Wait!' Nicole cried after him. 'That's foolish – how can you do any good – with your French?'

'At least I'll see they don't do anything outrageous to her.'

'They're certainly going to hold on to her,' Nicole assured him briskly. 'She *did* shoot the man. The best thing is to phone right away to Laura – she can do more than we can.'

Dick was unconvinced – also he was showing off for Rosemary.

'You wait,' said Nicole firmly, and hurried off to a telephone booth.

'When Nicole takes things into her hands,' he said with affectionate irony, 'there is nothing more to be done.'

He saw Rosemary for the first time that morning. They exchanged glances, trying to recognise the emotions of the day before. For a moment each seemed unreal to the other – then the slow warm hum of love began again.

'You like to help everybody, don't you?' Rosemary said.

'I only pretend to.'

'Mother likes to help everybody – of course she can't help as many people as you do.' She sighed. 'Sometimes I think I'm the most selfish person in the world.'

For the first time the mention of her mother annoyed rather than amused Dick. He wanted to sweep away her mother, remove the whole affair from the nursery footing upon which Rosemary persistently established it. But he realised that this impulse was a loss of control – what would become of Rosemary's urge towards him if, for even a moment, he relaxed. He saw, not without panic, that the affair was sliding to rest; it could not stand still, it must go on or go back; for the first time it occurred to him that Rosemary had her hand on the lever more authoritatively than he.

Before he had thought out a course of procedure, Nicole returned.

'I found Laura. It was the first news she had and her voice kept fading away and then getting loud again – as if she was fainting and then pulling herself together. She said she knew something was going to happen this morning.'

'Maria ought to be with Diaghilev,'[96] said Dick in a gentle tone, in order to bring them back to quietude. 'She has a nice sense of décor – not to say rhythm. Will any of us ever see a train out without hearing a few shots?'

They bumped down the wide steel steps. 'I'm sorry for the poor man,' Nicole said. 'Course that's why she talked so strange to me – she was getting ready to open fire.'

She laughed, Rosemary laughed too, but they were both horrified, and both of them deeply wanted Dick to make a moral comment on the matter and not leave it to them. This wish was not entirely conscious, especially on the part of Rosemary, who was accustomed to having shell fragments of such events shriek past her head. But a totality of shock had piled up in her too. For the moment, Dick was too shaken by the impetus of his newly recognised emotion to resolve things into the pattern of the holiday, so the women, missing something, lapsed into a vague unhappiness.

Then, as if nothing had happened, the lives of the Divers and their friends flowed out into the street.

However, everything had happened – Abe's departure and Mary's impending departure for Salzburg this afternoon had ended the time in Paris. Or perhaps the shots, the concussions that had finished God knew what dark matter, had terminated it. The shots had entered into all their lives: echoes of violence followed them out on to the pavement where two porters held a post-mortem beside them as they waited for a taxi.

'Tu as vu le revolver? Il était très petit, vrai perle – *un jouet*.' [97]

'Mais assez puissant!' said the other porter sagely. 'Tu as vu sa chemise? Assez de sang pour se croire à la guerre.' [98]

Chapter 20

IN THE SQUARE, as they came out, a suspended mass of gasoline exhaust cooked slowly in the July sun. It was a terrible thing – unlike pure heat it held no promise of rural escape but suggested only roads choked with the same foul asthma. During their luncheon, outdoors, across from the Luxembourg Gardens, Rosemary had cramps and felt fretful and full of impatient lassitude – it was the foretaste of this that had inspired her self-accusation of selfishness in the station.

Dick had no suspicion of the sharpness of the change; he was profoundly unhappy and the subsequent increase of egotism tended momentarily to blind him to what was going on round about him, and deprive him of the long ground-swell of imagination that he counted on for his judgments.

After Mary North left them, accompanied by the Italian singing teacher who had joined them for coffee and was taking her to her train, Rosemary, too, stood up, bound for an engagement at her studio: 'meet some officials.'

'And oh – ' she proposed ' – if Collis Clay, that Southern boy – if he comes while you are still sitting here, just tell him I couldn't wait; tell him to call me tomorrow.'

Too insouciant, in reaction from the late disturbance, she had assumed the privileges of a child – the result being to remind the Divers of their exclusive love for their own children; Rosemary was sharply rebuked in a short passage between the women: 'You'd better leave the message with a waiter,' Nicole's voice was stern and unmodulated, 'we're leaving immediately.'

Rosemary got it, took it without resentment.

'I'll let it go then. Goodbye, you darlings.'

Dick asked for the check; the Divers relaxed, chewing tentatively on toothpicks.

'Well – ' they said together.

He saw a flash of unhappiness on her mouth, so brief that only he would have noticed, and he could pretend not to have seen. What did Nicole think? Rosemary was one of a dozen people he had 'worked over' in the past years: these had included a French circus clown, Abe and Mary North, a pair of dancers, a writer, a painter, a comedienne from the Grand Guignol,[99] a half-crazy pederast from the Russian Ballet, a promising tenor they had staked to a year in Milan. Nicole well knew how seriously those people interpreted his interest and enthusiasm; but she realised also that, except while their children were being born, Dick had not spent a night apart from her since their marriage. On the other hand, there was a pleasingness about him that simply had to be used – those who possessed that pleasingness had to keep their hands in, and go along attaching people that they had no use to make of.

Now Dick hardened himself and let minutes pass without making any gestures of confidence, any representation of constantly renewed surprise that they were one together.

Collis Clay out of the South edged a passage between the closely packed tables and greeted the Divers cavalierly. Such salutations always astonished Dick – acquaintances saying 'Hi!' to them, or speaking only to one of them. He felt so intensely about people that in moments of apathy he preferred to remain concealed; that one could parade a casualness into his presence was a challenge to the key on which he lived.

Collis, unaware that he was without a wedding garment, heralded his arrival with: 'I reckon I'm late – the beyed[100] has flown.' Dick had to wrench something out of himself before he could forgive him for not having first complimented Nicole.

She left almost immediately and he sat with Collis, finishing the last of his wine. He rather like Collis – he was 'post-war'; less difficult than most of the Southerners he had known at New Haven a decade previously. Dick listened with amusement to the conversation that accompanied the slow, profound stuffing of a pipe. In the early afternoon children and nurses were trekking into the Luxembourg Gardens; it was the first time in months that Dick had let this part of the day out of his hands.

Suddenly his blood ran cold as he realised the content of Collis's confidential monologue.

' – she's not so cold as you'd probably think. I admit I thought she was cold for a long time. But she got into a jam with a friend of mine going from New York to Chicago at Easter – a boy named Hillis she thought was pretty nutsey[101] at New Haven – she had a compartment with a cousin of mine but she and Hillis wanted to be alone, so in the afternoon my cousin came and played cards in our compartment. Well, after about two hours we went back and there was Rosemary and Bill Hillis standing in the vestibule arguing with the conductor – Rosemary white as a sheet. Seems they locked the door and pulled down the blinds and I guess there was some heavy stuff going on when the conductor came for the tickets and knocked on the door. They thought it was us kidding them and wouldn't let him in at first, and when they did, he was plenty sore. He asked Hillis if that was his compartment and whether he and Rosemary were married that they locked the door, and Hillis lost his temper trying to explain there was nothing wrong. He said the conductor had insulted Rosemary and he wanted him to fight, but that conductor could have made trouble – and believe me I had an awful time smoothing it over.'

With every detail imagined, with even envy for the pair's community of misfortune in the vestibule, Dick felt a change taking place within him. Only the image of a third person, even a vanished one, entering into his relation with Rosemary was needed to throw him off his balance and send through him waves of pain, misery, desires, desperation. The vividly pictured hand on Rosemary's cheek, the quicker breath, the white excitement of the event viewed from outside, the inviolable secret warmth within.

– Do you mind if I pull down the curtain?

– Please do. It's too light in here.

Collis Clay was now speaking about fraternity politics at New Haven, in the same tone, with the same emphasis. Dick had gathered that he was in love with Rosemary in some curious way Dick could not have understood. The affair with Hillis seemed to have made no emotional impression on Collis save to give him a joyful conviction that Rosemary was 'human'.

'Bones[102] got a wonderful crowd,' he said. 'We all did, as a matter of fact. New Haven's so big now the sad thing is the men we have to leave out.'

– Do you mind if I pull down the curtain?

– Please do. It's too light in here.

. . . Dick went over Paris to his bank. Writing a cheque, he looked along the row of men at the desks deciding to which one he would present it for an OK. As he wrote he engrossed himself in the material act, examining meticulously the pen, writing laboriously upon the high glass-topped desk. Once he raised glazed eyes to look towards the mail department, then glazed his spirit again by concentration upon the objects he dealt with.

Still he failed to decide to whom the cheque should be presented, which man in the line would guess least of the unhappy predicament in which he found himself and, also, which one would be least likely to talk. There was Perrin, the suave New Yorker, who had asked him to luncheons at the American Club, there was Casasus, the Spaniard, with whom he usually discussed a mutual friend in spite of the fact that the friend had passed out of his life a dozen years before; there was Muchhause, who always asked him whether he wanted to draw upon his wife's money or his own.

As he entered the amount on the stub, and drew two lines under it, he decided to go to Pierce, who was young and for whom he would have to put on only a small show. It was often easier to give a show than to watch one.

He went to the mail desk first – as the woman who served him pushed up with her bosom a piece of paper that had nearly escaped the desk, he thought how differently women use their bodies from men. He took his letters aside to open. There was a bill for seventeen psychiatric books from a German concern, a bill from Brentano's,[103] a letter from Buffalo from his father, in a handwriting that year by year became more indecipherable; there was a card from Tommy Barban postmarked Fez and bearing a facetious communication; there were letters from doctors in Zurich, both in German; a disputed bill from a plasterer in Cannes; a bill from a furniture maker; a letter from the publisher of a medical journal in Baltimore, miscellaneous announcements, and an invitation to a showing of pictures by an incipient artist; also there were three letters for Nicole, and a letter for Rosemary sent in his care.

– Do you mind if I pull down the curtain?

He went towards Pierce but he was engaged with a woman, and Dick saw with his heels that he would have to present his cheque to Casasus at the next desk, who was free.

'How are you, Diver?' Casasus was genial. He stood up, his moustache spreading with his smile. 'We were talking about Featherstone the other day and I thought of you – he's out in California now.'

Dick widened his eyes and bent forward a little.

'In California?'

'That's what I heard.'

Dick held the cheque poised; to focus the attention of Casasus upon it he looked towards Pierce's desk, holding the latter for a moment in a friendly eye-play conditioned by an old joke of three years before when Pierce had been involved with a Lithuanian countess. Pierce played up with a grin until Casasus had authorised the cheque and had no further recourse to detain Dick, whom he liked, than to stand up holding his pince-nez and repeat, 'Yes, he's in California.'

Meanwhile Dick had seen that Perrin, at the head of the line of desks, was in conversation with the heavyweight champion of the world;[104] from a sidesweep of Perrin's eye Dick saw that he was considering calling him over and introducing him, but that he finally decided against it.

Cutting across the social mood of Casasus with the intensity he had accumulated at the glass desk – which is to say he looked hard at the cheque, studying it, and then fixed his eyes on grave problems beyond the first marble pillar to the right of the banker's head and made a business of shifting the cane, hat, and letters he carried – he said goodbye and went out. He had long ago purchased the door-man; his taxi sprang to the kerb.

'I want to go to the Films Par Excellence Studio[105] – it's on a little street in Passy.[106] Go to the Muette.[107] I'll direct you from there.'

He was rendered so uncertain by the events of the last forty-eight hours that he was not even sure of what he wanted to do; he paid off the taxi at the Muette and walked, in the direction of the studio, crossing to the opposite side of the street before he came to the building. Dignified in his fine clothes, with their fine accessories, he was yet swayed and driven as an animal. Dignity could come only with an overthrowing of his past, of the effort of the last six years. He went briskly around the block with the fatuousness of one of Tarkington's adolescents,[108] hurrying at the blind places lest he miss Rosemary's coming out of the studio. It was a melancholy neighbourhood. Next door to the place he saw a sign: '1000 Chemises'.[109] The shirts filled the window, piled, cravated, stuffed, or draped with shoddy grace on the showcase floor: '1000 Chemises' – count them! on either side he read: 'Papeterie', 'Pâtisserie', 'Solde', 'Réclame' – and Constance Talmadge in *Déjeuner de Soleil*, and farther away there were more sombre announcements: 'Vêtements Ecclésiastiques', 'Déclaration de Décès' and 'Pompes Funèbres'.[110] Life and death.

He knew that what he was now doing marked a turning point in his life – it was out of line with everything that had preceded it – even out of line with what effect he might hope to produce upon Rosemary. Rosemary saw him always as a model of correctness – his presence walking around this block was an intrusion. But Dick's necessity of behaving as he did was a projection of some submerged reality: he was compelled to walk there, or stand there, his shirt-sleeve fitting his wrist and his coat sleeve encasing his shirt-sleeve like a sleeve valve, his collar moulded plastically to his neck, his red hair cut exactly, his hand holding his briefcase like a dandy – just as another man once found it necessary to stand in front of a church in Ferrara,[111] in sackcloth and ashes. Dick was paying some tribute to things unforgotten, unshriven, unexpurgated.

Chapter 21

AFTER THREE-QUARTERS of an hour of standing around, he became suddenly involved in a human contact. It was just the sort of thing that was likely to happen to him when he was in the mood of not wanting to see anyone. So rigidly did he sometimes guard his exposed self-consciousness that frequently he defeated his own purposes; as an actor who underplays a part sets up a craning forward, a stimulated emotional attention in an audience, and seems to create in others an ability to bridge the gap he has left open. Similarly we are seldom sorry for those who need and crave our pity – we reserve this for those who, by other means, make us exercise the abstract function of pity.

So Dick might, himself, have analysed the incident that ensued. As he paced the Rue des Saints-Anges he was spoken to by a thin-faced American, perhaps thirty, with an air of being scarred and a slight but sinister smile. As Dick gave him the light he requested, he placed him as one of a type of which he had been conscious since early youth – a type that loafed about tobacco stores with one elbow on the counter and watched, through heaven knew what small chink of the mind, the people who came in and out. Intimate to garages, where he had vague business conducted in undertones, to barbershops, to the lobbies of theatres – in such places, at any rate, Dick placed him. Sometimes the face bobbed up in one of Tad's more savage cartoons[112] – in boyhood Dick had often thrown an uneasy glance at the dim borderland of crime on which he stood.

'How do you like Paris, Buddy?'

Not waiting for an answer the man tried to fit in his footsteps with Dick's: 'Where you from?' he asked encouragingly.

'From Buffalo.'

'I'm from San Antone[113] – but I been over here since the war.'

'You in the army?'

'*I'll* say I was. Eighty-fourth Division – ever heard of that outfit?'

The man walked a little ahead of him and fixed him with eyes that were practically menacing.

'Staying in Paris awhile, Buddy? or just passing through.'

'Passing through.'

'What hotel you staying at?'

Dick had begun laughing to himself – the party had the intention of rifling his room that night. His thoughts were read apparently without self-consciousness.

'With a build like yours you oughtn't to be afraid of me, Buddy. There's a lot of bums around just laying for American tourists, but you needn't be afraid of me.'

Becoming bored, Dick stopped walking: 'I just wonder why you've got so much time to waste.'

'I'm in business here in Paris.'

'In what line?'

'Selling papers.'

The contrast between the formidable manner and the mild profession was absurd – but the man amended it with: 'Don't worry; I made plenty money last year – ten or twenty francs for a *Sunny Times*[114]that cost six.'

He produced a newspaper clipping from a rusty wallet and passed it over to one who had become a fellow stroller – the cartoon showed a stream of Americans pouring from the gangplank of a liner freighted with gold.

'Two hundred thousand – spending ten million a summer.'

'What you doing out here in Passy?'

His companion looked around cautiously. 'Movies,' he said darkly. 'They got an American studio over there. And they need guys can speak English. I'm waiting for a break.'

Dick shook him off quickly and firmly.

It had become apparent that Rosemary either had escaped on one of his early circuits of the block or else had left before he came into the neighbourhood; he went into the bistro on the corner, bought a lead disc and, squeezed in an alcove between the kitchen and the foul toilet, he called the Roi George. He recognised Cheyne-Stokes tendencies[115] in his respiration – but like everything the symptom served only to turn him in towards his emotion. He gave the number of the hotel; then stood holding the phone and staring into the café; after a long while a strange little voice said hello.

'This is Dick – I had to call you.'

A pause from her – then bravely, and in key with his emotion: 'I'm glad you did.'

'I came to meet you at your studio – I'm out in Passy across the way from it. I thought maybe we'd ride around through the Bois.'[116]

'Oh, I only stayed there a minute! I'm so sorry.' A silence.

'Rosemary.'

'Yes, Dick.'

'Look, I'm in an extraordinary condition about you. When a child can disturb a middle-aged gent – things get difficult.'

'You're not middle-aged, Dick – you're the youngest person in the world.'

'Rosemary?' Silence while he stared at a shelf that held the humbler poisons of France – bottles of Otard, Rhum St James, Marie Brizard, Punch orangeade, André Fernet Blanca, Cherry Rocher, and Armagnac.[117]

'Are you alone?'

– *Do you mind if I pull down the curtain?*

'Who do you think I'd be with?'

'That's the state I'm in. I'd like to be with you now.'

Silence, then a sigh and an answer. 'I wish you were with me now.'

There was the hotel room where she lay behind a telephone number, and little gusts of music wailed around her –

> And two – for tea.
> And me for you,
> And you for me
> Alow-own.[118]

There was the remembered dust of powder over her tan – when he kissed her face it was damp around the corners of her hair; there was the flash of a white face under his own, the arc of a shoulder.

'It's impossible,' he said to himself. In a minute he was out in the street marching along towards the Muette, or away from it, his small briefcase still in his hand, his gold-headed stick held at a sword-like angle.

Rosemary returned to her desk and finished a letter to her mother.

' – I only saw him for a little while but I thought he was wonderful looking. I fell in love with him (of course I Do Love Dick Best but you know what I mean). He really is going to direct the picture and is leaving immediately for Hollywood, and I think we ought to leave, too. Collis Clay has been here. I like him all right but have not seen much of him because of the Divers, who really are divine, about the Nicest People I ever Knew. I am feeling not very well today and am taking the Medicine, though see No need for it. I'm not even Going to Try to tell you All that's Happened until I see You!!! So when you get this letter *wire, wire, wire!* Are you coming north or shall I come south with the Divers?'

At six Dick called Nicole.

'Have you any special plans?' he asked. 'Would you like to do something quiet – dinner at the hotel and then a play?'

'Would you? I'll do whatever you want. I phoned Rosemary a while ago and she's having dinner in her room. I think this upset all of us, don't you?'

'It didn't upset me,' he objected. 'Darling, unless you're physically tired let's do something. Otherwise we'll get south and spend a week wondering why we didn't see Boucher.[119] It's better than brooding – '

That was a blunder and Nicole took him up sharply.

'Brooding about what?'

'About Maria Wallis.'

She agreed to go to a play. It was a tradition between them that they should never be too tired for anything, and they found it made the days better on the whole and put the evenings more in order. When, inevitably, their spirits flagged they shifted the blame to the weariness and fatigue of others. Before they went out, as fine-looking a couple as could be found in Paris, they knocked softly at Rosemary's door. There was no answer; judging that she was asleep they walked into a warm strident Paris night, snatching a vermouth and bitters in the shadow by Fouquet's[120] bar.

Chapter 22

NICOLE AWOKE LATE, murmuring something back into her dream before she parted her long lashes tangled with sleep. Dick's bed was empty – only after a minute did she realise that she had been awakened by a knock at their salon door.

'*Entrez!*'[121] she called, but there was no answer, and after a moment she slipped on a dressing-gown and went to open it. A *sergent de ville*[122] confronted her courteously and stepped inside the door.

'Mr Afghan North – he is here?'

'What? No – he's gone to America.'

'When did he leave, madame?'

'Yesterday morning.'

He shook his head and waved his forefinger at her in a quicker rhythm.

'He was in Paris last night. He is registered here but his room is not occupied. They told me I had better ask at this room.'

'Sounds very peculiar to me – we saw him off yesterday morning on the boat train.'

'Be that as it may, he has been seen here this morning. Even his *carte d'identité*[123] has been seen. And there you are.'

'We know nothing about it,' she proclaimed in amazement.

He considered. He was an ill-smelling, handsome man.

'You were not with him at all last night?'

'But no.'

'We have arrested a Negro. We are convinced we have at last arrested the correct Negro.'

'I assure you that I haven't an idea what you're talking about. If it's the Mr Abraham North, the one we know, well, if he was in Paris last night we weren't aware of it.'

The man nodded, sucked his upper lip, convinced but disappointed.

'What happened?' Nicole demanded.

He showed his palms, puffing out his closed mouth. He had begun to find her attractive and his eyes flickered at her.

'What do you wish, madame? A summer affair. Mr Afghan North was robbed and he made a complaint. We have arrested the miscreant. Mr Afghan should come to identify him and make the proper charges.'

Nicole pulled her dressing-gown closer around her and dismissed him briskly. Mystified she took a bath and dressed. By this time it was after ten and she called Rosemary but got no answer – then she phoned the hotel office and found that Abe had indeed registered, at six-thirty this morning. His room, however, was still unoccupied. Hoping for a word from Dick she waited in the parlour of the suite; just as she had given up and decided to go out, the office called and announced: 'Meestaire Crawshow, *un nègre*.'

'On what business?' she demanded.

'He says he knows you and the doctaire. He says there is a Meestaire Freeman into prison that is a friend of all the world. He says there is injustice and he wishes to see Meestaire North before he himself is arrested.'

'We know nothing about it.' Nicole disclaimed the whole business with a vehement clap on the receiver. Abe's bizarre reappearance made it plain to her how fatigued she was with his dissipation. Dismissing him from her mind she went out, ran into Rosemary at the dressmaker's, and shopped with her for artificial flowers and all-coloured strings of coloured beads on the Rue de Rivoli.[124] She helped Rosemary choose a diamond for her mother, and some scarfs and novel cigarette cases to take home to business associates in California. For her son she bought Greek and Roman soldiers, a whole army of them, costing over a thousand francs. Once again they spent their money in different ways, and again Rosemary admired Nicole's method of spending. Nicole was sure that the money she spent was hers – Rosemary still thought her money was miraculously lent to her and she must consequently be very careful of it.

It was fun spending money in the sunlight of the foreign city, with healthy bodies under them that sent streams of colour up to their faces; with arms and hands, legs and ankles that they stretched out confidently, reaching or stepping with the confidence of women lovely to men.

When they got back to the hotel and found Dick, all bright and new in the morning, both of them had a moment of complete childish joy.

He had just received a garbled telephone call from Abe, who, so it appeared, had spent the forenoon in hiding.

'It was one of the most extraordinary telephone conversations I've ever held.'

Dick had talked not only to Abe but to a dozen others. On the phone these supernumeraries had been typically introduced as: ' – man wants to talk to you is in the teput dome, well he says he was in it – what is it?

'Hey, somebody, shut up – anyhow, he was in some shandel-scandal and he kaa *poss*ibly go home. My own *per*sonal is that – my personal is he's had a – ' Gulps sounded and thereafter what the party had, rested with the unknown.

The phone yielded up a supplementary offer: 'I thought it would appeal to you anyhow as a psychologist.' The vague personality who corresponded to this statement was eventually hung on to the phone; in the sequence he failed to appeal to Dick, as a psychologist, or indeed as anything else. Abe's conversation flowed on as follows:
'Hello.'
'Well?'
'Well, hello.'
'Who are you?'
'Well.' There were interpolated snorts of laughter.
'Well, I'll put somebody else on the line.'

Sometimes Dick could hear Abe's voice, accompanied by scufflings, droppings of the receiver, far-away fragments such as, 'No, I don't, Mr North . . . ' Then a pert decided voice had said: 'If you are a friend of Mr North you will come down and take him away.'

Abe cut in, solemn and ponderous, beating it all down with an overtone of earth-bound determination.

'Dick, I've launched a race riot in Montmartre.[125] I'm going over and get Freeman out of jail. If a Negro from Copenhagen that makes shoe polish – hello, can you hear me – well, look, if anybody comes there – ' once again the receiver was a chorus of innumerable melodies.

'Why are you back in Paris?' Dick demanded.

'I got as far as Evreux,[126] and I decided to take a plane back so I could compare it with St Sulpice. I mean I don't intend to bring St Sulpice back to Paris. I don't even mean Baroque! I mean St Germain.[127] For God's sake, wait a minute and I'll put the *chasseur* on the wire.'

'For God's sake, don't.'

'Listen – did Mary get off all right?'

'Yes.'

'Dick, I want you to talk with a man I met here this morning, the son of a naval officer that's been to every doctor in Europe. Let me tell you about him – '

Dick had rung off at this point – perhaps that was a piece of ingratitude, for he needed grist for the grinding activity of his mind.

'Abe used to be so nice,' Nicole told Rosemary. 'So nice. Long ago – when Dick and I were first married. If you had known him then. He'd come to stay with us for weeks and weeks and we scarcely knew he was in the house. Sometimes he'd play – sometimes he'd be in the library with a muted piano, making love to it by the hour – Dick, do you remember that maid? She thought he was a ghost and sometimes Abe used to meet her in the hall and moo at her, and it cost us a whole tea service once – but we didn't care.'

So much fun – so long ago. Rosemary envied them their fun, imagining a life of leisure unlike her own. She knew little of leisure but she had the respect for it of those who have never had it. She thought of it as a resting, without realising that the Divers were as far from relaxing as she was herself.

'What did this to him?' she asked. 'Why does he have to drink?'

Nicole shook her head right and left, disclaiming responsibility for the matter: 'So many smart men go to pieces nowadays.'

'And when haven't they?' Dick asked. 'Smart men play close to the line because they have to – some of them can't stand it, so they quit.'

'It must lie deeper than that.' Nicole clung to her conversation; also she was irritated that Dick should contradict her before Rosemary. 'Artists like – well, like Fernand[128] don't seem to have to wallow in alcohol. Why is it just Americans who dissipate?'

There were so many answers to this question that Dick decided to leave it in the air, to buzz victoriously in Nicole's ears. He had become intensely critical of her. Though he thought she was the most attractive human creature he had ever seen, though he got from her everything he needed, he scented battle from afar, and subconsciously he had been hardening and arming himself, hour by hour. He was not given to self-indulgence and he felt comparatively graceless at this moment of indulging himself, blinding his eyes with the hope that Nicole guessed at only an emotional excitement about Rosemary. He was not sure – last night at the theatre she had referred pointedly to Rosemary as a child.

The trio lunched downstairs in an atmosphere of carpets and padded waiters, who did not march at the stomping quick-step of those men who brought good food to the tables whereon they had recently dined. Here there were families of Americans staring around at families of Americans, and trying to make conversation with one another.

There was a party at the next table that they could not account for. It consisted of an expansive, somewhat secretarial, would-you-mind-repeating young man, and a score of women. The women were neither young nor old nor of any particular social class; yet the party gave the impression of a unit, held more closely together for example than a group of wives stalling through a professional congress of their husbands. Certainly it was more of a unit than any conceivable tourist party.

An instinct made Dick suck back the grave derision that formed on his tongue; he asked the waiter to find out who they were.

'Those are the gold-star muzzers,'[129] explained the waiter.

Aloud and in low voices they exclaimed. Rosemary's eyes filled with tears.

'Probably the young ones are the wives,' said Nicole.

Over his wine Dick looked at them again; in their happy faces, the dignity that surrounded and pervaded the party, he perceived all the maturity of an older America. For a while the sobered women who had come to mourn for their dead, for something they could not repair, made the room beautiful. Momentarily, he sat again on his father's knee, riding with Mosby[130] while the old loyalties and devotions fought on around him. Almost with an effort he turned back to his two women at the table and faced the whole new world in which he believed.

– Do you mind if I pull down the curtain?

Chapter 23

ABE NORTH WAS STILL IN THE RITZ BAR, where he had been since nine in the morning. When he arrived seeking sanctuary the windows were open and great beams were busy at pulling up the dust from smoky carpets and cushions. *Chasseurs* tore through the corridors, liberated and disembodied, moving for the moment in pure space. The sit-down bar for women, across from the bar proper, seemed very small – it was hard to imagine what throngs it could accommodate in the afternoon.

The famous Paul, the concessionaire, had not arrived, but Claude, who was checking stock, broke off his work with no improper surprise to make Abe a pick-me-up. Abe sat on a bench against a wall. After two drinks he began to feel better – so much better that he mounted to the barbershop and was shaved. When he returned to the bar Paul had arrived – in his custom-built motor, from which he had disembarked correctly at the Boulevard des Capucines.[131] Paul liked Abe and came over to talk.

'I was supposed to ship home this morning,' Abe said. 'I mean yesterday morning, or whatever this is.'

'Why din you?' asked Paul.

Abe considered, and happened finally to a reason: 'I was reading a serial in *Liberty*[132] and the next instalment was due here in Paris – so if I'd sailed I'd have missed it – then I never would have read it.'

'It must be a very good story.'

'It's a terr–r–rible story.'

Paul arose chuckling and paused, leaning on the back of a chair: 'If you really want to get off, Mr North, there are friends of yours going tomorrow on the *France*[133] – Mister what is his name – and Slim Pearson. Mister – I'll think of it – tall with a new beard.'

'Yardly,' Abe supplied.

'Mr Yardly. They're both going on the *France*.'

He was on his way to his duties but Abe tried to detain him: 'If I didn't have to go by way of Cherbourg. The baggage went that way.'

'Get your baggage in New York,' said Paul, receding.

The logic of the suggestion fitted gradually into Abe's pitch – he grew rather enthusiastic about being cared for, or rather of prolonging his state of irresponsibility.

Other clients had meanwhile drifted into the bar: first came a huge Dane whom Abe had somewhere encountered. The Dane took a seat across the room, and Abe guessed he would be there all the day, drinking, lunching, talking or reading newspapers. He felt a desire to outstay him. At eleven the college boys began to step in, stepping gingerly lest they tear one another bag from bag. It was about then he had the *chasseur* telephone to the Divers; by the time he was in touch with them he was in touch also with other friends – and his hunch was to put them all on different phones at once – the result was somewhat general. From time to time his mind reverted to the fact that he ought to go over and get Freeman out of jail, but he shook off all facts as parts of the nightmare.

By one o'clock the bar was jammed; amidst the consequent mixture of voices the staff of waiters functioned, pinning down their clients to the facts of drink and money.

'That makes two stingers . . . and one more . . . two martinis and one . . . nothing for you, Mr Quarterly . . . that makes three rounds. That makes seventy-five francs, Mr Quarterly. Mr Schaeffer said he had this – you had the last . . . I can only do what you say . . . thanks veramuch.'

In the confusion Abe had lost his seat; now he stood gently swaying and talking to some of the people with whom he had involved himself. A terrier ran a leash around his legs but Abe managed to extricate himself without upsetting and became the recipient of profuse apologies. Presently he was invited to lunch, but declined. It was almost Briglith,[134] he explained, and there was something he had to do at Briglith. A little later, with the exquisite manners of the alcoholic that are like the manners of a prisoner or a family servant, he said goodbye to an acquaintance, and turning around discovered that the bar's great moment was over as precipitately as it had begun.

Across from him the Dane and his companions had ordered luncheon. Abe did likewise but scarcely touched it. Afterward, he just sat, happy to live in the past. The drink made past happy things contemporary with the present, as if they were still going on, contemporary even with the future as if they were about to happen again.

At four the *chasseur* approached him: 'You wish to see a coloured fellow of the name Jules Peterson?'

'God! How did he find me?'

'I didn't tell him you were present.'

'Who did?' Abe fell over his glasses but recovered himself.

'Says he's already been around to all the American bars and hotels.'

'Tell him I'm not here – ' As the *chasseur* turned away Abe asked: 'Can he come in here?'

'I'll find out.'

Receiving the question Paul glanced over his shoulder; he shook his head, then seeing Abe he came over.

'I'm sorry; I can't allow it.'

Abe got himself up with an effort and went out to the Rue Cambon.[135]

Chapter 24

WITH HIS MINIATURE leather briefcase in his hand Richard Diver walked from the seventh *arrondissement* – where he left a note for Maria Wallis signed 'Dicole', the word with which he and Nicole had signed communications in the first days of love – to his shirt-makers where the clerks made a fuss over him out of proportion to the money he spent. Ashamed at promising so much to these poor Englishmen, with his fine manners, his air of having the key to security, ashamed of making a tailor shift an inch of silk on his arm. Afterward he went to the bar of the Crillon[136] and drank a small coffee and two fingers of gin.[137]

As he entered the hotel the halls had seemed unnaturally bright; when he left he realised that it was because it had already turned dark outside. It was a windy four-o'clock night with the leaves on the Champs-Élysées singing and falling, thin and wild. Dick turned down the Rue de Rivoli, walking two squares under the arcades to his bank where there was mail. Then he took a taxi and started up the Champs-Élysées through the first patter of rain, sitting alone with his love.

Back at two o'clock in the Roi George corridor the beauty of Nicole had been to the beauty of Rosemary as the beauty of Leonardo's girl[138] was to that of the girl of an illustrator. Dick moved on through the rain, demoniac and frightened, the passions of many men inside him and nothing simple that he could see.

Rosemary opened her door full of emotions no one else knew of. She was now what is sometimes called a 'little wild thing' – by twenty-four full hours she was not yet unified and she was absorbed in playing around with chaos; as if her destiny were a picture puzzle – counting benefits, counting hopes, telling off Dick, Nicole, her mother, the director she met yesterday, like stops on a string of beads.

When Dick knocked she had just dressed and had been watching the rain, thinking of some poem, and of full gutters in Beverly Hills. When she opened the door she saw him as something fixed and godlike as he had always been, as older people are to younger, rigid

and unmalleable. Dick saw her with an inevitable sense of disappointment. It took him a moment to respond to the unguarded sweetness
of her smile, her body calculated to a millimetre to suggest a bud yet
guarantee a flower. He was conscious of the print of her wet foot on
a rug through the bathroom door.

'Miss Television,'[139] he said with a lightness he did not feel. He put
his gloves, his briefcase on the dressing-table, his stick against the
wall. His chin dominated the lines of pain around his mouth, forcing
them up into his forehead and the corner of his eyes, like fear that
cannot be shown in public.

'Come and sit on my lap close to me,' he said softly, 'and let me see
about your lovely mouth.'

She came over and sat there and while the dripping slowed down
outside – drip–dri–i–p, she laid her lips to the beautiful cold image
she had created.

Presently she kissed him several times in the mouth, her face
getting big as it came up to him; he had never seen anything so
dazzling as the quality of her skin, and since sometimes beauty gives
back the images of one's best thoughts he thought of his responsibility about Nicole, and of the responsibility of her being two doors
down across the corridor.

'The rain's over,' he said. 'Do you see the sun on the slate?'

Rosemary stood up and leaned down and said her most sincere
thing to him.

'Oh, we're such *actors* – you and I.'

She went to her dresser and the moment that she laid her comb flat
against her hair there was a slow persistent knocking at the door.

They were shocked motionless; the knock was repeated insistently,
and in the sudden realisation that the door was not locked Rosemary
finished her hair with one stroke, nodded at Dick who had quickly
jerked the wrinkles out of the bed where they had been sitting, and
started for the door. Dick said in quite a natural voice, not too loud:
' – so if you don't feel up to going out, I'll tell Nicole and we'll have
a very quiet last evening.'

The precautions were needless for the situation of the parties
outside the door was so harassed as to preclude any but the most
fleeting judgments on matters not pertinent to themselves. Standing
there was Abe, aged by several months in the last twenty-four hours,
and a very frightened, concerned coloured man whom Abe introduced
as Mr Peterson of Stockholm.

'He's in a terrible situation and it's my fault,' said Abe. 'We need
some good advice.'

'Come in our rooms,' said Dick.

Abe insisted that Rosemary come too and they crossed the hall to the Divers' suite. Jules Peterson, a small, respectable Negro, on the suave model that heels the Republican party in the border states,[140] followed.

It appeared that the latter had been a legal witness to the early-morning dispute in Montparnasse;[141] he had accompanied Abe to the police station and supported his assertion that a thousand-franc note had been seized out of his hand by a Negro, whose identification was one of the points of the case. Abe and Jules Peterson, accompanied by an agent of police, returned to the bistro and too hastily identified as the criminal a Negro who, so it was established after an hour, had only entered the place after Abe left. The police had further complicated the situation by arresting the prominent Negro restaurateur, Freeman, who had only drifted through the alcoholic fog at a very early stage and then vanished. The true culprit, whose case, as reported by his friends, was that he had merely commandeered a fifty-franc note to pay for drinks that Abe had ordered, had only recently and in a somewhat sinister role, reappeared upon the scene.

In brief, Abe had succeeded in the space of an hour in entangling himself with the personal lives, consciences, and emotions of one Afro-European and three Afro-Americans inhabiting the French Latin quarter.[142] The disentanglement was not even faintly in sight and the day had passed in an atmosphere of unfamiliar Negro faces bobbing up in unexpected places and around unexpected corners, and insistent Negro voices on the phone.

In person, Abe had succeeded in evading all of them, save Jules Peterson. Peterson was rather in the position of the friendly Indian who had helped a white. The Negroes who suffered from the betrayal were not so much after Abe as after Peterson, and Peterson was very much after what protection he might get from Abe.

Up in Stockholm Peterson had failed as a small manufacturer of shoe polish and now possessed only his formula and sufficient trade tools to fill a small box; however, his new protector had promised in the early hours to set him up in business in Versailles. Abe's former chauffeur was a shoemaker there and Abe had handed Peterson two hundred francs on account.

Rosemary listened with distaste to this rigmarole; to appreciate its grotesquerie required a more robust sense of humour than hers. The little man with his portable manufactory, his insincere eyes that, from time to time, rolled white semicircles of panic into view; the figure of Abe, his face as blurred as the gaunt fine lines of it would permit – all this was as remote from her as sickness.

'I ask only a chance in life,' said Peterson with the sort of precise yet distorted intonation peculiar to colonial countries. 'My methods are simple, my formula is so good that I was drove away from Stockholm, ruined, because I did not care to dispose of it.'

Dick regarded him politely – interest formed, dissolved, he turned to Abe: 'You go to some hotel and go to bed. After you're all straight Mr Peterson will come and see you.'

'But don't you appreciate the mess that Peterson's in?' Abe protested.

'I shall wait in the hall,' said Mr Peterson with delicacy. 'It is perhaps hard to discuss my problems in front of me.'

He withdrew after a short travesty of a French bow; Abe pulled himself to his feet with the deliberation of a locomotive.

'I don't seem highly popular today.'

'Popular but not probable,' Dick advised him. 'My advice is to leave this hotel – by way of the bar, if you want. Go to the Chambord, or if you'll need a lot of service, go over to the Majestic.'[143]

'Could I annoy you for a drink?'

'There's not a thing up here,' Dick lied.

Resignedly Abe shook hands with Rosemary; he composed his face slowly, holding her hand a long time and forming sentences that did not emerge.

'You are the most – one of the most –'

She was sorry, and rather revolted at his dirty hands, but she laughed in a well-bred way, as though it were nothing unusual to her to watch a man walking in a slow dream. Often people display a curious respect for a man drunk, rather like the respect of simple races for the insane. Respect rather than fear. There is something awe-inspiring in one who has lost all inhibitions, who will do anything. Of course we make him pay afterward for his moment of superiority, his moment of impressiveness. Abe turned to Dick with a last appeal.

'If I go to a hotel and get all steamed and curry-combed, and sleep awhile, and fight off these Senegalese[144] – could I come and spend the evening by the fireside?'

Dick nodded at him, less in agreement than in mockery and said: 'You have a high opinion of your current capacities.'

'I bet if Nicole was here she'd let me come back.'

'All right.' Dick went to a trunk tray and brought a box to the central table; inside were innumerable cardboard letters.

'You can come if you want to play anagrams.'

Abe eyed the contents of the box with physical revulsion as though he had been asked to eat them like oats.

'What are anagrams? Haven't I had enough strange – '

'It's a quiet game. You spell words with them – any word except alcohol.'

'I bet you can spell alcohol,' Abe plunged his hand among the counters. 'Can I come back if I can spell alcohol?'

'You can come back if you want to play anagrams.'

Abe shook his head resignedly.

'If you're in that frame of mind there's no use – I'd just be in the way.' He waved his finger reproachfully at Dick. 'But remember what George the Third[145] said, that if Grant was drunk he wished he would bite the other generals.'

With a last desperate glance at Rosemary from the golden corners of his eyes, he went out. To his relief Peterson was no longer in the corridor. Feeling lost and homeless he went back to ask Paul the name of that boat.

Chapter 25

WHEN HE HAD TOTTERED OUT, Dick and Rosemary embraced fleetingly. There was a dust of Paris over both of them through which they scented each other: the rubber guard on Dick's fountain pen, the faintest odour of warmth from Rosemary's neck and shoulders. For another half-minute Dick clung to the situation; Rosemary was first to return to reality.

'I must go, youngster,' she said.

They blinked at each other across a widening space, and Rosemary made an exit that she had learned young, and on which no director had ever tried to improve.

She opened the door of her room and went directly to her desk where she had suddenly remembered leaving her wristwatch. It was there; slipping it on she glanced down at the daily letter to her mother; finishing the last sentence in her mind. Then, rather gradually, she realised without turning about that she was not alone in the room.

In an inhabited room there are refracting objects only half noticed: varnished wood, more or less polished brass, silver and ivory, and beyond these a thousand conveyors of light and shadow so mild that one scarcely thinks of them as that, the tops of picture-frames, the edges of pencils or ashtrays, of crystal or china ornaments; the totality of this refraction – appealing to equally subtle reflexes of the vision as well as to those associational fragments in the subconscious that we seem to hang on to, as a glass-fitter keeps the irregularly shaped pieces that may do some time – this fact might account for what Rosemary afterward mystically described as realising that there was some one in the room, before she could determine it. But when she did realise it she turned swift in a sort of ballet step and saw that a dead Negro was stretched upon her bed.

As she cried 'Aaouu!' and her still unfastened wristwatch banged against the desk she had the preposterous idea that it was Abe North. Then she dashed for the door and across the hall.

Dick was straightening up; he had examined the gloves worn that day and thrown them into a pile of soiled gloves in a corner of a trunk. He had hung up coat and vest and spread his shirt on another hanger – a trick of his own. 'You'll wear a shirt that's a little dirty where you won't wear a mussed shirt.' Nicole had come in and was dumping one of Abe's extraordinary ashtrays into the waste-basket when Rosemary tore into the room.

'*Dick! Dick!* Come and see!'

Dick jogged across the hall into her room. He knelt to Peterson's heart, and felt the pulse – the body was warm, the face, harassed and indirect in life, was gross and bitter in death; the box of materials was held under one arm but the shoe that dangled over the bedside was bare of polish and its sole was worn through. By French law Dick had no right to touch the body but he moved the arm a little to see something – there was a stain on the green coverlet, there would be faint blood on the blanket beneath.

Dick closed the door and stood thinking; he heard cautious steps in the corridor and then Nicole calling him by name. Opening the door he whispered: 'Bring the *couverture*[146] and top blanket from one of our beds – don't let anyone see you.' Then, noticing the strained look on her face, he added quickly, 'Look here, you mustn't get upset over this – it's only some nigger scrap.'

'I want it to be over.'

The body, as Dick lifted it, was light and ill-nourished. He held it so that further haemorrhages from the wound would flow into the man's clothes. Laying it beside the bed he stripped off the coverlet and top blanket and then opening the door an inch, listened – there was a clank of dishes down the hall followed by a loud patronising '*Merci, madame,*' but the waiter went in the other direction, towards the service stairway. Quickly Dick and Nicole exchanged bundles across the corridor; after spreading this covering on Rosemary's bed, Dick stood sweating in the warm twilight, considering. Certain points had become apparent to him in the moment following his examination of the body; first, that Abe's first hostile Indian had tracked the friendly Indian and discovered him in the corridor, and when the latter had taken desperate refuge in Rosemary's room, had hunted down and slain him; second, that if the situation were allowed to develop naturally, no power on earth could keep the smear off Rosemary – the paint was scarcely dry on the Arbuckle case.[147] Her contract was contingent upon an obligation to continue rigidly and unexceptionally as *Daddy's Girl*.

Automatically Dick made the old motion of turning up his sleeves though he wore a sleeveless undershirt, and bent over the body. Getting a purchase on the shoulders of the coat he kicked open the door with his heel, and dragged the body quickly into a plausible position in the corridor. He came back into Rosemary's room and smoothed back the grain of the plush floor rug. Then he went to the phone in his suite and called the manager-owner of the hotel.

'McBeth? – it's Dr Diver speaking – something very important. Are we on a more or less private line?'

It was good that he had made the extra effort which had firmly entrenched him with Mr McBeth. Here was one use for all the pleasingness that Dick had expended over a large area he would never retrace . . .

'Going out of the suite we came on a dead Negro . . . in the hall . . . no, no, he's a civilian. Wait a minute now – I knew you didn't want any guests to blunder on the body so I'm phoning you. Of course I must ask you to keep my name out of it. I don't want any French red tape just because I discovered the man.'

What exquisite consideration for the hotel! only because Mr McBeth, with his own eyes, had seen these traits in Dr Diver two nights before, could he credit the story without question.

In a minute Mr McBeth arrived and in another minute he was joined by a gendarme. In the interval he found time to whisper to Dick, 'You can be sure the name of any guest will be protected. I'm only too grateful to you for your pains.'

Mr McBeth took an immediate step that may only be imagined, but that influenced the gendarme so as to make him pull his moustaches in a frenzy of uneasiness and greed. He made perfunctory notes and sent a telephone call to his post. Meanwhile, with a celerity that Jules Peterson, as a business man, would have quite understood, the remains were carried into another apartment of one of the most fashionable hotels in the world.

Dick went back to his salon.

'What *hap*pened?' cried Rosemary. 'Do all the Americans in Paris just shoot at each other all the time?'

'This seems to be the open season,' he answered. 'Where's Nicole?'

'I think she's in the bathroom.'

She adored him for saving her – disasters that could have attended upon the event had passed in prophecy through her mind; and she had listened in wild worship to his strong, sure, polite voice making it all right. But before she reached him in a sway of soul and body his attention focused on something else: he went into the bedroom and towards the bathroom. And now Rosemary, too, could hear, louder and louder, a verbal inhumanity that penetrated the keyholes and the cracks in the doors, swept into the suite and in the shape of horror took form again.

With the idea that Nicole had fallen in the bathroom and hurt herself, Rosemary followed Dick. That was not the condition of affairs at which she stared before Dick shouldered her back and brusquely blocked her view.

Nicole knelt beside the tub swaying sideways and sideways. 'It's you!' she cried, ' – it's you come to intrude on the only privacy I have in the world – with your spread with red blood on it. I'll wear it for you – I'm not ashamed, though it was such a pity. On All Fools' Day[148] we had a party on the Zurichsee,[149] and all the fools were there, and I wanted to come dressed in a spread but they wouldn't let me – '

'Control yourself!'

' – so I sat in the bathroom and they brought me a domino[150] and said wear that. I did. What else could I do?'

'Control yourself, Nicole!'

'I never expected you to love me – it was too late – only don't come in the bathroom, the only place I can go for privacy, dragging spreads with red blood on them and asking me to fix them.'

'Control yourself. Get up – '

Rosemary, back in the salon, heard the bathroom door bang, and stood trembling: now she knew what Violet McKisco had seen in the bathroom at Villa Diana. She answered the ringing phone and almost cried with relief when she found it was Collis Clay, who had traced her to the Divers' apartment. She asked him to come up while she got her hat, because she was afraid to go into her room alone.

BOOK TWO

Chapter 1

IN THE SPRING OF 1917, when Dr Richard Diver first arrived in Zurich, he was twenty-six years old, a fine age for a man, indeed the very acme of bachelorhood. Even in war-time days, it was a fine age for Dick, who was already too valuable, to much of a capital investment to be shot off in a gun. Years later it seemed to him that even in this sanctuary he did not escape lightly, but about that he never made up his mind – in 1917 he laughed at the idea, saying apologetically that the war didn't touch him at all. Instructions from his local board[151] were that he was to complete his studies in Zurich and take a degree as he had planned.

Switzerland was an island, washed on one side by the waves of thunder around Gorizia[152] and on another by the cataracts along the Somme and the Aisne.[153] For once there seemed more intriguing strangers than sick ones in the cantons, but that had to be guessed at – the men who whispered in the little cafés of Berne and Geneva were as likely to be diamond salesmen or commercial travellers. However, no one had missed the long trains of blinded or one-legged men, or dying trunks, that crossed each other between the bright lakes of Constance and Neuchâtel. In the beer-halls and shop windows were bright posters presenting the Swiss defending their frontiers in 1914 – with inspiring ferocity young men and old men glared down from the mountains at phantom French and Germans; the purpose was to assure the Swiss heart that it had shared the contagious glory of those days. As the massacre continued the posters withered away, and no country was more surprised than its sister republic when the United States bungled its way into the war.

Dr Diver had seen around the edges of the war by that time: he was an Oxford Rhodes Scholar[154] from Connecticut in 1914. He returned home for a final year at Johns Hopkins,[155] and took his degree. In 1916 he managed to get to Vienna under the impression that, if he did not make haste, the great Freud[156] would eventually succumb to an airplane bomb. Even then Vienna was old with death but Dick managed to get enough coal and oil to sit in his room in the Damenstiftgasse[157] and write the pamphlets that he later destroyed, but that, rewritten, were the backbone of the book he published in Zurich in 1920.

Most of us have a favourite, a heroic period, in our lives and that was Dick Diver's. For one thing he had no idea that he was charming, that the affection he gave and inspired was anything unusual among healthy people. In his last year at New Haven some one referred to him as 'lucky Dick' – the name lingered in his head.

'Lucky Dick, you big stiff,' he would whisper to himself, walking around the last sticks of flame in his room. 'You hit it, my boy. Nobody knew it was there before you came along.'

At the beginning of 1917, when it was becoming difficult to find coal, Dick burned for fuel almost a hundred text books that he had accumulated; but only, as he laid each one on the fire, with an assurance chuckling inside him that he was himself a digest of what was within the book, that he could brief it five years from now, if it deserved to be briefed. This went on at any odd hour, if necessary, with a floor rug over his shoulders, with the fine quiet of the scholar which is nearest of all things to heavenly peace – but which, as will presently be told, had to end.

For its temporary continuance he thanked his body that had done the flying rings at New Haven, and now swam in the winter Danube. With Elkins, second secretary at the Embassy, he shared an apartment, and there were two nice girl visitors – which was that and not too much of it, nor too much of the Embassy either. His contact with Ed Elkins aroused in him a first faint doubt as to the quality of his mental processes; he could not feel that they were profoundly different from the thinking of Elkins – Elkins, who would name you all the quarterbacks in New Haven for thirty years.

' – And Lucky Dick can't be one of these clever men; he must be less intact, even faintly destroyed. If life won't do it for him it's not a substitute to get a disease, or a broken heart, or an inferiority complex, though it'd be nice to build out some broken side till it was better than the original structure.'

He mocked at his reasoning, calling it specious and 'American' – his criteria of uncerebral phrase-making was that it was American. He knew, though, that the price of his intactness was incompleteness.

'The best I can wish you, my child,' so said the Fairy Blackstick in Thackeray's *The Rose and the Ring*,[158] 'is a little misfortune.'

In some moods he griped at his own reasoning: Could I help it that

Pete Livingstone sat in the locker-room Tap Day when everybody looked all over hell for him? And I got an election when otherwise I wouldn't have got Elihu,[159] knowing so few men. He was good and right and I ought to have sat in the locker-room instead. Maybe I would, if I'd thought I had a chance at an election. But Mercer kept coming to my room all those weeks. I guess I knew I had a chance all right, all right. But it would have served me right if I'd swallowed my pin in the shower and set up a conflict.

After the lectures at the university he used to argue this point with a young Rumanian intellectual who reassured him: 'There's no evidence that Goethe[160] ever had a "conflict" in a modern sense, or a man like Jung,[161] for instance. You're not a romantic philosopher – you're a scientist. Memory, force, character – especially good sense. That's going to be your trouble – judgment about yourself – once I knew a man who worked two years on the brain of an armadillo, with the idea that he would sooner or later know more about the brain of an armadillo than any one. I kept arguing with him that he was not really pushing out the extension of the human range – it was too arbitrary. And sure enough, when he sent his work to the medical journal they refused it – they had just accepted a thesis by another man on the same subject.'

Dick got up to Zurich on fewer Achilles' heels than would be required to equip a centipede, but with plenty – the illusion of eternal strength and health, and of the essential goodness of people; illusions of a nation, the lies of generations of frontier mothers who had to croon falsely that there were no wolves outside the cabin door. After he took his degree, he received his orders to join a neurological unit forming in Bar-sur-Aube.[162]

In France, to his disgust, the work was executive rather than practical. In compensation he found time to complete the short text book and assemble the material for his next venture. He returned to Zurich in the spring of 1919 discharged.

The foregoing has the ring of a biography, without the satisfaction of knowing that the hero, like Grant, lolling in his general store in Galena,[163] is ready to be called to an intricate destiny. Moreover it is confusing to come across a youthful photograph of some one known in a rounded maturity and gaze with a shock upon a fiery, wiry, eagle-eyed stranger. Best to be reassuring – Dick Diver's moment now began.

Chapter 2

IT WAS A DAMP APRIL DAY, with long diagonal clouds over the Albishorn[164] and water inert in the low places. Zurich is not unlike an American city. Missing something ever since his arrival two days before, Dick perceived that it was the sense he had had in finite French lanes that there was nothing more. In Zurich there was a lot besides Zurich – the roofs up-led the eyes to tinkling cow pastures, which in turn modified hilltops farther up – so life was a perpendicular starting off to a postcard heaven. The Alpine lands, home of the toy and the funicular, the merry-go-round and the thin chime, were not a being *here*, as in France, with French vines growing over one's feet on the ground.

In Salzburg once Dick had felt the superimposed quality of a bought and borrowed century of music; once in the laboratories of the university in Zurich, delicately poking at the cervical of a brain, he had felt like a toy-maker rather than like the tornado who had hurried through the old red buildings of Hopkins, two years before, unstayed by the irony of the gigantic Christ in the entrance hall.

Yet he had decided to remain another two years in Zurich, for he did not underestimate the value of toy-making, of infinite precision, of infinite patience.

Today he went out to see Franz Gregorovious at Dohmler's clinic on the Zurichsee. Franz, resident pathologist at the clinic, a Vaudois by birth,[165] a few years older than Dick, met him at the tram stop. He had a dark and magnificent aspect of Cagliostro[166] about him, contrasted with holy eyes; he was the third of the Gregoroviouses – his grandfather had instructed Kraepelin[167] when psychiatry was just emerging from the darkness of all time. In personality he was proud, fiery, and sheep-like – he fancied himself as a hypnotist. If the original genius of the family had grown a little tired, Franz would without doubt become a fine clinician.

On the way to the clinic he said: 'Tell me of your experiences in the war. Are you changed like the rest? You have the same stupid and unageing American face, except I know you're not stupid, Dick.'

'I didn't see any of the war – you must have gathered that from my letters, Franz.'

'That doesn't matter – we have some shell-shocks who merely heard an air raid from a distance. We have a few who merely read newspapers.'

'It sounds like nonsense to me.'

'Maybe it is, Dick. But, we're a rich person's clinic – we don't use the word nonsense. Frankly, did you come down to see me or to see that girl?'

They looked sideways at each other; Franz smiled enigmatically.

'Naturally I saw all the first letters,' he said in his official basso. 'When the change began, delicacy prevented me from opening any more. Really it had become your case.'

'Then she's well?' Dick demanded.

'Perfectly well, I have charge of her, in fact I have charge of the majority of the English and American patients. They call me Dr Gregory.'

'Let me explain about that girl,' Dick said. 'I only saw her one time, that's a fact. When I came out to say goodbye to you just before I went over to France. It was the first time I put on my uniform and I felt very bogus in it – went around saluting private soldiers and all that.'

'Why didn't you wear it today?'

'Hey! I've been discharged three weeks. Here's the way I happened to see that girl. When I left you I walked down towards that building of yours on the lake to get my bicycle.'

' – towards the "Cedars"?'

' – a wonderful night, you know – moon over that mountain – '

'The Krenzegg.'[168]

' – I caught up with a nurse and a young girl. I didn't think the girl was a patient; I asked the nurse about tram times and we walked along. The girl was about the prettiest thing I ever saw.'

'She still is.'

'She'd never seen an American uniform and we talked, and I didn't think anything about it.' He broke off, recognising a familiar perspective, and then resumed: ' – except, Franz, I'm not as hard-boiled as you are yet; when I see a beautiful shell like that I can't help feeling a regret about what's inside it. That was absolutely all – till the letters began to come.'

'It was the best thing that could have happened to her,' said Franz dramatically, 'transference of the most fortuitous kind. That's why I came down to meet you on a very busy day. I want you to come into my office and talk a long time before you see her. In fact, I sent her into Zurich to do errands.' His voice was tense with enthusiasm. 'In fact, I sent her without a nurse, with a less stable patient. I'm intensely proud of this case, which I handled, with your accidental assistance.'

The car had followed the shore of the Zurichsee into a fertile region of pasture farms and low hills, steepled with châlets. The sun swam out into a blue sea of sky and suddenly it was a Swiss valley at its best – pleasant sounds and murmurs and a good fresh smell of health and cheer.

Professor Dohmler's plant consisted of three old buildings and a pair of new ones, between a slight eminence and the shore of the lake. At its founding, ten years before, it had been the first modern clinic for mental illness; at a casual glance no layman would recognise it as a refuge for the broken, the incomplete, the menacing, of this world, though two buildings were surrounded with vine-softened walls of a deceptive height. Some men raked straw in the sunshine; here and there, as they rode into the grounds, the car passed the white flag of a nurse waving beside a patient on a path.

After conducting Dick to his office, Franz excused himself for half an hour. Left alone Dick wandered about the room and tried to reconstruct Franz from the litter of his desk, from his books and the books of and by his father and grandfather; from the Swiss piety of a huge claret-coloured photo of the former on the wall. There was smoke in the room; pushing open a French window, Dick let in a cone of sunshine. Suddenly his thoughts swung to the patient, the girl.

He had received about fifty letters from her written over a period of eight months. The first one was apologetic, explaining that she had heard from America how girls wrote to soldiers whom they did not know. She had obtained the name and address from Dr Gregory and she hoped he would not mind if she sometimes sent word to wish him well, etc., etc.

So far it was easy to recognise the tone – from *Daddy-Long-Legs*[169] and *Molly-Make-Believe*, sprightly and sentimental epistolary collections enjoying a vogue in the States. But there the resemblance ended.

The letters were divided into two classes, of which the first class, up to about the time of the armistice, was of marked pathological turn, and of which the second class, running from thence up to the present, was entirely normal, and displayed a richly maturing nature. For these latter letters Dick had come to wait eagerly in the last dull months at Bar-sur-Aube – yet even from the first letters he had pieced together more than Franz would have guessed of the story.

MON CAPITAINE – I thought when I saw you in your uniform you were so handsome. Then I thought Je m'en fiche[170] French too and German. You thought I was pretty too but I've had that before and a long time I've stood it. If you come here again with that attitude base and criminal and not even faintly what I had been taught to associate with the role of gentleman then heaven help

(2)

you. However, you seem quieter than the others, all soft like a big cat. I have only gotten to like boys who are rather sissies. Are you a sissy? There were some somewhere.

Excuse all this, it is the third letter I have written you and will send immediately or will never send. I've thought a lot about moonlight too and there are many witnesses I could find if I could only be out of here.

(3)

They said you were a doctor, but so long as you are a cat it is different. My head aches so, so excuse this walking there like an ordinary with a white cat will explain, I think. I can speak three languages, four with English, and am sure I could be useful interpreting if you arrange such thing in France I'm sure I could control everything with the belts all bound around everybody like

(4)

it was Wednesday. It is now Saturday and you are far away, perhaps killed.

Come back to me some day, for I will be here always on this green hill. Unless they will let me write my father, whom I loved dearly.

Excuse this. I am not myself today. I will write when I feel better. Cheerio

NICOLE WARREN

Excuse all this.

CAPTAIN DIVER – I know introspection is not good for a highly nervous state like mine, but I would like you to know where I stand. Last year or whenever it was in Chicago when I got so I couldn't speak to servants or walk in the street I kept waiting for some one to tell me. It was the duty of some one who understood. The blind must be led. Only no one would tell me everything – they would just tell me half and I was already too muddled to put two and two together. One man was nice – he was a French officer and he understood. He gave me a flower and said it was 'plus petite et moins entendue'.[171] We were friends. Then he took it away. I grew sicker and there was no one to explain to me. They had a song

(2)

about Joan of Arc that they used to sing at me that was just mean – it would just make me cry, for there was nothing the matter with my head then. They kept making reference to sports, too, but I didn't care by that time. So there was that day I went walking on Michigan Boulevard[172] on and on for miles and finally they followed me in an

(3)

automobile, but I wouldn't get in. Finally they pulled me in and there were nurses. After that time I began to realise it all, because I could feel what was happening in others. So you see how I stand. And what good can it be for me to stay here with the doctors harping constantly in the things I was here to get over. So today I have written my father to come and take me away. I am glad you are

(4)

so interested in examining people and sending them back. It must be so much fun.

And again, from another letter:

You might pass up your next examination and write me a letter. They just sent me some phonograph records in case I should forget my lesson and I broke them all so the nurse won't speak to me. They were in English, so that the nurses would not understand. One doctor in Chicago said I was bluffing, but what he really meant was that I was a twin six[173] and he had never seen one before. But I was very busy being mad then, so I didn't care what he said, when I am very busy being mad I don't usually care what they say, not if I were a million girls.

You told me that night you'd teach me to play. Well, I think love

(2)

is all there is or should be. Anyhow I am glad your interest in examinations keeps you busy.

Tout à vous,[174]

NICOLE WARREN

There were other letters among whose helpless cæsuras lurked darker rhythms.

DEAR CAPTAIN DIVER – I write to you because there is no one else to whom I can turn and it seems to me if this farcical situation is apparent to one as sick as me it should be apparent to you. The mental trouble is all over and besides that I am completely broken and humiliated if that was what they wanted. My family have shamefully neglected me, there's no use asking them for help or pity. I have had enough and it is simply ruining my health and wasting my time pretending that what is the matter with my head is curable.

(2)

Here I am in what appears to be semi-insane-asylum, all because nobody saw fit to tell me the truth about anything. If I had only known what was going on like I know now I could have stood it I guess for I am pretty strong, but those who should have, did not see fit to enlighten me. And now, when I know and have paid such a price for knowing, they sit there with their dogs, lives and say I

(3)

should believe what I did believe. Especially one does but I know now. I am lonesome all the time far away from friends and family across the Atlantic I roam all over the place in a half daze. If you could get me a position as interpreter (I know French and German like a native, fair Italian and a little Spanish) or in the Red Cross

(4)

Ambulance or as a train nurse, though I would have to train you would prove a great blessing.

And again:

Since you will not accept my explanation of what is the matter you could at least explain to me what you think, because you have a kind cat's face, and not that funny look that seems to be so fashionable here. Dr Gregory gave me a snapshot of you, not as handsome as you are in your uniform, but younger looking.

Mon Capitaine – It was fine to have your postcard. I am so glad you take such interest in disqualifying nurses – oh, I understood your note very well indeed. Only I thought from the moment I met you that you were different.

Dear Capitaine – I think one thing today and another tomorrow. That is really all that's the matter with me, except a crazy defiance and a lack of proportion. I would gladly welcome any alienist[175] you might suggest. Here they lie in their bathtubs and sing Play in Your Own Backyard as if I had my backyard to play in or any hope which I can find by looking either backward or forward. They tried

(2)

it again in the candy store again and I almost hit the man with the weight, but they held me.

I am not going to write you any more. I am too unstable.

And then a month with no letters. And then suddenly the change.

– I am slowly coming back to life . . .
– Today the flowers and the clouds . . .

– The war is over and I scarcely knew there was a war . . .

– How kind you have been! You must be very wise behind your face like a white cat, except you don't look like that in the picture Dr Gregory gave me . . .

– Today I went to Zurich, how strange a feeling to see a city again.

– Today we went to Berne, it was so nice with the clocks.

– Today we climbed high enough to find asphodel and edelweiss . . .

After that the letters were fewer, but he answered them all. There was one:

I wish someone were in love with me like boys were ages ago before I was sick. I suppose it will be years, though, before I could think of anything like that.

But when Dick's answer was delayed for any reason, there was a fluttering burst of worry – like a worry of a lover: 'Perhaps I have bored you,' and: 'Afraid I have presumed,' and: 'I keep thinking at night you have been sick.'

In actuality Dick was sick with the flu. When he recovered, all except the formal part of his correspondence was sacrificed to the consequent fatigue, and shortly afterward the memory of her became overlaid by the vivid presence of a Wisconsin telephone girl at headquarters in Bar-sur-Aube. She was red-lipped like a poster, and known obscenely in the messes as 'The Switchboard'.

Franz came back into his office feeling self-important. Dick thought he would probably be a fine clinician, for the sonorous or staccato cadences by which he disciplined nurse or patient came not from his nervous system but from a tremendous and harmless vanity. His true emotions were more ordered and kept to himself.

'Now about the girl, Dick,' he said. 'Of course, I want to find out about you and tell you about myself, but first about the girl, because I have been waiting to tell you about it so long.'

He searched for and found a sheaf of papers in a filing cabinet, but after shuffling through them he found they were in his way and put them on his desk. Instead he told Dick the story.

Chapter 3

ABOUT A YEAR AND A HALF BEFORE, Dr Dohmler had some vague correspondence with an American gentleman living in Lausanne, a Mr Devereux Warren, of the Warren family of Chicago. A meeting was arranged and one day Mr Warren arrived at the clinic with his daughter Nicole, a girl of sixteen. She was obviously not well and the nurse who was with her took her to walk about the grounds while Mr Warren had his consultation.

Warren was a strikingly handsome man looking less than forty. He was a fine American type in every way, tall, broad, well made – 'un homme très chic',[176] as Dr Dohmler described him to Franz. His large grey eyes were sun-veined from rowing on Lake Geneva, and he had that special air about him of having known the best of this world. The conversation was in German, for it developed that he had been educated at Göttingen.[177] He was nervous and obviously very moved by his errand.

'Dr Dohmler, my daughter isn't right in the head. I've had lots of specialists and nurses for her and she's taken a couple of rest cures but the thing has grown too big for me and I've been strongly recommended to come to you.'

'Very well,' said Dr Dohmler. 'Suppose you start at the beginning and tell me everything.'

'There isn't any beginning, at least there isn't any insanity in the family that I know of, on either side. Nicole's mother died when she was eleven and I've sort of been father and mother both to her, with the help of governesses – father and mother both to her.'

He was very moved as he said this. Dr Dohmler saw that there were tears in the corners of his eyes and noticed for the first time that there was whiskey on his breath.

'As a child she was a darling thing – everybody was crazy about her, everybody that came in contact with her. She was smart as a whip and happy as the day is long. She liked to read or draw or dance or play the piano – anything. I used to hear my wife say she was the only one of our children who never cried at night. I've got an older girl, too, and there was a boy that died, but Nicole was – Nicole was – Nicole – '

He broke off and Dr Dohmler helped him.

'She was a perfectly normal, bright, happy child.'

'Perfectly.'

Dr Dohmler waited. Mr Warren shook his head, blew a long sigh, glanced quickly at Dr Dohmler and then at the floor again.

'About eight months ago, or maybe it was six months ago or maybe ten – I try to figure but I can't remember exactly where we were when she began to do funny things – crazy things. Her sister was the first one to say anything to me about it – because Nicole was always the same to me,' he added rather hastily, as if someone had accused him of being to blame, ' – the same loving little girl. The first thing was about a valet.'

'Oh, yes,' said Dr Dohmler, nodding his venerable head, as if, like Sherlock Holmes, he had expected a valet and only a valet to be introduced at this point.

'I had a valet – been with me for years – Swiss, by the way.' He looked up for Dr Dohmler's patriotic approval. 'And she got some crazy idea about him. She thought he was making up to her – of course, at the time I believed her and I let him go, but I know now it was all nonsense.'

'What did she claim he had done?'

'That was the first thing – the doctors couldn't pin her down. She just looked at them as if they ought to know what he'd done. But she certainly meant he'd made some kind of indecent advances to her – she didn't leave us in any doubt of that.'

'I see.'

'Of course, I've read about women getting lonesome and thinking there's a man under the bed and all that, but why should Nicole get such an idea? She could have all the young men she wanted. We were in Lake Forest – that's a summer place near Chicago where we have a place – and she was out all day playing golf or tennis with boys. And some of them pretty gone on her at that.'

All the time Warren was talking to the dried old package of Dr Dohmler, one section of the latter's mind kept thinking intermittently of Chicago. Once in his youth he could have gone to Chicago as fellow and docent at the university,[178] and perhaps become rich there and owned his own clinic instead of being only a minor shareholder in a clinic. But when he had thought of what he considered his own thin knowledge spread over that whole area, over all those wheat-fields, those endless prairies, he had decided against it. But he had heard about Chicago in those days, about the great feudal families of Armour, Palmer, Field, Crane, Warren, Swift, and McCormick[179] and many others, and since that time not a few patients had come to him from that stratum of Chicago and New York.

'She got worse,' continued Warren. 'She had a fit or something –

the things she said got crazier and crazier. Her sister wrote some of them down – ' He handed a much-folded piece of paper to the doctor. 'Almost always about men going to attack her, men she knew or men on the street – anybody – '

He told of their alarm and distress, of the horrors families go through under such circumstances, of the ineffectual efforts they had made in America, finally of the faith in a change of scene that had made him run the submarine blockade and bring his daughter to Switzerland.

' – on a United States cruiser,' he specified with a touch of hauteur. 'It was possible for me to arrange that, by a stroke of luck. And, may I add,' he smiled apologetically, 'that as they say: money is no object.'

'Certainly not,' agreed Dohmler dryly.

He was wondering why and about what the man was lying to him. Or, if he was wrong about that, what was the falsity that pervaded the whole room, the handsome figure in tweeds sprawling in his chair with a sportsman's ease? That was a tragedy out there, in the February day, the young bird with wings crushed somehow, and inside here it was all too thin, thin and wrong.

'I would like – to talk to her – a few minutes now,' said Dr Dohmler, going into English as if it would bring him closer to Warren.

Afterwards when Warren had left his daughter and returned to Lausanne, and several days had passed, the doctor and Franz entered upon Nicole's card:

Diagnostic: Schizophrénie. Phase aiguë en décroissance. La peur des hommes est un symptôme de la maladie, et n'est point constitutionelle . . . Le pronostic doit rester réservé.*

And then they waited with increasing interest as the days passed for Mr Warren's promised second visit.

It was slow in coming. After a fortnight Dr Dohmler wrote. Confronted with further silence he committed what was for those days *une folie*,[180] and telephoned to the Grand Hôtel at Vevey.[181] He learned from Mr Warren's valet that he was at the moment packing to sail for America. But reminded that the forty francs Swiss for the call would show up on the clinic books, the blood of the Tuileries Guard[182] rose to Dr Dohmler's aid and Mr Warren was got to the phone.

---

* Diagnosis: Divided Personality. Acute and downhill phase of the illness. The fear of men is a symptom of the illness and is not at all constitutional . . . The prognosis must be reserved.

'It is – absolutely necessary – that you come. Your daughter's health – all depends. I can take no responsibility.'

'But look here, doctor, that's just what you're for. I have a hurry call to go home!'

Dr Dohmler had never yet spoken to anyone so far away but he dispatched his ultimatum so firmly into the phone that the agonised American at the other end yielded. Half an hour after this second arrival on the Zurichsee, Warren had broken down, his fine shoulders shaking with awful sobs inside his easy-fitting coat, his eyes redder than the very sun on Lake Geneva, and they had the awful story.

'It just happened,' he said hoarsely. 'I don't know – I don't know.

'After her mother died when she was little she used to come into my bed every morning, sometimes she'd sleep in my bed. I was sorry for the little thing. Oh, after that, whenever we went places in an automobile or a train we used to hold hands. She used to sing to me. We used to say, "Now let's not pay any attention to anybody else this afternoon – let's just have each other – for this morning you're mine." ' A broken sarcasm came into his voice. 'People used to say what a wonderful father and daughter we were – they used to wipe their eyes. We were just like lovers – and then all at once we were lovers – and ten minutes after it happened I could have shot myself – except I guess I'm such a goddamned degenerate I didn't have the nerve to do it.'

'Then what?' said Dr Dohmler, thinking again of Chicago and of a mild pale gentleman with a pince-nez who had looked him over in Zurich thirty years before. 'Did this thing go on?'

'Oh, no! She almost – she seemed to freeze up right away. She'd just say, "Never mind, never mind, daddy. It doesn't matter, never mind." '

'There were no consequences?'

'No.' He gave one short convulsive sob and blew his nose several times. 'Except now there're plenty of consequences.'

As the story concluded, Dohmler sat back in the focal armchair of the middle class and said to himself sharply, 'Peasant!' – it was one of the few absolute worldly judgments that he had permitted himself for twenty years. Then he said: 'I would like for you to go to a hotel in Zurich and spend the night and come see me in the morning.'

'And then what?'

Dr Dohmler spread his hands wide enough to carry a young pig.

'Chicago,' he suggested.

Chapter 4

'THEN WE KNEW WHERE WE STOOD,' said Franz. 'Dohmler told Warren we would take the case if he would agree to keep away from his daughter indefinitely, with an absolute minimum of five years. After Warren's first collapse, he seemed chiefly concerned as to whether the story would ever leak back to America.

'We mapped out a routine for her and waited. The prognosis was bad – as you know, the percentage of cures, even so-called social cures, is very low at that age.'

'These first letters looked bad,' agreed Dick.

'Very bad – very typical. I hesitated about letting the first one get out of the clinic. Then I thought it will be good for Dick to know we're carrying on here. It was generous of you to answer them.'

Dick sighed. 'She was such a pretty thing – she enclosed a lot of snapshots of herself. And for a month there I didn't have anything to do. All I said in my letters was "Be a good girl and mind the doctors." '

'That was enough – it gave her somebody to think of outside. For a while she didn't have anybody – only one sister that she doesn't seem very close to. Besides, reading her letters helped us here – they were a measure of her condition.'

'I'm glad.'

'You see now what happened? She felt complicity – that's neither here nor there, except as we want to revalue her ultimate stability and strength of character. First came this shock. Then she went off to a boarding-school and heard the girls talking – so from sheer self-protection she developed the idea that she had had no complicity – and from there it was easy to slide into a phantom world where all men, the more you liked them and trusted them, the more evil – '

'Did she ever go into the – horror directly?'

'No, and as a matter of fact when she began to seem normal, about October, we were in a predicament. If she had been thirty years old we would have let her make her own adjustment, but she was so young we were afraid she might harden with it all twisted inside her. So Dr Dohmler said to her frankly, "Your duty now is to yourself. This doesn't by any account mean the end of anything for you – your life is just at its beginning," and so forth and so forth. She really has an excellent mind, so he gave her a little Freud to read, not too much, and she was very interested. In fact, we've made rather a pet of her around here. But she is reticent,' he added; he hesitated: 'We have wondered if in her recent letter to you which she mailed herself from Zurich, she has said anything that would be illuminating about her state of mind and her plans for the future.'

Dick considered.

'Yes and no – I'll bring the letters out here if you want. She seems hopeful and normally hungry for life – even rather romantic. Sometimes she speaks of "the past" as people speak who have been in prison. But you never know whether they refer to the crime or the imprisonment or the whole experience. After all I'm only a sort of stuffed figure in her life.'

'Of course, I understand your position exactly, and I express our gratitude once again. That was why I wanted to see you before you see her.'

Dick laughed.

'You think she's going to make a flying leap at my person?'

'No, not that. But I want to ask you to go very gently. You are attractive to women, Dick.'

'Then God help me! Well, I'll be gentle and repulsive – I'll chew garlic whenever I'm going to see her and wear a stubble beard. I'll drive her to cover.'

'Not garlic!' said Franz, taking him seriously. 'You don't want to compromise your career. But you're partly joking.'

' – and I can limp a little. And there's no real bathtub where I'm living, anyhow.'

'You're entirely joking.' Franz relaxed – or rather assumed the posture of one relaxed. 'Now tell me about yourself and your plans?'

'I've only got one, Franz, and that's to be a good psychologist – maybe to be the greatest one that ever lived.'

Franz laughed pleasantly, but he saw that this time Dick wasn't joking.

'That's very good – and very American,' he said. 'It's more difficult for us.' He got up and went to the French window. 'I stand here and I see Zurich – there is the steeple of the Gross-Münster.[183] In its vault my grandfather is buried. Across the bridge from it lies my ancestor Lavater,[184] who would not be buried in any church. Nearby is the statue of another ancestor, Heinrich Pestalozzi,[185] and one of Dr Alfred Escher.[186] And over everything there is always Zwingli[187] – I am continually confronted with a pantheon of heroes.'

'Yes, I see.' Dick got up. 'I was only talking big. Everything's just starting over. Most of the Americans in France are frantic to get home, but not me – I draw military pay all the rest of the year if I only attend lectures at the university. How's that for a government on the grand scale that knows its future great men? Then I'm going home for a month and see my father. Then I'm coming back – I've been offered a job.'

'Where?'

'Your rivals – Gisler's Clinic at Interlaken.'

'Don't touch it,' Franz advised him. 'They've had a dozen young men there in a year. Gisler's a manic-depressive himself, his wife and her lover run the clinic – of course, you understand that's confidential.'

'How about your old scheme for America?' asked Dick lightly. 'We were going to New York and start an up-to-date establishment for billionaires.'

'That was students' talk.'

Dick dined with Franz and his bride and a small dog with a smell of burning rubber, in the cottage on the edge of the grounds. He felt vaguely oppressed, not by the atmosphere of modest retrenchment, nor by Frau Gregorovious, who might have been prophesied, but by the sudden contracting of horizons to which Franz seemed so reconciled. For him the boundaries of asceticism were differently marked – he could see it as a means to an end, even as a carrying on with a glory it would itself supply, but it was hard to think of deliberately cutting life down to the scale of an inherited suit. The domestic gestures of Franz and his wife as they turned in a cramped space lacked grace and advantage. The post-war months in France, and the lavish liquidations taking place under the aegis of American splendour, had affected Dick's outlook. Also, men and women had made much of him, and perhaps what had brought him back to the centre of the great Swiss watch was an intuition that this was not too good for a serious man.

He made Kaethe Gregorovious feel charming, meanwhile becoming increasingly restless at the all-pervading cauliflower – simultaneously hating himself too for this incipience of he knew not what superficiality.

'God, am I like the rest after all?' – so he used to think starting awake at night – 'Am I like the rest?'

This was poor material for a socialist but good material for those who do much of the world's rarest work. The truth was that for some months he had been going through that partitioning of the things of youth wherein it is decided whether or not to die for what one no longer believes. In the dead white hours in Zurich staring into a stranger's pantry across the upshine of a street lamp, he used to think that he wanted to be good, he wanted to be kind, he wanted to be brave and wise, but it was all pretty difficult. He wanted to be loved, too, if he could fit it in.

Chapter 5

THE VERANDA OF THE CENTRAL BUILDING was illuminated from open French windows, save where the black shadows of stripling walls and the fantastic shadows of iron chairs slithered down into a gladiolus bed. From the figures that shuffled between the rooms Miss Warren emerged first in glimpses and then sharply when she saw him; as she crossed the threshold her face caught the room's last light and brought it outside with her. She walked to a rhythm – all that week there had been singing in her ears, summer songs of ardent skies and wild shade, and with his arrival the singing had become so loud she could have joined in with it.

'How do you do, Captain,' she said, unfastening her eyes from his with difficulty, as though they had become entangled. 'Shall we sit out here?' She stood still, her glance moving about for a moment. 'It's summer practically.'

A woman had followed her out, a dumpy woman in a shawl, and Nicole presented Dick: 'Señora – '

Franz excused himself and Dick grouped three chairs together.

'The lovely night,' the señora said.

'*Muy bella*,' agreed Nicole; then to Dick, 'Are you here for a long time?'

'I'm in Zurich for a long time, if that's what you mean.'

'This is really the first night of real spring,' the señora suggested.

'To stay?'

'At least till July.'

'I'm leaving in June.'

'June is a lovely month here,' the señora commented. 'You should stay for June and then leave in July when it gets really too hot.'

'You're going where?' Dick asked Nicole.

'Somewhere with my sister – somewhere exciting, I hope, because I've lost so much time. But perhaps they'll think I ought to go to a quiet place at first – perhaps Como.[188] Why don't you come to Como?'

'Ah, Como – ' began the señora.

Within the building a trio broke into Suppé's[189] 'Light Cavalry'. Nicole took advantage of this to stand up and the impression of her youth and beauty grew on Dick until it welled up inside him in a compact paroxysm of emotion. She smiled, a moving childish smile that was like all the lost youth in the world.

'The music's too loud to talk against – suppose we walk around. *Buenas noches, señora.*'

'G't night – g't night.'

They went down two steps to the path where in a moment a shadow cut across it. She took his arm.

'I have some phonograph records my sister sent me from America,' she said. 'Next time you come here I'll play them for you – I know a place to put the phonograph where no one can hear.'

'That'll be nice.'

'Do you know "Hindustan"?' she asked wistfully. 'I'd never heard it before, but I like it. And I've got "Why Do They Call Them Babies?" and "I'm Glad I Can Make You Cry".[190] I suppose you've danced to all those tunes in Paris?'

'I haven't been to Paris.'

Her cream-coloured dress, alternately blue or grey as they walked, and her very blonde hair, dazzled Dick – whenever he turned towards her she was smiling a little, her face lighting up like an angel's when they came into the range of a roadside arc. She thanked him for everything rather as if he had taken her to some party, and as Dick became less and less certain of his relation to her, her confidence increased – there was that excitement about her that seemed to reflect all the excitement of the world.

'I'm not under any restraint at all,' she said. 'I'll play you two good tunes called "Wait Till The Cows Come Home" and "Goodbye, Alexander".'[191]

He was late the next time, a week later, and Nicole was waiting for him at a point in the path which he would pass walking from Franz's house. Her hair, drawn back behind her ears, brushed her shoulders in such a way that the face seemed to have just emerged from it, as if this were the exact moment when she was coming from a wood into clear moonlight. The unknown yielded her up: Dick wished she had no background, that she was just a girl lost with no address save the night from which she had come. They went to the cache where she had left the phonograph, turned a corner by the workshop, climbed a rock, and sat down behind a low wall, facing miles and miles of rolling night.

They were in America now even Franz with his conception of Dick as an irresistible Lothario[192] would never have guessed that they had gone so far away. They were so sorry, dear; they went down to meet each other in a taxi, honey; they had preferences in smiles and had met in Hindustan, and shortly afterward they must have quarrelled, for nobody knew and nobody seemed to care – yet finally one of them had gone and left the other crying, only to feel blue, to feel sad.[193]

The thin tunes, holding lost times and future hopes in liaison, twisted upon the Valais[194] night. In the lulls of the phonograph a cricket held the scene together with a single note. By and by Nicole stopped playing the machine and sang to him.

> 'Lay a silver dollar
>   On the ground
> And watch it roll
>   Because it's round – '[195]

On the pure parting of her lips no breath hovered. Dick stood up suddenly.

'What's the matter, you don't like it?'

'Of course I do.'

'Our cook at home taught it to me:

> A woman never knows
>   What a good man she's got
> Till after she turns him down . . .

You like it?'

She smiled at him, making sure that the smile gathered up everything inside her and directed it towards him, making him a profound promise of herself for so little, for the beat of a response, the assurance of a complementary vibration in him. Minute by minute the sweetness drained down into her out of the willow trees, out of the dark world.

She stood up too, and stumbling over the phonograph, was momentarily against him, leaning into the hollow of his rounded shoulder.

'I've got one more record,' she said. 'Have you heard "So Long, Letty"?[196] I suppose you have.'

'Honestly, you don't understand – I haven't heard a thing.'

Nor known, nor smelt, nor tasted, he might have added; only hot-cheeked girls in hot secret rooms. The young maidens he had known at New Haven in 1914 kissed men, saying 'There!' hands at the man's chest to push him away. Now there was this scarcely saved waif of disaster bringing him the essence of a continent . . .

Chapter 6

IT WAS MAY when he next found her. The luncheon in Zurich was a council of caution; obviously the logic of his life tended away from the girl; yet when a stranger stared at her from a nearby table, eyes burning disturbingly like an uncharted light, he turned to the man with an urbane version of intimidation and broke the regard.

'He was just a peeper,' he explained cheerfully. 'He was just looking at your clothes. Why do you have so many different clothes?'

'Sister says we're very rich,' she offered humbly. 'Since Grandmother is dead.'

'I forgive you.'

He was enough older than Nicole to take pleasure in her youthful vanities and delights, the way she paused fractionally in front of the hall mirror on leaving the restaurant, so that the incorruptible quicksilver could give her back to herself. He delighted in her stretching out her hands to new octaves now that she found herself beautiful and rich. He tried honestly to divorce her from any obsession that he had stitched her together – glad to see her build up happiness and confidence apart from him; the difficulty was that, eventually, Nicole brought everything to his feet, gifts of sacrificial ambrosia, of worshipping myrtle.

The first week of summer found Dick re-established in Zurich. He had arranged his pamphlets and what work he had done in the army into a pattern from which he intended to make his revise of *A Psychology for Psychiatrists*. He thought he had a publisher; he had established contact with a poor student who would iron out his errors in German. Franz considered it a rash business, but Dick pointed out the disarming modesty of the theme.

'This is stuff I'll never know so well again,' he insisted. 'I have a hunch it's a thing that only fails to be basic because it's never had material recognition. The weakness of this profession is its attraction for the man a little crippled and broken. Within the walls of the profession he compensates by tending towards the clinical, the "practical" – he has won his battle without a struggle.

'On the contrary, you are a good man, Franz, because fate selected you for your profession before you were born. You'd better thank God you had no "bent" – I got to be a psychiatrist because there was a girl at St Hilda's in Oxford[197] that went to the same lectures. Maybe

I'm getting trite but I don't want to let my current ideas slide away with a few dozen glasses of beer.'

'All right,' Franz answered. 'You are an American. You can do this without professional harm. I do not like these generalities. Soon you will be writing little books called "Deep Thoughts for the Layman", so simplified that they are positively guaranteed not to cause thinking. If my father were alive he would look at you and grunt, Dick. He would take his napkin and fold it so, and hold his napkin ring, this very one – ' he held it up, a boar's head was carved in the brown wood – 'and he would say, "Well, my impression is – " then he would look at you and think suddenly, "What is the use?" then he would stop and grunt again; then we would be at the end of dinner.'

'I am alone today,' said Dick testily. 'But I may not be alone tomorrow. After that I'll fold up my napkin like your father and grunt.'

Franz waited a moment.

'How about our patient?' he asked.

'I don't know.'

'Well you should know about her by now.'

'I like her. She's attractive. What do you want me to do – take her up in the edelweiss?'

'No, I thought since you go in for scientific books you might have an idea.'

' – devote my life to her?'

Franz called his wife in the kitchen: 'Du lieber Gott! Bitte, bringe Dick noch ein Glas-Bier.'[198]

'I don't want any more if I've got to see Dohmler.'

'We think it's best to have a programme. Four weeks have passed away – apparently the girl is in love with you. That's not our business if we were in the world, but here in the clinic we have a stake in the matter.'

'I'll do whatever Dr Dohmler says,' Dick agreed.

But he had little faith that Dohmler would throw much light on the matter; he himself was the incalculable element involved. By no conscious volition of his own, the thing had drifted into his hands. It reminded him of a scene in his childhood when everyone in the house was looking for the lost key to the silver closet, Dick knowing he had hidden it under the handkerchiefs in his mother's top drawer; at that time he had experienced a philosophical detachment, and this was repeated now when he and Franz went together to Professor Dohmler's office.

The professor, his face beautiful under straight whiskers, like a vine-overgrown veranda of some fine old house, disarmed him. Dick knew some individuals with more talent, but no person of a class qualitatively superior to Dohmler.

Six months later he thought the same way when he saw Dohmler dead, the light out on the veranda, the vines of his whiskers tickling his stiff white collar, the many battles that had swayed before the chink-like eyes stilled for ever under the frail delicate lids –

' . . . Good-morning, sir.' He stood formally, thrown back to the army.

Professor Dohmler interlaced his tranquil fingers. Franz spoke in terms half of liaison officer, half of secretary, till his senior cut through him in mid-sentence.

'We have gone a certain way,' he said mildly. 'It's you, Dr Diver, who can best help us now.'

Routed out, Dick confessed: 'I'm not so straight on it myself.'

'I have nothing to do with your personal reactions,' said Dohmler. 'But I have much to with the fact that this so-called "transference",' he darted a short ironic look at Franz which the latter returned in kind, 'must be terminated. Miss Nicole does well indeed, but she is in no condition to survive what she might interpret as a tragedy.'

Again Franz began to speak, but Dr Dohmler motioned him silent.

'I realise that your position has been difficult.'

'Yes, it has.'

Now the professor sat back and laughed, saying on the last syllable of his laughter, with his sharp little grey eyes shining through: 'Perhaps you have got sentimentally involved yourself.'

Aware that he was being drawn on, Dick, too, laughed.

'She's a pretty girl – anybody responds to that to a certain extent. I have no intention – '

Again Franz tried to speak – again Dohmler stopped him with a question directed pointedly at Dick. 'Have you thought of going away?'

'I can't go away.'

Dr Dohmler turned to Franz: 'Then we can send Miss Warren away.'

'As you think best, Professor Dohmler,' Dick conceded. 'It's certainly a situation.'

Professor Dohmler raised himself like a legless man mounting a pair of crutches.

'But it is a professional situation,' he cried quietly.

He sighed himself back into his chair, waiting for the reverberating thunder to die out about the room. Dick saw that Dohmler had reached his climax, and he was not sure that he himself had survived it. When the thunder had diminished Franz managed to get his word in.

'Dr Diver is a man of fine character,' he said. 'I feel he only has to appreciate the situation in order to deal correctly with it. In my opinion Dick can co-operate right here, without anyone going away.'

'How do you feel about that?' Professor Dohmler asked Dick.

Dick felt churlish in the face of the situation; at the same time he realised in the silence after Dohmler's pronouncement that the state of inanimation could not be indefinitely prolonged; suddenly he spilled everything.

'I'm half in love with her – the question of marrying her has passed through my mind.'

'Tch! Tch!' uttered Franz.

'Wait.' Dohmler warned him. Franz refused to wait: 'What! And devote half your life to being doctor and nurse and all – never! I know what these cases are. One time in twenty it's finished in the first push – better never see her again!'

'What do you think?' Dohmler asked Dick.

'Of course Franz is right.'

Chapter 7

IT WAS LATE AFTERNOON when they wound up the discussion as to what Dick should do: he must be most kind and yet eliminate himself. When the doctors stood up at last, Dick's eyes fell outside the window to where a light rain was falling – Nicole was waiting, expectant, somewhere in that rain. When, presently, he went out buttoning his oilskin at the throat, pulling down the brim of his hat, he came upon her immediately under the roof of the main entrance.

'I know a new place we can go,' she said. 'When I was ill I didn't mind sitting inside with the others in the evening – what they said seemed like everything else. Naturally now I see them as ill and it's – it's – '

'You'll be leaving soon.'

'Oh, soon. My sister, Beth, but she's always been called Baby, she's coming in a few weeks to take me somewhere; after that I'll be back here for a last month.'

'The older sister?'

'Oh, quite a bit older. She's twenty-four – she's very English. She lives in London with my father's sister. She was engaged to an Englishman but he was killed – I never saw him.'

Her face, ivory gold against the blurred sunset that strove through the rain, had a promise Dick had never seen before: the high cheek-bones, the faintly wan quality, cool rather than feverish, was reminiscent of the frame of a promising colt – a creature whose life did not promise to be only a projection of youth upon a greyer screen, but instead, a true growing; the face would be handsome in middle life; it would be handsome in old age: the essential structure and the economy were there.

'What are you looking at?'

'I was just thinking that you're going to be rather happy.'

Nicole was frightened: 'Am I? All right – things couldn't be worse than they have been.'

In the covered woodshed to which she had led him, she sat cross-legged upon her golf shoes, her burberry[199] wound about her and her cheeks stung alive by the damp air. Gravely she returned his gaze, taking in his somewhat proud carriage that never quite yielded to the wooden post against which he leaned; she looked into his face that always tried to discipline itself into moulds of attentive seriousness, after excursions into joys and mockeries of its own. That part of him which seemed to fit his reddish Irish colouring she knew least; she was afraid of it, yet more anxious to explore – this was his more masculine side: the other part, the trained part, the consideration in the polite eyes, she expropriated without question, as most women did.

'At least this institution has been good for languages,' said Nicole. 'I've spoken French with two doctors, and German with the nurses, and Italian, or something like it, with a couple of scrub-women and one of the patients, and I've picked up a lot of Spanish from another.'

'That's fine.'

He tried to arrange an attitude but no logic seemed forthcoming.

' – Music too. Hope you didn't think I was only interested in ragtime. I practise every day – the last few months I've been taking a course in Zurich on the history of music. In fact it was all that kept me going at times – music and the drawing.' She leaned suddenly and twisted a loose strip from the sole of her shoe, and then looked up. 'I'd like to draw you just the way you are now.'

It made him sad when she brought out her accomplishments for his approval.

'I envy you. At present I don't seem to be interested in anything except my work.'

'Oh, I think that's fine for a man,' she said quickly. 'But for a girl I think she ought to have lots of minor accomplishments and pass them on to her children.'

'I suppose so,' said Dick with deliberated indifference.

Nicole sat quiet. Dick wished she would speak so that he could play the easy role of wet blanket, but now she sat quiet.

'You're all well,' he said. 'Try to forget the past; don't overdo things for a year or so. Go back to America and be a debutante and fall in love – and be happy.'

'I couldn't fall in love.' Her injured shoe scraped a cocoon of dust from the log on which she sat.

'Sure you can,' Dick insisted. 'Not for a year maybe, but sooner or later.' Then he added brutally: 'You can have a perfectly normal life with a houseful of beautiful descendants. The very fact that you could make a complete comeback at your age proves that the precipitating factors were pretty near everything. Young woman, you'll be pulling your weight long after your friends are carried off screaming.'

– But there was a look of pain in her eyes as she took the rough dose, the harsh reminder.

'I know I wouldn't be fit to marry anyone for a long time,' she said humbly.

Dick was too upset to say any more. He looked out into the grain field trying to recover his hard brassy attitude.

'You'll be all right – everybody here believes in you. Why, Dr Gregory is so proud of you that he'll probably – '

'I hate Dr Gregory.'

'Well, you shouldn't.'

Nicole's world had fallen to pieces, but it was only a flimsy and scarcely created world; beneath it her emotions and instincts fought on. Was it an hour ago she had waited by the entrance, wearing her hope like a corsage at her belt?

. . . Dresses stay crisp for him, button stay put, bloom narcissus – air stay still and sweet.

'It will be nice to have fun again,' she fumbled on. For a moment she entertained a desperate idea of telling him how rich she was, what big houses she lived in, that really she was a valuable property – for a moment she made herself into her grandfather, Sid Warren, the horse-trader. But she survived the temptation to confuse all values and shut these matters into the Victorian side-chambers – even though there was no home left to her, save emptiness and pain.

'I have to go back to the clinic. It's not raining now.'

Dick walked beside her, feeling her unhappiness, and wanting to drink the rain that touched her cheek.

'I have some new records,' she said. 'I can hardly wait to play them. Do you know – '

After supper that evening, Dick thought, he would finish the break; also he wanted to kick Franz's bottom for having partially introduced him to such a sordid business. He waited in the hall. His eyes followed a beret, not wet with waiting like Nicole's beret, but covering a skull recently operated on. Beneath it human eyes peered, found him and came over: 'Bonjour, docteur.'

'Bonjour, monsieur.'

'Il fait beau temps.'

'Oui, merveilleux.'

'Vous êtes ici maintenant?'

'Non, pour la journée seulement.'

'Ah, bon. Alors – au revoir, monsieur.'[200]

Glad at having survived another contact, the wretch in the beret moved away. Dick waited. Presently a nurse came downstairs and delivered him a message.

'Miss Warren asks to be excused, doctor. She wants to lie down. She wants to have dinner upstairs tonight.'

The nurse hung on his response, half expecting him to imply that Miss Warren's attitude was pathological.

'Oh, I see. Well – ' He rearranged the flow of his own saliva, the pulse of his heart. 'I hope she feels better. Thanks.'

He was puzzled and discontent. At any rate it freed him.

Leaving a note for Franz begging off from supper, he walked through the countryside to the tram station. As he reached the platform, with spring twilight gilding the rails and the glass in the slot machines, he began to feel that the station, the hospital, was hovering between being centripetal and centrifugal. He felt frightened. He was glad when the substantial cobblestones of Zurich clicked once more under his shoes.

He expected to hear from Nicole next day but there was no word. Wondering if she was ill, he called the clinic and talked to Franz.

'She came downstairs to luncheon yesterday and today,' said Franz. 'She seemed a little abstracted and in the clouds. How did it go off?'

Dick tried to plunge over the Alpine crevasse between the sexes.

'We didn't get to it – at least I didn't think we did. I tried to be distant, but I didn't think enough happened to change her attitude if it ever went deep.'

Perhaps his vanity had been hurt that there was no *coup de grâce* to administer.

'From some things she said to her nurse I'm inclined to think she understood.'

'All right.'

'It was the best thing that could have happened. She doesn't seem over-agitated – only a little in the clouds.'

'All right, then.'

'Dick, come soon and see me.'

Chapter 8

DURING THE NEXT WEEKS Dick experienced a vast dissatisfaction. The pathological origin and mechanistic defeat of the affair left a flat and metallic taste. Nicole's emotions had been used unfairly – what if they turned out to have been his own? Necessarily he must absent himself from felicity a while – in dreams he saw her walking on the clinic path swinging her wide straw hat . . .

One time he saw her in person; as he walked past the Palace Hôtel, a magnificent Rolls[201] curved into the half-moon entrance. Small within its gigantic proportions, and buoyed up by the power of a hundred superfluous horses, sat Nicole and a young woman whom he assumed was her sister. Nicole saw him and momentarily her lips parted in an expression of fright. Dick shifted his hat and passed, yet for a moment the air around him was loud with the circlings of all the goblins on the Gross-Münster.[202] He tried to write the matter out of his mind in a memorandum that went into detail as to the solemn regime before her; the possibilities of another 'push' of the malady under the stresses which the world would inevitably supply – in all a memorandum that would have been convincing to any one save to him who had written it.

The total value of this effort was to make him realise once more how far his emotions were involved; thenceforth he resolutely provided antidotes. One was the telephone girl from Bar-sur-Aube, now touring Europe from Nice to Coblenz, in a desperate round-up of the men she had known in her never-to-be-equalled holiday; another was the making of arrangements to get home on a government transport in August; a third was a consequent intensification of work on his proofs for the book that this autumn was to be presented to the German-speaking world of psychiatry.

Dick had outgrown the book; he wanted now to do more spade-work; if he got an exchange fellowship he could count on plenty of routine.

Meanwhile he had projected a new work: 'An attempt at a uniform and pragmatic classification of the neuroses and psychoses, based on an examination of fifteen hundred pre-Krapaelin and post-Krapaelin cases as they would be diagnosed in the terminology of the different contemporary schools' and another sonorous paragraph 'Together with a chronology of such subdivisions of opinion as have arisen independently'.

This title would look monumental in German.*

Going into Montreux Dick pedalled slowly, gaping at the Jugenhorn whenever possible, and blinded by glimpses of the lake through the alleys of the shore hotels. He was conscious of the groups of English, emergent after four years and walking with detective-story suspicion in their eyes, as though they were about to be assaulted in this questionable country by German train-bands. There was building and awakening everywhere on this mound of débris formed by a mountain torrent. At Berne and at Lausanne on the way south, Dick had been eagerly asked if there would be Americans this year. 'By August, if not in June?'

He wore leather shorts, an army shirt, mountain shoes. In his knapsack were a cotton suit and a change of underwear. At the Glion funicular[203] he checked his bicycle and took a small beer on the terrace of the station buffet, meanwhile watching the little bug crawl down the eighty-degree slope of the hill. His ear was full of dried blood from La Tour de Peilz,[204] where he had sprinted under the impression that he was a spoiled athlete. He asked for alcohol and cleared up the exterior while the funicular slid down into port. He saw his bicycle embarked, slung his knapsack into the lower compartment of the car, and followed it in.

Mountain-climbing cars are built on a slant similar to the angle of a hat-brim of a man who doesn't want to be recognised. As water gushed from the chamber under the car, Dick was impressed with the ingenuity of the whole idea – a complementary car was now taking on mountain water at the top and would pull the lightened car up by gravity, as soon as the brakes were released. It must have been a great inspiration. In the seat across, a couple of British were discussing the cable itself.

'The ones made in England always last five or six years. Two years ago the Germans underbid us, and how long do you think their cable lasted?'

---

* Ein Versuch die Neurosen und Psychosen gleichmässig und pragmatisch zu klassifizieren auf Grund der Untersuchung von fünfzehn hundert pre-Krapaelin und post-Krapaelin Fällen wie sie diagnostiziert sein würden in der Terminologie von den verschiedenen Schulen der Gegenwart, Zusammen mit einer Chronologie solcher Subdivisionen der Meinung welche unabhängig entstanden sind.

'How long?'

'A year and ten months. Then the Swiss sold it to the Italians. They don't have rigid inspections of cables.'

'I can see it would be a terrible thing for Switzerland if a cable broke.'

The conductor shut a door; he telephoned his confrère among the undulati, and with a jerk the car was pulled upward, heading for a pinpoint on an emerald hill above. After it cleared the low roofs, the skies of Vaud, Valais, Swiss Savoy, and Geneva spread around the passengers in cyclorama. On the centre of the lake, cooled by the piercing current of the Rhône, lay the true centre of the Western world. Upon it floated swans like boats and boats like swans, both lost in the nothingness of the heartless beauty. It was a bright day, with sun glittering on the grass beach below and the white courts of the Kursaal.[205] The figures on the courts threw no shadows.

When Chillon and the island palace of Salagnon[206] came into view Dick turned his eyes inward. The funicular was above the highest houses of the shore; on both sides a tangle of foliage and flowers culminated at intervals in masses of colour. It was a rail-side garden, and in the car was a sign: 'Défense de cueillir les fleurs.'[207]

Though one must not pick flowers on the way up, the blossoms trailed in as they passed – Dorothy Perkins roses[208] dragged patiently through each compartment slowly waggling with the motion of the funicular, letting go at the last to swing back to their rosy cluster. Again and again these branches went through the car.

In the compartment above and in front of Dick's, a group of English were standing up and exclaiming upon the backdrop of sky, when suddenly there was a confusion among them – they parted to give passage to a couple of young people who made apologies and scrambled over into the rear compartment of the funicular – Dick's compartment. The young man was a Latin with the eyes of a stuffed deer; the girl was Nicole.

The two climbers gasped momentarily from their efforts; as they settled into seats, laughing and crowding the English to the corners, Nicole said, 'Hel*lo*.' She was lovely to look at; immediately Dick saw that something was different; in a second he realised it was her fine-spun hair, bobbed like Irene Castle's[209] and fluffed into curls. She wore a sweater of powder blue and white tennis skirt – she was the first morning in May and every taint of the clinic was departed.

'Plunk!' she gasped. 'Whoo-oo, that guard. They'll arrest us at the next stop. Dr Diver, the Conte de Marmora.'[210]

'Gee-imminy!' She felt her new hair, panting. 'Sister bought first-class tickets – it's a matter of principle with her.' She and Marmora exchanged glances and shouted: 'Then we found that first-class is the hearse part behind the chauffeur – shut in with curtains for a rainy day, so you can't see anything. But Sister's very dignified – ' Again Nicole and Marmora laughed with young intimacy.

'Where you bound?' asked Dick.

'Caux.[211] You, too?' Nicole looked at his costume. 'That your bicycle they got up in front?'

'Yes. I'm going to coast down Monday.'

'With me on your handlebars? I mean, really – will you? I can't think of more fun.'

'But I will carry you down in my arms,' Marmora protested intensely. 'I will roller-skate you – or I will throw you and you will fall slowly like a feather.'

The delight in Nicole's face – to be a feather again instead of a plummet, to float not to drag. She was a carnival to watch – at times primly coy, posing, grimacing and gesturing – sometimes the shadow fell and the dignity of old suffering flowed down into her fingertips. Dick wished himself away from her, fearing that he was a reminder of a world well left behind. He resolved to go to the other hotel.

When the funicular came to rest, those new to it stirred in suspension between the blues of two heavens. It was merely for a mysterious exchange between the conductor of the car going up and the conductor of the car coming down. Then up and up over a forest path and a gorge – then again up a hill that became solid with narcissus, from passengers to sky. The people in Montreux playing tennis in the lakeside courts were pinpoints now. Something new was in the air; freshness – freshness embodying itself in music as the car slid into Glion and they heard the orchestra in the hotel garden.

When they changed to the mountain train the music was drowned by the rushing water released from the hydraulic chamber. Almost overhead was Caux, where the thousand windows of a hotel burned in the late sun.

But the approach was different – a leather-lunged engine pushed the passengers round and round in a corkscrew, mounting, rising; they chugged through low-level clouds and for a moment Dick lost Nicole's face in the spray of the slanting donkey-engine;[212] they skirted a lost streak of wind with the hotel growing in size at each spiral, until with a vast surprise they were there, on top of the sunshine.

In the confusion of arrival, as Dick slung his knapsack and started forward on the platform to get his bicycle, Nicole was beside him.

'Aren't you at our hotel?' she asked.

'I'm economising.'

'Will you come down and have dinner?' Some confusion with baggage ensued. 'This is my sister – Dr Diver from Zurich.'

Dick bowed to a young woman of twenty-five, tall and confident. She was both formidable and vulnerable, he decided, remembering other women with flower-like mouths grooved for bits.

'I'll drop in after dinner,' Dick promised. 'First I must get acclimated.'

He wheeled off his bicycle, feeling Nicole's eyes following him, feeling her helpless first love, feeling it twist around inside him. He went three hundred yards up the slope to the other hotel, he engaged a room and found himself washing without a memory of the intervening ten minutes, only a sort of drunken flush pierced with voices, unimportant voices that did not know how much he was loved.

Chapter 9

THEY WERE WAITING for him and incomplete without him. He was still the incalculable element; Miss Warren and the young Italian wore their anticipation as obviously as Nicole. The salon of the hotel, a room of fabled acoustics, was stripped for dancing, but there was a small gallery of Englishwomen of a certain age, with neckbands, dyed hair, and faces powdered pinkish grey; and of American women of a certain age, with snowy-white transformations, black dresses, and lips of cherry red. Miss Warren and Marmora were at a corner table – Nicole was diagonally across from them forty yards away, and as Dick arrived he heard her voice: 'Can you hear me? I'm speaking naturally.'

'Perfectly.'

'Hello, Dr Diver.'

'What's this?'

'You realise the people in the centre of the floor can't hear what I say, but you can?'

'A waiter told us about it,' said Miss Warren. 'Corner to corner – it's like wireless.'

It was exciting up on the mountain, like a ship at sea. Presently Marmora's parents joined them. They treated the Warrens with respect – Dick gathered that their fortunes had something to do with a bank in Milan that had something to do with the Warren fortunes. But Baby Warren wanted to talk to Dick, wanted to talk to him with the impetus that sent her out vagrantly towards all new men, as though she were on an inelastic tether and considered that she might as well get to the end of it as soon as possible. She crossed and recrossed her knees frequently in the manner of tall restless virgins.

' – Nicole told me that you took part care of her, and had a lot to do with her getting well. What I can't understand is what *we're* supposed to do – they were so indefinite at the sanatorium; they only told me she ought to be natural and gay. I knew the Marmoras were up here so I asked Tino to meet us at the funicular. And you see what happens – the very first thing Nicole has him crawling over the sides of the car as if they were both insane – '

'That was absolutely normal,' Dick laughed. 'I'd call it a good sign. They were showing off for each other.'

'But how can I tell? Before I knew it, almost in front of my eyes, she had her hair cut off, in Zurich, because of a picture in *Vanity Fair*.'[213]

'That's all right. She's a schizoid – a permanent eccentric. You can't change that.'

'What is it?'

'Just what I said – an eccentric.'

'Well, how can any one tell what's eccentric and what's crazy?'

'Nothing is going to be crazy – Nicole is all fresh and happy, you needn't be afraid.'

Baby shifted her knees about – she was a compendium of all the discontented women who had loved Byron[214] a hundred years before, yet, in spite of the tragic affair with the Guards officer, there was something wooden and onanistic about her.

'I don't mind the responsibility,' she declared, 'but I'm in the air. We've never had anything like this in the family before – we know Nicole had some shock and my opinion is it was about a boy, but we don't really know. Father says he would have shot him if he could have found out.'

The orchestra was playing 'Poor Butterfly';[215] young Marmora was dancing with his mother. It was a tune new enough to them all. Listening, and watching Nicole's shoulders as she chattered to the elder Marmora, whose hair was dashed with white like a piano keyboard, Dick thought of the shoulders of a violin, and then he thought of the dishonour, the secret. Oh, butterfly – the moments pass into hours –

'Actually *I* have a plan,' Baby continued with apologetic hardness. 'It may seem absolutely impractical to you but they say Nicole will need to be looked after for a few years. I don't know whether you know Chicago or not – '

'I don't.'

'Well, there's a North Side and a South Side and they're very much separated. The North Side is chic and all that, and we've always lived over there, at least for many years, but lots of old families, old Chicago families, if you know what I mean, still live on the South Side. The University[216] is there. I mean it's stuffy to some people, but anyhow it's different from the North Side. I don't know whether you understand.'

He nodded. With some concentration he had been able to follow her.

'Now of course we have lots of connections there – father controls certain chairs and fellowships and so forth at the University, and I thought if we took Nicole home and threw her with that crowd – you see she's quite musical and speaks all these languages – what could be better in her condition than if she fell in love with some good doctor – '

A burst of hilarity surged up in Dick, the Warrens were going to buy Nicole a doctor – You got a nice doctor you can let us use? There was no use worrying about Nicole when they were in the position of being able to buy her a nice young doctor, the paint scarcely dry on him.

'But how about the doctor?' he said automatically.

'There must be many who'd jump at the chance.'

The dancers were back, but Baby whispered quickly: 'This is the sort of thing I mean. Now where is Nicole – she's gone off somewhere. Is she upstairs in her room? What am I supposed to do? I never know whether it's something innocent or whether I ought to go find her.'

'Perhaps she just wants to be by herself – people living alone get used to loneliness.' Seeing that Miss Warren was not listening he stopped. 'I'll take a look around.'

For a moment all the outdoors shut in with mist was like spring with the curtains drawn. Life was gathered near the hotel. Dick passed some cellar windows where bus boys sat on bunks and played cards over a litre of Spanish wine. As he approached the promenade, the stars began to come through the white crests of the high Alps. On the horseshoe walk overlooking the lake Nicole was the figure motionless between two lampstands, and he approached silently across the grass. She turned to him with an expression of: 'Here you are,' and for a moment he was sorry he had come.

'Your sister wondered.'

'Oh!' She was accustomed to being watched. With an effort she explained herself: 'Sometimes I get a little – it gets a little too much.

I've lived so quietly. Tonight that music was too much. It made me want to cry – '

'I understand.'

'This has been an awfully exciting day.'

'I know.'

'I don't want to do anything antisocial – I've caused everybody enough trouble. But tonight I wanted to get away.'

It occurred to Dick suddenly, as it might occur to a dying man that he had forgotten to tell where his will was, that Nicole had been 're-educated' by Dohmler and the ghostly generations behind him; it occurred to him also that there would be so much she would have to be told. But having recorded this wisdom within himself, he yielded to the insistent face-value of the situation and said: 'You're a nice person – just keep using your own judgment about yourself.'

'You like me?'

'Of course.'

'Would you – ' They were strolling along towards the dim end of the horseshoe, two hundred yards ahead. 'If I hadn't been sick would you – I mean, would I have been the sort of girl you might have – oh, slush, you know what I mean.'

He was in for it now, possessed by a vast irrationality. She was so near that he felt his breathing change but again his training came to his aid in a boy's laugh and a trite remark.

'You're teasing yourself, my dear. Once I knew a man who fell in love with his nurse – ' The anecdote rambled on, punctuated by their footsteps. Suddenly Nicole interrupted in succinct Chicagoese: 'Bull!'

'That's a very vulgar expression.'

'What about it?' she flared up. 'You don't think I've got any common sense – before I was sick I didn't have any, but I have now. And if I don't know you're the most attractive man I ever met you must think I'm still crazy. It's my hard luck, all right – don't pretend I don't *know* – I know everything about you and me.'

Dick was at an additional disadvantage. He remembered the statement of the elder Miss Warren as to the young doctors that could be purchased in the intellectual stockyards of the South Side of Chicago, and he hardened for a moment. 'You're a fetching kid, but I couldn't fall in love.'

'You won't give me a chance.'

'What!'

The impertinence, the right to invade implied, astounded him. Short of anarchy he could not think of any chance that Nicole Warren deserved.

'Give me a chance now.'

The voice fell low, sank into her breast and stretched the tight bodice over her heart as she came up close. He felt the young lips, her body sighing in relief against the arm growing stronger to hold her. There were now no more plans than if Dick had arbitrarily made some indissoluble mixture, with atoms joined and inseparable; you could throw it all out but never again could they fit back into atomic scale. As he held her and tasted her, and as she curved in further and further towards him, with her own lips, new to herself, drowned and engulfed in love, yet solaced and triumphant, he was thankful to have an existence at all, if only as a reflection in her wet eyes.

'My God,' he gasped, 'you're fun to kiss.'

That was talk, but Nicole had a better hold on him now and she held it; she turned coquette and walked away, leaving him as suspended as in the funicular of the afternoon. She felt: There, that'll show him, how conceited; how he could do with me; oh, wasn't it wonderful! I've got him, he's mine. Now in the sequence came flight, but it was all so sweet and new that she dawdled, wanting to draw all of it in.

She shivered suddenly. Two thousand feet below she saw the necklace and bracelet of lights that were Montreux and Vevey, beyond them a dim pendant of Lausanne. From down there somewhere ascended a faint sound of dance music. Nicole was up in her head now, cool as cool, trying to collate the sentimentalities of her childhood, as deliberate as a man getting drunk after battle. But she was still afraid of Dick, who stood near her, leaning, characteristically, against the iron fence that rimmed the horseshoe; and this prompted her to say: 'I can remember how I stood waiting for you in the garden – holding all my self in my arms like a basket of flowers. It was that to me anyhow – I thought I was sweet – waiting to hand that basket to you.'

He breathed over her shoulder and turned her insistently about; she kissed him several times, her face getting big every time she came close, her hands holding him by the shoulders.

'It's raining hard.'

Suddenly there was a booming from the wine slopes across the lake; cannons were shooting at hail-bearing clouds in order to break them. The lights of the promenade went off, went on again. Then the storm came swiftly, first falling from the heavens, then doubly falling in torrents from the mountains and washing loud down the roads and stone ditches; with it came a dark, frightening sky and savage filaments of lightning and world-splitting thunder, while ragged, destroying clouds fled along past the hotel. Mountains and lake disappeared – the hotel crouched amid tumult, chaos and darkness.

By this time Dick and Nicole had reached the vestibule, where Baby Warren and the three Marmoras were anxiously awaiting them. It was exciting coming out of the wet fog – with the doors banging, to stand and laugh and quiver with emotion, wind in their ears and rain on their clothes. Now in the ballroom the orchestra was playing a Strauss waltz,[217] high and confusing.

. . . For Dr Diver to marry a mental patient? How did it happen? Where did it begin?

'Won't you come back after you've changed?' Baby Warren asked after a close scrutiny.

'I haven't got any change, except some shorts.'

As he trudged up to his hotel in a borrowed raincoat he kept laughing derisively in his throat.

'Big chance – oh, yes. My God! – they decided to buy a doctor? Well, they better stick to whoever they've got in Chicago.' Revolted by his harshness he made amends to Nicole, remembering that nothing had ever felt so young as her lips, remembering rain like tears shed for him that lay upon her softly shining porcelain cheeks . . . the silence of the storm ceasing woke him about three o'clock and he went to the window. Her beauty climbed the rolling slope, it came into the room, rustling ghost-like through the curtains . . .

. . . He climbed two thousand metres to Rochers de Naye[218] the following morning, amused by the fact that his conductor of the day before was using his day off to climb also.

Then Dick descended all the way to Montreux for a swim, got back to his hotel in time for dinner. Two notes awaited him.

I'm not ashamed about last night – it was the nicest thing that ever happened to me and even if I never saw you again, Mon Capitaine, I would be glad it happened.

That was disarming enough – the heavy shade of Dohmler retreated as Dick opened the second envelope:

DEAR DR DIVER – I phoned but you were out. I wonder if I may ask you a great big favour. Unforeseen circumstances call me back to Paris, and I find I can make better time by way of Lausanne. Can you let Nicole ride as far as Zurich with you, since you are going back Monday? and drop her at the sanatorium? Is this too much to ask?

Sincerely,

BETH EVAN WARREN

Dick was furious – Miss Warren had known he had a bicycle with him; yet she had so phrased her note that it was impossible to refuse. Throw us together! Sweet propinquity and the Warren money!

He was wrong; Baby Warren had no such intentions. She had looked Dick over with worldly eyes; she had measured him with the warped rule of an Anglophile and found him wanting – in spite of the fact that she found him toothsome. But for her he was too 'intellectual' and she pigeon-holed him with a shabby-snobby crowd she had once known in London – he put himself out too much to be really of the correct stuff. She could not see how he could be made into her idea of an aristocrat.

In addition to that he was stubborn – she had seen him leave her conversation and get down behind his eyes in that odd way that people did, half a dozen times. She had not liked Nicole's free and easy manner as a child and now she was sensibly habituated to thinking of her as a 'gone coon';[219] and anyhow Dr Diver was not the sort of medical man she could envisage in the family.

She only wanted to use him innocently as a convenience.

But her request had the effect that Dick assumed she desired. A ride in a train can be a terrible, heavy-hearted or comic thing; it can be a trial flight; it can be a prefiguration of another journey just as a given day with a friend can be long, from the taste of hurry in the morning up to the realisation of both being hungry and taking food together. Then comes the afternoon with the journey fading and dying, but quickening again at the end. Dick was sad to see Nicole's meagre joy; yet it was a relief for her, going back to the only home she knew. They made no love that day, but when he left her outside the sad door on the Zurichsee and she turned and looked at him he knew her problem was one they had together for good now.

Chapter 10

In Zurich in September Dr Diver had tea with Baby Warren.

'I think it's ill advised,' she said, 'I'm not sure I truly understand your motives.'

'Don't let's be unpleasant.'

'After all I'm Nicole's sister.'

'That doesn't give you the right to be unpleasant.' It irritated Dick that he knew so much that he could not tell her. 'Nicole's rich, but that doesn't make me an adventurer.'

'That's just it,' complained Baby stubbornly. 'Nicole's rich.'

'Just how much money has she got?' he asked.

She started; and with a silent laugh he continued, 'You see how silly this is? I'd rather talk to some man in your family – '

'Everything's been left to me,' she persisted. 'It isn't we think you're an adventurer. We don't know who you are.'

'I'm a doctor of medicine,' he said. 'My father is a clergyman, now retired. We lived in Buffalo and my past is open to investigation. I went to New Haven; afterward I was a Rhodes scholar. My great-grandfather was Governor of North Carolina and I'm a direct descendant of Mad Anthony Wayne.'[220]

'Who was Mad Anthony Wayne?' Baby asked suspiciously.

'Mad Anthony Wayne?'

'I think there's enough madness in this affair.'

He shook his head hopelessly, just as Nicole came out on the hotel terrace and looked around for them.

'He was too mad to leave as much money as Marshall Field,'[221] he said.

'That's all very well – '

Baby was right and she knew it. Face to face, her father would have it on almost any clergyman. They were an American ducal family without a title – the very name written in a hotel register, signed to an introduction, used in a difficult situation, caused a psychological metamorphosis in people, and in return this change had crystallised her own sense of position. She knew these facts from the English, who had known them for over two hundred years. But she did not know that twice Dick had come close to flinging the marriage in her face. All that saved it this time was Nicole finding their table and glowing away, white and fresh and new in the September afternoon.

How do you do, lawyer. We're going to Como tomorrow for a week and then back to Zurich. That's why I wanted you and sister to settle this, because it doesn't matter to us how much I'm allowed. We're going to live very quietly in Zurich for two years and Dick has enough to take care of us. No, Baby, I'm more practical than you think – It's only for clothes and things I'll need it . . . Why, that's more than – can the estate really afford to give me all that? I know I'll never manage to spend it. Do you have that much? Why do you have more – is it because I'm supposed to be incompetent? All right, let my share pile up then . . . No, Dick refuses to have anything whatever to do with it. I'll have to feel bloated for us both . . . Baby, you have no more idea of what Dick is like than, than – Now where do I sign? oh, I'm sorry.

. . . Isn't it funny and lovely being together, Dick? No place to go except close. Shall we just love and love? Ah, but I love the most, and I can tell when you're away from me, even a little. I think it's wonderful to be just like everybody else, to reach out and find you all warm beside me in the bed.

. . . If you will kindly call my husband at the hospital. Yes, the little book is selling everywhere – they want it published in six languages. I was to do the French translation but I'm tired these days – I'm afraid of falling, I'm so heavy and clumsy – like a broken roly-poly that can't stand up straight. The cold stethoscope against my heart and my strongest feeling '*Je m'en fiche de tout*'[222] – oh, that poor woman in the hospital with the blue baby, much better dead. Isn't it fine there are three of us now?

. . . That seems unreasonable, Dick – we have every reason for taking the bigger apartment. Why should we penalise ourselves just because there's more Warren money than Diver money? Oh, thank you, *camérière*,[223] but we've changed our minds. This English clergyman tells us that your wine here in Orvieto[224] is excellent. It doesn't travel? That must be why we have never heard of it, because we love wine.

The lakes are sunk in the brown clay and the slopes have all the creases of a belly. The photographer gave us the picture of me, my hair limp over the rail on the boat to Capri. 'Goodbye, Blue Grotto,'[225] sang the boatman, 'come again soo-oon.' And afterward tracing down the hot sinister shin of the Italian boot with the wind soughing around those eerie castles, the dead watching from up on those hills.

. . . This ship is nice, with our heels hitting the deck together. This is the blowy corner and each time we turn it I slant forward against the wind and pull my coat together without losing step with Dick. We are chanting nonsense:

                    'Oh–oh–oh–oh
                    Other flamingoes than me,
                    Oh–oh–oh–oh
                    Other flamingoes than me – '

Life is fun with Dick – the people in deck-chairs look at us, and a woman is trying to hear what we are singing. Dick is tired of singing it, so go on alone, Dick. You will walk differently alone, dear, through a thicker atmosphere, forcing your way through the shadows of chairs, through the dripping smoke of the funnels. You will feel your own reflection sliding along the eyes of those who look at you. You are no longer insulated; but I suppose you must touch life in order to spring from it.

Sitting on the stanchion of this lifeboat I look seaward and let my hair blow and shine. I am motionless against the sky and the boat is made to carry my form onward into the blue obscurity of the future, I am Pallas Athene[226] carved reverently on the front of a galley. The waters are lapping in the public toilets and the agate green foliage of spray changes and complains about the stern.

. . . We travelled a lot that year – from Woolloomooloo Bay to Biskra.[227] On the edge of the Sahara we ran into a plague of locusts and the chauffeur explained kindly that they were bumble-bees. The sky was low at night, full of the presence of a strange and watchful God. Oh, the poor little naked Ouled Naïl:[228] the night was noisy with drums from Senegal and flutes and whining camels, and the natives pattering about in shoes made of old automobile tyres.

But I was gone again by that time – trains and beaches they were all one. That was why he took me travelling, but after my second child, my little girl Topsy, was born everything got dark again.

. . . If I could get word to my husband who has seen fit to desert me here, to leave me in the hands of incompetents. You tell me my baby is black – that's farcical, that's very cheap. We went to Africa merely to see Timgad,[229] since my principal interest in life is archaeology. I am tired of knowing nothing and being reminded of it all the time.

. . . When I get well I want to be a fine person like you, Dick – I would study medicine except it's too late. We must spend my money and have a house – I'm tired of apartments and waiting for you. You're bored with Zurich and you can't find time for writing here and you say that it's a confession of weakness for a scientist not to write. And I'll look over the whole field of knowledge and pick out something and really know about it, so I'll have it to hang on to if I go to pieces again. You'll help me, Dick, so I won't feel so guilty. We'll live near a warm beach where we can be brown and young together.

. . . This is going to be Dick's work house. Oh, the idea came to us both at the same moment. We had passed Tarmes a dozen times and we rode up here and found the houses empty, except two stables. When we bought we acted through a Frenchman, but the navy sent spies up here in no time when they found that Americans had bought part of a hill village. They looked for cannons all through the building material, and finally Baby had to twitch wires for us at the Affaires Étrangères in Paris.[230]

No one comes to the Riviera in summer, so we expect to have a few guests and to work. There are some French people here – Mistinguett last week, surprised to find the hotel open, and Picasso and the man who wrote *Pas sur la Bouche*.[231]

. . . Dick, why did you register Mr and Mrs Diver instead of Dr and Mrs Diver? I just wondered – it just floated through my mind – You've taught me that work is everything and I believe you. You used to say a man knows things and when he stops knowing things he's like anybody else, and the thing is to get power before he stops knowing things. If you want to turn things topsy-turvy, all right, but must your Nicole follow you walking on her hands, darling?

. . . Tommy says I am silent. Since I was well the first time I talked a lot to Dick late at night, both of us sitting up in bed and lighting cigarettes, then diving down afterward out of the blue dawn and into the pillows, to keep the light from our eyes. Sometimes I sing, and play with the animals, and I have a few friends too – Mary, for instance. When Mary and I talk neither of us listens to the other. Talk is men. When I talk I say to myself that I am probably Dick. Already I have even been my son, remembering how wise and slow he is. Sometimes I am Dr Dohmler and one time I may even be an aspect of you, Tommy Barban. Tommy is in love with me, I think, but gently, reassuringly. Enough, though, so that he and Dick have begun to disapprove of each other. All in all, everything has never gone better. I am among friends who like me. I am here on this tranquil beach with my husband and two children. Everything is all right – if I can finish translating this damn recipe for chicken à la Maryland into French. My toes feel warm in the sand.

'Yes, I'll look. More new people – oh, that girl – yes. Who did you say she looked like . . . No, I haven't, we don't get much chance to see the new American pictures over here. Rosemary who? Well, we're getting very fashionable for July – seems very peculiar to me. Yes, she's lovely, but there can be too many people.'

Chapter 11

Dr Richard Diver and Mrs Elsie Speers sat in the Café des Alliés in August, under cool and dusty trees. The sparkle of the mica was dulled by the baked ground, and a few gusts of mistral from down the coast seeped through the Esterel[232] and rocked the fishing-boats in the harbour, pointing the masts here and there at a featureless sky.

'I had a letter this morning,' said Mrs Speers. 'What a terrible time you all must have had with those Negroes! But Rosemary said you were perfectly wonderful to her.'

'Rosemary ought to have a service stripe. It was pretty harrowing – the only person it didn't disturb was Abe North – he flew off to Havre[233] – he probably doesn't know about it yet.'

'I'm sorry Mrs Diver was upset,' she said carefully.

Rosemary had written:

Nicole seemed Out of her Mind. I didn't want to come South with them because I felt Dick had enough on his hands.

'She's all right now.' He spoke almost impatiently. 'So you're leaving tomorrow. When will you sail?'

'Right away.'

'My God, it's awful to have you go.'

'We're glad we came here. We've had a good time, thanks to you. You're the first man Rosemary ever cared for.'

Another gust of wind strained around the porphyry hills of La Napoule.[234] There was a hint in the air that the earth was hurrying on towards other weather; the lush midsummer moment outside of time was already over.

'Rosemary's had crushes, but sooner or later she always turned the man over to me – ' Mrs Speers laughed, ' – for dissection.'

'So I was spared.'

'There was nothing I could have done. She was in love with you before I ever saw you. I told her to go ahead.'

He saw that no provision had been made for him, or for Nicole, in Mrs Speers' plans – and he saw that her amorality sprang from the conditions of her own withdrawal. It was her right, the pension on which her own emotions had retired. Women necessarily capable of almost anything in their struggle for survival and can scarcely be convicted of such man-made crimes as 'cruelty'. So long as the shuffle of love and pain went on within proper walls Mrs Speers could view it with as much detachment and humour as a eunuch. She had not even allowed for the possibility of Rosemary's being damaged – or was she certain that she couldn't be?

'If what you say is true I don't think it did her any harm.' He was keeping up to the end the pretence that he could still think objectively about Rosemary. 'She's over it already. Still – so many of the important times in life begin by seeming incidental.'

'This wasn't incidental,' Mrs Speers insisted. 'You were the first man – you're an ideal to her. In every letter she says that.'

'She's so polite.'

'You and Rosemary are the politest people I've ever known, but she means this.'

'My politeness is a trick of the heart.'

This was partly true. From his father Dick had learned the somewhat conscious good manners of the young Southerner coming north after the Civil War. Often he used them and just as often he despised them because they were not a protest against how unpleasant selfishness was but against how unpleasant it looked.

'I'm in love with Rosemary,' he told her suddenly. 'It's a kind of self-indulgence saying that to you.'

It seemed very strange and official to him, as if the very tables and chairs in the Café des Alliés would remember it for ever. Already he felt her absence from these skies: on the beach he could only remember the sun-torn flesh of her shoulders; at Tarmes he crushed out her footprints as he crossed the garden; and now the orchestra launching into the 'Nice Carnival Song', an echo of last year's vanished gaieties, started the little dance that went on all about her. In a hundred hours she had come to possess all the world's dark magic; the blinding belladonna, the caffeine converting physical into nervous energy, the mandragora that imposes harmony.

With an effort he once more accepted the fiction that he shared Mrs Speers' detachment.

'You and Rosemary aren't really alike,' he said. 'The wisdom she got from you is all moulded up into her persona, into the mask she faces the world with. She doesn't think; her real depths are Irish and romantic and illogical.'

Mrs Speers knew too that Rosemary, for all her delicate surface, was a young mustang, perceptibly by Captain Dr Hoyt, USA Cross-sectioned, Rosemary would have displayed an enormous heart, liver and soul, all crammed close together under the lovely shell.

Saying goodbye, Dick was aware of Elsie Speers' full charm,

aware that she meant rather more to him than merely a last unwillingly relinquished fragment of Rosemary. He could possibly have made up Rosemary – he could never have made up her mother. If the cloak, spurs, and brilliants in which Rosemary had walked off were things with which he had endowed her, it was nice in contrast to watch her mother's grace knowing it was surely something he had not evoked. She had an air of seeming to wait, as if for a man to get through with something more important than herself, a battle or an operation, during which he must not be hurried or interfered with. When the man had finished she would be waiting, without fret or impatience, somewhere on a high stool, turning the pages of a newspaper.

'Goodbye – and I want you both to remember always how fond of you Nicole and I have grown.'

Back at the Villa Diana, he went to his workroom, and opened the shutters, closed against the midday glare. On his two long tables, in ordered confusion, lay the materials of his book. Volume I, concerned with Classification, had achieved some success in a small subsidised edition. He was negotiating for its reissue. Volume II was to be a great amplification of his first little book, *A Psychology for Psychiatrists*. Like so many men he had found that he had only one or two ideas – that his little collection of pamphlets now in its fiftieth German edition contained the germ of all he would ever think or know.

But he was currently uneasy about the whole thing. He resented the wasted years at New Haven, but mostly he felt a discrepancy between the growing luxury in which the Divers lived, and the need for display which apparently went along with it. Remembering his Rumanian friend's story, about the man who had worked for years on the brain of an armadillo, he suspected that patient Germans were sitting close to the libraries of Berlin and Vienna callously anticipating him. He had about decided to brief the work in its present condition and publish it in an undocumented volume of a hundred thousand words as an introduction to more scholarly volumes to follow.

He confirmed this decision walking around the rays of late afternoon in his workroom. With the new plan he could be through by spring. It seemed to him that when a man with his energy was pursued for a year by increasing doubts, it indicated some fault in the plan.

He laid the bars of gilded metal that he used as paperweights along the sheaves of notes. He swept up, for no servant was allowed in here, treated his washroom sketchily with Bon Ami,[235] repaired a screen, and sent off an order to a publishing house in Zurich. Then he drank an ounce of gin with twice as much water.

He saw Nicole in the garden. Presently he must encounter her and the prospect gave him a leaden feeling. Before her he must keep up a perfect front, now and tomorrow, next week and next year. All night in Paris he had held her in his arms while she slept light under the luminal;[236] in the early morning he broke in upon her confusion before it could form, with words of tenderness and protection, and she slept again with his face against the warm scent of her hair. Before she woke he had arranged everything at the phone in the next room. Rosemary was to move to another hotel. She was to be 'Daddy's Girl' and even to give up saying goodbye to them. The proprietor of the hotel, Mr McBeth, was to be the three Chinese monkeys.[237] Packing amid the piled boxes and tissue paper of many purchases, Dick and Nicole left for the Riviera at noon.

Then there was a reaction. As they settled down in the *wagon-lit* Dick saw that Nicole was waiting for it, and it came quickly and desperately, before the train was out of the *ceinture*[238] – his only instinct was to step off while the train was still going slow, rush back and see where Rosemary was, what she was doing. He opened a book and bent his pince-nez upon it, aware that Nicole was watching him from her pillow across the compartment. Unable to read, he pretended to be tired and shut his eyes, but she was still watching him, and though still she was half-asleep from the hangover of the drug, she was relieved and almost happy that he was hers again.

It was worse with his eyes shut for it gave a rhythm of finding and losing, finding and losing; but so as not to appear restless he lay like that until noon. At luncheon things were better – it was always a fine meal; a thousand lunches in inns and restaurants, *wagon-lits*, buffets, and aeroplanes were a mighty collation to have taken together. The familiar hurry of the train waiters, the little bottles of wine and mineral water, the excellent food of the Paris–Lyons–Méditerranée[239] gave them the illusion that everything was the same as before, but it was almost the first trip he had ever taken with Nicole that was a going away rather than a going towards. He drank a whole bottle of wine save for Nicole's single glass; they talked about the house and the children. But once back in the compartment a silence fell over them like the silence in the restaurant across from the Luxembourg. Receding from a grief, it seems necessary to retrace the same steps that brought us there. An unfamiliar impatience settled on Dick; suddenly Nicole said: 'It seemed too bad to leave Rosemary like that – do you suppose she'll be all right?'

'Of course. She could take care of herself anywhere – ' Lest this belittle Nicole's ability to do likewise, he added, 'After all, she's an actress, and even though her mother's in the background she *has* to look out for herself.'

'She's very attractive.'

'She's an infant.'

'She's attractive though.'

They talked aimlessly back and forth, each speaking for the other.

'She's not as intelligent as I thought,' Dick offered.

'She's quite smart.'

'Not very, though – there's a persistent aroma of the nursery.'

'She's very – very pretty,' Nicole said in a detached, emphatic way, 'and I thought she was very good in the picture.'

'She was well directed. Thinking it over, it wasn't very individual.'

'I thought it was. I can see how she'd be very attractive to men.'

His heart twisted. To what men? How many men?

– Do you mind if I pull down the curtain?

– Please do, it's too light in here.

Where now? And with whom?

'In a few years she'll look ten years older than you.'

'On the contrary. I sketched her one night on a theatre programme, I think she'll last.'

They were both restless in the night. In a day or two Dick would try to banish the ghost of Rosemary before it became walled up with them, but for the moment he had no force to do it. Sometimes it is harder to deprive oneself of a pain than of a pleasure, and the memory so possessed him that for the moment there was nothing to do but to pretend. This was more difficult because he was currently annoyed with Nicole, who, after all these years, should recognise symptoms of strain in herself and guard against them. Twice within a fortnight she had broken up: there had been the night of the dinner at Tarmes when he had found her in her bedroom dissolved in crazy laughter telling Mrs McKisco she could not go in the bathroom because the key was thrown down the well. Mrs McKisco was astonished and resentful, baffled and yet in a way comprehending. Dick had not been particularly alarmed then, for afterward Nicole was repentant. She called at Gausse's Hôtel but the McKiscos were gone.

The collapse in Paris was another matter, adding significance to the first one. It prophesied possibly a new cycle, a new *pousse*[240] of the malady. Having gone through unprofessional agonies during her long relapse following Topsy's birth, he had, perforce, hardened himself about her, making a cleavage between Nicole sick and Nicole well. This made it difficult now to distinguish between his self-protective professional detachment and some new coldness in his heart. As an indifference cherished, or left to atrophy, becomes an emptiness, to this extent he had learned to become empty of Nicole, serving her against his will with negations and emotional neglect. One writes of scars healed, a loose parallel to the pathology of the skin, but there is no such thing in the life of an individual. There are open wounds, shrunk sometimes to the size of a pin-prick, but wounds still. The marks of suffering are more comparable to the loss of a finger, or of the sight of an eye. We may not miss them, either, for one minute in a year, but if we should there is nothing to be done about it.

Chapter 12

HE FOUND NICOLE in the garden with her arms folded high on her shoulders. She looked at him with straight grey eyes, with a child's searching wonder.

'I went to Cannes,' he said. 'I ran into Mrs Speers. She's leaving tomorrow. She wanted to come up and say goodbye to you, but I slew the idea.'

'I'm sorry. I'd like to have seen her. I like her.'

'Who else do you think I saw – Bartholomew Tailor.'

'You didn't.'

'I couldn't have missed that face of his, the old experienced weasel. He was looking over the ground for Ciro's[241] Menagerie – they'll all be down next year. I suspected Mrs Abrams was a sort of outpost.'

'And Baby was outraged the first summer we came here.'

'They don't really give a damn where they are, so I don't see why they don't stay and freeze in Deauville.'

'Can't we start rumours about cholera or something?'

'I told Bartholomew that some categories died off like flies here – I told him the life of a suck was as short as the life of a machine-gunner in the war.'

'You didn't.'

'No, I didn't,' he admitted. 'He was very pleasant. It was a beautiful sight, he and I shaking hands there on the boulevard. The meeting of Sigmund Freud and Ward McAllister.'[242]

Dick didn't want to talk – he wanted to be alone so that his thoughts about work and the future would overpower his thoughts of love and today. Nicole knew about it but only darkly and tragically, hating him a little in an animal way, yet wanting to rub against his shoulder.

'The darling,' Dick said lightly.

He went into the house, forgetting something he wanted to do there, and then remembering it was the piano. He sat down whistling and played by ear:

> 'Just picture you upon my knee
> With tea for two and two for tea
> And me for you and you for me – '243

Through the melody flowed a sudden realisation that Nicole, hearing it, would guess quickly at a nostalgia for the past fortnight. He broke off with a casual chord and left the piano.

It was hard to know where to go. He glanced about the house that Nicole had made, that Nicole's grandfather had paid for. He owned only his work house and the ground on which it stood. Out of three thousand a year and what dribbled in from his publications he paid for his clothes and personal expenses, for cellar charges, and for Lanier's education, so far confined to a nurse's wage. Never had a move been contemplated without Dick's figuring his share. Living rather ascetically, travelling third-class when he was alone, with the cheapest wine, and good care of his clothes, and penalising himself for any extravagances, he maintained a qualified financial independence. After a certain point, though, it was difficult – again and again it was necessary to decide together as to the uses to which Nicole's money should be put. Naturally Nicole, wanting to own him, wanting him to stand still for ever, encouraged any slackness on his part, and in multiplying ways he was constantly inundated by a trickling of goods and money. The inception of the idea of the cliff villa which they had elaborated as a fantasy one day was a typical example of the forces divorcing them from the first simple arrangements in Zurich.

'Wouldn't it be fun if – ' it had been; and then, 'Won't it be fun when – '

It was not so much fun. His work became confused with Nicole's problems; in addition, her income had increased so fast of late that it seemed to belittle his work. Also, for the purpose of her cure, he had for many years pretended to a rigid domesticity from which he was drifting away, and this pretence became more arduous in this effortless immobility, in which he was inevitably subjected to microscopic examination. When Dick could no longer play what he wanted to play on the piano, it was an indication that life was being refined down to a point. He stayed in the big room a long time listening to the buzz of the electric clock, listening to time.

In November the waves grew black and dashed over the sea wall on to the shore road – such summer life as had survived disappeared and the beaches were melancholy and desolate under the mistral and rain. Gausse's Hôtel was closed for repairs and enlargement and the scaffolding of the summer Casino at Juan les Pins grew larger and more formidable. Going into Cannes or Nice, Dick and Nicole met new people – members of orchestras, restaurateurs, horticultural enthusiasts, shipbuilders – for Dick had bought an old dinghy – and members of the *Syndicat d'Initiative*.[244] They knew their servants well and gave thought to the children's education. In December, Nicole seemed well-knit again; when a month had passed without tension, without the tight mouth, the unmotivated smile, the unfathomable remark, they went to the Swiss Alps for the Christmas holidays.

Chapter 13

WITH HIS CAP, Dick slapped the snow from his dark blue ski-suit before going inside. The great hall, its floor pockmarked by two decades of hobnails, was cleared for the tea dance, and fourscore young Americans, domiciled in schools near Gstaad, bounced about to the frolic of 'Don't Bring Lulu',[245] or exploded violently with the first percussions of the Charleston.[246] It was a colony of the young, simple, and expensive – the *Sturmtruppen*[247] of the rich were at St Moritz. Baby Warren felt that she had made a gesture of renunciation in joining the Divers here.

Dick picked out the two sisters easily across the delicately haunted, soft-swaying room – they were poster-like, formidable in their snow costumes, Nicole's of cerulean blue, Baby's of brick red. The young Englishman was talking to them; but they were paying no attention, lulled to the staring point by the adolescent dance.

Nicole's snow-warm face lighted up further as she saw Dick. 'Where is he?'

'He missed the train – I'm meeting him later.' Dick sat down, swinging a heavy boot over his knee. 'You two look very striking together. Every once in a while I forget we're in the same party and get a big shock at seeing you.'

Baby was a tall, fine-looking woman, deeply engaged in being almost thirty. Symptomatically she had pulled two men with her from London, one scarcely down from Cambridge,[248] one old and hard with Victorian lecheries. Baby had certain spinster's characteristics – she was alien from touch, she started if she was touched suddenly, and such lingering touches as kisses and embraces slipped directly through the flesh into the forefront of her consciousness. She made few gestures with her trunk, her body proper – instead, she stamped her foot and tossed her head in almost an old-fashioned way. She relished the foretaste of death, prefigured by the catastrophes of friends – persistently she clung to the idea of Nicole's tragic destiny.

Baby's younger Englishman had been chaperoning the women down appropriate inclines and harrowing them on the bob-run. Dick, having turned an ankle in a too ambitious telemark,[249] loafed gratefully about the 'nursery slope' with the children or drank kvass[250] with a Russian doctor at the hotel.

'Please be happy, Dick,' Nicole urged him. 'Why don't you meet some of these ickle durls and dance with them in the afternoon?'

'What would I say to them?'

Her low almost harsh voice rose a few notes, simulating a plaintive coquetry: 'Say: "Ickle durl, oo is de pwettiest sing." What do you think you say?'

'I don't like ickle durls. They smell of Castile soap and peppermint. When I dance with them, I feel as if I'm pushing a baby carriage.'

It was a dangerous subject – he was careful, to the point of selfconsciousness, to stare far over the heads of young maidens.

'There's a lot of business,' said Baby. 'First place, there's news from home – the property we used to call the station property. The railroads only bought the centre of it at first. Now they've bought the rest, and it belonged to mother. It's a question of investing the money.'

Pretending to be repelled by this gross turn in the conversation, the Englishman made for a girl on the floor. Following him for an instant with the uncertain eyes of an American girl in the grip of a lifelong Anglophilia, Baby continued defiantly: 'It's a lot of money. It's three hundred thousand apiece. I keep an eye on my own investments but Nicole doesn't know anything about securities, and I don't suppose you do either.'

'I've got to meet the train,' Dick said evasively.

Outside he inhaled damp snowflakes that he could no longer see against the darkening sky. Three children sledding past shouted a warning in some strange language; he heard them yell at the next bend and a little farther on he heard sleighbells coming up the hill in the dark. The holiday station glittered with expectancy, boys and girls waiting for new boys and girls, and by the time the train arrived, Dick had caught the rhythm and pretended to Franz Gregorovious that he was clipping off a half-hour from an endless roll of pleasures. But Franz had some intensity of purpose at the moment that fought through any superimposition of mood on Dick's part. 'I may get up to Zurich for a day,' Dick had written, 'or you can manage to come to Lausanne.' Franz had managed to come all the way to Gstaad.

He was forty. Upon his healthy maturity reposed a set of pleasant official manners, but he was most at home in a somewhat stuffy safety from which he could despise the broken rich whom he re-educated. His scientific heredity might have bequeathed him a wider world but he seemed to have deliberately chosen the standpoint of a humbler class, a choice typified by his selection of a wife. At the hotel Baby Warren made a quick examination of him, and failing to find any of the hallmarks she respected, the subtler virtues or courtesies by which the privileged classes recognised one another, treated him thereafter with her second manner. Nicole was always a little afraid of him. Dick liked him, as he liked his friends, without reservations.

For the evening they were sliding down the hill into the village, on those little sleds which serve the same purpose as gondolas do in Venice. Their destination was a hotel with an old-fashioned Swiss tap-room, wooden and resounding, a room of clocks, kegs, steins, and antlers. Many parties at long tables blurred into one great party and ate fondue – a peculiarly indigestible form of Welsh rarebit, mitigated by hot spiced wine.

It was jolly in the big room; the younger Englishman remarked it and Dick conceded that there was no other word. With the pert heady wine he relaxed and pretended that the world was all put together again by the grey-haired men of the golden nineties who shouted old glees at the piano, by the young voices and the bright costumes toned into the room by the swirling smoke. For a moment he felt that they were in a ship with landfall just ahead; in the faces of all the girls was the same innocent expectation of the possibilities inherent in the situation and the night. He looked to see if that special girl was there and got an impression that she was at the table behind them – then he forgot her and invented a rigmarole and tried to make his party have a good time.

'I must talk to you,' said Franz in English. 'I have only twenty-four hours to spend here.'

'I suspected you had something on your mind.'

'I have a plan that is – so marvellous.' His hand fell upon Dick's knee. 'I have a plan that will be the making of us two.'

'Well?'

'Dick – there is a clinic we could have together – the old clinic of Braun on the Zugersee.[251] The plant is all modern except for a few points. He is sick – he wants to go up in Austria, to die probably. It is a chance that is just insuperable. You and me – what a pair! Now don't say anything yet until I finish.'

From the yellow glint in Baby's eyes, Dick saw she was listening.

'We must undertake it together. It would not bind you too tight – it would give you a base, a laboratory, a centre. You could stay in residence say no more than half the year, when the weather is fine. In winter you could go to France or America and write your texts fresh from clinical experience.' He lowered his voice. 'And for the convalescence of your family, there are the atmosphere and regularity of the clinic at hand.' Dick's expression did not encourage this note so Franz dropped it with the punctuation of his tongue leaving his lip quickly. 'We could be partners. I the executive manager, you the theoretician, the brilliant consultant and all that. I know myself – I know I have no genius and you have. But, in my way, I am thought very capable; I am utterly competent at the most modern clinical methods. Sometimes for months I have served as the practical head of the old clinic. The professor says this plan is excellent, he advises me to go ahead. He says he is going to live for ever, and work up to the last minute.'

Dick formed imaginary pictures of the prospect as a preliminary to any exercise of judgment.

'What's the financial angle?' he asked.

Franz threw up his chin, his eyebrows, the transient wrinkles of his forehead, his hands, his elbows, his shoulders; he strained up the muscles of his legs, so that the cloth of his trousers bulged, pushed up his heart into his throat and his voice into the roof of his mouth.

'There we have it! Money!' he bewailed. 'I have little money. The price in American money is two hundred thousand dollars. The innovation-ary – ' he tasted the coinage doubtfully, ' – steps, that you will agree are necessary, will cost twenty thousand dollars American. But the clinic is a gold-mine – I tell you, I have seen the books. For an investment of two hundred and twenty thousand dollars we have an assured income of – '

Baby's curiosity was such that Dick brought her into the conversation.

'In your experience, Baby,' he demanded, 'have you found that when a European wants to see an American very pressingly it is invariably something concerned with money?'

'What is it?' she said innocently.

'This young *Privatdozent*[252] thinks that he and I ought to launch into big business and try to attract nervous breakdowns from America.'

Worried, Franz stared at Baby as Dick continued: 'But who are we, Franz? You bear a big name and I've written two text books. Is that enough to attract anybody? And I haven't got that much money – I haven't got a tenth of it.' Franz smiled cynically. 'Honestly I haven't. Nicole and Baby are rich as Crœsus[253] but I haven't managed to get my hands on any of it yet.'

They were all listening now – Dick wondered if the girl at the table behind was listening too. The idea attracted him. He decided to let Baby speak for him, as one often lets women raise their voices over issues that are not in their hands. Baby became suddenly her grandfather, cool and experimental.

'I think it's a suggestion you ought to consider, Dick. I don't know what Dr Gregory was saying – but it seems to me – '

Behind him the girl had leaned forward into a smoke ring and was picking up something from the floor. Nicole's face, fitted into his own across the table – her beauty, tentatively nesting and posing, flowed into his love, ever braced to protect it.

'Consider it, Dick,' Franz urged excitedly. 'When one writes on psychiatry, one should have actual clinical contacts. Jung writes, Bleuler writes, Freud writes, Forel writes, Adler writes[254] – also they are in constant contact with mental disorder.'

'Dick has me,' laughed Nicole. 'I should think that'd be enough mental disorder for one man.'

'That's different,' said Franz cautiously.

Baby was thinking that if Nicole lived beside a clinic she would always feel quite safe about her.

'We must think it over carefully,' she said.

Though amused at her insolence, Dick did not encourage it.

'The decision concerns me, Baby,' he said gently. 'It's nice of you to want to buy me a clinic.'

Realising she had meddled, Baby withdrew hurriedly: 'Of course, it's entirely your affair.'

'A thing as important as this will take weeks to decide. I wonder how I like the picture of Nicole and me anchored to Zurich – ' He turned to Franz, anticipating: ' – I know. Zurich has a gashouse and running water and electric light – I lived there three years.'

'I will leave you to think it over,' said Franz. 'I am confident – '

One hundred pairs of five-pound boots had begun to clump towards the door, and they joined the press. Outside in the crisp moonlight, Dick saw the girl tying her sled to one of the sleighs ahead. They piled into their own sleigh and at the crisp-cracking whips the horses strained, breasting the dark air. Past them figures ran and scrambled, the younger ones shoving each other from sleds and runners, landing in the soft snow, then panting after the horses to drop exhausted on a sled or wail that they were abandoned. On either side the fields were beneficently tranquil; the space through which the cavalcade moved was high and limitless. In the country there was less noise as though they were all listening atavistically for wolves in the wide snow.

In Saanen,[255] they poured into the municipal dance, crowded with cow herders, hotel servants, shopkeepers, ski teachers, guides, tourists, peasants. To come into the warm enclosed place after the pantheistic animal feeling without, was to reassume some absurd and impressive knightly name, as thunderous as spurred boots in war, as football cleats on the cement of a locker-room floor. There was conventional yodelling, and the familiar rhythm of it separated Dick from what he had first found romantic in the scene. At first he thought it was because he had hounded the girl out of his conscious-ness; then it came to him under the form of what Baby had said: 'We must think it over carefully – ' and the unsaid lines back of that: 'We own you, and you'll admit it sooner or later. It is absurd to keep up the pretence of independence.'

It had been years since Dick had bottled up malice against a creature – since freshman year at New Haven when he had come upon a popular essay about 'mental hygiene'. Now he lost his temper at Baby and simultaneously tried to coop it up within him, resenting her cold rich insolence. It would be hundreds of years before any emergent Amazons would ever grasp the fact that a man is vulnerable only in his pride, but delicate as Humpty-Dumpty[256] once that is meddled with – though some of them paid the fact a cautious lip-service. Dr Diver's profession of sorting the broken shells of another sort of egg had given him a dread of breakage. But: 'There's too much good manners,' he said on the way back to Gstaad in the smooth sleigh.

'Well, I think that's nice,' said Baby.

'No, it isn't,' he insisted to the anonymous bundle of fur. 'Good manners are an admission that everybody is so tender that they have to be handled with gloves. Now, human respect – you don't call a man a coward or a liar lightly, but if you spend your life sparing people's feelings and feeding their vanity, you get so you can't distinguish what *should* be respected in them.'

'I think Americans take their manners rather seriously,' said the elder Englishman.

'I guess so,' said Dick. 'My father had the kind of manners he inherited from the days when you shot first and apologised afterward.

Men armed – why, you Europeans haven't carried arms in civil life since the beginning of the eighteenth century – '

'Not actually, perhaps – '

'Not *act*ually. Not really.'

'Dick, you've always had such beautiful manners,' said Baby conciliatingly.

The women were regarding him across the zoo of robes with some alarm. The younger Englishman did not understand – he was one of the kind who were always jumping around cornices and balconies, as if they thought they were in the rigging of a ship – and filled the ride to the hotel with a preposterous story about a boxing match with his best friend in which they loved and bruised each other for an hour, always with great reserve. Dick became facetious.

'So every time he hit you you considered him an even better friend?'

'I respected him more.'

'It's the premise I don't understand. You and your best friend scrap about a trivial matter – '

'If you don't understand, I can't explain it to you,' said the young Englishman coldly.

– This is what I'll get if I begin saying what I think, Dick said to himself.

He was ashamed at baiting the man, realising that the absurdity of the story rested in the immaturity of the attitude combined with the sophisticated method of its narration.

The carnival spirit was strong and they went with the crowd into the grill, where a Tunisian barman manipulated the illumination in a counterpoint, whose other melody was the moon off the ice rink staring in the big windows. In that light, Dick found the girl devitalised, and uninteresting – he turned from her to enjoy the darkness, the cigarette points going green and silver when the lights shone red, the band of white that fell across the dancers as the door to the bar was opened and closed.

'Now, tell me, Franz,' he demanded, 'do you think after sitting up all night drinking beer, you can go back and convince your patients that you have any character? Don't you think they'll see you're a gastropath?'

'I'm going to bed,' Nicole announced. Dick accompanied her to the door of the elevator.

'I'd come with you but I must show Franz that I'm not intended for a clinician.'

Nicole walked into the elevator.

'Baby has lots of common sense,' she said meditatively.

'Baby is one of – '

The door slashed shut – facing a mechanical hum, Dick finished the sentence in his mind, ' – Baby is a trivial, selfish woman.'

But two days later, sleighing to the station with Franz, Dick admitted that he thought favourably upon the matter.

'We're beginning to turn in a circle,' he admitted. 'Living on this scale, there's an unavoidable series of strains, and Nicole doesn't survive them. The pastoral quality down on the summer Riviera is all changing anyhow – next year they'll have a Season.'

They passed the crisp green rinks where Wiener waltzes[257] blared and the colours of many mountain schools flashed against the pale-blue skies.

' – I hope we'll be able to do it, Franz. There's nobody I'd rather try it with than you – '

Goodbye, Gstaad! Goodbye, fresh faces, cold sweet flowers, flakes in the darkness. Goodbye, Gstaad, goodbye!

Chapter 14

DICK AWOKE AT FIVE after a long dream of war, walked to the window and stared out at the Zugersee. His dream had begun in sombre majesty; navy-blue uniforms crossed a dark plaza behind bands playing the second movement of Prokofieff's 'Love of Three Oranges'.[258] Presently there were fire-engines, symbols of disaster, and a ghastly uprising of the mutilated in dressing station. He turned on his bedlamp light and made a thorough note of it ending with the half-ironic phrase: 'non-combatant's shell-shock'.

As he sat on the side of his bed, he felt the room, the house and the night as empty. In the next room Nicole muttered something desolate and he felt sorry for whatever loneliness she was feeling in her sleep. For him time stood still and then every few years accelerated in a rush, like the quick rewind of a film, but for Nicole the years slipped away by clock and calendar and birthday, with the added poignance of her perishable beauty.

Even this past year and a half on the Zugersee seemed wasted time for her, the seasons marked only by the workmen on the road turning pink in May, brown in July, black in September, white again in spring. She had come out of her first illness alive with new hopes, expecting so much, yet deprived of any subsistence except Dick, bringing up children she could only pretend gently to love, guided orphans. The people she liked, rebels mostly, disturbed her and were bad for her – she sought in them the vitality that had made them independent or creative or rugged, sought in vain – for their secrets were buried deep in childhood struggles they had forgotten. They were more interested in Nicole's exterior harmony and charm, the other face of her illness. She led a lonely life owning Dick, who did not want to be owned.

Many times he had tried unsuccessfully to let go his hold on her. They had many fine times together, fine talks between the loves of the white nights, but always when he turned away from her into himself he left her holding Nothing in her hands and staring at it, calling it many names, but knowing it was only the hope that he would come back soon.

He scrunched his pillow hard, lay down, and put the back of his neck against it as a Japanese does to slow the circulation, and slept again for a time. Later, while he shaved, Nicole awoke and marched around, giving abrupt, succinct orders to children and servants. Lanier came in to watch his father shave – living beside a psychiatric clinic he had developed an extraordinary confidence in and admiration for his father, together with an exaggerated indifference towards most other adults; the patients appeared to him either in their odd aspects, or else as devitalised, over-correct creatures without personality. He was a handsome, promising boy and Dick devoted much time to him, in the relationship of a sympathetic but exacting officer and a respectful enlisted man.

'Why,' Lanier asked, 'do you always leave a little lather on the top of your hair when you shave?'

Cautiously Dick parted soapy lips: 'I have never been able to find out. I've often wondered. I think it's because I get the first finger soapy when I make the line of my sideburn, but how it gets up on top of my head I don't know.'

'I'm going to watch it all tomorrow.'

'That's your only question before breakfast.'

'I don't really call it a question.'

'That's one on you.'

Half an hour later Dick started up to the administration building. He was thirty-eight – still declining a beard, he yet had a more medical aura about him than he had worn upon the Riviera. For eighteen months now he had lived at the clinic – certainly one of the best-appointed in Europe. Like Dohmler's it was of the modern type – no longer a single dark and sinister building but a small, scattered, yet deceitfully integrated village – Dick and Nicole had added much in the domain of taste, so that the plant was a thing of beauty, visited by every psychologist passing through Zurich. With the addition of a caddy house it might very well have been a country club. The Eglantine and the Beeches, houses for those sunk into eternal darkness, were screened by little copses from the main building, camouflaged strong-points. Behind was a large truck farm, worked partly by the patients. The workshops for ergo-therapy[259] were three, placed under a single roof, and there Dr Diver began his morning's inspection. The carpentry shop, full of sunlight, exuded the sweetness of sawdust, of a lost age of wood; always half a dozen men were there, hammering, planing, buzzing – silent men, who lifted solemn eyes from their work as he passed through. Himself a good carpenter, he discussed with them the efficiency of some tools for a moment in a quiet, personal, interested voice. Adjoining was the bookbindery, adapted to the most mobile of patients, who were not always, however, those who had the greatest chance for recovery. The last chamber was devoted to bead-work, weaving, and work in brass. The faces of the patients here wore the expression of one who has just sighed profoundly, dismissing something insoluble – but their sighs only marked the beginning of another ceaseless round of ratiocination, not in a line as with normal people but in the same circle. Round, round, and round. Around for ever. But the bright colours of the stuffs they worked with gave strangers a momentary illusion that all was well, as in a kindergarten. These patients brightened as Dr Diver came in. Most of them liked him better than they liked Dr Gregorovious. Those who had once lived in the great world invariably liked him better. There were a few who thought he neglected them, or that he was not simple, or that he posed. Their responses were not dissimilar to those that Dick evoked in non-professional life, but here they were warped and distorted.

One Englishwoman spoke to him always about a subject which she considered her own.

'Have we got music tonight?'

'I don't know,' he answered. 'I haven't seen Dr Lladislau. How did you enjoy the music that Mrs Sachs and Mr Longstreet gave us last night?'

'It was so-so.'

'I thought it was fine – especially the Chopin.'[260]

'I thought it was so-so.'

'When are you going to play for us yourself?'

She shrugged her shoulders, as pleased at this question as she had been for several years.

'Sometime. But I only play so-so.'

They knew that she did not play at all – she had had two sisters who were brilliant musicians, but she had never been able to learn the notes when they had been young together.

From the workshop Dick went to visit the Eglantine and the Beeches. Exteriorly these houses were as cheerful as the others; Nicole had designed the decoration and the furniture on a necessary base of concealed grilles and bars and immovable furniture. She had worked with so much imagination – the inventive quality, which she lacked, being supplied by the problem itself – that no instructed visitor would have dreamed that the light, graceful filigree work at a window was a strong unyielding end of a tether, that the pieces reflecting modern tubular tendencies were stauncher than the massive creations of the Edwardians – even the flowers lay in iron fingers and every casual ornament and fixture was as necessary as a girder in a skyscraper. Her tireless eyes had made each room yield up its greatest usefulness. Complimented, she referred to herself brusquely as a master plumber.

For those whose compasses were not depolarised there seemed many odd things in these houses. Dr Diver was often amused in the Eglantine, the men's building – here there was a strange little exhibitionist who thought that if he could walk unclothed and unmolested from the Étoile to the Place de la Concorde[261] he would solve many things – and, perhaps, Dick thought, he was quite right.

His most interesting case was in the main building. The patient was a woman of thirty who had been in the clinic six months; she was an American painter who had lived long in Paris. They had no very satisfactory history of her. A cousin had happened upon her all mad and gone and after an unsatisfactory interlude at one of the whoopee cures that fringed the city, dedicated largely to tourist victims of drug and drink, he had managed to get her to Switzerland. On her admittance she had been exceptionally pretty – now she was a living agonising sore. All blood tests had failed to give a positive reaction and the trouble was unsatisfactorily catalogued as nervous eczema. For two months she had lain under it, as if imprisoned in the Iron Maiden.[262] She was coherent, even brilliant, within the limits of her special hallucinations.

She was particularly his patient. During spells of over-excitement he was the only doctor who could 'do anything with her'. Several weeks ago, on one of many nights that she had passed in sleepless torture, Franz had succeeded in hypnotising her into a few hours of needed rest, but he had never again succeeded. Hypnosis was a tool that Dick distrusted and seldom used, for he knew that he could not always summon up the mood in himself – he had once tried it on Nicole and she had scornfully laughed at him.

The woman in room twenty could not see him when he came in – the area about her eyes was too tightly swollen. She spoke in a strong, rich, deep, thrilling voice.

'How long will this last? Is it going to be for ever?'

'It's not going to be very long now. Dr Lladislau tells me there are whole areas cleared up.'

'If I knew what I had done to deserve this I could accept it with equanimity.'

'It isn't wise to be mystical about it – we recognise it as a nervous phenomenon. It's related to the blush – when you were a girl, did you blush easily?'

She lay with her face turned to the ceiling.

'I have found nothing to blush for since I cut my wisdom teeth.'

'Haven't you committed your share of petty sins and mistakes?'

'I have nothing to reproach myself with.'

'You're very fortunate.'

The woman thought a moment; her voice came up through her bandaged face afflicted with subterranean melodies: 'I'm sharing the fate of the women of my time who challenged men to battle.'

'To your vast surprise it was just like all battles,' he answered adopting her formal diction.

'Just like all battles.' She thought this over. 'You pick a set-up, or else win a Pyrrhic victory,[263] or you're wrecked and ruined – you're a ghostly echo from a broken wall.'

'You are neither wrecked nor ruined,' he told her. 'Are you quite sure you've been in a real battle?'

'Look at me!' she cried furiously.

'You've suffered, but many women suffered before they mistook themselves for men.' It was becoming an argument and he retreated. 'In any case you mustn't confuse single failure with a final defeat.'

She sneered. 'Beautiful words,' and the phrase transpiring up through the crust of pain humbled him.

'We would like to go into the true reasons that brought you here – ' he began but she interrupted.

'I am here as a symbol of something. I thought perhaps you would know what it was.'

'You are sick,' he said mechanically.

'Then what was it I had almost found?'

'A greater sickness.'

'That's all?'

'That's all.' With disgust he heard himself lying, but here and now the vastness of the subject could only be compressed into a lie. 'Outside of that there's only confusion and chaos. I won't lecture to you – we have too acute a realisation of your physical suffering. But it's only by meeting the problems of every day, no matter how trifling and boring they seem, that you can make things drop back into place again. After that – perhaps you'll be able again to examine – '

He had slowed up to avoid the inevitable end of his thought: ' – the frontiers of consciousness.' The frontiers that artists must explore were not for her, ever. She was fine-spun, inbred – eventually she might find rest in some quiet mysticism. Exploration was for those with a measure of peasant blood, those with big thighs and thick ankles who could take punishment as they took bread and salt, on every inch of flesh and spirit.

– Not for you, he almost said. It's too tough a game for you.

Yet in the awful majesty of her pain he went out to her unreservedly, almost sexually. He wanted to gather her up in his arms, as he so often had Nicole, and cherish even her mistakes, so deeply were they part of her. The orange light through the drawn blind, the sarcophagus of her figure on the bed, the spot of face, the voice searching the vacuity of her illness and finding only remote abstractions.

As he arose the tears fled lava-like into her bandages.

'That is for something,' she whispered. 'Something must come out of it.'

He stooped and kissed her forehead.

'We must all try to be good,' he said.

Leaving her room he sent the nurse in to her. There were other patients to see: an American girl of fifteen who had been brought up on the basis that childhood was intended to be all fun – his visit was provoked by the fact that she had just hacked off all her hair with nail scissors. There was nothing much to be done for her – a family history of neurosis and nothing stable in her past to build on. The father, normal and conscientious himself, had tried to protect a nervous brood from life's troubles and had succeeded merely in preventing them from developing powers of adjustment to life's inevitable surprises. There was little that Dick could say: 'Helen, when you're in doubt you must ask a nurse, you must learn to take advice. Promise me you will.'

What was a promise with the head sick? He looked in upon a frail exile from the Caucasus buckled securely in a sort of hammock which in turn was submerged in a warm medical bath, and upon the three daughters of a Portuguese general who slid almost imperceptibly towards paresis.[264] He went into the room next to them and told a collapsed psychiatrist that he was better, always better, and the man tried to read his face for conviction, since he hung on the real world only through such reassurance as he could find in the resonance, or lack of it, in Dr Diver's voice. After that Dick discharged a shiftless orderly and by then it was the lunch hour.

Chapter 15

MEALS WITH THE PATIENTS were a chore he approached with apathy. The gathering, which of course did not include residents at the Eglantine or the Beeches, was conventional enough at first sight, but over it brooded always a heavy melancholy. Such doctors as were present kept up a conversation, but most of the patients, as if exhausted by their morning's endeavour, or depressed by the company, spoke little, and ate looking into their plates.

Luncheon over, Dick returned to his villa. Nicole was in the salon wearing a strange expression.

'Read that,' she said.

He opened the letter. It was from a woman recently discharged, though with scepticism on the part of the faculty. It accused him in no uncertain terms of having seduced her daughter, who had been at her mother's side during the crucial stage of the illness. It presumed that Mrs Diver would be glad to have this information and learn what her husband was 'really like'.

Dick read the letter again. Couched in clear and concise English he yet recognised it as the letter of a maniac. Upon a single occasion he had let the girl, a flirtatious little brunette, ride into Zurich with him, upon her request, and in the evening had brought her back to the clinic. In an idle, almost indulgent way, he kissed her. Later, she tried to carry the affair further, but he was not interested and subsequently, probably consequently, the girl had come to dislike him, and taken her mother away.

'This letter is deranged,' he said. 'I had no relations of any kind with that girl. I didn't even like her.'

'Yes, I've tried thinking that,' said Nicole.

'Surely you don't believe it?'

'I've been sitting here.'

He sank his voice to a reproachful note and sat beside her.

'This is absurd. This is a letter from a mental patient.'

'I was a mental patient.'

He stood up and spoke more authoritatively.

'Suppose we don't have any nonsense, Nicole. Go and round up the children and we'll start.'

In the car, with Dick driving, they followed the little promontories of the lake, catching the burn of light and water in the windshield, tunnelling through cascades of evergreen. It was Dick's car, a Renault so dwarfish that they all stuck out of it except the children, between whom Mademoiselle towered mast-like in the rear seat. They knew every kilometre of the road – where they would smell the pine needles and the black stove smoke. A high sun with a face traced on it beat fierce on the straw hats of the children.

Nicole was silent; Dick was uneasy at her straight hard gaze. Often he felt lonely with her, and frequently she tired him with the short floods of personal revelations that she reserved exclusively for him. 'I'm like this – I'm more like that,' but this afternoon he would have been glad had she rattled on in staccato for a while and given him glimpses of her thoughts. The situation was always most threatening when she backed up into herself and closed the doors behind her.

At Zug[265] Mademoiselle got out and left them. The Divers approached the Agiri Fair[266] through a menagerie of mammoth steamrollers that made way for them. Dick parked the car, and as Nicole looked at him without moving, he said: 'Come on, darl.' Her lips drew apart into a sudden awful smile, and his belly quailed, but as if he hadn't seen it he repeated: 'Come on. So the children can get out.'

'Oh, I'll come all right,' she answered, tearing the words from some story spinning itself out inside her, too fast for him to grasp. 'Don't worry about that. I'll come – '

'Then come.'

She turned from him as he walked beside her but the smile still flickered across her face, derisive and remote. Only when Lanier spoke to her several times did she manage to fix her attention upon an object, a Punch-and-Judy show, and to orient herself by anchoring to it.

Dick tried to think what to do. The dualism in his views of her – that of the husband, that of the psychiatrist – was increasingly paralysing his faculties. In these six years she had several times carried him over the line with her, disarming him by exciting emotional pity or by a flow of wit, fantastic and disassociated, so that only after the episode did he realise with the consciousness of his own relaxation from tension, that she had succeeded in getting a point against his better judgment.

A discussion with Topsy about the guignol – as to whether the Punch was the same Punch they had seen last year in Cannes – having

been settled, the family walked along again between the booths
under the open sky. The women's bonnets, perching over velvet
vests, the bright, spreading skirts of many cantons, seemed demure
against the blue and orange paint of the wagons and displays. There
was the sound of a whining, tinkling hootchy-kootchy show.[267]

Nicole began to run very suddenly, so suddenly that for a moment
Dick did not miss her. Far ahead he saw her yellow dress twisting
through the crowd, an ochre stitch along the edge of reality and
unreality, and started after her. Secretly she ran and secretly he
followed. As the hot afternoon went shrill and terrible with her flight
he had forgotten the children; then he wheeled and ran back to them,
drawing them this way and that by their arms, his eyes jumping from
booth to booth.

'Madame,' he cried to a young woman behind a white lottery
wheel, 'est-ce que je peux laisser ces petits avec vous deux minutes?
C'est très urgent – je vous donnerai dix francs.'

'Mais oui.'

He headed the children into the booth. 'Alors – restez avec cette
gentille dame.'

'Oui, Dick.'[268]

He darted off again but he had lost her; he circled the merry-go-
round, keeping up with it till he realised he was running beside it,
staring always at the same horse. He elbowed through the crowd in
the *buvette*;[269] then remembering a predilection of Nicole's he
snatched up an edge of a fortune-teller's tent and peered within. A
droning voice greeted him: 'La septième fille d'une septième fille née
sur les rives de Nil – entrez, monsieur – '[270]

Dropping the flap he ran along towards where the *Plaisance*
terminated at the lake and a small ferris wheel revolved slowly against
the sky. There he found her.

She was alone in what was momentarily the top boat of the wheel,
and as it descended he saw that she was laughing hilariously; he slunk
back in the crowd, a crowd which, at the wheel's next revolution,
spotted the intensity of Nicole's hysteria.

'Regardez-moi ça!'

'Regarde donc cette Anglaise!'[271]

Down she dropped again – this time the wheel and its music were
slowing and a dozen people were around her car, all of them impelled
by the quality of her laughter to smile in sympathetic idiocy. But
when Nicole saw Dick her laughter died – she made a gesture of
slipping by and away from him but he caught her arm and held it as
they walked away.

'Why did you lose control of yourself like that?'

'You know very well why.'

'No, I don't.'

'That's just preposterous – let me loose – that's an insult to my intelligence. Don't you think I saw that girl look at you – that little dark girl. Oh, this is farcical – a child, not more than fifteen. Don't you think I saw?'

'Stop here a minute and quiet down.'

They sat at a table, her eyes in a profundity of suspicion, her hand moving across her line of light as if it were obstructed. 'I want a drink – I want a brandy.'

'You can't have brandy – you can have a bock[272] if you want it.'

'Why can't I have a brandy?'

'We won't go into that. Listen to me – this business about a girl is a delusion, do you understand that word?'

'It's always a delusion when I see what you don't want me to see.'

He had a sense of guilt as in one of those nightmares where we are accused of a crime which we recognise as something undeniably experienced, but which upon waking we realise we have not committed. His eyes wavered from hers.

'I left the children with a gypsy woman in a booth. We ought to get them.'

'Who do you think you are?' she demanded. 'Svengali?'[273]

Fifteen minutes ago they had been a family. Now as she was crushed into a corner by his unwilling shoulder, he saw them all, child and man, as a perilous accident.

'We're going home.'

'Home!' she roared in a voice so abandoned that its louder tones wavered and cracked. 'And sit and think that we're all rotting and the children's ashes are rotting in every box I open? That filth!'

Almost with relief he saw that her words sterilised her, and Nicole, sensitised down to the corium[274] of the skin, saw the withdrawal in his face. Her own face softened and she begged, 'Help me, help me, Dick!'

A wave of agony went over him. It was awful that such a fine tower should not be erected, only suspended, suspended from him. Up to a point that was right; men were for that, beam and idea, girder and logarithm; but somehow Dick and Nicole had become one and equal, not opposite and complementary; she was Dick too, the drought in the marrow of his bones. He could not watch her disintegrations without participating in them. His intuition rilled out of him as tenderness and compassion – he could only take the characteristically modern course, to interpose – he would get a nurse from Zurich, to take her over tonight.

'You *can* help me.'

Her sweet bullying pulled him forward off his feet. 'You've helped me before – you can help me now.'

'I can only help you the same old way.'

'Someone can help me.'

'Maybe so. You can help yourself most. Let's find the children.'

There were numerous lottery booths with white wheels – Dick was startled when he enquired at the first and encountered blank disavowals. Evil-eyed, Nicole stood apart, denying the children, resenting them as part of a downright world she sought to make amorphous. Presently Dick found them, surrounded by women who were examining them with delight like fine goods, and by peasant children staring.

'Merci, monsieur, ah monsieur est trop généreux. C'était un plaisir, m'sieur, madame. Au revoir, mes petits.'[275]

They started back with a hot sorrow streaming down upon them; the car was weighted with their mutual apprehension and anguish, and the children's mouths were grave with disappointment. Grief presented itself in its terrible, dark unfamiliar colour. Somewhere around Zug, Nicole, with a convulsive effort, reiterated a remark she had made before about a misty yellow house set back from the road that looked like a painting not yet dry, but it was just an attempt to catch at a rope that was paying out too swiftly. Dick tried to rest – the struggle would come presently at home and he might have to sit a long time, restating the universe for her. A '*schizophrene*'[276] is well named as a split personality – Nicole was alternately a person to whom nothing need be explained and one to whom nothing *could* be explained. It was necessary to treat her with active and affirmative insistence, keeping the road to reality always open, making the road to escape harder going. But the brilliance, the versatility of madness is akin to the resourcefulness of water seeping through, over and around a dyke. It requires the united front of many people to work against it. He felt it necessary that this time Nicole cure herself; he wanted to wait until she remembered the other times, and revolted from them. In a tired way, he planned that they would again resume the regime relaxed a year before.

He had turned up a hill that made a short cut to the clinic, and now as he stepped on the accelerator for a short straightaway run parallel to the hillside the car swerved violently left, swerved right, tipped on two wheels and, as Dick, with Nicole's voice screaming in his ear, crushed down the mad hand clutching the steering wheel, righted itself, swerved once more and shot off the road; it tore through low underbrush, tipped again and settled slowly at an angle of ninety degrees against a tree.

The children were screaming and Nicole was screaming and cursing and trying to tear at Dick's face. Thinking first of the list of the car and unable to estimate it, Dick bent away Nicole's arm, climbed over the top side and lifted out the children; then he saw the car was in a stable position. Before doing anything else he stood there shaking and panting.

'You – ' he cried.

She was laughing hilariously, unashamed, unafraid, unconcerned. No one coming on the scene would have imagined that she had caused it; she laughed as after some mild escape of childhood.

'You were scared, weren't you?' she accused him. 'You wanted to live!'

She spoke with such force that in his shocked state Dick wondered if he had been frightened for himself – but the strained faces of the children, looking from parent to parent, made him want to grind her grinning mask into jelly.

Directly above them, half a kilometre by the winding road but only a hundred yards climbing, was an inn; one of its wings showed through the wooded hill.

'Take Topsy's hand,' he said to Lanier, 'like that, tight, and climb up that hill – see the little path? When you get to the inn tell them "*La voiture Divare est cassée*." [277] Someone must come right down.'

Lanier, not sure what had happened, but suspecting the dark and unprecedented, asked: 'What will you do, Dick?'

'We'll stay here with the car.'

Neither of them looked at their mother as they started off. 'Be careful crossing the road up there! Look both ways!' Dick shouted after them.

He and Nicole looked at each other directly, their eyes like blazing windows across a court of the same house. Then she took out a compact, looked in its mirror, and smoothed back the temple hair. Dick watched the children climbing for a moment until they disappeared among the pines halfway up; then he walked around the car to see the damage and plan how to get it back on the road. In the dirt he could trace the rocking course they had pursued for over a hundred feet; he was filled with a violent disgust that was not like anger.

In a few minutes the proprietor of the inn came running down.

'My God!' he exclaimed. 'How did it happen, were you going fast? What luck! Except for that tree you'd have rolled downhill!'

Taking advantage of Émile's reality, the wide black apron, the sweat upon the rolls of his face, Dick signalled to Nicole in a matter-of-fact way to let him help her from the car; whereupon she jumped over the lower side, lost her balance on the slope, fell to her knees and got up again. As she watched the men trying to move the car her expression became defiant. Welcoming even that mood Dick said: 'Go and wait with the children, Nicole.'

Only after she had gone did he remember that she had wanted cognac, and that there was cognac available up there – he told Émile never mind about the car; they would wait for the chauffeur and the big car to pull it up on the road. Together they hurried up to the inn.

Chapter 16

'I WANT TO GO AWAY,' he told Franz. 'For a month or so, as long as I can.'

'Why not, Dick? That was our original arrangement – it was you who insisted on staying. If you and Nicole – '

'I don't want to go away with Nicole. I want to go away alone. This last thing knocked me sideways – if I get two hours' sleep in twenty-four, it's one of Zwingli's miracles.'

'You wish a real leave of abstinence.'

'The word is "absence". Look here: if I go to Berlin to the Psychiatric Congress could you manage to keep the peace? For three months she's been all right and she likes her nurse. My God, you're the only human being in this world I can ask this of.'

Franz grunted, considering whether or not he could be trusted to think always of his partner's interest.

In Zurich the next week Dick drove to the airport and took the big plane for Munich. Soaring and roaring into the blue he felt numb, realising how tired he was. A vast persuasive quiet stole over him, and he abandoned sickness to the sick, sound to the motors, direction to the pilot. He had no intention of attending so much as a single session of the congress – he could imagine it well enough, new pamphlets by Bleuler and the elder Forel[278] that he could much better digest at home, the paper by the American who cured dementia præcox[279] by pulling out his patients' teeth or cauterising their tonsils, the half-derisive respect with which this idea would be greeted, for no more reason than that America was such a rich and powerful country. The other delegates from America – red-headed Schwartz with his saint's face and his infinite patience in straddling two worlds, as well as dozens of commercial alienists with hangdog faces, who would be present partly to increase their standing, and hence their reach for the big plums of the criminal practice, partly to master novel sophistries that they could weave into their stock-in-trade, to the infinite confusion of all values. There would be cynical Latins, and some man of Freud's from Vienna. Articulate among them would be the great Jung, bland, super-vigorous, on his rounds between the forests of anthropology and the neuroses of schoolboys. At first there would be an American cast to the congress, almost Rotarian in its forms and ceremonies, then the closer-knit European vitality would fight through, and finally the Americans would play their trump card, the announcement of colossal gifts and endowments, of great new plants and training schools, and in the presence of the figures the Europeans would blanch and walk timidly. But he would not be there to see.

They skirted the Vorarlberg Alps,[280] and Dick felt a pastoral delight in watching the villages. There were always four or five in sight, each one gathered around a church. It was simple looking at the earth from far off, simple as playing grim games with dolls and soldiers. This was the way statesmen and commanders and all retired people looked at things. Anyhow, it was a good draught of relief.

An Englishman spoke to him from across the aisle but he found something antipathetic in the English lately. England was like a rich man after a disastrous orgy who makes up to the household by chatting with them individually, when it is obvious to them that he is only trying to get back his self-respect in order to usurp his former power.

Dick had with him what magazines were available on the station quays: *The Century*, *The Motion Picture*, *L'Illustration*, and the *Fliegende Blätter*,[281] but it was more fun to descend in his imagination into the villages and shake hands with the rural characters. He sat in the churches as he sat in his father's church in Buffalo, amid the starchy must of Sunday clothes. He listened to the wisdom of the Near East, was Crucified, Died, and was Buried in the cheerful church, and once more worried between five or ten cents for the collection plate, because of the girl who sat in the pew behind.

The Englishman suddenly borrowed his magazines with a little small change of conversation, and Dick, glad to see them go, thought of the voyage ahead of him. Wolf-like under his sheep's clothing of long-staple Australian wool, he considered the world of pleasure –

the incorruptible Mediterranean with sweet old dirt caked in the olive trees, the peasant girl near Savona[282] with a face as green and rose as the colour of an illuminated missal. He would take her in his hands and snatch her across the border . . .

. . . But there he deserted her – he must press on towards the Isles of Greece, the cloudy waters of unfamiliar ports, the lost girl on shore, the moon of popular songs. A part of Dick's mind was made up of the tawdry souvenirs of his boyhood. Yet in that somewhat littered Five-and-Ten, he had managed to keep alive the low painful fire of intelligence.

Chapter 17

TOMMY BARBAN WAS A RULER, Tommy was a hero – Dick happened upon him in the Marienplatz[283] in Munich, in one of those cafés where small gamblers diced on 'tapestry' mats. The air was full of politics, and the slap of cards.

Tommy was at a table laughing his martial laugh: 'Um-buh-ha-ha! Um-buh-ha-ha!' As a rule, he drank little; courage was his game and his companions were always a little afraid of him. Recently an eighth of the area of his skull had been removed by a Warsaw surgeon and was knitting under his hair, and the weakest person in the café could have killed him with a flip of a knotted napkin.

' – This is Prince Chillicheff – ' a battered, powder-grey Russian of fifty ' – and Mr McKibben – and Mr Hannan – ' the latter was a lively ball of black eyes and hair, a clown; and he said immediately to Dick: 'The first thing before we shake hands – what do you mean by fooling around with my aunt?'

'Why, I – '

'You heard me. What are you doing here in Munich anyhow?'

'Um-bah-ha-ha!' laughed Tommy.

'Haven't you got aunts of your own? Why don't you fool with them?'

Dick laughed, whereupon the man shifted his attack: 'Now let's not have any more talk about aunts. How do I know you didn't make up the whole thing? Here you are a complete stranger with an acquaintance of less than half an hour, and you come up to me with a cock-and-bull story about your aunts. How do I know what you have concealed about you?'

Tommy laughed again, then he said good-naturedly, but firmly, 'That's enough, Carly. Sit down, Dick – how're you? How's Nicole?'

He did not like any man very much nor feel their presence with much intensity – he was all relaxed for combat; as a fine athlete playing secondary defence in any sport is really resting much of the time, while a lesser man only pretends to rest and is at a continual and self-destroying nervous tension.

Hannan, not entirely suppressed, moved to an adjoining piano, and with recurring resentment on his face whenever he looked at Dick, played chords, from time to time muttering, 'Your aunts,' and, in a dying cadence, 'I didn't say aunts anyhow. I said pants.'

'Well, how're you?' repeated Tommy. 'You don't look so – ' he fought for a word, ' – so jaunty as you used to, so spruce, you know what I mean.'

The remark sounded too much like one of those irritating accusations of waning vitality and Dick was about to retort by commenting on the extraordinary suits worn by Tommy and Prince Chillicheff, suits of a cut and pattern fantastic enough to have sauntered down Beale Street[284] on a Sunday – when an explanation was forthcoming.

'I see you are regarding our clothes,' said the Prince. 'We have just come out of Russia.'

'These were made in Poland by the court tailor,' said Tommy. 'That's a fact – Pilsudski's own tailor.'[285]

'You've been touring?' Dick asked.

They laughed, the Prince inordinately meanwhile clapping Tommy on the back.

'Yes, we have been touring. That's it, touring. We have made the Grand Tour of all the Russias. In state.'

Dick waited for an explanation. It came from Mr McKibben in two words.

'They escaped.'

'Have you been prisoners in Russia?'

'It was I,' explained Prince Chillicheff, his dead yellow eyes staring at Dick. 'Not a prisoner but in hiding.'

'Did you have much trouble getting out?'

'Some trouble. We left three Red Guards[286] dead at the border. Tommy left two – ' He held up two fingers like a Frenchman – 'I left one.'

'That's the part I don't understand,' said Mr McKibben. 'Why they should have objected to your leaving.'

Hannan turned from the piano and said, winking at the others: 'Mac thinks a Marxian is somebody who went to St Mark's school.'[287]

It was an escape story in the best tradition – an aristocrat hiding nine years with a former servant and working in a government bakery; the eighteen-year-old daughter in Paris who knew Tommy Barban . . . During the narrative Dick decided that this parched papier-mâché relic of the past was scarcely worth the lives of three young men. The question arose as to whether Tommy and Chillicheff had been frightened.

'When I was cold,' Tommy said. 'I always get scared when I'm cold. During the war I was always frightened when I was cold.'

McKibben stood up.

'I must leave. Tomorrow morning I'm going to Innsbruck by car with my wife and children – and the governess.'

'I'm going there tomorrow, too,' said Dick.

'Oh, are you?' exclaimed McKibben. 'Why not come with us? It's a big Packard[288] and there's only my wife and my children and myself – and the governess – '

'I can't possibly – '

'Of course she's not really a governess,' McKibben concluded, looking rather pathetically at Dick. 'As a matter of fact my wife knows your sister-in-law, Baby Warren.'

But Dick was not to be drawn in a blind contract.

'I've promised to travel with two men.'

'Oh,' McKibben's face fell. 'Well, I'll say goodbye.' He unscrewed two blooded wire-hairs from a nearby table and departed; Dick pictured the jammed Packard pounding towards Innsbruck with the McKibbens and their children and their baggage and yapping dogs – and the governess.

'The paper says they know the man who killed him,' said Tommy. 'But his cousins did not want it in the paper because it happened in a speakeasy. What do you think of that?'

'It's what's known as family pride.'

Hannan played a loud chord on the piano to attract attention to himself.

'I don't believe his first stuff holds up,' he said. 'Even barring the Europeans there are a dozen Americans can do what North did.'

It was the first indication Dick had had that they were talking about Abe North.

'The only difference is that Abe did it first,' said Tommy.

'I don't agree,' persisted Hannan. 'He got the reputation for being a good musician because he drank so much that his friends had to explain him away somehow – '

'What's this about Abe North? What about him? Is he in a jam?'

'Didn't you read the *Herald* this morning?'

'No.'

'He's dead. He was beaten to death in a speakeasy in New York. He just managed to crawl home to the Racquet Club[289] to die – '

'*Abe North?*'

'Yes, sure, they – '

'*Abe North?*' Dick stood up. 'Are you sure he's dead?'

Hannan turned around to McKibben: 'It wasn't the Racquet Club he crawled to – it was the Harvard Club.[290] I'm sure he didn't belong to the Racquet.'

'The paper said so,' McKibben insisted.

'It must have been a mistake. I'm quite sure.'

'*Beaten to death in a speakeasy.*'

'But I happen to know most of the members of the Racquet Club,' said Hannan. 'It *must* have been the Harvard Club.'

Dick got up, Tommy too. Prince Chillicheff started out of a wan study of nothing, perhaps of his chances of ever getting out of Russia, a study that had occupied him so long that it was doubtful if he could give it up immediately, and joined them in leaving.

'*Abe North beaten to death.*'

On the way to the hotel, a journey of which Dick was scarcely aware, Tommy said: 'We're waiting for a tailor to finish some suits so we can get to Paris. I'm going into stockbroking and they wouldn't take me if I showed up like this. Everybody in your country is making millions. Are you really leaving tomorrow? We can't even have dinner with you. It seems the Prince had an old girl in Munich. He called her up but she'd been dead five years and we're having dinner with the two daughters.'

The Prince nodded.

'Perhaps I could have arranged for Dr Diver.'

'No, no,' said Dick hastily.

He slept deep and awoke to a slow mournful march passing his window. It was a long column of men in uniform, wearing the familiar helmets of 1914, thick men in frock coats and silk hats, burghers, aristocrats, plain men. It was a society of veterans going to lay wreaths on the tombs of the dead. The column marched slowly with a sort of swagger for a lost magnificence, a past effort, a forgotten sorrow. The faces were only formally sad but Dick's lungs burst for a moment with regret for Abe's death, and his own youth of ten years ago.

Chapter 18

HE REACHED INNSBRUCK AT DUSK, sent his bags up to a hotel and walked into town. In the sunset the Emperor Maximilian[291] knelt in prayer above his bronze mourners; a quartet of Jesuit novices paced and read in the university garden. The marble souvenirs of old sieges, marriages, anniversaries, faded quickly when the sun was down, and he had *Erbsen-suppe* with *Würstchen* cut up in it, drank four *seidels* of Pilsner and refused a formidable dessert known as '*Kaiserschmarren*'.[292]

Despite the overhanging mountains Switzerland was far away, Nicole was far away. Walking in the garden later when it was dark he thought about her with detachment, loving her for her best self. He remembered once when the grass was damp and she came to him on hurried feet, her thin slippers drenched with dew. She stood upon his shoes nestling close and held up her face, showing it as a book open at a page.

'Think how you love me,' she whispered. 'I don't ask you to love me always like this, but I ask you to remember. Somewhere inside me there'll always be the person I am tonight.'

But Dick had come away for his soul's sake, and he began thinking about that. He had lost himself – he could not tell the hour when, or the day or the week, the month or the year. Once he had cut through things, solving the most complicated equations as the simplest problems of his simplest patients. Between the time he found Nicole flowering under a stone on the Zürichsee and the moment of his meeting with Rosemary the spear had been blunted.

Watching his father's struggles in poor parishes had wedded a desire for money to an essentially unacquisitive nature. It was not a healthy necessity for security – he had never felt more sure of himself, more thoroughly his own man, than at the time of his marriage to Nicole. Yet he had been swallowed up like a gigolo, and somehow permitted his arsenal to be locked up in the Warren safety-deposit vaults.

'There should have been a settlement in the Continental style; but it isn't over yet. I've wasted eight years teaching the rich the ABC's of human decency, but I'm not done. I've got too many unplayed trumps in my hand.'

He loitered among the fallow rose bushes and the beds of damp sweet indistinguishable fern. It was warm for October but cool enough to wear a heavy tweed coat buttoned by a little elastic tape at the neck. A figure detached itself from the black shape of a tree and he knew it was the woman whom he had passed in the lobby coming out. He was in love with every pretty woman he saw now, their forms at a distance, their shadows on a wall.

Her back was towards him as she faced the lights of the town. He scratched a match that she must have heard, but she remained motionless.

– Was it an invitation? or an indication of obliviousness? He had long been outside of the world of simple desires and their fulfilments, and he was inept and uncertain. For all he knew there might be some code among the wanderers of obscure spas by which they found each other quickly.

– Perhaps the next gesture was his. Strange children should smile at each other and say, 'Let's play.'

He moved closer, the shadow moved sideways. Possibly he would be snubbed like the scapegrace drummers[293] he had heard of in youth. His heart beat loud in contact with the unprobed, undissected, unanalysed, unacccounted for. Suddenly he turned away, and, as he did, the girl, too, broke the black frieze she made with the foliage, rounded a bench at a moderate but determined pace and took the path back to the hotel.

With a guide and two other men, Dick started up the Birkkar-spitze[294] next morning. It was a fine feeling once they were above the cowbells of the highest pastures – Dick looked forward to the night in the shack, enjoying his own fatigue, enjoying the captaincy of the guide, feeling a delight in his own anonymity. But at midday the weather changed to black sleet and hail and mountain thunder. Dick and one of the other climbers wanted to go on but the guide refused. Regretfully they struggled back to Innsbruck to start again tomorrow.

After dinner and a bottle of heavy local wine in the deserted dining-room, he felt excited, without knowing why, until he began thinking of the garden. He had passed the girl in the lobby before supper and this time she had looked at him and approved of him, but it kept worrying him: Why? When I could have had a good share of the pretty women of my time for the asking, why start that now? With a wraith, with a fragment of my desire? Why?

His imagination pushed ahead – the old asceticism, the actual unfamiliarity, triumphed: God, I might as well go back to the Riviera and sleep with Janice Caricamento or the Wilburhazy girl. To belittle all these years with something cheap and easy?

He was still excited, though, and he turned from the veranda and went up to his room to think. Being alone in body and spirit begets loneliness, and loneliness begets more loneliness.

Upstairs he walked around thinking of the matter and laying out his climbing clothes advantageously on the faint heater; he again encountered Nicole's telegram, still unopened, with which diurnally she accompanied his itinerary. He had delayed opening it before supper – perhaps because of the garden. It was a cablegram from Buffalo, forwarded through Zurich.

> Your father died peacefully tonight. HOLMES

He felt a sharp wince at the shock, a gathering of the forces of resistance; then it rolled up through his loins and stomach and throat.

He read the message again. He sat down on the bed, breathing and staring; thinking first the old selfish child's thought that comes with the death of a parent, how will it affect me now that this earliest and strongest of protections is gone?

The atavism passed and he walked the room still, stopping from time to time to look at the telegram. Holmes was formally his father's curate but actually, and for a decade, rector of the church. How did he die? Of old age – he was seventy-five. He had lived a long time.

Dick felt sad that he had died alone – he had survived his wife, and his brothers and sisters; there were cousins in Virginia but they were poor and not able to come north, and Holmes had had to sign the telegram. Dick loved his father – again and again he referred judgments to what his father would probably have thought or done. Dick was born several months after the death of two young sisters, and his father, guessing what would be the effect on Dick's mother, had saved him from a spoiling by becoming his moral guide. He was of tired stock yet he raised himself to that effort.

In the summer father and son walked downtown together to have their shoes shined – Dick in his starched duck sailor suit, his father always in beautifully cut clerical clothes – and the father was very proud of his handsome little boy. He told Dick all he knew about life, not much but most of it true, simple things, matters of behaviour that came within his clergyman's range. 'Once in a strange town when I was first ordained, I went into a crowded room and was confused as to who was my hostess. Several people I knew came towards me, but I disregarded them because I had seen a grey-haired woman sitting by a window far across the room. I went over to her and introduced myself. After that I made many friends in that town.'

His father had done that from a good heart – his father had been sure of what he was, with a deep pride of the two proud widows who had raised him to believe that nothing could be superior to 'good instincts', honour, courtesy, and courage.

The father always considered that his wife's small fortune belonged to his son, and in college and in medical school sent him a cheque for all of it four times a year. He was one of those about whom it was said with smug finality in the gilded age: 'Very much the gentleman, but not much get-up-and-go about him.'

. . . Dick sent down for a newspaper. Still pacing to and from the telegram open on his bureau, he chose a ship to go to America. Then he put in a call for Nicole in Zurich, remembering so many things as he waited, and wishing he had always been as good as he had intended to be.

Chapter 19

FOR AN HOUR, tied up with his profound reaction to his father's death, the magnificent façade of the homeland, the harbour of New York, seemed all sad and glorious to Dick, but once ashore the feeling vanished, nor did he find it again in the streets or the hotels or the trains that bore him first to Buffalo, and then south to Virginia with his father's body. Only as the local train shambled into the low-forested clayland of Westmoreland County, did he feel once more identified with his surroundings; at the station he saw a star he knew, and a cold moon bright over Chesapeake Bay; he heard the rasping wheels of buckboards[295] turning, the lovely fatuous voices, the sound of sluggish primeval rivers flowing softly under soft Indian names.

Next day at the churchyard his father was laid among a hundred Divers, Dorseys, and Hunters. It was very friendly leaving him there with all his relations around him. Flowers were scattered on the brown unsettled earth. Dick had no more ties here now and did not believe he would come back. He knelt on the hard soil. These dead, he knew them all, their weather-beaten faces with blue flashing eyes, the spare violent bodies, the souls made of new earth in the forest – heavy darkness of the seventeenth century.

'Goodbye, my father – goodbye, all my fathers.'

On the long-roofed steamship piers one is in a country that is no longer here and not yet there. The hazy yellow vault is full of echoing shouts. There are the rumble of trucks and the clump of trunks, the strident chatter of cranes, the first salt smell of the sea. One hurries through, even though there's time; the past, the continent, is behind;

the future is the glowing mouth in the side of the ship; the dim, turbulent alley is too confusedly the present.

Up the gangplank and the vision of the world adjusts itself, narrows. One is a citizen of a commonwealth smaller than Andorra, no longer sure of anything. The men at the purser's desk are as oddly shaped as the cabins; disdainful are the eyes of voyagers and their friends. Next the loud mournful whistles, the portentous vibration, and the boat, the human idea, is in motion. The pier and its faces slide by and for a moment the boat is a piece accidentally split off from them; the faces become remote, voiceless, the pier is one of many blurs along the water front. The harbour flows swiftly towards the sea.

With it flowed Albert McKisco, labelled by the newspapers as its most precious cargo. McKisco was having a vogue. His novels were pastiches of the work of the best people of his time, a feat not to be disparaged, and in addition he possessed a gift for softening and debasing what he borrowed, so that many readers were charmed by the ease with which they could follow him. Success had improved him and humbled him. He was no fool about his capacities – he realised that he possessed more vitality than many men of superior talent, and he was resolved to enjoy the success he had earned. 'I've done nothing yet,' he would say. 'I don't think I've got any real genius. But if I keep trying I may write a good book.' Fine dives have been made from flimsier springboards. The innumerable snubs of the past were forgotten. Indeed, his success was founded psychologically upon his duel with Tommy Barban, upon the basis of which, as it withered in his memory, he had created, afresh, a new self-respect.

Spotting Dick Diver the second day out, he eyed him tentatively, then introduced himself in a friendly way and sat down. Dick laid aside his reading and, after the few minutes that it took to realise the change in McKisco, the disappearance of the man's annoying sense of inferiority, found himself pleased to talk to him. McKisco was 'well-informed' on a range of subjects wider than Goethe's – it was interesting to listen to the innumerable facile combinations that he referred to as his opinions. They struck up an acquaintance, and Dick had several meals with them. The McKiscos had been invited to sit at the captain's table but with nascent snobbery they told Dick that they 'couldn't stand that bunch'.

Violet was very grand now, decked out by the grand *couturières*,[296] charmed about the little discoveries that well-bred girls make in their teens. She could, indeed, have learned them from her mother in Boise[297] but her soul was born dismally in the small movie houses

of Idaho, and she had had no time for her mother. Now she
'belonged' – together with several million other people – and she
was happy, though her husband still shushed her when she grew
violently naïve.

The McKiscos got off at Gibraltar. Next evening in Naples Dick
picked up a lost and miserable family of two girls and their mother in
the bus from the hotel to the station. He had seen them on the ship.
An overwhelming desire to help, or to be admired, came over him: he
showed them fragments of gaiety; tentatively he bought them wine,
with pleasure saw them begin to regain their proper egotism. He
pretended they were this and that, and falling in with his own plot,
and drinking too much to sustain the illusion, and all this time the
women thought only that this was a windfall from heaven. He
withdrew from them as the night waned and the train rocked and
snorted at Cassino and Frosinone.[298] After weird American partings
in the station at Rome, Dick went to the Hotel Quirinale,[299] somewhat exhausted.

At the desk he suddenly stared and upped his head. As if a drink
were acting on him, warming the lining of his stomach, throwing a
flush up into his brain, he saw the person he had come to see, the
person for whom he had made the Mediterranean crossing.

Simultaneously Rosemary saw him, acknowledging him before placing him; she looked back startled, and, leaving the girl she was with, she
hurried over. Holding himself erect, holding his breath, Dick turned to
her. As she came across the lobby, her beauty all groomed, like a young
horse dosed with Black-seed oil,[300] and hoofs varnished, shocked him
awake; but it all came too quick for him to do anything except conceal
his fatigue as best he could. To meet her starry-eyed confidence he
mustered an insincere pantomime implying, 'You *would* turn up here –
of all the people in the world.'

Her gloved hands closed over his on the desk; 'Dick – we're making
The Grandeur that was Rome – at least we think we are; we may quit
any day.'

He looked at her hard, trying to make her a little self-conscious, so
that she would observe less closely his unshaven face, his crumpled
and slept-in collar. Fortunately, she was in a hurry.

'We begin early because the mists rise at eleven – phone me at two.'

In his room Dick collected his faculties. He left a call for noon,
stripped off his clothes and dived literally into a heavy sleep.

He slept over the phone call but awoke at two, refreshed. Unpacking
his bag, he sent out suits and laundry. He shaved, lay for half an hour
in a warm bath and had breakfast. The sun had dipped into the Via

Nazionale and he let it through the portières with a jingling of old brass rings. Waiting for a suit to be pressed, he discovered from the *Corriere della Sera* that 'una novella di Sainclair Lewis Wall Street nella quale l'autore analizza la vita sociale di una piccola città Americana'.[301] Then he tried to think about Rosemary.

At first he thought nothing. She was young and magnetic, but so was Topsy. He guessed that she had had lovers and had loved them in the last four years. Well, you never knew exactly how much space you occupied in people's lives. Yet from this fog his affection emerged – the best contacts are when one knows the obstacles and still wants to preserve a relation. The past drifted back and he wanted to hold her eloquent giving-of-herself in its precious shell, till he enclosed it, till it no longer existed outside him. He tried to collect all that might attract her – it was less than it had been four years ago. Eighteen might look at thirty-four through a rising mist of adolescence, but twenty-two would see thirty-eight with discerning clarity. Moreover, Dick had been at an emotional peak at the time of the previous encounter; since then there had been a lesion of enthusiasm.

When the valet returned he put on a white shirt and collar and a black tie with a pearl; the cords of his reading-glasses passed through another pearl of the same size that swung a casual inch below. After sleep, his face had resumed the ruddy brown of many Riviera summers, and to limber himself up he stood on his hands on a chair until his fountain pen and coins fell out. At three he called Rosemary and was bidden to come up. Momentarily dizzy from his acrobatics, he stopped in the bar for a gin-and-tonic.

'Hi, Dr Diver!'

Only because of Rosemary's presence in the hotel did Dick place the man immediately as Collis Clay. He had his old confidence and an air of prosperity and big sudden jowls.

'Do you know Rosemary's here?' Collis asked.

'I ran into her.'

'I was in Florence and I heard she was here so I came down last week. You'd never know mama's little girl.' He modified the remark, 'I mean she was so carefully brought up and now she's a woman of the world – if you know what I mean. Believe me, has she got some of these Roman boys tied up in bags![302] And how!'

'You studying in Florence?'

'Me? Sure, I'm studying architecture there. I go back Sunday – I'm staying for the races.'

With difficulty Dick restrained him from adding the drink to the account he carried in the bar, like a stock-market report.

Chapter 20

WHEN DICK GOT OUT of the elevator he followed a tortuous corridor and turned at length towards a distant voice outside a lighted door. Rosemary was in black pyjamas; a luncheon table was still in the room; she was having coffee.

'You're still beautiful,' he said. 'A little more beautiful than ever.'

'Do you want coffee, youngster?'

'I'm sorry I was so unpresentable this morning.'

'You didn't look well – you all right now? Want coffee?'

'No, thanks.'

'You're fine again, I was scared this morning. Mother's coming over next month, if the company stays. She always asks me if I've seen you over here, as if she thought we were living next door. Mother always liked you – she always felt you were someone I ought to know.'

'Well, I'm glad she still thinks of me.'

'Oh, she does,' Rosemary reassured him. 'A very great deal.'

'I've seen you here and there in pictures,' said Dick. 'Once I had *Daddy's Girl* run off just for myself.'

'I have a good part in this one if it isn't cut.'

She crossed behind him, touching his shoulder as she passed. She phoned for the table to be taken away and settled in a big chair.

'I was just a little girl when I met you, Dick. Now I'm a woman.'

'I want to hear everything about you.'

'How is Nicole – and Lanier and Topsy?'

'They're fine. They often speak of you – '

The phone rang. While she answered it Dick examined two novels – one by Edna Ferber,[303] one by Albert McKisco. The waiter came for the table; bereft of its presence Rosemary seemed more alone in her black pyjamas.

' . . . I have a caller . . . No, not very well. I've got to go to the costumer's for a long fitting . . . No, not now . . . '

As though with the disappearance of the table she felt released, Rosemary smiled at Dick – that smile as if they two together had managed to get rid of all the trouble in the world and were now at peace in their own heaven . . .

'That's done,' she said. 'Do you realise I've spent the last hour getting ready for you?'

But again the phone called her. Dick got up to change his hat from the bed to the luggage stand, and in alarm Rosemary put her hand over the mouthpiece of the phone. 'You're not going!'

'No.'

When the communication was over he tried to drag the afternoon together, saying: 'I expect some nourishment from people now.'

'Me too,' Rosemary agreed. 'The man that just phoned me once knew a second cousin of mine. Imagine calling anybody up for a reason like that!'

Now she lowered the lights for love. Why else should she want to shut off his view of her? He sent his words to her like letters, as though they left him some time before they reached her.

'Hard to sit here and be close to you, and not kiss you.' Then they kissed passionately in the centre of the floor. She pressed against him, and went back to her chair.

It could not go on being merely pleasant in the room. Forward or backward; when the phone rang once more he strolled into the bedchamber and lay down on her bed, opening Albert McKisco's novel. Presently Rosemary came in and sat beside him.

'You have the longest eyelashes,' she remarked.

'We are now back at the Junior Prom. Among those present are Miss Rosemary Hoyt, the eyelash fancier – '

She kissed him and he pulled her down so that they lay side by side, and then they kissed till they were both breathless. Her breathing was young and eager and exciting. Her lips were faintly chapped but soft in the corners.

When they were still limbs and feet and clothes, struggles of his arms and back, and her throat and breasts, she whispered, 'No, not now – those things are rhythmic.'

Disciplined he crushed his passion into a corner of his mind, but bearing up her fragility on his arm until she was poised half a foot above him, he said lightly: 'Darling – that doesn't matter.'

Her face had changed with his looking up at it; there was the eternal moonlight in it.

'That would be poetic justice if it should be you,' she said. She twisted away from him, walked to the mirror, and boxed her disarranged hair with her hands. Presently she drew a chair close to the bed and stroked his cheek.

'Tell me the truth about you,' he demanded.

'I always have.'

'In a way – but nothing hangs together.'

They both laughed but he pursued.

'Are you actually a virgin?'

'No-o-!' she sang. 'I've slept with six hundred and forty men – if that's the answer you want.'

'It's none of my business.'

'Do you want me for a case in psychology?'

'Looking at you as a perfectly normal girl of twenty-two, living in the year nineteen twenty-eight, I guess you've taken a few shots at love.'

'It's all been – abortive,' she said.

Dick couldn't believe her. He could not decide whether she was deliberately building a barrier between them or whether this was intended to make an eventual surrender more significant.

'Let's go walk in the Pincio,'[304] he suggested.

He shook himself straight in his clothes and smoothed his hair. A moment had come and somehow passed. For three years Dick had been the ideal by which Rosemary measured other men and inevitably his stature had increased to heroic size. She did not want him to be like other men, yet here were the same exigent demands, as if he wanted to take some of herself away, carry it off in his pocket.

Walking on the greensward between cherubs and philosophers, fauns and falling water, she took his arm smugly, settling into it with a series of little readjustments, as if she wanted it to be right because it was going to be there forever. She plucked a twig and broke it, but she found no spring in it. Suddenly seeing what she wanted in Dick's face she took his gloved hand and kissed it. Then she cavorted childishly for him until he smiled and she laughed and they began having a good time.

'I can't go out with you tonight, darling, because I promised some people a long time ago. But if you'll get up early I'll take you out to the set tomorrow.'

He dined alone at the hotel, went to bed early, and met Rosemary in the lobby at half-past six. Beside him in the car she glowed away fresh and new in the morning sunshine. They went out through the Porta San Sebastiano and along the Appian Way[305] until they came to the huge set of the forum, larger than the forum itself. Rosemary turned him over to a man who led him about the great props; the arches and tiers of seats and the sanded arena. She was working on a stage which represented a guardroom for Christian prisoners, and presently they went there and watched Nicotera, one of many hopeful Valentinos,[306] strut and pose before a dozen female 'captives', their eyes melancholy and startling with mascara.

Rosemary appeared in a knee-length tunic.

'Watch this,' she whispered to Dick. 'I want your opinion. Everybody that's seen the rushes says – '

'What are the rushes?'

'When they run off what they took the day before. They say it's the first thing I've had sex appeal in.'

'I don't notice it.'

'You wouldn't! But I have.'

Nicotera in his leopard skin talked attentively to Rosemary while the electrician discussed something with the director, meanwhile leaning on him. Finally the director pushed his hand off roughly and wiped a sweating forehead, and Dick's guide remarked: 'He's on the hop again, and how!'[307]

'Who?' asked Dick, but before the man could answer the director walked swiftly over to them.

'Who's on the hop – you're on the hop yourself.' He spoke vehemently to Dick, as if to a jury. 'When he's on the hop he always thinks everybody else is, and how!' He glared at the guide a moment longer, then he clapped his hands: 'All right – everybody on the set.'

It was like visiting a great turbulent family. An actress approached Dick and talked to him for five minutes under the impression that he was an actor recently arrived from London. Discovering her mistake she scuttled away in panic. The majority of the company felt either sharply superior or sharply inferior to the world outside, but the former feeling prevailed. They were people of bravery and industry; they were risen to a position of prominence in a nation that for a decade had wanted only to be entertained.

The session ended as the light grew misty – a fine light for painters, but, for the camera, not to be compared with the clear California air. Nicotera followed Rosemary to the car and whispered something to her – she looked at him without smiling as she said goodbye.

Dick and Rosemary had luncheon at the Castelli dei Cæsari, a splendid restaurant in a high-terraced villa overlooking the ruined forum of an undetermined period of the decadence. Rosemary took a cocktail and a little wine, and Dick took enough so that his feeling of dissatisfaction left him. Afterward they drove back to the hotel, all flushed and happy, in a sort of exalted quiet. She wanted to be taken and she was, and what had begun with a childish infatuation on a beach was accomplished at last.

Chapter 21

ROSEMARY HAD ANOTHER DATE, a birthday party for a member of the company. Dick ran into Collis Clay in the lobby, but he wanted to dine alone, and pretended an engagement at the Excelsior.[308] He drank a cocktail with Collis and his vague dissatisfaction crystallised as impatience – he no longer had an excuse for playing truant to the clinic. This was less an infatuation than a romantic memory. Nicole was his girl – too often he was sick at heart about her, yet she was his girl. Time with Rosemary was self-indulgence – time with Collis was nothing plus nothing.

In the doorway of the Excelsior he ran into Baby Warren. Her large beautiful eyes, looking precisely like marbles, stared at him with surprise and curiosity. 'I thought you were in America, Dick! Is Nicole with you?'

'I came back by way of Naples.'

The black band on his arm reminded her to say: 'I'm so sorry to hear of your trouble.'

Inevitably they dined together.

'Tell me about everything,' she demanded.

Dick gave her a version of the facts, and Baby frowned. She found it necessary to blame some one for the catastrophe in her sister's life.

'Do you think Dr Dohmler took the right course with her from the first?'

'There's not much variety in treatment any more – of course you try to find the right personality to handle a particular case.'

'Dick, I don't pretend to advise you or to know much about it but don't you think a change might be good for her – to get out of that atmosphere of sickness and live in the world like other people?'

'But you were keen for the clinic,' he reminded her. 'You told me you'd never feel really safe about her – '

'That was when you were leading that hermit's life on the Riviera, up on a hill way off from anybody. I didn't mean to go back to that life. I meant, for instance, London. The English are the best-balanced race in the world.'

'They are not,' he disagreed.

'They are. I know them, you see. I mean it might be nice for you to take a house in London for the spring season – I know a dove of a house in Talbot Square you could get, furnished. I mean, living with sane, well-balanced English people.'

She would have gone on to tell him all the old propaganda stories of 1914 if he had not laughed and said: 'I've been reading a book by Michael Arlen[309] and if that's – '

She ruined Michael Arlen with a wave of her salad spoon.

'He only writes about degenerates. I mean the worthwhile English.'

As she thus dismissed her friends they were replaced in Dick's mind only by a picture of the alien, unresponsive faces that peopled the small hotels of Europe.

'Of course it's none of my business,' Baby repeated, as a preliminary to a further plunge, 'but to leave her alone in an atmosphere like that – '

'I went to America because my father died.'

'I understand that, I told you how sorry I was.' She fiddled with the glass grapes on her necklace. 'But there's *so much* money now. Plenty for everything, and it ought to be used to get Nicole well.'

'For one thing I can't see myself in London.'

'Why not? I should think you could work there as well as anywhere else.'

He sat back and looked at her. If she had ever suspected the rotted old truth, the real reason for Nicole's illness, she had certainly determined to deny it to herself, shoving it back in a dusty closet like one of the paintings she bought by mistake.

They continued the conversation in the Ulpia,[310] where Collis Clay came over to their table and sat down, and a gifted guitar player thrummed and rumbled 'Suona Fanfara Mia' in the cellar piled with wine casks.

'It's possible that I was the wrong person for Nicole,' Dick said. 'Still she would probably have married someone of my type, someone she thought she could rely on – indefinitely.'

'You think she'd be happier with somebody else?' Baby thought aloud suddenly. 'Of course it could be arranged.'

Only as she saw Dick bend forward with helpless laughter did she realise the preposterousness of her remark.

'Oh, you understand,' she assured him. 'Don't think for a moment that we're not grateful for all you've done. And we know you've had a hard time – '

'For God's sake,' he protested. 'If I didn't love Nicole it might be different.'

'But you do love Nicole?' she demanded in alarm.

Collis was catching up with the conversation now and Dick switched it quickly: 'Suppose we talk about something else – about you, for instance. Why don't you get married? We heard you were engaged to Lord Paley, the cousin of the – '

'Oh, no.' She became coy and elusive. 'That was last year.'

'Why don't you marry?' Dick insisted stubbornly.

'I don't know. One of the men I loved was killed in the war, and the other one threw me over.'

'Tell me about it. Tell me about your private life, Baby, and your opinions. You never do – we always talk about Nicole.'

'Both of them were Englishmen. I don't think there's any higher type in the world than a first-rate Englishman, do you? If there is I haven't met him. This man – oh, it's a long story. I hate long stories, don't you?'

'And how!' said Collis.

'Why, no – I like them if they're good.'

'That's something you do so well, Dick. You can keep a party moving by just a little sentence or a saying here and there. I think that's a wonderful talent.'

'It's a trick,' he said gently. That made three of her opinions he disagreed with.

'Of course I like formality – I like things to be just so, and on the grand scale. I know you probably don't but you must admit it's a sign of solidity in me.'

Dick did not even bother to dissent from this.

'Of course I know people say Baby Warren is racing around over Europe, chasing one novelty after another, and missing the best things in life, but I think on the contrary that I'm one of the few people who really go after the best things. I've known the most interesting people of my time.' Her voice blurred with the tinny drumming of another guitar number, but she called over it, 'I've made very few big mistakes – '

' – Only the very big ones, Baby.'

She had caught something facetious in his eyes and she changed the subject. It seemed impossible for them to hold anything in common. But he admired something in her, and he deposited her at the Excelsior with a series of compliments that left her shimmering.

Rosemary insisted on treating Dick to lunch next day. They went to a little *trattoria* kept by an Italian who had worked in America, and ate ham and eggs and waffles. Afterward, they went to the hotel. Dick's discovery that he was not in love with her, nor she with him, had added to rather than diminished his passion for her. Now that he knew he would not enter further into her life, she became the strange woman for him. He supposed many men meant no more than that when they said they were in love – not a wild submergence of soul, a dipping of all colours into an obscuring dye, such as his love for Nicole had been. Certain thoughts about Nicole, that she should die, sink into mental darkness, love another man, made him physically sick.

Nicotera was in Rosemary's sitting-room, chattering about a professional matter. When Rosemary gave him his cue to go, he left with humorous protests and a rather insolent wink at Dick. As usual the phone clamoured and Rosemary was engaged at it for ten minutes to Dick's increasing impatience.

'Let's go up to my room,' he suggested, and she agreed.

She lay across his knees on a big sofa; he ran his fingers through the lovely forelocks of her hair.

'Let me be curious about you again?' he asked.

'What do you want to know?'

'About men. I'm curious, not to say prurient.'

'You mean how long after I met you?'

'Or before.'

'Oh, no.' She was shocked. 'There was nothing before. You were the first man I cared about. You're still the only man I really care about.' She considered. 'It was about a year, I think.'

'Who was it?'

'Oh, a man.'

He closed in on her evasion.

'I'll bet I can tell you about it: the first affair was unsatisfactory and after that there was a long gap. The second was better, but you hadn't been in love with the man in the first place. The third was all right – '

Torturing himself he ran on. 'Then you had one real affair that fell of its own weight, and by that time you were getting afraid that you wouldn't have anything to give to the man you finally loved.' He felt increasingly Victorian. 'Afterwards there were half a dozen just episodic affairs, right up to the present. Is that close?'

She laughed between amusement and tears.

'It's about as wrong as it could be,' she said, to Dick's relief. 'But some day I'm going to find somebody and love him and love him and never let him go.'

Now his phone rang and Dick recognised Nicotera's voice, asking for Rosemary. He put his palm over the transmitter.

'Do you want to talk to him?'

She went to the phone and jabbered in a rapid Italian Dick could not understand.

'This telephoning takes time,' he said. 'It's after four and I have an engagement at five. You better go play with Signor Nicotera.'

'Don't be silly.'

'Then I think that while I'm here you ought to count him out.'

'It's difficult.' She was suddenly crying. 'Dick, I do love you, never anybody like you. But what have you got for me?'

'What has Nicotera got for anybody?'

'That's different.'

Because youth called to youth.

'He's a spic!' he said. He was frantic with jealousy, he didn't want to be hurt again.

'He's only a baby,' she said, sniffling. 'You know I'm yours first.'

In reaction he put his arms about her but she relaxed wearily backward; he held her like that for a moment as in the end of an adagio, her eyes closed, her hair falling straight back like that of a girl drowned.

'Dick, let me go. I never felt so mixed up in my life.'

He was a gruff red bird and instinctively she drew away from him as his unjustified jealousy began to snow over the qualities of consideration and understanding with which she felt at home.

'I want to know the truth,' he said.

'Yes, then. We're a lot together, he wants to marry me, but I don't want to. What of it? What do you expect me to do? You never asked me to marry you. Do you want me to play around for ever with half-wits like Collis Clay?'

'You were with Nicotera last night?'

'That's none of your business,' she sobbed. 'Excuse me, Dick, it is your business. You and mother are the only two people in the world I care about.'

'How about Nicotera?'

'How do I know?'

She had achieved the elusiveness that gives hidden significance to the least significant remarks.

'Is it like you felt towards me in Paris?'

'I feel comfortable and happy when I'm with you. In Paris it was different. But you never know how you once felt. Do you?'

He got up and began collecting his evening clothes – if he had to bring all the bitterness and hatred of the world into his heart, he was not going to be in love with her again.

'I don't care about Nicotera!' she declared. 'But I've got to go to Livorno[311] with the company tomorrow. Oh, why did this have to happen?' There was a new flood of tears. 'It's such a shame. Why did you come here? Why couldn't we just have the memory anyhow? I feel as if I'd quarrelled with mother.'

As he began to dress, she got up and went to the door.

'I won't go to the party tonight.' It was her last effort. 'I'll stay with you. I don't want to go anyhow.'

The tide began to flow again, but he retreated from it.

'I'll be in my room,' she said. 'Goodbye, Dick.'

'Goodbye.'

'Oh, such a shame, such a shame. Oh, such a shame. What's it all about anyhow?'

'I've wondered for a long time.'

'But why bring it to me?'

'I guess I'm the Black Death,'[312] he said slowly. 'I don't seem to bring people happiness any more.'

Chapter 22

THERE WERE FIVE PEOPLE in the Quirinale bar after dinner, a high-class Italian frail who sat on a stool making persistent conversation against the bartender's bored: 'Si . . . Si . . . Si', a light, snobbish Egyptian who was lonely but chary of the woman, and the two Americans.

Dick was always vividly conscious of his surroundings, while Collis Clay lived vaguely, the sharpest impressions dissolving upon a recording apparatus that had early atrophied, so the former talked and the latter listened, like a man sitting in a breeze.

Dick, worn away by the events of the afternoon, was taking it out on the inhabitants of Italy. He looked around the bar as if he hoped an Italian had heard him and would resent his words.

'This afternoon I had tea with my sister-in-law at the Excelsior. We got the last table and two men came up and looked around for a table and couldn't find one. So one of them came up to us and said, "Isn't this table reserved for the Princess Orsini?" and I said: "There was no sign on it," and he said: "But I think it's reserved for the Princess Orsini." I couldn't even answer him.'

'What'd he do?'

'He retired.' Dick switched around in his chair. 'I don't like these people. The other day I left Rosemary for two minutes in front of a store and an officer started walking up and down in front of her, tipping his hat.'

'I don't know,' said Collis after a moment. 'I'd rather be here than up in Paris with somebody picking your pocket every minute.'

He had been enjoying himself, and he held out against anything that threatened to dull his pleasure.

'I don't know,' he persisted. 'I don't mind it here.'

Dick evoked the picture that the few days had imprinted on his mind, and stared at it. The walk towards the American Express past the odorous confectioneries of the Via Nationale, through the foul tunnel up to the Spanish Steps,[313] where his spirit soared before the flower stalls and the house where Keats had died. He cared only about people; he was scarcely conscious of places except for their weather, until they had been invested with colour by tangible events. Rome was the end of his dream of Rosemary.

A bellboy came in and gave him a note.

'I did not go to the party,' it said. 'I am in my room. We leave for Livorno early in the morning.'

Dick handed the note and a tip to the boy.

'Tell Miss Hoyt you couldn't find me.' Turning to Collis he suggested the Bonbonieri.[314]

They inspected the tart at the bar, granting her the minimum of interest exacted by her profession, and she stared back with bright boldness; they went through the deserted lobby oppressed by draperies holding Victorian dust in stuffy folds, and they nodded at the night concierge, who returned the gesture with the bitter servility peculiar to night servants. Then in a taxi they rode along cheerless streets through a dank November night. There were no women in the streets, only pale men with dark coats buttoned to the neck, who stood in groups beside shoulders of cold stone.

'My God!' Dick sighed.

'What's a matter?'

'I was thinking of that man this afternoon: "This table is reserved for the Princess Orsini." Do you know what these old Roman families are? They're bandits, they're the ones who got possession of the temples and palaces after Rome went to pieces and preyed on the people.'

'I like Rome,' insisted Collis. 'Why won't you try the races?'

'I don't like races.'

'But all the women turn out – '

'I know I wouldn't like anything here. I like France, where everybody thinks he's Napoleon – down here everybody thinks he's Christ.'

At the Bonbonieri they descended to a panelled cabaret, hopelessly impermanent amid the cold stone. A listless band played a tango and a dozen couples covered the wide floor with those elaborate and dainty steps so offensive to the American eye. A surplus of waiters precluded the stir and bustle that even a few busy men can create;

over the scene as its form of animation brooded an air of waiting for something, for the dance, the night, the balance of forces which kept it stable, to cease. It assured the impressionable guest that whatever he was seeking he would not find it here.

This was plain as plain to Dick. He looked around, hoping his eye would catch on something, so that spirit instead of imagination could carry on for an hour. But there was nothing and after a moment he turned back to Collis. He had told Collis some of his current notions, and he was bored with his audience's short memory and lack of response. After half an hour of Collis he felt a distinct lesion of his own vitality.

They drank a bottle of Italian mousseux, and Dick became pale and somewhat noisy. He called the orchestra leader over to their table; this was a Bahama Negro, conceited and unpleasant, and in a few minutes there was a row.

'You asked me to sit down.'

'All right. And I gave you fifty lire, didn't I?'

'All right. All right. All right.'

'All right, I gave you fifty lire, didn't I? Then you came up and asked me to put some more in the horn!'

'You asked me to sit down, didn't you? Didn't you?'

'I asked you to sit down but I gave you fifty lire, didn't I?'

'All right. All right.'

The Negro got up sourly and went away, leaving Dick in a still more evil humour. But he saw a girl smiling at him from across the room and immediately the pale Roman shapes around him receded into decent, humble perspective. She was a young English girl, with blonde hair and a healthy, pretty English face, and she smiled at him again with an invitation he understood, that denied the flesh even in the act of tendering it.

'There's a quick trick or else I don't know bridge,' said Collis.

Dick got up and walked to her across the room.

'Won't you dance?'

The middle-aged Englishman with whom she was sitting said, almost apologetically: 'I'm going out soon.'

Sobered by excitement, Dick danced. He found in the girl a suggestion of all the pleasanter English things; the story of safe gardens ringed around by the sea was implicit in her bright voice, and as he leaned back to look at her, he meant what he said to her so sincerely that his voice trembled. When her current escort should leave, she promised to come and sit with them. The Englishman accepted her return with repeated apologies and smiles.

Back at his table Dick ordered another bottle of spumante.[315]

'She looks like somebody in the movies,' he said. 'I can't think who.' He glanced impatiently over his shoulder. 'Wonder what's keeping her?'

'I'd like to get in the movies,' said Collis thoughtfully. 'I'm supposed to go into my father's business but it doesn't appeal to me much. Sit in an office in Birmingham for twenty years – '

His voice resisted the pressure of materialistic civilisation.

'Too good for it?' suggested Dick.

'No, I don't mean that.'

'Yes, you do.'

'How do you know what I mean? Why don't you practise as a doctor, if you like to work so much?'

Dick had made them both wretched by this time, but simultaneously they had become vague with drink and in a moment they forgot; Collis left, and they shook hands warmly.

'Think it over,' said Dick sagely.

'Think what over?'

'You know.' It had been something about Collis going into his father's business – good sound advice.

Clay walked off into space. Dick finished his bottle and then danced with the English girl again, conquering his unwilling body with bold revolutions and stern determined marches down the floor. The most remarkable thing suddenly happened. He was dancing with the girl, the music stopped – and she had disappeared.

'Have you seen her?'

'Seen who?'

'The girl I was dancing with. Su'nly disappeared. Must be in the building.'

'No! No! That's the ladies' room.'

He stood up by the bar. There were two other men there, but he could think of no way of starting a conversation. He could have told them all about Rome and the violent origins of the Colonna and Gaetani families,[316] but he realised that as a beginning that would be somewhat abrupt. A row of Yenci[317] dolls on the cigar counter fell suddenly to the floor; there was a subsequent confusion and he had a sense of having been the cause of it, so he went back to the cabaret and drank a cup of black coffee. Collis was gone and the English girl was gone and there seemed nothing to do but go back to the hotel and lie down with his black heart. He paid his check and got his hat and coat.

There was dirty water in the gutters and between the rough

cobblestones; a marshy vapour from the Campagna, a sweat of exhausted cultures tainted the morning air. A quartet of taxi-drivers, their little eyes bobbing in dark pouches, surrounded him. One who leaned insistently in his face he pushed harshly away.

'Quanto a Hotel Quirinale?'

'Cento lire.'[318]

Six dollars. He shook his head and offered thirty lire which was twice the daytime fare, but they shrugged their shoulders as one pair, and moved off.

'Trenta-cinque lire e mancie,' he said firmly.

'Cento lire.'

He broke into English.

'To go half a mile? You'll take me for forty lire.'

'Oh, no.'

He was very tired. He pulled open the door of a cab and got in.

'Hotel Quirinale!' he said to the driver who stood obstinately outside the window. 'Wipe that sneer off your face and take me to the Quirinale.'

'Ah, no.'

Dick got out. By the door of the Bonbonieri someone was arguing with the taxi-drivers, someone who now tried to explain their attitude to Dick; again one of the men pressed close, insisting and gesticulating, and Dick shoved him away.

'I want to go the Quirinale Hotel.'

'He says wan huner lire,' explained the interpreter.

'I understand. I'll give him fifty lire. Go on away.' This last to the insistent man who had edged up once more. The man looked at him and spat contemptuously.

The passionate impatience of the week leaped up in Dick and clothed itself like a flash in violence, the honourable, the traditional resource of his land; he stepped forward and clapped the man's face.

They surged about him, threatening, waving their arms, trying ineffectually to close in on him – with his back against the wall Dick hit out clumsily, laughing a little, and for a few minutes the mock fight, an affair of foiled rushes and padded, glancing blows, swayed back and forth in front of the door. Then Dick tripped and fell; he was hurt somewhere but he struggled up again wrestling in arms that suddenly broke apart. There was a new voice and a new argument, but he leaned against the wall, panting, and furious at the indignity of his position. He saw there was no sympathy for him but he was unable to believe that he was wrong.

They were going to the police station and settle it there. His hat was retrieved and handed to him, and with some one holding his arm lightly he strode around the corner with the taxi-men and entered a bare barrack where *carabinieri* lounged under a single dim light.

At a desk sat a captain, to whom the officious individual who had stopped the battle spoke at length in Italian, at times pointing at Dick, and letting himself be interrupted by the taxi-men who delivered short bursts of invective and denunciation. The captain began to nod impatiently. He held up his hand and the hydra-headed address, with a few parting exclamations, died away. Then he turned to Dick.

'Spick Italiano?' he asked.

'No.'

'Spick Français?'

'Oui,' said Dick glowering.

'Alors. Écoute. Va au Quirinale. Espèce d'endormi. Écoute: vous êtes saoul. Payez ce que le chauffeur demande. Comprenez-vous?'[319]

Diver shook his head.

'Non, je ne veux pas.'

'Comment?'

'Je paierai quarante lires. C'est bien assez.'

The captain stood up.

'Écoute!' he cried portentously. 'Vous êtes saoul. Vous avez battu le chauffeur. Comme ci, comme ça.' He struck the air excitedly with right hand and left. 'C'est bon que je vous donne la liberté. Payez ce qu'il a dit – cento lire. Va au Quirinale.'[320]

Raging with humiliation, Dick stared back at him.

'All right.' He turned blindly to the door – before him, leering and nodding, was the man who had brought him to the police station. 'I'll go home,' he shouted, 'but first I'll fix this baby.'

He walked past the staring *carabinieri* and up to the grinning face, hit it with a smashing left beside the jaw. The man dropped to the floor.

For a moment he stood over him in savage triumph – but even as a first pang of doubt shot through him the world reeled; he was clubbed down, and fists and boots beat on him in a savage tattoo. He felt his nose break like a shingle and his eyes jerk as if they had snapped back on a rubber band into his head. A rib splintered under a stamping heel. Momentarily he lost consciousness, regained it as he was raised to a sitting position and his wrists jerked together with handcuffs. He struggled automatically. The plainclothes lieutenant whom he had knocked down stood dabbing his jaw with a handkerchief and looking into it for blood; he came over to Dick, poised himself, drew back his arm and smashed him to the floor.

When Dr Diver lay quite still a pail of water was sloshed over him. One of his eyes opened dimly as he was being dragged along by the wrists through a bloody haze, and he made out the human and ghastly face of one of the taxi-drivers.

'Go to the Excelsior Hotel,' he cried faintly. 'Tell Miss Warren. Two hundred lire! Miss Warren. *Due centi lire!* [321] Oh, you dirty – you god – '

Still he was dragged along through the bloody haze, choking and sobbing, over vague irregular surfaces into some small place where he was dropped upon a stone floor. The men went out, a door clanged, he was alone.

Chapter 23

UNTIL ONE O'CLOCK Baby Warren lay in bed, reading one of Marion Crawford's curiously inanimate Roman stories;[322] then she went to a window and looked down into the street. Across from the hotel two *carabinieri*, grotesque in swaddling capes and harlequin hats, swung voluminously from this side to that, like mains'ls coming about, and watching them she thought of the Guards officer who had stared at her so intensely at lunch. He had possessed the arrogance of a tall member of a short race, with no obligation save to be tall. Had he come up to her and said: 'Let's go along, you and I,' she would have answered: 'Why not?' – at least it seemed so now, for she was still disembodied by an unfamiliar background.

Her thoughts drifted back slowly through the guardsman to the two *carabinieri*, to Dick – she got into bed and turned out the light.

A little before four she was awakened by a brusque knocking.

'Yes – what is it?'

'It's the concierge, madame.'

She pulled on her kimono and faced him sleepily.

'You friend named Deever he's in a trouble. He had trouble with the police, and they have him in the jail. He sent a taxi up to tell, the driver says that he promised him two hundred lire.' He paused cautiously for this to be approved. 'The driver says Mr Deever in the bad trouble. He had a fight with the police and is terribly bad hurt.'

'I'll be right down.'

She dressed to an accompaniment of anxious heartbeats and ten minutes later stepped out of the elevator into the dark lobby. The chauffeur who brought the message was gone; the concierge hailed another one and told him the location of the jail. As they rode, the darkness lifted and thinned outside and Baby's nerves, scarcely awake, cringed faintly at the unstable balance between night and day. She began to race against the day; sometimes on the broad avenues she gained but whenever the thing that was pushing up paused for a moment, gusts of wind blew here and there impatiently and the slow creep of light began once more. The cab went past a loud fountain splashing in a voluminous shadow, turned into an alley so curved that the buildings were warped and strained following it, bumped and rattled over cobblestones, and stopped with a jerk where two sentry-boxes were bright against a wall of green damp. Suddenly from the violet darkness of an archway came Dick's voice, shouting and screaming.

'Are there any English? Are there any Americans? Are there any English? Are there any – oh, my God! You dirty Wops!'

His voice died away and she heard a dull sound of beating on the door. Then the voice began again.

'Are there any Americans? Are there any English?'

Following the voice she ran through the arch into a court, whirled about in momentary confusion and located the small guardroom whence the cries came. Two *carabinieri* started to their feet, but Baby brushed past them to the door of the cell.

'Dick!' she called. 'What's the trouble?'

'They've put out my eye,' he cried. 'They handcuffed me and then they beat me, the goddamn – the – '

Flashing around Baby took a step towards the two *carabinieri*.

'What have you done to him?' she whispered so fiercely that they flinched before her gathering fury.

'Non capisco inglese.'[323]

In French she execrated them; her wild, confident rage filled the room, enveloped them until they shrank and wriggled from the garments of blame with which she invested them. 'Do something! Do something!'

'We can do nothing until we are ordered.'

'Bene. Bay-nay! Bene!'

Once more Baby let her passion scorch around them until they sweated out apologies for their impotence, looking at each other with the sense that something had after all gone terribly wrong. Baby went to the cell door, leaned against it, almost caressing it, as if that could make Dick feel her presence and power, and cried: 'I'm going to the Embassy, I'll be back.' Throwing a last glance of infinite menace at the *carabinieri* she ran out.

She drove to the American Embassy where she paid off the taxi-driver upon his insistence. It was still dark when she ran up the steps and pressed the bell. She had pressed it three times before a sleepy English porter opened the door to her.

'I want to see someone,' she said. 'Anyone – but right away.'

'No one's awake, madame. We don't open until nine o'clock.'

Impatiently she waved the hour away.

'This is important. A man – an American has been terribly beaten. He's in an Italian jail.'

'No one's awake now. At nine o'clock – '

'I can't wait. They've put out a man's eye – my brother-in-law, and they won't let him out of jail. I must talk to some one – can't you see? Are you crazy? Are you an idiot, you stand there with that look in your face?'

'Hime[324] unable to do anything, madame.'

'You've got to wake someone up!' She seized him by the shoulders and jerked him violently. 'It's a matter of life and death. If you won't wake some one a terrible thing will happen to you – '

'Kindly don't lay hands on me, madame.'

From above and behind the porter floated down a weary Groton voice.[325]

'What is it there?'

The porter answered with relief.

'It's a lady, sir, and she has shaken me.' He had stepped back to speak and Baby pushed forward into the hall. On an upper landing, just aroused from sleep and wrapped in a white embroidered Persian robe, stood a singular young man. His face was of a monstrous and unnatural pink, vivid yet dead, and over his mouth was fastened what appeared to be a gag. When he saw Baby he moved his head back into a shadow.

'What is it?' he repeated.

Baby told him, in her agitation edging forward to the stairs. In the course of her story she realised that the gag was in reality a moustache bandage and that the man's face was covered with pink cold cream, but the fact fitted quietly into the nightmare. The thing to do, she cried passionately, was for him to come to the jail with her at once to get Dick out.

'It's a bad business,' he said.

'Yes,' she agreed conciliatingly. 'Yes?'

'This trying to fight the police.' A note of personal affront crept into his voice. 'I'm afraid there's nothing to be done until nine o'clock.'

'Till nine o'clock,' she repeated aghast. 'But you can do something, certainly! You can come to the jail with me and see that they don't hurt him any more.'

'We aren't permitted to do anything like that. The Consulate handles these things. The Consulate will be open at nine.'

His face, constrained to impassivity by the binding strap, infuriated Baby.

'I can't wait until nine. My brother-in-law says they've put his eye out – he's seriously hurt! I have to get to him. I have to find a doctor.' She let herself go and began to cry angrily as she talked, for she knew that he would respond to her agitation rather than her words. 'You've got to do something about this. It's your business to protect American citizens in trouble.'

But he was of the Eastern seaboard and too hard for her. Shaking his head patiently at her failure to understand his position he drew the Persian robe closer about him and came down a few steps.

'Write down the address of the Consulate for this lady,' he said to the porter, 'and look up Dr Colazzo's address and telephone number and write that down too.' He turned to Baby, with the expression of an exasperated Christ. 'My dear lady, the diplomatic corps represents the Government of the United States to the Government of Italy. It has nothing to do with the protection of citizens, except under specific instructions from the State Department. Your brother-in-law has broken the laws of this country and been put in jail, just as an Italian might be put in jail in New York. The only people who can let him go are the Italian courts and if your brother-in-law has a case you can get aid and advice from the Consulate, which protects the rights of American citizens. The Consulate does not open until nine o'clock. Even if it were my brother I couldn't do anything – '

'Can you phone the Consulate?' she broke in.

'We can't interfere with the Consulate. When the Consul gets there at nine – '

'Can you give me his home address?'

After a fractional pause the man shook his head. He took the memorandum from the porter and gave it to her.

'Now I'll ask you to excuse me.'

He had manœuvred her to the door: for an instant the violet dawn fell shrilly upon his pink mask and upon the linen sack that supported his moustache; then Baby was standing on the front steps alone. She had been in the Embassy ten minutes.

The piazza whereon it faced was empty save for an old man gathering cigarette butts with a spiked stick. Baby caught a taxi presently and went to the Consulate but there was no one there save a trio of wretched women scrubbing the stairs. She could not make them understand that she wanted the Consul's home address – in a sudden resurgence of anxiety she rushed out and told the chauffeur to take her to the jail. He did not know where it was, but by the use of words *semper diretto*, *dextra* and *sinestra* [326] she manœuvred him to its approximate locality, where she dismounted and explored a labyrinth of familiar alleys. But the buildings and the alleys all looked alike. Emerging from one trail into the Piazza di Spagna[327] she saw the American Express Company and her heart lifted at the word 'American' on the sign. There was a light in the window and hurrying across the square she tried the door, but it was locked, and inside the clock stood at seven. Then she thought of Collis Clay.

She remembered the name of his hotel, a stuffy villa sealed in red plush across from the Excelsior. The woman on duty at the office was not disposed to help her – she had no authority to disturb Mr Clay, and refused to let Miss Warren go up to his room alone; convinced finally that this was not an affair of passion she accompanied her.

Collis lay naked upon his bed. He had come in tight and, awakening, it took him some moments to realize his nudity. He atoned for it by an excess of modesty. Taking his clothes into the bathroom he dressed in haste, muttering to himself 'Gosh. She certainly musta got a good look at me.' After some telephoning, he and Baby found the jail and went to it.

The cell door was open and Dick was slumped on a chair in the guardroom. The *carabinieri* had washed some of the blood from his face, brushed him and set his hat concealingly upon his head. Baby stood in the doorway trembling.

'Mr Clay will stay with you,' she said. 'I want to get the Consul and a doctor.'

'All right.'

'Just stay quiet.'

'All right.'

'I'll be back.'

She drove to the Consulate; it was after eight now, and she was permitted to sit in the ante-room. Towards nine the Consul came in and Baby, hysterical with impotence and exhaustion, repeated her story. The Consul was disturbed. He warned her against getting into brawls in strange cities, but he was chiefly concerned that she should wait outside – with despair she read in his elderly eye that he wanted to be mixed up as little as possible in this catastrophe. Waiting on his action, she passed the minutes by phoning a doctor to go to Dick. There were other people in the ante-room and several were admitted to the Consul's office. After half an hour she chose the moment of someone's coming out and pushed past the secretary into the room.

'This is outrageous! An American has been beaten half to death and thrown into prison and you make no move to help.'

'Just a minute, Mrs – '

'I've waited long enough. You come right down to the jail and get him out!'

'Mrs – '

'We're people of considerable standing in America – ' Her mouth hardened as she continued. 'If it wasn't for the scandal we can – I shall see that your indifference to this matter is reported in the proper quarter. If my brother-in-law were a British citizen he'd have been free hours ago, but you're more concerned with what the police will think than about what you're here for.'

'Mrs – '

'You put on your hat and come with me right away.'

The mention of his hat alarmed the Consul, who began to clean his spectacles hurriedly and to ruffle his papers. This proved of no avail: the American Woman, aroused, stood over him; the clean-sweeping irrational temper that had broken the moral back of a race and made a nursery out of a continent, was too much for him. He rang for a vice-consul – Baby had won.

Dick sat in the sunshine that fell profusely through the guardroom window. Collis was with him and two *carabinieri*, and they were waiting for something to happen. With the narrowed vision of his one eye Dick could see the *carabinieri*; they were Tuscan peasants with short upper lips, and he found it difficult to associate them with the brutality of last night. He sent one of them to fetch him a glass of beer.

The beer made him light-headed and the episode was momentarily illuminated by a ray of sardonic humour. Collis was under the impression that the English girl had something to do with the catastrophe, but Dick was sure she had disappeared long before it happened. Collis was still absorbed by the fact that Miss Warren had found him naked on his bed.

Dick's rage had retreated into him a little and he felt a vast criminal irresponsibility. What had happened to him was so awful that nothing could make any difference unless he could choke it to death, and, as this was unlikely, he was hopeless. He would be a different person henceforward, and in his raw state he had bizarre feelings of what the new self would be. The matter had about it the impersonal quality of an act of God. No mature Aryan is able to profit by a humiliation; when he forgives, it has become part of his life, he has identified himself with the thing which has humiliated him – an upshot that in this case was impossible.

When Collis spoke of retribution, Dick shook his head and was silent. A lieutenant of *carabinieri*, pressed, burnished, vital, came into the room like three men and the guards jumped to attention. He seized the empty beer bottle and directed a stream of scolding at his men. The new spirit was in him, and the first thing was to get the beer bottle out of the guardroom. Dick looked at Collis and laughed.

The vice-consul, an overworked young man named Swanson, arrived, and they started to the court; Collis and Swanson on either side of Dick and the two *carabinieri* close behind. It was a yellow, hazy morning; the squares and arcades were crowded and Dick, pulling his hat low over his head, walked fast, setting the pace, until one of the short-legged *carabinieri* ran alongside and protested. Swanson arranged matters.

'I've disgraced you, haven't I?' said Dick jovially.

'You're liable to get killed fighting Italians,' replied Swanson sheepishly. 'They'll probably let you go this time, but if you were an Italian you'd get a couple of months in prison. And how!'

'Have you ever been in prison?'

Swanson laughed.

'I like him,' announced Dick to Clay. 'He's a very likeable young man and he gives people excellent advice, but I'll bet he's been to jail himself. Probably spent weeks at a time in jail.'

Swanson laughed.

'I mean you want to be careful. You don't know how these people are.'

'Oh, I know how they are,' broke out Dick, irritably. 'They're god-damn stinkers.' He turned around to the *carabinieri*: 'Did you get that?'

'I'm leaving you here,' Swanson said quickly. 'I told your sister-in-law I would – our lawyer will meet you upstairs in the court-room. You want to be careful.'

'Goodbye.' Dick shook hands politely. 'Thank you very much. I feel you have a future – '

With another smile Swanson hurried away, resuming his official expression of disapproval.

Now they came into a courtyard on all four sides of which outer stairways mounted to the chambers above. As they crossed the flags a groaning, hissing, booing sound went up from the loiterers in the courtyard, voices full of fury and scorn. Dick stared about.

'What's that?' he demanded, aghast.

One of the *carabinieri* spoke to a group of men and the sound died away.

They came into the court-room. A shabby Italian lawyer from the Consulate spoke at length to the judge while Dick and Collis waited aside. Someone who knew English turned from the window that gave on the yard and explained the sound that had accompanied their passage through. A native of Frascati[328] had raped and slain a five-year-old child and was to be brought in that morning – the crowd had assumed it was Dick.

In a few minutes the lawyer told Dick that he was freed – the court considered him punished enough.

'Enough!' Dick cried. 'Punished for what?'

'Come along,' said Collis. 'You can't do anything now.'

'But what did I do, except get into a fight with some taxi-men?'

'They claim you went up to a detective as if you were going to shake hands with him and hit him – '

'That's not true! I told him I was going to hit him – I didn't know he was a detective.'

'You better go along,' urged the lawyer.

'Come along.' Collis took his arm and they descended the steps.

'I want to make a speech,' Dick cried. 'I want to explain to these people how I raped a five-year-old girl. Maybe I did – '

'Come along.'

Baby was waiting with a doctor in a taxi-cab. Dick did not want to look at her and he disliked the doctor, whose stern manner revealed him as one of the least palatable of European types, the Latin moralist. Dick summed up his conception of the disaster, but no one had much to say. In his room in the Quirinale the doctor washed off the rest of the blood and the oily sweat, set his nose, his fractured ribs and fingers, disinfected the smaller wounds and put a hopeful dressing on the eye. Dick asked for a quarter of a grain of morphine, for he was still wide awake and full of nervous energy. With the morphine he fell asleep; the doctor and Collis left and Baby waited with him until a woman could arrive from the English nursing home. It had been a hard night but she had the satisfaction of feeling that, whatever Dick's previous record was, they now possessed a moral superiority over him for as long as he proved of any use.

BOOK THREE

Chapter 1

FRAU KAETHE GREGOROVIOUS overtook her husband on the path of their villa. 'How was Nicole?' she asked mildly; but she spoke out of breath, giving away the fact that she had held the question in her mind during her run.

Franz looked at her in surprise.

'Nicole's not sick. What makes you ask, dearest one?'

'You see her so much – I thought she must be sick.'

'We will talk of this in the house.'

Kaethe agreed meekly. His study was over in the administration building and the children were with their tutor in the living-room; they went up to the bedroom.

'Excuse me, Franz,' said Kaethe before he could speak. 'Excuse me, dear, I had no right to say that. I know my obligations and I am proud of them. But there is a bad feeling between Nicole and me.'

'Birds in their little nests agree,' Franz thundered. Finding the tone inappropriate to the sentiment, he repeated his command in the spaced and considered rhythm with which his old master, Dr Dohmler, could cast significance on the tritest platitude. 'Birds-in-their-nests-*agree*!'

'I realize that. You haven't seen me fail in courtesy towards Nicole.'

'I see you failing in common sense. Nicole is half a patient – she will possibly remain something of a patient all her life. In the absence of Dick I am responsible.' He hesitated; sometimes as a quiet joke he tried to keep news from Kaethe. 'There was a cable from Rome this morning. Dick has had grippe and is starting home tomorrow.'

Relieved, Kaethe pursued her course in a less personal tone: 'I think Nicole is less sick than anyone thinks – she only cherishes her illness as an instrument of power. She ought to be in the cinema, like your Norma Talmadge[329] – that's where all American women would be happy.'

'Are you jealous of Norma Talmadge, on a film?'

'I don't like Americans. They're selfish, *self*ish!'

'You like Dick?'

'I like him,' she admitted. 'He's different, he thinks of others.'

– And so does Norma Talmadge, Franz said to himself. Norma Talmadge must be a fine, noble woman beyond her loveliness. They must compel her to play foolish roles; Norma Talmadge must be a woman whom it would be a great privilege to know.

Kaethe had forgotten about Norma Talmadge, a vivid shadow that she had fretted bitterly upon one night as they were driving home from the movies in Zurich.

' – Dick married Nicole for her money,' she said. 'That was his weakness – you hinted as much yourself one night.'

'You're being malicious.'

'I shouldn't have said that,' she retracted. 'We must all live together like birds, as you say. But it's difficult when Nicole acts as – when Nicole pulls herself back a little, as if she were holding her breath – as if I *smelt* bad!'

Kaethe had touched a material truth. She did most of her work herself, and, frugal, she bought few clothes. An American shop-girl, laundering two changes of underwear every night, would have noticed a hint of yesterday's reawakened sweat about Kaethe's person, less a smell than an ammoniacal reminder of the eternity of toil and decay. To Franz this was as natural as the thick dark scent of Kaethe's hair, and he would have missed it equally; but to Nicole, born hating the smell of a nurse's fingers dressing her, it was an offence only to be endured.

'And the children,' Kaethe continued. 'She doesn't like them to play with our children – ' but Franz had heard enough: 'Hold your tongue – that kind of talk can hurt me professionally, since we owe this clinic to Nicole's money. Let us have lunch.'

Kaethe realised that her outburst had been ill-advised, but Franz's last remark reminded her that other Americans had money, and a week later she put her dislike of Nicole into new words.

The occasion was the dinner they tendered the Divers upon Dick's return. Hardly had their footfalls ceased on the path when she shut the door and said to Franz: 'Did you see around his eyes? He's been on a debauch!'

'Go gently,' Franz requested. 'Dick told me about that as soon as he came home. He was boxing on the trans-Atlantic ship. The American passengers box a lot on these trans-Atlantic ships.'

'I believe that?' she scoffed. 'It hurts him to move one of his arms and he has an unhealed scar on his temple – you can see where the hair's been cut away.'

Franz had not noticed these details.

'But what?' Kaethe demanded. 'Do you think that sort of thing does the clinic any good? The liquor I smelt on him tonight, and several other times since he's been back.'

She slowed her voice to fit the gravity of what she was about to say: 'Dick is no longer a serious man.'

Franz rocked his shoulders up the stairs, shaking off her persistence. In their bedroom he turned on her.

'He is most certainly a serious man and a brilliant man. Of all the men who have recently taken their degrees in neuro-pathology in Zurich, Dick has been regarded as the most brilliant – more brilliant than I could ever be.'

'For shame!'

'It's the truth – the shame would be not to admit it. I turn to Dick when cases are highly involved. His publications are still standard in their line – go into any medical library and ask. Most students think he's an Englishman – they don't believe that such thoroughness could come out of America.' He groaned domestically, taking his pyjamas from under the pillow, 'I can't understand why you talk this way, Kaethe – I thought you liked him.'

'For shame!' Kaethe said. 'You're the solid one, you do the work. It's a case of hare and tortoise – and in my opinion the hare's race is almost done.'

'Tch! Tch!'

'Very well, then. It's true.'

With his open hand he pushed down air briskly.

'Stop!'

The upshot was that they had exchanged viewpoints like debaters. Kaethe admitted to herself she had been too hard on Dick, whom she admired and of whom she stood in awe, who had been so appreciative and understanding of herself. As for Franz, once Kaethe's idea had had time to sink in, he never after believed that Dick was a serious person. And as time went on he convinced himself that he had never thought so.

Chapter 2

DICK TOLD NICOLE an expurgated version of the catastrophe in Rome – in his version he had gone philanthropically to the rescue of a drunken friend. He could trust Baby Warren to hold her tongue, since he had painted the disastrous effect of the truth upon Nicole. All this, however, was a low hurdle compared to the lingering effect of the episode upon him.

In reaction he took himself for an intensified beating in his work, so that Franz, trying to break with him, could find no basis on which to begin a disagreement. No friendship worth the name was ever destroyed in an hour without some painful flesh being torn – so Franz let himself believe with ever-increasing conviction that Dick travelled intellectually and emotionally at such a rate of speed that the vibrations jarred him – this was a contrast that had previously been considered a virtue in their relation. So, for the shoddiness of needs, are shoes made out of last year's hide.

Yet it was May before Franz found an opportunity to insert the first wedge. Dick came into his office white and tired one noon and sat down, saying: 'Well, she's gone.'

'She's dead?'

'The heart quit.'

Dick sat exhausted in the chair nearest the door. During three nights he had remained with the scabbed anonymous woman-artist he had come to love, formally to portion out the adrenalin, but really to throw as much wan light as he could into the darkness ahead.

Half appreciating his feeling, Franz travelled quickly over an opinion: 'It was neuro-syphilis. All the Wassermanns[330] we took won't tell me differently. The spinal fluid – '

'Never mind,' said Dick. 'Oh, God, never mind! If she cared enough about her secret to take it away with her, let it go at that.'

'You better lay off for a day.'

'Don't worry, I'm going to.'

Franz had his wedge; looking up from the telegram that he was writing to the woman's brother he enquired: 'Or do you want to take a little trip?'

'Not now.'

'I don't mean a vacation. There's a case in Lausanne. I've been on the phone with a Chilean all morning – '

'She was so damn brave,' said Dick. 'And it took her so long.' Franz shook his head sympathetically and Dick got himself together. 'Excuse me for interrupting you.'

'This is just a change – the situation is a father's problem with his son – the father can't get the son up here. He wants somebody to come down there.'

'What is it? Alcoholism? Homosexuality? When you say Lausanne – '

'A little of everything.'

'I'll go down. Is there any money in it?'

'Quite a lot, I'd say. Count on staying two or three days, and get the boy up here if he needs to be watched. In any case take your time, take your ease; combine business with pleasure.'

After two hours' train sleep Dick felt renewed, and he approached the interview with Señor Pardo y Ciudad Real in good spirits.

These interviews were much of a type. Often the sheer hysteria of the family representative was as interesting psychologically as the condition of the patient. This one was no exception: Señor Pardo y Ciudad Real, a handsome iron-grey Spaniard, noble of carriage, with all the appurtenances of wealth and power, raged up and down his suite in the Hôtel des Trois Mondes and told the story of his son with no more self-control than a drunken woman.

'I am at the end of my invention. My son is corrupt. He was corrupt at Harrow, he was corrupt at King's College, Cambridge.[331] He's incorrigibly corrupt. Now that there is this drinking it is more and more obvious how he is, and there is continual scandal. I have tried everything – I worked out a plan with a doctor friend of mine, sent them together for a tour of Spain. Every evening Francisco had an injection of cantharides[332] and then the two went together to a reputable bordello – for a week or so it seemed to work but the result was nothing. Finally last week in this very room, rather in that bathroom' – he pointed at it – 'I made Francisco strip to the waist and lashed him with a whip – '

Exhausted with his emotion he sat down and Dick spoke: 'That was foolish – the trip to Spain was futile also – ' He struggled against an upsurging hilarity – that any reputable medical man should have lent himself to such an amateurish experiment! ' – Señor, I must tell you that in these cases we can promise nothing. In the case of the drinking we can often accomplish something – with proper co-operation. The first thing is to see the boy, get enough of his confidence to find whether he has any insight into the matter.'

– The boy, with whom he sat on the terrace, was about twenty, handsome and alert.

'I'd like to know your attitude,' Dick said. 'Do you feel that the situation is getting worse? And do you want to do anything about it?'

'I suppose I do,' said Francisco, 'I am very unhappy.'

'Do you think it's from the drinking or from the abnormality?'

'I think the drinking is caused by the other.' He was serious for a while – suddenly an irrepressible facetiousness broke through and he laughed, saying, 'It's hopeless. At King's I was known as the Queen of Chile. That trip to Spain – all it did was to make me nauseated by the sight of a woman.'

Dick caught him up sharply.

'If you're happy in this mess, then I can't help you and I'm wasting my time.'

'No, let's talk – I despise most of the others so.' There was some manliness in the boy, perverted now into an active resistance to his father. But he had that typically roguish look in his eyes that homosexuals assume in discussing the subject.

'It's a hole-and-corner business at best,' Dick told him. 'You'll spend your life on it, and its consequences, and you won't have time or energy for any other decent or social act. If you want to face the world you'll have to begin by controlling your sensuality – and, first of all, the drinking that provokes it – '

He talked automatically, having abandoned the case ten minutes before. They talked pleasantly through another hour about the boy's home in Chile and about his ambitions. It was as close as Dick had ever come to comprehending such a character from any but the pathological angle – he gathered that this very charm made it possible for Francisco to perpetrate his outrages, and, for Dick, charm always had an independent existence, whether it was the mad gallantry of the wretch who had died in the clinic this morning, or the courageous grace which this lost young man brought to a drab old story. Dick tried to dissect it into pieces small enough to store away – realising that the totality of a life may be different in quality from its segments, and also that life during the forties seemed capable of being observed only in segments. His love for Nicole and Rosemary, his friendship with Abe North, with Tommy Barban in the broken universe of the war's ending – in such contacts the personalities had seemed to press up so close to him that he became the personality itself – there seemed some necessity of taking all or nothing; it was as if for the remainder of his life he was condemned to carry with him the egos of certain people, early met and early loved, and to be only as complete as they were complete themselves. There was some element of loneliness involved – so easy to be loved – so hard to love.

As he sat on the veranda with young Francisco, a ghost of the past swam into his ken. A tall, singularly swaying male detached himself from the shrubbery and approached Dick and Francisco with feeble resolution. For a moment he formed such an apologetic part of the vibrant landscape that Dick scarcely remarked him – then Dick was on his feet, shaking hands with an abstracted air, thinking, 'My God, I've stirred up a nest!' and trying to recollect the man's name.

'This is Dr Diver, isn't it?'

'Well, well – Mr Dumphry, isn't it?'

'Royal Dumphry. I had the pleasure of having dinner one night in that lovely garden of yours.'

'Of course.' Trying to dampen Mr Dumphry's enthusiasm, Dick went into impersonal chronology. 'It was in nineteen – twenty-four – or twenty-five – '

He had remained standing, but Royal Dumphry, shy as he had seemed at first, was no laggard with his pick and spade; he spoke to Francisco in a flip, intimate manner, but the latter, ashamed of him, joined Dick in trying to freeze him away.

'Dr Diver – one thing I want to say before you go. I've never forgotten that evening in your garden – how nice you and your wife were. To me it's one of the finest memories in my life, one of the happiest ones. I've always thought of it as the most civilised gathering of people that I have ever known.'

Dick continued a crab-like retreat towards the nearest door of the hotel.

'I'm glad you remembered it so pleasantly. Now I've got to see – '

'I understand,' Royal Dumphry pursued sympathetically. 'I hear he's dying.'

'Who's dying?'

'Perhaps I shouldn't have said that – but we have the same physician.'

Dick paused, regarding him in astonishment. 'Who're you talking about?'

'Why, your wife's father – perhaps I – '

'My *what*?'

'I suppose – you mean I'm the first person – '

'You mean my wife's father is here, in Lausanne?'

'Why, I thought you knew – I thought that was why you were here.'

'What doctor is taking care of him?'

Dick scrawled the name in a notebook, excused himself, and hurried to a telephone booth.

It was convenient for Dr Dangeu to see Dr Diver at his house immediately.

Dr Dangeu was a young *genevois*;[333] for a moment he was afraid that he was going to lose a profitable patient, but when Dick reassured him, he divulged the fact that Mr Warren was indeed dying.

'He is only fifty but the liver has stopped restoring itself; the precipitating factor is alcoholism.'

'Doesn't respond?'

'The man can take nothing except liquids – I give him three days, or at most, a week.'

'Does his elder daughter, Miss Warren, know his condition?'

'By his own wish no one knows except the manservant. It was only this morning I felt I had to tell him – he took it excitedly, although he has been in a very religious and resigned mood from the beginning of his illness.'

Dick considered: 'Well – ' he decided slowly, 'in any case I'll take care of the family angle. But I imagine they would want a consultation.'

'As you like.'

'I know I speak for them when I ask you to call in one of the best-known medical men around the lake – Herbrugge, from Geneva.'

'I was thinking of Herbrugge.'

'Meanwhile I'm here for a day at least and I'll keep in touch with you.'

That evening Dick went to Señor Pardo y Ciudad Real and they talked.

'We have large estates in Chile – ' said the old man. 'My son could well be taking care of them. Or I can get him in any one of a dozen enterprises in Paris – ' He shook his head and paced across the windows against a spring rain so cheerful that it didn't even drive the swans to cover. 'My only son! Can't you take him with you?'

The Spaniard knelt suddenly at Dick's feet.

'Can't you cure my only son? I believe in you – you can take him with you, cure him.'

'It's impossible to commit a person on such grounds. I wouldn't if I could.'

The Spaniard got up from his knees.

'I have been hasty – I have been driven – '

Descending to the lobby Dick met Dr Dangeu in the elevator.

'I was about to call your room,' the latter said. 'Can we speak out on the terrace?'

'Is Mr Warren dead?' Dick demanded.

'He is the same – the consultation is in the morning. Meanwhile he wants to see his daughter – your wife – with the greatest fervour. It seems there was some quarrel – '

'I know all about that.'

The doctors looked at each other, thinking.

'Why don't you talk to him before you make up your mind?' Dangeu suggested. 'His death will be graceful – merely a weakening and sinking.'

With an effort Dick consented.

'All right.'

The suite in which Charles Warren was gracefully weakening and sinking was of the same size as that of the Señor Pardo y Ciudad Real – throughout this hotel there were many chambers wherein rich ruins, fugitives from justice, claimants to the thrones of mediatised principalities,[334] lived on the derivatives of opium or barbital, listening eternally, as to an inescapable radio, to the coarse melodies of old sins. This corner of Europe does not so much draw people as accept them without inconvenient questions. Routes cross here – people bound for private sanatoriums or tuberculosis resorts in the mountains, people who are no longer *persona grata* in France or Italy.

The suite was darkened. A nun with a holy face was nursing the man whose emaciated fingers stirred a rosary on the white sheet. He was still handsome and his voice summoned up a thick burr of individuality as he spoke to Dick, after Dangeu had left them together.

'We get a lot of understanding at the end of life. Only now, Dr Diver, do I realise what it was all about.'

Dick waited.

'I've been a bad man. You must know how little right I have to see Nicole again, yet a Bigger Man than either of us says to forgive and to pity.' The rosary slipped from his weak hands and slid off the smooth bed-covers. Dick picked it up for him. 'If I could see Nicole for ten minutes I would go happy out of the world.'

'It's not a decision I can make for myself,' said Dick. 'Nicole is not strong.' He made his decision but pretended to hesitate. 'I can put it up to my professional associate.'

'What your associate says goes with me – very well, doctor. Let me tell you my debt to you is so large – '

Dick stood up quickly.

'I'll let you know the result through Dr Dangeu.'

In his room he called the clinic on the Zugersee. After a long time Kaethe answered from her own house.

'I want to get in touch with Franz.'

'Franz is up on the mountain. I'm going up myself – is it something I can tell him, Dick?'

'It's about Nicole – her father is dying here in Lausanne. Tell Franz that, to show him it's important; and ask him to phone me from up there.'

'I will.'

'Tell him I'll be in my room here at the hotel from three to five, and again from seven to eight, and after that to page me in the dining-room.'

In plotting these hours he forgot to add that Nicole was not to be told; when he remembered it he was talking into a dead telephone. Certainly Kaethe should realise.

. . . Kaethe had no exact intention of telling Nicole about the call when she rode up the deserted hill of mountain wild-flowers and secret winds, where the patients were taken to ski in winter and to climb in spring. Getting off the train she saw Nicole shepherding the children through some organised romp. Approaching, she drew her arm gently along Nicole's shoulder, saying: 'You are clever with children – you must teach them more about swimming in the summer.'

In the play they had grown hot, and Nicole's reflex in drawing away from Kaethe's arm was automatic to the point of rudeness. Kaethe's hand fell awkwardly into space, and then she too reacted, verbally and deplorably.

'Did you think I was going to embrace you?' she demanded sharply. 'It was only about Dick. I talked on the phone to him and I was sorry – '

'Is anything the matter with Dick?'

Kaethe suddenly realised her error, but she had taken a tactless course and there was no choice but to answer as Nicole pursued her with reiterated questions: '. . . then *why* were you sorry?'

'Nothing about Dick. I must talk to Franz.'

'It *is* about Dick.'

There was terror in her face and collaborating alarm in the faces of the Diver children, near at hand. Kaethe collapsed with: 'Your father is ill in Lausanne – Dick wants to talk to Franz about it.'

'Is he very sick?' Nicole demanded – just as Franz came up with his hearty hospital manner. Gratefully Kaethe passed the remnant of the buck to him – but the damage was done.

'I'm going to Lausanne,' announced Nicole.

'One minute,' said Franz. 'I'm not sure it's advisable. I must first talk on the phone to Dick.'

'Then I'll miss the train down,' Nicole protested, 'and then I'll miss the three o'clock from Zurich! If my father is dying I must – ' She left this in the air, afraid to formulate it. 'I *must* go. I'll have to run for the train.' She was running even as she spoke towards the sequence of flat cars that crowned the bare hill with bursting steam and sound. Over her shoulder she called back, 'If you phone Dick tell him I'm coming, Franz!'

. . . Dick was in his own room in the hotel reading the *New York Herald* when the swallow-like nun rushed in – simultaneously the phone rang.

'Is he dead?' Dick demanded of the nun, hopefully.

'Monsieur, il est parti – he has gone away.'

'Comment?'

'Il est parti – his man and his baggage have gone away too!'

It was incredible. A man in that condition to arise and depart.

Dick answered the phone call from Franz. 'You shouldn't have told Nicole,' he protested.

'Kaethe told her, very unwisely.'

'I suppose it was my fault. Never tell a thing to a woman till it's done. However, I'll meet Nicole . . . say, Franz, the craziest thing has happened down here – the old boy took up his bed and walked . . . '

'At what? What did you say?'

'I say he walked, old Warren – he walked!'

'But why not?'

'He was supposed to be dying of general collapse . . . He got up and walked away, back to Chicago, I guess . . . I don't know, the nurse is here now . . . I don't know, Franz – I've just heard about it . . . Call me later.'

He spent the better part of two hours tracing Warren's movements. The patient had found an opportunity between the change of day and night nurses to resort to the bar where he had gulped down four whiskies; he paid his hotel bill with a thousand-dollar note, instructing the desk that the change should be sent after him, and departed, presumably for America. A last-minute dash by Dick and Dangeu to overtake him at the station resulted only in Dick's failing to meet Nicole; when they did meet in the lobby of the hotel she seemed suddenly tired, and there was a tight purse to her lips that disquieted him.

'How's father?' she demanded.

'He's much better. He seemed to have a good deal of reserve energy after all.' He hesitated, breaking it to her easy. 'In fact, he got up and went away.'

Wanting a drink, for the chase had occupied the dinner hour, he led her, puzzled, towards the grill, and continued as they occupied two leather easy-chairs and ordered a highball[335] and a glass of beer: 'The man who was taking care of him made a wrong prognosis or something – wait a minute, I've hardly had time to think the thing out myself.'

'He's *gone*?'

'He got the evening train for Paris.'

They sat silent. From Nicole flowed a vast tragic apathy.

'It was instinct,' Dick said, finally. 'He was really dying, but he tried to get a resumption of rhythm – he's not the first person that ever walked off his deathbed – like an old clock – you know, you shake it and somehow from sheer habit it gets going again. Now your father – '

'Oh, don't tell me,' she said.

'His principal fuel was fear,' he continued. 'He got afraid, and off he went. He'll probably live till ninety – '

'Please don't tell me any more,' she said. 'Please don't – I couldn't stand any more.'

'All right. The little devil I came down to see is hopeless. We may as well go back tomorrow.'

'I don't see why you have to – come in contact with all this,' she burst forth.

'Oh, don't you? Sometimes I don't either.'

She put her hand on his.

'Oh, I'm sorry I said that, Dick.'

Someone had brought a phonograph into the bar and they sat listening to 'The Wedding of the Painted Doll'.[336]

Chapter 3

ONE MORNING A WEEK LATER, stopping at the desk for his mail, Dick became aware of some extra commotion outside: Patient Von Cohn Morris was going away. His parents, Australians, were putting his baggage vehemently into a large limousine, and beside them stood Dr Lladislau protesting with ineffectual attitudes against the violent gesturings of Morris, senior. The young man was regarding his embarkation with aloof cynicism as Dr Diver approached.

'Isn't this a little sudden, Mr Morris?'

Mr Morris started as he saw Dick – his florid face and the large checks on his suit seemed to turn off and on like electric lights. He approached Dick as though to strike him.

'High time we left, we and those who have come with us,' he began, and paused for breath. 'It is high time, Dr Diver. High time.'

'Will you come in my office?' Dick suggested.

'Not I! I'll talk to you, but I'm washing my hands of you and your place.'

'I'm sorry about that.'

He shook his finger at Dick. 'I was just telling this doctor here. We've wasted our time and our money.'

Dr Lladislau stirred in a feeble negative, signalling up a vague Slavic evasiveness. Dick had never liked Lladislau. He managed to walk the excited Australian along the path in the direction of his office, trying to persuade him to enter; but the man shook his head.

'It's you, Dr Diver, *you*, the very man. I went to Dr Lladislau because you were not to be found, Dr Diver, and because Dr Gregorovious is not expected until the nightfall, and I would not wait. No, sir! I would not wait a minute after my son told me the truth.'

He came up menacingly to Dick, who kept his hands loose enough to drop him if it seemed necessary. 'My son is here for alcoholism, and he told us he smelt liquor on your breath. Yes, sir!' He made a quick, apparently unsuccessful sniff. 'Not once, but twice Von Cohn says he has smelt liquor on your breath. I and my lady have never touched a drop of it in our lives. We hand Von Cohn to you to be cured, and within a month he twice smells liquor on your breath! What kind of cure is that there?'

Dick hesitated; Mr Morris was quite capable of making a scene on the clinic drive.

'After all, Mr Morris, some people are not going to give up what they regard as food because of your son – '

'But you're a doctor, man!' cried Morris furiously. 'When the workmen drink their beer that's bad 'cess to them[337] – but you're here supposing to cure – '

'This has gone too far. Your son came to us because of kleptomania.'

'What was behind it?' The man was almost shrieking. 'Drink – black drink. Do you know what colour black is? It's black! My own uncle was hung by the neck because of it, you hear! My son comes to a sanatorium, and a doctor reeks of it!'

'I must ask you to leave.'

'You *ask* me! We *are* leaving!'

'If you could be a little temperate we could tell you the results of the treatment to date. Naturally, since you feel as you do, we would not want your son as a patient – '

'You dare to use the word temperate to me?'

Dick called to Dr Lladislau and as he approached, said: 'Will you represent us in saying goodbye to the patient and to his family?'

He bowed slightly to Morris and went into his office, and stood rigid for a moment just inside the door. He watched until they drove away, the gross parents, the bland, degenerate offspring; it was easy to prophesy the family's swing around Europe, bullying their betters with hard ignorance and hard money. But what absorbed Dick after the disappearance of the caravan was the question as to what extent he had provoked this. He drank claret with each meal, took a nightcap, generally in the form of hot rum, and sometimes he tippled with gin in the afternoons – gin was the most difficult to detect on the breath. He was averaging a half-pint of alcohol a day, too much for his system to burn up.

Dismissing a tendency to justify himself, he sat down at his desk and wrote out, like a prescription, a regime that would cut his liquor in half. Doctors, chauffeurs, and Protestant clergymen could never smell of liquor, as could painters, brokers, cavalry leaders; Dick blamed himself only for indiscretion. But the matter was by no means clarified half an hour later when Franz, revivified by an Alpine fortnight, rolled up the drive, so eager to resume work that he was plunged in it before he reached his office. Dick met him there.

'How was Mount Everest?'

'We could very well have done Mount Everest the rate we were doing. We thought of it. How goes it all? How is my Kaethe, how is your Nicole?'

'All goes smooth domestically. But my God, Franz, we had a rotten scene this morning.'

'How? What was it?'

Dick walked around the room while Franz got in touch with his villa by telephone. After the family exchange was over, Dick said: 'The Morris boy was taken away – there was a row.'

Franz's buoyant face fell.

'I knew he'd left. I met Lladislau on the veranda.'

'What did Lladislau say?'

'Just that young Morris had gone – that you'd tell me about it. What about it?'

'The usual incoherent reasons.'

'He was a devil, that boy.'

'He was a case for anaesthesia,' Dick agreed. 'Anyhow, the father had beaten Lladislau into a colonial subject by the time I came along. What about Lladislau? Do we keep him? I say no – he's not much of a man, he can't seem to cope with anything.' Dick hesitated on the verge of the truth, swung away to give himself space within which to recapitulate. Franz perched on the edge of a desk, still in his linen duster and travelling gloves. Dick said: 'One of the remarks the boy made to his father was that your distinguished collaborator was a drunkard. The man is a fanatic, and the descendant seems to have caught traces of *vin du pays* on me.'

Franz sat down, musing on his lower lip. 'You can tell me at length,' he said finally.

'Why not now?' Dick suggested. 'You must know I'm the last man to abuse liquor.' His eyes and Franz's glinted on each other, pair on pair. 'Lladislau let the man get so worked up that I was on the defensive. It might have happened in front of patients, and you can imagine how hard it could be to defend yourself in a situation like that!'

Franz took off his gloves and coat. He went to the door and told the secretary, 'Don't disturb us.' Coming back into the room he flung himself at the long table and fooled with his mail, reasoning as little as is characteristic of people in such postures, rather summoning up a suitable mask for what he had to say.

'Dick, I know well that you are a temperate, well-balanced man, even though we do not entirely agree on the subject of alcohol. But a time has come – Dick, I must say frankly that I have been aware several times that you have had a drink when it was not the moment to have one. There is some reason. Why not try another leave of abstinence?'

'Absence,' Dick corrected him automatically. 'It's no solution for me to go away.'

They were both chafed, Franz at having his return marred and blurred.

'Sometimes you don't use your common sense, Dick.'

'I never understood what common sense meant applied to complicated problems – unless it means that a general practitioner can perform a better operation than a specialist.'

He was seized by an overwhelming disgust for the situation. To explain, to patch – these were not natural functions at their age – better to continue with the cracked echo of an old truth in the ears.

'This is no go,' he said suddenly.

'Well, that's occurred to me,' Franz admitted. 'Your heart isn't in this project any more, Dick.'

'I know. I want to leave – we could strike some arrangement about taking Nicole's money out gradually.'

'I have thought about that too, Dick – I have seen this coming. I am able to arrange other backing, and it will be possible to take all your money out by the end of the year.'

Dick had not intended to come to a decision so quickly, nor was he prepared for Franz's so ready acquiescence in the break, yet he was relieved. Not without desperation he had long felt the ethics of his profession dissolving into a lifeless mass.

Chapter 4

THE DIVERS WOULD RETURN to the Riviera, which was home. The Villa Diana had been rented again for the summer, so they divided the intervening time between German spas and French cathedral towns where they were always happy for a few days. Dick wrote a little with no particular method; it was one of those parts of life that is an awaiting; not upon Nicole's health, which seemed to thrive on travel, nor upon work, but simply an awaiting. The factor that gave purposefulness to the period was the children.

Dick's interest in them increased with their ages, now eleven and nine. He managed to reach them over the heads of employees on the principle that both the forcing of children and the fear of forcing them were inadequate substitutes for the long, careful watchfulness, the checking and balancing and reckoning of accounts, to the end that there should be no slip below a certain level of duty. He came to know them much better than Nicole did, and in expansive moods over the wines of several countries he talked and played with them at length. They had that wistful charm, almost sadness, peculiar to children who have learned early not to cry or laugh with abandon; they were apparently moved to no extremes of emotion, but content with a simple regimen and the simple pleasures allowed them. They lived on the even tenor found advisable in the experience of old families of the Western world, brought up rather than brought out. Dick thought, for example, that nothing was more conducive to the development of observation than compulsory silence.

Lanier was an unpredictable boy with an inhuman curiosity. 'Well, how many Pomeranians[338] would it take to lick a lion, father?' was typical of the questions with which he harassed Dick. Topsy was easier. She was nine and very fair and exquisitely made like Nicole, and in the past Dick had worried about that. Lately she had become as robust as any American child. He was satisfied with them both, but conveyed the fact to them only in a tacit way. They were not let off breaches of good conduct – 'Either one learns politeness at home,' Dick said, 'or the world teaches it to you with a whip and you may get hurt in the process. What do I care whether Topsy "adores" me or not? I'm not bringing her up to be my wife.'

Another element that distinguished this summer and autumn for the Divers was a plentitude of money. Due to the sale of their interest in the clinic, and to developments in America, there was now so much that the mere spending of it, the care of goods, was an absorption in itself. The style in which they travelled seemed fabulous.

Regard them, for example, as the train slows up at Boyen,[339] where they are to spend a fortnight visiting. The shifting from the *wagon-lit* has begun at the Italian frontier. The governess's maid and Madame Diver's maid have come up from second class to help with the baggage and the dogs. Mlle Bellois will superintend the hand-luggage, leaving the Sealyhams[340] to one maid and the pair of Pekinese[341] to the other. It is not necessarily poverty of spirit that makes a woman surround herself with life – it can be a superabundance of interest, and, except during her flashes of illness, Nicole was capable of being curator of it all. For example with the great quantity of heavy baggage – presently from the van would be unloaded four wardrobe trunks, a shoe trunk, three hat trunks, and two hat boxes, a chest of servants' trunks, a portable filing-cabinet, a medicine case, a spirit-lamp container, a picnic set, four tennis rackets in presses and cases, a phonograph, a typewriter. Distributed among the spaces reserved for family and entourage were two dozen supplementary grips, satchels and packages, each one numbered, down to the tag on the cane case. Thus all of it could be checked up in two minutes on any station platform, some for storage, some for accompaniment from the 'light trip list' or the 'heavy trip list', constantly revised, and carried on metal-edged plaques in Nicole's purse. She had devised the system as a child when travelling with her failing mother. It was equivalent to the system of a regimental supply officer who must think of the bellies and equipment of three thousand men.

The Divers flocked from the train into the early gathered twilight of the valley. The village people watched the debarkation with an awe akin to that which followed the Italian pilgrimages of Lord Byron a century before. Their hostess was the Contessa di Minghetti, lately Mary North. The journey that had begun in a room over the shop of a paperhanger in Newark had ended in an extraordinary marriage.

'Conte di Minghetti' was merely a papal title – the wealth of Mary's husband flowed from his being ruler-owner of manganese deposits in south-western Asia. He was not quite light enough to travel in a

Pullman south of Mason-Dixon;[342] he was of the Kabyle-Berber-Sabaean-Hindu[343] strain that belts across North Africa and Asia, more sympathetic to the European than the mongrel faces of the ports.

When these princely households, one of the East, one of the West, faced each other on the station platform, the splendour of the Divers seemed pioneer simplicity by comparison. Their hosts were accompanied by an Italian major-domo carrying a staff, by a quartet of turbaned retainers on motorcycles, and by two half-veiled females who stood respectfully a little behind Mary and salaamed[344] at Nicole, making her jump with the gesture.

To Mary as well as to the Divers the greeting was faintly comic; Mary gave an apologetic, belittling giggle; yet her voice, as she introduced her husband by his Asiatic title, flew proud and high.

In their rooms as they dressed for dinner, Dick and Nicole grimaced at each other in an awed way: such rich as want to be thought democratic pretend in private to be swept off their feet by swank.

'Little Mary North knows what she wants,' Dick muttered through his shaving cream. 'Abe educated her, and now she's married to a Buddha. If Europe ever goes Bolshevik she'll turn up as the bride of Stalin.'

Nicole looked around from her dressing-case. 'Watch your tongue, Dick, will you?' But she laughed. 'They're very swell. The warships all fire at them or salute them or something. Mary rides in the royal bus in London.'

'All right,' he agreed. As he heard Nicole at the door asking for pins, he called, 'I wonder if I could have some whiskey; I feel the mountain air!'

'She'll see to it,' presently Nicole called through the bathroom door. 'It was one of those women who were at the station. She has her veil off.'

'What did Mary tell you about life?' he asked.

'She didn't say so much – she was interested in high life – she asked me a lot of questions about my genealogy and all that sort of thing, as if I knew anything about it. But it seems the bridegroom has two very tan children by another marriage – one of them ill with some Asiatic thing they can't diagnose. I've got to warn the children. Sounds very peculiar to me. Mary will see how we'd feel about it.' She stood worrying a minute.

'She'll understand,' Dick reassured her. 'Probably the child's in bed.'

At dinner Dick talked to Hosain, who had been at an English public school. Hosain wanted to know about stocks and about Hollywood, and Dick, whipping up his imagination with champagne, told him preposterous tales.

'Billions?' Hosain demanded.

'Trillions,' Dick assured him.

'I didn't truly realise – '

'Well, perhaps millions,' Dick conceded. 'Every hotel guest is assigned a harem – or what amounts to a harem.'

'Other than the actors and directors?'

'Every hotel guest – even travelling salesmen. Why, they tried to send me up a dozen candidates, but Nicole wouldn't stand for it.'

Nicole reproved him when they were in their room alone. 'Why so many highballs? Why did you use your word spic in front of him?'

'Excuse me, I meant smoke.[345] The tongue slipped.'

'Dick, this isn't faintly like you.'

'Excuse me again. I'm not much like myself any more.'

That night Dick opened a bathroom window, giving on a narrow and tubular court of the château, grey as rats but echoing at the moment to plaintive and peculiar music, sad as a flute. Two men were chanting in an Eastern language or dialect full of k's and l's – he leaned out but he could not see them; there was obviously a religious significance in the sounds, and tired and emotionless he let them pray for him too, but what for, save that he should not lose himself in his increasing melancholy, he did not know.

Next day, over a thinly wooded hillside, they shot scrawny birds, distant poor relations to the partridge. It was done in a vague imitation of the English manner, with a corps of inexperienced beaters whom Dick managed to miss by firing only directly overhead.

On their return Lanier was waiting in their suite.

'Father, you said tell you immediately if we were near the sick boy.'

Nicole whirled about, immediately on guard.

' – so, mother,' Lanier continued, turning to her, 'the boy takes a bath every evening and tonight he took his bath just before mine and I had to take mine in his water, and it was dirty.'

'What? Now what?'

'I saw them take Tony out of it, and then they called me into it and the water was dirty.'

'But – did you take it?'

'Yes, mother.'

'Heavens!' she exclaimed to Dick.

He demanded: 'Why didn't Lucienne draw your bath?'

'Lucienne can't. It's a funny heater – it reached out and burned her arm last night and she's afraid of it, so one of those two women – '

'You go in this bathroom and take a bath now.'

'Don't say *I* told you,' said Lanier from the doorway.

Dick went in and sprinkled the tub with sulphur; closing the door he said to Nicole: 'Either we speak to Mary or we'd better get out.'

She agreed and he continued: 'People think their children are constitutionally cleaner than other people's, and their diseases are less contagious.'

Dick came in and helped himself from the decanter, chewing a biscuit savagely in the rhythm of the pouring water in the bathroom.

'Tell Lucienne that she's got to learn about the heater – ' he suggested. At that moment the Asiatic woman came in person to the door.

'El Contessa – '

Dick beckoned her inside and closed the door.

'Is the little sick boy better?' he enquired pleasantly.

'Better, yes, but he still has the eruptions frequently.'

'That's too bad – I'm very sorry. But you see our children mustn't be bathed in his water. That's out of the question – I'm sure your mistress would be furious if she had known you had done a thing like that.'

'I?' She seemed thunderstruck. 'Why, I merely saw your maid had difficulty with the heater – I told her about it and started the water.'

'But with a sick person you must empty the bathwater entirely out, and clean the tub.'

'I?'

Chokingly the woman drew a long breath, uttered a convulsed sob and rushed from the room.

'She mustn't get up on western civilisation at our expense,' he said grimly.

At dinner that night he decided that it must inevitably be a truncated visit: about his own country Hosain seemed to have observed only that there were many mountains and some goats and herders of goats. He was a reserved young man – to draw him out would have required the sincere effort that Dick now reserved for his family. Soon after dinner Hosain left Mary and the Divers to themselves, but the old unity was split – between them lay the restless social fields that Mary was about to conquer. Dick was relieved when, at nine-thirty, Mary received and read a note and got up.

'You'll have to excuse me. My husband is leaving on a short trip – and I must be with him.'

Next morning, hard on the heels of the servant bringing coffee,

Mary entered their room. She was dressed and they were not dressed, and she had the air of having been up for some time. Her face was toughened with quiet jerky fury.

'What is this story about Lanier having been bathed in a dirty bath?'

Dick began to protest, but she cut through: '*What* is this story that you commanded my husband's sister to clean Lanier's tub?'

She remained on her feet staring at them, as they sat impotent as idols in their beds, weighted by their trays. Together they exclaimed: 'His *sister!*'

'That you ordered one of his sisters to clean out a tub!'

'We didn't – ' their voices rang together saying the same thing, ' – I spoke to the native servant – '

'You spoke to Hosain's sister.'

Dick could only say: 'I supposed they were two maids.'

'You were told they were Himadoun.'[346]

'What?' Dick got out of bed and into a robe.

'I explained it to you at the piano night before last. Don't tell me you were too merry to understand.'

'Was that what you said? I didn't hear the beginning. I didn't connect the – we didn't make any connection, Mary. Well, all we can do is see her and apologise.'

'See her and apologise! I explained to you that when the oldest member of the family – when the oldest one marries, well, the two oldest sisters consecrate themselves to being Himadoun, to being his wife's ladies-in-waiting.'

'Was that why Hosain left the house last night?'

Mary hesitated; then nodded.

'He had to – they all left. His honour makes it necessary.'

Now both the Divers were up and dressing; Mary went on: 'And what's all that about the bathwater. As if a thing like that could happen in this house! We'll ask Lanier about it.'

Dick sat on the bedside indicating in a private gesture to Nicole that she should take over. Meanwhile, Mary went to the door and spoke to an attendant in Italian.

'Wait a minute,' Nicole said. 'I won't have that.'

'You accused us,' answered Mary, in a tone she had never used to Nicole before. 'Now I have a right to see.'

'I won't have the child brought in.' Nicole threw on her clothes as though they were chain mail.

'That's all right,' said Dick. 'Bring Lanier in. We'll settle this bathtub matter – fact or myth.'

Lanier, half clothed mentally and physically, gazed at the angered faces of the adults.

'Listen, Lanier,' Mary demanded, 'how did you come to think you were bathed in water that had been used before?'

'Speak up,' Dick added.

'It was just dirty, that was all.'

'Couldn't you hear the new water running, from your room next door?'

Lanier admitted the possibility but reiterated his point – the water was dirty. He was a little awed; he tried to see ahead: 'It couldn't have been running, because – '

They pinned him down.

'Why not?'

He stood in his little kimono arousing the sympathy of his parents and further arousing Mary's impatience – then he said: 'The water was dirty, it was full of soapsuds.'

'When you're not sure what you're saying – ' Mary began, but Nicole interrupted.

'Stop it, Mary. If there were dirty suds in the water it was logical to think it was dirty. His father told him to come – '

'There couldn't have been dirty suds in the water.'

Lanier looked reproachfully at his father, who had betrayed him. Nicole turned him about by the shoulders and sent him out of the room; Dick broke the tenseness with a laugh.

Then, as if the sound recalled the past, the old friendship, Mary guessed how far away from them she had gone and said in a mollifying tone: 'It's always like that with children.'

Her uneasiness grew as she remembered the past. 'You'd be silly to go – Hosain wanted to make this trip anyhow. After all, you're my guests and you just blundered into the thing.' But Dick, made more angry by this obliqueness and the use of the word blunder, turned away and began arranging his effects, saying: 'It's too bad about the young women. I'd like to apologise to the one who came in here.'

'If you'd only listened on the piano seat!'

'But you've gotten so damned dull, Mary. I listened as long as I could.'

'Be quiet!' Nicole advised him.

'I return his compliment,' said Mary bitterly. 'Goodbye, Nicole.' She went out.

After all that there was no question of her coming to see them off; the major-domo arranged the departure. Dick left formal notes for Hosain and the sisters. There was nothing to do except to go, but all of them, especially Lanier, felt bad about it.

'I insist,' insisted Lanier on the train, 'that it was dirty bathwater.'

'That'll do,' his father said. 'You better forget it – unless you want me to divorce you. Did you know there was a new law in France that you can divorce a child?'

Lanier roared with delight and the Divers were unified again – Dick wondered how many more times it could be done.

Chapter 5

NICOLE WENT TO THE WINDOW and bent over the sill to take a look at the rising altercation on the terrace; the April sun shone pink on the saintly face of Augustine, the cook, and blue on the butcher's knife she waved in her drunken hand. She had been with them since their return to Villa Diana in February.

Because of an obstruction of an awning she could see only Dick's head and his hand holding one of his heavy canes with a bronze knob on it. The knife and the cane, menacing each other, were like tripod and short sword in a gladiatorial combat. Dick's words reached her first: ' – care how much kitchen wine you drink but when I find you digging into a bottle of Chablis Moutonne – '[347]

'You talk about drinking!' Augustine cried, flourishing her sabre. 'You drink – all the time!'

Nicole called over the awning: 'What's the matter, Dick?' and he answered in English: 'The old girl has been polishing off the vintage wines. I'm firing her – at least I'm trying to.'

'Heavens! Well, don't let her reach you with that knife.'

Augustine shook her knife up at Nicole. Her old mouth was made of two small intersecting cherries.

'I would like to say, madame, if you knew that your husband drinks over at his Bastide[348] comparatively as a day labourer – '

'Shut up and get out!' interrupted Nicole. 'We'll get the gendarmes.'

'*You'll* get the gendarmes! With my brother in the corps! You – a disgusting American?'

In English Dick called up to Nicole: 'Get the children away from the house till I settle this.'

' – disgusting Americans who come here and drink up our finest wines,' screamed Augustine with the voice of the commune.

Dick mastered a firmer tone.

'You must leave now! I'll pay you what we owe you.'

'Very sure you'll pay me! And let me tell you – ' she came close and waved the knife so furiously that Dick raised his stick, whereupon she rushed into the kitchen and returned with the carving knife reinforced by a hatchet.

The situation was not prepossessing – Augustine was a strong woman and could be disarmed only at the risk of serious results to herself – and severe legal complications which were the lot of one who molested a French citizen. Trying a bluff Dick called up to Nicole: 'Phone the *poste de police*.' Then to Augustine, indicating her armament, 'This means arrest for you.'

'Ha-*ha!*' she laughed demoniacally; nevertheless she came no nearer. Nicole phoned the police but was answered with what was almost an echo of Augustine's laugh. She heard mumbles and passings of the word around – the connection was suddenly broken.

Returning to the window she called down to Dick: 'Give her something extra!'

'If I could get to that phone!' As this seemed impracticable, Dick capitulated. For fifty francs, increased to a hundred as he succumbed to the idea of getting her out hastily, Augustine yielded her fortress, covering the retreat with stormy grenades of '*Salaud!*' She would leave only when her nephew could come for her baggage. Waiting cautiously in the neighbourhood of the kitchen Dick heard a cork pop, but he yielded the point. There was no further trouble – when the nephew arrived, all apologetic, Augustine bade Dick a cheerful, convivial goodbye, and called up 'Au revoir, madame! Bonne chance!' to Nicole's window.

The Divers went to Nice and dined on a bouillabaisse, which is a stew of rock fish and small lobsters, highly seasoned with saffron, and a bottle of cold Chablis. He expressed pity for Augustine.

'I'm not sorry a bit,' said Nicole.

'I'm sorry – and yet I wish I'd shoved her over the cliff.'

There was little they dared talk about in these days; seldom did they find the right word when it counted, it arrived always a moment too late when one could not reach the other any more. Tonight Augustine's outburst had shaken them from their separate reveries; with the burn and chill of the spiced broth and the parching wine they talked.

'We can't go on like this,' Nicole suggested. 'Or can we? – what do you think?' Startled that for the moment Dick did not deny it, she continued, 'Some of the time I think it's my fault – I've ruined you.'

'So I'm ruined, am I?' he enquired pleasantly.

'I didn't mean that. But you used to want to create things – now you seem to want to smash them up.'

She trembled at criticising him in these broad terms – but his enlarging silence frightened her even more. She guessed that something was developing behind the silence, behind the hard, blue eyes, the almost unnatural interest in the children. Uncharacteristic bursts of temper surprised her – he would suddenly unroll a long scroll of contempt for some person, race, class, way of life, way of thinking. It was as though an incalculable story was telling itself inside him, about which she could only guess in the moments when it broke through the surface.

'After all, what do you get out of this?' she demanded.

'Knowing you're stronger every day. Knowing that your illness follows the law of diminishing returns.'

His voice came to her from far off, as though he were speaking of something remote and academic; her alarm made her exclaim, 'Dick!' and she thrust her hand forward to his across the table. A reflex pulled Dick's hand back and he added: 'There's the whole situation to think of, isn't there? There's not just you.' He covered her hand with his and said in the old pleasant voice of a conspirator for pleasure, mischief, profit, and delight: 'See that boat out there?'

It was the motor yacht of T. F. Golding lying placid among the little swells of the Nicean Bay,[349] constantly bound upon a romantic voyage that was not dependent upon actual motion. 'We'll go out there now and ask the people on board what's the matter with them. We'll find out if they're happy.'

'We hardly know him,' Nicole objected.

'He urged us. Besides, Baby knows him – she practically married him, doesn't she – didn't she?'

When they put out from the port in a hired launch it was already summer dusk and lights were breaking out in spasms along the rigging of the *Margin*. As they drew up alongside, Nicole's doubts reasserted themselves.

'He's having a party – '

'It's only a radio,' he guessed.

They were hailed – a huge white-haired man in a white suit looked down at them, calling: 'Do I recognise the Divers?'

'Boat ahoy, *Margin*!'

Their boat moved under the companionway; as they mounted, Golding doubled his huge frame to give Nicole a hand.

'Just in time for dinner.'

A small orchestra was playing astern.

I'm yours for the asking –
but till then you can't ask me to behave –

And as Golding's cyclonic arms blew them aft without touching them, Nicole was sorrier they had come, and more impatient at Dick. Having taken up an attitude of aloofness from the gay people here, at the time when Dick's work and her health were incompatible with going about, they had a reputation as refusers. Riviera replacements during the ensuing years interpreted this as a vague unpopularity. Nevertheless, having taken such a stand, Nicole felt it should not be cheaply compromised for a momentary self-indulgence.

As they passed through the principal salon they saw ahead of them figures that seemed to dance in the half-light of the circular stern. This was an illusion made by the enchantment of the music, the unfamiliar lighting, and the surrounding presence of water. Actually, save for some busy stewards, the guests loafed on a wide divan that followed the curve of the deck. There were a white, a red, a blurred dress, the laundered chests of several men, of whom one, detaching and identifying himself, brought from Nicole a rare little cry of delight.

'Tommy!'

Brushing aside the Gallicism of his formal dip at her hand, Nicole pressed her face against his. They sat, or rather lay down together on the Antoninian bench.[350] His handsome face was so dark as to have lost the pleasantness of deep tan, without attaining the blue beauty of Negroes – it was just worn leather. The foreignness of his pigmentation by unknown suns, his nourishment by strange soils, his tongue awkward with the curl of many dialects, his reactions attuned to odd alarms – these things fascinated and rested Nicole – in the moment of meeting she lay on his bosom, spiritually, going out and out . . . Then self-preservation reasserted itself and retiring to her own world she spoke lightly.

'You look just like all the adventurers in the movies – but why do you have to stay away so long?'

Tommy Barban looked at her, uncomprehending but alert; the pupils of his eyes flashed.

'Five years,' she continued, in throaty mimicry of nothing. '*Much* too long. Couldn't you only slaughter a certain number of creatures and then come back, and breathe air for a while?'

In her cherished presence Tommy Europeanised himself quickly.

'Mais pour nous héros,' he said, 'il nous faut de temps, Nicole. Nous ne pouvons pas faire de petits exercises d'héroisme – il faut faire les grandes compositions.'[351]

'Talk English to me, Tommy.'

'Parlez français avec moi, Nicole.'[352]

'But the meanings are different – in French you can be heroic and gallant with dignity, and you know it. But in English you can't be heroic and gallant without being a little absurd, and you know that too. That gives me an advantage.'

'But after all – ' He chuckled suddenly. 'Even in English I'm brave, heroic and all that.'

She pretended to be groggy with wonderment but he was not abashed.

'I only know what I see in the cinema,' he said.

'Is it all like the movies?'

'The movies aren't so bad – now this Ronald Colman – have you seen his pictures about the Corps d'Afrique du Nord?[353] They're not bad at all.'

'Very well, whenever I go to the movies I'll know you're going through just that sort of thing at that moment.'

As she spoke, Nicole was aware of a small, pale, pretty young woman with lovely metallic hair, almost green in the deck lights, who had been sitting on the other side of Tommy and might have been part either of their conversation or of the one next to them. She had obviously had a monopoly of Tommy, for now she abandoned hope of his attention with what was once called ill grace, and petulantly crossed the crescent of the deck.

'After all, I am a hero,' Tommy said calmly, only half joking. 'I have ferocious courage, *us*ually, something like a lion, something like a drunken man.'

Nicole waited until the echo of his boast had died away in his mind – she knew he had probably never made such a statement before. Then she looked among the strangers, and found, as usual, the fierce neurotics, pretending calm, liking the country only in horror of the city, of the sound of their own voices which had set the tone and pitch . . . She asked: 'Who is the woman in white?'

'The one who was beside me? Lady Caroline Sibley-Biers.' – They listened for a moment to her voice across the way: 'The man's a scoundrel, but he's a cat of the stripe. We sat up all night playing two-handed chemin-de-fer,[354] and he owes me a mille Swiss.'

Tommy laughed and said: 'She is now the wickedest woman in London – whenever I come back to Europe there is a new crop of the wickedest women from London. She's the very latest – though I believe there is now one other who's considered almost as wicked.'

Nicole glanced again at the woman across the deck – she was fragile, tubercular – it was incredible that such narrow shoulders, such puny arms could bear aloft the pennon of decadence, last ensign of the fading empire. Her resemblance was rather to one of John Held's flat-chested flappers[355] than to the hierarchy of tall languid blondes who had posed for painters and novelists since before the war.

Golding approached, fighting down the resonance of his huge bulk, which transmitted his will as through a gargantuan amplifier, and Nicole, still reluctant, yielded to his reiterated points: that the *Margin* was starting for Cannes immediately after dinner; that they could always pack in some caviare and champagne, even though they had dined; that in any case Dick was now on the phone, telling their chauffeur in Nice to drive their car back to Cannes and leave it in front of the Café des Alliés, where the Divers could retrieve it.

They moved into the dining salon and Dick was placed next to Lady Sibley-Biers. Nicole saw that his usually ruddy face was drained of blood; he talked in a dogmatic voice, of which only snatches reached Nicole: '. . . It's all right for you English, you're doing a dance of death . . . Sepoys in the ruined fort,[356] I mean Sepoys at the gate and gaiety in the fort and all that. The green hat, the crushed hat, no future.'

Lady Caroline answered him in short sentences spotted with the terminal 'What?' the double-edged 'Quite!' the depressing 'Cheerio!' that always had a connotation of imminent peril, but Dick appeared oblivious to the warning signals. Suddenly he made a particularly vehement pronouncement, the purport of which eluded Nicole, but she saw the young woman turn dark and sinewy, and heard her answer sharply: 'After all a chep's a chep and a chum's a chum.'

Again he had offended some one – couldn't he hold his tongue a little longer? How long? To death then.

At the piano, a fair-haired young Scotsman from the orchestra (entitled by its drum 'The Ragtime College Jazzes of Edinboro') had begun singing in a Danny Deever monotone, accompanying himself with low chords on the piano. He pronounced his words with great precision, as though they impressed him almost intolerably.

> 'There was a young lady from hell,
> Who jumped at the sound of a bell,
> Because she was bad – bad – bad,
> She jumped at the sound of a bell,
>   From hell (*Boomboom*)
>   From hell (*Toottoot*)
>   There was a young lady from hell –'

'What is all this?' whispered Tommy to Nicole.

The girl on the other side of him supplied the answer: 'Caroline Sibley-Biers wrote the words. He wrote the music.'

'Quelle enfantillage!' Tommy murmured as the next verse began, hinting at the jumpy lady's further predilections. 'On dirait qu'il récite Racine!' [357]

On the surface at least, Lady Caroline was paying no attention to the performance of her work. Glancing at her again Nicole found herself impressed, neither with the character nor the personality, but with the sheer strength derived from an attitude; Nicole thought that she was formidable, and she was confirmed in this point of view as the party rose from table. Dick remained in his seat wearing an odd expression; then he crashed into words with a harsh ineptness.

'I don't like innuendo in these deafening English whispers.'

Already halfway out of the room Lady Caroline turned and walked back to him; she spoke in a low clipped voice purposely audible to the whole company.

'You came to me asking for it – disparaging my countrymen, disparaging my friend, Mary Minghetti. I simply said you were observed associating with a questionable crowd in Lausanne. Is that a deafening whisper? or does it simply deafen *you*?'

'It's still all not loud enough,' said Dick, a little too late. 'So I am actually a notorious – '

Golding crushed out the phrase with his voice saying: 'What! What!' and moved his guests on out, with the threat of his powerful body. Turning the corner of the door Nicole saw that Dick was still sitting at the table. She was furious at the woman for her preposterous statement, equally furious at Dick for having brought them here, for having become fuddled, for having untipped the capped barbs of his irony, for having come off humiliated – she was a little more annoyed because she knew that her taking possession of Tommy Barban on their arrival had first irritated the Englishwoman.

A moment later she saw Dick standing in the gangway, apparently in complete control of himself as he talked with Golding; then for half an hour she did not see him anywhere about the deck and she broke out of an intricate Malay game, played with string and coffee beans, and said to Tommy: 'I've got to find Dick.'

Since dinner the yacht had been in motion westward. The fine night streamed away on either side, the diesel engines pounded softly, there was a spring wind that blew Nicole's hair abruptly when she reached the bow, and she had a sharp lesion of anxiety at seeing Dick standing in the angle by the flagstaff. His voice was serene as he recognised her.

'It's a nice night.'

'I was worried.'

'Oh, you were worried?'

'Oh, don't talk that way. It would give me so much pleasure to think of a little something I could do for you, Dick.'

He turned away from her, towards the veil of starlight over Africa.

'I believe that's true, Nicole. And sometimes I believe that the littler it was, the more pleasure it would give you.'

'Don't talk like that – don't say such things.'

His face, wan in the light that the white spray caught and tossed back to the brilliant sky, had none of the lines of annoyance she had expected. It was even detached; his eyes focused upon her gradually as upon a chessman to be moved; in the same slow manner he caught her wrist and drew her near.

'You ruined me, did you?' he enquired blandly. 'Then we're both ruined. So – '

Cold with terror she put her other wrist into his grip. All right, she would go with him – again she felt the beauty of the night vividly in one moment of complete response and abnegation – all right, then –

– But now she was unexpectedly free and Dick turned his back sighing, 'Tch! tch!'

Tears streamed down Nicole's face – in a moment she heard some one approaching; it was Tommy.

'You found him! Nicole thought maybe you jumped overboard, Dick,' he said, 'because that little English *poule*[358] slanged you.'

'It'd be a good setting to jump overboard,' said Dick mildly.

'Wouldn't it?' agreed Nicole hastily. 'Let's borrow life-preservers and jump over. I think we should do something spectacular. I feel that all our lives have been too restrained.'

Tommy sniffed from one to the other, trying to breathe in the situation with the night. 'We'll go ask the Lady Beer-and-Ale what to do – she should know the latest things. And we should memorise her song "There was a young lady from *l'enfer*". I shall translate it, and make a fortune from its success at the Casino.'

'Are you rich, Tommy?' Dick asked him, as they retraced the length of the boat.

'Not as things go now. I got tired of the brokerage business and went away. But I have good stocks in the hands of friends who are holding it for me. All goes well.'

'Dick's getting rich,' Nicole said. In reaction her voice had begun to tremble.

On the after-deck Golding had fanned three pairs of dancers into action with his colossal paws. Nicole and Tommy joined them and

Tommy remarked: 'Dick seems to be drinking.'

'Only moderately,' she said loyally.

'There are those who can drink and those who can't. Obviously Dick can't. You ought to tell him not to.'

'I!' she exclaimed in amazement. '*I* tell Dick what he should do or shouldn't do!'

But in a reticent way Dick was still vague and sleepy when they reached the pier at Cannes. Golding buoyed him down into the launch of the *Margin*, whereupon Lady Caroline shifted her place conspicuously. On the dock he bowed goodbye with exaggerated formality, and for a moment he seemed about to speed her with a salty epigram, but the bone of Tommy's arm went into the soft part of his and they walked to the attendant car.

'I'll drive you home,' Tommy suggested.

'Don't bother – we can get a cab.'

'I'd like to, if you can put me up.'

On the back seat of the car Dick remained quiescent until the yellow monolith of Golfe Juan was passed, and then the constant carnival at Juan les Pins, where the night was musical and strident in many languages. When the car turned up the hill towards Tarmes, he sat up suddenly, prompted by the tilt of the vehicle, and delivered a peroration: 'A charming representative of the – ' he stumbled momentarily, ' – a firm of – bring me Brains addled *à l'Anglaise*.' Then he went into an appeased sleep, belching now and then contentedly into the soft warm darkness.

Chapter 6

NEXT MORNING Dick came early into Nicole's room. 'I waited till I heard you up. Needless to say I feel badly about the evening – but how about no post-mortems?'

'I'm agreed,' she answered coolly, carrying her face to the mirror.

'Tommy drove us home? Or did I dream it?'

'You know he did.'

'Seems probable,' he admitted, 'since I just heard him coughing. I think I'll call on him.'

She was glad when he left her, for almost the first time in her life – his awful faculty of being right seemed to have deserted him at last.

Tommy was stirring in his bed, waking for *café au lait*.

'Feel all right?' Dick asked.

When Tommy complained of a sore throat he seized at a

professional attitude.

'Better have a gargle or something.'

'You have one?'

'Oddly enough I haven't – probably Nicole has.'

'Don't disturb her.'

'She's up.'

'How is she?'

Dick turned around slowly. 'Did you expect her to be dead because I was tight?' His tone was pleasant. 'Nicole is now made of – of Georgia pine, which is the hardest wood known, except lignum vitæ[359] from New Zealand – '

Nicole, going downstairs, heard the end of the conversation. She knew, as she had always known, that Tommy loved her; she knew he had come to dislike Dick, and that Dick had realised it before he did, and would react in some positive way to the man's lonely passion. This thought was succeeded by a moment of sheerly feminine satisfaction. She leaned over her children's breakfast table and told off instructions to the governess, while upstairs two men were concerned about her.

Later in the garden she was happy; she did not want anything to happen, but only for the situation to remain in suspension as the two men tossed her from one mind to another; she had not existed for a long time, even as a ball.

'Nice, Rabbits, isn't it – Or is it? Hey, Rabbit – hey you! Is it nice? – hey? – Or does it sound very peculiar to you?'

The rabbit, after an experience of practically nothing else and cabbage leaves, agreed after a few tentative shiftings of the nose.

Nicole went on through her garden routine. She left the flowers she cut in designated spots to be brought to the house later by the gardener. Reaching the sea wall she fell into a communicative mood and no one to communicate with; so she stopped and deliberated. She was somewhat shocked at the idea of being interested in another man – but other women have lovers – why not me? In the fine spring morning the inhibitions of the male world disappeared and she reasoned as gaily as a flower, while the wind blew her hair until her head moved with it. Other women have had lovers – the same forces that last night had made her yield to Dick up to the point of death, now kept her head nodding to the wind, content and happy with the logic of, Why shouldn't I?

She sat upon the low wall and looked down upon the sea. But from another sea, the wide swell of fantasy, she had fished out something tangible to lay beside the rest of her loot. If she need not, in her spirit, be for ever one with Dick as he had appeared last night, she must be something in addition, not just an image on his mind, condemned to endless parades around the circumference of a medal.

Nicole had chosen this part of the wall on which to sit, because the cliff shaded to a slanting meadow with a cultivated vegetable garden. Through a cluster of boughs she saw two men carrying rakes and spades and talking in a counterpoint of Niçois and Provençal.[360] Attracted by their words and gestures she caught the sense: 'I laid her down here.'

'I took her behind the vines there.'

'She doesn't care – neither does he. It was that sacred dog. Well, I laid her down here – '

'You got the rake?'

'You got it yourself, you clown.'

'Well, I don't care where you laid her down. Until that night I never even felt a woman's breast against my chest since I married – twelve years ago. And now you tell me – '

'But listen about the dog – '

Nicole watched them through the boughs; it seemed all right what they were saying – one thing was good for one person, another for another. Yet it was a man's world she had overheard; going back to the house she became doubtful again.

Dick and Tommy were on the terrace. She walked through them and into the house, brought out a sketch pad and began a head of Tommy.

'Hands never idle – distaff flying,' Dick said lightly. How could he talk so trivially with the blood still drained down from his cheeks so that the auburn lather of beard showed red as his eyes? She turned to Tommy saying: 'I can always do something. I used to have a nice active little Polynesian ape and juggle him around for hours till people began to make the most dismal rough jokes – '

She kept her eyes resolutely away from Dick. Presently he excused himself and went inside – she saw him pour himself two glasses of water, and she hardened further.

'Nicole – ' Tommy began, but interrupted himself to clear the harshness from his throat.

'I'm going to get you some special camphor rub,' she suggested. 'It's American – Dick believes in it. I'll be just a minute.'

'I must go, really.'

Dick came out and sat down. 'Believes in what?'

When she returned with the jar neither of them had moved, though she gathered they had had some sort of excited conversation about nothing.

The chauffeur was at the door, with a bag containing Tommy's clothes of the night before. The sight of Tommy in clothes borrowed from Dick moved her sadly, falsely, as though Tommy were not able to afford such clothes.

'When you get to the hotel rub this into your throat and chest and then inhale it,' she said.

'Say, there,' Dick murmured as Tommy went down the steps, 'don't give Tommy the whole jar – it has to be ordered from Paris – it's out of stock down here.'

Tommy came back within hearing and the three of them stood in the sunshine, Tommy squarely before the car so that it seemed by leaning forward he would tip it upon his back.

Nicole stepped down to the path.

'Now catch it,' she advised him. 'It's extremely rare.'

She heard Dick grow silent at her side; she took a step off from him and waved as the car drove off with Tommy and the special camphor rub. Then she turned to take her own medicine.

'There was no necessity for that gesture,' Dick said. 'There are four of us here – and for years whenever there's a cough – '

They looked at each other.

'We can always get another jar – ' then she lost her nerve and presently followed him upstairs where he lay down on his own bed and said nothing.

'Do you want lunch to be brought up to you?' she asked.

He nodded and continued to lie quiescent, staring at the ceiling. Doubtfully she went to give the order. Upstairs again she looked into his room – the blue eyes, like searchlights, played on a dark sky. She stood a minute in the doorway, aware of the sin she had committed against him, half afraid to come in . . . She put out her hand as if to rub his head, but he turned away like a suspicious animal. Nicole could stand the situation no longer; in a kitchen-maid's panic she ran downstairs, afraid of what the stricken man above would feed on while she must still continue dry suckling at his lean chest.

In a week Nicole forgot her flash about Tommy – she had not much memory for people and forgot them easily. But in the first hot blast of June she heard he was in Nice. He wrote a little note to them both – and she opened it under the parasol, together with other mail they had brought from the house. After reading it she tossed it over to Dick, and in exchange he threw a telegram into the lap of her beach pyjamas: 'Dears will be at Gausses tomorrow unfortunately without mother am counting on seeing you. ROSEMARY.'

'I'll be glad to see her,' said Nicole, grimly.

Chapter 7

BUT SHE WENT TO THE BEACH with Dick next morning with a renewal of her apprehension that Dick was contriving at some desperate solution. Since the evening on Golding's yacht she had sensed what was going on. So delicately balanced was she between an old foothold that had always guaranteed her security, and the imminence of a leap from which she must alight changed in the very chemistry of blood and muscle, that she did not dare bring the matter into the true forefront of consciousness. The figures of Dick and herself, mutating, undefined, appeared as spooks caught up into a fantastic dance. For months every word had seemed to have an overtone of some other meaning, soon to be resolved under circumstances that Dick would determine. Though this state of mind was perhaps more hopeful – the long years of sheer being had had an enlivening effect on the parts of her nature that early illness had killed, that Dick had not reached – through no fault of his but simply because no one nature can extend entirely inside another – it was still disquieting. The most unhappy aspect of their relations was Dick's growing indifference, at present personified by too much drink; Nicole did not know whether she was to be crushed or spared – Dick's voice, throbbing with insincerity, confused the issue; she couldn't guess how he was going to behave next upon the torturously slow unrolling of the carpet, nor what would happen at the end, at the moment of the leap.

For what might occur thereafter she had no anxiety – she suspected that that would be the lifting of a burden, an unblinding of eyes. Nicole had been designed for change, for flight, with money as fins and wings. The new state of things would be no more than if a racing chassis, concealed for years under the body of a family limousine, should be stripped to its original self. Nicole could feel the fresh breeze already – the wrench it was she feared, and the dark manner of its coming.

The Divers went out on the beach with her white suit and his white trunks very white against the colour of their bodies. Nicole saw Dick peer about for the children among the confused shapes and shadows of many umbrellas, and as his mind temporarily left her, ceasing to grip her, she looked at him with detachment, and decided that he was seeking his children, not protectively but for protection. Probably it was the beach he feared, like a deposed ruler secretly visiting an old court. She had come to hate his world with its delicate jokes and politenesses, forgetting that for many years it was the only world open to her. Let him look at it – his beach, perverted now to the tastes of the tasteless; he could search it for a day and find no stone of the Chinese wall he had once erected around it, no footprint of an old friend.

For a moment Nicole was sorry it was so; remembering the glass he had raked out of the old trash heap, remembering the sailor trunks and sweaters they had bought in a Nice back-street – garments that afterward ran through a vogue in silk among the Paris couturiers, remembering the simple little French girls climbing on the breakwaters crying, 'Dites donc! Dites donc!'[361] like birds, and the ritual of the morning time, the quiet restful extraversion towards sea and sun – many inventions of his, buried deeper than the sand under the span of so few years . . .

Now the swimming place was a 'club', though, like the international society it represented, it would be hard to say who was not admitted.

Nicole hardened again as Dick knelt on the straw mat and looked about for Rosemary. Her eyes followed his, searching among the new paraphernalia, the trapezes over the water, the swinging rings, the portable bath-houses, the floating towers, the searchlights from last night's fêtes, the modernistic buffet, white with a hackneyed motif of endless handlebars.

The water was almost the last place he looked for Rosemary, because few people swam any more in that blue paradise, children and one exhibitionistic valet who punctuated the morning with spectacular dives from a fifty-foot rock – most of Gausse's guests stripped the concealing pyjamas from their flabbiness for only a short hangover dip at one o'clock.

'There she is,' Nicole remarked.

She watched Dick's eyes following Rosemary's track from raft to raft; but the sigh that rocked out of her bosom was something left over from five years ago.

'Let's swim out and speak to Rosemary,' he suggested.

'You go.'

'We'll both go.' She struggled a moment against his pronouncement, but eventually they swam out together, tracing Rosemary by the school of little fish who followed her, taking their dazzle from her, the shining spoon of a trout hook.

Nicole stayed in the water while Dick hoisted himself up beside Rosemary, and the two sat dripping and talking, exactly as if they had never loved or touched each other. Rosemary was beautiful – her youth was a shock to Nicole, who rejoiced, however, that the young girl was less slender by a hairline than herself. Nicole swam around in little rings, listening to Rosemary, who was acting amusement, joy, and expectation – more confident than she had been five years ago.

'I miss mother so, but she's meeting me in Paris, Monday.'

'Five years ago you came here,' said Dick. 'And what a funny little thing you were, in one of those hotel peignoirs!'

'How you remember things! You always did – and always the nice things.'

Nicole saw the old game of flattery beginning again and she dove under water, coming up again to hear: 'I'm going to pretend it's five years ago and I'm a girl of eighteen again. You could always make me feel some you know, kind of, you know, kind of happy way – you and Nicole. I feel as if you're still on the beach there, under one of those umbrellas – the nicest people I'd ever known, maybe ever will.'

Swimming away, Nicole saw that the cloud of Dick's heartsickness had lifted a little as he began to play with Rosemary, bringing out his old expertness with people, a tarnished object of art; she guessed that with a drink or so he would have done his stunts on the swinging rings for her, fumbling through stunts he had once done with ease. She noticed that this summer, for the first time, he avoided high diving.

Later, as she dodged her way from raft to raft, Dick overtook her.

'Some of Rosemary's friends have a speedboat, the one out there. Do you want to aquaplane? I think it would be amusing.'

Remembering that once he could stand on his hands on a chair at the end of a board, she indulged him as she might have indulged Lanier. Last summer on the Zugersee they had played at that pleasant water game, and Dick had lifted a two-hundred-pound man from the board on to his shoulders and stood up. But women marry all their husbands' talents and naturally, afterward, are not so impressed with them as they may keep up the pretence of being. Nicole had not even pretended to be impressed, though she had said 'Yes' to him, and 'Yes, I think so too.'

She knew, though, that he was somewhat tired, that it was only the closeness of Rosemary's exciting youth that prompted the impending effort – she had seen him draw the same inspiration from the new bodies of her children and she wondered coldly if he would make a spectacle of himself. The Divers were older than the others in the boat – the young people were polite, deferential, but Nicole felt an undercurrent of 'Who are these Numbers anyhow?' and she missed

Dick's easy talent of taking control of situations and making them all right – he had concentrated on what he was going to try to do.

The motor throttled down two hundred yards from shore and one of the young men dove flat over the edge. He swam at the aimless twisting board, steadied it, climbed slowly to his knees on it – then got on his feet as the boat accelerated. Leaning back he swung his light vehicle ponderously from side to side in slow, breathless arcs that rode the trailing side-swell at the end of each swing. In the direct wake of the boat he let go his rope, balanced for a moment, then back-flipped into the water, disappearing like a statue of glory, and reappearing as an insignificant head while the boat made the circle back to him.

Nicole refused her turn; then Rosemary rode the board neatly and conservatively, with facetious cheers from her admirers. Three of them scrambled egotistically for the honour of pulling her into the boat, managing, among them, to bruise her knee and hip against the side.

'Now you, doctor,' said the Mexican at the wheel.

Dick and the last young man dove over the side and swam to the board. Dick was going to try his lifting trick and Nicole began to watch with smiling scorn. This physical showing-off for Rosemary irritated her most of all.

When the men had ridden long enough to find their balance, Dick knelt, and putting the back of his neck in the other man's crotch, found the rope through his legs, and slowly began to rise.

The people in the boat, watching closely, saw that he was having difficulties. He was on one knee; the trick was to straighten all the way up in the same motion with which he left his kneeling position. He rested for a moment, then his face contracted as he put his heart into the strain, and lifted.

The board was narrow, the man, though weighing less than a hundred and fifty, was awkward with his weight and grabbed clumsily at Dick's head. When, with a last wrenching effort of his back, Dick stood upright, the board slid sidewise and the pair toppled into the sea.

In the boat Rosemary exclaimed: 'Wonderful! They almost had it.'

But as they came back to the swimmers Nicole watched for a sight of Dick's face. It was full of annoyance as she expected, because he had done the thing with ease only two years ago.

The second time he was more careful. He rose a little, testing the balance of his burden, settled down again on his knee; then, grunting 'Alley oop!' began to rise – but before he could really straighten out, his legs suddenly buckled and he shoved the board away with his feet to avoid being struck as they fell off.

This time when the *Baby Gar*[362] came back it was apparent to all the passengers that he was angry.

'Do you mind if I try that once more?' he called, treading water. 'We almost had it then.'

'Sure. Go ahead.'

To Nicole he looked white-around-the-gills, and she cautioned him: 'Don't you think that's enough for now?'

He didn't answer. The first partner had had plenty and was hauled over the side, the Mexican driving the motorboat obligingly took his place.

He was heavier than the first man. As the boat gathered motion, Dick rested for a moment, belly-down on the board. Then he got beneath the man and took the rope, and his muscles flexed as he tried to rise.

He could not rise. Nicole saw him shift his position and strain upward again, but at the instant when the weight of his partner was full upon his shoulders he became immovable. He tried again – lifting an inch, two inches – Nicole felt the sweat glands of her forehead open as she strained with him – then he was simply holding his ground, then he collapsed back down on his knees with a smack, and they went over, Dick's head barely missing a kick of the board.

'Hurry back!' Nicole called to the driver; even as she spoke she saw him slide under water and she gave a little cry; but he came up again and turned on his back, and the Mexican swam near to help. It seemed for ever till the boat reached them, but when they came alongside at last and Nicole saw Dick floating exhausted and expressionless, alone with the water and the sky, her panic changed suddenly to contempt.

'We'll help you up, doctor . . . Get his foot . . . all right . . . now all together . . . '

Dick sat panting and looking at nothing.

'I knew you shouldn't have tried it,' Nicole could not help saying.

'He'd tired himself the first two times,' said the Mexican.

'It was a foolish thing,' Nicole insisted. Rosemary tactfully said nothing.

After a minute Dick got his breath, panting, 'I couldn't have lifted a paper doll that time.'

An explosive little laugh relieved the tension caused by his failure. They were all attentive to Dick as he disembarked at the dock. But Nicole was annoyed – everything he did annoyed her now.

She sat with Rosemary under an umbrella while Dick went to the buffet for a drink – he returned presently with some sherry for them.

'The first drink I ever had was with you,' Rosemary said, and with a spurt of enthusiasm she added, 'Oh, I'm so glad to see you and *know* you're all right. I was worried – ' Her sentence broke as she changed direction, ' – that maybe you wouldn't be.'

'Did you hear I'd gone into a process of deterioration?'

'Oh, no. I simply – just heard you'd changed. And I'm glad to see with my own eyes it isn't true.'

'It is true,' Dick answered, sitting down with them. 'The change came a long way back – but at first it didn't show. The manner remains intact for some time after the morale cracks.'

'Do you practise on the Riviera?' Rosemary demanded hastily.

'It'd be a good ground to find likely specimens.' He nodded here and there at the people milling about in the golden sand. 'Great candidates. Notice our old friend, Mrs Abrams, playing duchess to Mary North's queen? Don't get jealous about it – think of Mrs Abrams' long climb up the back stairs of the Ritz on her hands and knees and all the carpet dust she had to inhale.'

Rosemary interrupted him. 'But is that really Mary North?' She was regarding a woman sauntering in their direction followed by a small group who behaved as if they were accustomed to being looked at. When they were ten feet away, Mary's glance flickered fractionally over the Divers, one of those unfortunate glances that indicate to the glanced-upon that they have been observed but are to be overlooked, the sort of glance that neither the Divers nor Rosemary Hoyt had ever permitted themselves to throw at anyone in their lives. Dick was amused when Mary perceived Rosemary, changed her plans and came over. She spoke to Nicole with pleasant heartiness, nodded unsmilingly to Dick as if he were somewhat contagious – whereupon he bowed in ironic respect – as she greeted Rosemary.

'I heard you were here. For how long?'

'Until tomorrow,' Rosemary answered.

She, too, saw how Mary had walked through the Divers to talk to her, and a sense of obligation kept her unenthusiastic. No, she could not dine tonight.

Mary turned to Nicole, her manner indicating affection blended with pity.

'How are the children?' she asked.

They came up at the moment, and Nicole gave ear to a request that she overrule the governess on a swimming point.

'No,' Dick answered for her. 'What Mademoiselle says must go.'

Agreeing that one must support delegated authority, Nicole refused their request, whereupon Mary – who in the manner of an Anita Loos heroine[363] had dealings only with *faits accomplis*, who indeed could not have housebroken a French poodle puppy – regarded Dick as though he were guilty of a most flagrant bullying. Dick, chafed by the tiresome performance, enquired with mock solicitude: 'How are your children – and their aunts?'

Mary did not answer; she left them, first draping a sympathetic hand over Lanier's reluctant head. After she had gone Dick said: 'When I think of the time I spent working over her.'

'I like her,' said Nicole.

Dick's bitterness had surprised Rosemary, who had thought of him as all-forgiving, all-comprehending. Suddenly she recalled what it was she had heard about him. In conversation with some State Department people on the boat – Europeanised Americans who had reached a position where they could scarcely have been said to belong to any nation at all, at least not to any great power though perhaps to a Balkan-like state composed of similar citizens – the name of the ubiquitously renowned Baby Warren had occurred and it was remarked that Baby's younger sister had thrown herself away on a dissipated doctor. 'He's not received anywhere any more,' the woman said.

The phrase disturbed Rosemary, though she could not place the Divers as living in any relation to society where such a fact, if fact it was, could have any meaning, yet the hint of a hostile and organised public opinion rang in her ears. 'He's not received anywhere any more.' She pictured Dick climbing the steps of a mansion, presenting cards and being told by a butler: 'We're not receiving you any more'; then proceeding down an avenue only to be told the same thing by the countless other butlers of countless Ambassadors, Ministers, Chargés d'Affaires . . .

Nicole wondered how she could get away. She guessed that Dick, stung into alertness, would grow charming and would make Rosemary respond to him. Sure enough, in a moment his voice managed to qualify everything unpleasant he had said: 'Mary's all right – she's done very well. But it's hard to go on liking people who don't like you.'

Rosemary, falling into line, swayed towards Dick and crooned: 'Oh, you're so nice. I can't imagine anybody not forgiving you anything, no matter what you did to them.' Then feeling that her exuberance had transgressed on Nicole's rights, she looked at the sand exactly between them: 'I wanted to ask you both what you thought of my latest pictures – if you saw them.'

Nicole said nothing, having seen one of them and thought little about it.

'It'll take a few minutes to tell you,' Dick said. 'Let's suppose that

Nicole says to you that Lanier is ill. What do you do in life? What does any one do? They *act* – face, voice, words – the face shows sorrow, the voice shows shock, the words show sympathy.'

'Yes – I understand.'

'But, in the theatre, no. In the theatre all the best comédiennes have built up their reputation by burlesquing the correct emotional responses – fear and love and sympathy.'

'I see.' Yet she did not quite see.

Losing the thread of it, Nicole's impatience increased as Dick continued: 'The danger to an actress is in responding. Again, let's suppose that somebody told you, "Your lover is dead." In life you'd probably go to pieces. But on the stage you're trying to entertain – the audience can do the "responding" for themselves. First the actress has lines to follow, then she has to get the audience's attention back on herself, away from the murdered Chinese or whatever the thing is. So she must do something unexpected. If the audience thinks the character is hard she goes soft on them – if they think she's soft she goes hard. You go all *out* of character – you understand?'

'I don't quite,' admitted Rosemary. 'How do you mean out of character?'

'You do the unexpected thing until you've manœuvred the audience back from the objective fact to yourself. *Then* you slide into character again.'

Nicole could stand no more. She stood up sharply, making no attempt to conceal her impatience. Rosemary, who had been for a few minutes half-conscious of this, turned in a conciliatory way to Topsy.

'Would you like to be an actress when you grow up? I think you'd make a fine actress.'

Nicole stared at her deliberately and in her grandfather's voice said, slow and distinct: 'It's absolutely *out* to put such ideas in the heads of other people's children. Remember, we may have quite different plans for them.' She turned sharply to Dick. 'I'm going to take the car home. I'll send Michelle for you and the children.'

'You haven't driven for months,' he protested.

'I haven't forgotten how.'

Without a glance at Rosemary, whose face was responding violently, Nicole left the umbrella.

In the bath-house, she changed to pyjamas, her expression still hard as a plaque. But she turned into the road of arched pines and the atmosphere changed – with a squirrel's flight on a branch, a wind nudging at the leaves, a cock splitting distant air, with a creep of

sunlight transpiring through the immobility, then the voice of the
beach receded – Nicole relaxed and felt new and happy; her thoughts
were clear as good bells – she had a sense of being cured and in a new
way. Her ego began blooming like a great rich rose as she scrambled
back along the labyrinths in which she had wandered for years. She
hated the beach, resented the places where she had played planet to
Dick's sun.

'Why, I'm almost complete,' she thought. 'I'm practically standing
alone, without him.' And like a happy child, wanting the completion
as soon as possible, and knowing vaguely that Dick had planned for
her to have it, she lay on her bed as soon as she got home and wrote
Tommy Barban in Nice a short provocative letter.

But that was for the daytime – towards evening with the inevitable
diminution of nervous energy, her spirits flagged, and the arrows
flew a little in the twilight. She was afraid of what was in Dick's mind;
again she felt that a plan underlay his current actions and she was
afraid of his plans – they worked well and they had an all-inclusive
logic about them which Nicole was not able to command. She had
somehow given over the thinking to him, and in his absences her
every action seemed automatically governed by what he would like,
so that now she felt inadequate to match her intentions against his.
Yet think she must; she knew at last the number on the dreadful door
of fantasy, the threshold to the escape that was no escape; she knew
that for her the greatest sin now and in the future was to delude
herself. It had been a long lesson but she had learned it. Either you
think – or else others have to think for you and take power from you,
pervert and discipline your natural tastes, civilise and sterilise you.

They had a tranquil supper, with Dick drinking much beer and
being cheerful with the children in the dusky room. Afterwards he
played some Schubert songs[364] and some new jazz from America that
Nicole hummed in her harsh, sweet contralto over his shoulder.

> 'Thank y' father–r
> Thank y' mother–r
> Thanks for meeting up with one another – '

'I don't like that one,' Dick said, starting to turn the page.

'Oh, play it!' she exclaimed. 'Am I going through the rest of life
flinching at the word "father"?'

> ' – Thank the horse that pulled the buggy that night!
> Thank you both for being justabit tight – '[365]

Later they sat with the children on the Moorish roof and watched the fireworks of two casinos, far apart, far down on the shore. It was lonely and sad to be so empty-hearted towards each other.

Next morning, back from shopping in Cannes, Nicole found a note saying that Dick had taken the small car and gone up into Provence for a few days by himself. Even as she read it the phone rang – it was Tommy Barban from Monte Carlo, saying that he had received her letter and was driving over. She felt her lips' warmth in the receiver as she welcomed his coming.

Chapter 8

SHE BATHED AND ANOINTED HERSELF and covered her body with a layer of powder, while her toes crunched another pile on a bath towel. She looked microscopically at the lines of her flanks, wondering how soon the fine, slim edifice would begin to sink squat and earthward. In about six years, but now I'll do – in fact I'll do as well as any one I know.

She was not exaggerating. The only physical disparity between Nicole at present and the Nicole of five years before was simply that she was no longer a young girl. But she was enough ridden by the current youth worship, the moving pictures with their myriad faces of girl-children, blandly represented as carrying on the work and wisdom of the world, to feel a jealousy of youth.

She put on the first ankle-length day dress that she had owned for many years, and crossed herself reverently with Chanel Sixteen.[366] When Tommy drove up at one o'clock she had made her person into the trimmest of gardens.

How good to have things like this, to be worshipped again, to pretend to have a mystery! She had lost two of the great arrogant years in the life of a pretty girl – now she felt like making up for them; she greeted Tommy as if he were one of many men at her feet, walking ahead of him instead of beside him as they crossed the garden towards the market umbrella. Attractive women of nineteen and of twenty-nine are alike in their breezy confidence; on the contrary, the exigent womb of the twenties does not pull the outside world centripetally around itself. The former are ages of insolence, comparable the one to a young cadet, the other to a fighter strutting after combat.

But whereas a girl of nineteen draws her confidence from a surfeit of attention, a woman of twenty-nine is nourished on subtler stuff. Desirous, she chooses her *apéritifs* wisely, or, content, she enjoys the caviare of potential power. Happily she does not seem, in either case, to anticipate the subsequent years when her insight will often be blurred by panic, by the fear of stopping or the fear of going on. But on the landings of nineteen or twenty-nine she is pretty sure that there are no bears in the hall.

Nicole did not want any vague spiritual romance – she wanted an 'affair'; she wanted a change. She realised, thinking with Dick's thoughts, that from a superficial view it was a vulgar business to enter, without emotion, into an indulgence that menaced all of them. On the other hand, she blamed Dick for the immediate situation, and honestly thought that such an experiment might have therapeutic value. All summer she had been stimulated by watching people do exactly what they were tempted to do and pay no penalty for it – moreover, in spite of her intention of no longer lying to herself, she preferred to consider that she was merely feeling her way and that at any moment she could withdraw . . .

In the light shade Tommy caught her up in his white-duck arms and pulled her around to him, looking at her eyes.

'Don't move,' he said. 'I'm going to look at you a great deal from now on.'

There was some scent on his hair, a faint aura of soap from his white clothes. Her lips were tight, not smiling, and they both simply looked for a moment.

'Do you like what you see?' she murmured.

'Parle français.'

'Very well,' and she asked again in French. 'Do you like what you see?'

He pulled her closer.

'I like whatever I see about you.' He hesitated. 'I thought I knew your face but it seems there are some things I didn't know about it. When did you begin to have white crook's eyes?'

She broke away, shocked and indignant, and cried in English: 'Is that why you wanted to talk French?' Her voice quieted as the butler came with sherry. 'So you could be offensive more accurately?'

She parked her small seat violently on the cloth-of-silver chair cushion.

'I have no mirror here,' she said, again in French, but decisively, 'but if my eyes have changed it's because I'm well again. And being well perhaps I've gone back to my true self – I suppose my grandfather was a crook and I'm a crook by heritage, so there we are. Does that satisfy your logical mind?'

He scarcely seemed to know what she was talking about.

'Where's Dick – is he lunching with us?'

Seeing that his remark had meant comparatively little to him she suddenly laughed away its effect.

'Dick's on a tour,' she said. 'Rosemary Hoyt turned up, and either they're together or she upset him so much that he wants to go away and dream about her.'

'You know, you're a little complicated after all.'

'Oh no,' she assured him hastily. 'No, I'm not really – I'm just a – I'm just a whole lot of different simple people.'

Marius brought out melon and an ice pail, and Nicole, thinking irresistibly about her crook's eyes, did not answer; he gave one an entire nut to crack, this man, instead of giving it in fragments to pick at for meat.

'Why didn't they leave you in your natural state?' Tommy demanded presently. 'You are the most dramatic person I have known.'

She had no answer.

'All this taming of women!' he scoffed.

'In any society there are certain – ' She felt Dick's ghost prompting at her elbow but she subsided at Tommy's overtone: 'I've brutalised many men into shape but I wouldn't take a chance on half the number of women. Especially this "kind" bullying – what good does it do anybody? – you or him or anybody?'

Her heart leaped and then sank faintly with a sense of what she owed Dick.

'I suppose I've got – '

'You've got too much money,' he said impatiently 'That's the crux of the matter. Dick can't beat that.'

She considered while the melons were removed.

'What do you think I ought to do?'

For the first time in ten years she was under the sway of a personality other than her husband's. Everything Tommy said to her became part of her for ever.

They drank the bottle of wine while a faint wind rocked the pine needles and the sensuous heat of early afternoon made blinding freckles on the chequered luncheon cloth. Tommy came over behind her and laid his arms along hers, clasping her hands. Their cheeks touched and then their lips and she gasped, half with passion for him, half with the sudden surprise of its force . . .

'Can't you send the governess and the children away for the afternoon?'

'They have a piano lesson. Anyhow I don't want to stay here.'

'Kiss me again.'

A little later, riding towards Nice, she thought: So I have white crook's eyes, have I? Very well then, better a sane crook than a mad puritan.

His assertion seemed to absolve her from all blame or responsibility and she had a thrill of delight in thinking of herself in a new way. New vistas appeared ahead, peopled with the faces of many men, none of whom she need obey or even love. She drew in her breath, hunched her shoulders with a wriggle and turned to Tommy.

'Have we got to go all the way to your hotel at Monte Carlo?'

He brought the car to a stop with a squeak of tyres.

'No!' he answered. 'And my God, I have never been so happy as I am this minute.'

They had passed through Nice following the blue coast and begun to mount to the middling-high Corniche. Now Tommy turned sharply down to the shore, ran out a blunt peninsula, and stopped in the rear of a small shore hotel.

Its tangibility frightened Nicole for a moment. At the desk an American was arguing interminably with the clerk about the rate of exchange. She hovered, outwardly tranquil but inwardly miserable, as Tommy filled out the police blanks – his real, hers false. Their room was a Mediterranean room, almost ascetic, almost clean, darkened to the glare of the sea. Simplest of pleasures – simplest of places. Tommy ordered two cognacs, and when the door closed behind the waiter, he sat in the only chair, dark, scarred and handsome, his eyebrows arched and upcurling, a fighting Puck,[367] an earnest Satan.

Before they had finished the brandy they suddenly moved together and met standing up; then they were sitting on the bed and he kissed her hardy knees. Struggling a little still, like a decapitated animal, she forgot about Dick and her new white eyes, forgot Tommy himself and sank deeper into the minutes and the moment.

. . . When he got up to open a shutter and find out what caused the increasing clamour below their windows, his figure was darker and stronger than Dick's, with high lights along the rope-twists of muscle. Momentarily he had forgotten her too – almost in the second of his flesh breaking from hers she had a foretaste that things were going to be different than she had expected. She felt the nameless fear which precedes all emotions, joyous or sorrowful, inevitably as a hum of thunder precedes a storm.

Tommy peered cautiously from the balcony and reported.

'All I can see is two women on the balcony below this. They're talking about weather and tipping back and forth in American rocking-chairs.'

'Making all that noise?'

'The noise is coming from somewhere below them. Listen.'

> 'Oh, way down South in the land of cotton
> Hotels bum and business rotten
> Look away – '[368]

'It's Americans.'

Nicole flung her arms wide on the bed and stared at the ceiling; the powder had dampened on her to make a milky surface. She liked the bareness of the room, the sound of the single fly navigating overhead. Tommy brought the chair over to the bed and swept the clothes off it to sit down; she liked the economy of the weightless dress and espadrilles that mingled with his ducks upon the floor.

He inspected the oblong white torso joined abruptly to the brown limb and head, and said, laughing gravely: 'You are all new like a baby.'

'With white eyes.'

'I'll take care of that.'

'It's very hard taking care of white eyes – especially the ones made in Chicago.'

'I know all the old Languedoc[369] peasant remedies.'

'Kiss me, on the lips, Tommy.'

'That's so American,' he said, kissing her nevertheless. 'When I was in America last there were girls who would tear you apart with their lips, tear themselves too, until their faces were scarlet with the blood around the lips all brought out in a patch – but nothing further.'

Nicole leaned up on one elbow.

'I like this room,' she said.

He looked around.

'I find it somewhat meagre. Darling, I'm glad you wouldn't wait until we got to Monte Carlo.'

'Why only meagre? Why, this is a wonderful room, Tommy – like the bare tables in so many Cézannes and Picassos.'

'I don't know.' He did not try to understand her. 'There's that noise again. My God, has there been a murder?'

He went to the window and reported once more: 'It seems to be two American sailors fighting and a lot more cheering them on. They are from your battleship offshore.' He wrapped a towel around himself and went farther out on the balcony. 'They have *poules* with them. I have heard about this now – the women follow them from place to place wherever the ship goes. But what women! one would think with their pay they could find better women! Why the women who followed Korniloff!³⁷⁰ Why, we never looked at anything less than a ballerina!'

Nicole was glad he had known so many women, so that the word itself meant nothing to him; she would be able to hold him so long as the person in her transcended the universals of her body.

'Hit him where it hurts!'

'Yah-h-h-!'

'Hey, what I tell you get inside that right!'

'Come on, Dulschmit, you son!'

'Yaa-Yaa!'

'YAA-YEH-YAH!'

Tommy turned away.

'This place seems to have outlived its usefulness, you agree?'

She agreed, but they clung together for a moment before dressing, and then for a while longer it seemed as good enough a place as any . . .

Dressing at last Tommy exclaimed: '*My God*, those two women in the rocking-chairs on the balcony below us haven't moved. They're trying to talk this matter out of existence. They're here on an economical holiday, and all the American navy and all the whores in Europe couldn't spoil it.'

He came over gently and surrounded her, pulling the shoulder strap of her slip into place with his teeth; then a sound split the air outside: Cr-ACK-BOOM-m-*m*! It was the battleship sounding a recall.

Now, down below their window, it was pandemonium indeed – for the boat was moving to shores as yet unannounced. Waiters called accounts and demanded settlements in impassioned voices, there were oaths and denials; the tossing of bills too large and change too small; pass-outs were assisted to the boats, and the voices of the naval police chopped with quick commands through all voices. There were cries, tears, shrieks, promises as the first launch shoved off and the women crowded forward on the wharf, screaming and waving.

Tommy saw a girl rush out upon the balcony below waving a napkin, and before he could see whether or not the rocking English-women gave in at last and acknowledged her presence, there was a knock at their own door. Outside, excited female voices made them agree to unlock it, disclosing two girls, young, thin and barbaric, unfound rather than lost, in the hall. One of them wept chokingly.

'Kwee wave off your porch?'³⁷¹ implored the other in passionate American. 'Kwee please? Wave at the boy friends? Kwee, please. The other rooms is all locked.'

'With pleasure,' Tommy said.

The girls rushed out on the balcony and presently their voices struck a loud treble over the din.

' 'By, Charlie! Charlie, look *up!'*

'Send a wire gen'al alivery Nice!'

'Charlie! He don't see me.'

One of the girls hoisted her skirt suddenly, pulled and ripped at her pink step-ins and tore them to a sizable flag; then, screaming 'Ben! Ben!' she waved it wildly. As Tommy and Nicole left the room it still fluttered against the blue sky. Oh, say, can you see the tender colour of remembered flesh? – while at the stern of the battleship rose in rivalry the Star-Spangled Banner.[372]

They dined at the new Beach Casino at Monte Carlo . . . much later they swam in Beaulieu in a roofless cavern of white moonlight formed by a circlet of pale boulders about a cup of phosphorescent water, facing Monaco and the blur of Menton.[373] She liked his bringing her there to the eastward vision and the novel tricks of wind and water; it was all as new as they were to each other. Symbolically she lay across his saddle-bow as surely as if he had wolfed her away from Damascus and they had come out upon the Mongolian plain. Moment by moment all that Dick had taught her fell away and she was ever nearer to what she had been in the beginning, prototype of that obscure yielding up of swords that was going on in the world about her. Tangled with love in the moonlight she welcomed the anarchy of her lover.

They awoke together finding the moon gone down and the air cool. She struggled up demanding the time and Tommy called it roughly at three.

'I've got to go home then.'

'I thought we'd sleep in Monte Carlo.'

'No. There's a governess and the children. I've got to roll in before daylight.'

'As you like.'

They dipped for a second, and when he saw her shivering he rubbed her briskly with a towel. As they got into the car with their heads still damp, their skins fresh and glowing, they were loath to start back. It was very bright where they were and as Tommy kissed her she felt him losing himself in the whiteness of her cheeks and her white teeth and her cool brow and the hand that touched his face. Still attuned to Dick, she waited for interpretation or qualification; but none was forthcoming. Reassured sleepily and happily that none would be, she sank low in the seat and drowsed until the sound of the motor changed and she felt them climbing towards Villa Diana. At the gate she kissed him an almost automatic goodbye. The sound of her feet on the walk was changed, the night noises of the garden were suddenly in the past but she was glad, none the less, to be back. The day had progressed at a staccato rate, and in spite of its satisfactions she was not habituated to such strain.

Chapter 9

AT FOUR O'CLOCK next afternoon a station taxi stopped at the gate and Dick got out. Suddenly off-balance, Nicole ran from the terrace to meet him, breathless with her effort at self-control.

'Where's the car?' she asked.

'I left it in Arles. I didn't feel like driving any more.'

'I thought from your note that you'd be several days.'

'I ran into a mistral and some rain.'

'Did you have fun?'

'Just as much fun as anybody has running away from things. I drove Rosemary as far as Avignon and put her on her train there.' They walked towards the terrace together, where he deposited his bag. 'I didn't tell you in the note because I thought you'd imagine a lot of things.'

'That was very considerate of you.' Nicole felt surer of herself now.

'I wanted to find out if she had anything to offer – the only way was to see her alone.'

'Did she have – anything to offer?'

'Rosemary didn't grow up,' he answered. 'It's probably better that way. What have you been doing?'

She felt her face quiver like a rabbit's.

'I went dancing last night – with Tommy Barban. We went –'

He winced, interrupting her.

'Don't tell me about it. It doesn't matter what you do, only I don't want to know anything definitely.'

'There isn't anything to know.'

'All right, all right.' Then as if he had been away a week: 'How are the children?'

The phone rang in the house.

'If it's for me I'm not home,' said Dick turning away quickly. 'I've got some things to do over in the workroom.'

Nicole waited till he was out of sight behind the well; then she went into the house and took up the phone.

'Nicole, comment vas-tu?'[374]

'Dick's home.'

He groaned.

'Meet me here in Cannes,' he suggested. 'I've got to talk to you.'

'I can't.'

'Tell me you love me.' Without speaking she nodded at the receiver; he repeated, 'Tell me you love me.'

'Oh, I do,' she assured him. 'But there's nothing to be done right now.'

'Of course there is,' he said impatiently. 'Dick sees it's over between you two – it's obvious he has quit. What does he expect you to do?'

'I don't know. I'll have to – ' She stopped herself from saying ' – to wait until I can ask Dick,' and instead finished with: 'I'll write and I'll phone you tomorrow.'

She wandered about the house rather contentedly, resting on her achievement. She was a mischief, and that was a satisfaction; no longer was she a huntress of corralled game. Yesterday came back to her now in innumerable detail – detail that began to overlay her memory of similar moments when her love for Dick was fresh and intact. She began to slight that love, so that it seemed to have been tinged with sentimental habit from the first. With the opportunistic memory of women she scarcely recalled how she had felt when she and Dick had possessed each other in secret places around the corners of the world, during the month before they were married. Just so had she lied to Tommy last night, swearing to him that never before had she so entirely, so completely, so utterly . . .

. . . then remorse for this moment of betrayal, which so cavalierly belittled a decade of her life, turned her walk towards Dick's sanctuary.

Approaching noiselessly she saw him behind his cottage, sitting in a steamer chair by the cliff wall, and for a moment she regarded him silently. He was thinking, he was living a world completely his own and in the small motions of his face, the brow raised or lowered, the eyes narrowed or widened, the lips set and reset, the play of his hands, she saw him progress from phase to phase of his own story spinning out inside him, his own, not hers. Once he clenched his fists and leaned forward, once it brought into his face an expression of torment and despair – when this passed its stamp lingered in his eyes. For almost the first time in her life she was sorry for him – it is hard for those who have once been mentally afflicted to be sorry for those who are well, and though Nicole often paid lip-service to the fact that he had led her back to the world she had forfeited, she had thought of him really as an inexhaustible energy, incapable of fatigue – she forgot the troubles she caused him at the moment when she forgot the troubles of her own that had prompted her. That he no longer controlled her – did he know that? Had he willed it all? – she felt as sorry for him as she had sometimes felt for Abe North and his ignoble destiny, sorry as for the helplessness of infants and the old.

She went up to him and, putting her arm around his shoulder and touching their heads together said: 'Don't be sad.'

He looked at her coldly.

'Don't touch me!' he said.

Confused she moved a few feet away.

'Excuse me,' he continued abstractedly. 'I was just thinking what I thought of you – '

'Why not add the new classification to your book?'

'I have thought of it – "Furthermore and beyond the psychoses and neuroses – " '

'I didn't come over here to be disagreeable.'

'Then why *did* you come, Nicole? I can't do anything for you any more. I'm trying to save myself.'

'From my contamination?'

'My profession throws me in contact with questionable company sometimes.'

She wept with anger at the abuse.

'You're a coward! You've made a failure of your life, and you want to blame it on me.'

While he did not answer she began to feel the old hypnotism of his intelligence, sometimes exercised without power but always with substrata of truth under truth which she could not break or even crack. Again she struggled with it, fighting him with her small, fine eyes, with the plush arrogance of a top dog, with her nascent transference to another man, with the accumulated resentment of years; she fought him with her money and her faith that her sister disliked him and was behind her now; with the thought of the new enemies he was making with his bitterness, with her quick guile against his wining and dining slowness, her health and beauty against his physical deterioration, her unscrupulousness against his moralities – for this inner battle she used even her weaknesses – fighting bravely and courageously with the old cans and crockery and bottles, empty receptacles of her expiated sins, outrages, mistakes. And suddenly, in the space of two minutes, she achieved her victory and justified herself to herself without lie or subterfuge, cut the cord for ever. Then she walked, weak in the legs, and sobbing coolly, towards the household that was hers at last.

Dick waited until she was out of sight. Then he leaned his head forward on the parapet. The case was finished. Dr Diver was at liberty.

Chapter 10

AT TWO O'CLOCK that night the phone woke Nicole and she heard Dick answer it from what they called the restless bed, in the next room.

'Oui, oui . . . mais à qui est-ce-que je parle? . . . Oui . . .'[375] His voice woke up with surprise. 'But can I speak to one of the ladies, Sir the Officer? They are both ladies of the very highest prominence, ladies of connections that might cause political complications of the most serious . . . It is a fact, I swear to you . . . Very well, you will see.'

He got up and, as he absorbed the situation, his self-knowledge assured him that he would undertake to deal with it – the old fatal pleasingness, the old forceful charm, swept back with its cry of 'Use me!' He would have to go fix this thing that he didn't care a damn about, because it had early become a habit to be loved, perhaps from the moment when he had realised that he was the last hope of a decaying clan. On an almost parallel occasion, back in Dohmler's clinic on the Zürichsee, realising this power, he had made his choice, chosen Ophelia,[376] chosen the sweet poison and drunk it. Wanting above all to be brave and kind, he had wanted, even more than that, to be loved. So it had been. So it would ever be, he saw, simultaneously with the slow archaic tinkle from the phone box as he rang off.

There was a long pause. Nicole called, 'What is it? Who is it?'

Dick had begun to dress even as he hung up the phone.

'It's the *poste de police* in Antibes – they're holding Mary North and that Sibley-Biers. It's something serious – the agent wouldn't tell me; he kept saying "pas de mortes – pas d'automobiles",[377] but he implied it was just about everything else.'

'Why on earth did they call on you? It sounds very peculiar to me.'

'They've got to get out on bail to save their faces; and only some property owner in the Alpes Maritimes[378] can give bail.'

'They had their nerve.'

'I don't mind. However, I'll pick up Gausse at the hotel – '

Nicole stayed awake after he had departed, wondering what offence they could have committed; then she slept. A little after three when

Dick came in she sat up stark awake saying, 'What?' as if to a character in her dream.

'It was an extraordinary story – ' Dick said. He sat on the foot of her bed, telling her how he had roused old Gausse from an Alsatian coma,[379] told him to clean out his cash drawer, and driven him to the police station.

'I don't like to do something for that *Anglaise*,' Gausse grumbled.

Mary North and Lady Caroline, dressed in the costume of French sailors, lounged on a bench outside the two dingy cells. The latter had the outraged air of a Briton who momentarily expected the Mediterranean fleet to steam up to her assistance. Mary Minghetti was in a condition of panic and collapse – she literally flung herself at Dick's stomach as though that were the point of greatest association, imploring him to do something. Meanwhile the chief of police explained the matter to Gausse, who listened to each word with reluctance, divided between being properly appreciative of the officer's narrative gift and showing that, as the perfect servant, the story had no shocking effect on him.

'It was merely a lark,' said Lady Caroline with scorn. 'We were pretending to be sailors on leave, and we picked up two silly girls. They got the wind up and made a rotten scene in a lodging-house.'

Dick nodded gravely, looking at the stone floor, like a priest in the confessional – he was torn between a tendency to ironic laughter and another tendency to order fifty stripes of the cat and a fortnight of bread and water. The lack, in Lady Caroline's face, of any sense of evil, except the evil wrought by cowardly Provençal girls and stupid police, confounded him; yet he had long concluded that certain classes of English people lived upon a concentrated essence of the antisocial that, in comparison, reduced the gorgings of New York to something like a child contracting indigestion from ice cream.

'I've got to get out before Hosain hears about this,' Mary pleaded. 'Dick, you can always arrange things – you always could. Tell 'em we'll go right home, tell 'em we'll pay anything.'

'I shall not,' said Lady Caroline disdainfully. 'Not a shilling. But I shall jolly well find out what the Consulate in Cannes has to say about this.'

'No, no!' insisted Mary. 'We've got to get out tonight.'

'I'll see what I can do,' said Dick, and added, 'but money will certainly have to change hands.' Looking at them as though they were the innocents that he knew they were not, he shook his head: 'Of all the crazy stunts!'

Lady Caroline smiled complacently.

'You're an insanity doctor, aren't you? You ought to be able to help us – and Gausse has *got* to!'

At this point Dick went aside with Gausse and talked over the old man's findings. The affair was more serious than had been indicated – one of the girls whom they had picked up was of a respectable family. The family were furious, or pretended to be; a settlement would have to be made with them. The other girl, a girl of the port, could be more easily dealt with. There were French statutes that would make conviction punishable by imprisonment or, at the very least, public expulsion from the country. In addition to the difficulties, there was a growing difference in tolerance between such towns-people as benefited by the foreign colony and the ones who were annoyed by the consequent rise of prices. Gausse, having summarised the situation, turned it over to Dick. Dick called the chief of police into conference.

'Now you know that the French government wants to encourage American touring – so much so that in Paris this summer there's an order that Americans can't be arrested except for the most serious offences.'

'This is serious enough, my God.'

'But look now – you have their *cartes d'identité*?'

'They had none. They had nothing – two hundred francs and some rings. Not even shoe-laces that they could have hung themselves with!'

Relieved that there had been no *cartes d'identité* Dick continued.

'The Italian Countess is still an American citizen. She is the granddaughter – ' he told a string of lies slowly and portentously, 'of John D. Rockefeller Mellon.[380] You have heard of him?'

'Yes, oh heavens, yes. You mistake me for a nobody?'

'In addition she is the niece of Lord Henry Ford[381] and so connected with the Renault and Citroën companies – ' He thought he had better stop here. However, the sincerity of his voice had begun to affect the officer, so he continued: 'To arrest her is just as if you arrested a great royalty of England. It might mean – War!'

'But how about the Englishwoman?'

'I'm coming to that. She is affianced to the brother of the Prince of Wales – the Duke of Buckingham.'

'She will be an exquisite bride for him.'

'Now we are prepared to give – ' Dick calculated quickly, 'one thousand francs to each of the girls – and an additional thousand to the father of the "serious" one. Also two thousand in addition, for you to distribute as you think best – ' he shrugged his shoulders, ' –

among the men who made the arrest, the lodging-house keeper and so forth. I shall hand you the five thousand and expect you to do the negotiating immediately. Then they can be released on bail on some charge like disturbing the peace, and whatever fine there is will be paid before the magistrate tomorrow – by messenger.'

Before the officer spoke Dick saw by his expression that it would be all right. The man said hesitantly, 'I have made no entry because they have no *cartes d'identité*. I must see – give me the money.'

An hour later Dick and M. Gausse dropped the women by the Majestic Hotel, where Lady Caroline's chauffeur slept in her landau-let.[382]

'Remember,' said Dick, 'you owe Monsieur Gausse a hundred dollars apiece.'

'All right,' Mary agreed, 'I'll give him a cheque tomorrow – and something more.'

'Not I!' Startled, they all turned to Lady Caroline, who, now entirely recovered, was swollen with righteousness. 'The whole thing was an outrage. By no means did I authorise you to give a hundred dollars to those people.'

Little Gausse stood beside the car, his eyes blazing suddenly.

'You won't pay me?'

'Of course she will,' said Dick.

Suddenly the abuse that Gausse had once endured as a bus boy in London flamed up and he walked through the moonlight up to Lady Caroline.

He whipped a string of condemnatory words about her, and as she turned away with a frozen laugh, he took a step after her and swiftly planted his little foot in the most celebrated of targets. Lady Caroline, taken by surprise, flung up her hands like a person shot as her sailor-clad form sprawled forward on the sidewalk.

Dick's voice cut across her raging: 'Mary, you quiet her down! or you'll both be in leg-irons in ten minutes!'

On the way back to the hotel old Gausse said not a word, until they passed the Juan-les-Pins Casino, still sobbing and coughing with jazz; then he sighed forth, 'I have never seen women like this sort of women. I have known many of the great courtesans of the world, and for them I have much respect often, but women like these women I have never seen before.'

Chapter 11

DICK AND NICOLE were accustomed to go together to the barber, and have haircuts and shampoos in adjoining rooms. From Dick's side Nicole could hear the snip of shears, the count of change, the *voilàs* and *pardons*. The day after his return they went down to be shorn and washed in the perfumed breeze of the fans.

In front of the Carleton Hotel,[383] its windows as stubbornly blank to the summer as so many cellar doors, a car passed them and Tommy Barban was in it. Nicole's momentary glimpse of his expression, taciturn and thoughtful and, in the second of seeing her, wide-eyed and alert, disturbed her. She wanted to be going where he was going. The hour with the hairdresser seemed one of the wasteful intervals that composed her life, another little prison. The *coiffeuse* in her white uniform, faintly sweating lip-rouge and cologne, reminded her of many nurses.

In the next room Dick dozed under an apron and a lather of soap. The mirror in front of Nicole reflected the passage between the men's side and the women's, and Nicole started up at the sight of Tommy entering and wheeling sharply into the men's shop. She knew with a flush of joy that there was going to be some sort of showdown.

She heard fragments of its beginning.

'Hello, I want to see you.'

'. . . serious.'

'. . . serious.'

'. . . perfectly agreeable.'

In a minute Dick came into Nicole's booth, his expression emerging annoyed from behind the towel of his hastily rinsed face.

'Your friend has worked himself up into a state. He wants to see us together, so I agreed to have it over with. Come along!'

'But my hair – it's half-cut.'

'Never mind – come along!'

Resentfully she had the staring *coiffeuse* remove the towels.

Feeling messy and unadorned she followed Dick from the hotel. Outside Tommy bent over her hand.

'We'll go to the Café des Alliés,' said Dick.

'Where we can be alone,' Tommy agreed.

Under the arching trees, central in summer, Dick asked: 'Will you take anything, Nicole?'

'A *citron pressé*.'[384]

'For me a *demi*,' said Tommy.

'The Blackenwite with siphon,' said Dick.

'Il n'y a plus de Blackenwite. Nous n'avons que la Johnny Walkair.'

'Ça va.'[385]

> 'She's – not – wired for sound
> but on the quiet
> you ought to try it – '

'Your wife does not love you,' said Tommy suddenly. 'She loves me.'

The two men regarded each other with a curious impotence of expression. There can be little communication between men in that position, for their relation is indirect, and consists of how much each of them has possessed or will possess of the woman in question, so that their emotions pass through her divided self as through a bad telephone connection.

'Wait a minute,' Dick said. 'Donnez-moi du gin et du siphon.'[386]

'Bien, monsieur.'

'All right, go on, Tommy.'

'It's very plain to me that your marriage to Nicole has run its course. She is through. I've waited five years for that to be so.'

'What does Nicole say?'

They both looked at her.

'I've gotten very fond of Tommy, Dick.'

He nodded.

'You don't care for me any more,' she continued. 'It's all just habit. Things were never the same after Rosemary.'

Unattracted to this angle, Tommy broke in sharply with: 'You don't understand Nicole. You treat her always like a patient because she was once sick.'

They were suddenly interrupted by an insistent American, of sinister aspect, vending copies of the *Herald* and of the *Times* fresh from New York.

'Got everything here, buddies,' he announced. 'Been here long?'

'Cessez cela! Allez ouste!'[387] Tommy cried, and then to Dick, 'Now no woman would stand such – '

'Buddies,' interrupted the American again. 'You think I'm wasting my time – but lots of others don't.' He brought a grey clipping from his purse – and Dick recognised it as he saw it. It cartooned millions of Americans pouring from liners with bags of gold. 'You think I'm not going to get part of that? Well, I am. I'm just over from Nice for the Tour de France.'[388]

As Tommy got him off with a fierce 'allez-vous-en',[389] Dick identified him as the man who had once hailed him in the Rue des Saints-Anges, five years before.

'When does the Tour de France get here?' he called after him.

'Any minute now, buddy.'

He departed at last with a cheery wave and Tommy returned to Dick.

'Elle doit avoir plus avec moi qu'avec vous.'[390]

'Speak English! What do you mean "*doit avoir*"?'

' "Doit avoir"? Would have more happiness with me.'

'You'd be new to each other. But Nicole and I have had much happiness together, Tommy.'

'L'amour de famille,'[391] Tommy said, scoffing.

'If you and Nicole married won't that be "l'amour de famille"?' The increasing commotion made him break off; presently it came to a serpentine head on the promenade and a group, presently a crowd, of people sprung from hidden siestas, lined the kerbstone.

Boys sprinted past on bicycles, automobiles jammed with elaborate betasselled sportsmen slid up the street, high horns tooted to announce the approach of the race, and unsuspected cooks in undershirts appeared at restaurant doors as around a bend a procession came into sight. First was a lone cyclist in a red jersey, toiling intent and confident out of the westering sun, passing to the melody of a high chattering cheer. Then three together in a harlequinade of faded colour, legs caked yellow with dust and sweat, faces expressionless, eyes heavy and endlessly tired.

Tommy faced Dick, saying: 'I think Nicole wants a divorce – I suppose you'll make no obstacles?'

A troupe of fifty more swarmed after the first bicycle racers, strung out over two hundred yards; a few were smiling and self-conscious, a few obviously exhausted, most of them indifferent and weary. A retinue of small boys passed, a few defiant stragglers, a light truck carried the dupes of accident and defeat. They were back at the table. Nicole wanted Dick to take the initiative, but he seemed content to sit with his face half-shaved matching her hair half-cut.

'Isn't it true you're not happy with me any more?' Nicole continued. 'Without me you could get to your work again – you could work better if you didn't worry about me.'

Tommy moved impatiently.

'That is so useless. Nicole and I love each other, that's all there is to it.'

'Well, then,' said the doctor, 'since it's all settled, suppose we go back to the barbershop.'

Tommy wanted a row: 'There are several points – '

'Nicole and I will talk things over,' said Dick equitably. 'Don't worry – I agree in principal, and Nicole and I understand each other. There's less chance of unpleasantness if we avoid a three-cornered discussion.'

Unwillingly acknowledging Dick's logic, Tommy was moved by an irresistible racial tendency to chisel for an advantage.

'Let it be understood that from this moment,' he said, 'I stand in the position of Nicole's protector until details can be arranged. And I shall hold you strictly accountable for any abuse of the fact that you continue to inhabit the same house.'

'I never did go in for making love to dry loins,' said Dick.

He nodded, and walked off towards the hotel with Nicole's whitest eyes following him.

'He was fair enough,' Tommy conceded. 'Darling, will we be together tonight?'

'I suppose so.'

So it had happened – and with a minimum of drama; Nicole felt outguessed, realising that from the episode of the camphor-rub, Dick had anticipated everything. But also she felt happy and excited, and the odd little wish that she could tell Dick all about it faded quickly. But her eyes followed his figure until it became a dot and mingled with the other dots in the summer crowd.

Chapter 12

THE DAY BEFORE Dr Diver left the Riviera he spent all his time with his children. He was not young any more with a lot of nice thoughts and dreams to have about himself, so he wanted to remember them well. The children had been told that this winter they would be with their aunt in London and that soon they were going to come and see him in America. Fräulein was not to be discharged without his consent.

He was glad he had given so much to the little girl – about the boy he was more uncertain – always he had been uneasy about what he had to give to the ever-climbing, ever-clinging, breast-searching young. But, when he said goodbye to them, he wanted to lift their beautiful heads off their necks and hold them close for hours.

He embraced the old gardener who had made the first garden at Villa Diana six years ago; he kissed the Provençal girl who helped with the children. She had been with them for almost a decade and she fell on her knees and cried until Dick jerked her to her feet and gave her three hundred francs. Nicole was sleeping late, as had been agreed upon – he left a note for her, and one for Baby Warren, who was just back from Sardinia and staying at the house. Dick took a big drink from a bottle of brandy three feet high, holding ten quarts, that some one had presented them with.

Then he decided to leave his bags by the station in Cannes and take a last look at Gausse's beach.

The beach was peopled with only an advance guard of children when Nicole and her sister arrived that morning. A white sun, chivied of outline by a white sky, boomed over a windless day. Waiters were putting extra ice into the bar; an American photographer from the AP[392] worked with his equipment in a precarious shade and looked up quickly at every footfall descending the stone steps. At the hotel his prospective subjects slept late in darkened rooms upon their recent opiate of dawn.

When Nicole started out on the beach she saw Dick, not dressed for swimming, sitting on a rock above. She shrank back in the shadow of her dressing-tent. In a minute Baby joined her, saying: 'Dick's still there.'

'I saw him.'

'I think he might have the delicacy to go.'

'This is his place – in a way, he discovered it. Old Gausse always says he owes everything to Dick.'

Baby looked calmly at her sister.

'We should have let him confine himself to his bicycle excursions,' she remarked. 'When people are taken out of their depths they lose their heads, no matter how charming a bluff they put up.'

'Dick was a good husband to me for six years,' Nicole said. 'All that time I never suffered a minute's pain because of him, and he always did his best never to let anything hurt me.'

Baby's lower jaw projected slightly as she said: 'That's what he was educated for.'

The sisters sat in silence; Nicole wondering in a tired way about things; Baby considering whether or not to marry the latest candidate for her hand and money, an authenticated Hapsburg.[393] She was not quite *thinking* about it. Her affairs had long shared such a sameness, that, as she dried out, they were more important for their conversational value than for themselves. Her emotions had their truest existence in the telling of them.

'Is he gone?' Nicole asked after a while, 'I think his train leaves at noon.'

Baby looked.

'No. He's moved up higher on the terrace and he's talking to some women. Anyhow there are so many people now that he doesn't *have* to see us.'

He had seen them though, as they left their pavilion, and he followed them with his eyes until they disappeared again. He sat with Mary Minghetti, drinking anisette.[394]

'You were like you used to be the night you helped us,' she was saying, 'except at the end, when you were horrid about Caroline. Why aren't you nice like that always? You can be.'

It seemed fantastic to Dick to be in a position where Mary North could tell him about things.

'Your friends still like you, Dick. But you say awful things to people when you've been drinking. I've spent most of my time defending you this summer.'

'That remark is one of Dr Eliot's classics.'[395]

'It's true. Nobody cares whether you drink or not – ' She hesitated. 'Even when Abe drank hardest, he never offended people like you do.'

'You're all so dull,' he said.

'But we're all there is!' cried Mary. 'If you don't like nice people, try the ones who aren't nice, and see how you like that! All people want is to have a good time and if you make them unhappy you cut yourself off from nourishment.'

'Have I been nourished?' he asked.

Mary was having a good time, though she did not know it, as she had sat down with him only out of fear. Again she refused a drink and said: 'Self-indulgence is back of it. Of course, after Abe you can imagine how I feel about it – since I watched the progress of a good man towards alcoholism – '

Down the steps tripped Lady Caroline Sibley-Biers with blithe theatricality.

Dick felt fine – he was already well in advance of the day; arrived at where a man should be at the end of a good dinner, yet he showed only a fine, considered, restrained interest in Mary. His eyes, for the moment clear as a child's, asked her sympathy and stealing over him he felt the old necessity of convincing her that he was the last man in the world and she was the last woman.

. . . Then he would not have to look at those two other figures, a man and a woman, black and white and metallic against the sky . . .

'You once liked me, didn't you?' he asked.

'*Liked* you – I *loved* you. Everybody loved you. You could've had anybody you wanted for the asking – '

'There has always been something between you and me.'

She bit eagerly. 'Has there, Dick?'

'Always – I knew your troubles and how brave you were about them.' But the old interior laughter had begun inside him and he knew he couldn't keep it up much longer.

'I always thought you knew a lot,' Mary said enthusiastically. 'More about me than any one has ever known. Perhaps that's why I was so afraid of you when we didn't get along so well.'

His glance fell soft and kind upon hers, suggesting an emotion underneath; their glances married suddenly, bedded, strained together. Then as the laughter inside of him became so loud that it seemed as if Mary must hear it, Dick switched off the light and they were back in the Riviera sun.

'I must go,' he said. As he stood up he swayed a little; he did not feel well any more – his blood raced slow. He raised his right hand and with a papal cross he blessed the beach from the high terrace. Faces turned upward from several umbrellas.

'I'm going to him.' Nicole got to her knees.

'No, you're not,' said Tommy, pulling her down firmly. 'Let well enough alone.'

Chapter 13

NICOLE KEPT IN TOUCH with Dick after her new marriage; there were letters on business matters, and about the children. When she said, as she often did, 'I loved Dick and I'll never forget him,' Tommy answered, 'Of course not – why should you?'

Dick opened an office in Buffalo, but evidently without success. Nicole did not find what the trouble was, but she heard a few months later that he was in a little town named Batavia, New York, practising general medicine, and later that he was in Lockport,[396] doing the same thing. By accident she heard more about his life there than anywhere: that he bicycled a lot, was much admired by the ladies, and always had a big stack of papers on his desk that were known to be an important treatise on some medical subject, almost in process of completion. He was considered to have fine manners and once made a good speech at a public health meeting on the subject of drugs; but he became entangled with a girl who worked in a grocery store, and he was also involved in a lawsuit about some medical question; so he left Lockport.

After that he didn't ask for the children to be sent to America and didn't answer when Nicole wrote asking him if he needed money. In the last letter she had from him he told her that he was practising in Geneva, New York, and she got the impression that he had settled down with some one to keep house for him. She looked up Geneva in an atlas and found it was in the heart of the Finger Lakes Section[397] and considered a pleasant place. Perhaps, so she liked to think, his career was biding its time, again like Grant's in Galena;[398] his latest note was postmarked from Hornell,[399] New York, which is some distance from Geneva and a very small town; in any case he is almost certainly in that section of the country, in one town or another.

THE LAST
TYCOON

A Romance

———————— ◆ ————————

F. Scott Fitzgerald

Chapter 1

Though I haven't ever been on the screen I was brought up in pictures. Rudolph Valentino[400] came to my fifth birthday party – or so I was told. I put this down only to indicate that even before the age of reason I was in a position to watch the wheels go round.

I was going to write my memoirs once, *The Producer's Daughter*, but at eighteen you never quite get around to anything like that. It's just as well – it would have been as flat as an old column of Lolly Parsons'.[401] My father was in the picture business as another man might be in cotton or steel, and I took it tranquilly. At the worst I accepted Hollywood with the resignation of a ghost assigned to a haunted house. I knew what you were supposed to think about it but I was obstinately unhorrified.

This is easy to say, but harder to make people understand. When I was at Bennington[402] some of the English teachers who pretended an indifference to Hollywood[403] or its products, really *hated* it. Hated it way down deep as a threat to their existence. Even before that, when I was in a convent, a sweet little nun asked me to get her a script of a screenplay so she could 'teach her class about movie writing' as she had taught them about the essay and the short story. I got the script for her, and I suppose she puzzled over it and puzzled over it, but it was never mentioned in class, and she gave it back to me with an air of offended surprise and not a single comment. That's what I half expect to happen to this story.

You can take Hollywood for granted like I did, or you can dismiss it with the contempt we reserve for what we don't understand. It can be understood too, but only dimly and in flashes. Not half a dozen men have ever been able to keep the whole equation of pictures in their heads. And perhaps the closest a woman can come to the set-up is to try and understand one of those men.

The world from an aeroplane I knew. Father always had us travel back and forth that way from school and college. After my sister died when I was a junior, I travelled to and fro alone, and the journey always made me think of her, made me somewhat solemn and subdued. Sometimes there were picture people I knew on board the plane, and occasionally there was an attractive college boy – but not often during the Depression.[404] I seldom really fell asleep during the trip, what with thoughts of Eleanor and the sense of that sharp rip between coast and coast – at least not till we had left those lonely little airports in Tennessee.[405]

This trip was so rough that the passengers divided early into those who turned in right away and those who didn't want to turn in at all. There were two of these latter right across from me, and I was pretty sure from their fragmentary conversation that they were from Hollywood – one of them because he looked like it: a middle-aged Jew, who alternately talked with nervous excitement or else crouched as if ready to spring, in a harrowing silence; the other a pale, plain, stocky man of thirty, whom I was sure I had seen before. He had been to the house or something. But it might have been when I was a little girl, and so I wasn't offended that he didn't recognise me.

The stewardess – she was tall, handsome and flashing dark, a type that they seemed to run to – asked me if she could make up my berth.

' – and, dear, do you want an aspirin?' She perched on the side of the seat and rocked precariously to and fro with the June hurricane. ' – or nembutal?'[406]

'No.'

'I've been so busy with everyone else that I've had no time to ask you.' She sat down beside me and buckled us both in. 'Do you want some gum?'

This reminded me to get rid of the piece that had been boring me for hours. I wrapped it in a piece of magazine and put it into the automatic ash-holder.

'I can always tell people are nice,' the stewardess said approvingly, 'if they wrap their gum in paper before they put it in there.'

We sat for a while in the half-light of the swaying car. It was vaguely like a swanky restaurant at that twilight time between meals. We were all lingering – and not quite on purpose. Even the stewardess, I think, had to keep reminding herself why she was there.

She and I talked about a young actress I knew, whom she had flown West with two years before. It was in the very lowest time of the Depression, and the young actress kept staring out the window in such an intent way that the stewardess was afraid she was contemplating a leap. It appeared though that she was not afraid of poverty, but only of revolution.

'I know what mother and I are going to do,' she confided to the stewardess. 'We're coming out to the Yellowstone[407] and we're just going to live simply till it all blows over. Then we'll come back. They don't kill artists – you know?'

The proposition pleased me. It conjured up a pretty picture of the actress and her mother being fed by kind Tory bears[408] who brought them honey, and by gentle fawns who fetched extra milk from the does and then lingered near to make pillows for their heads at night. In turn I told the stewardess about the lawyer and the director who told their plans to father one night in those brave days. If the bonus army[409] conquered Washington, the lawyer had a boat hidden in the Sacramento River, and he was going to row upstream for a few months and then come back 'because they always needed lawyers after a revolution to straighten out the legal side'.

The director had tended more toward defeatism. He had an old suit, shirt and shoes in waiting – he never did say whether they were his own or whether he got them from the prop department – and he was going to Disappear into the Crowd. I remember father saying: 'But they'll look at your hands! They'll know you haven't done manual work for years. And they'll ask for your union card.' And I remember how the director's face fell, and how gloomy he was while he ate his dessert, and how funny and puny they sounded to me.

'Is your father an actor, Miss Brady?' asked the stewardess. 'I've certainly heard the name.'

At the name Brady, both the men across the aisle looked up. Sideways – that Hollywood look, that always seems thrown over one shoulder. Then the young, pale, stocky man unbuttoned his safety strap and stood in the aisle beside us.

'Are you Cecilia *Bra*dy?' he demanded accusingly, as if I'd been holding out on him. 'I *thought* I recognised you. I'm Wylie White.'

He could have omitted this – for at the same moment a new voice said, 'Watch your step, Wylie!', and another man brushed by him in the aisle and went forward in the direction of the cockpit. Wylie White started, and a little too late called after him defiantly: 'I only take orders from the pilot.'

I recognised the kind of pleasantry that goes on between the powers in Hollywood and their satellites.

The stewardess reproved him: 'Not so loud, please – some of the passengers are asleep.'

I saw now that the other man across the aisle, the middle-aged Jew, was on his feet also, staring with shameless economic lechery, after the man who had just gone by. Or rather at the back of the man, who gestured sideways with his hand in a sort of farewell, as he went out of my sight.

I asked the stewardess: 'Is he the as*sis*tant pilot?'

She was unbuckling our belt, about to abandon me to Wylie White.

'No. That's Mr Smith. He has the private compartment, the "bridal suite" – only he has it alone. The assistant pilot is always in uniform.' She stood up: 'I want to find out if we're going to be grounded in Nashville.'

Wylie White was aghast.

'Why?'

'It's a storm coming up in the Mississippi Valley.'

'Does that mean we'll have to stay here all *night*?'

'If this keeps up!'

A sudden dip indicated that it would. It tipped Wylie White into the seat opposite me, shunted the stewardess precipitately down in the direction of the cockpit, and plunked the Jewish man into a sitting position. After the studied, unruffled exclamations of distaste that befitted the air-minded, we settled down. There was an introduction.

'Miss Brady – Mr Schwartz,' said Wylie White. 'He's a great friend of your father's, too.'

Mr Schwartz nodded so vehemently that I could almost hear him saying: 'It's true. As God is my judge, it's true!'

He might have said this right out loud at one time in his life – but he was obviously a man to whom something had happened. Meeting him was like encountering a friend who has been in a fist fight or collision, and got flattened. You stare at your friend and say: 'What happened to you?' And he answers something unintelligible through broken teeth and swollen lips. He can't even tell you about it.

Mr Schwartz was physically unmarked; the exaggerated Persian nose and oblique eye-shadow were as congenital as the tip-tilted Irish redness around my father's nostrils.

'Nashville!' cried Wylie White. 'That means we go to an hotel. We don't get to the coast till tomorrow night – if then. My God! I was born in Nashville.'

'I should think you'd like to see it again.'

'Never – I've kept away for fifteen years. I hope I'll *never* see it again.'

But he would – for the plane was unmistakably going down, down, down, like Alice in the rabbit hole.[410] Cupping my hand against the window I saw the blur of the city far away on the left. The green sign 'Fasten your belts – No smoking' had been on since we first rode into the storm.

'Did you hear what he said?' said Schwartz from one of his fiery silences across the aisle.

'Hear what?' asked Wylie.

'Hear what he's calling himself,' said Schwartz. 'Mr *Smith*!'

'Why not?' asked Wylie.

'Oh, nothing,' said Schwartz quickly. 'I just thought it was funny. Smith.' I never heard a laugh with less mirth in it: 'Smith!'

I suppose there has been nothing like the airports since the days of the stage-stops – nothing quite as lonely, as sombre-silent. The old red-brick depots were built right into the towns they marked – people didn't get off at those isolated stations unless they lived there. But airports lead you way back in history like oases, like the stops on the great trade routes. The sight of air travellers strolling in ones and twos into midnight airports will draw a small crowd any night up to two. The young people look at the planes, the older ones look at the passengers with a watchful incredulity. In the big transcontinental planes we were the coastal rich, who casually alighted from our cloud in mid-America. High adventure might be among us, disguised as a movie star. But mostly it wasn't. And I always wished fervently that we looked more interesting than we did – just as I often have at premières, when the fans look at you with scornful reproach because you're not a star.

On the ground Wylie and I were suddenly friends because he held out his arm to steady me when I got out of the plane. From then on, he made a dead set for me – and I didn't mind. From the moment we walked into the airport it had become plain that if we were stranded here we were stranded here together. (It wasn't like the time I lost my boy – the time my boy played the piano with that girl Reina in a little New England farmhouse near Bennington, and I realised at last I wasn't wanted. Guy Lombardo[411] was on the air playing 'Top Hat' and 'Cheek to Cheek',[411] and she taught him the melodies. The keys falling like leaves and her hands splayed over his as she showed him a black chord. I was a freshman then.)

When we went into the airport Mr Schwartz was along with us, too, but he seemed in a sort of dream. All the time we were trying to get accurate information at the desk, he kept staring at the door that led out to the landing field, as if he were afraid the plane would leave without him. Then I excused myself for a few minutes and something happened that I didn't see, but when I came back he and White were standing close together, White talking and Schwartz looking twice as much as if a great truck had just backed up over him. He didn't stare at the door to the landing field any more. I heard the end of Wylie White's remark . . .

' – I told you to shut up. It serves you right.'

'I only said – '

He broke off as I came up and asked if there was any news. It was then half-past two in the morning.

'A little,' said Wylie White. 'They don't think we'll be able to start for three hours anyhow, so some of the softies are going to an hotel. But I'd like to take you out to the Hermitage, Home of Andrew Jackson.'[412]

'How could we see it in the dark?' demanded Schwartz.

'Hell, it'll be sunrise in two hours.'

'You two go,' said Schwartz.

'All right – you take the bus to the hotel. It's still waiting – *he*'s in there.' Wylie's voice had a taunt in it. 'Maybe it'd be a good thing.'

'No, I'll go along with you,' said Schwartz hastily.

We took a taxi in the sudden country dark outside, and he seemed to cheer up. He patted my kneecap encouragingly.

'I should go along,' he said, 'I should be chaperone. Once upon a time when I was in the big money, I had a daughter – a beautiful daughter.'

He spoke as if she had been sold to creditors as a tangible asset.

'You'll have another,' Wylie assured him. 'You'll get it all back. Another turn of the wheel and you'll be where Cecilia's papa is, won't he Cecilia?'

'Where is this Hermitage?' asked Schwartz presently. 'Far away at the end of nowhere? We will miss the plane?'

'Skip it,' said Wylie. 'We ought to've brought the stewardess along for you. Didn't you admire the stewardess? *I* thought she was pretty cute.'

We drove for a long time over a bright level countryside, just a road and a tree and a shack and a tree, and then suddenly along a winding twist of woodland. I could feel even in the darkness that the trees of the woodland were green – that it was all different from the dusty olive-tint of California. Somewhere we passed a Negro driving three cows ahead of him, and they mooed as he scattered them to the side of the road. They were real cows, with warm, fresh, silky flanks, and the Negro grew gradually real out of the darkness with his big brown eyes staring at us close to the car, as Wylie gave him a quarter. He said '*Thank* you – thank you,' and stood there, and the cows mooed again into the night as we drove off.

I thought of the first sheep I ever remember seeing – hundreds of them, and how our car drove suddenly into them on the back lot of the old Laemmle studio.[413] They were unhappy about being in pictures, but the men in the car with us kept saying: 'Swell!'

'Is that what you wanted, Dick?'

'Isn't that swell?' And the man named Dick kept standing up in the car as if he were Cortez or Balboa,[414] looking over that grey fleecy undulation. If I ever knew what picture they were in, I have long forgotten.

We had driven an hour. We crossed a brook over an old rattly iron bridge laid with planks. Now there were roosters crowing and blue-green shadows stirring every time we passed a farmhouse.

'I told you it'd be morning soon,' said Wylie. 'I was born near here – the son of impoverished southern paupers. The family mansion is now used as an outhouse. We had four servants – my father, my mother and my two sisters. I refused to join the guild, and so I went to Memphis to start my career, which has now reached a dead end.' He put his arm around me: 'Cecilia, will you marry me, so I can share the Brady fortune?'

He was disarming enough, so I let my head lie on his shoulder.

'What do you do, Cecilia. Go to school?'

'I go to Bennington. I'm a junior.'

'Oh, I beg your pardon. I should have known, but I never had the advantage of college training. But a *ju*nior – why I read in *Esquire*[415] that juniors have nothing to learn, Cecilia.'

'Why do people think that college girls – '

'Don't apologise – knowledge is power.'

'You'd know from the way you talk that we were on our way to Hollywood,' I said. 'It's always years and years behind the times.'

He pretended to be shocked.

'You mean girls in the East have no private lives?'

'That's the point. They *have* got private lives. You're bothering me, let go.'

'I can't. It might wake Schwartz, and I think this is the first sleep he's had for weeks. Listen, Cecilia: I once had an affair with the wife of a producer. A very short affair. When it was over she said to me in no uncertain terms, she said: "Don't you ever tell about this or I'll have you thrown out of Hollywood. My husband's a much more important man than you!" '

I liked him again now, and presently the taxi turned down a long lane fragrant with honeysuckle and narcissus, and stopped beside the great grey hulk of the Andrew Jackson house. The driver turned around to tell us something about it, but Wylie shushed him, pointing at Schwartz, and we tiptoed out of the car.

'You can't get into the Mansion now,' the taxi man told us politely.

Wylie and I went and sat against the wide pillars of the steps.

'What about Mr Schwartz?' I asked. 'Who is he?'

'To hell with Schwartz. He was the head of some combine once – First National? Paramount? United Artists?[416] Now he's down and out. But he'll be back. You can't flunk out of pictures unless you're a dope or a drunk.'

'You don't like Hollywood,' I suggested.

'Yes I do. Sure I do. Say! This isn't anything to talk about on the steps of Andrew Jackson's house – at dawn.'

'I *like* Hollywood,' I persisted.

'It's all right. It's a mining town in lotus land. Who said that? I did. It's a good place for toughies, but I went there from Savannah, Georgia. I went to a garden party the first day. My host shook hands and left me. It was all there – that swimming pool, green moss at two dollars an inch, beautiful felines having drinks and fun –

' – And nobody spoke to me. Not a soul. I spoke to half a dozen people but they didn't answer. That continued for an hour, two hours – then I got up from where I was sitting and ran out at a dog trot like a crazy man. I didn't feel I had any rightful identity until I got back to the hotel and the clerk handed me a letter addressed to me in my name.'

Naturally I hadn't ever had such an experience, but looking back on parties I'd been to, I realised that such things could happen. We don't go for strangers in Hollywood unless they wear a sign saying that their axe has been thoroughly ground elsewhere, and that in any case it's not going to fall on our necks – in other words, unless they're a celebrity. And they'd better look out even then.

'You should have risen above it,' I said smugly. 'It's not a slam at *you* when people are rude – it's a slam at the people they've met before.'

'Such a pretty girl – to say such wise things.'

There was an eager to-do in the eastern sky, and Wylie could see me plain – thin with good features and lots of style, and the kicking foetus of a mind. I wonder what I looked like in that dawn, five years ago. A little rumpled and pale, I suppose, but at that age, when one has the young illusion that most adventures are good, I needed only a bath and a change to go on for hours.

Wylie stared at me with really flattering appreciation – and then suddenly we were not alone. Mr Schwartz wandered apologetically into the pretty scene.

'I fell upon a large metal handle,' he said, touching the corner of his eye.

Wylie jumped up.

'Just in time, Mr Schwartz,' he said. 'The tour is just starting. Home of Old Hickory[417] – America's tenth president. The victor of

New Orleans, opponent of the National Bank, and inventor of the Spoils System.'

Schwartz looked towards me as towards a jury.

'There's a writer for you,' he said. 'Knows everything and at the same time he knows nothing.'

'What's that?' said Wylie, indignant.

It was my first inkling that he was a writer. And while I like writers – because if you ask a writer anything, you usually get an answer – still it belittled him in my eyes. Writers aren't people exactly. Or, if they're any good, they're a whole *lot* of people trying so hard to be one person. It's like actors, who try so pathetically not to look in mirrors, who lean *back*ward trying – only to see their faces in the reflecting chandeliers.

'Ain't writers like that, Cecilia?' demanded Schwartz. 'I have no words for them. I only know it's true.'

Wylie looked at him with slowly gathering indignation. 'I've heard that before,' he said. 'Look, Manny, I'm a more practical man than you any day! I've sat in an office and listened to some mystic stalk up and down for hours spouting tripe that'd land him on a nut-farm anywhere outside of California – and then at the end tell me how *practical* he was, and I was a dreamer – and would I kindly go away and make sense out of what he'd said.'

Mr Schwartz's face fell into its more disintegrated alignments. One eye looked upwards through the tall elms. He raised his hand and bit without interest at the cuticle on his second finger. There was a bird flying about the chimney of the house, and his glance followed it. It perched on the chimney pot like a raven, and Mr Schwartz's eyes remained fixed upon it as he said: 'We can't get in, and it's time for you two to go back to the plane.'

It was still not quite dawn. The Hermitage looked like a nice big white box, but a little lonely and vacated still after a hundred years. We walked back to the car. Only after we had gotten in, and Mr Schwartz had surprisingly shut the taxi door on us, did we realise he didn't intend to come along.

'I'm not going to the Coast – I decided that when I woke up. So I'll stay here, and afterwards the driver could come back for me.'

'Going back East?' said Wylie with surprise. 'Just because – '

'I have decided,' said Schwartz, faintly smiling. 'Once I used to be a regular man of decision – you'd be surprised.' He felt in his pocket, as the taxi driver warmed up the engine. 'Will you give this note to Mr Smith?'

'Shall I come in two hours?' the driver asked Schwartz.

'Yes . . . sure. I shall be glad to entertain myself looking around.'

I kept thinking of him all the way back to the airport – trying to fit him into that early hour and into that landscape. He had come a long way from some Ghetto to present himself at that raw shrine. Manny Schwartz and Andrew Jackson – it was hard to say them in the same sentence. It was doubtful if he knew who Andrew Jackson was as he wandered around, but perhaps he figured that if people had preserved his house Andrew Jackson must have been someone who was large and merciful, able to understand. At both ends of life man needed nourishment: a breast – a shrine. Something to lay himself beside when no one wanted him further, and shoot a bullet into his head.

Of course we did not know this for twenty hours. When we got to the airport we told the purser that Mr Schwartz was not continuing, and then forgot about him. The storm had wandered away into Eastern Tennessee and broken against the mountains, and we were taking off in less than an hour. Sleepy-eyed travellers appeared from the hotel, and I dozed a few minutes on one of those Iron Maidens[418] they use for couches. Slowly the idea of a perilous journey was recreated out of the débris of our failure: a new stewardess, tall, handsome, flashing dark, exactly like the other except she wore seersucker instead of French red-and-blue, went briskly past us with a suitcase. Wylie sat beside me as we waited.

'Did you give the note to Mr Smith?' I asked, half asleep.

'Yeah.'

'Who is Mr Smith? I suspect he spoiled Mr Schwartz's trip.'

'It was Schwartz's fault.'

'I'm prejudiced against steamrollers,' I said. 'My father tries to be a steamroller around the house, and I tell him to save it for the studio.'

I wondered if I was being fair; words are the palest counters at that time in the morning. 'Still, he steamrollered me into Bennington and I've always been grateful for that.'

'There would be quite a crash,' Wylie said, 'if steamroller Brady met steamroller Smith.'

'Is Mr Smith a competitor of father's?'

'Not exactly. I should say no. But if he was a competitor I know where my money would be.'

'On father?'

'I'm afraid not.'

It was too early in the morning for family patriotism. The pilot was at the desk with the purser and he shook his head as they regarded a prospective passenger who had put two nickels in the electric phonograph and lay alcoholically on a bench fighting off sleep. The first song he had chosen, 'Lost', thundered through the room, followed, after a slight interval, by his other choice, 'Gone', which was equally dogmatic and final. The pilot shook his head emphatically and walked over to the passenger.

'Afraid we're not going to be able to carry you this time, old man.'

'Wha'?'

The drunk sat up, awful-looking, yet discernibly attractive, and I was sorry for him in spite of his passionately ill-chosen music.

'Go back to the hotel and get some sleep. There'll be another plane tonight.'

'Only going up in ee *air*.'

'Not this time, old man.'

In his disappointment the drunk fell off the bench – and above the phonograph, a loudspeaker summoned us respectable people outside. In the corridor of the plane I ran into Monroe Stahr and fell all over him, or wanted to. There was a man any girl would go for, with or without encouragement. I was emphatically with*out* it, but he liked me and sat down opposite till the plane took off.

'Let's all ask for our money back,' he suggested. His dark eyes took me in, and I wondered what they would look like if he fell in love. They were kind, aloof, and, though they often reasoned with you gently, somewhat superior. It was no fault of theirs if they saw so much. He darted in and out of the role of 'one of the boys' with dexterity – but on the whole I should say he wasn't one of them. But he knew how to shut up, how to draw into the background, how to listen. From where he stood (and though he was not a tall man, it always seemed high up) he watched the multitudinous practicalities of his world like a proud young shepherd to whom night and day had never mattered. He was born sleepless, without a talent for rest or the desire for it.

We sat in unembarrassed silence – I had known him since he became father's partner a dozen years ago, when I was seven and Stahr was twenty-two. Wylie was across the aisle and I didn't know whether or not to introduce them, but Stahr kept turning his ring so abstractedly that he made me feel young and invisible, and I didn't care. I never dared look quite away from him or quite *at* him, unless I had something important to say – and I knew he affected many other people in the same manner.

'I'll *give* you this ring, Cecilia.'

'I beg your pardon. I didn't realise that I was – '

'I've got half a dozen like it.'

He handed it to me, a gold nugget with the letter S in bold relief. I had been thinking how oddly its bulk contrasted with his fingers, which were delicate and slender like the rest of his body, and like his slender face with the arched eyebrows and the dark curly hair. He looked spiritual at times, but he was a fighter – somebody out of his past knew him when he was one of a gang of kids in the Bronx,[419] and gave me a description of how he walked always at the head of his gang, this rather frail boy, occasionally throwing a command backward out of the corner of his mouth.

Stahr folded my hand over the ring, stood up, and addressed Wylie. 'Come up to the bridal suite,' he said. 'See you later, Cecilia.'

Before they went out of hearing, I heard Wylie's question: 'Did you open Schwartz's note?' And Stahr: 'Not yet.'

I must be slow, for only then did I realise that Stahr was Mr Smith. Afterwards Wylie told me what was in the note. Written by the headlights of the taxi, it was almost illegible.

DEAR MONROE – You are the best of them all I have always admired your mentality so when you turn against me I know it's no use! I must be no good and am not going to continue the journey let me warn you once again look out! I know.

Your friend

MANNY

Stahr read it twice, and raised his hand to the morning stubble on his chin.

'He's a nervous wreck,' he said. 'There's nothing to be done – absolutely nothing. I'm sorry I was short with him – but I don't like a man to approach me telling me it's for *my* sake.'

'Maybe it was,' said Wylie.

'It's poor technique.'

'I'd fall for it,' said Wylie. 'I'm vain as a woman. If anybody pretends to be interested in me, I'll ask for more. I like advice.'

Stahr shook his head distastefully. Wylie kept on ribbing him – he was one of those to whom this privilege was permitted.

'You fall for some kinds of flattery,' he said. 'This "little Napoleon stuff".'

'It makes me sick,' said Stahr, 'but it's not as bad as some man trying to help you.'

'If you don't like advice, why do you pay *me*?'

'That's a question of merchandise,' said Stahr. 'I'm a merchant. I want to buy what's in your mind.'

'You're no merchant,' said Wylie. 'I knew a lot of them when I was a publicity man, and I agree with Charles Francis Adams.'[420]

'What did he say?'

'He knew them all – Gould, Vanderbilt, Carnegie, Astor[421] – and he said there wasn't one he'd care to meet again in the hereafter. Well – they haven't improved since then, and that's why I say you're no merchant.'

'Adams was probably a sourbelly,'[422] said Stahr. 'He wanted to be head man himself, but he didn't have the judgement or else the character.'

'He had brains,' said Wylie rather tartly.

'It takes more than brains. You writers and artists poop out and get all mixed up, and somebody has to come in and straighten you out.' He shrugged his shoulders. 'You seem to take things so personally, hating people and worshipping them – always thinking people are so important – especially yourselves. You just ask to be kicked around. I like people and I like them to like me, but I wear my heart where God put it – on the inside.'

He broke off.

'What did I say to Schwartz in the airport? Do you remember – exactly?'

'You said, "Whatever you're after, the answer is No!" ' Stahr was silent.

'He was sunk,' said Wylie, 'but I laughed him out of it. We took Billy Brady's daughter for a ride.'

Stahr rang for the stewardess.

'That pilot,' he said, 'would he mind if I sat up in front with him a while?'

'That's against the rules, Mr Smith.'

'Ask him to step in here a minute when he's free.'

Stahr sat up front all afternoon. While we slid off the endless desert and over the tablelands, dyed with many colours like the white sands we dyed with colours when I was a child. Then in the late afternoon, the peaks themselves – the Mountains of the Frozen Saw[423] – slid under our propellers and we were close to home.

When I wasn't dozing I was thinking that I wanted to marry Stahr, that I wanted to make him love me. Oh, the conceit! What on earth did I have to offer? But I didn't think like that then. I had the pride of young women, which draws its strength from such sublime thoughts as 'I'm as good as *she* is.' For my purposes I was just as beautiful as the great beauties who must have inevitably thrown themselves at his head. My little spurt of intellectual interest was of course making me fit to be a brilliant ornament of any salon.

I know now it was absurd. Though Stahr's education was founded on nothing more than a night-school course in stenography, he had a long time ago run ahead through trackless wastes of perception into fields where very few men were able to follow him. But in my reckless conceit I matched my grey eyes against his brown ones for guile, my young golf-and-tennis heart-beats against his, which must be slowing a little after years of overwork. And I planned and I contrived and I plotted – any women can tell you – but it never came to anything, as you will see. I still like to think that if he'd been a poor boy and nearer my age I could have managed it, but of course the real truth was that I had nothing to offer that he didn't have; some of my more romantic ideas actually stemmed from pictures – *42nd Street*,[424] for example, had a great influence on me. It's more than possible that some of the pictures which Stahr himself conceived had shaped me into what I was.

So it was rather hopeless. Emotionally, at least, people can't live by taking in each other's washing.

But at that time it was different: father might help, the stewardess might help. She might go up in the cockpit and say to Stahr: 'If I ever saw love, it's in that girl's eyes.'

The pilot might help: 'Man, are you blind? Why don't you go back there?'

Wylie White might help – instead of standing in the aisle looking at me doubtfully, wondering whether I was awake or asleep.

'Sit down,' I said. 'What's new? – where are we?'

'Up in the air.'

'Oh, so that's it. Sit down.' I tried to show a cheerful interest: 'What are you writing?'

'Heaven help me, I am writing about a Boy Scout – *The* Boy Scout.'

'Is it Stahr's idea?'

'I don't know – he told me to look into it. He may have ten writers working ahead of me or behind me, a system which he so thoughtfully invented. So you're in love with him?'

'I should say not,' I said indignantly. 'I've known him all my life.'

'Desperate, eh? Well, I'll arrange it if you'll use all your influence to advance me. I want a unit of my own.'

I closed my eyes and drifted off. When I woke up, the stewardess was putting a blanket over me.

'Almost there,' she said.

Out the window I could see by the sunset that we were in a greener land.

'I just heard something funny,' she volunteered, 'up in the cockpit – that Mr Smith – or Mr Stahr – I never remember seeing his name – '

'It's never on any pictures,' I said.

'Oh. Well, he's been asking the pilots a lot about flying – I mean he's interested? You *know*?'

'I know.'

'I mean one of them told me he bet he could teach Mr Stahr solo flying in ten minutes. He has such a fine mentality, that's what he said.'

I was getting impatient.

'Well, what was so funny?'

'Well, finally one of the pilots asked Mr Smith if he liked his business, and Mr Smith said, "Sure. Sure I like it. It's nice being the only sound nut in a hatful of cracked ones." '

The stewardess doubled up with laughter – and I could have spat at her.

'I mean calling all those people a hatful of nuts. I mean *cracked* nuts.' Her laughter stopped with unexpected suddenness, and her face was grave as she stood up. 'Well, I've got to finish my chart.'

'Goodbye.'

Obviously Stahr had put the pilots right up on the throne with him and let them rule with him for a while. Years later I travelled with one of those same pilots and he told me one thing Stahr had said.

He was looking down at the mountains.

'Suppose you were a railroad man,' he said. 'You have to send a train through there somewhere. Well, you get your surveyors' reports, and you find there's three or four or half a dozen gaps, and not one is better than the other. You've got to decide – on what basis? you can't test the best way – except by doing it. So you just do it.'

The pilot thought he had missed something.

'How do you mean?'

'You choose some one way for no reason at all – because that mountain's pink or the blueprint is a better blue. You see?'

The pilot considered that this was very valuable advice. But he doubted if he'd ever be in a position to apply it.

'What I wanted to know,' he told me ruefully, 'is how he ever got to be Mr Stahr.'

I'm afraid Stahr could never have answered that one; for the embryo is not equipped with a memory. But I could answer a little. He had flown up very high to see, on strong wings, when he was young. And while he was up there he had looked on all the kingdoms, with the kind of eyes that can stare straight into the sun. Beating his wings tenaciously – finally frantically – and keeping on beating them, he had stayed up there longer than most of us, and then, remembering all he had seen from his great height of how things were, he had settled gradually to earth.

The motors were off, and all our five senses began to readjust themselves for landing. I could see a line of lights for the Long Beach Naval Station[425] ahead and to the left, and on the right a twinkling blur for Santa Monica. The California moon was out, huge and orange over the Pacific. However I happened to feel about these things – and they were home, after all – I know that Stahr must have felt much more. These were the things I had first opened my eyes on, like the sheep on the back lot of the old Laemmle studio; but this was where Stahr had come to earth after that extraordinary illuminating flight where he saw which way we were going, and how we looked doing it, and how much of it mattered. You could say that this was where an accidental wind blew him, but I don't think so. I would rather think that in a 'long shot' he saw a new way of measuring our jerky hopes and graceful rogueries and awkward sorrows, and that he came here from choice to be with us to the end. Like the plane coming down into the Glendale airport,[426] into the warm darkness.

Chapter 2

IT WAS NINE O'CLOCK of a July night and there were still some extras in the drugstore across from the studio – I could see them bent over the pin-games inside – as I parked my car. 'Old' Johnny Swanson stood on the corner in his semi-cowboy clothes, staring gloomily past the moon. Once he had been as big in pictures as Tom Mix or Bill Hart[427] – now it was too sad to speak to him, and I hurried across the street and through the front gate.

There is never a time when a studio is absolutely quiet. There is always a night shift of technicians in the laboratories and dubbing-rooms and people on the maintenance staff dropping in at the commissary. But the sounds are all different – the padded hush of tyres, the quiet tick of a motor running idle, the naked cry of a soprano singing into a nightbound microphone. Around a corner I came upon a man in rubber boots washing down a car in a wonderful white light – a fountain among the dead industrial shadows. I slowed up as I saw Mr Marcus being hoisted into his car in front of the administration building, because he took so long to say anything, even good-night – and while I waited I realised that the soprano was singing, *Come, come, I love you only*[428] over and over; I remember this because she kept singing the same line during the earthquake.[429] That didn't come for five minutes yet.

Father's offices were in the old building with the long balconies and iron rails with their suggestion of a perpetual tightrope. Father was on the second floor, with Stahr on one side and Mr Marcus on the other – this evening there were lights all along the row. My stomach dipped a little at the proximity to Stahr, but that was in pretty good control now – I'd seen him only once in the month I'd been home.

There were a lot of strange things about father's office, but I'll make it brief. In the outer part were three poker-faced secretaries who had sat there like witches ever since I could remember – Birdy Peters, Maude something, and Rosemary Schmiel; I don't know whether this was her name, but she was the dean of the trio, so to speak, and under her desk was the kick-lock that admitted you to father's throne room. All three of the secretaries were passionate capitalists, and Birdy had invented the rule that if typists were seen eating together more than once in a single week, they were hauled up on the carpet. At that time the studios feared mob rule.

I went on in. Nowadays all chief executives have huge drawing-rooms, but my father's was the first. It was also the first to have one-way glass in the big French windows, and I've heard a story about a trap in the floor that would drop unpleasant visitors to an oubliette below, but believe it to be an invention. There was a big painting of Will Rogers,[430] hung conspicuously and intended, I think, to suggest father's essential kinship with Hollywood's St Francis; there was a signed photograph of Minna Davis, Stahr's dead wife, and photos of other studio celebrities and big chalk drawings of mother and me. Tonight the one-way French windows were open and a big moon, rosy-gold with a haze around, was wedged helpless in one of them. Father and Jacques La Borwitz and Rosemary Schmiel were down at the end around a big circular desk.

What did father look like? I couldn't describe him except for once in New York when I met him where I didn't expect to; I was aware of a bulky, middle-aged man who looked a little ashamed of himself, and I wished he'd move on – and then I saw he was father. Afterwards I was shocked at my impression. Father can be very magnetic – he had a tough jaw and an Irish smile.

But as for Jacques La Borwitz, I shall spare you. Let me just say he was an assistant producer, which is something like a commissar, and let it go at that. Where Stahr picked up such mental cadavers or had them forced upon him – or especially how he got any use out of them – has always amazed me, as it amazed everyone fresh from the East who slapped up against them. Jacques La Borwitz had his points, no doubt, but so have the sub-microscopic protozoa, so has a dog prowling for a bitch and a bone. Jacques La – oh my!

From their expressions I was sure they had been talking about Stahr. Stahr had ordered something or forbidden something, or defied father or junked one of La Borwitz's pictures or something catastrophic, and they were sitting there in protest at night in a community of rebellion and helplessness. Rosemary Schmiel sat pad in hand, as if ready to write down their dejection.

'I'm to drive you home dead or alive,' I told father. 'All those birthday presents rotting away in their packages!'

'A birthday!' cried Jacques in a flurry of apology. 'How old? I didn't know.'

'Forty-three,' said father distinctly.

He was older than that – four years – and Jacques knew it; I saw him note it down in his account book to use sometime. Out here these account books are carried open in the hand. One can see the entries being made without recourse to lip-reading, and Rosemary Schmiel was compelled in emulation to make a mark on her pad. As she rubbed it out, the earth quaked under us.

We didn't get the full shock like at Long Beach, where the upper storeys of shops were spewed into the streets and small hotels drifted out to sea – but for a full minute our bowels were one with the bowels of the earth – like some nightmare attempt to attach our navel cords again and jerk us back to the womb of creation.

Mother's picture fell off the wall, revealing a small safe – Rosemary and I grabbed frantically for each other and did a strange screaming waltz across the room. Jacques fainted or at least disappeared, and father clung to his desk and shouted, 'Are you all right?' Outside the window the singer came to the climax of 'I Love You Only', held it a moment and then, I swear, started it all over. Or maybe they were playing it back to her from the recording machine.

The room stood still, shimmying a little. We made our way to the door, suddenly including Jacques, who had reappeared, and tottered out dizzily through the ante-room on to the iron balcony. Almost all the lights were out, and from here and there we could hear cries and calls. Momentarily we stood waiting for a second shock – then, as with a common impulse, we went into Stahr's entry and through to his office.

The office was big, but not as big as father's. Stahr sat on the side of his couch rubbing his eyes. When the quake came he had been asleep, and he wasn't sure yet whether he had dreamed it. When we convinced him he thought it was all rather funny – until the telephones began to ring. I watched him as unobtrusively as possible. He was grey with fatigue while he listened to the phone and dictagraph;[431] but as the reports came in, his eyes began to pick up shine.

'A couple of water mains have burst,' he said to father, ' – they're heading into the back lot.'

'Gray's shooting in the French Village,' said father.

'It's flooded around the Station, too, and in the Jungle and the City Corner. What the hell – nobody seems to be hurt.' In passing, he shook my hands gravely: 'Where've you been, Cecilia?'

'You going out there, Monroe?' father asked.

'When all the news is in. One of the power lines is off, too – I've sent for Robinson.'

He made me sit down with him on the couch and tell about the quake again.

'You look tired,' I said, cute and motherly.

'Yes,' he agreed, 'I've got no place to go in the evenings, so I just work.'

'I'll arrange some evenings for you.'

'I used to play poker with a gang,' he said thoughtfully, 'before I was married. But they all drank themselves to death.'

Miss Doolan, his secretary, came in with fresh bad news.

'Robby'll take care of everything when he comes,' Stahr assured father. He turned to me. 'Now there's a man – that Robinson. He was a trouble-shooter – fixed the telephone wires in Minnesota blizzards – nothing stumps him. He'll be here in a minute – you'll like Robby.' He said it as if it had been his life-long intention to bring us together, and he had arranged the whole earthquake with just that in mind. 'Yes, you'll like Robby,' he repeated. 'When do you go back to college?'

'I've just come home.'

'You get the whole summer?'

'I'm sorry,' I said. 'I'll go back as soon as I can.'

I was in a mist. It hadn't failed to cross my mind that he might have some intention about me, but if it was so, it was in an exasperatingly early stage – I was merely 'a good property'. And the idea didn't seem so attractive at that moment – like marrying a doctor. He seldom left the studio before eleven.

'How long,' he asked my father, 'before she graduates from college. That's what I was trying to say.'

And I think I was about to sing out eagerly that I needn't go back at all, that I was quite educated already – when the totally admirable Robinson came in. He was a bow-legged young redhead, all ready to go.

'This is Robby, Cecilia,' said Stahr. 'Come on, Robby.'

So I met Robby. I can't say it seemed like fate – but it was. For it was Robby who later told me how Stahr found his love that night.

*   *   *

Under the moon the back lot was thirty acres of fairyland – not because the locations really looked like African jungles and French châteaux and schooners at anchor and Broadway at night, but because they looked like the torn picture books of childhood, like fragments of stories dancing in an open fire. I never lived in a house with an attic, but a back lot must be something like that, and at night of course in an enchanted distorted way, it all comes true.

When Stahr and Robby arrived, clusters of lights had already picked out the danger spots in the flood.

'We'll pump it out into the swamp on Thirty-Sixth Street,' said Robby after a moment. 'It's city property – but isn't this an act of God? Say – look there!'

On top of a huge head of the Goddess Siva,[432] two women were floating down the current of an impromptu river. The idol had come unloosed from a set of Burma, and it meandered earnestly on its way, stopping sometimes to waddle and bump in the shallows with the other débris of the tide. The two refugees had found sanctuary along a scroll of curls on its bald forehead and seemed at first glance to be sightseers on an interesting bus-ride through the scene of the flood.

'Will you look at that, Monroe!' said Robby. 'Look at those dames!'

Dragging their legs through sudden bogs, they made their way to the bank of the stream. Now they could see the women, looking a little scared but brightening at the prospect of rescue.

'We ought to let 'em drift out to the waste pipe,' said Robby gallantly, 'but DeMille[433] needs that head next week.'

He wouldn't have hurt a fly, though, and presently he was hip deep in the water, fishing for them with a pole and succeeding only in spinning it in a dizzy circle. Help arrived, and the impression quickly got around that one of them was very pretty, and then that they were people of importance. But they were just strays, and Robby waited disgustedly to give them hell while the thing was brought finally into control and beached.

'Put that head back!' he called up to them. 'You think it's a souvenir?'

One of the women came sliding smoothly down the cheek of the idol, and Robby caught her and set her on solid ground; the other one hesitated and then followed. Robby turned to Stahr for judgement.

'What'll we do with them, chief?'

Stahr did not answer. Smiling faintly at him from not four feet away was the face of his dead wife, identical even to the expression. Across the four feet of moonlight, the eyes he knew looked back at him, a curl blew a little on a familiar forehead; the smile lingered, changed a little according to pattern; the lips parted – the same. An awful fear went over him, and he wanted to cry aloud. Back from the still sour room, the muffled glide of the limousine hearse, the falling concealing flowers, from out there in the dark – here now warm and glowing. The river passed him in a rush, the great spotlights swooped and blinked – and then he heard another voice speak that was not Minna's voice.

'We're sorry,' said the voice. 'We followed a truck in through a gate.'

A little crowd had gathered – electricians, grips, truckers, and Robby began to nip at them like a sheep dog.

'. . . get the big pumps on the tanks on Stage 4 . . . put a cable around this head . . . raft it up on a couple of two by fours . . . get the water out of the jungle first, for Christ's sake . . . that big "A" pipe, lay it down . . . all that stuff is plastic . . .'

Stahr stood watching the two women as they threaded their way after a policeman towards an exit gate. Then he took a tentative step to see if the weakness had gone out of his knees. A loud tractor came bumping through the slush, and men began streaming by him – every second one glancing at him, smiling, speaking: 'Hello, Monroe . . . Hello, Mr Stahr . . . wet night, Mr Stahr . . . Monroe . . . Monroe . . . Stahr . . . Stahr . . . Stahr.'

He spoke and waved back as the people streamed by in the darkness, looking, I suppose, a little like the Emperor and the Old Guard.[434] There is no world so but it has its heroes, and Stahr was the hero. Most of these men had been here a long time – through the beginnings and the great upset, when sound came, and the three years of Depression, he had seen that no harm came to them. The old loyalties were trembling now, there were clay feet everywhere; but still he was their man, the last of the princes. And their greeting was a sort of low cheer as they went by.

Chapter 3

BETWEEN THE NIGHT I got back and the quake, I'd made many observations.

About father, for example. I loved father – in a sort of irregular graph with many low swoops – but I began to see that his strong will didn't fill him out as a passable man. Most of what he accomplished boiled down to shrewd. He had acquired with luck and shrewdness a quarter interest in a booming circus – together with young Stahr. That was his life's effort – all the rest was an instinct to hang on. Of course, he talked that double talk to Wall Street about how mysterious it was to make a picture, but father didn't know the ABCs of dubbing or even cutting. Nor had he learned much about the feel of America as a bar boy in Ballyhegan, nor did he have any more than a drummer's sense[435] of a story. On the other hand, he didn't have concealed paresis like – ; he came to the studio before noon, and, with a suspiciousness developed like a muscle, it was hard to put anything over on him.

Stahr had been his luck – and Stahr was something else again. He was a marker in industry like Edison and Lumière and Griffith and Chaplin.[436] He led pictures way up past the range and power of the theatre, reaching a sort of golden age, before the censorship.

Proof of his leadership was the spying that went on around him – not just for inside information or patented process secrets – but spying on his scent for a trend in taste, his guess as to how things were going to be. Too much of his vitality was taken by the mere parrying of these attempts. It made his work secret in part, often devious, slow – and hard to describe as the plans of a general, where the psychological factors become too tenuous and we end by merely adding up the successes and failures. But I have determined to give you a glimpse of him functioning, which is my excuse for what follows. It is drawn partly from a paper I wrote in college on *A Producer's Day* and partly from my imagination. More often I have blocked in the ordinary events myself, while the stranger ones are true.

*   *   *

In the early morning after the flood, a man walked up to the outside balcony of the Administration Building. He lingered there some time, according to an eyewitness, then mounted to the iron railing and dove head first to the pavement below. Breakage – one arm.

Miss Doolan, Stahr's secretary, told him about it when he buzzed for her at nine. He had slept in his office without hearing the small commotion.

'Pete Zavras!' Stahr exclaimed, ' – the cameraman?'

'They took him to a doctor's office. It won't be in the paper.'

'Hell of a thing,' he said. 'I knew he'd gone to pot – but I don't know why. He was all right when we used him two years ago – why should he come here? How did he get in?'

'He bluffed it with his old studio pass,' said Catherine Doolan. She was a dry hawk, the wife of an assistant director. 'Perhaps the quake had something to do with it.'

'He was the best cameraman in town,' Stahr said. When he had heard of the hundreds dead at Long Beach, he was still haunted by the abortive suicide at dawn. He told Catherine Doolan to trace the matter down.

The first dictagraph messages blew in through the warm morning. While he shaved and had coffee, he talked and listened. Robby had left a message: 'If Mr Stahr wants me tell him to hell with it I'm in bed.' An actor was sick or thought so; the Governor of California was bringing a party out; a supervisor had beaten up his wife for the prints and must be 'reduced to a writer' – these three affairs were father's job – unless the actor was under personal contract to Stahr. There was early snow on a location in Canada with the company already there – Stahr raced over the possibilities of salvage, reviewing the story of the picture. Nothing. Stahr called Catherine Doolan.

'I want to speak to the cop who put two women off the back lot last night. I think his name's Malone.'

'Yes, Mr Stahr. I've got Joe Wyman – about the trousers.'

'Hello, Joe,' said Stahr. 'Listen – two people at the sneak preview complained that Morgan's fly was open for half the picture . . . of course they're exaggerating, but even if it's only ten feet . . . no, we can't find the people, but I want that picture run over and over until you find that footage. Get a lot of people in the projection room – somebody'll spot it.'

'Tout passe. L'art robuste
Seul à l'éternité.'[437]

'And there's the Prince from Denmark,'[438] said Catherine Doolan. 'He's very handsome.' She was impelled to add pointlessly, ' – for a tall man.'

'Thanks,' Stahr said. 'Thank you, Catherine, I appreciate it that I am now the handsomest small man on the lot. Send the Prince out on the sets and tell him we'll lunch at one.'

'And Mr George Boxley – looking very angry in a British way.'

'I'll see him for ten minutes.'

As she went out, he asked: 'Did Robby phone in?'

'No.'

'Call sound, and if he's been heard from, call him and ask him this. Ask him this – did he hear that woman's name last night? Either of those women. Or anything so they could be traced.'

'Anything else?'

'No, but tell him it's important while he still remembers. What were they? I mean what kind of people – ask him that, too. I mean were they – '

She waited, scratching his words on her pad without looking.

' – oh, were they – questionable? Were they theatrical? Never mind – skip that. Just ask if he knows how they can be traced.'

The policeman, Malone, had known nothing. Two dames, and he had hustled 'em, you betcha. One of them was sore. Which one? One of them. They had a car, a Chevvy[439] – he thought of taking the licence. Was it – the good looker who was sore? It was one of them.

Not which one – he had noticed nothing. Even on the lot here Minna was forgotten. In three years. So much for that, then.

Stahr smiled at Mr George Boxley. It was a kindly fatherly smile Stahr had developed inversely when he was a young man pushed into high places. Originally it had been a smile of respect towards his elders, then as his own decisions grew rapidly to displace theirs, a smile so that they should not feel it – finally emerging as what it was: a smile of kindness – sometimes a little hurried and tired, but always there – towards anyone who had not angered him within the hour. Or anyone he did not intend to insult, aggressive and outright.

Mr Boxley did not smile back. He came in with the air of being violently dragged, though no one apparently had a hand on him. He stood in front of a chair, and again it was as if two invisible attendants seized his arms and set him down forcibly into it. He sat there morosely. Even when he lit a cigarette on Stahr's invitation, one felt that the match was held to it by exterior forces he disdained to control.

Stahr looked at him courteously.

'Something not going well, Mr Boxley?'

The novelist looked back at him in thunderous silence.

'I read your letter,' said Stahr. The tone of the pleasant young headmaster was gone. He spoke as to an equal, with a faint two-edged deference.

'I can't get what I write on paper,' broke out Boxley. 'You've all been very decent, but it's a sort of conspiracy. Those two hacks you've teamed me with listen to what I say, but they spoil it – they seem to have a vocabulary of about a hundred words.'

'Why don't you write it yourself?' asked Stahr.

'I have. I sent you some.'

'But it was just talk, back and forth,' said Stahr mildly. 'Interesting talk but nothing more.'

Now it was all the two ghostly attendants could do to hold Boxley in the deep chair. He struggled to get up; he uttered a single quiet bark which had some relation to laughter but none to amusement, and said: 'I don't think you people read things. The men are duelling when the conversation takes place. At the end one of them falls into a well and has to be hauled up in a bucket.'

He barked again and subsided.

'Would you write that in a book of your own, Mr Boxley?'

'What? Naturally not.'

'You'd consider it too cheap.'

'Movie standards are different,' said Boxley, hedging.

'Do you ever go to them?'

'No – almost never.'

'Isn't it because people are always duelling and falling down wells?'

'Yes – and wearing strained facial expressions and talking incredible and unnatural dialogue.'

'Skip the dialogue for a minute,' said Stahr. 'Granted your dialogue is more graceful than what these hacks can write – that's why we brought you out here. But let's imagine something that isn't either bad dialogue or jumping down a well. Has your office got a stove in it that lights with a match?'

'I think it has,' said Boxley stiffly, ' – but I never use it.'

'Suppose you're in your office. You've been fighting duels or writing all day and you're too tired to fight or write any more. You're sitting there staring – dull, like we all get sometimes. A pretty stenographer that you've seen before comes into the room and you watch her – idly. She doesn't see you, though you're very close to her. She takes off her gloves, opens her purse and dumps it out on a table – '

Stahr stood up, tossing his key-ring on his desk.

'She has two dimes and a nickel – and a cardboard matchbox. She leaves the nickel on the desk, puts the two dimes back into her purse and takes her black gloves to the stove, opens it and puts them inside. There is one match in the matchbox and she starts to light it kneeling by the stove. You notice that there's a stiff wind blowing in the window – but just then your telephone rings. The girl picks it up, says hello – listens – and says deliberately into the phone, "I've never owned a pair of black gloves in my life." She hangs up, kneels by the stove again, and just as she lights the match, you glance around very suddenly and see that there's another man in the office, watching every move the girl makes – '

Stahr paused. He picked up his keys and put them in his pocket.

'Go on,' said Boxley, smiling. 'What happens?'

'I don't know,' said Stahr. 'I was just making pictures.'

Boxley felt he was being put in the wrong.

'It's just melodrama,' he said.

'Not necessarily,' said Stahr. 'In any case, nobody has moved violently or talked cheap dialogue or had any facial expression at all. There was only one bad line, and a writer like you could improve it. But you were interested.'

'What was the nickel for?' asked Boxley evasively.

'I don't know,' said Stahr. Suddenly he laughed. 'Oh, yes – the nickel was for the movies.'

The two invisible attendants seemed to release Boxley. He relaxed, leaned back in his chair and laughed.

'What in hell do you pay me for?' he demanded. 'I don't understand the damn stuff.'

'You will,' said Stahr grinning, 'or you wouldn't have asked about the nickel.'

*   *   *

A dark saucer-eyed man was waiting in the outer office as they came out.

'Mr Boxley, this is Mr Mike Van Dyke,' Stahr said. 'What is it, Mike?'

'Nothing,' Mike said. 'I just came up to see if you were real.'

'Why don't you go to work?' Stahr said. 'I haven't had a laugh in the rushes for days.'

'I'm afraid of a nervous breakdown.'

'You ought to keep in form,' Stahr said. 'Let's see you peddle your stuff.' He turned to Boxley: 'Mike's a gag man – he was out here when I was in the cradle. Mike, show Mr Boxley a double wing, clutch, kick and scram.'

'Here?' asked Mike.

'Here.'

'There isn't much room. I wanted to ask you about – '

'There's lots of room.'

'Well,' he looked around tentatively. 'You shoot the gun.'

Miss Doolan's assistant, Katy, took a paper bag, blew it open.

'It was a routine,' Mike said to Boxley, ' – back in the Keystone days.'[440] He turned to Stahr: 'Does he know what a routine is?'

'It means an act,' Stahr explained. 'Georgie Jessel talks about "Lincoln's Gettysburg routine".'[441]

Katy poised the neck of the blown-up bag in her mouth. Mike stood with his back to her.

'Ready?' Katy asked. She brought her hands down on the side. Immediately Mike grabbed his bottom with both hands, jumped in the air, slid his feet out on the floor one after the other, remaining in place and flapping his arms twice like a bird –

'Double wing,' said Stahr.

– and then ran out the screen-door which the office boy held open for him and disappeared past the window of the balcony.

'Mr Stahr,' said Miss Doolan, 'Mr Hanson is on the phone from New York.'

Ten minutes later he clicked his dictagraph, and Miss Doolan came in. There was a male star waiting to see him in the outer office, Miss Doolan said.

'Tell him I went out by the balcony,' Stahr advised her.

'All right. He's been in four times this week. He seems very anxious.'

'Did he give you any hint of what he wanted? Isn't it something he can see Mr Brady about?'

'He didn't say. You have a conference coming up. Miss Meloney and Mr White are outside. Mr Broaca is next door in Mr Reinmund's office.'

'Send Mr Roderiguez in,' said Stahr. 'Tell him I can see him only for a minute.'

When the handsome actor came in, Stahr remained standing.

'What is it that can't wait?' he asked pleasantly.

The actor waited carefully till Miss Doolan had gone out.

'Monroe, I'm through,' he said. 'I had to see you.'

'Through!' said Stahr. 'Have you seen *Variety*?[442] Your picture's held over at Roxy's[443] and did thirty-seven thousand in Chicago last week.'

'That's the worst of it. That's the tragedy. I get everything I want, and now it means nothing.'

'Well, go on, explain.'

'There's nothing between Esther and me any more. There never can be again.'

'A row.'

'Oh, no – worse – I can't bear to mention it. My head's in a daze. I wander around like a madman. I go through my part as if I was asleep.'

'I haven't noticed it,' said Stahr. 'You were great in your rushes yesterday.'

'Was I? That just shows you nobody ever guesses.'

'Are you trying to tell me that you and Esther are separating?'

'I suppose it'll come to that. Yes – inevitably – it will.'

'What was it?' demanded Stahr impatiently. 'Did she come in without knocking?'

'Oh, there's nobody else. It's just – me. I'm through.'

Stahr got it suddenly.

'How do you know?'

'It's been true for six weeks.'

'It's your imagination,' said Stahr. 'Have you been to a doctor?'

The actor nodded.

'I've tried everything. I even – one day in desperation I went down to – to Claris. But it was hopeless. I'm washed up.'

Stahr had an impish temptation to tell him to go to Brady about it. Brady handled all matters of public relations. Or was this private relations. He turned away for a moment, got his face in control, turned back.

'I've been to Pat Brady,' said the star, as if guessing the thought. 'He gave me a lot of phoney advice and I tried it all, but nothing doing. Esther and I sit opposite each other at dinner, and I'm ashamed to look at her. She's been a good sport about it, but I'm ashamed. I'm ashamed all day long. I think *Rainy Day* grossed twenty-five thousand in Des Moines and broke all records in St Louis and did twenty-seven thousand in Kansas City. My fan mail's way up, and there I am afraid to go home at night, afraid to go to bed.'

Stahr began to be faintly oppressed. When the actor first came in, Stahr had intended to invite him to a cocktail party, but now it scarcely seemed appropriate. What would he want with a cocktail party with this hanging over him? In his mind's eye he saw him wandering haunted from guest to guest with a cocktail in his hand and his grosses up twenty-seven thousand.

'So I came to you, Monroe. I never saw a situation where you didn't know a way out. I said to myself: even if he advises me to kill myself, I'll ask Monroe.'

The buzzer sounded on Stahr's desk – he switched on the dictagraph and heard Miss Doolan's voice.

'Five minutes, Mr Stahr.'

'I'm sorry,' said Stahr. 'I'll need a few minutes more.'

'Five hundred girls marched to my house from the high school,' the actor said gloomily, 'and I stood behind the curtains and watched them. I couldn't go out.'

'You sit down,' said Stahr. 'We'll take plenty of time and talk this over.'

In the outer office, two members of the conference group had already waited ten minutes – Wylie White and Jane Meloney. The latter was a dried-up little blonde of fifty about whom one could hear the fifty assorted opinions of Hollywood – 'a sentimental dope', 'the best writer on construction in Hollywood', 'a veteran', 'that old hack', 'the smartest woman on the lot', 'the cleverest plagiarist in the biz'; and, of course, in addition she was variously described as a nymphomaniac, a virgin, a pushover, a Lesbian, and a faithful wife. Without being an old maid, she was, like most self-made women, rather old maidish. She had ulcers of the stomach, and her salary was over a hundred thousand a year. A complicated treatise could be written on whether she was 'worth it' or more than that or nothing at all. Her value lay in such ordinary assets as the bare fact that she was a woman and adaptable, quick and trustworthy, 'knew the game', and was without egotism. She had been a great friend of Minna's, and over a period of years Stahr had managed to stifle what amounted to a sharp physical revulsion.

She and Wylie waited in silence – occasionally addressing a remark to Miss Doolan. Every few minutes Reinmund, the supervisor, called up from his office, where he and Broaca, the director, were waiting. After ten minutes Stahr's button went on, and Miss Doolan called Reinmund and Broaca; simultaneously Stahr and the actor came out of Stahr's office with Stahr holding the man's arm. He was so wound up now that when Wylie White asked him how he was he opened his mouth and began to tell him then and there.

'Oh, I've had an awful time,' he said, but Stahr interrupted sharply.

'No, you haven't. Now you go along and do the role the way I said.'

'Thank you, Monroe.'

Jane Meloney looked after him without speaking.

'Somebody been catching flies on him?' she asked – a phrase for stealing scenes.

'I'm sorry I kept you waiting,' Stahr said. 'Come on in.'

*　　*　　*

It was noon already and the conferees were entitled to exactly an hour of Stahr's time. No less, for such a conference could only be interrupted by a director who was held up in his shooting; seldom much more, because every eight days the company must release a production as complex and costly as Reinhardt's *Miracle*.[444]

Occasionally, less often than five years ago, Stahr would work all through the night on a single picture. But after such a spree he felt badly for days. If he could go from problem to problem, there was a certain rebirth of vitality with each change. And like those sleepers who can wake whenever they wish, he had set his psychological clock to run one hour.

The cast assembled included, besides the writers, Reinmund, one of the most favoured of the supervisors, and John Broaca, the picture's director.

Broaca, on the surface, was all engineer – large and without nerves, quietly resolute, popular. He was an ignoramus, and Stahr often caught him making the same scenes over and over – one scene about a rich young girl occurred in all his pictures with the same action, the same business. A bunch of large dogs entered the room and jumped around the girl. Later the girl went to a stable and slapped a horse on the rump. The explanation was probably not Freudian; more likely that at a drab moment in youth he had looked through a fence and seen a beautiful girl with dogs and horses. As a trademark for glamour it was stamped on his brain forever.

Reinmund was a handsome young opportunist, with a fairly good education. Originally a man of some character, he was being daily forced by his anomalous position into devious ways of acting and thinking. He was a bad man now, as men go. At thirty he had none of the virtues which either gentile Americans or Jews are taught to think admirable. But he got his pictures out in time, and by manifesting an almost homosexual fixation on Stahr, seemed to have dulled Stahr's usual acuteness. Stahr liked him – considered him a good all-round man.

Wylie White, of course, in any country would have been recognisable as an intellectual of the second order. He was civilised and voluble, both simple and acute, half dazed and half saturnine. His jealousy of Stahr showed only in unguarded flashes, and was mingled with admiration and even affection.

'The production date for this picture is two weeks from Saturday,' said Stahr. 'I think basically it's all right – much improved.'

Reinmund and the two writers exchanged a glance of congratulation.

'Except for one thing,' said Stahr, thoughtfully. 'I don't see why it should be produced at all, and I've decided to put it away.'

There was a moment of shocked silence – and then murmurs of protest, stricken queries.

'It's not your fault,' Stahr said. 'I thought there was something there that wasn't there – that was all.' He hesitated, looking regretfully at Reinmund: 'It's too bad – it was a good play. We paid fifty thousand for it.'

'What's the matter with it, Monroe?' asked Broaca bluntly.

'Well, it hardly seems worth while to go into it,' said Stahr.

Reinmund and Wylie White were both thinking of the professional effect on them. Reinmund had two pictures to his account this year – but Wylie White needed a credit to start his comeback to the scene. Jane Meloney was watching Stahr closely from little skull-like eyes.

'Couldn't you give us some clue,' Reinmund asked. 'This is a good deal of a blow, Monroe.'

'I just wouldn't put Margaret Sullavan in it,' said Stahr. 'Or Colman[445] either. I wouldn't advise them to play it – '

'Specifically, Monroe,' begged Wylie White. 'What didn't you like? The scenes? the dialogue? the humour? construction?'

Stahr picked up the script from his desk, let it fall as if it were, physically, too heavy to handle.

'I don't like the people,' he said. 'I wouldn't like to meet them – if I knew they were going to be somewhere, I'd go somewhere else.'

Reinmund smiled, but there was worry in his eyes.

'Well, that's a damning criticism,' he said. 'I thought the people were rather interesting.'

'So did I,' said Broaca. 'I thought Em was very sympathetic.'

'Did you?' asked Stahr sharply. 'I could just barely believe she was alive. And when I came to the end, I said to myself, "So what?" '

'There must be something to do,' Reinmund said. 'Naturally we feel bad about this. This is the structure we agreed on – '

'But it's not the story,' said Stahr. 'I've told you many times that the first thing I decide is the *kind* of story I want. We change in every other regard, but once that is set we've got to work towards it with every line and movement. This is not the kind of story I want. The story we bought had shine and glow – it was a happy story. This is all full of doubt and hesitation. The hero and heroine stop loving each other over trifles – then they start up again over trifles. After the first sequence, you don't care if she never sees him again or he her.'

'That's my fault,' said Wylie suddenly. 'You see, Monroe, I don't think stenographers have the same dumb admiration for their bosses they had in 1929. They've been laid off – they've seen their bosses jittery. The world has moved on, that's all.'

Stahr looked at him impatiently, gave a short nod.

'That's not under discussion,' he said. 'The premise of this story is that the girl did have a dumb admiration for her boss, if you want to call it that. And there wasn't any evidence that he'd ever been jittery. When you make her doubt him in any way, you have a different kind of story. Or rather you haven't anything at all. These people are extraverts – get that straight – and I want them to extravert all over the lot. When I want to do a Eugene O'Neill[446] play, I'll buy one.'

Jane Meloney, who had never taken her eyes off Stahr, knew it was going to be all right now. If he had really been going to abandon the picture, he wouldn't have gone at it like this. She had been in this game longer than any of them except Broaca, with whom she had had a three-day affair twenty years ago.

Stahr turned to Reinmund.

'You ought to have understood from the casting, Reiny, what kind of a picture I wanted. I started marking the lines that Corliss and McKelway couldn't say and got tired of it. Remember this in the future – if I order a limousine, I want that kind of car. And the fastest midget racer you ever saw wouldn't do. Now – ' He looked around. ' – shall we go any further? Now that I've told you I don't even like the kind of picture this is? Shall we go on? We've got two weeks. At the end of that time I'm going to put Corliss and McKelway into this or something else – is it worth while?'

'Well, naturally,' said Reinmund, 'I think it is. I feel bad about this. I should have warned Wylie. I thought he had some good ideas.'

'Monroe's right,' said Broaca bluntly. 'I felt this was wrong all the time, but I couldn't put my finger on it.'

Wylie and Rose looked at him contemptuously and exchanged a glance.

'Do you writers think you can get hot on it again?' asked Stahr, not unkindly. 'Or shall I try somebody fresh?'

'I'd like another shot,' said Wylie.

'How about you, Jane?'

She nodded briefly.

'What do you think of the girl?' asked Stahr.

'Well – naturally I'm prejudiced in her favour.'

'You better forget it,' said Stahr warningly. 'Ten million Americans would put thumbs down on that girl if she walked on the screen. We've got an hour and twenty-five minutes on the screen –

you show a woman being unfaithful to a man for one-third of that time and you've given the impression that she's one-third whore.'

'Is that a big proportion?' asked Jane slyly, and they laughed.

'It is for me,' said Stahr thoughtfully, 'even if it wasn't for the Hays office.[447] If you want to paint a scarlet letter on her back, it's all right, but that's another story. Not this story. This is a future wife and mother. However – *however* – '

He pointed his pencil at Wylie White.

' – this has as much passion as that Oscar on my desk.'

'What the hell!' said Wylie. 'She's full of it. Why she goes to – '

'She's loose enough,' said Stahr, ' – but that's all. There's one scene in the play better than all this you cooked up, and you've left it out. When she's trying to make the time pass by changing her watch.'

'It didn't seem to fit,' Wylie apologised.

'Now,' said Stahr, 'I've got about fifty ideas. I'm going to call Miss Doolan.' He pressed a button. ' – And if there's anything you don't understand, speak up – '

Miss Doolan slid in almost imperceptibly. Pacing the floor swiftly, Stahr began. In the first place he wanted to tell them what kind of girl she was – what kind of a girl he approved of here. She was a perfect girl with a few small faults as in the play, but a perfect girl not because the public wanted her that way but because it was the kind of girl that he, Stahr, liked to see in this sort of picture. Was that clear? It was no character role. She stood for health, vitality, ambition, and love. What gave the play its importance was entirely a situation in which she found herself. She became possessed of a secret that affected a great many lives. There was a right thing and a wrong thing to do – at first it was not plain which was which, but when it was, she went right away and did it. That was the kind of story this was – thin, clean, and shining. No doubts.

'She has never heard the word labour troubles,' he said with a sigh. 'She might be living in 1929. Is it plain what kind of girl I want?'

'It's very plain, Mónroe.'

'Now about the things she does,' said Stahr. 'At all times, at all moments when she is on the screen in our sight, she wants to sleep with Ken Willard. Is that plain, Wylie?'

'Passionately plain.'

'Whatever she does, it is in place of sleeping with Ken Willard. If she walks down the street she is walking to sleep with Ken Willard, if she eats her food it is to give her strength to sleep with Ken Willard. *But* at no time do you give the impression that she would even consider sleeping with Ken Willard unless they were properly sanctified. I'm ashamed of having to tell you these kindergarten facts, but they have somehow leaked out of the story.'

He opened the script and began to go through it page by page. Miss Doolan's notes would be typed in quintuplicate and given to them, but Jane Meloney made notes of her own. Broaca put his hand up to his half-closed eyes – he could remember 'when a director was something out here', when writers were gag-men or eager and ashamed young reporters full of whiskey – a director was all there was then. No supervisor – no Stahr.

He started wide-awake as he heard his name.

'It would be nice, John, if you could put the boy on a pointed roof and let him walk around and keep the camera on him. You might get a nice feeling – not danger, not suspense, not pointing for anything – a kid on the roof in the morning.'

Broaca brought himself back in the room.

'All right,' he said, ' – just an element of danger.'

'Not exactly,' said Stahr. 'He doesn't start to fall off the roof. Break into the next scene with it.'

'Through the window,' suggested Jane Meloney. 'He could climb in his sister's window.'

'That's a good transition,' said Stahr. 'Right into the diary scene.'

Broaca was wide-awake now.

'I'll shoot up at him,' he said. 'Let him go away from the camera. Just a fixed shot from quite a distance – let him go away from the camera. Don't follow him. Pick him up in a close shot and let him go away again. No attention on him except against the whole roof and the sky.' He liked the shot – it was a director's shot that didn't come up on every page any more. He might use a crane – it would be cheaper in the end than building the roof on the ground with a process sky. That was one thing about Stahr – the literal sky was the limit. He had worked with Jews too long to believe legends that they were small with money.

'In the third sequence have him hit the priest,' Stahr said.

'What!' Wylie cried, ' – and have the Catholics on our neck.'

'I've talked to Joe Breen.[448] Priests have been hit. It doesn't reflect on them.'

His quiet voice ran on – stopped abruptly as Miss Doolan glanced at the clock.

'Is that too much to do before Monday?' he asked Wylie.

Wylie looked at Jane and she looked back, not even bothering to nod. He saw their weekend melting away, but he was a different man from when he entered the room. When you were paid fifteen hundred a week, emergency work was one thing you did not skimp, not when your picture was threatened. As a 'free lance' writer Wylie had failed from lack of caring, but here was Stahr to care, for all of them. The effect would not wear off when he left the office – nor anywhere within the walls of the lot. He felt a great purposefulness. The mixture of common sense, wise sensibility, theatrical ingenuity, and a certain half-naïve conception of the common weal which Stahr had just stated aloud, inspired him to do his part, to get his block of stone in place, even if the effort were foredoomed, the result as dull as a pyramid.

Out of the window Jane Meloney watched the trickle streaming towards the commissary. She would have her lunch in her office and knit a few rows while it came. The man was coming at one-fifteen with the French perfume smuggled over the Mexican border. That was no sin – it was like Prohibition.

Broaca watched as Reinmund fawned upon Stahr. He sensed that Reinmund was on his way up. He received seven hundred and fifty a week for his partial authority over directors, writers, and stars who got much more. He wore a pair of cheap English shoes he had bought near the Beverly Wilshire,[449] and Broaca hoped they hurt his feet, but soon now he would order his shoes from Peel's[450] and put away his little green Alpine hat with a feather. Broaca was years ahead of him. He had a fine record in the war, but he had never felt quite the same with himself since he had let Ike Franklin strike him in the face with his open hand.

There was smoke in the room, and behind it, behind his great desk, Stahr was withdrawing further and further, in all courtesy, still giving Reinmund an ear and Miss Doolan an ear. The conference was over.

*   *   *

[*Stahr was to have received the Danish Prince Agge, who wanted 'to learn about pictures from the beginning' and who in the author's cast of characters is described as an 'early Fascist'.*]

'Mr Marcus calling from New York,' said Miss Doolan.

'What do you mean?' demanded Stahr. 'Why, I saw him here last night.'

'Well, he's on the phone – it's a New York call and Miss Jacobs' voice. It's his office.'

Stahr laughed.

'I'm seeing him at lunch,' he said. 'There's no aeroplane fast enough to take him there.'

Miss Doolan returned to the phone. Stahr lingered to hear the outcome.

'It's all right,' said Miss Doolan presently. 'It was a mistake. Mr Marcus called East this morning to tell them about the quake and the flood on the back lot, and it seems he asked them to ask you about it. It was a new secretary who didn't understand Mr Marcus. I think she got mixed up.'

'I think she did,' said Stahr grimly.

Prince Agge did not understand either of them, but, looking for the fabulous, he felt it was something triumphantly American. Mr Marcus, whose quarters could be seen across the way, had called his New York office to ask Stahr about the flood. The Prince imagined some intricate relationship without realising that the transaction had taken place entirely within the once brilliant steel-trap mind of Mr Marcus, which was intermittently slipping.

'I think she was a very new secretary,' repeated Stahr. 'Any other messages?'

'Mr Robinson called in,' Miss Doolan said, as she started for the commissary. 'One of the women told him her name, but he's forgotten it – he thinks it was Smith or Brown or Jones.'

'That's a great help.'

'And he remembers she says she just moved to Los Angeles.'

'I remember she had a silver belt,' Stahr said, 'with stars cut out of it.'

'I'm still trying to find out more about Pete Zavras. I talked to his wife.'

'What did she say?'

'Oh, they've had an awful time – given up their house – she's been sick – '

'Is the eye-trouble hopeless?'

'She didn't seem to know anything about the state of his eyes. She didn't even know he was going blind.'

'That's funny.'

He thought about it on the way to luncheon, but it was as confusing as the actor's trouble this morning. Troubles about people's health didn't seem within his range – he gave no thought to his own. In the lane beside the commissary he stepped back as an open electric truck crammed with girls in the bright costumes of the Regency came rolling in from the back lot. The dresses were fluttering in the wind, the young painted faces looked at him curiously, and he smiled as it went by.

*   *   *

Eleven men and their guest, Prince Agge, sat at lunch in the private dining-room of the studio commissary. They were the money men – they were the rulers; and unless there was a guest, they ate in broken silence, sometimes asking questions about each other's wives and children, sometimes discharging a single absorption from the forefront of their consciousness. Eight out of the ten were Jews – five of the ten were foreign-born, including a Greek and an Englishman; and they had all known each other for a long time: there was a rating in the group, from old Marcus down to old Leanbaum, who had bought the most fortunate block of stock in the business and never was allowed to spend over a million a year producing.

Old Marcus still managed to function with disquieting resilience. Some never-atrophying instinct warned him of danger, of gangings up against him – he was never so dangerous himself as when others considered him surrounded. His grey face had attained such immobility that even those who were accustomed to watch the reflex of the inner corner of his eye could no longer see it. Nature had grown a little white whisker there to conceal it; his armour was complete.

As he was the oldest, Stahr was the youngest of the group – not by many years at this date, though he had first sat with most of these men when he was a boy wonder of twenty-two. Then, more than now, he had been a money man among money men. Then he had been able to figure costs in his head with a speed and accuracy that dazzled them – for they were not wizards or even experts in that regard, despite the popular conception of Jews in finance. Most of them owed their success to different and incompatible qualities. But in a group a tradition carries along the less adept, and they were content to look at Stahr for the sublimated auditing, and experience a sort of glow as if they had done it themselves, like rooters at a football game.

Stahr, as will presently be seen, had grown away from that particular gift, though it was always there.

Prince Agge sat between Stahr and Mort Fleishacker, the company lawyer, and across from Joe Popolos the theatre owner. He was hostile to Jews in a vague general way that he tried to cure himself of. As a turbulent man, serving his time in the Foreign Legion,[451] he thought that Jews were too fond of their own skins. But he was willing to concede that they might be different in America under different circumstances, and certainly he found Stahr was much of a man in every way. For the rest – he thought most business men were dull dogs – for final reference he reverted always to the blood of Bernadotte[452] in his veins.

My father – I will call him Mr Brady, as Prince Agge did when he told me of this luncheon – was worried about a picture, and when Leanbaum went out early, he came up and took his chair opposite.

'How about the South America picture idea, Monroe?' he asked.

Prince Agge noticed a blink of attention towards them as distinct as if a dozen pairs of eyelashes had made the sound of batting wings. Then silence again.

'We're going ahead with it,' said Stahr.

'With that same budget?' Brady asked.

Stahr nodded.

'It's out of proportion,' said Brady. 'There won't be any miracle in these bad times – no *Hell's Angels* or *Ben Hur*,[453] when you throw it away and get it back.'

Probably the attack was planned, for Popolos, the Greek, took up the matter in a sort of double talk.

'It's not adoptable, Monroe, in as we wish adopt to this times in as it changes. It what could be done as we run the gamut of prosperity is scarcely conceptuable now.'

'What do you think, Mr Marcus?' asked Stahr.

All eyes followed his down the table, but, as if forewarned, Mr Marcus had already signalled his private waiter behind him that he wished to rise, and was even now in a basket-like position in the waiter's arms. He looked at them with such helplessness that it was hard to realise that in the evenings he sometimes went dancing with his young Canadian girl.

'Monroe is our production genius,' he said. 'I count upon Monroe and lean heavily upon him. I have not seen the flood myself.'

There was a moment of silence as he moved from the room.

'There's not a two million dollar gross in the country now,' said Brady.

'Is not,' agreed Popolos. 'Even as if so you could grab them by the head and push them by and in, is not.'

'Probably not,' agreed Stahr. He paused as if to make sure that all were listening. 'I think we can count on a million and a quarter from the road-show. Perhaps a million and a half altogether. And a quarter of a million abroad.'

Again there was silence – this time puzzled, a little confused. Over his shoulder Stahr asked the waiter to be connected with his office on the phone.

'But your budget?' said Fleishacker. 'Your budget is seventeen hundred and fifty thousand, I understand. And your expectations only add up to that without profits.'

'Those aren't my expectations,' said Stahr. 'We're not sure of more than a million and a half.'

The room had grown so motionless that Prince Agge could hear a grey chunk of ash fall from a cigar in mid-air. Fleishacker started to speak, his face fixed with amazement, but a phone had been handed over Stahr's shoulder.

'Your office, Mr Stahr.'

'Oh, yes – oh, hello, Miss Doolan. I've figured it out about Zavras. It's one of those lousy rumours – I'll bet my shirt on it . . . Oh, you did. Good . . . good. Now here's what to do: send him to my oculist this afternoon – Dr John Kennedy – and have him get a report and have it photostatted – you understand?'

He hung up – turned with a touch of passion to the table at large.

'Did any of you ever hear a story that Pete Zavras was going blind?'

There were a couple of nods. But most of those present were poised breathlessly on whether Stahr had slipped on his figures a minute before.

'It's pure bunk. He says he's never even been to an oculist – never knew why the studios turned against him,' said Stahr. 'Somebody didn't like him or somebody talked too much, and he's been out of work for a year.'

There was a conventional murmur of sympathy. Stahr signed the check and made as though to get up.

'Excuse me, Monroe,' said Fleishacker persistently, while Brady and Popolos watched. 'I'm fairly new here, and perhaps I fail to comprehend implicitly and explicitly.' He was talking fast, but the veins on his forehead bulged with pride at the big words from NYU.[454] 'Do I understand you to say you expect to gross a quarter million short of your budget?'

'It's a quality picture,' said Stahr with assumed innocence.

It had dawned on them all now, but they still felt there was a trick in it. Stahr really thought it would make money. No one in his senses –

'For two years we've played safe,' said Stahr. 'It's time we made a picture that'll lose some money. Write it off as goodwill – this'll bring in new customers.'

Some of them still thought he meant it was a flyer and a favourable one, but he left them in no doubt.

'It'll lose money,' he said as he stood up, his jaw just slightly out and his eyes smiling and shining. 'It would be a bigger miracle than *Hell's Angels* if it broke even. But we have a certain duty to the public, as Pat Brady has said at Academy dinners.[455] It's a good thing for the production schedule to slip in a picture that'll lose money.'

He nodded at Prince Agge. As the latter made his bows quickly, he tried to take in with a last glance the general effect of what Stahr had said, but he could tell nothing. The eyes, not so much downcast as fixed upon an indefinite distance just above the table, were all blinking quickly now, but there was not a whisper in the room.

*   *   *

Coming out of the private dining-room they passed through a corner of the commissary proper. Prince Agge drank it in – eagerly. It was gay with gypsies and with citizens and soldiers, with the sideburns and braided coats of the First Empire.[456] From a little distance they were men who lived and walked a hundred years ago, and Agge wondered how he and the men of his time would look as extras in some future costume picture.

Then he saw Abraham Lincoln, and his whole feeling suddenly changed. He had been brought up in the dawn of Scandinavian socialism when Nicolay's biography[457] was much read. He had been told Lincoln was a great man whom he should admire, and he hated him instead, because he was forced upon him. But now seeing him sitting here, his legs crossed, his kindly face fixed on a forty-cent dinner, including dessert, his shawl wrapped around him as if to protect himself from the erratic air-cooling – now Prince Agge, who was in America at last, stared as a tourist at the mummy of Lenin in the Kremlin.[458] This, then, was Lincoln. Stahr had walked on far ahead of him, turned waiting for him – but still Agge stared.

This, then, he thought, was what they all meant to be.

Lincoln suddenly raised a triangle of pie and jammed it in his mouth, and, a little frightened, Prince Agge hurried to join Stahr.

'I hope you're getting what you want,' said Stahr, feeling he had neglected him. 'We'll have some rushes in half an hour and then you can go on to as many sets as you want.'

'I should rather stay with you,' said Prince Agge.

'I'll see what there is for me,' said Stahr. 'Then we'll go on together.'

There was the Japanese consul on the release of a spy story which might offend the national sensibilities of Japan. There were phone calls and telegrams. There was some further information from Robby.

'Now he remembers the name of the woman. He's sure it was Smith,' said Miss Doolan. 'He asked her if she wanted to come on the lot and get some dry shoes, and she said no – so she can't sue.'

'That's pretty bad for a total recall – "Smith". That's a great help.'

He thought a moment: 'Ask the phone company for a list of Smiths that have taken new phones here in the last month. Call them all.'

'All right.'

Chapter 4

'How ARE YOU, Monroe,' said Red Ridingwood. 'I'm glad you came down.'

Stahr walked past him, heading across the great stage towards the set of a brilliant room that would be used tomorrow. Director Ridingwood followed, realising after a moment that, however fast he walked Stahr managed to be a step or two ahead. He recognised the indication of displeasure – he had used it himself. He had had his own studio once and he had used everything. There was no stop Stahr could pull that would surprise him. His task was the delivery of situations, and Stahr by effective business could not outplay him on his own grounds. Goldwyn[459] had once interfered with him, and Ridingwood had led Goldwyn into trying to act out a part in front of fifty people – with the result that he had anticipated: his own authority had been restored.

Stahr reached the brilliant set and stopped.

'It's no good,' said Ridingwood. 'No imagination. I don't care how you light it – '

'Why did you call me about it?' Stahr asked, standing close to him. 'Why didn't you take it up with Art?'

'I didn't ask you to come down, Monroe.'

'You wanted to be your own supervisor.'

'I'm sorry, Monroe,' said Ridingwood patiently, 'but I didn't ask you to come down.'

Stahr turned suddenly and walked back towards the camera set-up. The eyes and open mouths of a group of visitors moved momentarily off the heroine of the picture, took in Stahr, and then moved vacantly back to the heroine again. They were Knights of Columbus.[460] They had seen the host carried in procession, but this was the dream made flesh.

Stahr stopped beside her chair. She wore a low gown which displayed the bright eczema of her chest and back. Before each take, the blemished surface was plastered over with an emollient, which was removed immediately after the take. Her hair was of the colour and viscosity of drying blood, but there was starlight that actually photographed in her eyes.

Before Stahr could speak, he heard a helpful voice behind him: 'She's radiant. Absolutely radiant.'

It was an assistant director, and the intention was delicate compliment. The actress was being complimented so that she did not have to strain her poor skin to bend and hear. Stahr was being complimented for having her under contract. Ridingwood was being remotely complimented.

'Everything all right?' Stahr asked her pleasantly.

'Oh, it's fine,' she agreed, ' – except for the —ing publicity men.'

He winked at her gently.

'We'll keep them away,' he said.

Her name had become currently synonymous with the expression 'bitch'. Presumably she had modelled herself after one of those queens in the Tarzan comics[461] who rule mysteriously over a nation of blacks. She regarded the rest of the world as black. She was a necessary evil, borrowed for a single picture.

Ridingwood walked with Stahr towards the door of the stage.

'Everything's all right,' the director said. 'She's as good as she can be.'

They were out of hearing range, and Stahr stopped suddenly and looked at Red with blazing eyes.

'You've been photographing crap,' he said. 'Do you know what she reminds me of in the rushes – "Miss Foodstuffs".'

'I'm trying to get the best performance – '

'Come along with me,' said Stahr abruptly.

'With you? Shall I tell them to rest?'

'Leave it as it is,' said Stahr, pushing the padded outer door.

His car and chauffeur waited outside. Minutes were precious most days.

'Get in,' said Stahr.

Red knew now it was serious. He even knew all at once what was the matter. The girl had got the whip hand on him the first day with her cold lashing tongue. He was a peace-loving man and he had let her walk through her part cold rather than cause trouble.

Stahr spoke into his thoughts.

'You can't handle her,' he said. 'I told you what I wanted. I wanted her *mean* – and she comes out bored. I'm afraid we'll have to call it off, Red.'

'The picture?'

'No. I'm putting Harley on it.'

'All right, Monroe.'

'I'm sorry, Red. We'll try something else another time.'

The car drew up in front of Stahr's office.

'Shall I finish this take?' said Red.

'It's being done now,' said Stahr grimly. 'Harley's in there.'

'What the hell –'

'He went in when we came out. I had him read the script last night.'

'Now listen, Monroe –'

'It's my busy day, Red,' said Stahr, tersely. 'You lost interest about three days ago.'

It was a sorry mess, Ridingwood thought. It meant he would have slight, very slight loss of position – it probably meant that he could not have a third wife just now as he had planned. There wasn't even the satisfaction of raising a row about it – if you disagreed with Stahr, you did not advertise it. Stahr was his world's great customer, who was always – almost always – right.

'How about my coat?' he asked suddenly. 'I left it over a chair on the set.'

'I know you did,' said Stahr. 'Here it is.'

He was trying so hard to be charitable about Ridingwood's lapse that he had forgotten that he had it in his hand.

*   *   *

'Mr Stahr's Projection Room' was a miniature picture theatre with four rows of over-stuffed chairs. In front of the front row ran long tables with dim lamps, buzzers, and telephones. Against the wall was an upright piano, left there since the early days of sound. The room had been redecorated and reupholstered only a year before, but already it was ragged again with work and hours.

Here Stahr sat at two-thirty and again at six-thirty watching the lengths of film taken during the day. There was often a savage tensity about the occasion – he was dealing with *faits accomplis* – the net results of months of buying, planning, writing and rewriting, casting, constructing, lighting, rehearsing, and shooting – the fruit of brilliant hunches or of counsels of despair, of lethargy, conspiracy, and sweat. At this point the tortuous manoeuvre was staged and in suspension – there were reports from the battle-line.

Besides Stahr, there were present the representatives of all technical departments, together with the supervisors and unit managers of the pictures concerned. The directors did not appear at these showings – officially because their work was considered done, actually because few punches were pulled here as money ran out in silver spools. There had evolved a delicate staying away.

The staff was already assembled. Stahr came in and took his place quickly, and the murmur of conversation died away. As he sat back and drew his thin knee up beside him in the chair, the lights in the room went out. There was the flare of a match in the back row – then silence.

On the screen a troop of French Canadians pushed their canoes up a rapids. The scene had been photographed in a studio tank, and at the end of each take, after the director's voice could be heard saying 'Cut,' the actors on the screen relaxed and wiped their brows and sometimes laughed hilariously – and the water in the tank stopped flowing and the illusion ceased. Except to name his choice from each set of takes and to remark that it was 'a good process', Stahr made no comment.

The next scene, still in the rapids, called for dialogue between the Canadian girl (Claudette Colbert) and the *courrier du bois* (Ronald Colman),[462] with her looking down at him from a canoe. After a few strips had run through, Stahr spoke up suddenly.

'Has the tank been dismantled?'

'Yes, sir.'

'Monroe – they needed it for – '

Stahr cut in peremptorily.

'Have it set up again right away. Let's have that second take again.'

The lights went on momentarily. One of the unit managers left his chair and came and stood in front of Stahr.

'A beautifully acted scene thrown away,' raged Stahr quietly. 'It wasn't centred. The camera was set up so it caught the beautiful top of Claudette's head all the time she was talking. That's just what we want, isn't it? That's just what people go to see – the top of a beautiful girl's head. Tell Tim he could have saved wear and tear by using her stand-in.'

The lights went out again. The unit manager squatted by Stahr's chair to be out of the way. The take was run again.

'Do you see now?' asked Stahr. 'And there's a hair in the picture – there on the right, see it? Find out if it's in the projector or the film.'

At the very end of the take, Claudette Colbert slowly lifted her head, revealing her great liquid eyes.

'That's what we should have had all the way,' said Stahr. 'She gave a fine performance too. See if you can fit it in tomorrow or late this afternoon.'

Pete Zavras would not have made a slip like that. There were not six cameramen in the industry you could entirely trust.

The lights went on; the supervisor and unit manager for that picture went out.

'Monroe, this stuff was shot yesterday – it came through late last night.'

The room darkened. On the screen appeared the head of Siva, immense and imperturbable, oblivious to the fact that in a few hours it was to be washed away in a flood. Around it milled a crowd of the faithful.

'When you take that scene again,' said Stahr suddenly, 'put a couple of little kids up on top. You better check about whether it's reverent or not, but I think it's all right. Kids'll do anything.'

'Yes, Monroe.'

A silver belt with stars cut out of it . . . Smith, Jones, or Brown . . . Personal – will the woman with the silver belt who –?

With another picture the scene shifted to New York, a gangster story, and suddenly Stahr became restive.

'That scene's trash,' he called suddenly in the darkness. 'It's badly written, it's miscast, it accomplishes nothing. Those types aren't tough. They look like a lot of dressed-up lollipops – what the hell is the matter, Lee?'

'The scene was written on the set this morning,' said Lee Kapper. 'Burton wanted to get all the stuff on Stage 6.'

'Well – it's trash. And so is this one. There's no use printing stuff like that. She doesn't believe what she's saying – neither does Cary.[463] "I love you" in a close-up – they'll cluck you out of the house! And the girl's overdressed.'

In the darkness a signal was given, the projector stopped, the lights went on. The room waited in utter silence. Stahr's face was expressionless.

'Who wrote the scene?' he asked after a minute.

'Wylie White.'

'Is he sober?'

'Sure he is.'

Stahr considered. 'Put about four writers on that scene tonight,' he said. 'See who we've got. Is Sidney Howard[464] here yet?'

'He got in this morning.'

'Talk to him about it. Explain to him what I want there. The girl is in deadly terror – she's stalling. It's as simple as that. People don't have three emotions at once. And Kapper – '

The art director leaned forward out of the second row.

'Yeah.'

'There's something the matter with that set.'

There were little glances exchanged all over the room.

'What is it, Monroe?'

'You tell *me*,' said Stahr. 'It's crowded. It doesn't carry your eye out. It looks cheap.'

'It wasn't.'

'I know it wasn't. There's not much the matter, but there's something. Go over and take a look tonight. It may be too much furniture – or the wrong kind. Perhaps a window would help. Couldn't you force the perspective in that hall a little more?'

'I'll see what I can do.' Kapper edged his way out of the row, looking at his watch.

'I'll have to get at it right away,' he said. 'I'll work tonight and we'll put it up in the morning.'

'All right. Lee, you can shoot around those scenes, can't you?'

'I think so, Monroe.'

'I take the blame for this. Have you got the fight stuff?'

'Coming up now.'

Stahr nodded. Kapper hurried out, and the room went dark again. On the screen four men staged a terrific socking match in a cellar. Stahr laughed.

'Look at Tracy,'[465] he said. 'Look at him go down after that guy. I bet he's been in a few.'

The men fought over and over. Always the same fight. Always at the end they faced each other smiling, sometimes touching the opponent in a friendly gesture on the shoulder. The only one in danger was the stunt man, a pug who could have murdered the other three. He was in danger only if they swung wild and didn't follow the blows he had taught them. Even so, the youngest actor was afraid for his face and the director had covered his flinches with ingenious angles and interpositions.

And then two men met endlessly in a door, recognised each other, and went on. They met, they started, they went on.

Then a little girl read underneath a tree with a boy reading on a limb of the tree above. The little girl was bored and wanted to talk to the boy. He would pay no attention. The core of the apple he was eating fell on the little girl's head.

A voice spoke up out of the darkness: 'It's pretty long, isn't it, Monroe?'

'Not a bit,' said Stahr. 'It's nice. It has nice feeling.'

'I just thought it was long.'

'Sometimes ten feet can be too long – sometimes a scene two hundred feet long can be too short. I want to speak to the cutter before he touches this scene – this is something that'll be remembered in the picture.'

The oracle had spoken. There was nothing to question or argue. Stahr must be right always, not most of the time, but always – or the structure would melt down like gradual butter.

Another hour passed. Dreams hung in fragments at the far end of the room, suffered analysis, passed – to be dreamed in crowds, or else discarded. The end was signalled by two tests, a character man and a girl. After the rushes, which had a tense rhythm of their own, the tests were smooth and finished; the observers settled in their chairs; Stahr's foot slipped to the floor. Opinions were welcome. One of the technical men let it be known that he would willingly cohabit with the girl; the rest were indifferent.

'Somebody sent up a test of that girl two years ago. She must be getting around – but she isn't getting any better. But the man's good. Can't we use him as the old Russian Prince in *Steppes*?'

'He *is* an old Russian Prince,' said the casting director, 'but he's ashamed of it. He's a Red. And that's one part he says he wouldn't play.'

'It's the only part he could play,' said Stahr.

The lights went on. Stahr rolled his gum into its wrapper and put it in an ashtray. He turned questioningly to his secretary.

'The processes on Stage 2,' she said.

He looked in briefly at the processes, moving pictures taken against a background of other moving pictures by an ingenious device. There was a meeting in Marcus' office on the subject of *Manon*[466] with a happy ending, and Stahr had his say on that as he had had before – it had been making money without a happy ending for a century and a half. He was obdurate – at this time in the afternoon he was at his most fluent and the opposition faded into another subject: they would lend a dozen stars to the benefit for those the quake had made homeless at Long Beach. In a sudden burst of giving, five of them all at once made up a purse of twenty-five thousand dollars. They gave well, but not as poor men give. It was not charity.

At his office there was word from the oculist to whom he had sent Pete Zavras that the cameraman's eyes were 19–20: approximately perfect. He had written a letter that Zavras was having photostated. Stahr walked around his office cockily while Miss Doolan admired him. Prince Agge had dropped in to thank him for his afternoon on the sets, and while they talked, a cryptic word came from a supervisor that some writers named Tarleton had 'found out' and were about to quit.

'These are good writers,' Stahr explained to Prince Agge, 'and we don't have good writers out here.'

'Why, you can hire anyone!' exclaimed his visitor in surprise.

'Oh, we hire them, but when they get out here, they're not good writers – so we have to work with the material we have.'

'Such as what?'

'Anybody that'll accept the system and stay decently sober – we have all sorts of people – disappointed poets, one-hit playwrights – college girls – we put them on an idea in pairs, and if it slows down, we put two more writers working behind them. I've had as many as three pairs working independently on the same idea.'

'Do they like that?'

'Not if they know about it. They're not geniuses – none of them could make as much any other way. But these Tarletons are a husband and wife team from the East – pretty good playwrights. They've just found out they're not alone on the story and it shocks them – shocks their sense of unity – that's the word they'll use.'

'But what does make the – the unity?'

Stahr hesitated – his face was grim except that his eyes twinkled.

'I'm the unity,' he said. 'Come and see us again.'

He saw the Tarletons. He told them he liked their work, looking at Mrs Tarleton as if he could read her handwriting through the typescript. He told them kindly that he was taking them from the picture and putting them on another, where there was less pressure, more time. As he had half expected, they begged to stay on the first picture, seeing a quicker credit, even though it was shared with others. The system was a shame, he admitted – gross, commercial, to be deplored. He had originated it – a fact that he did not mention.

When they had gone, Miss Doolan came in triumphant.

'Mr Stahr, the lady with the belt is on the phone.'

Stahr walked into his office alone and sat down behind his desk and picked up the phone with a great sinking of his stomach. He did not know what he wanted. He had not thought about the matter as he had thought about the matter of Pete Zavras. At first he had only wanted to know if they were 'professional' people, if the woman was an actress who had got herself up to look like Minna, as he had once had a young actress made up like Claudette Colbert and photographed her from the same angles.

'Hello,' he said.

'Hello.'

As he searched the short, rather surprised word for a vibration of last night, the feeling of terror began to steal over him, and he choked it off with an effort of will.

'Well – you were hard to find,' he said. '*Smith* – and you moved here recently. That was all we had. And a silver belt.'

'Oh, yes,' the voice said, still uneasy, unpoised, 'I had on a silver belt last night.'

Now, where from here?

'Who *are* you?' the voice said, with a touch of flurried bourgeois dignity.

'My name is Monroe Stahr,' he said.

A pause. It was a name that never appeared on the screen, and she seemed to have trouble placing it.

'Oh, yes – yes. You were the husband of Minna Davis.'

'Yes.'

Was it a trick? As the whole vision of last night came back to him – the very skin with that peculiar radiance as if phosphorus had touched it – he thought whether it might not be a trick to reach him from somewhere. Not Minna and yet Minna. The curtains blew suddenly into the room, the papers whispered on his desk, and his heart cringed faintly at the intense reality of the day outside his window. If he could go out now this way, what would happen if he saw her again – the starry veiled expression, the mouth strongly formed for poor brave human laughter.

'I'd like to see you. Would you like to come to the studio?'

Again the hesitancy – then a blank refusal.

'Oh, I don't think I ought to. I'm awfully sorry.'

This last was purely formal, a brush-off, a final axe. Ordinary skin-deep vanity came to Stahr's aid, adding persuasion to his urgency.

'I'd like to see you,' he said. 'There's a reason.'

'Well – I'm afraid that – '

'Could I come and see you?'

A pause again, not from hesitation, he felt, but to assemble her answer.

'There's something you don't know,' she said finally.

'Oh, you're probably married,' he was impatient. 'It has nothing to do with that. I asked you to come here openly, bring your husband if you have one.'

'It's – it's quite impossible.'

'Why?'

'I feel silly even talking to you, but your secretary insisted – I thought I'd dropped something in the flood last night and you'd found it.'

'I want very much to see you for five minutes.'

'To put me in the movies?'

'That wasn't my idea.'

There was such a long pause that he thought he had offended her.

'Where could I meet you?' she asked unexpectedly.

'Here? At your house?'

'No – somewhere outside.'

Suddenly Stahr could think of no place. His own house – a restaurant. Where did people meet? – a house of assignation, a cocktail bar?

'I'll meet you somewhere at nine o'clock,' she said.

'That's impossible, I'm afraid.'

'Then never mind.'

'All right, then, nine o'clock, but can we make it near here? There's a drugstore on Wilshire – '[467]

*   *   *

It was a quarter to six. There were two men outside who had come every day at this time only to be postponed. This was an hour of fatigue – the men's business was not so important that it must be seen to, nor so insignificant that it could be ignored. So he postponed it again and sat motionless at his desk for a moment, thinking about Russia. Not so much about Russia as about the picture about Russia[468] which would consume a hopeless half-hour presently. He knew there were many stories about Russia, not to mention The Story, and he had employed a squad of writers and research men for over a year, but all the stories involved had the wrong feel. He felt it could be told in terms of the American thirteen states,[469] but it kept coming out different, in new terms that opened unpleasant possibilities and problems. He considered he was very fair to Russia – he had no desire to make anything but a sympathetic picture, but it kept turning into a headache.

'Mr Stahr – Mr Drummon's outside, and Mr Kirstoff and Mrs Cornhill, about the Russian picture.'

'All right – send them in.'

Afterwards from six-thirty to seven-thirty he watched the afternoon rushes. Except for his engagement with the girl, he would ordinarily have spent the early evening in the projection room or the dubbing-room, but it had been a late night with the earthquake, and he decided to go to dinner. Coming in through his front office, he found Pete Zavras waiting, his arm in a sling.

'You are the Aeschylus and the Euripides of the moving picture,' said Zavras simply. 'Also the Aristophanes and the Menander.'[470]

He bowed.

'Who are they?' asked Stahr smiling.

'They are my countrymen.'

'I didn't know you made pictures in Greece.'

'You're joking with me, Monroe,' said Zavras. 'I want to say you are as dandy a fellow as they come. You have saved me one hundred per cent.'

'You feel all right now?'

'My arm is nothing. It feels like someone kisses me there. It was worth doing what I did, if this is the outcome.'

'How did you happen to do it here?' Stahr asked curiously.

'Before the Delphic oracle,'[471] said Zavras. 'The Oedipus who solved the riddle. I wish I had my hands on the son-of-a-bitch who started the story.'

'You make me sorry I didn't get an education,' said Stahr.

'It isn't worth a damn,' said Pete. 'I took my baccalaureate in Salonika[472] and look how I ended up.'

'Not quite,' said Stahr.

'If you want anybody's throat cut any time day or night,' said Zavras, 'my number is in the book.'

Stahr closed his eyes and opened them again. Zavras's silhouette had blurred a little against the sun. He hung on to the table behind him and said in an ordinary voice, 'Good luck, Pete.'

The room was almost black, but he made his feet move, following a pattern, into his office and waited till the door clicked shut before he felt for the pills. The water decanter clattered against the table; the glass clacked. He sat down in a big chair, waiting for the benzedrine to take effect before he went to dinner.

*　　*　　*

As Stahr walked back from the commissary, a hand waved at him from an open roadster.[473] From the heads showing over the back he recognised a young actor and his girl, and watched them disappear through the gate, already part of the summer twilight. Little by little he was losing the feel of such things, until it seemed that Minna had taken their poignancy with her; his appreciation of splendour was fading so that presently the luxury of eternal mourning would depart. A childish association of Minna with the material heavens made him, when he reached his office, order out his roadster for the first time this year. The big limousine seemed heavy with remembered conferences or exhausted sleep.

Leaving the studio, he was still tense, but the open car pulled the summer evening up close, and he looked at it. There was a moon down at the end of the boulevard, and it was a good illusion that it was a different moon every evening, every year. Other lights shone in

Hollywood since Minna's death: in the open markets lemons and grapefruit and green apples slanted a misty glare into the street. Ahead of him the stop-signal of a car winked violet and at another crossing he watched it wink again. Everywhere floodlights raked the sky. On an empty corner two mysterious men moved a gleaming drum in pointless arcs over the heavens.

In the drugstore a woman stood by the candy counter. She was tall, almost as tall as Stahr, and embarrassed. Obviously it was a situation for her, and if Stahr had not looked as he did – most considerate and polite – she would not have gone through with it. They said hello, and walked out without another word, scarcely a glance – yet before they reached the curb Stahr knew: this was just exactly a pretty American woman and nothing more – no beauty like Minna.

'Where are we going?' she asked. 'I thought there'd be a chauffeur. Never mind – I'm a good boxer.'

'Boxer?'

'That didn't sound very polite.' She forced a smile. 'But you people are supposed to be such *horrors*.'

The conception of himself as sinister amused Stahr – then suddenly it failed to amuse him.

'Why did you want to see me?' she asked as she got in.

He stood motionless, wanting to tell her to get out immediately. But she had relaxed in the car, and he knew the unfortunate situation was of his own making – he shut his teeth and walked round to get in. The street lamp fell full upon her face, and it was difficult to believe that this was the girl of last night. He saw no resemblance to Minna at all.

'I'll run you home,' he said. 'Where do you live?'

'Run me home?' She was startled. 'There's no hurry – I'm sorry if I offended you.'

'No. It was nice of you to come. I've been stupid. Last night I had an idea that you were an exact double for someone I knew. It was dark and the light was in my eyes.'

She was offended – he had reproached her for not looking like someone else.

'It was just that!' she said. 'That's funny.'

They rode in silence for a minute.

'You were married to Minna Davis, weren't you?' she said with a flash of intuition. 'Excuse me for referring to it.'

He was driving as fast as he could without making it conspicuous.

'I'm quite a different type from Minna Davis,' she said, ' – if that's who you meant. You might have referred to the girl who was with me. She looks more like Minna Davis than I do.'

That was of no interest now. The thing was to get this over quick and forget it.

'Could it have been her?' she asked. 'She lives next door.'

'Not possibly,' he said. 'I remember the silver belt you wore.'

'That was me all right.'

They were northwest of Sunset, climbing one of the canyons through the hills. Lighted bungalows rose along the winding road, and the electric current that animated them sweated into the evening air as radio sound.

'You see that last highest light – Kathleen lives there. I live just over the top of the hill.'

A moment later she said, 'Stop here.'

'I thought you said over the top.'

'I want to stop at Kathleen's.'

'I'm afraid I'm – '

'I want to get out here myself,' she said impatiently.

Stahr slid out after her. She started towards a new little house almost roofed over by a single willow tree, and automatically he followed her to the steps. She rang a bell and turned to say good-night.

'I'm sorry you were disappointed,' she said.

He was sorry for her now – sorry for them both.

'It was my fault. Good-night.'

A wedge of light came out the opening door, and as a girl's voice enquired, 'Who is it?' Stahr looked up.

There she was – face and form and smile against the light from inside. It was Minna's face – the skin with its peculiar radiance as if phosphorus had touched it, the mouth with its warm line that never counted costs – and over all the haunting jollity that had fascinated a generation.

With a leap his heart went out of him as it had the night before, only this time it stayed out there with a vast beneficence.

'Oh, Edna, you can't come in,' the girl said. 'I've been cleaning and the house is full of ammonia smell.'

Edna began to laugh, bold and loud. 'I believe it was you he wanted to see, Kathleen,' she said.

Stahr's eyes and Kathleen's met and tangled. For an instant they made love as no one ever dares to do after. Their glance was slower than an embrace, more urgent than a call.

'He telephoned me,' said Edna. 'It seems he thought – '

Stahr interrupted, stepping forward into the light.

'I was afraid we were rude at the studio, yesterday evening.'

But there were no words for what he really said. She listened closely without shame. Life flared high in them both – Edna seemed at a distance and in darkness.

'You weren't rude,' said Kathleen. A cool wind blew the brown curls around her forehead. 'We had no business there.'

'I hope you'll both,' Stahr said, 'come and make a tour of the studio.'

'Who are you? Somebody important?'

'He was Minna Davis's husband, he's a producer,' said Edna, as if it were a rare joke, ' – and this isn't at all what he just told me. I think he has a crush on you.'

'Shut up, Edna,' said Kathleen sharply.

As if suddenly realising her offensiveness, Edna said, 'Phone me, will you?' and stalked away towards the road. But she carried their secret with her – she had seen a spark pass between them in the darkness.

'I remember you,' Kathleen said to Stahr. 'You got us out of the flood.'

Now what? The other woman was more missed in her absence. They were alone and on too slim a basis for what had passed already. They existed nowhere. His world seemed far away – she had no world at all except the idol's head, the half-open door.

'You're Irish,' he said, trying to build one for her.

She nodded.

'I've lived in London a long time – I didn't think you could tell.'

The wild green eyes of a bus sped up the road in the darkness. They were silent until it went by.

'Your friend Edna didn't like me,' he said. 'I think it was the word Producer.'

'She's just come out here, too. She's a silly creature who means no harm. *I* shouldn't be afraid of you.'

She searched his face. She thought, like everyone, that he seemed tired – then she forgot it at the impression he gave of a brazier out of doors on a cool night.

'I suppose the girls are all after you to put them on the screen.'

'They've given up,' he said.

This was an understatement – they were all there, he knew, just over the threshold, but they had been there so long that their clamouring voices were no more than the sound of the traffic in the street. But his position remained more than royal: a king could make only one queen; Stahr, at least so they supposed, could make many.

'I'm thinking that it would turn you into a cynic,' she said. 'You didn't want to put me in pictures?'

'No.'

'That's good. I'm no actress. Once in London a man came up to me in the Carlton[474] and asked me to make a test, but I thought a while and finally I didn't go.'

They had been standing nearly motionless, as if in a moment he would leave and she would go in. Stahr laughed suddenly.

'I feel as if I had my foot in the door – like a collector.'

She laughed, too. 'I'm sorry I can't ask you in. Shall I get my reefer[475] and sit outside?'

'No.' He scarcely knew why he felt it was time to go. He might see her again – he might not. It was just as well this way.

'You'll come to the studio?' he said. 'I can't promise to go around with you, but if you come, you must be sure to send word to my office.'

A frown, the shadow of a hair in breadth, appeared between her eyes. 'I'm not sure,' she said. 'But I'm very much obliged.'

He knew that, for some reason, she would not come – in an instant she had slipped away from him. They both sensed that the moment was played out. He must go, even though he went nowhere, and it left him with nothing. Practically, vulgarly, he did not have her telephone number – or even her name; but it seemed impossible to ask for them now.

She walked with him to the car, her glowing beauty and her unexplored novelty pressing up against him; but there was a foot of moonlight between them when they came out of the shadow.

'Is this all?' he said spontaneously.

He saw regret in her face – but there was a flick of the lip, also, a bending of the smile towards some indirection, a momentary dropping and lifting of a curtain over a forbidden passage.

'I do hope we'll meet again,' she said almost formally.

'I'd be sorry if we didn't.'

They were distant for a moment. But as he turned his car in the next drive, and came back with her still waiting, and waved and drove on, he felt exalted and happy. He was glad that there was beauty in the world that would not be weighed in the scales of the casting department.

But at home he felt a curious loneliness as his butler made him tea in the samovar. It was the old hurt come back, heavy and delightful. When he took up the first of two scripts that were his evening stint, that presently he would visualise line by line on the screen, he waited a moment, thinking of Minna. He explained to her that it was really nothing, that no one could ever be like she was, that he was sorry.

*　　*　　*

That was substantially a day of Stahr's. I don't know about the illness, when it started, etc., because he was secretive, but I know he fainted a couple of times that month because father told me. Prince Agge is my authority for the luncheon in the commissary where he told them he was going to make a picture that would lose money – which was something, considering the men he had to deal with and that he held a big block of stock and had a profit-sharing contract.

And Wylie White told me a lot, which I believed because he felt Stahr intensely with a mixture of jealousy and admiration. As for me, I was head over heels in love with him then, and you can take what I say for what it's worth.

Chapter 5

FRESH AS THE MORNING, I went up to see him a week later. Or so I thought; when Wylie called for me, I had gotten into riding clothes to give the impression I'd been out in the dew since early morning.

'I'm going to throw myself under the wheel of Stahr's car, this morning,' I said.

'How about this car?' he suggested. 'It's one of the best cars Mort Fleishacker ever sold second-hand.'

'Not on your flowing veil,' I answered like a book. 'You have a wife in the East.'

'She's the past,' he said. 'You've got one great card, Celia – your valuation of yourself. Do you think anybody would look at you if you weren't Pat Brady's daughter?'

We don't take abuse like our mothers would have. Nothing – no remark from a contemporary means much. They tell you to be smart, they're marrying you for your money, or you tell them. Everything's simpler. Or is it? as we used to say.

But as I turned on the radio and the car raced up Laurel Canyon to 'The Thundering Beat Of My Heart',[476] I didn't believe he was right. I had good features except my face was too round, and a skin they seemed to love to touch, and good legs, and I didn't have to wear a brassière. I haven't a sweet nature, but who was Wylie to reproach me for that?

'Don't you think I'm smart to go in the morning?' I asked.

'Yeah. To the busiest man in California. He'll appreciate it. Why didn't you wake him up at four?'

'That's just it. At night he's tired. He's been looking at people all day, and some of them not bad. I come in in the morning and start a train of thought.'

'I don't like it. It's brazen.'

'What have you got to offer? And don't be rough.'

'I love you,' he said without much conviction. 'I love you more than I love your money, and that's plenty. Maybe your father would make me a supervisor.'

'I could marry the last man tapped for Bones[477] this year and live in Southampton.'

I turned the dial and got either 'Gone' or 'Lost' – there were good songs that year. The music was getting better again. When I was young during the Depression, it wasn't so hot, and the best numbers were from the twenties, like Benny Goodman playing 'Blue Heaven' or Paul Whiteman[478] with 'When Day Is Done'.[479] There were only the bands to listen to. But now I liked almost everything except father singing 'Little Girl, You've Had A Busy Day'[480] to try to create a sentimental father-and-daughter feeling.

'Lost' and 'Gone' were the wrong mood, so I turned again and got 'Lovely To Look At',[481] which was my kind of poetry. I looked back as we crossed the crest of the foothills – with the air so clear you could see the leaves on Sunset Mountain two miles away. It's startling to you sometimes – just air, unobstructed, uncomplicated air.

'*Lovely to look at – de-lightful to know-w,*' I sang.

'Are you going to sing for Stahr?' Wylie said. 'If you do, get in a line about my being a good supervisor.'

'Oh, this'll be only Stahr and me,' I said. 'He's going to look at me and think, "I've never really seen her before".'

'We don't use that line this year,' he said.

' – Then he'll say "Little Cecilia", like he did the night of the earthquake. He'll say he never noticed I have become a woman.'

'You won't have to do a thing.'

'I'll stand there and bloom. After he kisses me as you would a child – '

'That's all in my script,' complained Wylie, 'and I've got to show it to him tomorrow.'

' – he'll sit down and put his face in his hands and say he never thought of me like that.'

'You mean you get in a little fast work during the kiss?'

'I bloom, I told you. How often do I have to tell you I bloom.'

'It's beginning to sound pretty randy to me,' said Wylie. 'How about laying off – I've got to work this morning.'

'Then he says it seems as if he was always meant to be this way.'

'Right in the industry. Producer's blood.' He pretended to shiver. 'I'd hate to have a transfusion of that.'

'Then he says – '

'I know all his lines,' said Wylie. 'What I want to know is what you say.'

'Somebody comes in,' I went on.

'And you jump up quickly off the casting couch, smoothing your skirts.'

'Do you want me to walk out and get home?'

We were in Beverly Hills, getting very beautiful now with the tall Hawaiian pines. Hollywood is a perfectly zoned city, so you know exactly what kind of people economically live in each section, from executives and directors, through technicians in their bungalows, right down to extras. This was the executive section and a very fancy lot of pastry. It wasn't as romantic as the dingiest village of Virginia or New Hampshire, but it looked nice this morning.

'They asked me how I knew,' sang the radio, ' *– my true love was true.* [482]

My heart was fire, and smoke was in my eyes and everything, but I figured my chance at about fifty-fifty. I would walk right up on him as if I was either going to walk through him or kiss him on the mouth – and stop a bare foot away and say 'Hello' with disarming understatement.

And I did – though of course it wasn't like I expected: Stahr's beautiful dark eyes looking back into mine, knowing, I am dead sure, everything I was thinking – and not a bit embarrassed. I stood there an hour, I think, without moving, and all he did was twitch the side of his mouth and put his hands in his pockets.

'Will you go with me to the ball tonight?' I asked.

'What ball?'

'The screenwriters' ball down at the Ambassador.' [483]

'Oh, yes.' He considered. 'I can't go with you. I might just come in late. We've got a sneak preview in Glendale.'

How different it all was from what you'd planned. When he sat down, I went over and put my head among his telephones, like a sort of desk appendage, and looked at him; and his dark eyes looked back so kind and nothing. Men don't often know those times when a girl could be had for nothing. All I succeeded in putting into his head was: 'Why don't you get married, Celia?'

Maybe he'd bring up Robby again, try to make a match there.

'What could I do to interest an interesting man?' I asked him.

'Tell him you're in love with him.'

'Should I chase him?'

'Yes,' he said smiling.

'I don't know. If it isn't there, it isn't there.'

'I'd marry you,' he said unexpectedly. 'I'm lonesome as hell. But I'm too old and tired to undertake anything.'

I went around the desk and stood beside him.

'Undertake me.'

He looked up in surprise, understanding for the first time that I was in deadly earnest.

'Oh, no,' he said. He looked almost miserable for a minute. 'Pictures are my girl. I haven't got much time – ' He corrected himself quickly, 'I mean any time.'

'You couldn't love me.'

'It's not that,' he said and – right out of my dream but with a difference: 'I never thought of you that way, Celia. I've known you so long. Somebody told me you were going to marry Wylie White.'

'And you had – no reaction.'

'Yes, I did. I was going to speak to you about it. Wait till he's been sober for two years.'

'I'm not even considering it, Monroe.'

We were way off the track, and just as in my daydream, somebody came in – only I was quite sure Stahr had pressed a concealed button.

I'll always think of that moment, when I felt Miss Doolan behind me with her pad, as the end of childhood, the end of the time when you cut out pictures. What I was looking at wasn't Stahr but a picture of him I cut out over and over: the eyes that flashed a sophisticated understanding at you and then darted up too soon into his wide brow with its ten thousand plots and plans; the face that was ageing from within, so that there were no casual furrows of worry and vexation but a drawn asceticism as if from a silent self-set struggle – or a long illness. It was handsomer to me than all the rosy tan from Coronado to Del Monte.[484] He was my picture, as sure as if he had been pasted on the inside of my old locker in school. That's what I told Wylie White, and when a girl tells the man she likes second best about the other one – then she's in love.

*   *   *

I noticed the girl long before Stahr arrived at the dance. Not a pretty girl, for there are none of those in Los Angeles – one girl can be pretty, but a dozen are only a chorus. Nor yet a professional beauty – they do all the breathing for everyone, and finally even the men have to go outside for air. Just a girl, with the skin of one of Raphael's corner angels[485] and a style that made you look back twice to see if it were something she had on.

I noticed her and forgot her. She was sitting back behind the pillars at a table whose ornament was a faded semi-star, who, in hopes of being noticed and getting a bit, rose and danced regularly with some scarecrow males. It reminded me shamefully of my first party, where mother made me dance over and over with the same boy to keep in the spotlight. The semi-star spoke to several people at our table, but we were busy being Café Society and she got nowhere at all.

From our angle it appeared that they all wanted something.

'You're expected to fling it around,' said Wylie, ' – like in the old days. When they find out you're hanging on to it, they get discouraged. That's what all this brave gloom is about – the only way to keep their self-respect is to be Hemingway characters.[486] But underneath they hate you in a mournful way, and you know it.'

He was right – I knew that since 1933 the rich could only be happy alone together.

I saw Stahr come into the half-light at the top of the wide steps and stand there with his hands in his pockets, looking around. It was late and the lights seemed to have burned a little lower, though they were the same. The floor show was finished, except for a man who still wore a placard which said that at midnight in the Hollywood Bowl[487] Sonja Henie[488] was going to skate on hot soup. You could see the sign as he danced becoming less funny on his back. A few years before there would have been drunks around. The faded actress seemed to be looking for them hopefully over her partner's shoulder. I followed her with my eyes when she went back to her table –

– and there, to my surprise, was Stahr talking to the other girl. They were smiling at each other as if this was the beginning of the world.

*   *   *

Stahr had expected nothing like this when he stood at the head of the steps a few minutes earlier. The 'sneak preview' had disappointed him, and afterwards he had had a scene with Jacques La Borwitz right in front of the theatre, for which he was now sorry. He had started towards the Brady party when he saw Kathleen sitting in the middle of a long white table alone.

Immediately things changed. As he walked towards her, the people shrank back against the walls till they were only murals; the white table lengthened and became an altar where the priestess sat alone. Vitality swelled up in him, and he could have stood a long time across the table from her, looking and smiling.

The incumbents of the table were crawling back – Stahr and Kathleen danced.

When she came close, his several visions of her blurred; she was momentarily unreal. Usually a girl's skull made her real, but not this time – Stahr continued to be dazzled as they danced out along the floor – to the last edge, where they stepped through a mirror into another dance with new dancers whose faces were familiar but nothing more. In this new region he talked, fast and urgently.

'What's your name?'

'Kathleen Moore.'

'Kathleen Moore,' he repeated.

'I have no telephone, if that's what you're thinking.'

'When will you come to the studio?'

'It's not possible. Truly.'

'Why isn't it? Are you married?'

'No.'

'You're not married?'

'No, nor never have been. But then I may be.'

'Someone there at the table.'

'No.' She laughed. 'What curiosity!'

But she was deep in it with him, no matter what the words were. Her eyes invited him to a romantic communion of unbelievable intensity. As if she realised this, she said, frightened: 'I must go back now. I promised this dance.'

'I don't want to lose you. Couldn't we have lunch or dinner?'

'It's impossible.' But her expression helplessly amended the words to, 'It's just possible. The door is still open by a chink, if you could squeeze past. But quickly – so little time.'

'I must go back,' she repeated aloud. Then she dropped her arms, stopped dancing, and looked at him, a laughing wanton.

'When I'm with you, I don't breathe quite right,' she said.

She turned, picked up her long dress, and stepped back through the mirror. Stahr followed until she stopped near her table.

'Thank you for the dance,' she said, 'and now really, good-night.'

Then she nearly ran.

Stahr went to the table where he was expected and sat down with the Café Society group – from Wall Street, Grand Street, Loudon County, Virginia, and Odessa, Russia. They were all talking with enthusiasm about a horse that had run very fast, and Mr Marcus was the most enthusiastic of all. Stahr guessed that the Jews had taken over the worship of horses as a symbol – for years it had been the Cossacks mounted and the Jews on foot. Now the Jews had horses, and it gave them a sense of extraordinary well-being and power. Stahr sat pretending to listen and even nodding when something was referred to him, but all the time watching the table behind the pillars. If everything had not happened as it had, even to his connecting the silver belt with the wrong girl, he might have thought it was some elaborate frame-up. But the elusiveness was beyond suspicion. For there in a moment he saw that she was escaping again – the pantomime at the table indicated goodbye. She was leaving, she was gone.

'There,' said Wylie White with malice, 'goes Cinderella. Simply bring the slipper to the Regal Shoe Company, 812 South Broadway.'

Stahr overtook her in the long upper lobby, where middle-aged women sat behind a roped-off space, watching the ballroom entrance.

'Am I responsible for this?' he asked.

'I was going, anyhow.' But she added almost resentfully, 'They talked as if I'd been dancing with the Prince of Wales. They all stared at me. One of the men wanted to draw my picture, and another one wanted to see me tomorrow.'

'That's just what I want,' said Stahr gently, 'but I want to see you much more than he does.'

'You insist so,' she said wearily. 'One reason I left England was that men always wanted their own way. I thought it was different here. Isn't it enough that I don't want to see you?'

'Ordinarily,' agreed Stahr. 'Please believe me, I'm way out of my depth already. I feel like a fool. But I must see you again and talk to you.'

She hesitated.

'There's no reason for feeling like a fool,' she said. 'You're too good a man to feel like a fool. But you should see this for what it is.'

'What is it?'

'You've fallen for me – completely. You've got me in your dreams.'

'I'd forgotten you,' he declared, ' – till the moment I walked in that door.'

'Forgotten me with your head perhaps. But I knew the first time I saw you that you were the kind that likes me – '

She stopped herself. Near them a man and woman from the party were saying goodbye: 'Tell her hello – tell her I love her dearly,' said the woman, ' – you both – all of you – the children.' Stahr could not talk like that, the way everyone talked now. He could think of nothing further to say as they walked towards the elevator except: 'I suppose you're perfectly right.'

'Oh, you admit it?'

'No, I don't,' he retracted. 'It's just the whole way you're made. What you say – how you walk – the way you look right this minute – ' He saw she had melted a little, and his hopes rose. 'Tomorrow is Sunday, and usually I work on Sunday, but if there's anything you're curious about in Hollywood, any person you want to meet or see, please let me arrange it.'

They were standing by the elevator. It opened, but she let it go.

'You're very modest,' she said. 'You always talk about showing me the studio and taking me around. Don't you ever stay alone?'

'Tomorrow I'll feel very much alone.'

'Oh, the poor man – I could weep for him. He could have all the stars jumping around him and he chooses me.'

He smiled – he had laid himself open to that one.

The elevator came again. She signalled for it to wait.

'I'm a weak woman,' she said. 'If I meet you tomorrow, will you leave me in peace? No, you won't. You'll make it worse. It wouldn't do any good but harm, so I'll say no and thank you.'

She got into the elevator. Stahr got in too, and they smiled as they dropped two floors to the hall, cross-sectioned with small shops. Down at the end, held back by police, was the crowd, their heads and shoulders leaning forward to look down the alley. Kathleen shivered.

'They looked so strange when I came in,' she said, ' – as if they were furious at me for not being someone famous.'

'I know another way out,' said Stahr.

They went through a drugstore, down an alley, and came out into the clear cool California night beside the car park. He felt detached from the dance now, and she did, too.

'A lot of picture people used to live down here,' he said. 'John Barrymore and Pola Negri in those bungalows. And Connie Talmadge[489] lived in that tall thin apartment house over the way.'

'Doesn't anybody live here now?'

'The studios moved out into the country,' he said, ' – what used to be the country. I had some good times around here, though.'

He did not mention that ten years ago Minna and her mother had lived in another apartment over the way.

'How old are you?' she asked suddenly.

'I've lost track – almost thirty-five, I think.'

'They said at the table you were the boy wonder.'

'I'll be that when I'm sixty,' he said grimly. 'You will meet me tomorrow, won't you?'

'I'll meet you,' she said. 'Where?'

Suddenly there was no place to meet. She would not go to a party at anyone's house, nor to the country, nor swimming, though she hesitated, nor to a well-known restaurant. She seemed hard to please, but he knew there was some reason. He would find out in time. It occurred to him that she might be the sister or daughter of someone well-known who was pledged to keep in the background. He suggested that he come for her and they could decide.

'That wouldn't do,' she said. 'What about right here? – the same spot.'

He nodded – pointing up at the arch under which they stood.

He put her into her car, which would have brought eighty dollars from any kindly dealer, and watched it rasp away. Down by the entrance a cheer went up as a favourite emerged, and Stahr wondered whether to show himself and say good-night.

*   *   *

This is Celia taking up the narrative in person. Stahr came back finally – it was about half-past three – and asked me to dance.

'How are you?' he asked me, just as if he hadn't seen me that morning. 'I got involved in a long conversation with a man.'

It was secret, too – he cared that much about it.

'I took him for a drive,' he went on innocently. 'I didn't realise how much this part of Hollywood had changed.'

'Has it changed?'

'Oh, yes,' he said, ' – changed completely. Unrecognisable. I couldn't tell you exactly, but it's all changed – everything. It's like a new city.' After a moment he amplified: 'I had no idea how much it had changed.'

'Who was the man?' I ventured.

'An old friend,' he said vaguely, ' – someone I knew a long time ago.'

I had made Wylie try to find out quietly who she was. He had gone over and the ex-star had asked him excitedly to sit down. No: she didn't know who the girl was – a friend of a friend of someone – even the man who had brought her didn't know.

So Stahr and I danced to the beautiful music of Glenn Miller[490] playing 'I'm On A See-Saw'. It was good dancing now, with plenty of room. But it was lonely – lonelier than before the girl had gone. For me, as well as for Stahr, she took the evening with her, took along the stabbing pain I had felt – left the great ballroom empty and without emotion. Now it was nothing, and I was dancing with an absent-minded man who told me how much Los Angeles had changed.

*   *   *

They met, next afternoon, as strangers in an unfamiliar country. Last night was gone, the girl he had danced with was gone. A misty rose-and-blue hat with a trifling veil came along the terrace to him, and paused, searching his face. Stahr was strange, too, in a brown suit and a black tie that blocked him out more tangibly than a formal dinner coat, or when he was simply a face and voice in the darkness the night they had first met.

He was the first to be sure it was the same person as before: the upper part of the face that was Minna's, luminous, with creamy temples and opalescent brown – the cool-coloured curly hair. He could have put his arm around her and pulled her close with an almost family familiarity – already he knew the down on her neck, the very set of her backbone, the corners of her eyes, and how she breathed – the very texture of the clothes that she would wear.

'Did you wait here all night,' she said, in a voice that was like a whisper.

'I didn't move – didn't stir.'

Still the problem remained, the same one – there was no special place to go.

'I'd like tea,' she suggested, ' – if it's some place you're not known.'

'That sounds as if one of us had a bad reputation.'

'Doesn't it?' she laughed.

'We'll go to the shore,' Stahr suggested. 'There's a place there where I got out once and was chased by a trained seal.'

'Do you think the seal could make tea?'

'Well – he's trained. And I don't think he'll talk – I don't think his training got that far. What in *hell* are you trying to hide?'

After a moment she said lightly: 'Perhaps the future,' in a way that might mean anything or nothing at all.

As they drove away, she pointed at her jalopy in the parking lot.

'Do you think it's safe?'

'I doubt it. I noticed some black-bearded foreigners snooping around.'

Kathleen looked at him alarmed.

'Really?' She saw he was smiling. 'I believe everything you say,' she said. 'You've got such a gentle way about you that I don't see why they're all so afraid of you.' She examined him with approval – fretting a little about his pallor, which was accentuated by the bright afternoon. 'Do you work very hard? Do you really always work on Sundays?'

He responded to her interest – impersonal yet not perfunctory.

'Not always. Once we had – we had a house with a pool and all –

and people came on Sunday. I played tennis and swam. I don't swim any more.'

'Why not? It's good for you. I thought all Americans swam.'

'My legs got very thin – a few years ago, and it embarrassed me. There were other things I used to do – lots of things: I used to play handball when I was a kid, and sometimes out here – I had a court that was washed away in a storm.'

'You have a good build,' she said in formal compliment, meaning only that he was made with thin grace.

He rejected this with a shake of his head.

'I enjoy working most,' he said. 'My work is very congenial.'

'Did you always want to be in movies?'

'No. When I was young I wanted to be a chief clerk – the one who knew where everything was.'

She smiled.

'That's odd. And now you're much more than that.'

'No, I'm still a chief clerk,' Stahr said. 'That's my gift, if I have one. Only when I got to be it, I found out that no one knew where anything was. And I found out that you had to know why it was where it was, and whether it should be left there. They began throwing it all at me, and it was a very complex office. Pretty soon I had all the keys. And they wouldn't have remembered what locks they fitted if I'd given them back.'

They stopped for a red light, and a newsboy bleated at him: 'Mickey Mouse Murdered! Randolph Hearst [491] declares war on China!'

'We'll have to buy this paper,' she said.

As they drove on, she straightened her hat and preened herself. Seeing him looking at her, she smiled.

She was alert and calm – qualities that were currently at a premium. There was lassitude in plenty – California was filling up with weary desperados. And there were tense young men and women who lived back East in spirit while they carried on a losing battle against the climate. But it was everyone's secret that sustained effort was difficult here – a secret that Stahr scarcely admitted to himself. But he knew that people from other places spurted a pure rill of new energy for a while.

They were very friendly now. She had not made a move or a gesture that was out of keeping with her beauty, that pressed it out of its contour one way or another. It was all proper to itself. He judged her as he would a shot in a picture. She was not trash, she was not confused but clear – in his special meaning of the word, which implied balance, delicacy and proportion, she was 'nice'.

They reached Santa Monica, where there were the stately houses of a dozen picture stars, penned in the middle of a crawling Coney Island. They turned downhill into the wide blue sky and sea and went on along the sea till the beach slid out again from under the bathers in a widening and narrowing yellow strand.

'I'm building a house out here,' Stahr said, ' – much farther on. I don't know why I'm building it.'

'Perhaps it's for me,' she said.

'Maybe it is.'

'I think it's splendid for you to build a big house for me without even knowing what I looked like.'

'It isn't too big. And it hasn't any roof. I didn't know what kind of roof you wanted.'

'We don't want a roof. They told me it never rained here. It – '

She stopped so suddenly that he knew she was reminded of something. 'Just something that's past,' she said.

'What was it?' he demanded, ' – another house without a roof?'

'Yes. Another house without a roof.'

'Were you happy there?'

'I lived with a man,' she said, 'a long, long time – too long. It was one of those awful mistakes people make. I lived with him a long time after I wanted to get out, but he couldn't let me go. He'd try, but he couldn't. So finally I ran away.'

He was listening, weighing but not judging. Nothing changed under the rose and blue hat. She was twenty-five or so. It would have been a waste if she had not loved and been loved.

'We were too close,' she said. 'We should probably have had children – to stand between us. But you can't have children when there's no roof to the house.'

All right, he knew something of her. It would not be like last night when something kept saying, as in a story conference: 'We know nothing about the girl. We don't have to know much – but we have to know something.' A vague background spread behind her, something more tangible than the head of Siva in the moonlight.

They came to the restaurant, forbidding with many Sunday automobiles. When they got out, the trained seal growled reminiscently at Stahr. The man who owned it said that the seal would never ride in the back seat of his car but always climbed over the back and up in front. It was plain that the man was in bondage to the seal, though he had not yet acknowledged it to himself.

'I'd like to see the house you're building,' said Kathleen. 'I don't want tea – tea is the past.'

Kathleen drank a coke[492] instead and they drove on ten miles into a sun so bright that he took out two pairs of cheaters[493] from a compartment. Five miles further on they turned down a small promontory and came to the fuselage of Stahr's house.

A headwind blowing out of the sun threw spray up the rocks and over the car. Concrete mixer, raw yellow wood and builders' rubble waited, an open wound in the seascape for Sunday to be over. They walked around front, where great boulders rose to what would be the terrace.

She looked at the feeble hills behind and winced faintly at the barren glitter, and Stahr saw –

'No use looking for what's not here,' he said cheerfully. 'Think of it as if you were standing on one of those globes with a map on it – I always wanted one when I was a boy.'

'I understand,' she said after a minute. 'When you do that, you can feel the earth turn, can't you?'

He nodded. 'Yes. Otherwise it's all just *mañana* – waiting for the morning or the moon.'

They went in under the scaffolding. One room, which was to be the chief salon, was completed even to the built-in book shelves and the curtain rods and the trap in the floor for the motion picture projection machine. And to her surprise, this opened out to a porch with cushioned chairs in place and a ping-pong table. There was another ping-pong table on the newly laid sod beyond.

'Last week I gave a premature luncheon,' he admitted, 'I had some props brought out – some grass and things. I wanted to see how the place felt.'

She laughed suddenly. 'Isn't that real grass?'

'Oh yes – it's grass.'

Beyond the strip of anticipatory lawn was the excavation for a swimming pool, patronised now by a crowd of seagulls, which saw them and took flight.

'Are you going to live here all alone?' she asked him, ' – not even dancing girls?'

'Probably. I used to make plans, but not any more. I thought this would be a nice place to read scripts. The studio is really home.'

'That's what I've heard about American business men.'

He caught a tilt of criticism in her voice.

'You do what you're born to do,' he said gently. 'About once a month somebody tries to reform me, tells me what a barren old age I'll have when I can't work any more. But it's not so simple.'

The wind was rising. It was time to go, and he had his car keys out of his pocket, absent-mindedly jingling them in his hand. There was the silvery 'hey!' of a telephone, coming from somewhere across the sunshine.

It was not from the house, and they hurried here and there around the garden, like children playing warmer and colder – closing in finally on a tool shack by the tennis court. The phone, irked with delay, barked at them suspiciously from the wall. Stahr hesitated.

'Shall I let the damn thing ring?'

'I couldn't. Unless I was sure who it was.'

'Either it's for somebody else or they've made a wild guess.'

He picked up the receiver.

'Hello . . . Long distance from where? Yes, this is Mr Stahr.'

His manner changed perceptibly. She saw what few people had seen for a decade: Stahr impressed. It was not discordant, because he often pretended to be impressed, but it made him momentarily a little younger.

'It's the President,' he said to her, almost stiffly.

'Of your company?'

'No, of the United States.'

He was trying to be casual for her benefit, but his voice was eager.

'All right, I'll wait,' he said into the phone, and then to Kathleen: 'I've talked to him before.'

She watched. He smiled at her and winked, as an evidence that while he must give this his best attention, he had not forgotten her.

'Hello,' he said presently. He listened. Then he said 'Hello' again. He frowned.

'Can you talk a little louder,' he said politely, and then: 'Who? . . . What's that?'

She saw a disgusted look come into his face.

'I don't want to talk to him,' he said. 'No!'

He turned to Kathleen: 'Believe it or not, it's an orang-utan.'

He waited while something was explained to him at length; then he repeated: 'I don't want to talk to it, Lew. I haven't got anything to say that would interest an orang-utan.'

He beckoned to Kathleen, and when she came close to the phone, he held the receiver so that she heard odd breathing and a gruff growl. Then a voice: 'This is no phoney, Monroe. It can talk and it's a dead ringer for McKinley.[494] Mr Horace Wickersham is with me here with a picture of McKinley in his hand – '

Stahr listened patiently.

'We've got a chimp,' he said, after a minute. 'He bit a chunk out of John Gilbert[495] last year . . . All right, put him on again.'

He spoke formally as if to a child.

'Hello, orang-utan.'

His face changed, and he turned to Kathleen.

'He said "Hello".'

'Ask him his name,' suggested Kathleen.

'Hello, orang-utan – God, what a thing to be! – Do you know your name? . . . He doesn't seem to know his name . . . Listen, Lew. We're not making anything like *King Kong*, and there is no monkey in *The Hairy Ape* . . . Of course I'm sure. I'm sorry, Lew, goodbye.'

He was annoyed with Lew because he had thought it was the President and had changed his manner, acting as if it were. He felt a little ridiculous, but Kathleen felt sorry and liked him better because it had been an orang-utan.

*   *   *

They started back along the shore with the sun behind them. The house seemed kindlier when they left it, as if warmed by their visit – the hard glitter of the place was more endurable if they were not bound there like people on the shiny surface of a moon. Looking back from a curve of the shore, they saw the sky growing pink behind the indecisive structure, and the point of land seemed a friendly island, not without promise of fine hours on a further day.

Past Malibu with its gaudy shacks and fishing barges they came into the range of human kind again, the cars stacked and piled along the road, the beaches like ant hills without a pattern, save for the dark drowned heads that sprinkled the sea.

Goods from the city were increasing in sight – blankets, matting, umbrellas, cook stoves, reticules full of clothing – the prisoners had laid out their shackles beside them on this sand. It was Stahr's sea if he wanted it, or knew what to do with it – only by sufferance did these others wet their feet and fingers in the wild cool reservoirs of man's world.

Stahr turned off the road by the sea and up a canyon and along a hill road, and the people dropped away. The hill became the outskirts of the city. Stopping for gasoline, he stood beside the car.

'We could have dinner,' he said almost anxiously.

'You have work you could do.'

'No – I haven't planned anything. Couldn't we have dinner?'

He knew that she had nothing to do either – no planned evening or special place to go.

She compromised.

'Do you want to get something in that drugstore across the street?'

He looked at it tentatively.

'Is that really what you want?'

'I like to eat in American drugstores. It seems so queer and strange.'

They sat on high stools and had tomato broth and hot sandwiches. It was more intimate than anything they had done, and they both felt a dangerous sort of loneliness, and felt it in each other. They shared in varied scents of the drugstore, bitter and sweet and sour, and the mystery of the waitress, with only the outer part of her hair dyed and black beneath, and, when it was over, the still life of their empty plates – a sliver of potato, a sliced pickle, and an olive stone.

*   *   *

It was dusk in the street, it seemed nothing to smile at him now when they got into the car.

'Thank you so much. It's been a nice afternoon.'

It was not far from her house. They felt the beginning of the hill, and the louder sound of the car in second was the beginning of the end. Lights were on in the climbing bungalows – he turned on the headlights of the car. Stahr felt heavy in the pit of his stomach.

'We'll go out again.'

'No,' she said quickly, as if she had been expecting this. 'I'll write you a letter. I'm sorry I've been so mysterious – it was really a compliment because I like you so much. You should try not to work so hard. You ought to marry again.'

'Oh, that isn't what you should say,' he broke out protestingly. 'This has been you and me today. It may have meant nothing to you – it meant a lot to me. I'd like time to tell you about it.'

But if he were to take time it must be in her house, for they were there and she was shaking her head as the car drew up to the door.

'I must go now. I do have an engagement. I didn't tell you.'

'That's not true. But it's all right.'

He walked to the door with her and stood in his own footsteps of that other night, while she felt in her bag for the key.

'Have you got it?'

'I've got it,' she said.

That was the moment to go in, but she wanted to see him once more and she leaned her head to the left, then to the right, trying to catch his face against the last twilight. She leaned too far and too long, and it was natural when his hand touched the back of her upper arm and shoulder and pressed her forward into the darkness of his throat. She shut her eyes, feeling the bevel of the key in her tightclutched hand. She said 'Oh' in an expiring sigh, and then 'Oh' again, as he pulled her in close and his chin pushed her cheek around gently. They were both smiling just faintly, and she was frowning, too, as the inch between them melted into darkness.

When they were apart, she shook her head still, but more in wonder than in denial. It came like this then, it was your own fault, now far back, when was the moment? It came like this, and every instant the burden of tearing herself away from them together, from it, was heavier and more unimaginable. He was exultant; she resented and could not blame him, but she would not be part of his exultation, for it was a defeat. So far it was a defeat. And then she thought that if she stopped it being a defeat, broke off and went inside, it was still not a victory. Then it was just nothing.

'This was not my idea,' she said, 'not at all my idea.'

'Can I come in?'

'Oh, no – no.'

'Then let's jump in the car and drive somewhere.'

With relief, she caught at the exact phrasing – to get away from here immediately, that was accomplishment or sounded like it – as if she were fleeing from the spot of a crime. Then they were in the car, going down hill with the breeze cool in their faces, and she came slowly to herself. Now it was all clear in black and white.

'We'll go back to your house on the beach,' she said.

'Back there?'

'Yes – we'll go back to your house. Don't let's talk. I just want to ride.'

* * *

When they got to the coast again the sky was grey, and at Santa Monica a sudden gust of rain bounced over them. Stahr halted beside the road, put on a raincoat, and lifted the canvas top. 'We've got a roof,' he said.

The windshield wiper ticked domestically as a grandfather's clock. Sullen cars were leaving the wet beaches and starting back into the city. Further on they ran into fog – the road lost its boundaries on either side, and the lights of cars coming towards them were stationary until just before they flared past.

They had left a part of themselves behind, and they felt light and free in the car. Fog fizzed in at a chink, and Kathleen took off the rose-and-blue hat in a calm, slow way that made him watch tensely, and put it under a strip of canvas in the back seat. She shook out her hair and, when she saw Stahr was looking at her, she smiled.

The trained seal's restaurant was only a sheen of light off towards the ocean. Stahr cranked down a window and looked for landmarks, but after a few more miles the fog fell away, and just ahead of them the road turned off that led to his house. Out here a moon showed behind the clouds. There was still a shifting light over the sea.

The house had dissolved a little back into its elements. They found the dripping beams of a doorway and groped over mysterious waist-high obstacles to the single finished room, odorous of sawdust and wet wood. When he took her in his arms, they could just see each other's eyes in the half darkness. Presently his raincoat dropped to the floor.

'Wait,' she said.

She needed a minute. She did not see how any good could come from this, and though this did not prevent her from being happy and desirous, she needed a minute to think how it was, to go back an hour and know how it had happened. She waited in his arms, moving her head a little from side to side as she had before, only more slowly, and never taking her eyes from his. Then she discovered that he was trembling.

He discovered it at the same time, and his arms relaxed. Immediately she spoke to him coarsely and provocatively, and pulled his face down to hers. Then, with her knees she struggled out of something, still standing up and holding him with one arm, and kicked it off beside the coat. He was not trembling now and he held her again, as they knelt down together and slid to the raincoat on the floor.

*   *   *

Afterwards they lay without speaking, and then he was full of such tender love for her that he held her tight till a stitch tore in her dress. The small sound brought them to reality.

'I'll help you up,' he said, taking her hands.

'Not just yet. I was thinking of something.'

She lay in the darkness, thinking irrationally that it would be such a bright indefatigable baby, but presently she let him help her up . . . When she came back into the room, it was lit from a single electric fixture.

'A one-bulb lighting system,' he said. 'Shall I turn it off?'

'No. It's very nice. I want to see you.'

They sat in the wooden frame of the window seat, with the soles of their shoes touching.

'You seem far away,' she said.

'So do you.'

'Are you surprised?'

'At what?'

'That we're two people again. Don't you always think – hope that you'll be one person, and then find you're still two?'

'I feel very close to you.'

'So do I to you,' she said.

'Thank you.'

'Thank *you*.'

They laughed.

'Is this what you wanted?' she asked. 'I mean last night.'

'Not consciously.'

'I wonder when it was settled,' she brooded. 'There's a moment when you needn't, and then there's another moment when you know nothing in the world could keep it from happening.'

This had an experienced ring, and to his surprise he liked her even more. In his mood, which was passionately to repeat yet not recapitulate the past, it was right that it should be that way.

'I *am* rather a trollop,' she said, following his thoughts. 'I suppose that's why I didn't get on to Edna.'

'Who is Edna?'

'The girl you thought was me. The one you phoned to – who lived across the road. She's moved to Santa Barbara.'

'You mean she was a tart?'

'So it seems. She went to what you call call-houses.'⁴⁹⁶

'That's funny.'

'If she had been English, I'd have known right away. But she seemed like everyone else. She only told me just before she went away.'

He saw her shiver and got up, putting the raincoat around her shoulders. He opened a closet and a pile of pillows and beach mattress fell out on the floor. There was a box of candles, and he lit them around the room, attaching the electric heater where the bulb had been.

'Why was Edna afraid of me?' he asked suddenly.

'Because you were a producer. She had some awful experience or a friend of hers did. Also, I think she was extremely stupid.'

'How did you happen to know her?'

'She came over. Maybe she thought I was a fallen sister. She seemed quite pleasant. She said "Call me Edna" all the time – "Please call me Edna," so finally I called her Edna and we were friends.'

She got off the window seat so he could lay pillows along it and behind her.

'What can I do?' she said. 'I'm a parasite.'

'No, you're not.' He put his arms around her. 'Be still. Get warm.'

They sat for a while quiet.

'I know why you liked me at first,' she said. 'Edna told me.'

'What did she tell you?'

'That I looked like – Minna Davis. Several people have told me that.'

He leaned away from her and nodded.

'It's here,' she said, putting her hands on her cheekbones and distorting her cheeks slightly. 'Here and here.'

'Yes,' said Stahr. 'It was very strange. You look more like she actually *looked* than how she was on the screen.'

She got up, changing the subject with her gesture as if she were afraid of it.

'I'm warm now,' she said. She went to the closet and peered in, came back wearing a little apron with a crystalline pattern like a snowfall. She stared around critically.

'Of course we've just moved in,' she said, ' – and there's a sort of echo.'

She opened the door of the veranda and pulled in two wicker chairs, drying them off. He watched her move, intently, yet half afraid that her body would fail somewhere and break the spell. He had watched women in screen-tests and seen their beauty vanish second by second, as if a lovely statue had begun to walk with the meagre joints of a paper doll. But Kathleen was ruggedly set on the balls of her feet – the fragility was, as it should be, an illusion.

'It's stopped raining,' she said. 'It rained the day I came. Such an awful rain – so loud – like horses weeing.'

He laughed.

'You'll like it. Especially if you've got to stay here. Are you going to stay here? Can't you tell me now? What's the mystery?'

She shook her head.

'Not now – it's not worth telling.'

'Come here then.'

She came over and stood near him, and he pressed his cheek against the cool fabric of the apron.

'You're a tired man,' she said, putting her hand in his hair.

'Not that way.'

'I didn't mean that way,' she said hastily. 'I meant you'll work yourself sick.'

'Don't be a mother,' he said.

Be a trollop, he thought. He wanted the pattern of his life broken.

If he was going to die soon, like the two doctors said, he wanted to stop being Stahr for a while and hunt for love like men who had no gifts to give, like young nameless men who looked along the streets in the dark.

'You've taken off my apron,' she said gently.

'Yes.'

'Would anyone be passing along the beach? Shall we put out the candles?'

'No, don't put out the candles.'

Afterwards she lay half on a white cushion and smiled up at him.

'I feel like Venus on the half shell,' she said.

'What made you think of that?'

'Look at me – isn't it Botticelli?'[497]

'I don't know,' he said smiling. 'It is if you say so.'

She yawned.

'I've had such a good time. And I'm very fond of you.'

'You know a lot, don't you?'

'What do you mean?'

'Oh, from little things you've said. Or perhaps the way you say them.'

She deliberated.

'Not much,' she said. 'I never went to a university, if that's what you mean. But the man I told you about knew everything and he had a passion for educating me. He made out schedules and made me take courses at the Sorbonne[498] and go to museums. I picked up a little.'

'What was he?'

'He was a painter of sorts and a hell-cat. And a lot besides. He wanted me to read Spengler[499] – everything was for that. All the history and philosophy and harmony was all so I could read Spengler, and then I left him before we got to Spengler. At the end I think that was the chief reason he didn't want me to go.'

'Who was Spengler?'

'I tell you we didn't get to him,' she laughed, 'and now I'm forgetting everything very patiently, because it isn't likely I'll ever meet anyone like him again.'

'Oh, but you shouldn't forget,' said Stahr, shocked. He had an intense respect for learning, a racial memory of the old *schules*.[500] 'You shouldn't forget.'

'It was just in place of babies.'

'You could teach your babies,' he said.

'Could I?'

'Sure you could. You could give it to them while they were young.

When I want to know anything, I've got to ask some drunken writer. Don't throw it away.'

'All right,' she said, getting up. 'I'll tell it to my children. But it's so endless – the more you know, the more there is just beyond, and it keeps on coming. This man could have been anything if he hadn't been a coward and a fool.'

'But you were in love with him.'

'Oh, yes – with all my heart.' She looked through the window, shading her eyes. 'It's light out there. Let's go down to the beach.'

He jumped up, exclaiming: 'Why, I think it's the grunion!'[501]

'What?'

'It's tonight. It's in all the papers.' He hurried out the door, and she heard him open the door of the car. Presently he returned with a newspaper.

'It's at ten-sixteen. That's five minutes.'

'An eclipse or something?'

'Very punctual fish,' he said. 'Leave your shoes and stockings and come with me.'

It was a fine blue night. The tide was at the turn, and the little silver fish rocked off shore waiting for 10.16. A few seconds after the time they came swarming in with the tide, and Stahr and Kathleen stepped over them barefoot as they flicked slip-slop on the sand. A Negro man came along the shore towards them, collecting the grunion quickly, like twigs, into two pails. They came in twos and threes and platoons and companies, relentless and exalted and scornful, round the great bare feet of the intruders, as they had come before Sir Francis Drake[502] had nailed his plaque to the boulder on the shore.

'I wish for another pail,' the Negro man said, resting a moment.

'You've come a long way out,' said Stahr.

'I used to go to Malibu, but they don't like it, those moving picture people.'

A wave came in and forced them back, receded swiftly, leaving the sand alive again.

'Is it worth the trip?' Stahr asked.

'I don't figure it that way. I really come out to read some Emerson.[503] Have you ever read him?'

'I have,' said Kathleen. 'Some.'

'I've got him inside my shirt. I got some Rosicrucian[504] literature with me, too, but I'm fed up with them.'

The wind had changed a little – the waves were stronger further down, and they walked along the foaming edge of the water.

'What's your work?' the Negro asked Stahr.

'I work for the pictures.'

'Oh.' After a moment he added, 'I never go to movies.'

'Why not?' asked Stahr sharply.

'There's no profit. I never let my children go.'

Stahr watched him, and Kathleen watched Stahr protectively.

'Some of them are good,' she said, against a wave of spray; but he did not hear her. She felt she could contradict him and said it again, and this time he looked at her indifferently.

'Are the Rosicrucian brotherhood against pictures?' asked Stahr.

'Seems as if they don't know what they *are* for. One week they for one thing and next week for another.'

Only the little fish were certain. Half an hour had gone, and still they came. The Negro's two pails were full, and finally he went off over the beach towards the road, unaware that he had rocked an industry.

Stahr and Kathleen walked back to the house, and she thought how to drive his momentary blues away.

'Poor old Sambo,' she said.

'What?'

'Don't you call them poor old Sambo?'

'We don't call them anything especially.' After a moment, he said, 'They have pictures of their own.'

In the house she drew on her shoes and stockings before the heater.

'I like California better,' she said deliberately. 'I think I was a bit sex-starved.'

'That wasn't quite all, was it?'

'You know it wasn't.'

'It's nice to be near you.'

She gave a little sigh as she stood up, so small that he did not notice it.

'I don't want to lose you now,' he said. 'I don't know what you think of me or whether you think of me at all. As you've probably guessed, my heart's in the grave – ' He hesitated, wondering if this was quite true. ' – but you're the most attractive woman I've met since I don't know when. I can't stop looking at you. I don't know now exactly the colour of your eyes, but they make me sorry for everyone in the world – '

'Stop it, stop it!' she cried laughing. 'You'll have me looking in the mirror for weeks. My eyes aren't any colour – they're just eyes to see with, and I'm just as ordinary as I can be. I have nice teeth for an English girl – '

'You have beautiful teeth.'

' – but I couldn't hold a candle to these girls I see here – '

'*You* stop it,' he said. 'What I said is true, and I'm a cautious man.'

She stood motionless a moment – thinking. She looked at him, then she looked back into herself, then at him again – then she gave up her thought.

'We must go,' she said.

*   *   *

Now they were different people as they started back. Four times they had driven along the shore road today, each time a different pair. Curiosity, sadness, and desire were behind them now; this was a true returning – to themselves and all their past and future and the encroaching presence of tomorrow. He asked her to sit close in the car, and she did, but they did not seem close, because for that you have to seem to be growing closer. Nothing stands still. It was on his tongue to ask her to come to the house he rented and sleep there tonight – but he felt that it would make him sound lonely. As the car climbed the hill to her house, Kathleen looked for something behind the seat cushion.

'What have you lost?'

'It might have fallen out,' she said, feeling through her purse in the darkness.

'What was it?'

'An envelope.'

'Was it important?'

'No.'

But when they got to her house and Stahr turned on the dashboard light, she helped take the cushions out and look again.

'It doesn't matter,' she said, as they walked to the door. 'What's your address where you really live?'

'Just Bel Air. There's no number.'

'Where is Bel Air?'

'It's a sort of development, near Santa Monica.[505] But you'd better call me at the studio.'

'All right . . . good-night, Mr Stahr.'

'*Mister* Stahr,' he repeated, astonished.

She corrected herself gently.

'Well, then, good-night, Stahr. Is that better?'

He felt as though he had been pushed away a little.

'As you like,' he said. He refused to let the aloofness communicate itself. He kept looking at her and moved his head from side to side in her own gesture, saying without words: 'You know what's happened to me.' She sighed. Then she came into his arms and for a moment was his again completely. Before anything could change, Stahr whispered good-night and turned away and went to his car.

Winding down the hill, he listened inside himself as if something by an unknown composer, powerful and strange and strong, was about to be played for the first time. The theme would be stated presently, but because the composer was always new, he would not recognise it as the theme right away. It would come in some such guise as the auto horns from the technicolor boulevards below, or be barely audible, a tattoo on the muffled drum of the moon. He strained to hear it, knowing only that music was beginning, new music that he liked and did not understand. It was hard to react to what one could entirely compass – this was new and confusing, nothing one could shut off in the middle and supply the rest from an old score.

Also, and persistently, and bound up with the other, there was the Negro on the sand. He was waiting at home for Stahr, with his pails of silver fish, and he would be waiting at the studio in the morning. He had said that he did not allow his children to listen to Stahr's story. He was prejudiced and wrong, and he must be shown somehow, some way. A picture, many pictures, a decade of pictures, must be made to show him he was wrong. Since he had spoken, Stahr had thrown four pictures out of his plans – one that was going into production this week. They were borderline pictures in point of interest, but at least he submitted the borderline pictures to the Negro and found them trash. And he put back on his list a difficult picture that he had tossed to the wolves, to Brady and Marcus and the rest, to get his way on something else. He rescued it for the Negro man.

When he drove up to his door, the porch lights went on, and his Filipino came down the steps to put away the car. In the library, Stahr found a list of phone calls:[506]

> La Borwitz
> Marcus
> Harlow
> Reinmund
> Fairbanks
> Brady
> Colman
> Skouras
> Fleishacker, *etc.*

The Filipino came into the room with a letter.

'This fell out of the car,' he said.

'Thanks,' said Stahr. 'I was looking for it.'

'Will you be running a picture tonight, Mr Stahr?'

'No, thanks – you can go to bed.'

The letter, to his surprise, was addressed to Monroe Stahr, Esq. He started to open it – then it occurred to him that she had wanted to recapture it, and possibly to withdraw it. If she had had a phone, he would have called her for permission before opening it. He held it for a moment. It had been written before they met – it was odd to think that whatever it said was now invalidated; it possessed the interest of a souvenir by representing a mood that was gone.

Still he did not like to read it without asking her. He put it down beside a pile of scripts and sat down with the top script in his lap. He was proud of resisting his first impulse to open the letter. It seemed to prove that he was not 'losing his head'. He had never lost his head about Minna, even in the beginning – it had been the most appropriate and regal match imaginable. She had loved him always and just before she died, all unwilling and surprised, his tenderness had burst and surged forward and he had been in love with her. In love with Minna and death together – with the world in which she looked so alone that he wanted to go with her there.

But 'falling for dames' had never been an obsession – his brother had gone to pieces over a dame, or rather over dame after dame after dame. But Stahr, in his younger days, had them once and never more than once – like one drink. He had quite another sort of adventure reserved for his mind – something better than a series of emotional sprees. Like many brilliant men, he had grown up dead cold. Beginning at about twelve, probably, with the total rejection common to those of extraordinary mental powers, the 'See here: this is all wrong – a mess – all a lie – and a sham – ', he swept it all away, everything, as men of his type do; and then instead of being a son-of-a-bitch as most of them are, he looked around at the barrenness that was left and said to himself, '*This* will never do.' And so he had learned tolerance, kindness, forbearance, and even affection like lessons.

The Filipino boy brought in a carafe of water and bowls of nuts and fruit, and said good-night. Stahr opened the first script and began to read.

He read for three hours – stopping from time to time, editing without a pencil. Sometimes he looked up, warm from some very vague happy thought that was not in the script, and it took him a minute each time to remember what it was. Then he knew it was Kathleen, and he looked at the letter – it was nice to have a letter.

It was three o'clock when a vein began to bump in the back of his hand, signalling that it was time to quit. Kathleen was really far away now with the waning night – the different aspects of her telescoped into the memory of a single thrilling stranger, bound to him only by a few slender hours. It seemed perfectly all right to open the letter.

DEAR MR STAHR – In half an hour I will be keeping my date with you. When we say goodbye I will hand you this letter. It is to tell you that I am to be married soon and that I won't be able to see you after today.

I should have told you last night but it didn't seem to concern you. And it would seem silly to spend this beautiful afternoon telling you about it and watching your interest fade. Let it fade all at once – now. I will have told you enough to convince you that I am Nobody's Prize Potato. (I have just learned that expression – from my hostess of last night, who called and stayed an hour. She seems to believe that everyone is Nobody's Prize Potato – except you. I think I am supposed to tell you she thinks this, so give her a job if you can.)

I am very flattered that anyone who sees so many lovely women – I can't finish this sentence but you know what I mean. And I will be late if I don't go to meet you right now.

With all good wishes

KATHLEEN MOORE

Stahr's first feeling was like fear; his second thought was that the letter was invalidated – she had even tried to retrieve it. But then he remembered 'Mr Stahr' just at the end, and that she had asked him his address – she had probably already written another letter which would also say goodbye. Illogically he was shocked by the letter's indifference to what had happened later. He read it again, realising that it foresaw nothing. Yet in front of the house she had decided to let it stand, belittling everything that had happened, curving her mind away from the fact that there had been no other man in her consciousness that afternoon. But he could not even believe this now, and the whole adventure began to peel away even as he recapitulated it searchingly to himself. The car, the hill, the hat, the music, the letter itself, blew off like the scraps of tar paper from the rubble of his house. And Kathleen departed, packing up her remembered gestures, her softly moving head, her sturdy eager body, her bare feet in the wet swirling sand. The skies paled and faded – the wind and rain turned dreary, washing the silver fish back to sea. It was only one more day, and nothing was left except the pile of scripts upon the table.

He went upstairs. Minna died again on the first landing, and he forgot her lingeringly and miserably again, step by step to the top. The empty floor stretched around him – the doors with no one sleeping behind. In his room, Stahr took off his tie, untied his shoes, and sat on the side of his bed. It was all closed out, except for something that he could not remember; then he remembered: her car was still down in the parking lot of the hotel. He set his clock to give him six hours' sleep.

*   *   *

This is Cecilia taking up the story. I think it would be most interesting to follow my own movements at this point, as this is a time in my life that I am ashamed of. What people are ashamed of usually makes a good story.

When I sent Wylie over to Martha Dodd's table, he had no success in finding out who the girl was, but it had suddenly become my chief interest in life. Also, I guessed – correctly – that it would be Martha Dodd's. To have had at your table a girl who is admired by royalty, who may be tagged for a coronet in our little feudal system – and not even know her name!

I had only a speaking acquaintance with Martha, and it would be too obvious to approach her directly, but I went out to the studio Monday and dropped in on Jane Meloney.

Jane Meloney was quite a friend of mine. I thought of her rather as a child thinks of a family dependant. I knew she was a writer, but I grew up thinking that writer and secretary were the same, except that a writer usually smelled of cocktails and came more often to meals. They were spoken of the same way when they were not around – except for a species called playwrights, who came from the East. These were treated with respect if they did not stay long – if they did, they sank with the others into the white collar class.

Jane's office was in the 'old writers' building'. There was one on every lot, a row of iron maidens left over from silent days and still resounding with the dull moans of cloistered hacks and bums. There was the story of the new producer who had gone down the line one day and then reported excitedly to the head office.

'Who are those men?'

'They're supposed to be writers.'

'I thought so. Well, I watched them for ten minutes and there were two of them that didn't write a line.'

Jane was at her typewriter, about to break off for lunch. I told her frankly that I had a rival.

'It's a dark horse,' I said. 'I can't even find out her name.'

'Oh,' said Jane. 'Well, maybe I know something about that. I heard something from somebody.'

The somebody, of course, was her nephew, Ned Sollinger, Stahr's office boy. He had been her pride and hope. She had sent him through New York University, where he played on the football team. Then in his first year at medical school, after a girl turned him down, he dissected out the least publicised section of a lady corpse and sent it to the girl. Don't ask me why. In disgrace with fortune and men's eyes, he had begun life at the bottom again, and was still there.

'What do you know?' I asked.

'It was the night of the earthquake. She fell into the lake on the back lot, and he dove in and saved her life. Someone else told me it was his balcony she jumped off of and broke her arm.'

'Who was she?'

'Well, that's funny, too – '

Her phone rang, and I waited restlessly during a long conversation she had with Joe Reinmund. He seemed to be trying to find out over the phone how good she was or whether she had ever written any pictures at all. And she was reputed to have been on the set the day Griffith[507] invented the close-up! While he talked she groaned silently, writhed, made faces into the receiver, held it all in her lap so that the voice reached her faintly – and kept up a side chatter to me.

'What is *he* doing – killing time between appointments? . . . He's asked me every one of these questions ten times . . . that's all on a memorandum I sent him . . .'

And into the phone: 'If this goes up to Monroe, it won't be my doing. I want to go right through to the end.'

She shut her eyes in agony again.

'Now he's casting it . . . he's casting the minor characters . . . he's going to have Buddy Ebson . . . My God, he just hasn't anything to do . . . now he's on Walter Davenport – he means Donald Crisp[508] . . . he's got a big casting directory open in his lap and I can hear him turn the pages . . . he's a big important man this morning, a second Stahr, and for Christ sake I've got two scenes to do before lunch.'

Reinmund quit finally or was interrupted at his end. A waiter came in from the commissary with Jane's luncheon and a Coca-Cola for me – I wasn't lunching that summer. Jane wrote down one sentence on her typewriter before she ate. It interested me the way she wrote. One day I was there when she and a young man had just lifted a story out of the *Saturday Evening Post*[509] – changing the characters and all. Then they began to write it, making each line answer the line before it, and of course it sounded just like people do in life when they're straining to be anything – funny or gentle or brave. I always wanted to see that one on the screen, but I missed it somehow.

I found her as lovable as a cheap old toy. She made three thousand a week, and her husbands all drank and beat her nearly to death. But today I had an axe to grind.

'You don't know her name?' I persisted.

'Oh – ' said Jane, 'that. Well, he kept calling her up afterwards, and he told Katy Doolan it was the wrong name after all.'

'I think he found her,' I said. 'Do you know Martha Dodd?'

'Hasn't that little girl had a tough break, though!' she exclaimed with ready theatrical sympathy.

'Could you possibly invite her to lunch tomorrow?'

'Oh, I think she gets enough to eat all right. There's a Mexican – '

I explained that my motives were not charitable. Jane agreed to co-operate. She called Martha Dodd.

We had lunch next day at the Bev Brown Derby,[510] a languid restaurant, patronised for its food by clients who always look as if they'd like to lie down. There is some animation at lunch, where the women put on a show for the first five minutes after they eat, but we were a tepid threesome. I should have come right out with my curiosity. Martha Dodd was an agricultural girl, who had never quite understood what had happened to her and had nothing to show for it except a washed-out look about the eyes. She still believed that the life she had tasted was reality and this was only a long waiting.

'I had a beautiful place in 1928,' she told us, ' – thirty acres, with a miniature golf course and a pool and a gorgeous view. All spring I was up to my ass in daisies.'

I ended by asking her to come over and meet father. This was pure penance for having had 'a mixed motive' and being ashamed of it. One doesn't mix motives in Hollywood – it is confusing. Everybody understands, and the climate wears you down. A mixed motive is conspicuous waste.

Jane left us at the studio gate, disgusted by my cowardice. Martha had worked up inside to a pitch about her career – not a very high pitch, because of seven years of neglect, but a sort of nervous acquiescence, and I was going to speak strongly to father. They never did anything for people like Martha, who had made them so much money at one time. They let them slip away into misery eked out with extra work – it would have been kinder to ship them out of town. And father was being so proud of me this summer. I had to keep him from telling everybody just how I had been brought up so as to produce such a perfect jewel. And Bennington – oh, what an exclusive – dear God, my heart. I assured him there was the usual proportion of natural-born skivvies and biddies tastefully concealed by throw-overs from sex Fifth Avenue;[511] but father had worked himself up to practically an alumnus. 'You've had everything,' he used to say happily. Everything included roughly the two years in Florence, where I managed against heavy odds to be the only virgin in school, and the courtesy début in Boston, Massachusetts. I was a veritable flower of the fine old cost-and-gross aristocracy.

So I knew he would do something for Martha Dodd, and as he went into his office, I had great dreams of doing something for Johnny Swanson, the cowboy, too, and Evelyn Brent, and all sorts of discarded flowers. Father was a charming and sympathetic man – except for that time I had seen him unexpectedly in New York – and there was something touching about his being my father. After all, he was *my* father – he would do anything in the world for me.

Only Rosemary Schmiel was in the outer office, and she was on Birdy Peters's phone. She waved for me to sit down, but I was full of my plans and, telling Martha to take it easy, I pressed the clicker under Rosemary's desk and went towards the opened door.

'Your father's in conference,' Rosemary called. 'Not in conference, but I ought to – '

By this time I was through the door and a little vestibule and another door, and caught father in his shirtsleeves, very sweaty and trying to open a window. It was a hot day, but I hadn't realised it was that hot, and thought he was ill.

'No, I'm all right,' he said. 'What is it?'

I told him. I told him the whole theory of people like Martha Dodd, walking up and down his office. How could he use them and guarantee them regular employment? He seemed to take me up excitedly and kept nodding and agreeing, and I felt closer to him than I had for a long time. I came close and kissed him on his cheek. He was trembling and his shirt was soaked through.

'You're not well,' I said, 'or you're in some sort of stew.'

'No, I'm not at all.'

'What is it?'

'Oh, it's Monroe,' he said. 'That goddam little Vine Street Jesus![512] He's in my hair night and day!'

'What's happened?' I asked, very much cooler.

'Oh, he sits like a little goddam priest or rabbi and says what he'll do and he won't do. I can't tell you now – I'm half crazy. Why don't you go along?'

'I won't have you like this.'

'Go along, I tell you!' I sniffed, but he never drank.

'Go and brush your hair,' I said. 'I want you to see Martha Dodd.'

'In here! I'd never get rid of her.'

'Out there then. Go wash up first. Put on another shirt.'

With an exaggerated gesture of despair, he went into the little bathroom adjoining. It was hot in the office as if it had been closed for hours, and maybe that was making him sick, so I opened two more windows.

'You go along,' father called from behind the closed door of the bathroom. 'I'll be there presently.'

'Be awfully nice to her,' I said. 'No charity.'

As if it were Martha speaking for herself, a long low moan came from somewhere in the room. I was startled – then transfixed, as it came again, not from the bathroom where father was, not from outside, but from a closet in the wall across from me. How I was brave enough I don't know, but I ran across to it and opened it, and father's secretary, Birdy Peters, tumbled out stark naked – just like a corpse in the movies. With her came a gust of stifling, stuffy air. She flopped sideways on the floor, with the one hand still clutching some clothes, and lay on the floor bathed in sweat – just as father came in from the bathroom. I could feel him standing behind me, and without turning I knew exactly how he looked, for I had surprised him before.

'Cover her up,' I said, covering her up myself with a rug from the couch. 'Cover her *up*!'

I left the office. Rosemary Schmiel saw my face as I came out and responded with a terrified expression. I never saw her again or Birdy Peters either. As Martha and I went out, Martha asked: 'What's the matter, dear?' – and when I didn't say anything: 'You did your best. Probably it was the wrong time. I'll tell you what I'll do. I'll take you to see a very nice English girl. Did you see the girl that Stahr danced with at our table the other night?'

So at the price of a little immersion in the family drains I had what I wanted.

*   *   *

I don't remember much about our call. She wasn't at home was one reason. The screen-door of her house was unlocked, and Martha went in calling 'Kathleen' with bright familiarity. The room we saw was bare and formal as an hotel; there were flowers about, but they did not look like sent flowers. Also, Martha found a note on the table, which said: 'Leave the dress. Have gone looking for a job. Will drop by tomorrow.'

Martha read it twice but it didn't seem to be for Stahr, and we waited five minutes. People's houses are very still when they are gone. Not that I expect them to be jumping around, but I leave the observation for what it's worth. Very still. Prim almost, with just a fly holding down the place and paying no attention to you, and the corner of a curtain blowing.

'I wonder what kind of a job,' said Martha. 'Last Sunday she went somewhere with Stahr.'

But I was no longer interested. It seemed awful to be here – producer's blood, I thought in horror. And in quick panic I pulled her out into the placid sunshine. It was no use – I felt just black and awful. I had always been proud of my body – I had a way of thinking of it as geometric which made everything it did seem all right. And there was probably not any kind of place, including churches and office and shrines, where people had not embraced – but no one had ever stuffed me naked into a hole in the wall in the middle of a business day.

* * *

'If you were in a drugstore,' said Stahr, ' – having a prescription filled – '

'You mean a chemist's?' Boxley asked.

'If you were in a chemist's,' conceded Stahr, 'and you were getting a prescription for some member of your family who was very sick – '

' – Very ill?' queried Boxley.

'Very ill. *Then* whatever caught your attention through the window, whatever distracted you and held you would probably be material for pictures.'

'A murder outside the window, you mean.'

'There you go,' said Stahr, smiling. 'It might be a spider working on the pane.'

'Of course – I see.'

'I'm afraid you don't, Mr Boxley. You see it for *your* medium, but not for ours. You keep the spiders for yourself and you try to pin the murders on us.'

'I might as well leave,' said Boxley. 'I'm no good to you. I've been here three weeks and I've accomplished nothing. I make suggestions, but no one writes them down.'

'I want you to stay. Something in you doesn't like pictures, doesn't like telling a story this way – '

'It's such a damned bother,' exploded Boxley. 'You can't let yourself go – '

He checked himself. He knew that Stahr, the helmsman, was finding time for him in the middle of a constant stiff blow – that they were talking in the always creaking rigging of a ship sailing in great awkward tacks along an open sea. Or else – it seemed at times – they were in a huge quarry – where even the newly-cut marble bore the tracery of old pediments, half-obliterated inscriptions of the past.

'I keep wishing you could start over,' Boxley said. 'It's this mass production.'

'That's the condition,' said Stahr. 'There's always some lousy condition. We're making a life of Rubens – suppose I asked you to do portraits of rich dopes like Bill Brady and me and Gary Cooper[513] and Marcus when you wanted to paint Jesus Christ? Wouldn't you feel you had a condition? Our condition is that we have to take people's own favourite folklore and dress it up and give it back to them. Anything beyond that is sugar. So won't you give us some sugar, Mr Boxley?'

Boxley knew he could sit with Wylie White tonight at the Troc[514] raging at Stahr, but he had been reading Lord Charnwood[515] and he recognised that Stahr like Lincoln was a leader carrying on a long war on many fronts; almost single-handed he had moved pictures sharply forward through a decade, to a point where the content of the 'A productions' was wider and richer than that of the stage. Stahr was an artist only, as Mr Lincoln was a general, perforce and as a layman.

'Come down to La Borwitz's office with me,' said Stahr. 'They sure need some sugar there.'

In La Borwitz's office, two writers, a shorthand secretary and a hushed supervisor, sat in a tense smoky stalemate, where Stahr had left them three hours before. He looked at the faces one after another and found nothing. La Borwitz spoke with awed reverence for his defeat.

'We've just got too many characters, Monroe.'

Stahr snorted affably.

'That's the principal idea of the picture.'

He took some change out of his pocket, looked up at the suspended light and tossed up half a dollar, which clanked into the bowl. He looked at the coins in his hands and selected a quarter.

La Borwitz watched miserably; he knew this was a favourite trick of Stahr's and he saw the sands running out. At the moment everyone's back was towards him. Suddenly he brought up his hands from their placid position under the desk and threw them high in the air, so high that they seemed to leave his wrist – and then he caught them neatly as they were descending. After that he felt better. He was in control.

One of the writers had taken out some coins, also, and presently rules were defined. 'You have to toss your coin through the chains without hitting them. Whatever falls into the light is the kitty.'

They played for half an hour – all except Boxley, who sat aside and dug into the script, and the secretary, who kept tally. She calculated the cost of the four men's time, arriving at a figure of sixteen hundred dollars. At the end, La Borwitz was winner by $5.50, and a janitor brought in a stepladder to take the money out of the light.

Boxley spoke up suddenly.

'You have the stuffings of a turkey here,' he said.

'What!'

'It's not pictures.'

They looked at him in astonishment. Stahr concealed a smile.

'So we've got a real picture man here!' exclaimed La Borwitz.

'A lot of beautiful speeches,' said Boxley boldly, 'but no situations. After all, you know, it's not going to be a novel. And it's too long. I can't exactly describe how I feel, but it's not quite right. And it leaves me cold.'

He was giving them back what had been handed him for three weeks. Stahr turned away, watching the others out of the corner of his eye.

'We don't need *less* characters,' said Boxley. 'We need *more*. As I see it, that's the idea.'

'That's the idea,' said the writers.

'Yes – that's the idea,' said La Borwitz.

Boxley was inspired by the attention he had created.

'Let each character see himself in the other's place,' he said. 'The policeman is about to arrest the thief when he sees that the thief actually has *his* face. I mean, show it that way. You could almost call the thing *Put Yourself in My Place*.'

Suddenly they were at work again – taking up this new theme in turn like hepcats in a swing band and going to town with it. They might throw it out again tomorrow, but life had come back for a moment. Pitching the coins had done it as much as Boxley. Stahr had recreated the proper atmosphere – never consenting to be a driver of the driven, but feeling like and acting like and even sometimes looking like a small boy getting up a show.

He left them, touching Boxley on the shoulder in passing – a deliberate accolade – he didn't want them to gang up on him and break his spirit in an hour.

*   *   *

Dr Baer was waiting in his inner office. With him was a coloured man with a portable cardiograph like a huge suitcase. Stahr called it the lie detector. Stahr stripped to the waist, and the weekly examination began.

'How've you been feeling?'

'Oh – the usual,' said Stahr.

'Been hard at it? Getting any sleep?'

'No – about five hours. If I go to bed early, I just lie there.'

'Take the sleeping pills.'

'The yellow one gives me a hangover.'

'Take two red ones, then.'

'That's a nightmare.'

'Take one of each – the yellow first.'

'All right – I'll try. How've *you* been?'

'Say – I take care of myself, Monroe, I save myself.'

'The hell you do – you're up all night sometimes.'

'Then I sleep all next day.'

After ten minutes, Baer said: 'Seems OK. The blood pressure's up five points.'

'Good,' said Stahr. 'That's good, isn't it?'

'That's good. I'll develop the cardiographs tonight. When are you coming away with me?'

'Oh, sometime,' said Stahr lightly. 'In about six weeks things'll ease up.'

Baer looked at him with a genuine liking that had grown over three years.

'You got better in thirty-three when you laid up,' he said. 'Even for three weeks.'

'I will again.'

No he wouldn't, Baer thought. With Minna's help he had enforced a few short rests years ago and lately he had hinted around, trying to find who Stahr considered his closest friends. Who could take him away and keep him away? It would almost surely be useless. He was due to die very soon now. Within six months one could say definitely. What was the use of developing the cardiograms? You couldn't persuade a man like Stahr to stop and lie down and look at the sky for six months. He would much rather die. He said differently, but what it added up to was the definite urge towards total exhaustion that he had run into before. Fatigue was a drug as well as a poison, and Stahr apparently derived some rare almost physical pleasure from working light-headed with weariness. It was a perversion of the life force he had seen before, but he had almost stopped trying to interfere with it. He had cured a man or so – a hollow triumph of killing and preserving the shell.

'You hold your own,' he said.

They exchanged a glance. Did Stahr know? Probably. But he did not know when – he did not know how soon now.

'If I hold my own, I can't ask more,' said Stahr.

The coloured man had finished packing the apparatus.

'Next week same time?'

'OK, Bill,' said Stahr. 'Goodbye.'

As the door closed, Stahr switched open the dictagraph. Miss Doolan's voice came through immediately.

'Do you know a Miss Kathleen Moore?'

'What do you mean?' he asked startled.

'A Miss Kathleen Moore is on the line. She said you asked her to call.'

'Well, my God!' he exclaimed. He was swept with indignant rapture. It had been five days – this would never do at all.

'She's on now?'

'Yes.'

'Well, all right then.'

In a moment he heard the voice up close to him.

'Are you married?' he asked, low and surly.

'No, not yet.'

His memory blocked out her face and form – as he sat down, she seemed to lean down to his desk, keeping level with his eyes.

'What's on your mind?' he asked in the same surly voice. It was hard to talk that way.

'You did find the letter?' she asked.

'Yes. It turned up that night.'

'That's what I want to speak to you about.'

He found an attitude at length – he was outraged.

'What is there to talk about?' he demanded.

'I tried to write you another letter, but it wouldn't write.'

'I know that, too.'

There was a pause.

'Oh, cheer up!' she said surprisingly. 'This doesn't sound like you. It *is* Stahr, isn't it? That very nice Mr Stahr?'

'I feel a little outraged,' he said almost pompously. 'I don't see the use of this. I had at least a pleasant memory of you.'

'I don't believe it's you,' she said. 'Next thing you'll wish me luck.' Suddenly she laughed: 'Is this what you planned to say? I know how awful it gets when you plan to say anything – '

'I never expected to hear from you again,' he said with dignity; but it was no use, she laughed again – a woman's laugh that is like a child's, just one syllable, a crow and a cry of delight.

'Do you know how you make me feel?' she demanded. 'Like a day in London during a caterpillar plague when a hot furry thing dropped in my mouth.'

'I'm sorry.'

'Oh, please wake up,' she begged. 'I want to see you. I can't explain things on the phone. It was no fun for me either, you understand.'

'I'm very busy. There's a sneak preview in Glendale tonight.'

'Is that an invitation?'

'George Boxley, the English writer, is going with me.' He surprised himself. 'Do you want to come along?'

'How could we talk?'

She considered. 'Why don't you call for me afterwards,' she suggested. 'We could ride around.'

Miss Doolan on the huge dictagraph was trying to cut in on the line with a shooting director – the only interruption ever permitted. He flipped the button and called 'Wait' impatiently into the machine.

'About eleven?' Kathleen was saying confidentially.

The idea of 'riding around' seemed so unwise that if he could have thought of the words to refuse her he would have spoken them, but he did not want to be the caterpillar. Suddenly he had no attitude left except the sense that the day, at least, was complete. He had an evening – a beginning, a middle, and an end.

*   *   *

He rapped on the screen-door, heard her call from inside, and stood waiting where the level fell away. From below came the whir of a lawn mower – a man was cutting his grass at midnight. The moon was so bright that Stahr could see him plainly, a hundred feet off and down, as he stopped and rested on the handle before pushing it back across his garden. There was a midsummer restlessness abroad – early August with imprudent loves and impulsive crimes. With little more to expect from summer, one tried anxiously to live in the present – or, if there was no present, to invent one.

She came at last. She was all different and delighted. She wore a suit with a skirt that she kept hitching up as they walked down to the car with a brave, gay, stimulating, reckless air of 'Tighten up your belt, baby. Let's get going.' Stahr had brought his limousine with the chauffeur, and the intimacy of the four walls whisking them along a new curve in the dark took away any strangeness at once. In its way, the little trip they made was one of the best times he had ever had in his life. It was certainly one of the times when, if he knew he was going to die, it was not tonight.

She told him her story. She sat beside him cool and gleaming for a while, spinning on excitedly, carrying him to far places with her, meeting and knowing the people she had known. The story was vague at first. 'This Man' was the one she had loved and lived with. 'This American' was the one who had rescued her when she was sinking into a quicksand.

'Who is he – the American?'

Oh, names – what did they matter? No one important like Stahr, not rich. He had lived in London and now they would live out here. She was going to be a good wife, a real person. He was getting a divorce – not just on account of her – but that was the delay.

'But the first man?' asked Stahr. 'How did you get into that?'

Oh, that was a blessing at first. From sixteen to twenty-one the thing was to eat. The day her stepmother presented her at Court they had one shilling to eat with so as not to feel faint. Sixpence apiece, but the stepmother watched while she ate. After a few months the stepmother died, and she would have sold out for that shilling but she was too weak to go into the streets. London can be harsh – oh, quite.

Was there nobody?

There were friends in Ireland who sent butter. There was a soup kitchen. There was a visit to an uncle, who made advances to her when she had a full stomach, and she held out and got fifty pounds out of him for not telling his wife.

'Couldn't you work?' Stahr asked.

'I worked. I sold cars. Once I sold a car.'

'But couldn't you get a regular job?'

'It's hard – it's different. There was a feeling that people like me forced other people out of jobs. A woman struck me when I tried to get a job as chambermaid in an hotel.'

'But you were presented at Court?'

'That was my stepmother who did that – on an off-chance. I was nobody. My father was shot by the Black-and-Tans in twenty-two[516] when I was a child. He wrote a book called *Last Blessing*. Did you ever read it?'

'I don't read.'

'I wish you'd buy it for the movies. It's a good little book. I still get a royalty from it – ten shillings a year.'

Then she met 'The Man' and they travelled the world around. She had been to all the places that Stahr made movies of, and lived in cities whose name he had never heard. Then The Man went to seed, drinking and sleeping with the housemaids and trying to force her off on his friends. They all tried to make her stick with him. They said she had saved him and should cleave to him longer now, indefinitely, to the end. It was her duty. They brought enormous pressure to bear. But she had met The American, and so finally she ran away.

'You should have run away before.'

'Well, you see, it was difficult.' She hesitated, and plunged. 'You see, I ran away from a king.'

His moralities somehow collapsed – she had managed to top him. A confusion of thoughts raced through his head – one of them a faint old credo that all royalty was diseased.

'It wasn't the King of England,' she said. 'My king was out of a job as he used to say. There are lots of kings in London.' She laughed – then added almost defiantly, 'He was very attractive until he began drinking and raising hell.'

'What was he king of?'

She told him – and Stahr visualised the face out of old newsreels.

'He was a very learned man,' she said. 'He could have taught all sorts of subjects. But he wasn't much like a king. Not nearly as much as you. None of them were.'

This time Stahr laughed.

'You know what I mean. They all felt old-fashioned. Most of them tried so hard to keep up with things. They were always advised to keep up with things. One was a syndicalist,[517] for instance. And one used to carry around a couple of clippings about a tennis tournament when he was in the semi-finals. I saw those clippings a dozen times.'

They rode through Griffith Park and out past the dark studios of Burbank, past the airports, and along the way to Pasadena past the neon signs of roadside cabarets. Up in his head he wanted her, but it was late and just the ride was an overwhelming joy. They held hands and once she came close into his arms saying, 'Oh, you're *so* nice. I *do* like to be with you.' But her mind was divided – this was not his night as the Sunday afternoon had been his. She was absorbed in herself, stung into excitement by telling of her own adventures; he could not help wondering if he was getting the story she had saved up for The American.

'How long have you known The American?' he asked.

'Oh, I knew him for several months. We used to meet. We understood each other. He used to say, "It looks like a cinch from now on." '

'Then why did you call me up?'

She hesitated.

'I wanted to see you once more. Then, *too* – he was supposed to arrive today, but last night he wired that he'd be another week. I wanted to talk to a friend – after all, you *are* my friend.'

He wanted her very much now, but one part of his mind was cold and kept saying: She wants to see if I'm in love with her, if I want to marry her. Then she'd consider whether or not to throw this man over. She won't consider it till I've committed myself.

'Are you in love with The American?' he asked.

'Oh, yes. It's absolutely arranged. He saved my life and my reason. He's moving halfway round the world for me. I insisted on that.'

'But are you in love with him?'

'Oh, yes. I'm in love with him.'

The 'Oh, yes,' told him she was not – told him to speak for himself – that she would see. He took her in his arms and kissed her deliberately on the mouth and held her for a long time. It was so warm.

'Not tonight,' she whispered.

'All right.'

They passed over suicide bridge with the high new wire.[518]

'I know what it is,' she said, 'but how stupid. English people don't kill themselves when they don't get what they want.'

They turned around in the driveway of an hotel and started back. It was a dark night with no moon. The wave of desire had passed and neither spoke for a while. Her talk of kings had carried him oddly back in flashes to the pearly White Way[519] of Main Street in Erie, Pennsylvania, when he was fifteen. There was a restaurant with lobsters in the window and green weeds and bright lights on a shell cavern, and beyond behind a red curtain the terribly strange brooding mystery of people and violin music. That was just before he left for New York. This girl reminded him of the fresh iced fishes and lobsters in the window. She was Beautiful Doll. Minna had never been Beautiful Doll.

They looked at each other and her eyes asked, 'Shall I marry The

American?' He did not answer. After a while he said: 'Let's go somewhere for the weekend.'

She considered.

'Are you talking about tomorrow?'

'I'm afraid I am.'

'Well, I'll tell you tomorrow,' she said.

'Tell me tonight. I'd be afraid – '

' – find a note in the car?' she laughed. 'No there's no note in the car. You know almost everything now.'

'Almost everything.'

'Yes – almost. A few little things.'

He would have to know what they were. She would tell him tomorrow. He doubted – he wanted to doubt – if there had been a maze of philandering: a fixation had held her to The Man, the king, firmly and long. Three years of a highly anomalous position – one foot in the palace and one in the background. 'You had to laugh a lot,' she said. 'I learned to laugh a lot.'

'He could have married you – like Mrs Simpson,'[520] Stahr said in protest.

'Oh, he was married. And he wasn't a romantic.' She stopped herself.

'Am I?'

'Yes,' she said, unwillingly, as if she were laying down a trump. 'Part of you is. You're three or four different men but each of them out in the open. Like all Americans.'

'Don't start trusting Americans too implicitly,' he said smiling. 'They may be out in the open, but they change very fast.'

She looked concerned.

'Do they?'

'Very fast and all at once,' he said, 'and nothing ever changes them back.'

'You frighten me. I always had a great sense of security with Americans.'

She seemed suddenly so alone that he took her hand.

'Where will we go tomorrow?' he said. 'Maybe up in the mountains. I've got everything to do tomorrow, but I won't do any of it. We can start at four and get there by afternoon.'

'I'm not sure. I seem to be a little mixed up. This doesn't seem to be quite the girl who came out to California for a new life.'

He could have said it then, said, 'It *is* a new life,' for he knew it was, he knew he could not let her go now; but something else said to sleep on it as an adult, no romantic. And not to tell her till tomorrow. Still she was looking at him, her eyes wandering from his forehead to his chin and back again, and then up and down once more, with that odd slowly-waving motion of her head.

. . . It is your chance, Stahr. Better take it now. This is your girl. She can save you, she can worry you back to life. She will take looking after and you will grow strong to do it. But take her now – tell her and take her away. Neither of you knows it, but far away over the night The American has changed his plans. At this moment his train is speeding through Albuquerque; the schedule is accurate. The engineer is on time. In the morning he will be here.

. . . The chauffeur turned up the hill to Kathleen's house. It seemed warm even in darkness – wherever he had been near here was by way of being an enchanted place for Stahr: this limousine, the rising house at the beach, the very distances they had already covered together over the sprawled city. The hill they climbed now gave forth a sort of glow, a sustained sound that struck his soul alert with delight.

As he said goodbye he felt again that it was impossible to leave her, even for a few hours. There were only ten years between them, but he felt that madness about it akin to the love of an ageing man for a young girl. It was a deep and desperate time-need, a clock ticking with his heart, and it urged him, against the whole logic of his life, to walk past her into the house now and say, 'This is forever.'

Kathleen waited, irresolute herself – pink and silver frost waiting to melt with spring. She was a European, humble in the face of power, but there was a fierce self-respect that would only let her go so far. She had no illusions about the considerations that swayed princes.

'We'll go to the mountains tomorrow,' said Stahr. Many thousands of people depended on his balanced judgement – you can suddenly blunt a quality you have lived by for twenty years.

He was very busy the next morning, Saturday. At two o'clock when he came from luncheon, there was a stack of telegrams – a company ship was lost in the Arctic; a star was in disgrace; a writer was suing for one million dollars. Jews were dead miserably beyond the sea.[521] The last telegram stared up at him: 'I was married at noon today. Goodbye'; and on a sticker attached, 'Send your answer by Western Union Telegram'.

Chapter 6

I KNEW NOTHING about any of this. I went up to Lake Louise,[522] and when I came back didn't go near the studio. I think I would have started East in mid-August – if Stahr hadn't called me up one day at home.

'I want you to arrange something, Celia – I want to meet a Communist Party member.'

'Which one?' I asked, somewhat startled.

'Any one.'

'Haven't you got plenty out there?'

'I mean one of their organisers – from New York.'

The summer before I had been all politics – I could probably have arranged a meeting with Harry Bridges.[523] But my boy had been killed in an auto accident after I went back to college, and I was out of touch with such things. I had heard there was a man from *The New Masses*[524] around somewhere.

'Will you promise him immunity?' I asked, joking.

'Oh, yes,' Stahr answered seriously. 'I won't hurt him. Get one that can talk – tell him to bring one of his books along.'

He spoke as if he wanted to meet a member of the 'I am' cult.[525]

'Do you want a blonde or a brunette?'

'Oh, get a man,' he said hastily.

Hearing Stahr's voice cheered me up – since I had barged in on father it had all seemed a paddling about in thin spittle. Stahr changed everything about it – changed the angle from which I saw it, changed the very air.

'I don't think your father ought to know,' he said. 'Can we pretend the man is a Bulgarian musician or something?'

'Oh, they don't dress up any more,' I said.

It was harder to arrange than I thought – Stahr's negotiations with the Writers' Guild,[526] which had continued over a year, were approaching a dead end. Perhaps they were afraid of being corrupted, and I was asked what Stahr's 'proposition' was. Afterwards Stahr told me that he prepared for the meeting by running off the Russian Revolutionary films that he had in his film library at home. He also ran off *Dr Caligari* and Salvador Dali's *Le Chien Andalou*,[527] possibly suspecting that they had a bearing on the matter. He had been startled by the Russian films back in the twenties, and on Wylie White's suggestion he had had the script department get him up a two-page 'treatment' of the *Communist Manifesto*.

But his mind was closed on the subject. He was a rationalist who did his own reasoning without benefit of books – and he had just managed to climb out of a thousand years of Jewry into the late eighteenth century. He could not bear to see it melt away – he cherished the parvenu's passionate loyalty to an imaginary past.

The meeting took place in what I called the 'processed leather room' – it was one of six done for us by a decorator from Sloane's[528] years ago, and the term stuck in my head. It was *the* most decorator's room: an angora wool carpet the colour of dawn, the most delicate grey imaginable – you hardly dared walk on it; and the silver panelling and leather tables and creamy pictures and slim fragilities looked so easy to stain that we could not breathe hard in there, though it was wonderful to look into from the door when the windows were open and the curtains whimpered querulously against the breeze. It was a lineal descendant of the old American parlour that used to be closed except on Sundays. But it was exactly the room for the occasion, and I hoped that whatever happened would give it character and make it henceforth part of our house.

Stahr arrived first. He was white and nervous and troubled – except for his voice, which was always quiet and full of consideration. There was a brave personal quality in the way he would meet you – he would walk right up to you and put aside something that was in the way, and grow to know you all over as if he couldn't help himself. I kissed him for some reason, and took him into the processed leather room.

'When do you go back to college?' he asked.

We had been over this fascinating ground before.

'Would you like me if I were a little shorter?' I asked, 'I could wear low heels and plaster down my hair.'

'Let's have dinner tonight,' he suggested. 'People will think I'm your father but I don't mind.'

'I *love* old men,' I assured him. 'Unless the man has a crutch, I feel it's just a boy and girl affair.'

'Have you had many of those?'

'Enough.'

'People fall in and out of love all the time, don't they?'

'Every three years or so, Fanny Brice[529] says. I just read it in the paper.'

'I wonder how they manage it,' he said. 'I know it's true because I see them. But they look so con*vinced* every time. And then suddenly they don't look convinced. But they get convinced all over.'

'You've been making too many movies.'

'I wonder if they're as convinced the second time or the third time or the fourth time,' he persisted.

'More each time,' I said. 'Most of all the last time.'

He thought this over and seemed to agree.

'I suppose so. Most of all the last time.'

I didn't like the way he said this, and I suddenly saw that under the surface he was miserable.

'It's a great nuisance,' he said. 'It'll be better when it's over.'

'Wait a *min*ute! Perhaps pictures are in the wrong hands.'

Brimmer, the Party Member, was announced, and going to meet him I slid over to the door on one of those gossamer throw-rugs and practically into his arms.

He was a nice-looking man, this Brimmer – a little on the order of Spencer Tracy, but with a stronger face and a wider range of reactions written up in it. I couldn't help thinking as he and Stahr smiled and shook hands and squared off, that they were two of the most alert men I had ever seen. They were very conscious of each other immediately – both as polite to me as you please, but with a softening of the ends of their sentences when they turned in my direction.

'What are you people trying to do?' demanded Stahr. 'You've got my young men all upset.'

'That keeps them awake, doesn't it?' said Brimmer.

'First we let half a dozen Russians study the plant,' said Stahr. 'As a model plant, you understand. And then you try to break up the unity that makes it a model plant.'

'The unity?' Brimmer repeated. 'Do you mean what's known as The Company Spirit?'

'Oh, not that,' said Stahr, impatiently. 'It seems to be *me* you're after. Last week a writer came into my office – a drunk – a man who's been floating around for years just two steps out of the bughouse – and began telling me my business.'

Brimmer smiled.

'You don't look to me like a man who could be told his business, Mr Stahr.'

They would both have tea. When I came back, Stahr was telling a story about the Warner Brothers and Brimmer was laughing with him.

'I'll tell you another one,' Stahr said. 'Balanchine[530] the Russian dancer had them mixed up with the Ritz Brothers.[531] He didn't know which ones he was training and which ones he was working for. He used to go around saying, "I cannot train these Warner Brothers[532] to dance." '

It looked like a quiet afternoon. Brimmer asked him why the producers didn't back the anti-Nazi League.[533]

'Because of you people,' said Stahr. 'It's your way of getting at the writers. In the long view you're wasting your time. Writers are children – even in normal times they can't keep their minds on their work.'

'They're the farmers in this business,' said Brimmer pleasantly. 'They grow the grain but they're not in at the feast. Their feeling towards the producer is like the farmers' resentment of the city fellow.'

I was wondering about Stahr's girl – whether it was all over between them. Later, when I heard the whole thing from Kathleen, standing in the rain in a wretched road called Goldwyn Avenue,[534] I figured out that this must have been a week after she sent him the telegram. She couldn't help the telegram. The man got off the train unexpectedly and walked her to the registry office without a flicker of doubt that this was what she wanted. It was eight in the morning, and Kathleen was in such a daze that she was chiefly concerned about how to get the telegram to Stahr. In theory you could stop and say, 'Listen, I forgot to tell you but I met a man.' But this track had been laid down so thoroughly, with such confidence, such struggle, such relief, that when it came along, suddenly cutting across the other, she found herself on it like a car on a closed switch. He watched her write the telegram, looking directly at it across the table, and she hoped he couldn't read it upside down . . .

When my mind came back into the room, they had destroyed the poor writers – Brimmer had gone so far as to admit they were 'unstable'.

'They are not equipped for authority,' said Stahr. 'There is no substitute for will. Sometimes you have to fake will when you don't feel it at all.'

'I've had that experience.'

'You have to say, "It's got to be like this – no other way" – even if you're not sure. A dozen times a week that happens to me. Situations where there is no real reason for anything. You pretend there is.'

'All leaders have felt that,' said Brimmer. 'Labour leaders, and certainly military leaders.'

'So I've had to take an attitude in this Guild matter. It looks to me like a try for power, and all I am going to give the writers is money.'

'You give some of them very little money. Thirty dollars a week.'

'Who gets that?' asked Stahr, surprised.

'The ones that are commodities and easy to replace.'

'Not on my lot,' said Stahr.

'Oh, yes,' said Brimmer. 'Two men in your shorts department get thirty dollars a week.'

'Who?'

'Man named Ransome – man named O'Brien.'

Stahr and I smiled together.

'Those are not writers,' said Stahr. 'Those are cousins of Cecilia's father.'

'There are some in other studios,' said Brimmer.

Stahr took his teaspoon and poured himself some medicine from a little bottle.

'What's a fink?' he asked suddenly.

'A fink? That's a strike-breaker or a company tec.'

'I thought so,' said Stahr. 'I've got a fifteen-hundred-dollar writer that every time he walks through the commissary keeps saying "Fink!" behind other writers' chairs. If he didn't scare hell out of them, it'd be funny.'

Brimmer laughed. 'I'd like to see that,' he said.

'You wouldn't like to spend a day with me over there?' suggested Stahr.

Brimmer laughed with genuine amusement.

'No, Mr Stahr. But I don't doubt but that I'd be impressed. I've heard you're one of the hardest working and most efficient men in the entire West. It'd be a privilege to watch you, but I'm afraid I'll have to deny myself.'

Stahr looked at me.

'I like your friend,' he said. 'He's crazy, but I like him.' He looked closely at Brimmer: 'Born on this side?'

'Oh, yes. Several generations.'

'Many of them like you?'

'My father was a Baptist minister.'

'I mean are many of them Reds. I'd like to meet this big Jew that tried to blow over the Ford factory. What's his name – '

'Frankensteen?'[535]

'That's the man. I guess some of you believe in it.'

'Quite a few,' said Brimmer dryly.

'Not you,' said Stahr.

A shade of annoyance floated across Brimmer's face.

'Oh, yes,' he said.

'Oh, no,' said Stahr. 'Maybe you did once.'

Brimmer shrugged his shoulders.

'Perhaps the boot's on the other foot,' he said. 'At the bottom of your heart, Mr Stahr, you know I'm right.'

'No,' said Stahr, 'I think it's a bunch of tripe.'

' – you think to yourself, "He's right," but you think the system will last out your time.'

'You don't really think you're going to overthrow the government.'

'No, Mr Stahr. But we think perhaps you are.'

They were nicking at each other – little pricking strokes like men do sometimes. Women do it, too; but it is a joined battle then with no quarter. But it is not pleasant to watch men do it, because you never know what's next. Certainly it wasn't improving the tonal associations of the room for me, and I moved them out the french window into our golden-yellow California garden.

It was midsummer, but fresh water from the gasping sprinklers made the lawn glitter like spring. I could see Brimmer look at it with a sigh in his glance – a way they have. He opened up big outside – inches taller than I thought and broad-shouldered. He reminded me a little of Superman[536] when he takes off his spectacles. I thought he was as attractive as men can be who don't really care about women as such. We played a round robin game of ping-pong, and he handled his bat well. I heard father come into the house singing that damned 'Little Girl, You've Had A Busy Day', and then breaking off, as if he remembered we weren't speaking any more. It was half-past six – my car was standing in the drive, and I suggested we go down to the Trocadero for dinner.

Brimmer had that look that Father O'Ney had that time in New York when he turned his collar around and went with father and me to the Russian Ballet. He hadn't quite ought to be here. When Bernie, the photographer, who was waiting there for some big game or other, came up to our table, he looked trapped – Stahr made Bernie go away, and I would like to have had the picture.

Then, to my astonishment, Stahr had three cocktails, one after the other.

'Now I know you've been disappointed in love,' I said.

'What makes you think that, Cecilia?'

'Cocktails.'

'Oh, I never drink, Cecilia. I get dyspepsia – I've never been tight.'

I counted them: ' – two – *three*.'

'I didn't realise. I couldn't taste them. I thought there was something the matter.'

A silly glassy look darted into his eye – then passed away.

'This is my first drink in a week,' said Brimmer. 'I did my drinking in the Navy.'

The look was back in Stahr's eye – he winked fatuously at me and said: 'This soap-box son-of-a-bitch has been working on the Navy.'

Brimmer didn't know quite how to take this. Evidently he decided to include it with the evening, for he smiled faintly, and I saw Stahr was smiling, too. I was relieved when I saw it was safely in the great American tradition, and I tried to take hold of the conversation, but Stahr seemed suddenly all right.

'Here's my typical experience,' he said very succinctly and clearly to Brimmer. 'The best director in Hollywood – a man I never interfere with – has some streak in him that wants to slip a pansy into every picture, or something on that order. Something offensive. He stamps it in deep like a watermark so I can't get it out. Every time he does it the Legion of Decency[537] moves a step forward, and something has to be sacrificed out of some honest film.'

'Typical organisational trouble,' agreed Brimmer.

'Typical,' said Stahr. 'It's an endless battle. So now this director tells me it's all right because he's got a Directors' Guild and I can't oppress the poor. That's how you add to my troubles.'

'It's a little remote from us,' said Brimmer smiling. 'I don't think we'd make much headway with the directors.'

'The directors used to be my pals,' said Stahr proudly.

It was like Edward VII's boast that he had moved in the best society in Europe.

'But some of them have never forgiven me,' he continued, 'for bringing out stage directors when sound came in. It put them on their toes and made them learn their jobs all over, but they never did really forgive me. That time we imported a whole new hogshead full of writers, and I thought they were great fellows till they all went red.'

Gary Cooper came in and sat down in a corner with a bunch of men who breathed whenever he did and looked as if they lived off him and weren't budging. A woman across the room looked around and turned out to be Carole Lombard[538] – I was glad that Brimmer was at least getting an eyeful.

Stahr ordered a whiskey-and-soda and, almost immediately, another. He ate nothing but a few spoonfuls of soup and he said all the awful things about everybody being lazy so-and-so's and none of it mattered to *him* because he had lots of money – it was the kind of talk you heard whenever father and his friends were together. I think Stahr realised that it sounded pretty ugly outside of the proper company – maybe he had never heard how it sounded before. Anyhow he shut up and drank off a cup of black coffee. I loved him, and what he said didn't change that, but I hated Brimmer to carry off this impression. I wanted him to see Stahr as a sort of technological virtuoso, and here Stahr had been playing the wicked overseer to a point he would have called trash if he had watched it on the screen.

'I'm a production man,' he said, as if to modify his previous attitude. 'I like writers – I think I understand them. I don't want to kick anybody out if they do their work.'

'We don't want you to,' said Brimmer pleasantly. 'We'd like to take you over as a going concern.'

Stahr nodded grimly.

'I'd like to put you in a roomful of my partners. They've all got a dozen reasons for having Fitts[539] run you fellows out of town.'

'We appreciate your protection,' said Brimmer with a certain irony. 'Frankly we *do* find you difficult, Mr Stahr – precisely because you are a paternalistic employer and your influence is very great.'

Stahr was only half listening.

'I never thought,' he said, 'that I had more brains than a writer has. But I always thought that his brains *belonged* to me – because I knew how to use them. Like the Romans – I've heard that they never invented things but they knew what to do with them. Do you see? I don't say it's right. But it's the way I've always felt – since I was a boy.'

This interested Brimmer – the first thing that had interested him for an hour.

'You know yourself very well, Mr Stahr,' he said.

I think he wanted to get away. He had been curious to see what kind of man Stahr was, and now he thought he knew. Still hoping things would be different, I rashly urged him to ride home with us, but when Stahr stopped by the bar for another drink I knew I'd made a mistake.

It was a gentle, harmless, motionless evening with a lot of Saturday cars. Stahr's hand lay along the back of the seat touching my hair. Suddenly I wished it had been about ten years ago – I would have been nine, Brimmer about eighteen and working his way through some mid-western college, and Stahr twenty-five, just having inherited the world and full of confidence and joy. We would both have looked up to Stahr so, without question. And here we were in an adult conflict, to which there was no peaceable solution, complicated now with the exhaustion and drink.

We turned in at our drive, and I drove around to the garden again.

'I must go along now,' said Brimmer. 'I've got to meet some people.'

'No, stay,' said Stahr. 'I never have said what I wanted. We'll play ping-pong and have another drink, and then we'll tear into each other.'

Brimmer hesitated. Stahr turned on the floodlight and picked up his ping-pong bat, and I went into the house for some whiskey – I wouldn't have dared disobey him.

When I came back, they were not playing, but Stahr was batting a whole box of new balls across to Brimmer, who turned them aside. When I arrived, he quit and took the bottle and retired to a chair just out of the floodlight, watching in dark dangerous majesty. He was pale – he was so transparent that you could almost watch the alcohol mingle with the poison of his exhaustion.

'Time to relax on Saturday night,' he said.

'You're not relaxing,' I said.

He was carrying on a losing battle with his instinct towards schizophrenia.

'I'm going to beat up Brimmer,' he announced after a moment. 'I'm going to handle this thing personally.'

'Can't you pay somebody to do it?' asked Brimmer.

I signalled him to keep quiet.

'I do my own dirty work,' said Stahr. 'I'm going to beat hell out of you and put you on a train.'

He got up and came forward, and I put my arms around him, gripping him.

'Please *stop* this!' I said. 'Oh, you're being so bad.'

'This fellow has an influence over you,' he said darkly. 'Over all you young people. You don't know what you're doing.'

'Please go home,' I said to Brimmer.

Stahr's suit was made of slippery cloth and suddenly he slipped away from me and went for Brimmer. Brimmer retreated backwards around the table. There was an odd expression in his face, and afterwards I thought it looked as if he were saying, 'Is *this* all? This frail half-sick person holding up the whole thing.'

Then Stahr came close, his hands going up. It seemed to me that Brimmer held him off with his left arm a minute, and then I looked away – I couldn't bear to watch.

When I looked back, Stahr was out of sight below the level of the table, and Brimmer was looking down at him.

'Please go home,' I said to Brimmer.

'All right.' He stood looking down at Stahr as I came around the table. 'I always wanted to hit ten million dollars, but I didn't know it would be like this.'

Stahr lay motionless.

'Please go,' I said.

'I'm sorry. Can I help –'

'No. Please go. I understand.'

He looked again, a little awed at the depths of Stahr's repose, which he had created in a split second. Then he went quickly away over the grass, and I knelt down and shook Stahr. After a moment he came awake with a terrific convulsion and bounced up on his feet.

'Where is he?' he shouted.

'Who?' I asked innocently.

'That American. Why in hell did you have to marry him, you damn fool?'

'Monroe – he's gone. I didn't marry anybody.'

I pushed him down in a chair.

'He's been gone half an hour,' I lied.

The ping-pong balls lay around in the grass like a constellation of stars. I turned on a sprinkler and came back with a wet handkerchief, but there was no mark on Stahr – he must have been hit in the side of the head. He went off behind some trees and was sick, and I heard him kicking up some earth over it. After that he seemed all right, but he wouldn't go into the house till I got him some mouthwash, so I took back the whiskey bottle and got a mouthwash bottle. His wretched essay at getting drunk was over. I've been out with college freshmen, but for sheer ineptitude and absence of the Bacchic spirit it unquestionably took the cake. Every bad thing happened to him, but that was all.

*　　　*　　　*

We went in the house; the cook said father and Mr Marcus and Fleishacker were on the veranda, so we stayed in the 'processed leather room'. We both sat down in a couple of places and seemed to slide off, and finally I sat on a fur rug and Stahr on a footstool beside me.

'Did I hit him?' he asked.

'Oh, yes,' I said. 'Quite badly.'

'I don't believe it.' After a minute he added: 'I didn't want to hurt him. I just wanted to chase him out. I guess he got scared and hit me.'

If this was his interpretation of what had happened, it was all right with me.

'Do you hold it against him?'

'Oh, no,' he said. 'I was drunk.' He looked around. 'I've never been in here before – who did this room? – somebody from the studio?

'Well, I'll have to get out of here,' he said in his old pleasant way. 'How would you like to go out to Doug Fairbanks' ranch and spend the night?' he asked me. 'I know he'd love to have you.'

That's how the two weeks started that he and I went around together. It only took one of them for Louella to have us married.

* * *

This is the point at which Fitzgerald's manuscript, in what is something like its penultimate draft stage, stops. Max Perkins, Fitzgerald's editor, reported that the manuscript ran to 56,000 words, though Matthew Bruccoli, in his scholarly edition, counts it at something closer to 44,000 words.

Fitzgerald's Plans for *The Last Tycoon*

Fitzgerald was invariably meticulous in the planning of his novels and at his death left extensive notes, character sketches, outlines, letters and various *obiter dicta* from which scholars such as Edmund Wilson and Matthew J. Bruccoli Jr have adumbrated their sense of how the rest of the novel was to unfold. A particularly important document in this respect is the letter of 29 September 1939 that Fitzgerald sent to Kenneth Littauer, a fiction editor at *Collier's* magazine and a New York literary agent, with a copy to Max Perkins, in which he develops the plan for his novel at some length (the letter can be found in the editions of Bruccoli and Wilson listed in the Bibliography). What follows here draws on Bruccoli's and Wilson's researches but is guided also by what his other fiction tells us about his methods. This summary is presented as a straightforward narrative of what might be called 'the fictional facts', but makes some attempt to surmise how these 'facts' would be rendered. The words in quotation marks come from Fitzgerald's notes and outlines.

SUMMARY

After the interview with Brimmer, Stahr travels to the East Coast in late August to discuss with the stockholders both the wage-cut at the studio and the wider consequences of his struggle with Brady. From New York he goes to Washington, his first visit to the city, where he is taken ill, in part because of the suffocating heat of the place. With Stahr acting as the 'centre of consciousness', the city of Washington ties in with the evocation of Andrew Jackson's home in Chapter 1, the two images linking the founding principles of American republican democracy to the meretriciousness of Hollywood. Stahr almost dies and thinks of leaving the movie-business altogether, but he returns to Hollywood and finds that Brady has implemented a fifty-per-cent wage cut for their studio staff. Though star is opposed to the Hollywood unions he is, as Fitzgerald says, a 'paternalistic employer' who feels that those who work for him should be properly rewarded, even if the times are tough economically. The pay cut provokes a quarrel with Wylie White and Stahr is morally exercised by the disloyalty of White (Stahr's holding to essentially conservative views of business relations based on trust and probity), but he is persuaded of the force of White's proposal that the only way to counteract the unions is to establish company unions (that is union membership co-extensive with the employers and not with the craft).

Cecilia's father (Brady) finds out about Stahr's relationship with Kathleen (their love is consummated in Chapter 5) and attempts to blackmail him, in part to gain control over the company. The novel was now to dramatise the conflict between Stahr and both Brady and the unions. Stahr is able to retaliate because of his knowledge of the philandering Brady's involvement in the death of his mistress's husband. His meeting with Brimmer, the union organiser, in Chapter 6, confirms for Stahr his increasing loss of power and thus speaks to the novel's reference to him as the 'last' tycoon. Despite his love for Kathleen, Stahr 'cannot bring himself to marry her' and their relationship is temporarily broken off. Cecilia, who is in love with Stahr, 'throws herself at his head', but he is indifferent to her. 'Stahr throws over Cecilia who tells her father' and has 'one last fling with Kathleen'. Now Brady, seeking control of the management of the studio, sides with the unions, and with the help of Kathleen's husband, W. Bronson Smith, a studio technician who is active in the technicians' union, plots to have Stahr murdered. Stahr discovers Brady's plan and, as Fitzgerald notes, 'resorts to Brady's own methods' by hiring a thug to murder his competitor. Fitzgerald gave no indication of how the murder was to be planned and executed but in order to be away from the crime Stahr arranges a trip to New York. At the airport from which he is to leave he sees Kathleen for the last time and also runs into Cecilia (his narrator) who is returning to Bennington College. Stahr's plane crashes and in the synopsis he sent to Littauer and Perkins Fitzgerald makes reference to the death on 6 May 1933 of Bronson M. Cutting, a progressive Republican senator from New Mexico, in a plane crash near Atlanta, Missouri. Travelling with Cutting on the onward eastbound flight from Albuquerque were members of the film crew from Paramount

Studios. Fitzgerald was struck by a detail of the accident (though it is not confirmed in the histories) – the fact that the bodies of the dead were rifled by those who lived near to the site of the crash. In his fictionalisation of this, the bodies are discovered by three children, two boys and a girl, who 'on a Sunday picnic discover the wreckage'; it is one of the boys who finds Stahr's briefcase and it is he who, a week later, reports their discovery of the bodies to a local judge. Stahr's death in the air crash brings the novel around to its beginning where Cecilia and Stahr travel to Los Angeles on the same plane, and is evidence of the degree of 'through composition' to be found in Fitzgerald's last novel. Stahr's 'aerial adventure' becomes a 'dying fall', the accident ironically excluding him from the experience of that other 'crash' which is to come from the irretrievable wreckage of his film empire.

The final scene describes Stahr's funeral and would, no doubt, have been rendered with the same effects of *diminuendo* that Fitzgerald had employed so effectively at the conclusion of *The Great Gatsby* and *Tender is the Night*. An added effect was to come from the ironic appearance of the cowboy actor 'Old' Johnny Swanson (introduced in Chapter 2, but not developed) at Stahr's funeral; Swanson is based on Harry Carney who was a pallbearer at Thalberg's funeral, though the invitation sent to him was a mistake, and Swanson's presence at Stahr's funeral is also the consequence of a mistaken invitation. Fitzgerald was hoping to expose the hypocrisy, insincerity and sentimentalism of Hollywood at the end of his novel. One of the concluding scenes (it might well have been placed before the funeral) is a glimpse of the future in the character of Mort Flieshacker, the company lawyer who has opposed Stahr and who now, with his death, assumes great influence in the motion-picture industry.

NOTES TO
TENDER IS THE NIGHT

Tender is the Night is the most allusive of Fitzgerald's novels. The Notes here cover cinematic, geographical, historical, literary, medical, scientific and technological allusions and proper names, among others, and are intended to expedite the reader's understanding of the novel, rather than to offer interpretive or critical glosses. The reader might want to have a good map of France handy to track Fitzgerald's evocation of the environs of the French Riviera in Book One; similarly a good map of Paris for the many Parisian episodes in the novel, and a good dictionary of psychology will be of considerable use in the reading of Book Two. Fitzgerald's errors (by which I mean external errors of correspondence between the facts of the novel and the facts of life, not internal errors of inconsistency in characterisation or narration) are of interest and I have tried to comment briefly on these (where I have detected them) in the Notes. Matthew J. Bruccoli and Judith S. Baughman's *Reader's Companion to F. Scott Fitzgerald's 'Tender is the Night'* is an invaluable resource for information on the novel's composition, background, textual history, emendations, deletions, etc., as well as for its body of explanatory notes.

1 (title page) *Tender is the Night*   The title and quotation are from the fourth stanza of John Keats's 'Ode to a Nightingale' (1819).

2 (p. 2) *To Gerald and Sara . . .*   Gerald (1888–1964) and Sara (1883–1975) Murphy, who lived at Cap d'Antibes and were the centre of a network of expatriate writers, musicians and artists, were close friends of Scott and Zelda Fitzgerald; Gerald Murphy was a painter.

3 (p. 3) *Gausses Hôtel des Étrangers*   an imaginative location, but almost certainly the Grand Hôtel du Cap D'Antibes. Dean Christian Gauss taught Fitzgerald when Fitzgerald was an undergraduate at Princeton University

4 (p. 3) *Maures*   a mountain range at the western edge of the French Riviera

5 (p. 5) *the flotte at Golfe Juan*   the French fleet

6 (p. 9) *Antheil and Joyce*   George Antheil (1900–59), an American composer; James Joyce (1882–1941), the great Irish writer whom Fitzgerald met in Paris in 1928

7 (p. 9) *Ulysses*   the novel by James Joyce first published in Paris in 1922. It was banned in the United States until 1933 and in Britain until 1937.

8 (p. 11) *Daddy's Girl*   the title, of course, is fictional but some of Fitzgerald's commentators suggest the film is based on *Stella Dallas* (1925). Lois Moran (1909–90), an actress Fitzgerald met in Hollywood in 1927, played the part of Laurel Dallas in this silent movie.

9 (p. 11) *Earl Brady*   a fictional film director, probably based on Rex Ingram (1893–1950), the Irish-born director

10 (p. 12) *the Pont du Gard at Arles, the Amphitheatre at Orange, winter sports at Chamonix*   The Pont du Gard is, correctly, at Nîmes and is part of the Roman aqueduct; the amphitheatre at Orange in Provence is one of the finest examples of Roman architecture in France; Chamonix is a ski resort in the French Alps.

11 (p. 13) *the Croisette*   The Boulevard de la Croisette is the main seafront thoroughfare in Cannes.

12 (p. 13) *Le Temps and the Saturday Evening Post*   The former is a French national newspaper, the latter an American weekly magazine to which Fitzgerald contributed many stories.

13 (p. 13) *Ivan the Terrible*   Ivan the Terrible (1530–84) was the first Russian ruler to be crowned 'Tsar'.

14 (p. 14) *country estaminets*   small cafés, often a country cottage with a bar-room

15 (p. 14) *Corniche d'Or*   the coastal road between Cannes, St Raphael and Fréjus

16 (p. 14) *plage*   the beach

17 (p. 15) *Rodinesque*   in the manner of Auguste Rodin (1840–1917), French sculptor

18 (p. 15) *a garçon and a chasseur*   a waiter and a porter, respectively

19 (p. 15) *New York Herald*   a reference to the European edition of the *New York Herald* newspaper, more commonly known in the 1920s as the *Paris Herald*

20 (p. 17) *the Book of Etiquette*   This appears to be a generic reference to the etiquette books, and various other guides to good social behaviour, popular in the 1920s.

21 (p. 19) *a pansy's trick*   pansy (or 'pansy-boy') was a slang term for homosexual

22 (p. 20) *La Turbie*   a village on the French Riviera, close to Monaco

23 (p. 20) *an old Gaumont lot*   Gaumont is one of the oldest of the French film companies

24 (p. 21) *First National . . . Famous*   two Hollywood studios of the early years of the film industry. Famous Players-Lasky later became Paramount Pictures.

25 (p. 21) *Connie Talmadge*   Constance Talmadge (1900–73), American actress of the silent cinema. She appeared in D. W. Griffith's *Intolerance* (1916).

26 (p. 24) *cabinet de toilette*   bathroom

27 (p. 25) *Mon ami Pierrot*   better known as 'Au clair de la lune', a famous children's song composed by Jean-Baptiste Lully (1632–87). The stanza translates thus:

> By the moonlight
>   My friend Pierre
> Lend me your pen
>   So that I might write a word
> My candle is dead
>   I have no more fire
> Open the door
>   For the love of God

28 (p. 29) *Van Buren Denby*   This is a fictional character, but Martin Van Buren (1782–1862) was President of the United States from 1837 to 1841.

29 (p. 29) *Veuve Cliquot*   a *grande marque* champagne. Fitzgerald misspells the name (properly 'Veuve Clicquot').

30 (p. 30) *one of Mrs Burnett's vicious tracts*   a reference to the famous writer of children's books, Frances Hodgson Burnett (1849–1924)

31 (p. 31) *the Riff*   the Riff (or Rif) Mountains in Northern Morocco, visible from Gibraltar

32 (p. 31) *I fought against the Riff . . .*   Barban's remark here suggests he fought against the Berbers in the Rif War of 1919–26 between the Spanish army and the Rif and Jabala tribes of Morocco.

33 (p. 32) *Îles des Lérins*   two small islands in the Mediterranean off Cannes

34 (p. 34) *the Divers' big Isotta*   a car made by the Isotta Fraschini Motori of Bari, Italy, noted for its luxury

35 (p. 34) *Aix-les-Bains*   a spa town in the Savoy department of France, south of Geneva

36 (p. 37) *cuckoo*   here in the sense of 'barmy' or 'unbelievable'

37 (p. 38) *code duello*   the rules regulating the conduct of a duel

38 (p. 40) *forty-fives*   probably a reference to Colt .45 pistols

39 (p. 40) *a novel of Pushkin's*   Alexander Pushkin (1799–1837), Russian poet, author of *Eugene Onegin* (1833). It is not clear what work Abe is referring to here. Bruccoli and Baughman suggest it is a reference to Mikhail Lermontov's *A Hero of Our Time* (1840).

40 (p. 42) *Juan les Pins*   resort west of Antibes

41 (p. 44) *Pardon, messieurs . . . chez lui*   'Excuse me, gentlemen. Would you like to pay my honorarium? It's only for medical expenses, of course. M. Barban only has a thousand-franc note and isn't able to pay, while the other gentleman has left his wallet at home.'

42 (p. 44) *Combien?*   How much?

43 (p. 44) *Voisins*   a Parisian restaurant

44 (p. 45) *West Point*   United States Military Academy in New York State

45 (p. 45) *a Mayfair party in Hollywood*   The now defunct Mayfair Club in Hollywood was noted for its annual ball.

46 (p. 46) *a Count of the House of Lippe Weissenfeld*   Nicole's ancestry is here traced back through one of the great European royal houses.

47 (p. 46) *President Tyler*   John Tyler (1790–1862), President of the United States 1841–5; he was never elected but succeeded William Henry Harrison who died of pneumonia after one month in office. (There is probably a joke here: Tyler had more children than any other president in American history, fifteen, by two wives.)

48 (p. 46) *Franco-American Films . . . Rue des Saintes Anges*   Both the company and the street are fictional.

49 (p. 46) *vestiaire*   cloakroom

50 (p. 47) *Hermès*   the fashionable shop on the Rue du Faubourg-Sainte-Honoré in Paris

51 (p. 47) *Five-and-Tens*   'nickel and dime' stores, so-called because their goods were all priced at five or ten cents

52 (p. 48) *Beaumont-Hamel*   the site of one of the most terrible battles of the Somme offensive of 1916. On the morning of 1 July

1916 British troops attempted to break through German defences at Beaumont-Hamel, north-east of Amiens and close to the French–Belgian border. The 1st Newfoundland Regiment (fighting as part of the British army) was virtually eliminated by German machine-gun fire: of the 800 men who marched into battle only 68 returned after little more than half an hour of fighting.

53 (p. 48) *the tragic hill of Thiepval* Thiepval lies slightly south-east of Beaumont-Hamel and was, at the beginning of the Somme offensive, just behind German lines.

54 (p. 49) *just quit over in Turkey* The Graeco-Turkish War of 1919–22 was effectively concluded with the Turkish capture of Smyrna (Izmir) in 1922, thus ending the Greek presence in Anatolia.

55 (p. 49) *Morocco* See Note 32 above.

56 (p. 49) *the first Marne again* the River Marne, east of Paris, where the first German offensive of World War I came to a halt

57 (p. 49) *Valence . . . Unter der Linden . . . Derby* Valence is a city on the Rhône River, south of Lyon; the Unter der Linden is one of the main thoroughfares of Berlin; the Derby is an annual horse race held at Epsom Downs in southern England.

58 (p. 49) *General Grant . . . Petersburg* Ulysses S. Grant (1822–85), later President of the United States (1869–77), commanded Union forces at Petersburg, Virginia, during the American Civil War (1861–5), where trenches were dug for infantrymen.

59 (p. 49) *Lewis Carroll* the pen name of Charles Dodgson (1832–98), the author of *Alice's Adventures in Wonderland* (1865)

60 (p. 49) *Jules Verne* popular French novelist (1825–1905), author of many works of *voyages extraordinaires*, among them *Journey to the Centre of the Earth* (1864) and *Twenty Thousand Leagues under the Sea* (1870)

61 (p. 49) *Undine* a tale by the German author Friedrich de la Motte-Fouqué (1777–1843), published in 1811

62 (p. 49) *marraines* godmothers

63 (p. 49) *D. H. Lawrence* the English writer (1885–1930), author of *Sons and Lovers* (1913), *Women in Love* (1920) and *Lady Chatterley's Lover* (1928)

64 (p. 50) *the Newfoundland dead* See Note 52 above.

65 (p. 50) *Amiens* a city on the River Somme

66 (p. 51) *Gare du Nord and Waterloo station*   railway stations in Paris and London, respectively

67 (p. 51) *'Yes, We Have No Bananas'*   a popular comic song from 1922

68 (p. 51) *Württemburgers, Prussian Guards, Chasseurs Alpins*   regiments in the German and French armies

69 (p. 51) *Beaujolais*   a red wine from the Beaujolais district of southern Burgundy

70 (p. 52) *the Decorative Arts Exposition*   L'Exposition Internationale des Arts Décoratifs et Industriels Modernes opened in Paris in 1925 and was influential in promoting the architectural and decorative style known as 'Art Deco'.

71 (p. 52) *Hôtel Roi George*   a fictional location

72 (p. 52) *Suresnes*   a suburb (municipality) west of the city centre of Paris

73 (p. 58) *Rue des Saints-Pères*   Here the Parisian street is real; it is close to the church of St Germain des Prés on the left bank of the River Seine.

74 (p. 58) *Lake Forest*   a wealthy suburb about thirty miles north of Chicago

75 (p. 58) *Luxembourg Gardens*   Les Jardins du Luxembourg, the great baroque gardens and palace on the Boulevard St-Michel in Paris

76 (p. 59) *New Haven*   the town in Connecticut where Yale University is situated

77 (p. 59) *Tanagra*   a city in Ancient Greece and the site of one of the battles of the Peloponnesian War

78 (p. 59) *Duncan Phyfe*   Scottish-born American cabinet-maker (1768–1854)

79 (p. 61) *Lutetia*   a hotel on the Boulevard Raspail in Paris

80 (p. 61) *Cardinal de Retz's palace in the Rue Monsieur*   Cardinal Jean-François-Paul-Gondi de Retz (1614–79), Archbishop of Paris; the Rue Monsieur is near the church of St Jean de Dieu in the seventh *arrondissement* of Paris.

81 (p. 61) *Louisa M. Alcott or Madame de Ségur*   the American author (1832–88) of *Little Women* (1868) and the Comtesse de Ségur (1799–1874), a French author of children's books

82 (p. 63) *Place de la Concorde*   the plaza at the south-eastern end of the Champs-Élysées in Paris

83 (p. 66) *the Shah of Persia*   the King of Persia (now Iran)

84 (p. 66) *Teheran* Tehran, capital of Persia (Iran)

85 (p. 66) *Major Hengist and Mr Horsa* comic references to the brothers Hengist and Horsa who led the Jutish (a Low German tribe) invasion of England in the fifth century AD and established the kingdom of Kent

86 (p. 67) *the Ritz* one of the most luxurious hotels in Paris. Fitzgerald's friend and contemporary Ernest Hemingway (1898–1961) said, 'When I dream of afterlife in heaven, the action always takes place at the Ritz Paris.'

87 (p. 67) *General Pershing* John J. Pershing (1860–1948), commander of American forces in Europe in World War I

88 (p. 67) *a Goldberg cartoon* Reuben Lucius Goldberg (1883–1970), American cartoonist

89 (p. 67) *the Halles* Les Halles, the market district of Paris

90 (p. 68) *Saint-Sulpice* the church in the Place St-Sulpice, just north of the Jardins du Luxembourg. See Note 75 above.

91 (p. 69) *Gare Saint-Lazare* railway station to the north-west of the city centre of Paris

92 (p. 70) *St Genèvieve's* a dance hall near the College de France on the Left Bank in Paris. St Genèvieve was a patroness of the city in the fifth century AD.

93 (p. 71) *survivant* an archaic form of 'surviving'

94 (p. 72) *a Pullman entrance* a railway coach manufactured by the Pullman Company in Illinois

95 (p. 72) *poste de police* police station

96 (p. 73) *Diaghilev* Serge Diaghilev (1872–1929), Russian choreographer and impresario, founder of the Ballets Russes

97 (p. 74) *'Tu as vu . . . un jouet'* 'Did you see the revolver? It was very small, a real beauty – a toy.'

98 (p. 74) *'Mais assez puissant . . . la guerre'* 'But very powerful. Did you see his shirt? Enough blood to make you think it was a war.'

99 (p. 75) *Grand Guignol* a Paris theatre famous for its horror productions, thus the association of the name with the horrific and sensational

100 (p. 75) *beyed* Fitzgerald renders Collis's very Southern pronunciation of 'bird' phonetically

101 (p. 75) *nutsey* good-looking

102 (p. 76) *Bones* Collis is referring to the Skull and Bones, the most prestigious and secretive of Yale's undergraduate societies.

103 (p. 77) *Brentano's*   a bookshop on l'Avenue de l'Opéra in Paris that sold English-language texts

104 (p. 78) *the heavyweight champion of the world*   Jack Dempsey (1895–1983) was heavyweight boxing champion from 1919 until 1926.

105 (p. 78) *Films Par Excellence Studio*   a fictional company

106 (p. 78) *Passy*   a residential district of Paris near the Bois de Boulogne

107 (p. 78) *Muette*   la Porte de le Muette, near the Bois de Boulogne

108 (p. 78) *one of Tarkington's adolescents*   a reference to the American author Booth Tarkington (1869–1946) who wrote novels of adolescent life in the American midwest

109 (p. 78) *'1000 chemises'*   a thousand shirts, but probably a reference to the Parisian chain-store, Au Cent Mille Chemises

110 (p. 78) *'Papeterie' . . . 'Pompe Funèbres'*   stationery shop; cake shop; sales (goods reduced in price); advertising; *Breakfast at Sunrise* (a film starring Constance Talmadge, see Note 25 above); ecclesiastical robes; death notices; funeral homes

111 (p. 79) *Ferrara*   a town in northern Italy between Bologna and Padua

112 (p. 79) *Tad's more savage cartoons*   the American cartoonist Thomas Aloysius Dorgan (1877–1929) whose pseudonym was 'Tad'

113 (p. 79) *San Antone*   San Antonio, Texas

114 (p. 80) *Sunny Times*   the *Sunday New York Times* newspaper

115 (p. 80) *Cheyne-Stokes tendencies*   a pathological breathing condition named after the two doctors who identified the disorder

116 (p. 81) *the Bois*   Bois de Boulogne

117 (p. 81) *Otard . . . Armagnac*   names of rums and brandies, and other drinks

118 (p. 81) *'And two – for tea . . .'*   'Tea For Two', a popular song from 1924

119 (p. 82) *Boucher*   François Boucher (1703–70), French painter

120 (p. 82) *Fouquet's*   a restaurant and bar on the Champs-Elysées

121 (p. 82) *'Entrez!'*   'Come in!'

122 (p. 82) *sergent de ville*   policeman

123 (p. 83) *carte d'identité*   identity card

124 (p. 83) *Rue de Rivoli*   a street bordering the Jardin des Tuileries in Paris

125 (p. 85) *Montmartre*   a district of Paris noted for its night-life

126 (p. 85) *Evreux*   a town in Normandy with a great twelfth-century cathedral

127 (p. 85) *St Germain*   the church of St Germain-des-Prés on the Boulevard St-Germain in Paris

128 (p. 85) *artists like ... Fernand*   possibly a reference to the Cubist painter Fernand Leger (1881–1955)

129 (p. 86) *the gold-star muzzers*   The waiter means the American Gold Star Mothers whose membership was made up (at the time of the novel's publication) of mothers who had lost a son or daughter in World War I.

130 (p. 86) *Mosby*   John Singleton Mosby (1833–1916), the commander of a group of partisan rangers in western and northern Virginia who fought against the Union Army during the American Civil War

131 (p. 87) *Boulevard des Capucines*   a street in the centre of Paris

132 (p. 87) *Liberty*   a weekly American magazine of news, international affairs and political and social commentary. Fitzgerald had planned to have *Tender is the Night* published in *Liberty*.

133 (p. 87) *France*   a passenger vessel

134 (p. 88) *Briglith*   Bruccoli and Baughman suggest this might be a corruption of 'brillig', four o'clock in the afternoon, from Lewis Carroll's *Through the Looking-Glass* (1871).

135 (p. 89) *Rue Cambon*   a street in central Paris near la Place Vendôme

136 (p. 89) *the bar of the Crillon*   the Hôtel de Crillon

137 (p. 89) *two fingers of gin*   a measurement of spirits (here gin) roughly equivalent to the distance between the joint and the tip of the nail on the longest forefinger (a little short of two inches)

138 (p. 89) *Leonardo's girl*   a portrait by Leonardo da Vinci (1452–1519)

139 (p. 90) *'Miss Television'*   the word was in use by 1909, before the invention of television; Dick uses the word here in the sense of 'televisual' or 'photogenic'. See, also, the story 'Outside the Cabinet-Maker's'.

140 (p. 91) *on the suave model that heels the Republican party in the border states*   Jules is described as being like one of the black Americans who joined the Republican party in the 'border states' (those states that bordered the secessionist states of the South in the American Civil War, such as Delaware and

Maryland) because the Democratic party was the party of 'white supremacy' in the southern states where the black American was disenfranchised.

141 (p. 91) *Montparnasse*   the bohemian district south of Les Jardins du Luxembourg and east of Gare Montparnasse (named after Mount Parnassus) on the Left Bank in Paris

142 (p. 91) *the French Latin quarter*   the district near the University of Paris V (formerly Sorbonne) and St Germain des Prés. The name comes from the Latin habitually spoken by students during the medieval period.

143 (p. 92) *Chambord . . . Majestic*   two luxury hotels in central Paris

144 (p. 92) *fight off these Senegalese*   Senegal was a French colony until 1960

145 (p. 93) *George the Third*   Hanoverian king of Great Britain (1760–1820) at the time of the American War of Independence

146 (p. 94) *couverture* bedspread

147 (p. 95) *the Arbuckle case*   The silent-screen comedian Roscoe 'Fatty' Arbuckle (1887–1933) was charged with the murder of Virginia Rappe, who had been attending a party in his suite at the St Francis Hotel in San Francisco in September 1921. Though Arbuckle was acquitted, the scandal ruined his film career.

148 (p. 96) *All Fools' Day*   1st April

149 (p. 96) *Zurichsee*   Lake Zurich

150 (p. 96) *domino*   loose cloak of the kind worn to a masked ball

151 (p. 97) *local board*   Dick Diver's draft (conscription) board in the United States

152 (p. 97) *the waves of thunder around Gorizia*   a reference to the battle between Austro-Hungary and Italy in August 1916 fought at Gorizia in north-eastern Italy, near the border with Slovenia

153 (p. 97) *Somme and Aisne*   two rivers in France associated with some of the most terrible battles of World War I

154 (p. 97) *an Oxford Rhodes scholar*   Dick Diver had had a scholarship to attend Oxford University. The scholarship was funded by Cecil Rhodes (1853–1902), the Victorian imperialist who founded the De Beers Mining Company in South Africa, and was open to candidates from the United States.

155 (p. 97) *Johns Hopkins*   here, specifically, the School of Medicine at Johns Hopkins University in Baltimore, Maryland. Gertrude Stein studied medicine at Johns Hopkins between 1897 and 1901.

156 (p. 97) *Freud*   Sigmund Freud (1856–1939), Austrian physician and psychoanalyist

157 (p. 98) *Damenstiftgasse*   There is no such street in present-day Vienna

158 (p. 98) *The Rose and the Ring*   a novel (1855) by William Makepeace Thackeray (1811–63)

159 (p. 99) *Tap Day ... Elihu*   undergraduate societies at Yale select their members by tapping them on the shoulder

160 (p. 99) *Goethe*   Johann Wolfgang von Goethe (1749–1832), German poet, novelist, playwright and philosopher, author of *Faust*

161 (p. 99) *Jung*   Carl Jung (1875–1961), Swiss psychiatrist and colleague of Freud

162 (p. 99) *Bar-sur-Aube*   a town in France, south-east of Paris

163 (p. 99) *Galena*   a small town in Illinois where Ulysses S. Grant (see Note 58 above) worked in his family's general store

164 (p. 100) *Albishorn*   a mountain near Zurich

165 (p. 100) *a Vaudois by birth*   someone from the Swiss canton of Vaud

166 (p. 100) *Cagliostro*   Alessandro, Count di Cagliostro (1743–93), Italian alchemist and charlatan

167 (p. 100) *Kraepelin*   Emil Kraepelin (1856–1926), German pyschiatrist

168 (p. 101) *the Krenzegg*   a mountain near Zurich

169 (p. 102) *Daddy-Long-Legs ... Molly-Make-Believe*   in the style of popular sentimental novels of the pre-World War I years

170 (p. 102) *Je m'en fiche*   I don't care

171 (p. 103) *'plus petite et moins entendue'*   smaller and less significant

172 (p. 104) *Michigan Boulevard*   one of the main shopping streets in Chicago (now Michigan Avenue)

173 (p. 104) *twin six*   a twelve-cylinder (two rows of six) motor-car engine

174 (p. 104) *Tout à vous*   Yours, always

175 (p. 105) *alienist*   here in the sense of one who treats mental disorders

176 (p. 107) *'un homme très chic'*   a very fashionably dressed man

177 (p. 107) *Göttingen*   a town in Germany, in the province of Hanover, with a distinguished university

178 (p. 108) *docent at the university* in American universities a recognised teacher who is not on the salaried staff

179 (p. 108) *Armour . . . McCormick* a list of great Chicago companies and businesses, each named after its founder

180 (p. 109) *une folie* a mistaken, or reckless, act

181 (p. 109) *Vevey* a resort on Lake Geneva (Lac Leman) in Switzerland, near Montreux

182 (p. 109) *Tuileries Guard* A unit of Swiss guards defended the French royal family against French revolutionaries in the Tuileries Palace in Paris in August 1792; all were massacred.

183 (p. 112) *Gross-Münster* (Grossmünster) a cathedral in Zurich where Zwingli preached. See also Note 187 below.

184 (p. 112) *Lavater* Johann Kaspar Lavater (1741–1801), Swiss theologian noted for his work on physiognomy

185 (p. 112) *Pestalozzi* Johann Heinrich Pestalozzi (1746–1827), Swiss educational theorist noted for his progressive ideas of how children learn by activity

186 (p. 112) *Dr Alfred Escher* Here Fitzgerald seems to be referring to Alfred Escher (1819–82), the founder of Crédit Suisse; he was not a doctor.

187 (p. 112) *Zwingli* Huldreich Zwingli (1484–1531), Swiss Protestant reformer who preached at the Grossmünster in Zurich

188 (p. 114) *Como* Lake Como in northern Italy

189 (p. 114) *Suppé* Franz von Suppé (1820–95), Austrian composer

190 (p. 115) *'Hindustan' . . . 'I'm Glad I Can Make You Cry'* all popular songs from around the end of World War I

191 (p. 115) *'Wait Till The Cows Come Home' and 'Goodbye, Alexander'* popular songs from 1917 and 1918

192 (p. 115) *Lothario* a rake or libertine; the name comes from the character in Nicholas Rowe's *The Fair Penitent* (1703)

193 (p. 115) *They were so sorry, dear . . . to feel sad* these 'pop song' phrases are all taken from popular songs of the day

194 (p. 116) *Valais* a Swiss canton; Fitzgerald's geography seems to have gone awry at this point

195 (p. 116) *'Lay a silver dollar . . . its round'* lyrics from the popular song 'Silver Dollar'

196 (p. 116) *'So Long, Letty'* a popular song from 1916

197 (p. 117) *St Hilda's in Oxford* St Hilda's Hall (now St Hilda's College), a college for women at Oxford University

198 (p. 118) *'Du lieber Gott! . . . Glas-Bier'* 'Dear God! Please bring Dick another glass of beer.'

199 (p. 121) *burberry* a raincoat (usually one manufactured by the Thomas H. Burberry Company)

200 (p. 123) *'Bonjour, docteur . . . au revoir, monsieur'* 'Hello, doctor.' 'Hello, sir.' 'Lovely weather.' 'Yes, marvellous.' 'Are you staying here?' 'No, just visiting.' 'Ah, yes. Well then, goodbye, sir.'

201 (p. 124) *a magnificent Rolls* a Rolls-Royce motor car

202 (p. 124) *goblins on the Gross-Münster* the Gothic gargoyles on the outer walls of the cathedral

203 (p. 125) *the Glion funicular* the funicular railway providing access to Glion, a resort above Montreux

204 (p. 125) *La Tour de Peilz* a resort on Lake Geneva

205 (p. 126) *the white courts of the Kursaal* the tennis-courts of the health resort (Kursaal)

206 (p. 126) *Chillon and the island palace of Salagnon* islands near Montreux

207 (p. 126) *'Défense de cueillir les fleurs'* 'Do not pick the flowers.'

208 (p. 126) *Dorothy Perkins roses* an American rambling rose

209 (p. 126) *like Irene Castle's* Irene Castle (1893–1969), a dancer from the Ragtime period who, with her husband Vernon, did much to popularise ballroom dancing

210 (p. 126) *the Conte de Marmora* in the Piedmont region of north-western Italy

211 (p. 127) *Caux* a ski resort near Montreux

212 (p. 127) *donkey-engine* a small steam engine (usually used of the hoisting machine of a merchant ship)

213 (p. 129) *Vanity Fair* American fashion and style magazine

214 (p. 129) *Byron* Lord Byron (1788–1824), English Romantic poet

215 (p. 129) *'Poor Butterfly'* a popular song from 1916

216 (p. 130) *the University* the University of Chicago

217 (p. 133) *a Strauss waltz* Johann Strauss II (1825–99), the Viennese composer, was known as 'the Waltz king'.

218 (p. 133) *Rochers de Naye* mountain peaks above Montreux

219 (p. 134) *a 'gone-coon'* in the sense of one whose case is hopeless

220 (p. 135) *Mad Anthony Wayne* Anthony Wayne (1745–96), American general who distinguished himself in the American War of Independence and was popularly known as 'Mad Anthony'

221 (p. 135) *Marshall Field*   Chicago tycoon (1834–1906) who founded the Marshall Field's Department Store in Chicago

222 (p. 136) *'Je m'en fiche de tout'*   'I don't care at all.'

223 (p. 136) *camérière*   chambermaid (archaic)

224 (p. 136) *Orvieto*   a city in central Italy noted for its white wine

225 (p. 136) *Blue Grotto*   The caves on the island of Capri, near Naples, are noted for their light.

226 (p. 137) *Pallas Athene*   Athena, the daughter of Zeus and goddess of Athens

227 (p. 137) *from Woolloomooloo Bay to Biskra*   Biskra is a town in Algeria, but Woolloomooloo Bay is off Sydney in Australia and thus the geography seems confused

228 (p. 137) *Ouled Naïl*   an Algerian tribe. The term is also used to describe a form of belly-dancing.

229 (p. 137) *Timgad*   a walled city in Algeria built by the Roman emperor Trajan around 100 AD

230 (p. 138) *Affaires Étrangères in Paris*   Ministry of Foreign Affairs

231 (p. 138) *Mistinguette . . . Pas sur la Bouche*   Jeanne Bourgeois (1875–1956), known as Mistinguett, French singer; Pablo Picasso (1881–1973), Spanish painter; Maurice Yvain (1891–1965), author of *Pas sur la Bouche* ('Not on the Lips'), a musical comedy first performed in 1925

232 (p. 139) *Esterel*   a mountain range above Cannes

233 (p. 139) *Havre*   Le Havre, French port in Normandy

234 (p. 139) *La Napoule*   seaside resort near Cannes

235 (p. 141) *Bon Ami*   a cleansing powder (the company is American, not French or Swiss)

236 (p. 142) *luminal*   a sedative

237 (p. 142) *the three Chinese monkeys*   i.e. 'see no evil, speak no evil, hear no evil', the context, of course, suggesting that the proprietor of the hotel is to keep quiet about the circumstances of the murder, thus protecting Rosemary's career

238 (p. 142) *ceinture*   a circle of railway tracks

239 (p. 142) *Paris-Lyon-Méditerranée*   a railway service between Paris and the French Riviera (also known as PLM)

240 (p. 143) *pousse*   bout or outbreak

241 (p. 144) *Ciro's*   a Parisian nightclub

242 (p. 144) *Ward McAllister*   American lawyer (1827–95) who became a leading figure in New York's refined society

243 (p. 145) *'Just picture you upon my knee . . . for me'*   lyrics from the song 'Tea For Two'

244 (p. 146) *Syndicat d'Initiative*   organisation for promoting tourism

245 (p. 146) *'Don't Bring Lulu'*   a popular song from 1925

246 (p. 146) *the Charleston*   the dance routine associated with the 'flappers' of the 1920s

247 (p. 146) *Sturmtruppen*   storm-troopers

248 (p. 146) *scarcely down from Cambridge*   i.e. recently graduated from the University of Cambridge

249 (p. 147) *telemark*   a sharp turn in downhill skiing

250 (p. 147) *kvass*   a Russian beer made from fermented bread

251 (p. 148) *Zugeresee*   one of the smaller Swiss lakes near Lucerne

252 (p. 149) *Privatdocent*   an unsalaried university teacher. See Note 178 above.

253 (p. 150) *Croesus*   King of Lydia in Asia Minor, *c.*560–546BC, whose wealth was legendary

254 (p. 150) *Bleuler writes . . . Adler writes*   Eugene Bleuler (1857–1939), Swiss psychiatrist; Oscar Forel (1891–1982), Swiss psychiatrist and physician; Alfred Adler (1870–1937), Austrian psychiatrist and psychotherapist

255 (p. 151) *Saanen*   resort near Gstaad

256 (p. 151) *Humpty-Dumpty*   the personified egg of the nursery rhyme 'Humpty Dumpty sat on a wall'. Fitzgerald may be thinking of the Humpty Dumpty of Chapter 6 of Lewis Carroll's *Through the Looking-Glass* (1871).

257 (p. 153) *Wiener waltzes*   Viennese waltzes

258 (p. 153) *Prokofieff's 'Love of Three Oranges'*   an opera (1921) by the Russian composer Sergei Prokofiev (1891–1955)

259 (p. 155) *ergo-therapy*   form of psychiatric therapy based on the idea that physical labour is therapeutic

260 (p. 155) *the Chopin*   piano music by the Polish composer Frederick Chopin (1810–49)

261 (p. 156) *from the Étoile to the Place de la Concorde*   i.e. the length of the Champs-Élysées

262 (p. 156) *the Iron Maiden*   instrument of torture shaped to the human body

263 (p. 157) *Pyrrhic victory*   victory gained at too great a cost

264 (p. 159) *paresis*   partial paralysis

265 (p. 160) *Zug*   town (and canton) in Switzerland on the Zugersee

266 (p. 160) *the Agiri Fair*   a religious festival held annually in the canton of Zug

267 (p. 161) *hootchy-kootchy show*   a show with provocative or sensual dancing

268 (p. 161) *'Madame . . . Oui, Dick'*   'Madam, can I leave the children with you for two minutes? It's very urgent – I'll give you ten francs.' 'Of course.' 'Stay with this nice lady.' 'Yes, Dick.'

269 (p. 161) *buvette*   refreshment stall

270 (p. 161) *'La septième . . . monsieur'*   'The seventh daughter of a seventh daughter born on the banks of the Nile – come in, sir – '

271 (p. 161) *'Regardez-moi . . . cette Anglaise!'*   'Look ! Look at that Englishwoman!'

272 (p. 162) *bock*   a German beer

273 (p. 162) *Svengali*   a hypnotist or mesmerist, from the character of the same name in *Trilby* (1894), a novel by George du Maurier (1834–96).

274 (p. 162) *corium*   the layer of skin under the epidermis

275 (p. 163) *'Merci, monsieur . . . mes petits'*   'Thank you, sir, you're very generous. It was a pleasure, sir, madam. Bye bye, children.'

276 (p. 163) *'schizophrene'*   schizophrenic

277 (p. 164) *'La voiture Divare est cassée'*   'The Divers' motor car has broken down.' (Fitzgerald has Dick render his surname as he thinks a Frenchman would, but 'Divare' is infelicitous.)

278 (p. 165) *the elder Forel*   Auguste Forel (1848–1931), Swiss physician and psychiatrist, father of Oscar Forel. See Note 254 above.

279 (p. 165) *dementia praecox*   form of insanity characterised by feebleness of mind

280 (p. 166) *Vorarlberg Alps*   mountainous region of western Austria bordering Lichtenstein and Switzerland

281 (p. 166) *The Century . . . Fliegende Blätter*   names of magazines

282 (p. 167) *Savona*   Italian province and port west of Genoa

283 (p. 167) *Marienplatz*   the main square in Munich

284 (p. 168) *Beale Street*   street in Memphis, Tennessee, regarded by some as the 'birthplace' of the Blues

285 (p. 168) *Pilsudski's own tailor*   Jozef Klemens Pilsudski (1867–1935) was Polish head of state of the independent Polish republic for two periods of office in the 1920s and 1930s.

286 (p. 168) *Red Guards*   Soviet soldiers (the references here are to the Soviet-Polish War of 1920)

287 (p. 168) *St Mark's School*   a boys' school in Southborough, Massachusetts (now co-educational)

288 (p. 169) *a big Packard*   an American motor car

289 (p. 170) *Racquet Club*   a private club in New York City

290 (p. 170) *Harvard Club*   a private club in New York City for the alumni of Harvard University

291 (p. 171) *the Emperor Maximilian*   the statue of the Emperor Maximilian (1459–1519) in the centre of Innsbruck, Austria

292 (p. 171) *Erbsen-suppe with Würstchen . . . Kaiserschmarren*   pea-soup; small sausages; mugs of Pilsner beer; pancake with raisins

293 (p. 172) *scapegrace drummers*   travelling salesman (who 'drum up' business)

294 (p. 172) *Birkkarspitze*   a mountain peak near Innsbruck

295 (p. 174) *buckboards*   open, horse-drawn, wagons

296 (p. 175) *couturières*   the best fashion designers

297 (p. 175) *Boise*   the state capital of Idaho

298 (p. 176) *Cassino and Frosinone*   two stops on the railway journey between Naples and Rome. (The monastery at Monte Cassino was destroyed in a famous battle of World War II.)

299 (p. 176) *Hotel Quirinale*   a hotel in Rome

300 (p. 176) *Black-seed oil*   the oil of black cumin seed, widely used in the treatment of coughs and other respiratory infections, but here the context indicates it is used to dose horses

301 (p. 177) *'una novella . . . Americana'*   Dick reads in the Italian newspaper, *Corriere della Sera*, of the publication of 'a novel by Sainclair Lewis, *Wall Street*, in which the author analyses the social life of a small American town'. The reference, presumably, is to Lewis's *Main Street* (1920). The spelling 'Sainclair' is deliberate.

302 (p. 177) *'tied up in bags'*   i.e. enamoured of her, attracted to her

303 (p. 178) *Edna Ferber*   Edna Ferber (1885–1968), American novelist, author of *Showboat* (1926)

304 (p. 180) *Pincio*   a district of Rome, to the north of the city

305 (p. 180) *Porta San Sebastiano . . . Appian Way*   a gateway into Rome; one of the principal land routes of Italy

306 (p. 180) *hopeful Valentinos*   a reference to actors seeking to emulate the style (and success) of Rudolph Valentino (1895–1926), one of the most popular film stars of the day

307 (p. 181) *'He's on the hop again, and how!'*   To be 'hopped up' is an American idiom for being 'high', that is, on drugs (here, presumably, marijuana or cocaine).

308 (p. 182) *the Excelsior*   a luxury hotel

309 (p. 183) *Michael Arlen*   English novelist (1895–1956), author of *The Green Hat* (1924)

310 (p. 183) *the Ulpia*   a restaurant in Rome

311 (p. 186) *Livorno*   a port (also known as Leghorn) in Tuscany in central Italy

312 (p. 187) *the Black Death*   the common name for the great bubonic plague that ravaged Europe in the latter half of the fourteenth century

313 (p. 188) *the Spanish Steps*   the Scalinata di Spagna, the flight of steps that leads to the church of Trinita dei Monti in Rome

314 (p. 188) *Bonbonieri*   the word translates as 'candy-box'

315 (p. 190) *spumante*   Italian sparkling wine

316 (p. 190) *Colonna and Gaetani families*   politically powerful families (and organisations) in medieval Rome

317 (p. 190) *Yenci*   dolls made of felt and manufactured in Italy

318 (p. 191) *'Quanto a Hotel Quirinale? . . . Cento lire'*   'How much to the Hotel Quirinale?' 'One hundred lire.' 'Thirty-five lire and a tip, too.' 'One hundred lire.'

319 (p. 192) *'Alors . . . Comprenez-vous?'*   'OK. Listen. Go to the Quirinale. Listen: you're drunk. Pay what the chauffeur asks for. Do you understand?'

320 (p. 192) *'Non . . . au Quirinale'*   'No, I don't want to.' 'What?' 'I'll pay forty lire. That's more than enough.' 'Listen . . . You are drunk. You punched the chauffeur. Like this; like that. You're lucky that I'm letting you go. Pay him what he asks for – one hundred lire. Go to the Quirinale.'

321 (p. 193) *due centi lire*   two hundred lire

322 (p. 193) *Marion Crawford's curiously inanimate Roman stories*   The American novelist Francis Marion Crawford (1854–1909) set a number of his stories in Italy, such as *A Roman Singer* (1884).

323 (p. 194) *'Non capisco inglese'*   'I don't speak English.'

324 (p. 195) *'Hime'*   I'm (phonetic)

325 (p. 195) *Groton voice*   Groton is a private boarding and preparatory school in Groton, Massachusetts; the accent is upper class.

326 (p. 197) *semper diretto . . . sinestra*   straight ahead; right and left

327 (p. 197) *Plaza di Spagna*   the Spanish Plaza in Rome

328 (p. 200) *Frascati*   a town in the hills south of Rome, often associated with its white wine of the same name

329 (p. 201) *Norma Talmadge*   American film actress (1897–1957), sister of Constance. See Note 25 above.

330 (p. 204) *Wassermanns*   a test for syphilis named after the German bacteriologist August von Wassermann (1866–1925) who developed it

331 (p. 205) *Harrow . . . King's College, Cambridge*   a public school at Harrow in north London and one of the most distinguished colleges at Cambridge University

332 (p. 205) *cantharides*   the insect known as Spanish Fly, but here the reference is to the pharmacological product (dried beetle) taken as an aphrodisiac

333 (p. 208) *Gènevois*   someone from Geneva

334 (p. 209) *mediatised principalities*   a state (or principality) annexed to another state, usually in an arrangement that gives the former ruler some rights and privileges

335 (p. 212) *a highball*   whiskey with water or soda water

336 (p. 212) *The Wedding of the Painted Doll*   a popular song from 1929

337 (p. 213) *that's bad 'cess to them*   i.e. that's bad luck

338 (p. 216) *Pomeranians*   small dogs with long, silky hair

339 (p. 217) *Boyen*   Bolzano in the Tyrolean Alps of Italy was ceded to Italy in 1919, having previously been part of the Austro-Hungarian Empire and known as Bozen or Boyen.

340 (p. 217) *Sealyhams*   a breed of terrier

341 (p. 217) *Pekinese*   small Chinese lapdog

342 (p. 218) *Mason-Dixon*   The Mason-Dixon line (named after the English astronomers Jeremiah Dixon and Charles Mason) distinguishes 'free' states to the North from 'slave' states to the South in the United States

343 (p. 218) *Kabyle-Berber-Sabaean-Hindu*   ethnic, linguistic and religious categories

344 (p. 218) *salaamed*   bowed obsequiously

345 (p. 219) *I meant smoke*   'Smoke' or 'Smokey' is a pejorative term (or descriptive adjective) for a black man

346 (p. 221) *Himadoun*   ladies-in-waiting. The context suggests the word is oriental in origin (see Note 343 above).

347 (p. 223) *Chablis Moutonne*   Moutonne is one of the Grands Crus of Chablis, the white wine of the region north-west of Dijon in France.

348 (p. 223) *Bastide*   a French country-house

349 (p 225) *the Nicean Bay*   the Bay of Nice

350 (p. 226) *Antoninian bench*   of the Antonine period in the decorative arts, after the Roman Emperor Antonius Pius (AD86–161)

351 (p. 226) '*Mais pour . . . grandes compositions*'   'But for us heroes . . . we need time, Nicole. We can't engage in minor acts of heroism; we have to do things on the grand scale.'

352 (p. 227) '*Parlez français . . . Nicole*'   'Speak to me in French, Nicole.'

353 (p. 227) *Ronald Colman . . . Corps d'Afrique du Nord*   Ronald Colman (1891–1958), the English actor, appeared in the 1926 film of P. C. Wren's *Beau Geste*, a novel about the French Foreign Legion (here Fitzgerald confuses the Corps d'Afrique du Nord with the Legion Étrangère).

354 (p. 227) *two-handed chemin-de-fer*   a form of baccarat, a card game frequently played in casinos (known in the United States as 'chemmy')

355 (p. 228) *John Held's flat-chested flappers*   John Held (1889–1958), the American cartoonist and illustrator was famed for his depictions of the 'flappers' of the 1920s

356 (p. 228) *Sepoys in the ruined fort*   Sepoys were natives of India employed as soldiers by European (usually British) colonial powers.

357 (p. 229) '*Quelle enfanterie! . . . Racine!*'   'What childishness! It sounds as if he's reciting Racine!'; Jean Racine (1639–99), French tragic dramatist

358 (p. 230) *poule*   prostitute, harlot

359 (p. 232) *lignum vitae*   literally 'wood of life'; trees and shrubs generally of hard wood (though not common in New Zealand)

360 (p. 233) *Niçoise and Provençal*   the spoken French accents of Nice and Provence

361 (p. 236) '*Dîtes donc! Dîtes donc!*'   'Hey! Hey there!'

362 (p. 239) *Baby Gar*   the brand name of a small motorboat

363 (p. 240) *an Anita Loos heroine*   American author (1893–1981) of *Gentlemen Prefer Blondes* (1925), noted for her satirical portraits of *femmes fatales* of the Jazz Age

364 (p. 243) *Schubert songs*   the Austrian composer Franz Schubert (1797–1828) is noted for his *lieder* (songs)

365 (p. 243) *'Thank the horse . . . Thank you both for being justabit tight'* lyrics from a popular song

366 (p. 244) *Chanel Sixteen*   a perfume supposedly manufactured by the House of Chanel in Paris (but Fitzgerald seems to be confusing it with Chanel No. 5)

367 (p. 247) *a fighting Puck*   the character Puck in Shakespeare's *A Midsummer Night's Dream*, but here in the sense of any mischief-maker

368 (p. 248) *'Oh, way down South . . . Look away'*   The lines parody 'Dixie', the song associated with the Southern cause during the American Civil War.

369 (p. 248) *Languedoc*   coastal region of southern France

370 (p. 249) *Korniloff*   Lavr Georgyevich Kornilov (1870–1918), Russian general accused of plotting to overthrow the provisional Russian government of February 1917

371 (p. 249) *'Kwee wave off your porch?'*   'Can we wave off your porch?' ('Kwee' is rendered phonetically.)

372 (p. 250) *Star-Spangled Banner*   The national anthem of the United States was composed by Francis Scott Key (1780–1843), a lawyer and amateur poet: he was a distant relation of F. Scott Fitzgerald.

373 (p. 250) *Beaulieu . . . Menton*   Beaulieu-sur-Mer is a resort on the French Riviera; Menton is a resort east of Monaco on the border with Italy.

374 (p. 252) *'Nicole, comment vas-tu?'*   Nicole, how are you?'

375 (p. 254) *'Oui, oui . . . Oui . . . '*   'Yes, yes . . . but who am I speaking to ? . . . Yes . . . '

376 (p. 254) *chosen Ophelia*   a reference to the character in Shakespeare's *Hamlet*

377 (p. 254) *"pas de mortes – pas d'automobiles"*   "not death – nothing to do with motor cars"

378 (p. 254) *Alpes Maritimes*   The resorts of the French Riviera fall within the administrative jurisdiction of the department of the Alpes Maritimes.

379 (p. 255) *roused old Gausse from an Alsatian coma*   Gausse is from the Alsace region of France.

380 (p. 256) *John D. Rockefeller Mellon*   Dick Diver conflates the

names of two great American business tycoons, John D. Rockefeller (1839–1937) and Andrew Mellon (1855–1937).

381 (p. 256) *Lord Henry Ford*   Here Dick Diver gives the American car manufacturer Henry Ford (1863–1947) the rank of a nobleman.

382 (p. 257) *landaulet*   a convertible motor car

383 (p. 258) *Carleton Hotel*   Fitzgerald probably intends the Carlton Hotel in Cannes

384 (p. 258) *citron pressé*   lemon juice

385 (p. 259) *'Il n'y a plus . . . Ça va.'*   'We don't have any Blackenwhite. We only have Johnny Walker.' 'OK.'

386 (p. 259) *'Donnez moi du gin et du siphon'*   'Give me gin and some soda water.'

387 (p. 259) *'Cessez cela! Allez ouste!'*   'Stop this! And get out of here!'

388 (p. 259) *Tour de France*   the annual bicycle race

389 (p. 259) *'allez-vous-en'*   'go away'

390 (p. 260) *'Elle doit . . . vous'*   'She'll have more with me than she does with you.'

391 (p. 260) *l'amour de famille*   domestic love (or domestic bliss)

392 (p. 262) *photographer from the AP*   the Associated Press, an American news organisation akin to Reuters

393 (p. 262) *authenticated Hapsburg*   a member of the royal Hapsburg family, one of the great family dynasties of Central and Western Europe

394 (p. 263) *anisette*   an aniseed-flavoured liqueur

395 (p. 263) *Dr Eliot's classics*   Charles W. Eliot (1834–1926), President of Harvard University, edited *The Harvard Classics*, one of the most comprehensive, multi-volume collections of its time.

396 (p. 264) *Batavia . . . Lockport*   small towns in New York State

397 (p. 265) *Finger Lakes Section*   a group of lakes in western New York State, so-called because they resemble the fingers of the human hand. Geneva is at the north end of Seneca Lake.

398 (p. 265) *like Grant's in Galena*   See Note 163 above.

399 (p. 265) *Hornell*   a town in New York State about fifty miles south-west of Geneva

NOTES TO
THE LAST TYCOON

The Title

In the Cambridge Edition of the Works of F. Scott Fitzgerald, this novel is entitled *The Loves of the Last Tycoon: A Western* (Cambridge University Press, Cambridge, 1994). The editor, Matthew Bruccoli Jr, a distinguished Fitzgerald scholar, has favoured this title on the grounds that recent scholarship has concluded that this is what Fitzgerald intended to call the novel. Edmund Wilson's edition, however, gave it Fitzgerald's temporary working title of *The Last Tycoon*, and Sheilah Graham, Fitzgerald's English lover whom he had met in Hollywood in the summer of 1937, took the view that this was the title that Fitzgerald would finally favour, in part because of its rhythmical affinity with *The Great Gatsby*. This title is retained in this new edition for Wordsworth. Wilson divided the manuscript into six chapters, largely by following the arrangement of the episodes and their assignment to chapters (Fitzgerald identified them as A, B, C, etc.) in Fitzgerald's last diagrammatic outline. Bruccoli's scholarly text, however, offers only one chapter with seventeen episode divisions. This is accurate with respect to the state of the manuscript in its unfinished form but it makes for a somewhat disconcerting and alien reading experience; the effect, indeed, it to make the novel 'episodic' in the worst sense. This new edition for Wordsworth Classics follows Wilson's text and the reader interested in the more recondite aspects of textual scholarship might want to compare this text with that offered in Matthew J. Bruccoli's edition.

400 (p. 269) *Rudolph Valentino* Rodolfo Alfonso Valentina d'Antonguolla (1895–1926), Italian actor and leading male star of the silent film era, widely known as 'the Latin Lover'

401 (p. 269) *Lolly Parsons* Louella Parason (1880–1972), one of the most well-known of the Hollywood 'gossip columnists'

402 (p. 269) *Bennington* Bennington College, a private girls' college in Bennington, Vermont. The college became co-educational in 1969.

403 (p. 269) *Hollywood* Strictly speaking, the location of the movie industry in Southern California is not coextensive with Hollywood; many production studios now extend into the nearby area of Westside.

404 (p. 269) *the Depression* The period of economic downturn in the United States that began with 'the Panic of 1929', triggered by the stock-market crash, and which, in effect, only concluded with America's entry into World War II in 1941, is known as the Great Depression; Fitzgerald's reference to this and his dating of the events of the novel in his final outline suggest that he loosely connected his story with the summer of 1935.

405 (p. 270) *lonely little airports in Tennessee* Air travel in the 1930s between New York and Los Angeles usually necessitated re-fuelling stops *en route*, often at airports in Tennessee and Arizona.

406 (p. 270) *Nembutal* a barbiturate drug

407 (p. 270) *Yellowstone* Yellowstone National Park, 3,500 square miles in area, located in the state of Wyoming but extending into Montana and Idaho

408 (p. 271) *Tory bears* American colonists loyal to King George III of Great Britain during the American War of Independence were called 'Tories'.

409 (p. 271) *the bonus army* The 'Bonus Expeditionary Army', made up of veterans of World War I, many of them jobless, marched on Washington in the spring and summer of 1932 demanding immediate cash payment of their veterans' bonuses .

410 (p. 272) *Alice in the rabbit-hole* in Lewis Carroll's *Alice's Adventures in Wonderland* (1865)

411 (p. 273) *Guy Lombardo . . . to Cheek* Gaetano Alberto ('Guy') Lombardo (1902–77), Canadian-born American bandleader and violinist; 'Top Hat' and 'Cheek To Cheek', songs by Irving Berlin (1888 –1989), American popular song composer, for the film *Top Hat* (1935), starring Fred Astaire and Ginger Rogers

412 (p. 274) *Hermitage, Home of Andrew Jackson* Andrew Jackson (1767–1845), seventh president of the United States; his home near Nashville, Tennessee, was named 'The Hermitage'. See Introduction.

413 (p. 274) *old Laemmle studio* Carl Laemmle (1867–1939), German-born founder of Universal Pictures

414 (p. 275) *Cortez or Balboa* Hernan Cortez de Monroy y Pizzaro (1485–1547) and Vasco Núñez de Balboa (1475–1519), Spanish explorers and conquistadors; the sentence is also a veiled reference to 'On First Looking into Chapman's Homer' (1816), a poem by John Keats (1795–1821), a poet whom Fitzgerald held in high regard.

415 (p. 275) *Esquire*   an American 'men's' magazine, largely concerned with fashion and lifestyle, founded in 1932

416 (p. 276) *First National? Paramount? United Artists?* Hollywood movie studios

417 (p. 276) *Old Hickory*   the nickname of Andrew Jackson (see Note 412). Jackson led the American troops that defeated British forces at the Battle of New Orleans (1815). Fitzgerald mistakenly refers to him as the tenth president.

418 (p. 278) *Iron Maidens*   instruments of torture; an iron cabinet that drives spikes though its victim as it closes

419 (p. 280) *the Bronx*   a borough of New York City

420 (p. 280) *Charles Francis Adams*   Fitzgerald's reference is clearly to Charles Francis Adams II (1835–1915), the grandson of John Quincy Adams (1735–1826), sixth president of the United States; he was chairman of government directors of the Union Pacific Railroad and later president of the railroad.

421 (p. 281) *Gould, Vanderbilt, Carnegie, Astor*   Jason 'Jay' Gould (1836–92), American railroad 'baron' and speculator; Cornelius Vanderbilt (1794–1877), American railroad and shipping magnate; Andrew Carnegie (1835–1919), Scottish-born American industrialist and businessman, founder of the Carnegie Steel Company, later US Steel; John Jacob Astor (1763–1848), German-born American businessman and investor, founder of the American Fur Company

422 (p. 281) *sourbelly*   someone who is invariably complaining or miserable

423 (p. 281) *Mountains of the Frozen Saw*   the Sawtooth mountain range in the state of Idaho; this is an 'internal' error of Fitzgerald's

424 (p. 282) *42nd Street*   a Warner Brothers musical of 1933

425 (p. 284) *Long Beach Naval Station*   the naval base at Long Beach in Greater Los Angeles, home to the United States Pacific Fleet

426 (p. 284) *Glendale airport*   Glendale is a city in Greater Los Angeles County; the airport is now called the Bob Hope Airport after the American actor and comedian.

427 (p. 284) *Tom Mix or Bill Hart*   Thomas Edwin ('Tom') Mix (1880–1940) and William St Hart (1864–1946), American film actors of the silent era noted for their appearances in Westerns

428 (p. 284) *Come, come, I love you only*   a song from the operetta *The Chocolate Soldier* (1908) by Oscar Nathan Straus (1860–1954)

429 (p. 284) *the earthquake*   An earthquake of a magnitude of 6.4 on the Richter Scale struck Long Beach, California, on 11 March 1933, but Fitzgerald's description of the damage done and his diagram of the novel suggests that what is described is more consistent with the minor shocks of June and July 1935, especially with the reference to 1935 in the synopsis of the novel he sent to Kenneth Littauer and Max Perkins; the earthquake of 13 July 1935 shook the Greater Los Angeles area, including Hollywood, and extended north-west to Pasadena and east to San Bernadino.

430 (p. 285) *Will Rogers*   William Penn Adair Rogers (1879–1935), American film actor, humorist and social commentator; one of the most famous American entertainers of the inter-war years

431 (p. 287) *dictograph*   a sound-recording instrument

432 (p. 288) *the Goddess Siva*   Shiva, a Hindu deity, the god of destruction and death

433 (p. 288) *DeMille*   Cecil Blount DeMille (1881–1959), American film producer and director

434 (p. 289) *the Emperor and the Old Guard*   Napoleon Bonaparte (1769–1821) was Emperor of France from 1804–15; his Imperial Guard was made up of veteran soldiers.

435 (p. 290) *drummer's sense . . .*   Drummers were travelling salesmen: they 'drummed up' business.

436 (p. 290) *Edison . . . Lumière . . . Griffith . . . Chaplin*   Thomas Edison (1847–1931), American businessman, inventor and scientist, known above all for his invention of the light bulb; the Lumière brothers, Auguste Marie Louis Nicholas (1862–1964) and Louis Jean (1864–1948), are numbered among the earliest cinematographers; David Lewelyn Wark Griffith (1875–1948), American film director; Sir Charles Spencer ('Charlie') Chaplin (1889–1977), English silent film comic actor and film director

437 (p. 291) *'Tout passe . . . l'éternité'*   'Everything dies but great art lasts for ever' (French); from the poem 'L'Art' (1858) by the French *symboliste* poet Théophile Gautier (1811–72)

438 (p. 291) *the Prince from Denmark*   Agge, Count of Rosenborg (1887–1940), is an historical figure: he was the eldest child of Prince Valdemar of Denmark and Princess Marie d'Orléans, and was an officer in the French Foreign Legion. He died in Taza, Morocco. Fitzgerald is probably in error in later attributing his ancestry to the Swedish House of Bernadotte.

439 (p. 292) *a Chevvy* (usually 'Chevy') a car manufactured by the Chevrolet Motor Company, a company acquired by General Motors in 1917

440 (p. 295) *the Keystone Days* the Keystone Cops, a group of actors (many of them remain unknown) who played incompetent policemen in a series of silent films made between 1912 and 1917; the films were produced by Mack Sennett (1880–1960)

441 (p. 295) *Georgie Jessel . . . Lincoln's Gettysburg routine* George Jessel (1889–1981), American actor, singer and songwriter, whose reputation was, above all, built on his comedy sketches. He also produced a number of musicals for Twentieth-Century Fox. Abraham Lincoln, sixteenth president of the United States, delivered the 'Gettysburg Address' at the dedication of the Soldiers' National Cemetery in Gettysburg, Pennsylvania (the site of a decisive victory for the Union Army during the American Civil War) on 19 November 1863.

442 (p. 295) *Variety* the leading American entertainment trade-magazine, founded in 1905

443 (p. 295) *Roxy's* the Roxy, a cinema in New York City

444 (p. 298) *Reinhardt's 'Miracle'* Max Reinhardt (1873–1943), Austrian-born American film director. *The Miracle* (1912), which Reinhardt co-directed with Cherry Kearton, was an early attempt to add sound to the moving image.

445 (p. 299) *Margaret Sullavan . . . Colman* Margaret Sullavan (1911–1960), American film actress; Ronald Colman (1891–1958), English actor who starred in many Hollywood films

446 (p. 300) *Eugene O'Neill* Eugene Gladstone O'Neill (1888–1953), American dramatist, author of *Mourning Becomes Elektra* (1931) and *A Long Day's Journey into Night* (1941). See below.

447 (p. 301) *Hays Office* William Harrison Hays (1879–1954) gave his name to the industry-written Hays Production Code that oversaw censorship matters for the motion-picture industry.

448 (p. 302) *Joe Breen* Joseph Breen (1890–1965), American film censor who worked for the Hays Production Code

449 (p. 303) *Beverly Wilshire* a hotel at 9500 Wilshire Boulevard, Los Angeles, completed in 1928

450 (p. 303) *Peel's* probably Peal and Company, an English manufacturer of luxury shoes and boots

451 (p. 305) *the Foreign Legion* a military unit of the French Army founded in 1831 and recruited entirely from foreign nationals. For much of its history the Legion's homeland has been Algeria.

452 (p. 305) *Bernadotte*   the current royal house of the Swedish monarchy, briefly also the royal house of Norway. Fitzgerald is in error in attributing the 'blood of Bernadotte' to Prince Agge, who is Danish.

453 (p. 306) *Hell's Angels ... Ben Hur*   *Hell's Angels* (1930), an American war film directed by Howard Hughes; *Ben-Hur* (1925), a silent film directed by Fred Niblo

454 (p. 307) *NYU*   New York University, a private university in New York City

455 (p. 307) *Academy dinners*   the dinners held during the award ceremonies of the American Academy of Motion Picture Arts and Sciences (the awards are more widely known as the 'Oscars')

456 (p. 308) *First Empire*   the empire of Napoleon 1 in France, 1804–15

457 (p. 308) *Nicolay's biography*   *Abraham Lincoln: A History* (1917), a ten-volume biography of Lincoln by John George Nicolay and John Hay

458 (p. 308) *Lenin in the Kremlin*   Vladimir Ilich Lenin (1870–1924), revolutionary leader of the Soviet Communist Party that took power in Russian after the October Revolution of 1917. Lenin's mausoleum in Red Square, Moscow, is located just outside the walls of the Kremlin Palace and houses Lenin's embalmed body.

459 (p. 309) *Goldwyn*   Samuel Goldwyn (1879–1974), Polish-born American film producer, founder of the Goldwyn Pictures Corporation

460 (p. 309) *Knights of Columbus*   a Roman Catholic fraternal society established in Connecticut in February 1882, its mission to promote Catholic education and charitable giving

461 (p. 310) *Tarzan comics*   Edgar Rice Burroughs' (1875–1950) jungle hero, Tarzan, was depicted in comic strips as well as in feature films of the period.

462 (p. 312) *Claudette Colbert ... Ronald Colman*   Claudette Colbert (1903–66), French-born American stage and film actress; Ronald Charles Colman (1891–1958), English actor (see Note 445 above); *courrer du bois* (French), correctly 'coureur', French-Canadian woodsman

463 (p. 313) *Cary*   Cary Grant (1904–86), born Archibald Alexander Leach, English-born American film actor

464 (p. 313) *Sidney Howard* Sidney Coe Howard (1891–1939), American playwright and screenwriter, was the credited screenwriter for *Gone with the Wind* (1939).

465 (p. 314) *Tracy* Spencer Tracy (1900–67), American film actor

466 (p. 315) *Manon* Manon Lescaut (1731), a novel by Antoine François Prevost (1697–1763)

467 (p. 318) *a drugstore on Wilshire* American drugstores are pharmacies but they often sell sweets, magazines and cosmetics, and many have restaurant facilities (like those of a diner); Wilshire Boulevard is one of the main east-west streets in Los Angeles.

468 (p. 318) *the picture about Russia* Stahr's real-life counterpart, Irving Thalberg (see Introduction), had for several years planned a film about Russia.

469 (p. 318) *the American thirteen states* the original thirteen British colonies on the Atlantic seaboard of North America

470 (p. 318) *Aeschylus ... Euripides ... Aristophanes ... Menander* respectively tragic and comic dramatists of ancient Greece: Aeschylus (525–456 BC), author of *The Oresteia*; Euripides (480–406 BC), author of *Elektra* and *The Trojan Women*; Aristophanes (446–386 BC), author of *The Frogs*; Menander (342–291 BC), author of *Dyskolos* (*The Grouch*)

471 (p. 319) *Delphic oracle ... Oedipus* The Oracle of Delphi (Pythia), an oracle being a person, thing or place taken as a source of prophesy or wise counsel; in Sophocles' play *Oedipus the King* (429 BC), Oedipus solves the riddle of the Sphinx.

472 (p. 319) *Salonika* the city of Thessaloniki in Greece

473 (p. 319) *open roadster* a two-seater sports car, usually without a fixed roof

474 (p. 323) *the Carlton* an error: Fitzgerald intends an exclusive hotel and no London hotel, so named, existed at the time

475 (p. 323) *reefer* a reefing-jacket, a close-fitting jacket made of heavy cloth

476 (p. 324) *The Thundering Beat Of My Heart* 'The Beat Of My Heart' (1934), a popular song, lyrics by Johnny Burke to music by Harold Spence

477 (p. 325) *Bones* Skull and Bones, a prestigious secret society at Yale University, New Haven, Connecticut, is generally referred to as 'Bones'.

478 (p. 325) *Benny Goodman ... Paul Whiteman* Benjamin David ('Benny') Goodman (1909–86), American jazz clarinettist

and jazz band leader; Paul Samuel Whiteman (1890–1967), American bandleader, composer and orchestral director

479 (p. 325) *When Day Is Done* a popular song from 1926, English lyrics by B. G. DeSylva to music by the Austrian composer Robert Katscher (1894–1942)

480 (p. 325) *Little Girl, You've Had A Busy Day* Cecilia's father alters the title of the popular song 'Little Man, You've Had A Busy Day' (1934), lyrics by Maurice Sigler and Al Hoffman to music by Mabel Wayne.

481 (p. 325) *Lovely To Look At* a popular song of 1935, lyrics by Dorothy Fields and Jimmy McHugh to music by Jerome Kern

482 (p. 326) *They asked me how I knew . . . was true* the first lines of 'Smoke Gets In Your Eyes' (1933), a popular song, lyrics by Oscar Harbach to music by Jerome Kern

483 (p. 326) *Ambassador* the Ambassador Hotel at 3400 Wilshire Boulevard, Los Angeles

484 (p. 327) *Coronado . . . Del Monte* towns in California

485 (pp. 327–8) *Raphael's corner angels* Raffaello Sanzio da Urbino (1483–1520), Italian Renaissance painter and architect

486 (p. 328) *Hemingway characters* Ernest Hemingway (1899–1961), American novelist and close friend of Fitzgerald's; the reference is to the fortitude of Hemingway's characters in the face of danger.

487 (p. 328) *Hollywood Bowl* an outdoor concert arena

488 (p. 328) *Sonja Henie* Sonja Henie (1912–69), Norwegian World and Olympic champion figure skater and Hollywood film star

489 (p. 331) *John Barrymore, Pola Negri . . . Connie Talmadge* John Sidney Blyth Barrymore (1882–1942), American film actor, paternal grandfather of Drew Barrymore; Pola Negri (1897–1987), Polish-born American actress of the 'golden era' of Hollywood film-making; Constance Talmadge (1898–1973), American film actress of the silent era

490 (p. 332) *Glenn Miller* Alton Glenn Miller (1904–44), American bandleader, who went missing in an aircraft over the English Channel on 15 December 1944 and whose body has never been found. 'I'm On A See-Saw' (1934) was a song played by the Glenn Miller Orchestra, lyrics by Desmond Carter to music by Vivian Ellis.

491 (p. 334) *Randolph Hearst* William Randolph Hearst (1863–1951), American publisher and newspaper magnate, head of

Hearst Newspapers. He is fictionally recreated in Orson Welles's film, *Citizen Kane* (1941).

492 (p. 336) *Coke* Coca-Cola

493 (p. 336) *cheaters* sunglasses

494 (p. 337) *McKinley* William McKinley (1843–1901), twenty-fifth president of the United States. McKinley was assassinated in 1901 and was succeeded by Theodore Roosevelt (1858–1919), his vice president.

495 (p. 337) *John Gilbert* John Cecil Pringle (1899–1936), stage name John Gilbert, American film actor, star of many silent films, known as 'the Great Lover'

496 (p. 342) *call-houses* brothels that send prostitutes to their clients in response to telephone calls

497 (p. 344) *Botticelli* Sandro Botticelli (1445–1510), Italian Renaissance painter. 'The Birth of Venus' depicts Venus standing in a scallop shell.

498 (p. 344) *Sorbonne* the University of Paris at the Sorbonne, located in the Latin Quarter

499 (p. 344) *Spengler* Oswald Spengler (1880–1936), German philosopher and historian, author of *The Decline of the West* (1918)

500 (p. 344) *schules* schools, also synagogues (Yiddish)

501 (p. 345) *grunion* a small Pacific fish

502 (p. 345) *Sir Francis Drake* Francis Drake (1540–96), English sea-captain and explorer, knighted by Queen Elizabeth I in 1581

503 (p. 345) *Emerson* Ralph Waldo Emerson (1803–82), American writer and philosopher

504 (p. 345) *Rosicrucians* a religious group claiming various forms of secret and magical knowledge

505 (p. 347) *Bel-Air . . . Santa Monica* exclusive residential districts of west Los Angeles

506 (p. 348) *list of phone calls* the list in Stahr's library mixes real people with fictional characters from the novel: Jean Harlow (1911–37), Hollywood actress known as 'the Blonde Bombshell'; Douglas Fairbanks (1883–1939), American actor, director and producer; Colman, see Note 462 above; Spyros Skouras (1893–1971), Greek-born American motion-picture executive

507 (p. 352) *Griffith* See Note 436 above.

508 (p. 352) *Buddy Ebsen . . . Walter Davenport . . . Donald Crisp* American character actors. Ebsen went on to star in the TV series *The Beverly Hillbillies* that ran from 1962 until 1971.

509 (p. 353) *the Saturday Evening Post* at the time a weekly mass-circulation magazine that published many of Fitzgerald's early stories

510 (p. 353) *Bev Brown Derby* one of the Brown Derby restaurants in Los Angeles

511 (p. 354) *skivvies and biddies . . . Sex Fifth Avenue* colloquial words for maids and chambermaids; a pun on Saks Fifth Avenue, the New York department store

512 (p. 354) *Vine Street Jesus* Vine Street intersects with Hollywood Boulevard

513 (p. 357) *Gary Cooper* Frank James 'Gary' Cooper (1901–61), American film actor

514 (p. 357) *Troc* the Trocadero nightclub in Hollywood

515 (p. 357) *Lord Charnwood* Godfrey Rathbone Benson (1864–1945), 1st Baron Charnwood, politician and historian, author of *Abraham Lincoln* (1916)

516 (p. 363) *the Black-and-Tans in twenty-two* temporary constables of the Royal Irish Constabulary employed to quell the Irish uprising again British rule. Their name refers to the colour of their uniform.

517 (p. 363) *syndicalist* Syndicalists advocated the ownership of factories and businesses by their workers.

518 (p. 364) *suicide bridge . . . new wire* high wire was attached to some California bridges to deter suicide attempts

519 (p. 364) *White Way* a brightly lit street

520 (p. 365) *Mrs Simpson* Wallis Simpson (1896–1986), Duchess of Windsor, wife to Prince Edward, Duke of Windsor, briefly King Edward VIII

521 (p. 366) *Jews were dead . . . sea* a reference to German anti-Semitism in the 1930s

522 (p. 367) *Lake Louise* a ski resort in Alberta, Canada

523 (p. 367) *Harry Bridges* Alfred Renton Bridges (1901–90), Australian-born American labour leader

524 (p. 367) *The New Masses* American Marxist publication that ran from 1926 until 1948

525 (p. 367) *the 'I am' cult* an occult religious movement in the United States that mixed alchemy and theosophy

526 (p. 367) *Writers' Guild* the Screen Writers' Guild established in 1920 to represent the interests of screenwriters and scriptwriters

527 (p. 367) *Doctor Caligari . . . Le Chien Andalou*   The Cabinet of Dr Caligari, a horror film of 1920 directed by Robert Weine; *Un Chien Andalou*, a short surrealist film directed by Luis Buñuel (1900–83) and Salvador Dali (1904–89)

528 (p. 368) *Sloane's*   a New York department store

529 (p. 368) *Fanny Brice*   the stage name of Fania Borach (1891–1951), American singer, comedienne and film actress

530 (p. 369) *Balanchine*   George Balanchine (1904–83), Russian ballet-dancer and choreographer

531 (p. 369) *the Ritz Brothers*   three brothers, Al, Jimmy and Harry Ritz, an American comedy team

532 (p. 369) *Warner Brothers*   the American film studio founded in 1923

533 (p. 370) *the anti-Nazi league*   The Hollywood Anit-Nazi League, or the Hollywood League Against Nazi-ism, was established in 1936 and at its height had in excess of 4,000 members.

534 (p. 370) *Goldwyn Avenue*   correctly Goldwyn Terrace, a street in Los Angeles named after Samuel Goldwyn

535 (p. 371) *Frankensteen*   Richard Frankensteen (1907–77), union leader, President of the United Autoworkers' Union

536 (p. 372) *Superman*   the American comic-book hero introduced in 1939

537 (p. 373) *the Legion of Decency*   The National Legion of Decency, established in 1933, was a Roman Catholic organisation that sought to combat immorality in motion pictures.

538 (p. 373) *Carole Lombard*   the stage name of Jane Alice Peters (1908–42), American film actress noted for her comedy roles

539 (p. 374) *Fitts*   Buron Rogers Fitts (1895–1973) was District Attorney for the State of California from 1928 until 1940; some historians have asserted that he was bribed by officials from MGM studios in the mid-1930s.